CW00825431

# Leaving the Land

Anne Ewing

iUniverse, Inc.
Bloomington

## Leaving the Land



*iUniverse books may be ordered through booksellers or by contacting:*

*iUniverse*
*1663 Liberty Drive*
*Bloomington, IN 47403*
*www.iuniverse.com*
*1-800-Authors (1-800-288-4677)*



*ISBN: 978-1-4502-9634-2 (sc)*
*ISBN: 978-1-4502-9635-9 (ebk)*

*Printed in the United States of America*

*iUniverse rev. date: 3/9/2011*

# Preface

This chronicle is dedicated to the memory of my parents, Joey and Jim Rutherford. It is an account of their lives and those of their parents and grandparents. It is based on my memories, partly of the stories they told, partly of the events that happened, and partly of the characters that peopled my childhood and young life. It is a true record but, naturally, technically accurate only to the extent that the reliability of my memory allows. While I accept that others may have a different interpretation of events and individuals described, I trust that nothing in its telling will cause offence or unhappiness to anyone. It may be that time and distance have lent enchantment to the view, but my intention was always to portray my parents as truthfully and objectively as possible.

The title of this account, *Leaving the Land*, is also the title of a song by the Scottish-Australian singer-songwriter, Eric Bogle. Joey and Jim left the land, of course, when they left Pitkinny in 1976—an experience so closely mirrored in the words of that song—and their links to the land were broken finally when they died, Joey in 1999 and Jim in 2000. In a wider context, the family history of most people born in Scotland over the last three hundred years has involved a leaving of the land, as economic and social conditions necessitated a move from the country to the towns and cities, and from work on the land to work in an increasingly industrial and urban landscape. Jim and his family were among those who had retained their links to the land, and Joey came to love the farm life she shared with Jim. I have grown to value my upbringing at Pitkinny more and more and to feel privileged to be part of that continuum, and of a way of life that has become ever rarer.

*Pitkinny Farm*

# Acknowledgements

I am indebted to my family: my husband, Bill; my son Calum and his wife, Maria; and my son Donald and his wife, Aoife, for their unfailing encouragement and enthusiasm for this project; to my sister Margaret, brother-in-law John, and my three nieces, Pamela, Alison, and Lynda, for their invaluable contributions. The cover for this book was painted beautifully by my daughter-in-law, Maria. In addition, thanks are due to the many people who have related their memories of Mum and Dad—in particular, to Lena Imrie and her late husband, Robbie; the late Dougie Imrie and his wife, Chrissie, who all worked at Pitkinny over many years; and in general to the numerous family members, friends, and acquaintances who have, either directly or indirectly, shared their recollections of Jim and Joey.

Shortly after the house at Cadham was sold following Dad's death, Betty and Jim Henderson, dear lifelong friends of Joey and Jim, described how, in passing the house one day, they felt, not for the first time, the acute pain of losing close friends, as they realised they would never again be welcomed in that home. "All the doors are closing," said Betty. At the time I felt that was such a sorrowful but inevitable accompaniment of increasing age and frailty. But now, nearly a decade later, I am aware that as the years pass a new generation is growing up. Joey and Jim's grandchildren and great-grandchildren are creating new homes of their own with new doors opening up to their families and friends, and the spirit of my parents lives on in them. If some of their progeny, however occasionally, dip into this account of the lives of their antecedents, recall their experiences, and mention them by name, my motivation in making this record will have been vindicated and my time and effort well spent.

I would like to thank, in absentia, Eric Bogle, the Scottish-born Australian song writer and folk singer, who graciously granted me his permission to use the name of one of his songs, "Leaving the Land" as the title of this work. It mirrors so closely the experience of Joey and Jim as they left behind their farming years at Pitkinny. Only her name, Jenny, and her constant battle with the dust differ from that of Joey and her perennial war with the mud. In every other detail the song represents so vividly the emotions that must have accompanied them as they drove along the farm loan for the last time.

I appreciate the kindness of the late Dan Imrie in allowing me to reproduce some of the photographs from his publication, *Around the Farms*, in which some of the folk who worked at Pitkinny over the years are featured.

Also, I wish to express my gratitude in acknowledging, in memoriam, the debt I personally owe to Lewis Grassic Gibbon, aka James Leslie Mitchell, the author of *Sunset Song*. By way of paying homage to him, I have used his arrangement of headings and chapters, which follows the farming calendar. The inscription on his headstone in Arbuthnot churchyard stands as my introductory quotation. But more than that, *Sunset Song*, his seminal work, with his heroine Chris Guthrie and his description of her growing up in the farming community of the Howe o' the Mearns, had a great and lasting impact on me as a young woman and perhaps subconsciously inspired me in later life when I came to write this chronicle. Like Chris, I can see I am a product of the conflict between the pull of the land, with its timeless and unchanging quality, on the one hand and the lure of the academic and intellectual life and its insistent modernity on the other. That, and the nature I inherited from my parents and their forebears, combined with the wholesome and selfless nurturing I enjoyed, when set against the unparalleled economic, social, and political changes of the second half of the twentieth century, made me the person I became.

Finally, I am immensely grateful to my husband, Bill, who has been a wonderful emotional and practical support in all aspects involved in the production of the text and images in this work.

# Contents

# Introduction

"The kindness of friends,
The warmth of toil,
The peace of rest."

My father, James Rutherford (Jim), died on 7 July 2000 and was buried five days later. He had lived for eighty-three and a half years, surviving into the first year of the twenty-first century and of the third millennium. He had been widowed eighteen months before, on 15 January 1999. My mother, Johann Barclay Mitchell (Joey), was buried then in mid-winter, the grief that day raw and cruel for her family: her husband denied his life partner after nearly sixty years of marriage; her children, my sister and I, bereft of a mother after more than fifty years of selfless parenting; her grandchildren, three girls and two boys, adults now and conscious of her influence on them, but still young enough to remember her unconditional joy in them, their births, and their growing; her great-grandchildren, three generations removed from her and too young to be aware of the pain and finality of this parting, unaware of the significance of their existence in relation to hers.

In contrast, my father's funeral was on a summer's day of benign warmth, calm air, and gentle sunshine, as the passing clouds would allow. Accordingly, the harsh edges of that day's sorrow were softened by a sense of a circle closed, a journey completed, a resolution achieved. My parents lay together now for all time, sheltered by the earth that bore them, nurtured their growth, and sustained their endeavours and achievements. In turn, they had tilled that same earth, treasured its fruits, and now finally enriched it, as they had enriched the lives of their family and friends.

My mother and father were back where they belonged. There could be no more fitting resting place, and we left the flower-shrouded grave reassuring each other of that comfort.

A few weeks later, I stood alone looking at the freshly inscribed addition to the words on the headstone, so brief a description of two lives: their names, their ages, the dates of their deaths. One word to describe my father's occupation: farmer. Another to name their home: Pitkinny. It seemed so little to convey the range of experiences they shared: success and disaster, joy and tragedy, love and antipathy, health and sickness. My insights into my mother's and father's lives are of necessity those of a child to a parent. I never knew them as a lover or friend, neighbour or adversary; still, what they were, I am, to a greater or lesser degree, and the older I grow, the more acutely conscious of that I become. Of course, my life was very different from theirs. That is an incontrovertible fact, determined by the vastly different social and economic influences which were brought to bear on my generation through the second half of the twentieth century.

Nevertheless, I appreciate more and more their legacy, which helped shape my values, my understanding of the world, and the people in it, and my aspirations for myself and for my own family. I do not wish to idealise my parents. They were real, three-dimensional characters with as many foibles and failings as strengths and successes, and they remain as vital and essential to me now in death as they ever were in life. I consequently feel compelled in some way to make a record of their lives, to make a statement about how they lived and how, in living, they touched so many other lives.

*Johann Barclay Mitchell 1941*

*James Rutherford 1941*

*Headstone in St. Drostan's cemetery, Markinch*

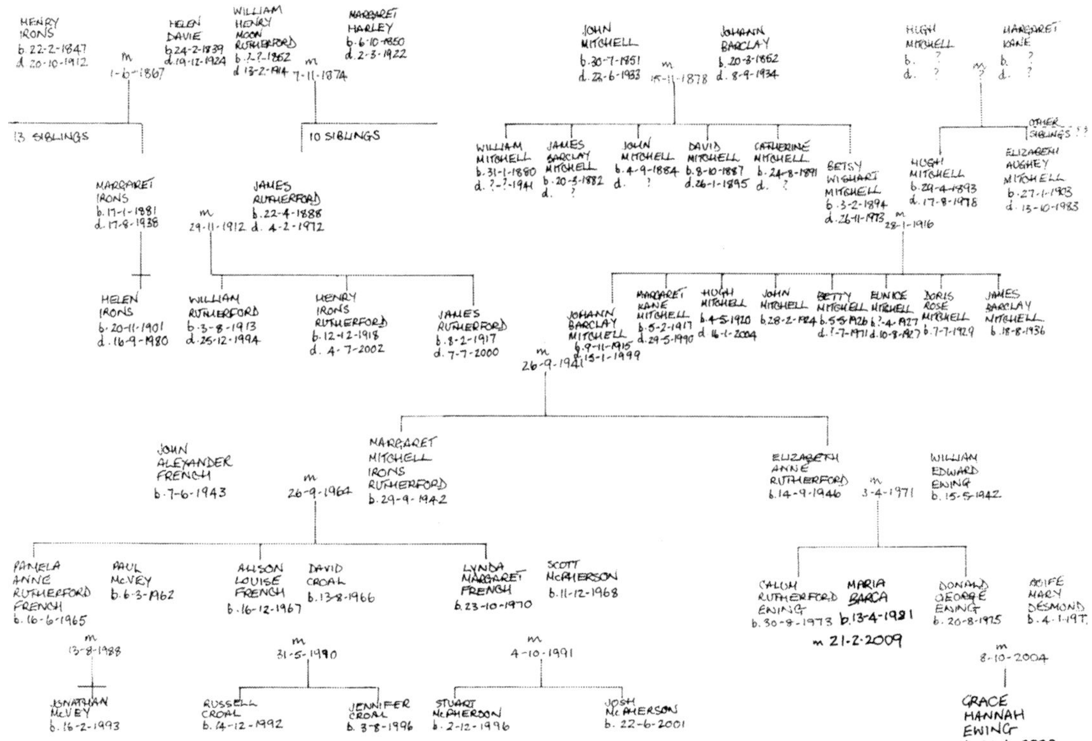


*Rutherford-Mitchell Family Tree*

# PRELUDE

## THE UNFURROWED FIELD

# Chapter 1

"My granny's number is 681."

My parents, Joey and Jim, lie together in the cemetery named for the parish church of Markinch: St. Drostan's, a few hundred yards from my mother's birthplace in that small town and three miles from my father's in the little village of Star—a satellite of Markinch indeed, as its more definitive name, Star of Markinch, suggests.

The cemetery is on the crest of a ridge to the east of the town, and from it you can look in all directions. To the west is the town, with its fine and imposing Romanesque church tower on a small hill, the oldest part of the town clustered round as if for warmth and sustenance. From there a track leads northeast over the Cuinin Hill to Star, and from the cemetery you can trace its tree-marked ridge. Along that track my father walked almost every day of his life as a schoolboy, a messenger for his mother and father, a home-guardsman in the early days of the Second World War, and as a hopeful suitor as he courted my mother. Further west stand the Lomond Hills, west and east, but more familiarly called West Law and Falkland Hill, the objectives of many summer expeditions for my mother and her family. These features marked a physical and perhaps a symbolic boundary to their adventures, the villages of Leslie and Falkland the limit of their walking.

To the southwest you can see the new town of Glenrothes, already more than sixty years old, and much less obtrusive to the eye than you might expect, as it has bedded down amidst an imaginative and generous planning of greenery and mixed woodland landscaping. You might suppose that this development, and the passage of time, would have assuaged the affront to the farming community represented by this urban imposition on the rural landscape, but my father never forgave the sacrifice of some wonderful farms, which gave their names to the precincts of the new town: Bighty, Auchmuty, Pitteuchar, Macedonia, South Parks, and Warout. This adoption of the farm names was but an insult added to injury as far as he was concerned.

As you look eastwards from the cemetery, the land gradually descends towards the coast of Fife, the widening estuary of the River Forth with Largo Law in the distance, and beyond that the North Sea. To the southeast the Isle of May and the Bass Rock rise from the firth, with the Lothian coast on the other shore of the estuary. My maternal grandmother was born and spent her early childhood there in Abbeyhill, on the eastern fringe of the capital, before her family returned to Fife to live. My mother worked for a time in domestic service in Broughty Ferry, a suburb of

Dundee, across the other estuary of the Tay to the north of Fife, and then as a newly married woman moved within the county but to the western edge, near the boundary with Kinross-shire. As a young woman and a newly qualified teacher, I travelled across the North Sea to work in Sweden, a venture which brought a challenging and lasting new dimension to my life. With each succeeding generation, as we have become more affluent and technology has made travel so much easier, our personal horizons have widened. My mother and my grandmother crossed firths, I crossed the sea, and my two sons in turn have crossed continents and oceans to live and work in the United States, Hong Kong, and Japan.

Across the boundary wall near my parents' grave, the land slopes steeply to the south, to the valley of the River Leven, its course marked by the line of the Leven Woods, a favourite playground for my mother and her brothers and sisters. From there a formerly well-used access to the town lies now sadly forgotten and overgrown: the sixty-three steps, a wooden staircase cut into the steep slope up towards the railway station. Nearby is the "Haigs of Markinch" whisky blending and bottling plant, long closed down and the buildings subdivided and given over to alternative enterprises, but at least still in existence as a landmark near the station for rail passengers familiar with the east coast main line north from Edinburgh to Dundee and beyond. The railway was a lifeline for the traditional industries of the area (whisky, wool and paper mills), for the farming community's trade, and for the commerce of the town. It crosses the valley of the River Leven on an impressive viaduct, which has a little brother no longer used, further west, which carried a branch line towards Woodside, the site of Glenrothes new town. From the station the main line skirts round the eastern edge of Markinch, past the old and long unused St. Drostan's kirkyard, and north towards Ladybank and Cupar, Fife's county town.

So my parents now lie together in the centre of what was their known world as children: the primary school my mother attended; the "advance division" or secondary school they both went to; the John Dixon Park gifted to the town in 1919 by John Dixon, paper mill owner and benefactor—who was later a town councillor and provost for many years and had a keen interest in physical fitness and sport; the many and varied shops in the town with their flagship, the Markinch and District Co-operative Society with its various branches in the area, the cornerstone of many peoples' daily lives, providing jobs, services, and the wherewithal to sustain them and their families. I can picture this small town, tracing its familiar streets and its immediate surroundings almost as well as my parents could, because so much of my childhood was spent there.

My grandparents' home was a magnet for my own family—my aunts, uncles, and cousins—as we visited almost every weekend. Balbirnie Estate, belonging to the Balfour family, began on the other side of our grandparents' garden wall and was a favourite, if illicit, playground for us. In springtime we used to help ourselves to the profusely growing "wild" daffodils, and our mother and aunts went home with armfuls of the yellow blooms. The Back Burn was a favourite picnic spot, and we loved paddling in its water. On the way there we always stopped to look at Stob's Cross, a standing stone of great antiquity which used to make me feel slightly uneasy, as it stood in sinister dark shadow on a dank north-facing aspect. Markinch Hill with its war memorial was clearly a place deserving of reverence and respect, while the John Dixon Park held wonderful promise of hours spent on the swings, roundabout, and chute—very basic equipment, but well loved and well used. We never aspired to the tennis courts, but for a few summers we were regular patrons of the putting green—a wonderful addition to the attractions of the park. The only drawback to that was that you had to pay, so we had to make our meagre pocket money stretch that bit further.

Another hedonistic—and at sixpence a time for children, affordable—delight of Markinch was "the pictures" every Wednesday and Saturday. The town hall was turned into a cinema on those evenings. I seem to remember wooden benches at the front, with rows of wooden seats at the back. A few proper cinema seats were available upstairs on the balcony, but they were beyond our means. The whole enterprise was managed by a strict disciplinarian, Aund Wallace, who kept all the children in order as he strolled up and down with his torch. Any misbehaviour was subject to summary justice, and his warnings, "Ah'll see your faither the morn!" were taken very seriously, as he knew everyone there. With threepenny worth of "aromatics," small pink and brown scented sweets, purchased at Sharp's sweet shop on the way there and another threepenny worth of chips on the way home, what better way to spend my one shilling pocket money? The other great indulgence was ice cream from Malocco's café, usually a cone or a slider with raspberry sauce or, very occasionally as funds would allow, from a "silver" dish while sitting down at one of the tables—the height of sophistication that Markinch had to offer children on a summer's day!

My older sister Margaret and I, of course, were simply enjoying the kind of thing that town children took for granted. It was wonderful for us to have all these activities on our doorstep, which were denied to us at home on the farm. We could not go into our nearest village, Cardenden, other than to and from school, on our own until we were much older, whereas in Markinch everything was so close to our Gran and Grandad's house that we were quite safe. Also, we often had the company of cousins or neighbouring children on our outings and adventures. We would stay for a few days at a time during school holidays. We used to love running errands for our Gran, and one of the favourite messages was to go down to Mason the baker's at the bottom of the road to buy rolls in the early mornings. The bake-house was beside the shop, and the wonderful smells emanating from there were only surpassed by the taste of a warm roll spread with butter and then dipped in sugar, a treat we were allowed by Gran, but never at home.

Our Gran was a keen member of "the Store," or the Co-op, where she did most of her food shopping. She kept her receipts on a spike in the larder and always knew exactly how much dividend she was due when the half-yearly discount was paid out. One day she wanted some meat from the butcher's, and I pleaded with her to be allowed to go on my own. Eventually she agreed, but only after ascertaining that I most definitely knew where the "store" butcher's shop was located and that I had memorised her store number. I felt so proud of myself as I set out with shopping bag, purse, and message line in hand. When I had been served and was paying the butcher, I announced loudly and clearly, "My gran's number is 681." At that the butcher looked slightly puzzled, but when I repeated this information, no doubt with the beginnings of a tremor in my voice, the penny dropped, and he said, "This is no the store, hen." I was afraid to go home and tell my Gran that she would not be getting any dividend for the meat I had bought, and I knew there was no fooling her, because she would be waiting for the receipt to stick on her spike. So I trailed up the road, walking more and more slowly, dreading the reaction I would get. In the event, once Gran got over the realisation that some of her hard-earned income had gone into the till at Brunton's, the private butcher's shop she had never patronised on principle, the storm was short-lived and soon forgotten by Gran, who, I realise now, looking back all those years, had great forbearance and usually put up with her school holiday visitors with patience and good humour.

Another example of this was when her grandchildren were responsible for the loss of her prized wedding china. It was Markinch Highland Games day, a red-letter day for us all. The whole family would turn up at Gran and Grandad's. We usually got to wear our new summer dress for the occasion, and it was the day that our new season's Clarks sandals got their first airing, invariably resulting in painfully skinned heels until they were broken in. We would spend much of the day at the Games, watching all the events in the arena, but the best part for the children was "the shows," the fun fair with the usual stalls and the swing-boats and roundabouts, which always accompanied the Games. A favourite was Jock's shop, a stall that sold all manner of little toys and games and the kind of rubbishy sweets that we loved. The candy floss seller was always well-patronised too, and once our appetites were well and truly jaded we would all come back to Gran's for tea. One year we persuaded her to use her "best cheenie." We had paid a quick visit "over the wall" into Balbirnie, and, the daffodil season being long past, we decided to pick rhododendrons instead, as we were sure our gran, mum, and aunts would welcome a change of flower. Later, after we had all gone home and Gran was returning her wedding china to the china cabinet, she slipped on some rhodie leaves, which had fallen on the floor. Suffice it to say that some of the "guid cheenie" did not survive the resulting crash, but happily Gran did, and we were all back again the following weekend and for many more Highland Games days to come.

The village of Star of Markinch has always had its name both shortened and lengthened in common usage. Locally, it is referred to as The Star in the same way as other villages are prefixed by the definite article, such as The Coaltown (Coaltown of Balgonie) or The Milton (Milton of Balgonie). (When my brother-in-law first knew my sister and heard us referring to The Star, he thought it must be a pub!) The name derives from "starr," a word common to old Scots and Swedish, meaning sedge or peat. Peats cut from the nearby Star Moss were a valuable source of fuel and were also used to impart flavour to the locally distilled Cameron Brig whisky. In the early part of the nineteenth century, most of the inhabitants were handloom weavers, but with the collapse of that industry on the introduction of power looms, most of the population concentrated on the cultivation of the little crofts adjoining the cottages.

In my father's childhood and youth, it might have been more accurate to refer to Star as a hamlet, as it was very small, and was somewhat unique in that it was entirely a farming village, but it included a primary school, a pub, and a post office. My father's family occupied the small holding and dairy at the west end of the village and were later tenants of Broomfield Farm further to the west, which formed part of the Balbirnie Estate. My memories of The Star are much less detailed than those of Markinch, mainly because we spent much less time there. Apart from short visits, we only once stayed for a couple of days with an aunt and uncle there. I do remember wondering when I was very young if the name had some biblical significance, as the phrases "Star of Markinch" and "Star of Bethlehem" had a similarity, but somehow I realised that there was nothing fanciful or remotely spiritual about The Star. It was a place to be taken seriously, and the most valued quality there was seen to be hard work. There never seemed, in my memory, to be much in the way of fun or light-heartedness to be had there, and innovation and modernity were clearly to be discouraged at all costs. We were very conscious of this even at a young age, although it was never spoken about. We did not consider our parents to be trendsetters, but we realised that they were not as old-fashioned as our grandfather, who ruled our aunts and uncles and fashioned their attitudes in the same way. We were very fortunate to have parents who had a sense of humour, who did their very best to give us a warm and comfortable home, and who had ambitions to improve their and our living conditions—but our grandfather did not see the point of enjoying the benefits of his hard work and did his best to deny them to his immediate family as well.

We did not feel valued as grandchildren, although our aunts and uncles were always kind to us, and we got on well with our three cousins. The main reason for this lack of warmth was our grandfather, who really had no time for us because we were girls and consequently more or less useless. My mother told us later that when we were very young he would look at us and point at us, saying, "What are they?" as if he didn't know our gender! I am sure that our mother soon reminded him in no uncertain fashion, but my sister remembers that she was at The Star when the present Princess Royal was born; when the news was being spoken of, our grandfather said that "Lassie bairns should be thrown into the Leven (river)!" Young as she was, Margaret remembers being shocked and horrified that he could say such a thing, and even worse, seem to mean it!

We would usually pay a visit just before Christmas time, and, although there would be a discreet exchange of small gifts for the children between my mother and our aunts, there was never a mention of the impending festival. Of course, in those days no one—unless they were very well off—celebrated Christmas to any great extent, and certainly not in the way that it is celebrated nowadays; still, I used to hope year after year that someone would at least say "Merry Christmas" as we left to go home, but it never happened. I wondered what the reaction would be if I said it, but I never had the courage. There was no time or space for sentiment or for any of the finer things in life with my grandfather, and I suppose everyone in his immediate family took a lead from him in this regard. He had undoubtedly had a hard life and had many admirable qualities, but I could never imagine him having a softer side to his nature. My maternal grandparents had very little in the way of material possessions, and had had no education either, but they did have more human warmth and affection for us as grandchildren.

So the town of Markinch, the village of Star, and their immediate environs were central features of our childhood. I now realise that another, more powerful reason is that we grew up hearing stories about my parents and their families' lives, lived of necessity—given the limits to their ability to travel—entirely within their home area. Many of the features of my recollections of The Star and Markinch had also influenced the lives of former generations.

*Markinch Games (1949 approx.)*
*(Middle Row from left) Auntie Betty with cousin Eunice, Gran Betsy with sister Margaret, Mum Joey with Anne*
*(Front Row from left) Cathy Webster, Irene Webster, and Uncle James.*

*Playtime at 83 Croft Crescent, Markinch (1950)*
*(Left to right front) Eunice Mitchell, Willie Lindsay, Anne Rutherford*
*(Left to right back) Margaret Rutherford, Margaret Lindsay*

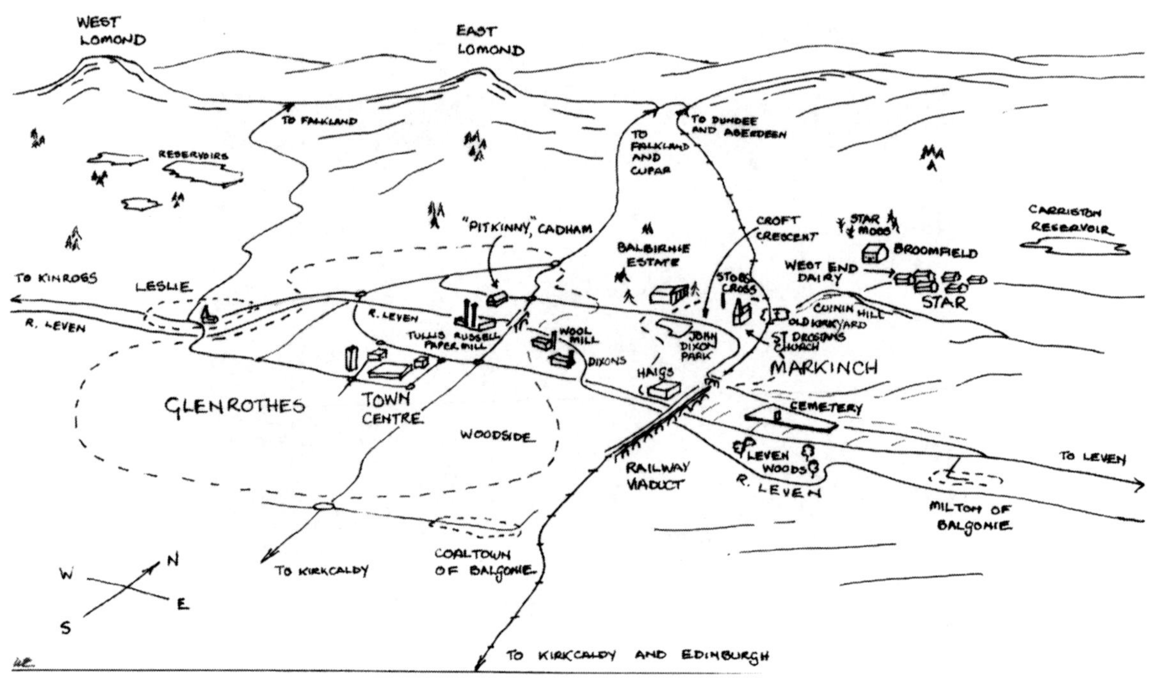


*Map of the Markinch area*

# Chapter 2

## "Ye'll be in Cupar by denner time!"

My mother died in the very early morning of 15 January 1999. We understood that her life was drawing to a close, and we decided that my sister, Margaret, would be with her in hospital while I stayed with my father at home in Cadham. Although we had tried to prepare him, he was completely devastated by the fact of my mother's passing; it was only later that day that the reality of the situation gradually began to sink in, as the rest of the family began to gather at my parents' home. Our older son, Calum, was at that time working in Hong Kong, and my mother left us in no doubt that she didn't want him to fly halfway round the world on her account. Accordingly, we persuaded him not to rush home for the funeral, but to wait until his planned visit home the following month. Our younger son, Donald, who was in his post-graduate year at Edinburgh University, travelled by train to Markinch; as I sat in my car waiting for him at the station, I thought of several events which had happened there, and which were recounted to me by my parents.

A misty succession of ghosts passed before me. I could picture Jim as a young boy, sent to the station by his mother to dispatch a gift to her sister. He had walked over the Cuinin Hill, carrying a freshly killed young cockerel, grasping it by its feet tied together with string, and bearing a prominently displayed address label. He hated this task and was tempted to dump it somewhere, but knew better. Punishment would be certain to follow, as experience had taught him. As I looked across the street to Joey's childhood home, in a block of houses named Mitchell Place, coincidentally the same name as her surname, I thought of the retribution visited on her as a young girl one cold winter's morning. While her parents lived in Mitchell Place, her grandparents lived in Landel Street, just a few minutes walk away. Living space was limited in her parents' home to a room and kitchen with a small scullery and an outside toilet, as was the norm in working-class homes of that time, so as the oldest sibling, my mother usually slept at her granny's. On this particular morning, while on some errand between the two houses, she passed the station forecourt as the pupils who attended the High School in Cupar were waiting for their train. As youngsters have always done on frosty days, they had made a slide on the sloping icy pavement. On her return journey, after the slide-makers had departed for school, my mother could not resist having a few "shots" on the slide. Hardly had she begun than she felt a heavy hand on her shoulder. It was Davie Moyes, the local bobby. "If there's no a ha'penny worth o' saut on there by the time I come back this wye, ye'll be in Cupar by denner time!"

Joey knew exactly what he meant: She would be arrested and taken to the Sheriff Court in the county town that very morning unless she could destroy the offending danger to public safety. She raced to her granny's house and begged a ha'penny, then to "the Store" (the Co-op) for the salt, then sprinkled it on the slide before going to school and quaking in her shoes for the rest of the day, fearing that her efforts would be in vain. When I hear my contemporaries bemoan the absence of the "friendly" community policemen on the beat, I understand why they hark back to a situation which, on the face of it, did engender respect for the law. But I also think of the level of terror this example inspired in a wee girl, who was neither the perpetrator of the offence nor worldly enough to realise that the bobby's threat was probably not meant to be taken seriously, and that his tongue was probably very firmly in his cheek. Joey, in common with most folk of her generation, certainly retained a very healthy respect for the law throughout her life. How often as children she would tell us: "Never steal, never smoke, and never tell lies!" Significantly, making ice slides was never mentioned!

This was the era when the vast majority of journeys, both passenger and freight, were by train. Sometimes the station was the scene of happy occasions. In a time when leisure was severely limited and social events very rare, I see in my mind's eye excited expeditions of families converging on the station to embark on Sunday school trips, suitably festooned with balloons and streamers and carrying buckets and spades for the beach. A large number of pipe bands arrived by train for the Highland Games, to take part in the prestigious competition there, and would alight, assemble, and march down the High Street to the John Dixon Park to the skirl of the pipes and the beat of the drums.

I have a picture of an earlier occasion when the pipes were heard in the High Street, an altogether more sombre though probably exciting time, when the HLI (Highland Light Infantry) regiment marched off to the First World War and the Gallipoli disaster, having been in camp in the Play Field. Those soldiers in kilts—from so long ago and yet still young and bright-eyed, before the hellish experience of war dimmed their eyes and stole their youth and indeed, for many, their lives—numbered among them my grandfather. It is impossible to identify him in the picture, but there is one young kiltie at the rear of the column seen talking to a young woman in a straw hat. It is tempting to believe that they could be my grandparents and to imagine what their conversation might be. We will never know, but given the circumstances of my mother's birth, it will always remain an intriguing scenario for me to wonder about.

A generation and one world war later, the same station saw another sad and fearful farewell for my family, as the oldest of Joey's brothers, a second Hugh Mitchell, four years her junior and named after his father, left to become part of the British Expeditionary Force in France, before the outbreak of the Second World War. He had joined the RAF Reserve at the age of eighteen the previous September during the Munich Crisis at the Leuchars Air Show, along with some of his friends. The inducement of an enlistment fee of thirty shillings, a free "holiday" at camp, and the excitement and glamour of donning a uniform, was enough to entice them into an adventure in which, by volunteering, they had some choice of regiment and service. Had he waited for the call-up, he would have had to go where he was sent. Despite their reservations—"Ye're a young fool, Hugh, don't you know there's going to be a war?" thundered his father—his parents had to be content with this justification for his actions. Off he went, a young man of nineteen, to play his part, as a member of the RAF Regiment, in many of the dramatic actions of that awful conflict.

He did not escape from Dunkirk during the fall of France but made his way with his unit along the north coast of France to Brest, where they were rescued by French fishing boats and taken to the Irish Republic, where they travelled in sealed trains (Ireland being a neutral country). He was able to throw a briefly worded postcard from the train, addressed to his parents. Some kind Irish person posted it, and my mother used to show it to us. A French soldier who had escaped with Hughie had added some words, "To our so sympathetic British friends."

The torment his family must have lived through during those days before they knew that Hughie had survived must have been awful, and it is illustrated by the experience my mother had one morning as she saw the telegram boy come up the garden path. She met him and opened the telegram quickly before her mother could see it. She remembered that she read the words, "The War Office regret to inform you…" Her sister Greta found her crying on the doorstep and on asking her what was wrong and seeing the telegram, she also feared the worst—until, that is, she read it and saw that it was in fact from their Uncle Wullie, telling them to expect him for a visit the next day! This shows that my Mum was so keyed up by worry about her brother that she actually read words that were not there!

As the war progressed, Hughie returned to France and, on D-day +2, had an amusing experience amid all the drama and dread of being part of such a historic event. He was directing lorries as they were disembarking on the beach from a landing craft and recognised one of the drivers as a former schoolmate from Markinch. He tried to attract this lad's attention, but the driver was concentrating so hard on staying within the white lines which demarcated the safe, mine-free areas from those still to be cleared that he didn't see Hughie until long after the war when my uncle greeted him with the words, "Dae yo no let on tae yer friends when ye meet them abroad?" Later, towards the end of the conflict, Hughie was in one of the first contingents to cross the Rhine into Germany.

Having married a girl he had met while stationed in East Anglia, he returned only briefly to live in Markinch and resume his job as a paper mill engineer in Dickson's mill, where he had served his time as an apprentice. Thereafter, he and his family lived and worked in various parts of England before finally emigrating to the United States in 1968 to join my aunt's sister, who had gone to New Hampshire as a GI war bride. As many former soldiers do, my uncle made light of his wartime experiences, and it is with some regret that I realise I could have made more of an effort to encourage him to share his experience, and similarly with my maternal grandfather, who had fought and been wounded in Gallipoli in the First World War. Sadly, it is only when it is too late that we realise we have lost a golden opportunity to learn firsthand what these life-changing experiences meant to the people who underwent them. Many years later, just after we retired, Bill and I were to spend ANZAC (Australia and New Zealand Army Corps) Day, 25 April 2002, in Albany, southwest Australia, during our long-planned world tour. As we watched the old men marching and the younger generations saluting them, I thought of the common destiny that united them with my grandfather on a beach at Suvla Bay, so far away from their homes on opposite sides of the world, and of the thousands of others who shared that fate but never returned to their families and never had the chance of having children and grandchildren to remember them.

Before the war, in 1935, another stressful departure at that same station was when my mother left home to work in service as an under-nursery maid for a family in Broughty Ferry. Her employers were a commander in the Royal Navy and his wife, who was a member of the D.C. Thomson publishing dynasty in Dundee. They lived in a large white mansion which we looked for and found years later, once when my mother spent the day with me in Dundee while I was a student there. She felt desperately unhappy and was indeed terrified at the prospect of leaving everything familiar and dear to her in order to "better" herself by launching out on this venture. She was miserably homesick all the time she was there and tried to console herself by picturing every aspect of her home and imagining in detail what would be happening at any given time of day. She wrote home constantly, sometimes asking for descriptions of everyday objects and patterns, the more clearly to visualise them. Although the lifestyle of her employers was initially totally alien to my mother, she did realise that she was learning many new housewifery and child care skills, albeit in a household where there seemed to be no limit to material wealth, a situation she had never experienced before and was unlikely to ever again.

I was aware as I grew up that Mum's political affiliations were somewhat to the left of Dad's. She disliked intensely any ostentatious show of wealth and hated injustice or prejudice of any kind. I wonder if this short experience of life in domestic service informed these principles. I do remember her irritation when describing how none of the servants was allowed to remain on the staircase if or when one of the family was there and had to retreat either upwards or downwards until their "betters" had passed. She was also affronted when she learned that the lady's maid had to perform the most intimate of services for her mistress, a young and fit woman, which my mother and I, for my part, would have considered at best unnecessary and at worst demeaning and humiliating. On another occasion the head nursery maid suffered terrible bruising to her shins when she was kicked by the oldest of the children in her care during a temper tantrum. She saw this as an occupational hazard, but Mum was outraged on her behalf and would have found it difficult or even impossible to restrain herself from administering some kind of firm admonishment to the recalcitrant young rascal! So, she said, it was just as well that the situation never arose.

What is clear to me now is that my mother had great innate ability to relate to children regardless of background or situation. Always the oldest sister at home and a mainstay of help for her mother and granny in caring for her younger siblings, she worked equally hard at looking after these privileged youngsters and would in time become an excellent mother to her own two girls and a wonderful grandmother to their children in turn. She often thought later in her life that perhaps she would have in time overcome her desolation at being separated from her family and might have made a career in some kind of child care, but suddenly a letter from home changed all that. My grandmother was going to have a late baby at the age of forty-two, and my mother was needed at home. So, in early 1936 she returned on the train to Markinch and a new phase in her life.

*51st battalion of the Highland Light Infantry leaving for Gallipoli in early 1915*
*(© William Fiet 1998)*

*The paper sack department of Dixon's mill 1922. Joey would work here ten years later.*
*(© William Fiet 1998)*

*The workshop at Dixon's mill in the 1920s. This was Hugh's workplace for many years.*
*(© William Fiet 1998)*

*Markinch and District Co-operative Society branches in High Street*
*(© William Fiet 1998)*

*Haig's whisky blending and bottling plant*
*(© William Fiet 1998)*

*View of Markinch railway station*
*(© William Fiet 1998)*

TELEGRAMS,
PAPER MARKINCH.

M.G., M.F., GLAZED SULPHITES & KRAFTS.
BLEACHED, UNBLEACHED & COLOURED.
MAXIMUM DECKLES M.G. 88". M.F. 78".

PROPRIETORS
FIFE PAPER MILLS LTD.

FIFE PAPER MILLS LTD
INCORPORATING
MILL No 14
J. & W. DIXON, BALBIRNIE, MARKINCH
&
MILL No 16
MILLFIELD, LEVEN
MARKINCH, FIFE

TELEPHONE
50 MARKINCH.

PAPER BAG MANUFACTURERS
PLAIN & PRINTED.
FLAT, SATCHEL & ROSE SHAPES.

YOUR REF. ............ OUR REF. FHG/MW.

13th September, 1935.

TO WHOM IT MAY CONCERN.

This is to certify that Joan Mitchell has been in our employ for the past three years, during which time she has given us every satisfaction. We have no hesitation in recommending her as an honest and trustworthy worker.

Yours faithfully,

FIFE PAPER MILLS LIMITED.

F H Gover

Manager, Bag-making Dept.

ALL QUOTATIONS ARE BASED ON FREIGHT BY CHEAPEST ROUTE.

*Joey's reference from Fife Paper Mills for her post in service in Broughty Ferry*

*Uncle Hughie in RAF Reserve uniform*

*Uncle Hughie in RAF Regiment (bottom left)*

# Chapter 3

"You'll never be fit enough to play tennis, lassie."

I cannot remember when or how I became aware of some irregularity in the matter of my mother's birth, but I do remember her talking about it to me at some point after the death of her parents. She was very matter-of-fact about her less than ideal start in life, but how I wish I had tried to find out more about the circumstances of her birth. It was not in her nature to make a fuss about something for which she could not be held to account, or about which nothing could be remedied. As one of a generation who seemed able to patiently accept whatever life threw at them, she saw this for what it was: an "accident of birth." My generation has grown up used to the generally accepted wisdom that it is healthier to openly discuss traumatic events in life, in order to be able to deal successfully with them, but previous generations preferred to keep their own counsel, and private family matters often remained secret.

According to her birth certificate, Joey was born at thirty minutes past midnight on 9 November 1915. The space designated for "Name and maiden surname of mother" reads "Betsy Mitchell," and there is the addition of her occupation, "paper-mill worker." The space for "Name, surname and rank or profession of father" has been left blank. Thus, by omission, was my mother declared illegitimate. Her parents shared the same surname, and had the details of her father been inserted there, they might have read "Hugh Mitchell, soldier." There is no doubt about my mother's paternity, but her parents were not married until 28 January 1916.

I will never know exactly the sequence of events, but the facts speak for themselves. When my grandmother was two months pregnant, in April 1915, my grandfather was fighting in Gallipoli in the HLI regiment as part of Churchill's ill-fated First World War campaign against the Turks. He was wounded in the arm by shrapnel from a shell-burst which killed outright the next man in line, so he must have been back in Scotland sometime later in the year. My mother told me that two of Betsy's brothers traced my grandfather, who was at that time billeted in Reid Street in Dunfermline, where they informed him of my grandmother's condition and "persuaded" him to do the decent thing by her. It is possible to interpret these events in various ways. Did my grandparents meet and fall in love, only to be torn apart by war? Did Betsy send her young man off to war with a wonderful memory of love fulfilled? Did Hugh know of his girl's condition and enlist (conscription did not begin until 1916) to escape a romantic entanglement he did not welcome? I will never know the answer to these questions and it really doesn't matter now, but this is what makes that HLI photograph so intriguing. Could that young couple have been Betsy and Hugh and if so, what might they have been saying to each other?

Whatever the precise events, they married and went on to have seven more children, six of whom survived into adulthood; seventeen grandchildren; and nine great-grandchildren before Betsy died in 1973 and Hugh in 1978. The circumstances of Joey's birth were by no means exceptional, especially at a time when women generally had little or no control over their fertility and when external events could intervene to prevent a timely solution to a resulting outcome. Had my grandfather not been in the army, perhaps they would have married quickly, and so avoided the stigma of illegitimacy for their firstborn in a society where the technicalities of your parentage were very significant; unlike today, when the nuclear family is fast becoming the minority lifestyle of choice.

So my mother's early days were spent with her mother and her maternal grandparents in their home at 31 Landel Street, Markinch, and later between there and her parents' home in Mitchell Place, a few minutes' walk away. My great-grandparents were John (Jeck) Mitchell and his wife Johann (Hann) (nee Barclay), who had married in Markinch in 1878. He was for a short time a policeman in Lochgelly, but clearly he was not cut out for that line of work. After a few weeks in his job he was interviewed by his inspector, who asked him to explain why he had no arrests to his credit. He honestly declared that he had not encountered anyone who had worse character than himself, so he didn't feel justified in making an arrest! Needless to say, his career in the police was thereafter rather short-lived. He then began to work on the railway. This took the family to Edinburgh, to the district of Canongate, where my grandmother was born, the youngest of the family, before they moved to Begg's Buildings in Abbeyhill and thereafter back to Markinch and to a job on the railway there. The rapidly developing whisky blending and bottling plant of John Haig & Co. demanded an expansion of the station facilities, and Jeck's post was in connection with that.

Hann was the "howdie wife" in Markinch. As was usual in the early days of the twentieth century, most communities relied on the services of women who, although they had no formal nursing qualifications, acted as midwives and nurses in cooperation with the family doctors who served these communities. Hann was highly respected and well-known by most of the people in the town. She had the reputation of being a very strict matriarch, but was an excellent wife and mother and was much-loved by her family. In addition to my grandmother who, as the youngest in the family, was somewhat spoiled by her older siblings, Hann and Jeck had another daughter, Kate, and four sons, William (Wullie), John (Johnny), James (Jim), and David, who sadly died in his eighth year.

My mother spent much of her time with her granny, and although she died twelve years before I was born, I have always felt that I knew her because of the many vivid recollections of her which my mother shared with us. Every Sunday in the summertime Hann would don a clean black dress and a fresh white apron and go for a walk through Markinch. Most households in those days kept a garden, vegetables at the back and flowers at the front. As she progressed through the small town, she would help herself to a bloom from the occasional garden, returning home with a lovely bouquet. No one objected, perhaps because this was a way for the townsfolk to acknowledge the debt they owed to this woman who had brought most of the bairns into the world and would see most of the folk out, hopefully, but sadly not always, as old men and women. I assume that Hann must have been paid for her work, but whether this came directly from her clients or indirectly via the family doctors I have no way of knowing.

Her grandfather Jeck was remembered by Joey as a quiet, patient man, who deferred to his wife in most matters. He was not a man to drink, but their son John, who lived in Edinburgh was a bit of a "wide boy" and was always up to something. He had been quite a successful professional athlete in his younger day, but had somewhat gone to seed and would lead his father astray on those occasions when he paid them a surprise visit. On one such day Hann had "killed the fatted calf," or rather Jeck's fatted calf when, without consulting her husband, she gave Johnny the piece of steak she had intended for Jeck. (As was usually the case in those days, the meat was reserved for the man of the house and there would have been no question of my great-granny having steak as well.) After the dinner was over, Johnny persuaded his father to accompany him to the pub. Unused as he was to the drink, Jeck became ill when he returned home and called for a basin wherein he was duly sick. As he sat there staring into the basin, feeling very sorry for himself, he said ruefully, "Well, Hann I dinnae ken what's in there, but there's ae thing shair, there's nae steak!"

Uncle Johnny later "emigrated" to Australia, but my mother always harboured a suspicion that in fact he had to "clear out" of Scotland as he may have fallen foul of the law in some regard. Something else we will never be able to ascertain, but perhaps somewhere Down Under we have relatives with a liking for steak and the pub; probably a fitting description of a large proportion of Australian manhood!

Emigration has been a feature of Scottish life common to many families throughout the last few hundred years. One of Hann and Jeck's other sons, Jim, emigrated to Canada as a young man. There he married a young woman who had also emigrated from Fife and they had a son whom they named John. Jim returned to Markinch with his family when his wife became pregnant again. Sadly, she died giving birth to twin boys, James and William. Jim decided his future still lay in Canada and he asked his mother to care for his sons until he could get established, when he would come for them. She agreed, but with some reservations as William, the weaker of the twins, was a very delicate child. Hann's cousin offered to help, and she took the baby into her home and cared for him. When Jim returned from Canada to claim his sons a few years later, by which time he had remarried, his mother's cousin refused to give up the little boy, to whom she had become very attached. Jim apparently accepted the situation and returned to Canada with the older boy, John and the other twin, James. A photograph of those two little boys, taken with their grandparents shortly before they left, is a poignant testament to a very unhappy prospect. Those boys would never again see the grandparents who had looked after them, the twins would never meet each other at all, and William would meet his older brother only once, when John paid a flying visit to Fife in 1958 while en route home to Canada from a business trip to Denmark.

It seems so sad to us that any siblings, let alone twins, should be separated so arbitrarily, given the importance we place on familial bonding; certainly later in life, William became somewhat embittered by the experience. Despite having led an apparently satisfactory life, he told my mother that he was sure he would have been more successful had he been taken to Canada, as his two brothers had become very prosperous and prominent businessmen. His father Jim, ironically, returned to Scotland after he retired and died in Markinch, and I wonder what kind of a relationship he had in his remaining few years with the son he had left behind and hardly knew. Given the huge numbers who emigrated from Scotland, I am sure this kind of family experience is far from unique, and for succeeding generations, economic success may have been assured, but for others, it must have been at great personal loss and heartbreak. This is further exemplified by the way John Mitchell, whom we had met in 1958, began to correspond with my mother in the last few years of his life. As increasing frailty rendered him incapable of writing himself, he would communicate through his second wife, Buddy.

He was desperate to know details of the years he had lived as a young boy with his grandparents Hann and Jeck in Markinch; details which my mother sometimes found difficult to supply at such a great distance in years and space. It was clear that he had a great need to remember those days and to understand more about his antecedents in Scotland. This further sad tale of lost opportunities and misplaced memories helps to explain my reasons for writing this account of my parents' lives, so that some day in the future some of their descendants will satisfy that need to know, at least to some degree. It was with a sense of satisfactory completion that my sister Margaret met Buddy Mitchell as a very old lady in Kamloops, British Columbia in 2000, and that I sent her a copy of that photograph of her late husband as a wee boy about to leave Scotland.

My great-granny must have witnessed more than her fair share of grief and hardship in her daily work. Infant mortality was still a common feature of family life for most people. Many children succumbed to deadly childhood illnesses like diphtheria and scarlet fever. A stay in the fever hospital, of which there were many in all parts of the country, was a common experience of childhood, accompanied always by fumigation if not destruction of household bedding and other treasured personal possessions. Young adults, who were said to "go into a decline," would die slow painful deaths from consumption (tuberculosis), or in the case of galloping consumption, would die in a shockingly short time. People still had a fear of the workhouse, and all their waking hours were spent in a ceaseless struggle to make ends meet and to maintain the basic wherewithal for survival. Leisure was an unknown concept for most people; childhood was short and responsibilities were shouldered early by most youngsters. This applied very much to my mother as the oldest sibling. She and Greta, her younger sister by fifteen months, were expected to help with housework and the care of the younger children.

My grandparents, in common with many—if not most—families at that time, lost one of their children in infancy. Eunice was born in 1928, coming between Betty and Doris in the family. She died of meningitis when only a few weeks old. Up to that time, the family had little or no contact with any form of organised religion, but the dying baby was baptised in the house by the local minister, James Bryden. In accordance with accepted doctrine and popular belief, an unbaptised baby would be denied the kingdom of heaven and a life after death. Consequently the sacrament of baptism was sought for Eunice, and the rest of the children were also christened at the same time. I assume that there was little further involvement with the church, beyond some sporadic Sunday school attendance, because as far as I am aware, none of the family was confirmed as full communicant members of the local parish church as they became adults.

Indeed, the lack of familiarity with religious matters is illustrated by the story of my Uncle John, nine years younger than Joey, who as a small boy came rushing into the house one day in sheer terror to report that "God is walking up the street!" He had, in fact, seen the minister who, as was usual in those days, dressed in a long black coat and a big black hat. However, Joey was eventually to join the Church of Scotland in 1957 at the age of forty-two in circumstances which illustrate in a very telling way the depth of her character.

In those days education, no matter how elementary, was a serious business, and my mother loved school and learning. She was a bookworm all of her life and when as a child she borrowed books from the school library, she would irritate her granny, who did not see the value in reading when there was so much work to be done. "Ye've aye got yer heid atween the pages o' a book! I'll pit a stop to your nonsense!" Soon after that warning, Joey could not find the library book when it was time to return it to the school and, with much trepidation, had to own up to the teacher to having lost it. She got no sympathy at home, of course, and much as she loved her granny, she privately suspected that Hann had disposed of the time-wasting publication. Joey was careful after that not to let her granny catch her reading!

Life in the 1920s was hard for families like my mother's. There was no social security safety net for people when misfortune befell them. Economic recession meant short time work or the complete loss of jobs, experiences which affected my grandfather more than once. As Joey became a teenager, Hann and Betsy were naturally looking forward to the day she could leave school and start work to earn money to supplement the household income. There was the awful day when they realised that they had anticipated her fourteenth birthday by a whole year and that she was in fact approaching only her thirteenth birthday and would have one more year to attend school!

It is hard to believe that such a mistake was possible when we now as parents have the luxury of celebrating birthdays, and consciously involve ourselves in the development and education of our families. But in those days there was neither the time nor the money to do either, and with a growing family snapping at her heels, there was never any possibility of Joey being able to continue her education beyond the minimum school leaving age of fourteen. Pleas by the headmaster, Mr Stevens, to my grandfather to allow her to go on to high school fell on deaf ears. She showed great promise at school and certainly had the intelligence, enthusiasm, and motivation to achieve academic success, but the realities of the situation were that, although some working-class families at that time could educate their children by making great sacrifices, my grandparents were not able to follow that pattern.

I remember thirty-five years later, as I was about to start at university, my grandfather Hugh expressed regrets about that decision. Joey replied, with some irritation, "An' Ah would hae done well at high school, wi'nae shain for my feet or the richt claes for my back!" I felt sadness for both my mother and my grandfather, and realised for the first time how aware my mother was of her missed opportunity and how much she cared about it. We always knew that our parents, and particularly my mother, were determined that we should benefit from maximum educational opportunity and have the choices she never had in life.

If education proved a cost more than many families could bear, so health was often also a matter of what you could afford. There was no National Health Service, and doctors' consultations had to be paid for. I assume that although some, if not most, of the old-style family practitioners were probably altruistic up to a point where poor families were concerned, they also had to make a living. In addition, the perception of patients was that sending for the doctor was very much a last resort, when home remedies and nursing failed to effect a cure. Such a situation arose when Joey twice became ill with rheumatic fever. She had a raging temperature and acute joint pains and swelling. After many wakeful nights, a neighbour of my grandparents—a kindly soul by the name of Mrs Neil—came in and put a ten-shilling note on the table. "Ye'll get the doctor for Joey, Ah'm no listening to her greetin' another nicht." Sadly, the damage had already been done, and my mother suffered from diseased heart valves for the rest of her life. Despite many alarms at various times of her life, she learned to live with the condition, and although it may have ultimately contributed to the cause of her death, she led a full and active life to the age of eighty-three.

She never let her health stand in her way, but there were times when her condition led doctors to force her to courses of action which, in retrospect, and knowing what we know now about heart disease, were ill-advised. The first of these was when she was fourteen and was desperate to learn to play tennis. Tennis courts had been opened in the John Dixon Park and somehow Joey managed to save up enough of the hard-earned pennies she acquired by running errands and doing jobs for neighbours to buy herself tennis shoes and a racquet. It was at this point that the family doctor, Dr. Wight, intervened. "You'll never be fit enough to play tennis, lassie!" So her hopes were dashed, and her young brother Hughie wore her shoes, and the other younger children amused themselves with her racquet. Nowadays corrective heart surgery might be an option, or at least an awareness of the benefits of physical exercise would lead to a different outcome. Later in her life, mismanagement of her health would lead to much more devastating consequences, but as she once remarked to me, the one thing she was not dissuaded from was the need to work hard, which she did all her life.

Her first job at fourteen years old was in the Balbirnie Wool Mill, which involved long shifts of hard labour, with long walks in all weather to and from work. This was often despite great pain in her joints, to the degree that she had difficulty fitting her swollen feet into her shoes and had to wear hand-me-down men's shoes. No doctor or anyone else ever held their hands up in horror at her plight then! Not that Joey would have welcomed that either, as she always relished hard work and never seemed to get tired, even when she was well on in years and was in more or less constant pain from spondylosis and osteoarthritis. It was only in the last year or two of her life that her physical strength deserted her, and then she was very unhappy and frustrated to be unable to keep busy and to have to depend on others to do what she saw as her work: running her house and cooking for her and my father.

There was very little entertainment, and very few treats for working-class children in the 1920s, beyond what was offered by the school, the Sunday school, and the Band of Hope. This was a temperance society where every child was encouraged to "sign the pledge" to forswear alcohol for life, in exchange for a bag of buns and a cup of tea at the occasional soiree it offered. One event that stood out in Joey's memory was a school party when she was leaving primary school and going into the advance division, as secondary school was called. At half past eight that evening, just as the fun and games reached their climax, she was called to the door of the school. There she met her grandad in a state of great anxiety. As she often did, she was staying with her grandparents, and Jeck was furious that she was out so late. "This is a terrible state o' affairs," he ranted, "keeping bairns oot o' their beds at this time o' nicht! Come awa' hame noo!" He was so upset that he considered reporting the school for encouraging youngsters towards a life of sinful ease and irresponsible frivolity. At half-past eight in the evening! How things have changed.

Hann Barclay Mitchell had a great influence on the community she served. This is well illustrated by my mother's account of her first day at work in the Balbirnie Wool Mill. She and the other new girls had to give their names to their new boss; four of them, including Joey, gave the same name, "Johann." One of the others was her cousin, Johann Webster, a daughter of her Aunt Kate, who lived at Woodside. When the other two also gave the same Christian name, the manager said, "So! You're all Hann Barclay's bairns," meaning that they were all brought into the world by, and named after, my great-granny.

After her husband Jeck died in 1932, Hann began to fail too. "Oh, Ah miss yer faither," she would often say. She was happier than ever to have Joey stay with her. One morning she sent her to fetch her daughter Betsy. Then she told her that she had noticed blood in her urine and declared, "Well that's the end o' me then!" The doctor was consulted, but Hann refused all treatment with the warning, "And none o' yer needles, doctor!" She declined day by day, refusing all food and drinking very little. Her son Johnny was summoned and, on the advice of the doctor, suggested,

"You could get better, mother, if you would take some nourishment." Her reply was, "That would be a great peety, noo that I've come this far." She gradually slipped into unconsciousness, and at the end was given an injection to ease her way. It was as if she had made up her mind that her time had come and no one would deny her wish to be gone. How annoyed she would have been, had she known that the doctor at the end ignored her instruction about the needles! No one knew what the injection was, but I am sure that many well-meaning doctors in the past would do what they could to end suffering, and allow for a dignified and peaceful death. This situation is light years away from that of the present, with vexed questions relating to the grey area between palliative care and euthanasia.

A final testimony to the respect and affection in which Hann was held in Markinch came with her funeral. In those days Sunday funerals were common, and hers coincided with Armistice Day, 11 November 1934. The mourners came on to her burial from the remembrance service at the war memorial and her coffin was carried by her bairns, all young men she had brought into the world. I have often wondered how many of the young men she delivered had died in the Great War and could not be there that day to perform a service to a woman who had been so closely identified with the community she served.

My mother desperately missed her granny, and as many young people find with their first experience of bereavement, couldn't understand how life went on as if nothing significant had happened. "Don't you miss my granny?" she would ask her mother. "Aye, but at least she's no' here to tell me what tae dae!" came the answer. My mother could certainly remember times when, on the day Betsy had her turn for the wash-house, her mother would arrive bright and early. "A' richt, Betsy, I'll mind the bairns, you get doon to the wash-hoose and licht the biler." She kept her daughter on her toes, and it wasn't always welcome assistance, as my own granny Betsy had a much more relaxed approach to housework, cooking, and child care than her hard-working mother. After the washing was done, and it took all day, then the bairns would have their weekly dook in the hot, soapy water, so making maximum use of the wash-house facilities and the hard-won hot water.

Joey was greatly influenced by her granny's example in very many ways. They shared the same high principles and integrity. They were hard-working women who always put their families first. Neither would suffer fools gladly, but at the same time had a great empathy for people and their trials and tribulations, of which they were very aware. I never knew my great-granny but wish that I had, although through my mother's recollections we were allowed a glimpse of her life, the world she inhabited, and the people she loved, and felt greatly enriched by that opportunity.

EXTRACT OF AN ENTRY IN A REGISTER OF **BIRTHS,** of 17° & 18° VICTORIÆ,

kept in the undermentioned PARISH or DISTRICT, in terms Cap. 80, §§ 56 & 58.

| (1) Name and Surname. | (2) When and Where Born. | (3) Sex. | (4) Name, Surname, and Rank or Profession of Father. Name, and Maiden Surname of Mother. Date and Place of Marriage. | (5) Signature and Qualification of Informant, and Residence, if out of the House in which the Birth occurred. | (6) When and Where Regist and Signature of Regist |
|---|---|---|---|---|---|
| Johan Barclay Mitchell | 1915 November Ninth 0h. 30m. P.M. 31 Landel Street Markinch | F | — Betsy Mitchell Papermill Worker | (signed) Betsy Mitchell Mother | 1915. November 2 At Markinch (signed) Geo G. N. D. Registrar |

EXTRACTED from the REGISTER BOOK OF BIRTHS, for the DISTRICT of MARKINCH, COUNTY of FIFE, this 13th day of September 19.

; of Births, Deaths, and Marriages pertaining to every Registration District in Scotland are kept in *duplicate* for each year; xamined and compared, one of the duplicates is retained by the Local Registrar, while the other is transmitted to the Registrar-urgh. Every person is entitled to search the alphabetical Indexes of the duplicate Registers in the custody of the Registrar, d during the hours of business fixed by the Sheriff, or, where no special regulation has been made by him upon the subject, at rs on any lawful day, on payment of a fee of 2s. for a General, and 1s. for a Particular Search, and to have an Extract of any Registers for the further sum of 2s. 1d., including Stamp Duty. In the case of a *Particular* Search, the applicant must indicate a entry; while in the case of a *General* Search, he does not require to specify the object of such search. Every Extract of any Entry in , kept under the provisions of the Registration Acts (17 & 18 Vict. c. 80, 18 & 19 Vict. c. 29, and 23 & 24 Vict. c. 85), duly authenticated Registrar, is admissible as evidence in all parts of His Majesty's dominions without any other or further proof of such Entry.

The 62d Section of the Statute 17 & 18 Vict. c. 80 enacts that "every person who shall wilfully destroy, obliterate, erase "or cause to be destroyed, obliterated, erased, or injured any such Register, or Duplicate thereof, or any Minute, Notice, or Ce "pursuant to this Act, or shall falsely make or counterfeit, or cause to be falsely made or counterfeited, any part of any such "or any such Minute, Notice, or Certificate, or shall wilfully insert or make or cause to be inserted or made in any such "any false or fictitious Entry of or any false statement touching any Birth, Death, or Marriage, or shall wilfully give an "falsify any Certificate, or shall certify any Writing to be an Extract of any such Register, knowing the same to be fals "part thereof, shall be deemed guilty of an offence, and on conviction thereof be liable to be punished by Transportatio "ceeding Seven Years, or by Imprisonment for a period not exceeding Two Years."

*Joey's birth certificate*

*Joey as a baby*

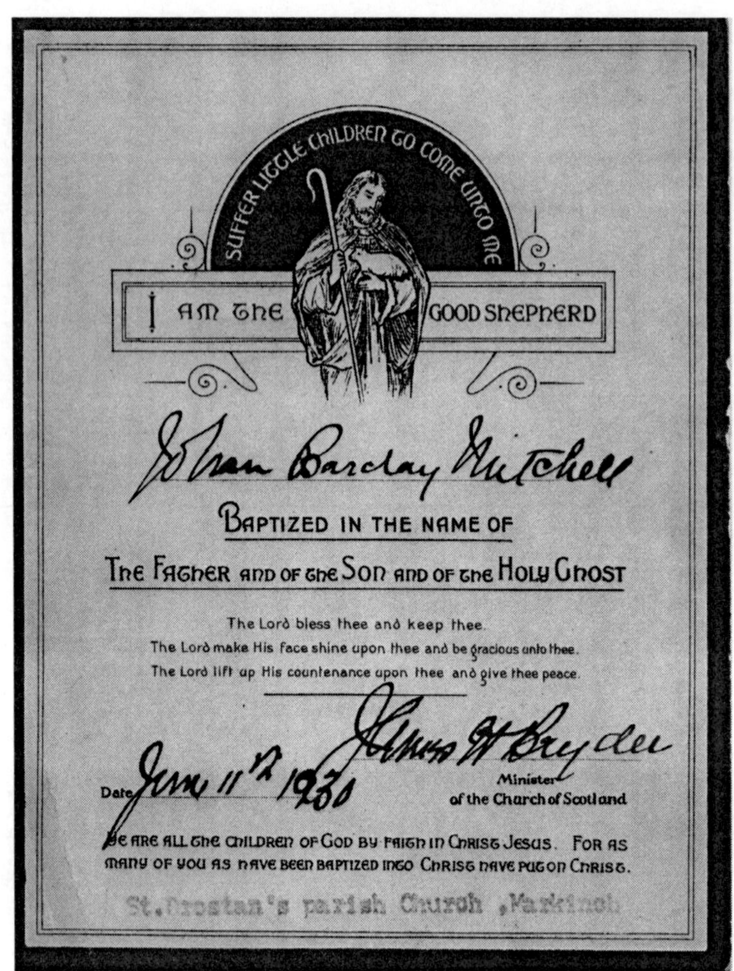

SUFFER LITTLE CHILDREN TO COME UNTO ME

I AM THE GOOD SHEPHERD

Johan Barclay Mitchell

BAPTIZED IN THE NAME OF

THE FATHER AND OF THE SON AND OF THE HOLY GHOST

The Lord bless thee and keep thee.
The Lord make His face shine upon thee and be gracious unto thee.
The Lord lift up His countenance upon thee and give thee peace.

Date June 11th 1930

Minister of the Church of Scotland

YE ARE ALL THE CHILDREN OF GOD BY FAITH IN CHRIST JESUS. FOR AS MANY OF YOU AS HAVE BEEN BAPTIZED INTO CHRIST HAVE PUT ON CHRIST.

St.Drostan's parish Church ,Markinch

*Joey's baptismal certificate*

*Great Gran Hann Barclay with niece Etta Kirk (on left)*

*John Mitchell and Johann Barclay Mitchell with their grandsons John (older) and James (younger) prior to the boys' departure for Canada with their father James*

*Joey's school photograph around 1926 (back row third from the right)*

# Chapter 4

## "So, is this the wan wha's gaun tae be a meenister?"

As Joey was growing up in Markinch, Jim's young life was spent within and around the hamlet of Star. He was born there in the small holding which would become known as The Dairy, at the west end of the straggle of houses with their gardens and small fields, on 8 February 1917, fifteen months after Joey's birth. He was the middle son of three; his elder brother was William (Wullie), and the younger was Henry (Harry). In accordance with tradition at that time, as the second-born son, Dad ought to have been named Henry, after his maternal grandfather. However, it was decided to break with tradition on this occasion and name the new baby after his father, as there was a possibility that James might have to go to fight in the First World War, which still had more than eighteen months to run at that stage. Conscription had begun in 1916, and for some reason, it was feared that his occupation as part-time smallholder would not keep him at home, so the second son was given his father's name in case he did not survive the war. In the event, he avoided the call-up and never left home. As a result, the name Henry was in turn given to the third and youngest son, who was born in December 1918. The boys had an elder sister named Helen (Nellie), who was just over fifteen years older than Jim. As I grew up, I became aware at some stage that my aunt, although she was Dad's sister, had a different surname: Irons. Gradually, I came to understand that she was actually his half-sister, but the actual circumstances of her birth eluded me until much later, when my mother explained it to me.

As our grandmother had died before our parents were married, Auntie Nellie, who had never herself been married, kept house for our grandfather, and in a way seemed like a granny figure to us. She also worked very hard at the dairy, milking twice a day, and fulfilling all the other roles demanded of a farm wife, which our own mother also had. We ourselves at Pitkinny in those days certainly did not live in the lap of luxury, but we had the basic comforts of warmth, cleanliness, and order, thanks to our mother's skill as a homemaker and to her unceasing hard work. In contrast, it was clear to us that conditions at the dairy house were far from satisfactory. There was no bathroom; the scullery (kitchen) was a bare, primitive place in which to work; and the kitchen (living room) always seemed cold and dark. The only bright spots I can remember in the house were the lovely red geraniums, which filled the kitchen windowsills and presented a cheerful face to the farmyard. Nellie must have enjoyed some pleasure tending her plants, but I remember when my mum admired the flowers, the compliment was dismissed, almost as if to acknowledge it would be an admission that she had spent time on something unnecessary and frivolous.

The only source of heat, as in most homes then, was the coal fire and it was never lit, even in winter, until after the afternoon milking was done. Likewise, the lights were never switched on until you could barely see each other. Auntie Nellie and Grandad lived a comfortless existence in conditions which suggested penury, if not actual poverty. She always wore a wrap-around peenie (apron) and wellington boots and as the years passed, she became more and more bent, her hands terribly calloused with painful-looking hacks, caused by working in the dairy with wet hands in the cold all the time. But she was always glad to see us and very interested in our lives as we grew up. As a child, I remember she would upend a big bag of sweeties on the table and urge us to help ourselves. But it was also made very clear that she had no time to linger over social niceties, even if she had wanted to, as Grandad was always in the background and we knew only too well that he would not allow anything to interfere with the work of the dairy.

When she died in 1980, eight years after our grandfather, my uncle and aunt passed on some of her personal effects and papers. Among those were some photographs, obviously taken in a studio, of Auntie Nellie as a small girl. She looked like a little princess, beautifully dressed and, in one case, sitting on a lovely rocking horse against an exquisite setting. Even allowing for the liking in those days for extremely flamboyant backgrounds in photographic studios, and the very serious countenance of those being photographed, these examples spoke volumes: here was a little girl who was much thought of and clearly cherished by whoever had arranged and paid for these pictures. This did not equate with our image of Auntie Nellie as we remembered her. Nor did the beautiful drawings we found in her school sketchbook, which we discovered in her schoolbag, a beautifully made leather satchel with her initials "N.I." stamped on the front. Dad had never seen it before, but she had kept this memento of her school days. The intricate pencil drawings, the watercolours of flowers and plants, and the examples of her handwriting illustrate her artistic and academic potential. She clearly was a skilled and gifted young artist and, like my mother, she always displayed an interest in the world. After she and my grandfather got a television, which in itself was surprising given his general distrust of anything at all innovative, she would often express interest in what she had seen and was, even with increasing age, intensely curious about things outside her experience.

So what had happened to Helen, that much-loved little girl in the photograph? What had changed her into the care-worn, prematurely aged Auntie Nellie we knew? My mother was able to trace the events that shaped that unhappy transformation. Only my father had memories of his mother, our paternal grandmother, as she had died in 1938, not long before he began to court my mother, when he was twenty-one and Nellie nearly thirty-seven. Our granny was Margaret (Maggie) Irons, the youngest of fourteen children. She was born to Henry Irons and his wife Helen Davie in Auchtertool in 1881. As a young woman she went into domestic service and eventually worked as a housemaid to a family named Donaldson, who lived in a big house at Crombie Point on the north shore of the River Forth, west of Rosyth and east of Torryburn. In photographs, Maggie is seen as a tall, strikingly handsome young woman, and it is perhaps understandable that she became romantically involved with one of the sons of the family she worked for. In due course she became pregnant by him—something of an occupational hazard for young women in domestic service in those days. It was generally believed by her family that the young man in question wanted to marry her, but of course that was deemed impossible by his father. So, by way of compensation, some money was settled on Maggie and she returned to, and was apparently welcomed by, her family in Auchtertool. Amongst Auntie Nellie's photographs were some taken of the Donaldson family. She had once told my mother that her father was "one of the young men in bowler hats in the pony and trap," and that photograph is as much as we know about her paternity. Less than that is evidenced in her birth certificate, which is even more brutal than my mother's, in the insertion of the actual word: "illegitimate."

In due course, Helen Irons was born and it seems certain that she grew up a loved and wanted child and grandchild. When she was eleven years old, in 1912, her mother Maggie married my grandfather, James Rutherford, who was one of eleven surviving children of William Rutherford and Janet Harley. He had been born in 1888 at Glenduckie Cotton, Dunbog, in the parish of Flisk, in northeast Fife. As a young man, he must have shown early signs of the industry, determination, and ambition which motivated him to hold down a night-shift job in the whisky distillery at Cameron Bridge, near Windygates, and a daytime enterprise to establish and develop a small holding of a few acres, and later a dairy, in Star. He met Maggie, who was seven years older than he, and I suspect that he saw her as quite a catch, owing to the bit of money she had.

I have not been able to discover a connection between Maggie's eligibility and his purchase of the smallholding, but I believe that such a connection is probable. In return for Maggie's suitability as a wife, he could offer the security of marriage, but I can't help but feel that James got the best of the bargain. My father told me that his mother's family had concerns about her welfare in marrying our grandfather. She was the youngest of a big family and was probably a favourite of her older siblings, so they must have had qualms about the life to which she was about to commit herself and Nellie. These doubts were realised six years later, when one of her brothers went to visit her and her family just before she gave birth to her last son in 1918. He was appalled to find her pushing a full wheelbarrow load of neeps, no doubt at the behest of her husband, despite the advanced stage of her pregnancy.

Thereafter, there was less and less contact between Maggie and her family, and I can only assume that this was what my grandfather wanted. His one concern was that his family could work hard—a laudable quality in normal circumstances, but in his case, it superseded everything else. Within a short time of his marriage, he had Maggie and Nellie working as hard as he did himself. One of Nellie's jobs as a young girl was to deliver milk daily, in a pony and trap, to the Cameron Bridge Distillery and to Buckhaven Co-operative Society, a round trip of about twenty miles. There were many links between the distillery and the Rutherford family: peat from the Star Moss was dug to fuel the distillery and to flavour its whisky; James worked there as a young man; Nellie drove there every day; finally, she died near there in the hospital of the same name; and on the day of her funeral in 1980, a bottle of Cameron Brig was drunk in her memory by the men of the family. She had kept it for years with that very purpose in mind. Not a drop of the hard stuff would ever have been crossed her lips, of course, but she had made her wishes known in this regard.

It was "all hands to the pump" on the smallholding and dairy and in addition, sometime in the late twenties James acquired the tenancy of Broomfield, one of the farms on Balbirnie Estate, located nearby the west end of Star. Maggie had given birth to three boys within five years, all of whom would grow up to work with their father, but sadly, her capacity for hard work was compromised by failing health. She developed pernicious anaemia, for which there was no effective treatment and which James saw as a great weakness on her part. Her increasing inability to fulfil his requirement for hard graft further alienated him from his wife, and there was very little in the way of sympathy or understanding from her husband. His self-denial and diligence may be seen as admirable, but he expected nothing less from those around him, and he had no respect for any other human qualities. He did not work hard to provide any kind of improvement in his or their standard of living; rather, the unceasing toil became an end in itself. The accumulation of wealth was his one objective, not for what it could make possible, but for its intrinsic value.

As Maggie's health deteriorated further, she told her children that when she died, she wanted to be buried beside her parents in Auchtertool. When she passed away on 17 August, 1938, Jim told his father what she had said, only to be told sharply, "She'll go where I put her. She wisnae a clean tattie onywye." In other words, James refused to respect his wife's dying wish and clearly had never accepted the fact that she had had an illegitimate child. Instead, he had Maggie buried in St Drostan's cemetery and erected an impressive headstone in her memory. So to the outside world, here lay the beloved wife of James Rutherford, and it might be supposed that he had loved her and cared for her, but the family knew a different story. It is probably true that in every life there are two stories, one for public consumption and the other true one known only to those involved. My maternal grandmother described some men of her generation as "kerbside angels and fireside devils," and I think to some extent that applied to my paternal grandfather.

I have often looked at that headstone and thought of the grandmother I never knew, and have felt such sadness that she had such a loveless and sterile life with my grandfather. I hope that she had pleasure in her four children, but even that must have been tainted by the way James condemned them to a thankless existence of penury and toil. My sister Margaret once asked Aunt Nellie if we could have some little keepsake that had belonged to our granny, and despite obviously not understanding, or indeed sharing the sentiment with which we made the request, after some thought she produced two gold rings, one her mother's wedding ring and the other a "keeper" ring. I have worn the latter every day since then and often think of the granny I never knew. Nellie, the illegitimate child so resented by her stepfather, was the woman who worked for him every day of her adult life, and who looked after him in his old age. She never, to our knowledge, had a day of ease or pleasure. Neither she nor Grandad would attend any of our weddings, because he would never contemplate a day off for such a trivial reason. "We dinnae hae five day week coos! They need milked every day!"

I have often thought of how Maggie must have been sorely missed by her children, and how little attention was paid to their emotional well-being as they mourned their mother. The only clues I have are that my father obviously remembered the slight to his mother in the choice of her final resting place, and that when he was courting Joey, he said that he found it hard to contemplate marriage and family life, as he had witnessed the unhappiness his father had caused his mother. I believe that his early upbringing did affect my father, probably more than it affected his brothers, because I am sure that he took after his mother in having a softer side to his nature than most of the Rutherfords. I often heard my own mother say that he had the thrawn-ness and bad temper of his father's nature and, while he could erupt in fury at times and could turn the air blue with no "expletives deleted" at all, he was basically very likeable and had a kindly and humane personality.

Dad had a natural charm and people were drawn to him. He could be described as "pawky" and would go to great lengths to try to please everyone. Mum had a very pragmatic and realistic appreciation of personal qualities in people, not least my father, and she once said to me, in exasperation at something Dad had said or done, "Yer faither must have a deep crease across his backside!" When I asked her what she meant, she continued, "From spending so much time sitting on the fence!" As a young man considering marrying and settling down, he could not face living and working with his father any longer, and was desperate to break away and set up his own farm. How he ever plucked up the courage to suggest this to James I don't know, but we were always grateful for that decision, as we appreciated that we had a much happier young life and a better material upbringing in a much less narrow-minded environment than we would have had at the Star, under the watchful gaze of our grandad.

I would not want to paint too dark and gloomy a picture of Jim's childhood; although they had a hard life, he had many happy memories too. Their mother must have shown them affection, and their childhood must have had its lighter moments. Their maternal grandmother, Helen Davie Irons, spent a short time before her death living with Maggie and her family in Star. It appears that she had a modest pension, so presumably James was agreeable to having his mother-in-law in his home, as she would be able to pay her way. A photograph shows Jim, with his brothers Wullie and Harry, as wee boys with their granny, and they each have a kitten in their arms. Maggie and, hopefully, James, must have been proud of their sons. It would appear that Dad did well at Star school, according to his report cards. In those days the school grades were E (Excellent), VG (Very Good), G (Good), FG (Fairly Good), F (Fair), and U (Unsatisfactory). Throughout his school career he had only one or two F or U grades, the majority being of a higher order. However, in 1925 he excelled at Bible Study, scoring a VG, and he remembered a visit from some of his aunts at about that time. When the boys appeared and were being introduced, and it came Jim's turn, one of the ladies said, "So is this the wan wha's gaun tae be a meenister?" Anyone who knew Dad in later life would doubtless be amused by that! Nevertheless, Maggie must have had ambitions for her family, and the sad fact that they were probably all unrealistic was the fault of my grandfather, who could never see beyond the tough daily grind he knew himself and to which he condemned all around him.

The Star school my father went to is still in use today, albeit with some changes and additions. His headmaster was Mr Rodger, a very strict disciplinarian, whose one professional aim was to get his charges successfully through seven years of elementary education and safely on their way to the advance division, the secondary school in Markinch. Occasionally he would despair of some of the slower pupils, and was often heard to say in exasperation, "I think I'll have to borrow some tattie bags from Mr Rutherford. It's the only way I'm going to get some of you dunderheids down to Markinch!" Many years later, in 2003, our younger son Donald visited that same school during his placement with Fife council as he completed his master's course in educational psychology. Sadly his grandfather would never know that he had revived our family's connection with that old village school.

When Jim had successfully completed the transfer to Markinch School without, in his case, the need for a tattie bag, he had a long walk there and back every day over the Ciunin Hill to be faced in all weathers. He was tempted, only once fortunately, to play truant. Of course he couldn't go anywhere he might be seen and had to skulk around the fields and lanes between the Star and Markinch, and then live in dread for a guilt-ridden week or two in case he had been spotted and reported to the school or, even worse, to his father. He remembered it as one of the most miserable days of his young life, and it was no doubt a valuable lesson. A similar experience is described vividly in the poem "Conscience" by Walter Wingate:

> "An' Ah joukit hame frae tree tae tree,
> Fur Ah kent that Ah was whaur Ah sudna be."

Maggie was one of fourteen children and James one of eleven, so by the time they were all married, Dad had more than forty aunts and uncles and innumerable cousins. When our own boys were young, and heard this, their reaction was, "It must have been wonderful on your birthday and at Christmas, Grandad." How my dad laughed and how unbelieving they were, when he told them that there were no presents on either day, except an apple and an orange in your stocking at Christmas, but only as long as you believed in Santa. "Thereafter, nothing!" "What? Nothing?!" He described one Christmas, when his younger brother Harry was still a believer. While he was still asleep, Jim and Wullie removed the orange and apple and substituted two neeps. When he woke up, Harry was initially thrilled by the size of the bulging stocking, only to be bitterly disappointed by Santa's surprise!

The three boys had many chores to complete, even at a young age. One of the more pleasant ones was to walk the three miles to Markinch every Saturday at teatime. The purpose of this long walk was to buy the Saturday evening paper, the *Sporting Post*, and six tea bread. These were buns and cookies, and it was the highlight of the week to enjoy the vicarious thrill of shop-bought goodies instead of homemade, plain fare. Harry was longing to be considered old enough for this important errand, and when the much-anticipated day came, he set out with great enthusiasm. He was very late in returning, and his mother was getting more and more worried that something had happened to him. At last he turned up, looking very shame-faced and clearly in dread of a row. When his mother opened the paper bag of tea bread it was to find only five, and each of those had had a bite removed from it. The temptation had proved too much in the course of the long walk home, and having eaten his own bun, he obviously thought that a bite out of each of the others might not be noticed! I think the family saw the funny side of Harry's misdemeanour, and his only punishment was that he had to wait a bit longer and develop more self-restraint before he was allowed another opportunity to try the tea bread run!

There was a time when the boys were young when they enjoyed briefly the pleasures of motoring. James had bought a Model T Ford and removed the back seats, in order to use it as a pickup to transport two milk churns. I am not sure whether this relieved Nellie of the pony and trap milk delivery, but he sometimes would put the seats back in the car on a Sunday and take the family for a run. On one such occasion, Jim recalled that they had gone quite far afield, perhaps to the area around Dunning in Perthshire. Grandad got rather lost and when they came to a crossroads he could see, at the far side, an old-fashioned signpost in the form of a pointing arm. It was very old and had probably been there since the times of coach travel. Unable to make it out, he sent Jim to read it. My dad could remember it very clearly as reading "London: 442 miles." When he returned to the car and reported this fact, Grandad reacted with horror. "Get back in the car and let's get hame. Shairly we're no near London!" He quickly found his way back to Star and never went touring again. Perhaps James had such a shock that he never dared repeat the experience, and perhaps that was where Dad got his love of cars and of driving. In later life, he owned many cars and there were few parts of Scotland that Joey and Jim did not travel around at one time or another.

Both of my parents were born during the First World War, and, although they had no personal memory of that conflict, they well remembered its aftermath and the losses that were suffered by so many in the course of the "war to end wars," including some in their own family. My dad spoke of his uncle and a cousin who were killed, and after he died and we were looking through his papers, we came across a souvenir Margaret and I had brought to my parents from a school holiday in Paris in 1959. It was a cheap little trinket box and it was closely sealed with sticky tape. When opened, it revealed a number of tiny newspaper cuttings, which I assume were collected by either Auntie Nellie or my granny. Each one is a death notice, in some cases accompanied by a photograph, of a young man killed in the Great War. Some of them were Fife men who were presumably known to the Rutherfords. The roll of honour is as follows:

Private David Ronaldson of the Black Watch, from Burntisland, died of wounds. Private James Brewster of the Black Watch, from Kennoway, was killed in action. Private Robert White of Ballinkirk, Star, died of pneumonia in Salonika. Attached is this moving tribute:

"Sleep on, dear son, in a lonely grave,
A grave we will never see,
As long as life and memory last,
We will remember thee."

Two brothers are listed among the fallen. Private S. Bayne Lawson, a Cameron Highlander from Innerleith, was missing and believed killed, and his brother Private Herriot Bayne Lawson from Methil was killed. He was twenty-six years old and had been at the front for two years and three months and left a widow and three children.

Others were related to Dad's family. One, presumably, was Gunner J. Rutherford from Kennoway, who was killed in action, but I have not been able to determine his exact relationship. A second was the uncle Dad knew of, Lance Corporal Duncan Grant Rutherford. He was the youngest of my grandfather's brothers, and he was married to an Agnes Rodger. He was killed in Cambrai on 30 September 1918, less than two months before the war came to an end. Her tribute to him reads:

"One of the many to answer the call,
For those he loved he gave his all,
Somewhere afar, in a soldier's grave,
Lies my dear husband amongst the brave."

An even sadder footnote to his death was the fate of his only child, a daughter, Margaret, who some time after her father's death in action, developed scarlet fever. This was a notifiable disease and as her mother Agnes could not bear for her to be taken away to the fever hospital, she refused to call a doctor, believing that she could cure her at home. Sadly, her confidence was misplaced and Margaret died within a very short time.

My grandmother lost a nephew, Private Henry Irons of the Black Watch, the firstborn son of her oldest brother John (Jeck) Irons and his wife. His obituary reads:

"In civil life he was employed as a milk salesman with the Dunfermline Co-operative Society Ltd. He was the eldest son of Mr and Mrs John Irons, Coal Road, Dunfermline. He leaves a widow who resides at 115 Baldridgeburn Street, Dunfermline."

Henry's father Jeck was a frequent visitor to Star, where he came to see his sister Maggie and his mother in the last days of her life, and my Dad remembered his uncle well as on old man. We have a photograph which had belonged to Auntie Nellie of him with his young family, and it is so sad to think of the heartbreak that was to come to them with the loss of that lovely boy, young Henry, in the war. In those days they lived in the village of Cairneyhill, the same village I lived in with my family and where our two boys spent their entire childhood. I tried to find where they lived in Cairneyhill and eventually discovered that their house was part of a building that, ironically, was demolished to make way for the war memorial at some time after the Great War. An old man in the village remembered that site as having the name "Irons's Buildings." I recall one Remembrance Day when our son Calum was one of the colour party of Boy Scouts in attendance at that war memorial, thinking how fateful is seemed that there was this link between my family and that of Jeck Irons, and yet we were separated by more than a century and our lives were so entirely different in every way. By the time of the First War Henry was married and living in Dunfermline. His name appears on the Dunfermline War Memorial and we often stop there and think of him.

Dad had sometimes spoken of these two young men, an uncle from his father's side and a cousin from his mother's, who lost their lives in the dreadful waste of the Great War, as he had heard about them from his parents, but I never knew that he had these original newspaper cuttings. It may be that they were saved by his mother or sister without the knowledge of his father, who would not have approved of the sentiment or the emotional involvement implied by their existence. I find it very touching to think of my father at some time after 1959 continuing to save them and sealing them in that little trinket box we had brought from France. What thoughts of his family, and especially of his mother, went through his mind at that moment? I only wish that I had known about them and shared Dad's memories and feelings, but being a man of his generation, perhaps he would have found such a wish an intrusion into some private and precious place in his heart. Rather, I should be content to hope that in some other dimension, he knows that in a special place in my heart I feel for him as a young boy growing into manhood, bereft of his mother's love and without even the slightest sign of affection from his father, and then in his middle age reflecting on these mementoes of past heartbreaks and tragedies.

So Jim and Joey were growing up a few miles from each other, vaguely aware of each other at school in Markinch, although separated by a year. Joey always thought Jim's name was John and if she ever thought of him it was with that name. She left school and went to work in the Balbirnie Wool Mill, and a year later he began to work full time for his father. These were to be difficult years for them both, but there were lightsome moments too. In time they would meet again and the rest, as they say, is history.

## Dear Ancestor

Your tombstone stands among the rest,
neglected and alone. The name
and date are chiselled out,
on polished marble stone.
It reaches out to all who care,
it is too late to mourn.
You did not know that I exist,
you died and I was born.

Yet each of us are cells of you,
In flesh, in blood and bone.
Our blood contracts and beats a pulse,
entirely our own.

Dear Ancestor, the place you filled
one hundred years ago,
spreads out amongst the ones you left
who would have loved you so.
I wonder if you lived and loved,
I wonder if you knew,
that someday I would find this spot,
and come and visit you.

Anon.

EXTRACT ENTRY OF BIRTH: 17 & 18 Victoriæ Cap. 80, § 37.

| (1) Name and Surname. | (2) When and Where Born. | (3) Sex. | (4) Name, Surname, and Rank or Profession of Father. Name, and Maiden Surname of Mother. Date and Place of Marriage. | (5) Signature and Qualification of Informant, and Residence, if out of the House in which the Birth occurred. | (6) When and Where Registered, and Signature of Registrar. |
|---|---|---|---|---|---|
| James Rutherford | 1917. February Eighth. 4h. 45m. A.M. Star, Kennoway. | M. | James Rutherford, Crofter. Margaret Rutherford, M.S. Irons. 1912. November 29th. Buckhaven. | (Signed) James Rutherford. Father. (Present) | 1917. February 20th At Kennoway (Signed) A.H. Rintoul. Registrar. |

XTRACTED from the REGISTER BOOK OF BIRTHS, for the Parish of Kennoway in the unty of Fife, this 20th day of February 1917. A.H. Rintoul. Registrar.

*Jim's birth certificate*

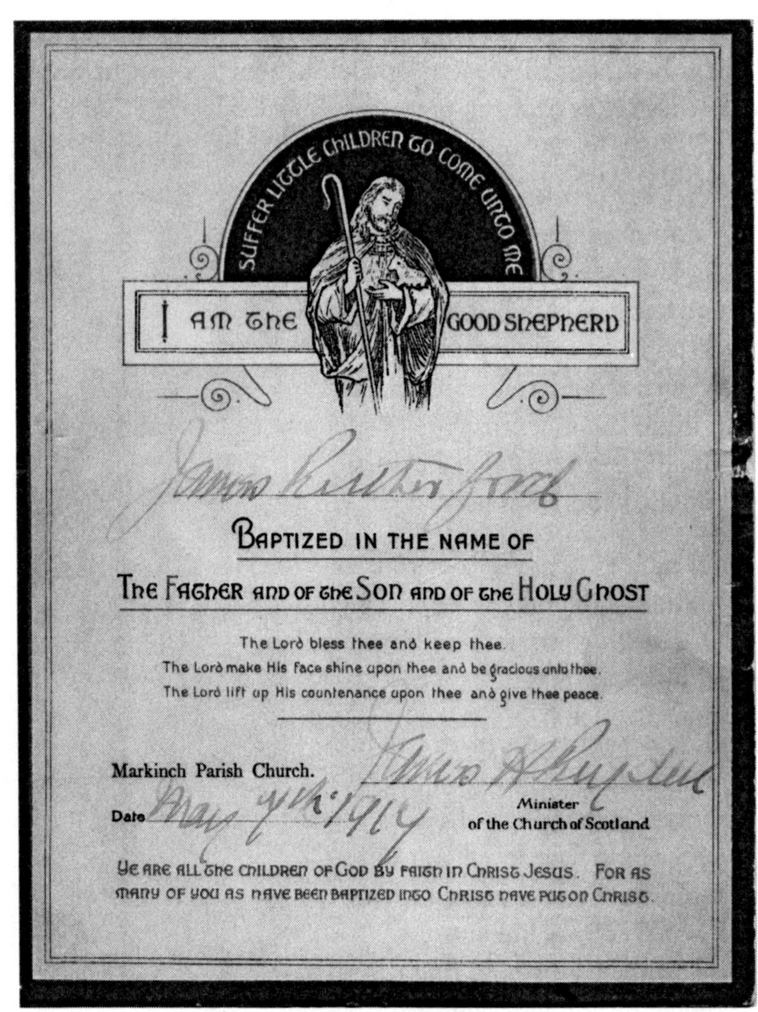
SUFFER LITTLE CHILDREN TO COME UNTO ME

I AM THE GOOD SHEPHERD

James Rutherford

BAPTIZED IN THE NAME OF

THE FATHER AND OF THE SON AND OF THE HOLY GHOST

The Lord bless thee and keep thee.
The Lord make His face shine upon thee and be gracious unto thee.
The Lord lift up His countenance upon thee and give thee peace.

Markinch Parish Church.

Date May 7th 1917

Minister of the Church of Scotland

YE ARE ALL THE CHILDREN OF GOD BY FAITH IN CHRIST JESUS. FOR AS MANY OF YOU AS HAVE BEEN BAPTIZED INTO CHRIST HAVE PUT ON CHRIST.

*Jim's baptismal certificate*

*Maggie Irons, housemaid*

*Maggie's employer and his sons, one of whom was Nellie's father*

*Maggie and Nellie*

*Maggie cutting neeps at the dairy*

*James and his Model T Ford milk delivery vehicle*

*Wullie, Jim, and Harry (Ages 9, 5, and 3 years)*

*Star School—Wullie (back row; aged 9 years), Jim (front row; aged 5 years)*

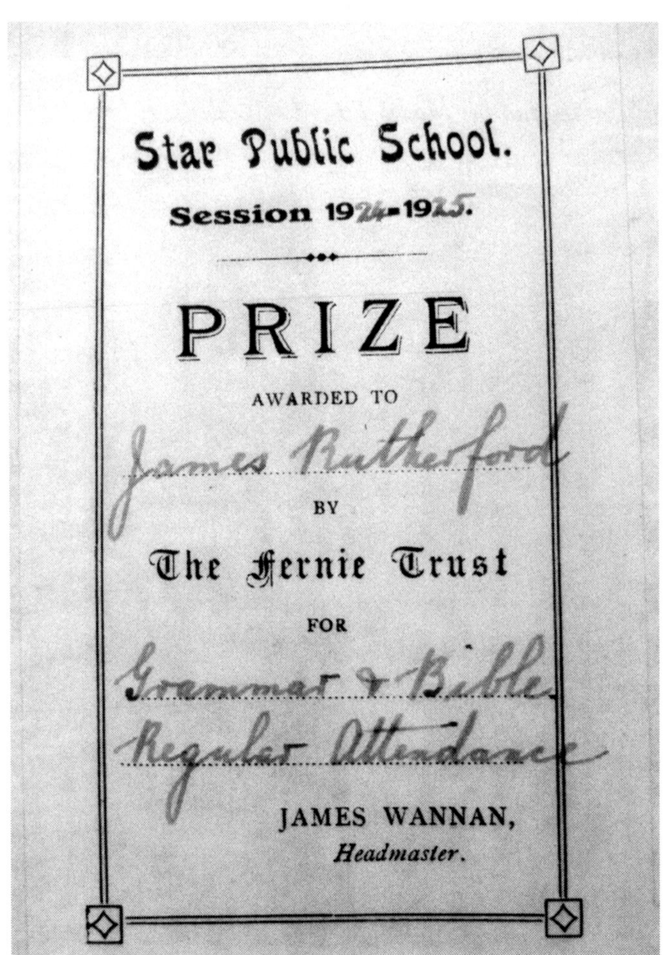

Star Public School.

Session 1924-1925.

PRIZE

AWARDED TO

James Rutherford

BY

The Fernie Trust

FOR

Grammar & Bible

Regular Attendance

JAMES WANNAN,
*Headmaster.*

*Jim's Star School prize, 1925*

*Wullie, Jim, and Harry with Granny Irons (Helen Davie)*

# Day School Certificate (Lower).

The Lords of the Committee of the Privy Council on Education in Scotland have been pleased, in terms of the Day School Code, Article 18 (i) (*b*), to sanction the award of this Certificate by the Education Authority of Fife to James Rutherford a pupil in Markinch Public School, who has successfully completed an approved course of instruction, extending over two years, in an Advanced Division, and in respect of studies, character and conduct has been awarded the general marks :—

(*a*) Studies G.

(*b*) Character and Conduct V.G.

Gregor MacGregor. *Director of Education or other officer of the Education Authority.*

*Date* 4th May 1931. EDUCATION OFFICER.

| Subjects of Study. | Degree of Proficiency. |
| --- | --- |
| English. | G. |
| History. | G. |
| Geography. | G. |
| Mathematics. including arithmetic | G. |
| Arithmetic. | |
| Science | G. |
| Drawing | F.G. |
| Benchwork | F.G. |
| French | F. |

*Head Teacher.*

*Jim's school leaving certificate (14 years old)*

Gnr. J. Rutherford, R.F.A., Kennoway, killed.

L.-Cpl. Adam Arnott, Scots Guards, Dunfermline, killed.

Pte. Henry Irons, Black Watch, Dunfermline, killed.

RUTHERFORD.—Killed in action on 1st Oct., in France, Lance-Corpl. Duncan Rutherford, beloved husband of Agnes Rodger, and youngest son of the late Wm. Rutherford, and of Mrs Rutherford, Starr, Markinch.

One of the many to answer the call,
For those he loved he gave his all;
Somewhere afar in a soldier's grave,
Lies my dear husband amongst the brave.

**DUNFERMLINE.**

Pte. Henry Irons, Black Watch, killed. In civil life he was employed as a milk salesman with the Dunfermline Co-Operative Society, Ltd. He was the eldest son of Mr and Mrs John Irons, Coal Rd., Dunfermline. He leaves a widow, who resides at 115 Baldridgeburn St., Dunfermline.

*Obituaries of Jim's uncle and cousin killed in the Great War, 1914–1918*

*Jim's Uncle John Irons and his family. The older son Henry's obituary is seen above*

# PART 1

# PLOUGHING

# Chapter 5

## "And what do you think you're doing, young man?"

Throughout the nineteenth and for most of the twentieth century, the overwhelming economic and social trend was for increasing industrialisation and urbanisation. Thus, in any family over the course of those generations it should be possible to discern a move away from the farm to the factory and away from the country to the town. This was certainly true for my mother's family, while my father's remained closely associated with the land. Joey's grandfather started his working life as a ploughman in Fife, but spent most of his time working on the railways, firstly in Edinburgh, then in Markinch, apart from his brief abortive spell in the police force! Her father was born into a rural farming community in Drumheglis, Northern Ireland, but moved to Glasgow as a boy, subsequently serving his time in engineering. Where his apprenticeship was, I have no way of knowing, and how he came to be in Fife is no clearer. Was he here only because of the HLI camp in Markinch in 1914–1915 when he met Betsy?

Although I remember my mother mentioning that he had a half-brother who died in the Great War, the only sibling of his that I know of with any certainty was Elizabeth, ten years his junior. She worked in the St Enoch Hotel in Glasgow, one of the British Railway hotel chain, before being transferred to Gleneagles where she met and married a young man from Perth, Tommy Shields. They later moved to live in Falkland, where Tommy found work in the linoleum factory. He suffered a serious industrial injury when he lost an ear, and an old friend of my parents, who also worked there and was qualified in first aid, remembers being sent for and nearly fainting when he saw poor Tommy's severed ear lying in the sink in the medical room!

The socioeconomic trend that saw people move away from the land into urban and industrial surroundings and work is reflected in the working lives of both my maternal great-grandfather and my maternal grandfather. The former worked on the new railway facility, which served John Haig and Sons, while the latter spent most of his career in paper manufacture, the two industries which provided most of the jobs in the Markinch district.

In common with many of her contemporaries, Joey's first job was in the Balbirnie Wool Mill, which was located on the banks of the River Leven between Markinch and Woodside. She would later work nearby at Dixon's paper mill near Preston Hall, where her father Hugh was an engineer. These two and many other mills on the course of the river would use its water power to drive their machinery in the early days, and I can remember, as a child, seeing the remains of disused water wheels and mill lades. Later, as first steam and then oil, gas, and electrical energy were utilised, water was still needed in vast quantities in the manufacture of both wool and paper. Historically, mills lined the course of the Leven from Leslie to Markinch and beyond. The course of the river itself was altered by the digging of "the cut," from where it leaves Loch Leven to the bridging point at Auchmuir, to ensure a necessarily regular flow of water for these industrial processes.

Thus Joey left school on a Friday and started work on the Monday. She had to walk more than a mile and put in a ten-hour shift for five days a week and a five-hour shift on a Saturday. The work was hard and Joey battled often with poor health, especially when she suffered a second bout of rheumatic fever. She and her sister Greta, who started work a year later, often knew what it was like to be hungry and to feel the cold. As children, they remembered going barefoot in the summer, and even in the winter their shoes would often be "letting in." The sisters automatically kept to the insides of the pavements nearest to the walls of the buildings, where the rain didn't reach. Joey could vividly recall vowing to herself that if she was ever lucky enough to have children of her own, they would never know hunger or cold. This was a vow which she kept assiduously as she brought us up; sometimes (it seemed to us as we grew older) to our cost, as keeping us warm and well-clad was more important than the appearance of the clothes, which we didn't always appreciate. Having raised a family of my own, I can now understand completely my mother's drive to look after us well and the lengths to which she went to achieve that purpose. I have no doubt that my own sons often felt that I fussed too much over their well-being. Perhaps it is the same with every generation; my mother had bitter personal experience of physical hardship in her childhood, while my sister Margaret and I can remember children we knew in school who had very little in the way of home comforts. The saddest thing of all is that child neglect and cruelty have not altogether vanished with the so-called affluent society, and indeed in some ways the emotional security of many children may be as lacking as it ever was, in an era of increasing instability in family relationships, albeit in the context of apparent affluence.

Many years later, in the 1990s, my mother was genuinely perplexed to see the then- current fashion amongst young people for blue jeans with tears and holes in them. Although she remembered her granny Hann say, many years before, that if you're not in the fashion, you might as well be dead, she thought it ridiculous that it was actually possible—and that people really did —buy them like that! She knew what it was to have few decent clothes to wear, but had always tried hard not to appear to be poor, whereas her grandsons, who could have lovely clothes to wear, were choosing to dress in rags. Proof perhaps that Hann had been right after all! It was similar in a way to the outrage that my father expressed when, at about the same time, on ordering his meal in a restaurant with us, saw that one of the starters was potato skins. "Dae ye mean to tell me that they're expectin' us tae eat the skins noo?"

In addition to working hard in the mill, Joey and Greta, as the oldest siblings, had to work hard at home. Housework, cooking and looking after their younger brothers and sisters made great demands on their time, and after a year or two, they felt as if they had little or no opportunity to improve their condition. They had to hand over their unopened pay packets to their mother, in exchange for a small amount of pocket money. Eventually, they managed to get Betsy to agree that they should "pay their meat." In other words, they would give Betsy enough money for their food and board, and keep the rest of their wages to look after themselves. In this way, they were able to save a little and could manage to clothe themselves better, and generally have more control over their everyday lives, so hoping to improve their standard of living.

Joey's family was undeniably poor. As she was starting to contribute to the family income at the age of fourteen in 1929, Greta was nearly thirteen and still had one more year at school. Hughie was nine, John five, and Betty only two. The next child, Eunice, had died at a few weeks old the year before, and now Doris was the new baby in the family. In an era when sex education was nonexistent, my mother recalled how she had for a long time assumed that each new baby in the family arrived in the doctor's Gladstone bag!

The Great Depression was at its height, and a secure job was a scarce and precious commodity. It is easy to understand the huge impact one more wage could have on a family budget which was only just managing to maintain the precarious balance between well-being and destitution. There was no social security, no financial safety net apart from the charity of the parish, and beyond that, the threat of the "puirs' hoose" always hovered. Given these circumstances, I have always been greatly impressed by how hard people strove to maintain a semblance of self-sufficiency in making ends meet. In common with so many, my mother had an enormous drive to always keep, above all, her self-respect, no matter how little she had. I think this was a reflection of a general principle which prevailed throughout society, and in her particular case she had absorbed the high moral standards of her granny, Hann Barclay.

There did undoubtedly exist an underclass of people who had inadequate material and personal resources to cope with life's harsh demands. This would lead to, at worst, criminality, or at best, to dependence on charity, but above this group, the vast majority of people subscribed to a general standard of moral decency and financial probity. The extended family was, of course, of enormous support to most, while for many the Church imposed a code of behaviour. Society was much more hierarchical than now. People knew their place and few would, or could, attempt to "get above their station." It is a commonly held belief that the working and middle classes were always more moral in their behaviour than the upper class and the aristocracy. In this sense, perhaps a cynical view would be that the class system succeeded as a means of social and political control over the mass of the population, while those with money and position could do as they pleased!

Whatever the sociological rationale, the outcome was that despite financial struggle and physical hardship, my mother's family, by and large, lived by this generally accepted code of conduct. Honesty was still commonly regarded as the best policy. The threat of a very severe penal code deterred most people from dishonesty, stealing, or worse. In some cases, people who were "sailing close to the wind" would suddenly emigrate, as my mother suspected her Uncle Johnny did.

In terms of sexual morality, marriage was clearly the regulatory convention. While sex before or outside marriage was, of course, a fact of life, and birth control an extremely inexact science, more often than not, young men would do the decent thing by marrying the young woman "in trouble." This must have led to many unhappy marriages in which such couples had to "grin and bear it," as divorce was almost unknown amongst working-class families with limited means, and carried a huge stigma. (The war would bring change in that area as in so many others. My Aunt Betty married a Polish officer who was stationed locally and had a daughter a few months older than me. The marriage was not happy and she divorced him some years later—a fact that was never spoken of in the family, to my knowledge. Her daughter was largely brought up by my grandparents, but I feel she was never a happy girl and clearly felt the stigma of not having a father. Many years later she would trace her father, but I have no way of knowing if that was a happy experience for her or for him.)

Where children were born out of wedlock—either because one parent was already married or where paternity could not be determined—the "nateral bairn" (natural child) was usually brought up as one more sibling, sometimes, sadly, never knowing the truth about his or her parentage. So their real mother purported to be their sister, and their real granny their mother. In large families this could almost go unnoticed, but where the truth was eventually discovered and acknowledged, there must have been great emotional confusion and unhappiness. In the worst-case scenario, illegitimate children might be completely unwanted by the family, and my parents remembered cases of children or young adults who were "boarded out" or fostered with other families, some happily, others less so. An intermediate solution would be adoption, sometimes officially but often unofficially, which would no doubt have equally variable result in terms of personal happiness.

On the face of it, although society seemed to regulate sexual morality quite satisfactorily, nowadays we would be concerned about the effects these solutions would have on the emotional well-being and social adjustment of the adults and children involved. At that time, there was neither the awareness nor the resources to consider the psychological trauma that could be caused by the stigma of illegitimacy or divorce, the uncertainty of paternity, the alienation of children from their natural parents, and the subsequent effects of their perceived rejection. I think of that cousin of my mother's, William Mitchell, who grew up in Fife without knowing his twin, his older brother, or his father in Canada. We now have an awareness of human psychology and child development which might lead us to question the "morality" which prevailed during Joey's young life. But have we really come so far along the road to social cohesion now that sexual freedom, the free availability of contraception, abortion, divorce, and the increasingly accepted variety of sexual preference and lifestyle have led to issues of physical and mental health and well-being unheard of three generations ago?

So as the "roaring twenties" gave way to the "hungry thirties," Joey and Greta were working in the paper mill and striving at home to improve the family's standard of living. They had moved from Mitchell Place near the top of the High Street to a new house in Queen's Crescent. This was part of a new development, the first social/public housing scheme to be built in Markinch, a result of the 1924 Housing Act, and represented an enormous improvement in living conditions. They had three bedrooms, one for the boys, one for the girls, and one for Betsy and Hugh. The house had a kitchen (living room), a scullery (kitchen) and a bathroom—indoor plumbing for the first time! They would subsequently move again to another new house at 83 Croft Crescent—with four bedrooms this time—in a newer council scheme at the west end of the town.

Betsy welcomed the help from her two eldest daughters in running the house and caring for the younger children. She herself had grown up as the spoiled youngest child in her family, and had never really adjusted to the demands of being a housewife and mother, and after the death of her own mother Hann in 1934, came to rely more and more on her girls. Hugh, perhaps initially an unwilling young husband and father, exercised a high degree of self-interest and was never really a committed family man. Joey and Greta knew that he "played away from home" after they were informed by children at school that they had a half-sister in another village. What must their thoughts and feelings have been then? How did they make sense of that revelation? This is another example of the hard knocks that came the way of children in an era when they were expected to be "seen and not heard," and when their emotional welfare was so often ignored. When they later worked at the same mill as their father did, they became aware of the fact that, although Hugh was known to be a very good engineer and a very hard worker, he also had the reputation as the "boss's man." He would never be party to any collective action by the workers in making representation of any of their concerns to their employer. I certainly remember my grandfather being very well-spoken and having something of a patrician air about him. He impressed strangers as being a "real gentleman," which did not always sit well with his personal standards of behaviour, as they were known to his close family.

Some years after he retired from Dixon's mill, he was visited one day by one of the managers, who asked Hugh for his help. They had acquired a new bag-making machine from Germany and it was defying all attempts to get it working properly. Would Hugh come to the mill and see if he could help? My grandfather complied with this request and, in a few days, he had solved their problem. He was rightly proud of this achievement and of the fact that his reputation as an engineer had been vindicated, but there was no question of him having any remuneration from Dixon's for his efforts. He was horrified when Betsy suggested that he should have been paid for his work. It says everything about the characters of my grandparents that for one, the pride in the achievement of a job well done was enough, while for the other, more practical recognition in the form of hard cash would have been more appreciated. I have sympathy for both points of view in this case, but if I had to choose, I am afraid that I would, as my mother did, tend to side with Betsy, as the burden of making ends meet always fell on her shoulders—after, that is, Hugh had kept his pocket money before giving her the rest of his wage.

Hugh was, in common with most fathers at that time, a strict disciplinarian, and would often resort to physical punishment of his children. Betsy and Hugh did not have a happy marriage, and this inevitably impinged on the family. Betsy suffered from occasional seizures which were assumed to be epileptic in nature, but my mother came to believe that they were a psychosomatic response to stress and deep frustration, as they always happened when she was lashing out in a temper tantrum, usually re-directed at one or another of the children. Perhaps Hugh felt that he had been trapped into marriage; he had been heard to declare that Joey was not in fact his child. However, anyone who knew them in later life would easily see the clear physical resemblance between Joey and her father. Despite these difficulties in their early relationship, they became very close in later life, and it was Joey who did most for her parents in their old age. This was welcomed and appreciated by Hugh, and speaks volumes for Joey's patient nature that she was able to forgive the harsh treatment meted out to her by Hugh when she was young. In later years, Betsy accepted Joey's help also, but more reluctantly and often with poor grace; an example, perhaps, of role reversal, where Gran took the part of the petulant and recalcitrant child, and Mum became the caring parent, humouring and coaxing the unwilling offspring.

With their very tight budget, Joey and Greta could not afford to buy clothes, and soon learned to make their own dresses. Girls then learned to sew, knit, and crochet from their mothers, grandmothers, and other older members of their family, just as they were trained in other domestic skills such as cooking, cleaning, and washing. My sister Margaret and I also learned all these skills, mostly at home and some at school, because in those days, society at large and families in particular were anxious that girls should be equipped to become wives and mothers. In a similar way, boys learned practical skills like gardening and woodwork at home; they were also part of the school curriculum, even in the 1950s and '60s, when girls did domestic science and boys learned technical subjects and gardening. Every school had a garden and often had a little furnished flat where girls could practise homecraft skills. In my early childhood, as in most families, there was a set of cobbler's lasts, and our mother would hammer seggs into the heels and toes of our school shoes to make them last longer. Margaret hated this as it made your footsteps very loud and your approach very conspicuous. So as we waited for the school bus in the morning, she would knock the seggs out with a stone but always to no avail, as Mum would repeat the cobbling operation as often as necessary!

Thus most people were engaged in a wide variety of activities, which illustrated the continuing links with a self-sufficient and more rural way of life which persisted long after they had left the land and became town dwellers. But it was also indicative of economic necessity, when making your own clothes, cooking meals daily from fresh ingredients, and growing much of your own food was much more affordable than buying everything ready-made. So we grew up learning how to make soup, preserve fruit and vegetables, bake, knit, sew, and mend clothes. Nowadays it hardly makes economic sense, when we live in a global market based on the principle of division of labour and it is often more expensive to "do it yourself" when raw materials are expensive to buy. Nevertheless, I believe that we have lost an important link with the land, even to the extent that many children have now no real understanding of the origin of the food they eat. Also, as practical skills are lost, with no hope of their being passed on from generation to generation, we have also lost the sense of achievement and creativity which they fostered. The day may come when these skills are really needed in a post-industrial world where we can no longer count indefinitely on the global market to supply all our needs.

Although most of their time was accounted for by work either at home or at the mill, Joey and Greta had some leisure time. They had been in the habit of visiting their aunt and uncle, Kate and Jock Webster, at Woodside. They had five cousins there, Johann the eldest girl who had started work the same day as Joey, her two older brothers Charlie and Jack, and two younger sisters Grace and Cathy. With their workmates and cousins, Joey and Greta began to spread their wings and started to go dancing. The local villages and small towns all had halls where dances would be held regularly on Fridays and Saturdays. Thonrton, Kirkton of Fues, Leslie, and Falkland were the usual venues and less frequently and further away, Gallatown (Kirkcaldy) and Cupar. They knew that their father would not allow them to go to these dances, because he had a very puritanical attitude to many forms of entertainment. Having been brought up in a very strict Protestant culture in Ulster, he also had strong sectarian attitudes where religion was concerned, although he had little or no religious faith himself. He would not allow playing cards in the house, and would not use or tolerate bad language or blue jokes. This strict ethos did not, of course, extend to his own personal conduct, but he was in no way unique in being something of a hypocrite in this regard. A typical case of "Do as I say, not as I do!"

As their mother Betsy and their Aunt Kate had a more flexible attitude to the girls' social activities, they complied in a subterfuge to allow them to the dancing. They told Hugh that they were going to visit the Websters at Woodside. Of course they could not wear their dance dresses, so they packed their glad rags in a bag and persuaded their young brother John to lower it to them out of the staircase window. They would then change at a friend's house, or at Woodside, and then repeat the exercise in reverse on returning home, when the bag would be secreted outside in the garden until it was safe to retrieve it. This plan worked quite successfully for some time, but of course they knew they could never stay out too late, as their father was always waiting up for them. Greta, being much more timid then Joey, was always in a dreadful state of nerves on the way home, in case they would be found out, and would often suffer terrible bouts of diarrhoea as a result. She was on the point of giving up on dancing, as she felt it was more trouble than it was worth, when one evening they were caught red-handed. As John was lowering the bag out of the window, he heard the words behind him, "And what do you think you're doing, young man?" Hugh was standing there, and the cat (and the dance dresses) was well and truly out of the bag!

Joey stood her ground, however, and insisted that she and her sister would go dancing. She assured Hugh that they would not let the family down and that they would behave with propriety. He must have been impressed with Joey's forthright stand; from that time on they began to enjoy more freedom. They later learned that their Aunt Kate had intervened on their behalf by telling Hugh that his daughters were well thought of and that their reputations were safe. She warned him that by insisting on denying the girls their freedom, they were more likely to stray from the straight and narrow in defiance of him. Hugh must have seen sense in this view and as a result, Joey and Greta were able to lead a much more satisfactory social life. It was during some of these evenings at the dancing that Joey met Jim and later, Greta met her future husband Bobby.

As their social life looked up and they became more skilled as dressmakers, they were able to be more ambitious in their choice of style and fabric. They aspired to dresses made of crêpe de chine, blue for Greta and pink for Joey. This fabric was more expensive and sophisticated than their usual choice, but it creased very easily. However, they wore the new dresses once or twice to the dancing and they stood up quite well. They were invited to go to the pictures in Kirkcaldy by two young men they had met at the dancing. It was the first time they had actually gone on a date, but felt that they would be safe in a foursome. That was their first mistake; the second was the decision to wear the crêpe de chine dresses. In the event, they both had a dreadful time and each had a terrific tussle with their respective dates in the cinema, struggling to defend their virtue. The hemlines and necklines of their dresses were under siege and when they eventually made their escape from the pictures, their reputations were still intact, but they looked as if they had been pulled through a hedge backwards. The dresses had a million creases and they had to sit through a very embarrassing bus journey back to Markinch, enduring the stares of the other passengers!

During one of the slumps in the economic cycle in the 1930s Dixon's mill put some of their workers on short time, which had a drastic effect on Joey's income. She showed typical initiative in making good this shortfall, by advertising her skills as an interior decorator. She had learned how to wallpaper and paint, and for the princely sum of £1, she would decorate a room. This involved distempering the ceiling (no emulsion paint then!), putting up the wallpaper (sometimes with decorative corners and/or borders), and gloss-painting the woodwork. Even now, when young people are often encouraged to consider setting up their own business, this would seem to be a very enterprising move by a young woman who had no family example to follow or encouragement to spread her wings.

When the family moved into 83 Croft Crescent, in the early days of the Second World War, the new house had a large garden. It was about that time that Betsy's brother Wullie came to stay with my grandparents. He had owned a nursery in Alloa, but sadly the business had gone to the wall, helped in no small way by his fondness for the bottle. I don't remember if he had been widowed or if his wife had given up on him, but he was alone and virtually homeless, so he came to live in Markinch. He brought his time and his horticultural skills to bear on the garden, and soon had made a vegetable plot at the back (Dig for Victory!) and created a beautiful terraced rockery full of a lovely selection of plants at the front. There was a rose-covered arch over the garden path as it approached the front door, and there was a series of meandering paths through the rockery. The garden was a talking point in the town, and Uncle Wullie certainly paid his way as a lodger. This was to be the family home until the early 1950s, when Betsy and Hugh made their final move to a smaller house further round the crescent after all the children but Doris and James had left home.

I remember when I was very small, playing with my sister and cousins in the rockery. The large rocks were the school desks when we played "schoolies," and the dried astilbe flower heads would be crumpled to make "brown sugar" when we played "shoppies." Similarly, small details of the house come to mind. Gran used a gas poker to light the coal fire in the kitchen (living room). There was an inner glass door in the hall, with small panes of bevelled glass, which produced brightly coloured squares on the hall linoleum. The light switch in the scullery (kitchen) had a brass cover and inside it, the bakelite lever which operated the switch was cracked. Sometimes when you operated the switch, you got a slight electric shock. This used to give us a vicarious thrill; no one ever seemed concerned that it might be dangerous! Years later I remember Grandad would impress us by being able to hold on to the electric fence in the field at Pitkinny without ever getting a shock, so perhaps that was why he was never aware of the faulty switch in his house at number 83! When I consider this house it seems that it was a very substantial, spacious, and quite well-appointed home, albeit a council house, but built to a very high standard, especially when compared to the much more poorly constructed public housing of the 1960s and 70s, when budget restraints in local councils determined a much poorer build quality, as illustrated by some of the housing in the New Town of Glenrothes, which was built much later than Croft Crescent.

It was in that house that I had my first encounter with Santa Claus. I must have been about four or five years old and we were at our grandparents' around Christmas with some of our aunts and uncles and cousins, when all of a sudden the Great Man unexpectedly arrived. We were all completely terrified. My cousin Jim Drennan tried to disappear up the front of his Dad's pullover, Margaret slid down off her chair to hide under the table, and I (as was my habit, being a bit of a cry-baby or "torn-face") promptly burst into tears! Santa, it turned out, was Betsy, who unknown to anyone had borrowed a Santa suit, complete with beard and whiskers. Although we continued to believe in Santa for a long time afterwards, what really frightened me about this apparition in red was that Gran was wearing her dentures in honour of the occasion. I was transfixed by these awful, big, white, sparkling teeth, and even if I had known it was Gran, I would still have been terrified. She hardly ever wore her teeth, except for weddings and funerals (and Santa impersonations!), and when she did, she wasn't like our Gran at all. So the family all discouraged her from this vanity, and she did it less and less as the years passed.

Betsy had an aunt, Hann's sister, known to the family as Granny Irvine, who lived in Daisy Street in Glasgow. (Greta was actually born there in February 1917, but I don't know what circumstances led to that.) Very occasionally, as the years passed and scarce funds would allow, an expedition to visit her would be undertaken by Betsy, and once Mum remembered going there with Greta. Glasgow, even when I was young, always seemed like the other side of the moon to us. It was somehow an alien location, and the people there seemed to be very exotic and exciting but, in some undefined way, rather dangerous. Dad used to sing a song "The Big Kilmarnock Bunnet," which included the line "stravaigin' through the muckle streets o' Glesca." Perhaps that was what gave the city a metropolitan atmosphere on our rare visits there when we were children; an air that Edinburgh, much more familiar to us, never had. Certainly the streets in Glasgow were very wide and somewhat intimidating and, we were led to believe, full of "keelies," whatever they were! Even when I did my postgraduate teaching year in Glasgow in the late 1960s, I still had a rather nervous and uncertain approach to living there, so it is understandable that Joey and Greta were both quite overwhelmed by the experience of visiting their extended family there a generation earlier. One of Granny Irvine's grandsons, John, came to stay once with Betsy and her family; he was equally unsure of this strange and alien place, Markinch. The two sets of cousins were very conscious of their mutually strange accents, and soon realised that in fact not only did John speak with a different rhythm and intonation, but seemed to speak almost a different language entirely, using different words for familiar things! The first evening, having set the table in the kitchen, Betsy realised that she had forgotten to bring the milk. She asked John to fetch it, and when he asked her where it was, she told him he would find it in the scullery. He went to get it but after a long time came back to say that he couldn't find it. When Betsy took him into the scullery and pointed to the milk jug on the table, he said in astonishment, "But in Glesca' we ca' that a joog, no a scullery!"

Another amusing incident happened when Uncle Wullie first came to stay with Betsy and Hugh. As explained earlier, he'd had an unhappy time, losing his battle with the bottle and shortly afterwards, as a consequence, his business and his wife. His health was not good, and Betsy was concerned about him. He decided to go out for a walk one cold and dark evening, and his sister made sure he was well wrapped up, with his hat pulled well down over his ears and a big muffler wrapped round his neck. I suspect that he was making for the pub, but whether or not that had occurred to Betsy, I don't know. After a long time when he hadn't returned, she was getting very worried when a knock at the door revealed what had happened. It was the police, with a very annoyed Uncle Wullie in tow! It was the very early days of the war and the Home Guard, recently formed and very enthusiastic, had arrested him as a suspected fifth columnist. As he was a stranger to Markinch, they of course didn't recognise him and when they challenged him, "Halt! Who goes there?" as they had been trained to do, he didn't take them seriously, so they arrested him as a suspicious character and took him to the police station. There he explained who he was, but they had to bring him to the house and ask Betsy and Hugh to vouch for him. What an introduction to his new home town! On a more serious note, he was actually lucky that he survived the incident unscathed. It was only shortly after, in the north of Fife, where a home guardsman actually shot and killed a challenged suspect who did not immediately halt and tell him who went there!

As the "phoney war" of the first few months of conflict gave way to the full fury of the German blitzkreig on the Low Countries and Belgium, and the fall of France and the Dunkirk evacuation brought the desperate fear that Hughie might not survive, Joey could remember the dawning realisation that the war was not confined to other countries, as the first air raids were visited on Scotland. She remembered holding her young brother James in her arms as the family sheltered in the hallway of their home, which, having no windows, was the safest place in the absence of any actual air raid shelter. As she cringed under the coats hanging on the wall, listening to the unmistakable drone of the enemy planes, and comforted her wee brother, she must have wondered what the future held for them all.

So Joey, a young woman in her early twenties, working hard to improve her lot in life, one evening at the dancing met a young man she had not seen since their school days. She remembered him as John Rutherford, but learned that his name was actually Jim. He was fifteen months younger than she, having been in the year below her at school, and Joey was not thinking in terms of settling down. But sometimes Fate takes a hand in our lives when we least expect it. War was looming and the future was very uncertain for everyone, and perhaps at times like that there is an imperative to get on with living and affirming life. In choosing a life partner, it is not only a question of finding the right person, but of finding him or her at the right time. For Joey, I think the time was right.

*Back row, left to right, Joey, her cousin Johann Webster*
*Front row, left to right, Greta, their Uncle Jim from Canada, and their cousin Grace Webster*

*Joey and Greta with workmates on a mill outing*

*Joey's Uncle Wullie with her brother John, aged 15 years, and James, aged 3 years, at 83 Croft Crescent, Markinch*

*Joey and her friend Jean Watson*

*Queen's Crescent home in the late 1920s*

# FIFE EDUCATION AUTHORITY.

## RECORD OF WORK CERTIFICATE.

IT is hereby certified that Johan Mitchell having passed the Qualifying Examination at Markinch 1928, was enrolled as a Pupil in the Advanced Division of Markinch Public School, followed the Domestic Course for a period of 1 years 9 months, and left School on January 1930.

During that time his/her General Proficiency in the work of the Course was G.

The following statement shows the standard of proficiency attained in the several subjects of the Course undertaken :—

| SUBJECTS. | Average Marks. |
|---|---|
| English (including History and Geography), | G. |
| Arithmetic, | G. |
| Mathematics, | |
| Art, | G. |
| Practical Science, | G. |
| Technical Drawing, | |
| Benchwork, | |
| | |
| French, | |
| | |
| Commercial Subjects—Book-Keeping, | |
| Shorthand, | |
| Domestic Subjects—Cookery and Laundry, | G+ |
| Housewifery, | |
| Needlework, | V.G. |
| Music, | G. |
| Hand-Writing, | G. |

J. Starns Head Teacher.

IN NAME OF THE EDUCATION AUTHORITY,

GREGOR MACGREGOR,
*Director of Education and Executive Officer.*

NOTE.—The "Record of Work" Certificate does not replace the Day School Certificate, which constitutes the main end of attainment for pupils in an Advanced Division Course.

This Certificate should be used as a passport to the Preparatory Classes of the Continuation School, and as evidence to employers of the state of advancement in an Advanced Division of scholars when freed from the obligation to attend Day School.

*Joey's school leaving certificate, aged 14 years*

# Chapter 6

"Tell yer faither Ah'll pey 'im the morn."

When Jim left school, he followed his older brother Wullie into working for their father. He became a ploughman, working the land that came with their tenancy of Broomfield Farm. I never asked my father if he had any other ambition. Even if he had, it would probably have been pointless to consider it. While Joey's parents were anxious for the small addition to the family income which she could earn, Jim's father was equally desperate for the extra labour his second son could contribute.

Dad worked long hours on the land, tilling Broomfield's arable acres with Wullie and his father, while his mother and Nellie concentrated on the work of the dairy. Dad handled the two Clydesdale horses as they pulled the plough and other implements. It was hard work in all kinds of weather. The horses had to be fed, watered, and groomed every morning before he himself could have his breakfast, and likewise at the end of the day's work, before he could consider his labour over for the day. The days in the field were as long as the daylight lasted: preparation of the ground and the sowing and planting of the crops filled the lengthening days from spring into summer. High summer saw the climax of the harvest of the hay and later the grain. As the days began to grow shorter, threshing of the grain and the potato harvest would be followed by ploughing and the harvesting of the turnips, which would persist well into the early winter. Although, as the twentieth century reached its third decade, mechanisation of some agricultural activities was developing, little of this was to be found at Broomfield, as my grandfather was very reluctant to contemplate the necessary expense which investment in machinery would involve.

So in the dairy, the cows were still milked by hand in the byre, and the heavy milk churns manhandled (or rather, woman-handled) into the dairy, the milk poured through the cooler and into the churns again, to await delivery to the various customers. Hand broadcasting of the seed was still done, although some sowing was done by the seed-drill, pulled by the horses. Hay was mown by a horse-drawn mower and piled by hand into ricks, tied by ropes weighed down by heavy stones. Potatoes were entirely planted and lifted by hand, back-breaking work, but the oats, barley, and wheat were harvested by the horse-drawn binder which could now also tie the sheaves. However, they still had to be stooked in groups in the fields to dry and completely ripen, and then had to be manhandled by pitchforks onto trailers and transported into the stackyard, where they were built into stacks until threshing time. Turnips had to be lifted and shawed by hand in the fields using sickles, and then loaded onto trailers, a job often done in cold and wet weather. The fodder crops such as turnips and hay were grown to feed the cattle in the winter when they were kept indoors, while barley was sold to the whisky industry and potatoes, a staple food for both animals and humans alike, sold locally. The oats went to the porridge oats factory at Cupar, and some sugar beet was grown for the sugar refining plant, also in the county town. The milk produced at the dairy was driven to the Buckhaven Co-operative Society shop and to the Cameron Bridge distillery, in the early days by pony and trap by Aunt Nellie and later by model T Ford by Grandad.

Milking was done twice a day, usually starting between three and four in the morning and again at the same time in the afternoon. In the winter, the cows were in the byre all the time, so mucking out took a lot of time, whereas in the summer the cows had to be brought in from the fields. The beasts knew their place and would always go to their own stall in the byre. As with the Clydesdales, the welfare of the animals was of paramount importance, and in some ways seemed to matter more to my grandfather than the well-being of his own family. It has always been interesting to me that the working day was referred to in terms of the animals as well. For example, the start of the working day was "yoking time." This was related to the operation of putting the yoke on the horse, while the end of the working day was known as "lousing time," which referred to the loosening or unharnessing of the horse. The care of the horses and their equipment was central to the work of the farm, and involved many and varied chores in the stable. So even when bad weather and the long hours of winter darkness limited the outdoor work, there was still plenty to keep everyone occupied, and the animals still had to be fed and milked twice a day, all of this done by the light of paraffin-fuelled tilly and hurricane lamps. Electricity was still decades away. When at last we were connected to the electricity supply in 1953, I remember Dad remarking that he had spent the first half of his life in the cold and the dark and he was determined to make up for it! In fact I can never remember Dad nagging us about wasting electricity, because he never begrudged its cost, having known what it was like not to have it. There came a time, however, in the early 1960s, when there was to be another reason for Dad's profligacy, but that is another story for another time.

It is easy to see why spare time was an unknown concept in the life of a ploughman, and the unsocial hours of a dairyman meant that when Jim and Wullie, and then a couple of years later, Harry, were not working or eating, they were sleeping. They received no wage from their father, only their keep and pocket money of half a crown on a Saturday. Jim never considered himself to be a real "horsey man," whereas Wullie was naturally inclined to working with the big patient Clydesdales. Jim's memories of his early days as a ploughman, of endless hours spent trudging behind the plough with nothing to look at but "twa big horses' erses," were not happy ones. I find myself wondering what his thoughts were in those days. I can be sure of one thing. He longed to be master of his own fate. He never succumbed graciously to being at the beck and call of his father, and didn't see eye to eye with him on anything, whereas Wullie and Harry seemed much more content to do their father's bidding. To that extent Dad was, in his father's eyes, the black sheep of the family, and was to turn out to be the prodigal son. But only to a limited extent, because once he broke away on his own he made a success of his life, and there was certainly never a joyous return or a killing of the fatted calf!

Jim was to become in time a very innovative and successful farmer and businessman, but I don't think he owed any of his business acumen to genetic inheritance. A rare early opportunity to indulge his entrepreneurial instincts came when an old man in the village asked Jim for a "bag o' tatties." Dad promised to deliver one to him after teatime, in the hope that he would get the money for it without anyone, especially his father, being any the wiser. Normally Dad would have hefted the one-hundredweight bag onto his back but, it still being daylight, he knew he would be seen from the house. So he had an enormous struggle to crouch beneath the level of the garden wall, dragging the heavy contraband on the ground until it was safe to lift it onto his back. Having succeeded in delivering the tatties, he was dumbfounded to hear the old man say, "That's awfu' guid o' ye Jimmy. Tell yer faither Ah'll pey 'im the morn." Not only did Jim not get his expected reward for all his trouble, he would have to explain to his father why he hadn't told him about the request for the tatties in the first place!

While Maggie, James, and Nellie lived in the dairy house at the west end of Star, the three boys "bothied," or looked after themselves, in the farmhouse at Broomfield about half a mile away. They slept there and saw to their own breakfast and supper, but would have their main meals prepared by their mother at the dairy house. The three young brothers must have had some happy times there when some of their pals from the village would join them, albeit in the very limited free time they had. Wullie learned to play the pipes and Harry would play tunes on the melodion, while Jim started to learn and sing the songs that would build over the years into a large and varied repertoire. Learning long tracts of epic poems and Bible passages by heart was an integral part of the school and Sunday school curriculum, and as a schoolboy Jim was very adept at this and, more to the point, enjoyed it. Even as an old man, he could remember the words of all the songs he knew and could even recite whole poems, such as "The Boy Stood on the Burning Deck" and "The Burial of Sir John Moore." Less edifying was the pornographic version of the latter, which he would occasionally begin after he had had a few too many "bold John Barleycorns." As to the content of this particular rendition, I couldn't pass comment, as my mother never let him get past the first verse! His father's brother Wull had gone to work as a farm manager in Yorkshire, and he and his daughter Margaret would write to Jim from time to time. He seems to have been a self-educated man who enjoyed poetry and literature in general. He took an interest in his nephew Jim, and once sent him the poem "The Howe o' the Mearns" which he, or perhaps Margaret, had copied in a beautiful copperplate hand. Jim was fond of his uncle and cousin, and I am sure they represented a glimmer of light and affection which he so badly missed during his mother's long illness, and even more so after she died.

Living conditions at the dairy and Broomfield were fairly primitive, even by the standards of the time, with no running water or inside sanitation. Water was pumped from the outside well and ablutions were of necessity very basic and rudimentary. The family was reasonably well fed in quantity and quality, and Jim did not remember being hungry in the same way as Joey did. Country folk could always count on an assured and plentiful supply of home-grown food, and were able to fill up on staple carbohydrates like potatoes and porridge, although the protein-rich foods like milk, eggs, and meat would be less available to the family, as they represented a valuable source of cash income. If Jim was quite well fed there were few home comforts, with little or no attention paid to the physical or emotional well-being of the family. This situation was exacerbated by Maggie's deteriorating health, and James's correspondingly increased dominance over his children.

The death of a mother must always be a devastating blow to a family, and so it was with Maggie's untimely passing at the age of only fifty-seven. She must have had some comfort from the fact that, despite her failing strength over many years, she had at least seen her boys grown up. I am fairly sure that the deepest emotional impact of her death was felt by Jim, because he was, of the three boys, the most sensitive and the one most like his mother. He remembered very clearly how his father refused to grant his wife's dying wish to be buried beside her parents in Auchtertool. He later admitted to Joey that, as a result, he had a rather jaundiced attitude to marriage and family life: his only role model as a husband was his father. Although this may always be the case, in other families there may well be the leavening effect of the example of other men. In Jim's case, his father's personality did not encourage familial and social relationships, and consequently the family led a somewhat isolated life, devoid of much in the way of social graces and interpersonal skills. It is probably only due to his mother's influence that Jim had the opportunity to grow up to be a popular and socially well-adjusted adult.

The trauma of his mother's death and his father's reaction to it, coupled with the lack of parental affection and approval over many years, certainly affected Jim in his adult life and relationships. On the one hand, he was extremely affable and friendly, hospitable, generous, and gregarious, but on the other, he could be very short-tempered and volatile; as is so often the way, these traits were most often experienced by those who were nearest and dearest to him. He was inclined to put his own needs first, before those of his immediate family, which often competed with his freedom of action and his desire to escape from the daily grind and the responsibilities of running a business. To Dad, these often appeared in the form of a whisky bottle and the attraction and approbation of his drinking friends. So there were times when he would return late from the cattle markets, or when the curling matches would be a mere excuse for a prolonged session at the bar.

Jim's sister Nellie told Joey before they were married that as a youngster Jim was inclined to suffer from "nervous debility." Perhaps this was due to some emotional frailty as a child, which must have been exacerbated by the harshness of his upbringing. As a consequence, a lack of self-esteem may well have found expression in a craving for approval and affection from friends and acquaintances rather than in seeking them from a close and loving family. As with many men of his generation and, given his early experiences, perhaps more than most, he grew up believing that the function and status of women derived from their relationship to, and duties towards, the men of their family. When his mother died, Aunt Nellie fulfilled that function; then he looked to Joey to look after him. He expected the women in his life to satisfy his physical needs but in terms of emotional fulfilment, he found that with his friends.

Many years later, I believe that Dad came subconsciously to realise that, and as a consequence he developed close, warm, and more demonstrative ties with his two sons-in-law and his three granddaughters and two grandsons. This was true to a lesser extent of his relationship with my sister and me, but for us it came rather late in the day and I regret that I did not have a closer bond with him when I was young. Having said that, our experience of fathering, while infinitely more rewarding than the one Jim had with his father, was still of a more remote paternal figure than the closely involved relationship our sons have with Bill. To a large extent, this can be explained in generational terms, but in addition to that, there is the specific nature of my parents' relationship as it impinged on my consciousness while I was growing up. I was quite aware, from a fairly young age, of the hurt and disappointment which Jim would often cause Joey, most often in the context of his drinking. As I became more aware, I could understand the effect of his childhood as the source of his selfishness, and could forgive his shortcomings and rationalise his behaviour. It was much harder for Mum to accept his failings. She found this to be increasingly difficult as she grew older, given her own very high standard of behaviour, perhaps because she came to realise that in all probability he would never change. Equally, she refused to compromise her ideals, and as a consequence my parents had a somewhat stormy and occasionally highly volatile relationship. Not in the early days of their marriage, of course, but over time, as Joey began to assert herself more and more, and to increasingly question Jim's right to put himself and his needs before hers and her daughters'.

Having said that, Joey and Jim also had many happy times together and I believe that fundamentally they cared deeply about each other. They always had a very open door to many people—some who had been close friends since their childhood and youth, others who became friends in the course of their adult lives, and some only in their last few years. They never lost the knack of making friends, and they were very well liked. They both had the gift of a sense of humour, and there was much laughter, even when—to all intents and purposes—there wasn't much to laugh about! They could always see the funny side of things, and some of my happiest memories as a child are of the times when, after we were in bed, we would hear Mum and Dad laughing uproariously together. There were other times, of course, when voices raised in anger would give rise to other, less happy memories, but one invaluable lesson we learned was that you keep trying, even when things are hard. You don't just give up on each other. One feeling there never was between Jim and Joey was indifference; in fact, I used to think there was too much emotion. They may have had their bad times, but they were balanced by the good times. They really lived and they really interacted, not only with each other but with other people, in such a way that I know they are remembered with affection by many people who came into contact with them over the years. I can safely assert that no one who ever came to Pitkinny left feeling depressed or bored. There were certainly some who left with a flea in their ear, because neither of my parents would suffer fools gladly, or others who were glad to get away, with Jim's curses ringing in their ears. (Very often these were unwanted commercial travellers, who wasted his time.) Many drove along the loan still chuckling or laughing out loud over some story or other, but invariably they had all been stimulated, cheered, or entertained to some degree!

As the autumn of 1938 passed and the family tried to adjust to the loss of their mother, on the wider world stage the Munich Crisis of September gave way to an uneasy "peace for our time" settlement of the international situation, which could only postpone the inevitable descent into world war. Jim's world must have seemed insecure and lonelier than ever, and it is perhaps no coincidence that he and his brothers all joined the Church of Scotland two months after Maggie's death. At whose instigation this rite of passage was embarked upon, I don't know, but having been baptised as babies, the boys became full communicant members of St. Drostan's Church in Markinch in October 1938. The only reference I can remember Dad making to this event was an irreverent description of how Wullie tripped spectacularly while mounting the steps in front of the communion table on his way to shake hands with the assembled kirk elders, and landed his full length in front of the minister!

War was declared on 3 September 1939 and, five months later, while the country was still in the "phoney war" stage, Jim received his call-up papers. For some reason, despite being in a reserved occupation, he still went in front of the Kirkcaldy Medical Board of 10 February 1940, two days after his twenty-third birthday. In the course of the following interview he mentioned that he could drive. When he passed Grade 1, as fit for service, he was told he could expect to be drafted straightaway and posted to the south coast of England, where the army was desperate for drivers. When he was asked in the passing how he had learned to drive, still a rather unusual accomplishment for young men, he said he had always driven on the farm. At that the officer in charge looked very disappointed and asked how Jim didn't know that he was a reserved occupation, that he should never have reached that stage of the selection procedure at all, and that he could not be compulsorily conscripted. He hopefully also pointed out to Jim that he could, of course, volunteer! Jim would be the first to admit that he had a very well-developed sense of self-preservation, and it took him no time at all to decide to decline that particular invitation. To be fair, by then he had met Joey and had a clear idea what his intentions towards her were likely to be. He was realistic enough to realise that he should be grateful for an honourable way to avoid active service, unlike most young men, who had no choice but to "take the king's shilling."

He had, of course, to join the Civil Defence Force, commonly known as the Home Guard. This really was, in my case, "Dad's army," and Jim did his bit by turning up for duty at the Star hall, where their "Captain Mainwaring" was a retired brigadier. Jim would do guard duty as ordered, but with no great enthusiasm, often at Carrieston Water Works. He did admit to dereliction of duty on occasion—but only when the weather was very bad—by sleeping in someone's coal shed. One could be forgiven for supposing that our wartime government had some intelligence that the Star area was a prime target for invasion by the Third Reich, judging by the number of roadblocks, pillboxes, and earthworks around the village, the remains of some of which can still be seen. If that was the case, it's just as well that they didn't decide to invade on one of those nights!

Eventually, the home guardsmen were issued with rifles, but initially they had to make do with broomsticks and pitchforks. As their weaponry became ever more sophisticated, one evening the CO demonstrated the use of a bazooka for anti-tank action, unaware that there was a live round in the chamber. When it went off, everyone dived to the ground, and not one of them moved for a few seconds after the blast. Apparently the brigadier thought they had all been hit, whereas in fact they were all clean terrified and, having got down safely, were determined not to get up again in case they had another nasty surprise. Dad always said he was a lucky man. Not only did he never hear a shot fired in anger, he only heard one shot fired at all in the whole course of the war, and that was a case of so-called friendly fire! He did sometimes find spent incendiary bombs and resulting damage to the crops in the mornings when he went to the fields to start work. German bombers returning from raids on Clydebank would discard their remaining unused ordnance before heading home over the North Sea.

Another abiding memory from those days was when the news came through, on 22 June 1941, that Germany had invaded their erstwhile ally, the Soviet Union. Their CO declared that "Civilisation is yet to dawn on the world." Jim and his cohorts were reminded that beyond their relatively safe corner of a world at war, where they were "playin' at sojers," great and tragic events were being played out on the world stage which would ultimately affect all their futures. As with many young people living in such uncertain times, both Jim and Joey were reluctant to waste time and felt an impulse to settle down. Having met each other at the dancing and, as events progressed in those early days of the war, finding that their relationship was becoming ever more serious, they decided to take the plunge and get married.

## The Howe o' the Mearns

Laddie, my lad, when ye gang at the tail o' the plough
An' the days draw in,
When the burnin' yellow's awa' that was aince a-lowe
On the braes o' whin,
Do ye mind o' me that's deaved wi' the wearyfu' south
An' its puir concairns,
While the weepies fade on the knowes at the river's mouth
In the Howe o' the Mearns?

There was nae twa lads frae the Grampians doon to the Tay
That could best us twa;
At bothie or dance, or the field on a fitba' day
We could sort them a';
An' at courtin'-time when the stars keeked doon on the glen
An' its theek o' fairns,
It was you an' me got the pick o' the basket then
In the Howe o' the Mearns.

London is fine, an' for ilk o' the lassies at hame
There'll be saxty here,
But the springtime comes, an' the hairst, an' its aye the same
Through the changefu' year.
O, a lad thinks lang o' hame ere he thinks his fill
As his breid he airns –
An' they're thrashin' noo at the white farm up on the hill
In the Howe o' the Mearns.

Gin I mind mysel' an' toil for the lave o' my days
While I've een to see,
When I'm auld an' done wi' the fash o' their English wyes
I'll come hame to dee.
For the lad dreams aye o' the prize that the man'll get
But he lives and lairns,
An' it's far, far ayont him still, bit it's farther yet
To the Howe o' the Mearns.

Laddie, my lad, when the hair is white on yer pow
An' the work's put past,
When yer hand's owre auld an' heavy to haud the plough
I'll win hame at last,
An' we'll bide our time on the knowes whaur the broom stands braw
An' we played as bairns,
Till the last lang gloamin' shall creep on us baith an fa'
On the Howe o' the Mearns.

Violet Jacob

*Jim sowing*

*Jim with Clydesdales*

*Jim, Harry, and the Tumblin Tam hay rake*

*Nellie the milkmaid*

*Jim, aged 22 years (1939)*

I AM THE BREAD OF LIFE: HE THAT COMETH TO ME SHALL NEVER HUNGER, AND HE THAT BELIEVETH ON ME SHALL NEVER THIRST. ✠

Mr James Rutherford

did this day ratify the vows of his Baptism and was admitted to the Communion of

The Lord's Supper

Date 9th Oct. 1938.

Edwin M.M. Davidson, M.A., B.D.
Minister
of the Church of Scotland

Abide in Me, and I in you. As the branch cannot bear fruit of itself except it abide in the vine; no more can ye, except ye abide in Me.

*Jim's confirmation certificate*

*Jim in Home Guard uniform (1940)*

*Jim and friend at the Empire Exhibition in Glasgow (1938)*

# NATIONAL SERVICE (ARMED FORCES) ACT, 1939

GRADE CARD

(10)

Registration No. LGH193.

Mr. James Rutherford

whose address on his registration card is Broomfold Farm

Chat, Markinch.

was medically examined at KIRKCALDY

on 12 FEB 1940

and placed in

GRADE* I (one)

~~E.D. Until*~~ ............ KIRKCALDY MEDICAL BOARD (Medical Board stamp.)

Chairman of Board [illegible]

Man's Signature James Rutherford

*The roman numeral denoting the man's Grade (with number also spelt out) will be entered in RED ink by the Chairman himself, e.g., Grade I (one), Grade II (two) (a) (Vision). If the examination is deferred the Chairman will enter a date after the words " E.D. Until ", and cross out " Grade " ; alternatively, the words " E.D. Until......... " will be struck out.

N.S. 55 [P.T.O.

*Jim's call-up paper*

KEEP THIS CARD SAFELY

NATIONAL SERVICE (ARMED FORCES) ACTS

Certificate of Registration

Occ Classn. No. 210·10. Registration No. LGH. 193.

Holder's Name RUTHERFORD. James.

Home Address South Bogside Farm, Glencraig, Lochgelly.

Date of Birth 8/2/1917.

Holder's Signature James Rutherford.

READ THIS CAREFULLY

Care should be taken not to lose this certificate, but in the event of loss, application for a duplicate should be made to the nearest office of the Ministry of Labour and National Service.

**If you change your address, etc., at any time between the date of registration and the date of being called up for military service, you must complete the appropriate space on the other side of this certificate and post it at once.** A new Certificate of Registration will then be sent to you.

If you voluntarily join H.M. Forces you should hand this certificate to the appropriate Service Officer.

You should not voluntarily give up your employment because you have been registered for military service.

**This certificate must be produced on request to a constable in uniform.**

**A person who uses or lends this certificate or allows it to be used by any other person with intent to deceive, renders himself liable to heavy penalties.**

N.S.2. Wt.37642/4471 1000M 1/41 T. & W. Ltd. A95426 51-8478

*Jim's registration document*

# PART 2

# DRILLING

# Chapter 7

## "Whaur's yer half-croon comin' frae next Setterday?"

The courtship of Joey and Jim coincided with the first two years of the Second World War. This conflict was to mark a unique watershed in terms of political and military history as, for the first time ever, the civilian population was exposed directly and indirectly to the dangers of war. The demands this made on the daily lives of people were to change forever the fabric of our society. In economic, social, and political terms, the impact of the war was enormous and all-pervading for all levels of society, and examples of these changes can be seen in the lives of my mother and father as they prepared to get married.

To some extent these developments had been foreshadowed by innovations towards the end of the Great War, with the beginnings of war in the air and the start of chemical warfare, including the use of gas as a weapon on the western front. Later events would give more dire warnings of things to come: the Spanish Civil War, when the famous Picasso painting illustrated the bombing of Guernica, and the Japanese aggression against the Chinese, with the wholesale annihilation of many of the citizens of Nanjing.

Everyone in Britain, particularly those who lived in areas of strategic importance or in the major cities, could expect to be the targets of air raids, so ARP precautions involved civilians in blackout and fire-watching duties. Buildings everywhere had to be fitted with blackout shutters or curtains, while motor vehicles were allowed only minimal lights that could not be seen from the sky, and street lights were forbidden. So everyone had to get used to finding their way with little or no light. There was a great fear that air raids would constitute not only explosive and incendiary bombs, but would deliver gas attacks on the civilian population, so everyone was equipped with, and had to carry at all times, a gas mask. Even babies had specially designed masks and my sister Margaret, born in 1942, had one of these.

The government quickly began to disseminate public information, and people were bombarded with posters and newspaper and magazine advertisements. The newsreels in the cinema were a very effective means of reaching the population, at a time when it was estimated that each week thirty million people attended five thousand cinemas countrywide. In all these ways, the government was able to educate the population in necessary wartime behaviour. Warnings about the danger of spies abounded: "Even the walls have ears"; "Careless talk costs lives." The great need for increased domestic food production resulted in the "dig for victory" campaign. Suddenly life seemed saturated with regulations, rules, and directions. When it came from our own government it was seen as public information; only the enemy used propaganda! An example of this might be the drive to get people to hand in all their unused metal such as pots and pans, and housewives everywhere sacrificed many of their cooking utensils. Iron railings were removed from most public buildings and old bicycles were to be recycled, but it was shown later that by the end of the war much of this material was stockpiled and had never seen active service. The effect of these campaigns, of course, was to mobilise the public in the war effort.

The most keenly-felt regulations involved rationing. As an island nation, in time of war we could no longer count on an assured supply of imported food and raw materials, and strict control had to be exercised, so most commodities were subject to rationing. "Dig for victory" meant that all available land had to be cultivated, and everyone had to turn their hands to growing vegetables in their gardens. This was not easy for city dwellers, who had long lost the habit of gardening for food; but for many, certainly in Fife, their link with the land had never really been broken and they had always been used to that activity. Workers in primary industries like farming and mining were exempt from military service. These men, of course, had to join the Home Guard or Civil Defence Volunteer units along with those beyond the age for conscription. Country people, on the whole, found rationing much less onerous than those in the urban areas, and an informal barter system soon became established. With this and the inevitable black market (everyone knew someone who always seemed able to procure and deal in contraband), there were ways to supplement the food supply. The overall effect was that the lives of ordinary people were subject to a very high degree of control, and sacrifices had to be made by everyone in the desperate situation which Britain faced when, after Dunkirk in the summer of 1940, she stood alone against Hitler's Germany until the end of 1941, when the Americans joined the war after Pearl Harbour.

This explains why, as I was growing up, my parents and grandparents remembered events in relation to the war. Things happened before, during, or after the war, even events that were quite unconnected to the conflict—a testament to the huge impact the war had on peoples' lives, even those who, thankfully, were not directly involved in the fighting. Apart from Joey's two brothers, Hughie and John, all of our family were in that fortunate position, but despite that, everyone felt they had a part to play in the war. "There's a war on, you know," became a watchword for putting up with the hardships and shortages. Inventiveness and ingenuity on the part of all kinds of people seemed to have no limits for a generation who were used to "make do and mend," to tolerating what could not be changed, and to coping without the things they couldn't have. This pervaded all levels of society, from the highly innovative and ingenious ground-breaking technical achievements of "the boffins" in the government and armed services, to the day-to-day struggle to improvise solutions and circumvent shortages.

Silk stockings soon became unobtainable; young women would use gravy-browning to give their legs some colour, and draw pencil lines up the back of their legs to simulate the seams that all stockings had then. Jim and his brothers grew parsnips at Broomfield. They were used, with the addition of tinned fruit puree, to make a type of jam. In the absence of bananas, which could not be obtained from the Caribbean, housewives would mash cooked parsnips, which had a similar consistency to bananas, and add artificial banana flavouring, to create an ersatz version of the fruit. However, Joey said you had to have a very active imagination to believe that you were eating a banana! (It is interesting that after the war, parsnips seemed to vanish from Scottish fields and became strangers to the greengrocer's and the table in Scotland. I never remember seeing them or tasting them until I visited the family of a student boyfriend in Bristol in the 1960s. Perhaps people in Scotland had seen enough of that vegetable masquerading as a fruit during the war.) Also, Scottish farmers were encouraged to grow flax, a crop that had not been seen in Scottish fields for generations, to produce linen as a substitute for imported cotton.

In these days when we are very sensitive to the preservation of our civil liberties, I wonder how we would cope with the wartime demands which people tolerated with a remarkable degree of good cheer and forbearance. I believe it was a measure of the belief that people had in the necessity for war. There was an unequivocal acceptance that if there was ever a just war, this was it. The alternative to standing up against Hitler was unthinkable and made opposition to the war effort unimaginable. Despite the tragedy the war represented to many families who lost dear ones in the conflict, or to those whose lives were changed forever by it—and in a way that must have applied to almost everyone—there must have been some comfort to be gained from knowing that it was simply a matter of a struggle for national survival. I wonder if we could ever again have that degree of national unity based on such a clear, unambiguous international situation. That is not in any way to wish for war in any form, but comes from an understanding of the infinitely more complex and subtle nature of international relations in the twenty-first century.

So the war loomed large over my parents' courtship and, as suggested earlier, may have had the effect of encouraging them to get on with their lives, given the precarious state of the world. There was no formal engagement, but they "came to an understanding." There was no engagement ring, and certainly no joyful celebration of their intention to marry. Jim had no money he could call his own; Joey was not, and never would be, interested in outward shows of affection, and would have seen an engagement ring as an unnecessary and ostentatious display. Jim was introduced to Joey's family, and I believe that he was made welcome by Hugh and Betsy, and by Joey's brothers and sisters. Although they were certainly not well off, and there were tensions between her parents, Joey's home almost certainly represented a warmer and more affectionate family environment than the one Jim came from, especially now his mother had died. Betsy declared, "Ah've never seen onybody less like a plooman than Jim. He's that thin and peely-wally!" Hugh took to Jim from the start and they would always get on well together in the years to come.

Hughie was in the Air Force by then, and serving with the BEF in France, while John would not be called up until much later in the war. Greta would later join the ATS when conscription began to apply to young women. (This did not affect Joey because by then she was married and was working on the land.) Greta had the choice of going to work in munitions factories or joining the Auxiliary Territorial Service. Either way it meant that she would have to leave home, so she chose the latter as the lesser of two evils, but in the event she had a miserable time. She was never stationed further from home than Redford Barracks in Edinburgh, but being very shy and timid, she was desperately homesick and found the whole experience traumatising.

While Jim's induction into Joey's family went off smoothly, and he was soon starting to get his feet under the table at 83 Croft Crescent, the same could not be said about Joey's introduction to her prospective in-laws. She was aware of Jim's reluctance to take her to the Star for the first time, and it was only at her insistence that she was eventually to meet James and Nellie and her two future brothers-in-law. Years later, she was to remember the experience as a terrible ordeal, as she certainly was not made to feel welcome as a new member of the Rutherford family. Of course, she was a town girl and had no experience of farm life, so on her first visit she was subjected to an inquisition: "Can ye milk?" "Can ye thin neeps?" They must have known that she could do neither, but when she answered in the negative, she was quickly told, "Ye're no goin' tae be ony yaise tae Jimmy if ye canna dae thae things, so ye'll better learn!"

So she would go up to the Star at the weekends and after work, to be put through her paces by Nellie, while James had very little to do with her. Mum told us that she supposed she must have been very keen on Dad, otherwise she would have run a mile that very first day. We would say, "Do you mean you were in love with Dad?" She would answer, "In love? What does that mean?" Joey had a very sceptical attitude to the concept of romantic love, perhaps due to her awareness of the less-than-happy marriage of her own parents, and I suppose we felt that she was too dismissive of our interpretation of her feelings for Jim in those early days of their relationship. Joey was nothing if not realistic when it came to human nature and relationships, sometimes to the point of cynicism, and if we found it hard to appreciate when we were young, I am sure it made us more likely to be somewhat wary of, and alert to, insincere expressions of affection in our own dealings with the opposite sex!

The bush telegraph, of course, was at work in Markinch and the Star. The Co-op baker's van was a great conduit for news and gossip, and the baker asked Betsy one day, "Does yer lassie ken what she's daen, getting' in tow wi' thae Rutherfords at the Star? They're hard nuts tae crack!" He told her that Nellie had asked him what he knew about Jimmy's lass. She had remarked, "She'll be the kind o' mill lassie that'll only hae wan pair o' breeks tae her name!" Betsy was, of course, angry and worried that Jim's family were so unkind about Joey, as they clearly thought her a poor prospect as a daughter-in-law, coming as she did from the town and working in the mill. There could be no hope of any kind of dowry. They were to be proved wrong, of course, as what Joey brought to her marriage was a determination to learn all she could about farm life, and the ability to work as hard, if not harder, than Jim himself in making a success of their life together and of their eventual business. The fact that she turned out to be a better farmer's wife than most women who were born to life on the farm could not have been lost on James and Nellie, but it was a measure of their meanness of spirit that they never acknowledged the fact, or gave Joey any credit for her achievement over the years, although in the fullness of time, Nellie would come to be kind to her in her way, and I am sure had a grudging respect for her.

There was little or no contact between the two families during the courtship, but one day, Joey took her little brother James to visit Nellie. James was the late baby whose imminent arrival in 1936 had precipitated Joey's return from her brief career in service in Broughty Ferry. She was needed at home to help Betsy with the new addition to the family, and it was Joey who virtually brought him up in his early years. Greta, on the other hand, was horrified that her mother should have a child at the advanced age of forty-two. Knowing by then that babies did not arrive in the doctor's Gladstone bag, she told her parents that they would be the "speak o' the place!" She declared that she would have nothing to do with the new baby and she largely carried out that promise in James's early life, although she would later be very fond of him. James was a rather delicate wee boy and had several bouts of pneumonia in his early childhood. At one time, after Joey was married and living at Bogside, her young sister Doris, seven years older than James, came to visit and announced that their mother Betsy could not join her because James was ill with "consumption." Joey spent a frantic week worrying about him, until the following weekend, when she was able to establish that he had, in fact, "congestion" of the lungs, still a serious condition, but not the potential death sentence TB might have been. Joey looked after him very well, though, and he survived these illnesses. He was one of the first patients of the family doctor, Dr Wight, to be treated with M&B, the new, early antibiotic medication.

On that first visit to the Star, the wee boy asked to go to the toilet. Nellie directed Joey to the outside lavatory at the bottom of the garden. It was never used by the family, whose toilet routine was even more primitive than that afforded by the "dry lavvy." James was fascinated by the whole situation! The little wooden structure was very picturesque, covered as it was by rambling roses and honeysuckle. As he sat there, wide-eyed and somewhat overawed, he asked Joey in a hushed whisper, "Is this whaur the coos come?"

A wedding date was set in due course and it was with great trepidation that Joey and Jim faced the prospect of marriage. After all, it was not as if they had witnessed much in the way of matrimonial bliss in any of their parents' lives, but one thing they were sure of: they had to set up their own home, away from the Star. Jim could not face continuing to live and work in his father's shadow, and Joey had seen enough of life at the Star to know that she did not want that either. Jim was so determined on this course of action that he made up his mind that, if his father would not help him, he would leave Broomfield anyway and get a job as a lorry driver. However—quite how it came about, I am not sure—James agreed that Jim should look for a farm to rent for himself. Perhaps he felt that his business could not sustain all of his sons should they all take wives, but as things turned out, Wullie and Harry were not to follow Jim's example. Instead they continued to work in partnership with their father and Nellie after they married—Harry in 1943 and Wullie in 1946—both, incidentally, to farmers' daughters.

After looking around for some time for a potential tenancy, one was found at South Bogside Farm, between Cardenden and Glencraig, just inside the Fife boundary with Kinross-shire. It was one of many farms owned by the Fife Coal Company, which would be subsumed into the National Coal Board after the war. James stood as guarantor to the tune of £500, a lot of money then, and it was agreed that the lease would not begin until Martinmas (November) the following agricultural term. (The other terms were Candlemas [February], Whitsun [May], and Lammas [August].) Jim and Joey would stay and work at Broomfield for the first three months of their marriage.

It was made very clear by James that the financial help he was giving Jim was all he could ever expect in the way of an inheritance: "What ye get noo, ye dinna get later on." He also stressed that once Jim had made his bed he would have to lie on it, and that as he was choosing to leave Broomfield he could expect no assistance in the future. Jim was grateful for his father's grudging help and only too happy to agree to that; on 3 June 1941 the tenancy was drawn up, and the lease duly signed in September of that year. I don't know whether Jim really understood how strongly his father meant these warnings, or whether he realised that James had very little confidence in his son's ability, but events were to show that his father would never relent in his future refusal to help in any way, but kept a very critical and watchful eye on everything Joey and Jim did in their farming.

As the wedding date approached, Joey—with Greta's help—had many preparations to make. Because it was wartime and everything was in short supply and on ration, and of course because money was very limited, the wedding had to be a very modest affair. They were married on 26 September by the Markinch minister, Rev Davidson, in the living room of Hugh and Betsy's house at 83 Croft Crescent. Joey and Greta worked hard to have the house look its best with the limited resources to hand. It was impossible to buy elaborate bridal outfits, so Joey made her wedding dress and Greta's bridesmaid's dress. They were day dresses, and they had hats and corsages instead of veils and bouquets, which was common for wartime weddings. Jim and his best man Wullie wore lounge suits; the only celebratory concessions were flowers in their buttonholes.

Mum and Dad's wedding photograph shows them to be very young and extremely nervous. No one in the bridal party is smiling; Joey looks completely terrified, and you can almost see tears in her eyes! Both she and Jim were very aware of the seriousness of the step they were taking. Grandad Rutherford surprised everyone by breaking down after the ceremony as, in tears, he asked Jim, "Whaur's yer half-croon comin' frae next Setterday!" Thankfully, some of the younger members of the family and some friends of Joey and Jim helped to break the ice, and there followed a fairly happy, if understated, reception. One telegram was received from Isa and Jean Scott, which included the deliberate ambiguity, "May yer bags aye be fu' o' seed." When the (hopefully by now) happy couple left on honeymoon, they were accompanied through the blackout by their brothers and sisters and friends to the bus stop in Markinch where they had a happy and noisy send-off as they embarked on the first stage of their honeymoon. The first bus took them out to Markinch road-end where they would catch the Kirkcaldy bus. It was when they were waiting there at Cadham that Joey realised that she had left the key for her suitcase on her dressing table. There was nothing else for it but to walk the half mile back into number 83, where Jim slipped unseen into the house and up the stairs to get the key as the party continued in the living room. They then walked down to the bus stop for the second time, but this time, of course, alone. As they waited again at the same bus stop as before, they heard their friends coming down the street from the house. The party had obviously ended and they were all chatting about the wedding. Comments like "I wonder if they're in their hotel room by now" and other more ribald ones issued forth in the darkness, but thankfully the blackout hid Joey and Jim's blushes and they were spared the indignity of being spotted and having to explain themselves! So they restarted their journey to Kirkcaldy and the Station Hotel, where they would spend their first night of married life. They were not to know that exactly twenty-three years later, to the day, their elder daughter Margaret and her new husband John French would have their wedding reception in that same hotel. When Jim made his speech that day, and he mentioned the fact that he and Joey had spent the first night of their honeymoon just upstairs, they got a huge cheer from the assembled guests!

The next day, the honeymoon couple caught the train to Stirling, where Jim bought Joey her wedding present: a pair of crystal candlesticks, which now adorn our mantlepiece. They are a beautiful reminder of their wedding day and honeymoon and were very special to Mum, who kept them on her dressing table throughout their married life. From Stirling they went to Thornhill and stayed a night with Jim's Auntie Lizzie and Uncle Bob, his father's brother, before returning next day to the Star. The very short honeymoon was over, and real life was about to be resumed.

Joey proceeded to keep house for Jim and his two brothers in Broomfield farmhouse. It was an old house with little in the way of comfort, but I am sure that it benefited from a woman's touch, as Joey brought her homemaking skills to bear on it during the three months they lived there. She and Jim had received some wedding presents, although they were limited in number and variety due to wartime shortages. There was a lovely pair of white linen sheets—a handsome present in those days—which was a gift from Isa Scott, a good friend of Joey's family and a supervisor at Dixon's mill. Joey was very proud of those sheets, but was brought down to earth with a bump when Nellie, on seeing them, insisted that they should not be used, but should be set aside as their "dead sheets." At first Joey did not understand what Nellie meant, but then realised with horror that they were to be reserved for use as shrouds! When Jim heard, he lost his rag with Nellie: "God, Nellie, we're just starting our life and you're talking about us ending it!" This was typical of the harshness with which Nellie and James approached life, and the insensitivity they showed to the people they should have cared most about, and Joey must have longed for the day they could leave the Star.

Another thing she found hard to deal with was that they had to vacate the farmhouse for a day each time the Balfour family from Balbirnie House wanted the use of it for their shooting parties. This really offended her sense of natural justice and reinforced her egalitarian instincts. She despised the way Jim's family were happy to "touch the forelock" and "bend the knee" to their landlords. Soon she and Jim would also be tenant farmers, but it seemed easier to countenance a landlord in the form of a coal company than in the embodiment of the landed gentry. It would not be long until she had an example of the degree of control any landlord has over the lives of their tenants, when the National Coal Board exercised a disproportionately severe reprimand to Jim in response to his attempt to exercise his democratic rights.

So, in November 1941, Joey and Jim moved to South Bogside Farm. The fourteen intervening miles might as well have been forty or four hundred, as it seemed very far away from their familiar surroundings. The landscape and settlement patterns of west Fife were very different from the Markinch area, because it was largely on the coal field and the villages all owed their existence to the coal mines. While Joey was delighted to be in her own home and Jim relieved to be his own boss, their happiness was tinged with an awareness of the strangeness of their new situation and the weight of responsibility for each other and for the success or failure of their life together.

When I remember my mother describing their wedding day and the early months of their marriage, the image that I hold most vividly is that of Joey and Jim waiting together that night for the bus at Cadham. Little did they know when they stood there on the threshold of their new life together that they would end their lives in a house, not yet built, only a hundred yards along the road. I never pass that spot but I think of them, two young people, fearful of the future and yet hopeful and excited about what it might bring. They were on the brink of a journey; not only one that would start them on their honeymoon, but one that would mark the beginning of a long life together. It would see them return almost to the same spot, within a mile or two of where they were born and of where their life together started, a circle completed, encompassing a marriage of nearly sixty years. I want to capture the essence of those years as I remember them and from the memories of many other people who shared the journey with Mum and Dad, just as their early years, as I have described them, are a distillation of the memories they shared with me in the course of my life as their daughter.

## Certificate of Proclamation of Banns.

At Markinch the Sixteenth day of September One thousand nine hundred and ~~thirty~~ forty-one

*It is hereby certified that* James Rutherford, Broomfold, Markinch.

*and* Johan Barclay Mitchell, 83 Croft Crescent, Markinch. *have been duly proclaimed in the Church of* St Drostan's Parish.

*on* 14th September 1941 *in order to marriage,*

*and that no objections have been offered.*

Archd. Mitchell Jr. { ~~Minister or~~ Session-Clerk.

## Certificate of Marriage.

At 83 Croft Cresc. Markinch *the* Twenty Sixth *day of* September *One thousand nine hundred and* ~~*thirty*~~ Forty One

*It is hereby certified that the above parties were this day married by me,*

Edwin M. M. Davidson, M.A., B.D.

*Minister at* Markinch

*Proclamation of banns*

**EXTRACT OF AN ENTRY IN A REGISTER OF MARRIAGES** **1922 - 1965**

kept under the Registration of Births, Deaths and Marriages (Scotland) Act 1965

| (1) When, Where, and How Married | (2) Names (in full) of Parties, with Signatures; Rank or Profession, and whether Bachelor, Spinster, Widower, Widow, or Divorced | (3) Age | (4) Usual Residence | (5) Name, Surname, and Rank or Profession of Father; Name, and Maiden Surname of Mother | (6) If a Regular Marriage, Signature and Designation of Officiating Minister or Registrar, and Signatures and Addresses of Witnesses; If an Irregular Marriage, Date of Decree of Declarator, or of Sheriff's Warrant | (7) When and Where Registered and Signature of Registrar |
|---|---|---|---|---|---|---|
| 1941 | (Name in Full) James Rutherford | 24 | Broomfield | James Rutherford | (Signed) Edwin M.M. Davidson | 1941 |
| n the Twenty-sixth | | | Star | Farmer | Minister at St. Drostan's | September 29th |
| ay of September | (Signature) James Rutherford | | | Margaret Rutherford | Parish Church, Markinch | |
| t 83 Croft Crescent | Farmer | | | m.s. Irons | | At Markinch |
| rkinch | (Bachelor) | | | (deceased) | (Signed) Margaret Mitchell | |
| fter Banns | (Name in Full) Johan Barclay Mitchell | 25 | 83 | Betsy Mitchell | 83 Croft Crescent | (Signed) |
| ccording to the Forms | | | Croft Crescent | Papermill Worker | Markinch Witness | W.B. Morris |
| f the Church of | (Signature) Johan B. Mitchell | | Markinch | afterwards married to | William Rutherford | Registrar |
| cotland | Papermill Worker | | | Hugh Mitchell | Broomfield | |
| | (Spinster) | | | Papermill Engineer | Star Witness | |

ED from the Register of Marriages for the District of Markinch
County of Fife this 10th day of March 1980 — wmiller

*ATTENTION IS DIRECTED TO THE NOTES OVERLEAF*

*Marriage certificate*

*The wedding of Joey and Jim; bridesmaid, Greta; best man, Wullie*

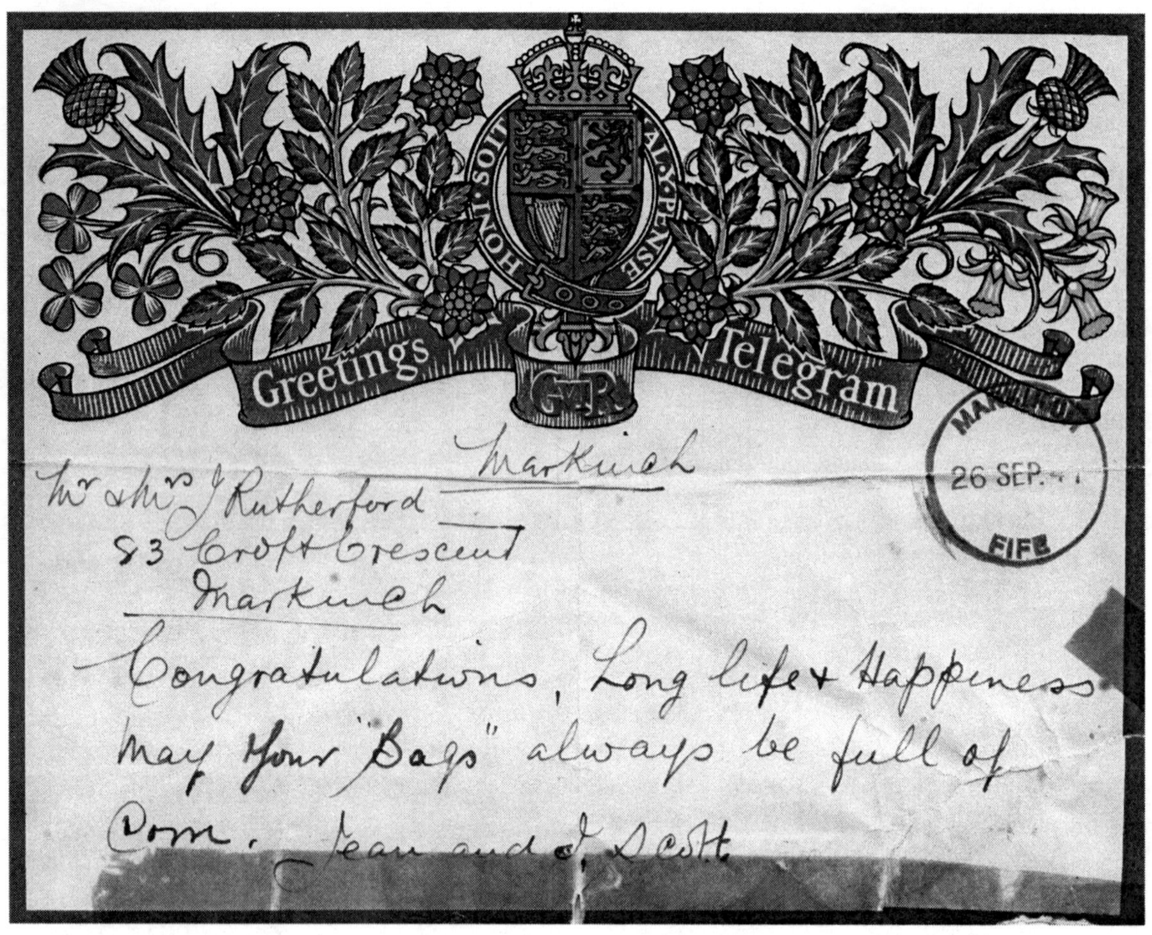
HONI SOIT QUI MAL Y PENSE

Greetings Telegram

GR

26 SEP.

FIFE

Markinch

Mr & Mrs J Rutherford
83 Croft Crescent
Markinch

Congratulations, Long life & Happiness
May your "Bags" always be full of
Corn. Jean and I. Scott

*Wedding telegram from Jean and Isa Scott ("May your bags always be full of corn")*

# Chapter 8

"See that he gets some denner afore he gets awa' hame."

Joey and Jim began their life as tenant farmers to the Fife Coal Company, when they took up residence at South Bogside Farm in November 1941. Jim had made an offer for the fourteen-year lease in May of that year, it was accepted in June, and the agreement countersigned by James senior, as guarantor for the first five years' rent at £100 per annum, on 9 September. Much as they had longed to be away from Broomfield and to be masters of their own destiny, they were very aware of the burden of responsibility they now bore for themselves and for each other. They had to make a go of their enterprise or face the inevitable "I told you so," which James would be only too ready to vent on them if they failed.

Added to this, was the sense of isolation and the strangeness of their new surroundings, particularly for Joey. The landscape and the people of West Fife were very different from those of their home area, and she couldn't help feeling homesick as she found the complete stillness unnerving, used as she was to the hustle and bustle of her old home. On their very first morning, Jim as usual went outside immediately, leaving Joey to start turning their new abode into a home. Bogside farmhouse was old and inclined to be damp. It had no electricity and came complete with its own colony of mice, but it did have some amenities that Broomfield and many other farmhouses at that time lacked. There was hot and cold running water, the open range in the kitchen having a back-boiler, which heated the water. In addition, there was an indoor toilet. These, and the later installation of a bath in one end of the scullery, were immense advantages. If the house needed a lot of hard work to add some comfort to the basic shelter it offered, Joey was very satisfied with its potential.

So as she wired in to the task, she was surprised to see a hen, one of a flock left behind according to the terms of the lease by the previous tenant, Sandy Lindsay, come into the kitchen, flap up onto one of the hand-me-down armchairs, and proceed to lay an egg! Joey was so glad to see this living creature—which obviously felt very much at home—that she immediately cheered up, and by the time Jim came in for his breakfast, the house was already beginning to feel less strange. That hen repeated her performance every morning, laying its daily egg on the chair, clearly accepting and approving of her new owners. As the days and weeks passed, Joey would gradually feel at home at Bogside, but she was always conscious of the distance that separated her from her old home. On the odd occasion when she went down to Cardenden, she could see from Woodend, far away to the east, the vague outline of the Roundall, a group of large trees on the ridge near St Drostan's cemetery, to the east of Markinch. That always made her feel better, to know that home wasn't so far away after all. This illustrates how, in the absence of personal transport in the form of cars, a few miles were a real barrier to movement, especially for those living in the country far from bus routes.

The reaction to Mum and Dad of their new neighbours was somewhat restrained, to say the least. A number of farms marched with Bogside: to the west was Capeldrae, tenanted by Lowry McFarlane; and to the east was Westfield, occupied by Matthie Black; beyond which, on the way to Cardenden, was Redhouse, tenanted by Huggy Buick. Between Cardenden and Kinglassie lay the farms of Hairstanes, occupied by Jim Wilson; and Strathruddie, farmed by Lowry's brother Sandy. On the brae to the southwest was North Pitkinny, where Montgomery and subsequently (briefly) Stevenson were tenants, and which would later become their second farm and our home, with South Pitkinny beyond that. It was attached to the farm of Pitcairn, further southwest again, on the main road to Lochgelly, where Tam Smith was the farmer.

To these older, well-established farmers Joey and Jim must have seemed a pair of young upstarts and, even worse, outsiders from a different part of the county. This also goes to show how in those days people did not as a rule move far outwith their original area, and although only a few miles distant, west and central Fife were poles apart in terms of culture and experience. No doubt the wives of these farmers knew that Joey was new to farm life, and a few were very quick to pass on advice to her. Some was kindly meant but others less so, and Joey was confirmed in her determination to develop her own independent and individual approach to her role. This did not win her friends easily, but it did earn her respect from all but the most intransigent new acquaintances. Likewise, some of his new neighbours found Jim's innovative and sometimes apparently cavalier approach to farming difficult to get used to, but in time they would all come to accept that he really did know what he was doing and, like his own father, most of them would find themselves following his lead, although they would never have admitted to it! All in all, over the years, there developed a solid foundation of mutual respect and support; the Black family at Westfield, in particular, would become valued friends.

In the early days of their occupancy, Bogside was part of the parish and postal district of Glencraig, but would later become part of Auchterderran Parish, with Cardenden their postal address. Bogside was on the road which ran northwest from Cardenden to Ballingry and across the county border to Kinross. To the north and parallel to the road was the Lochty Burn and the branch railway line of the same name. Halfway between Bogside and Capeldrae to the west was Capeldrae Row, a group of seventeen houses in three blocks of five, six, and six, which like most of the farms, belonged to the Fife Coal Company. One of these houses was allocated to Bogside as a "cottar hoose," a home for a farm worker at Bogside. The others were the homes of miners and other employees of the company, many of whom would work as casual labour on the nearby farms, especially in the labour-intensive harvest times.

Beyond Capeldrae, on the north side of the road, there was a prisoner-of-war camp, built to house German prisoners. Later, after the end of hostilities, it was used as a DP (displaced persons) camp for poor souls who had lost their homes and families as a result of the war, and were temporarily housed there until they could be either reunited with their relatives or found more permanent locations. From time to time, prisoners were brought to work at Bogside, and Joey always found this very stressful. They had strict instructions regarding non-fraternisation and, of course, the prisoners were forbidden to communicate with the other workers beyond the needs of the job, but Joey felt very sorry for them. Normally she provided food and drink for folk working on the place, but when she tried to include the prisoners, they would shake their heads and shy away from this attempt at basic human contact. I suppose she was thinking of her brother Hughie, and hoping that if he were in a similar position, someone somewhere would take pity on him.

Many years later, as I worked as a teacher of English as a second language, sometimes with children and young adults who had recently arrived in Scotland from far-flung regions of the world, with little or no English and clearly homesick and bewildered by their new surroundings, I wondered how it would be for one of my sons if he found himself in that situation. I hoped that he would encounter warm and friendly people to help him, and of course they were both to have exactly that experience when they went to work abroad, one in Hong Kong and one in Japan. I had had a similar experience when I went to work in Sweden when I was twenty-two, and found myself having to make my way in a strange environment, albeit one not that far removed in distance or culture from my own, and with people who could more or less all speak at least some English. As a result, I could understand Joey's urge to make some human contact with these poor men who found themselves prisoners in an alien land. That her overtures were met with polite but firm refusal was a measure of their awareness that to accept would have landed all of them in trouble with the authorities.

In a sense it was the existence of that camp that later led Jim into another kind of trouble with authority—namely his landlord, the Fife Coal Company. The DP camp was connected to the public electricity supply, and he enquired on behalf of himself and the other coal company tenants why the same amenity was denied to the local farms and Capeldrae Row, despite their close proximity to the camp. He felt the explanation he was given was not satisfactory, and decided to address the question to their local MP, who was about to hold a public meeting for his constituents. This was Willie Gallacher, the first Communist member of the House of Commons, who had been elected to represent West Fife in the 1945 election. Jim may have been somewhat politically naïve in thinking that he was entitled to exercise his democratic right by asking a question of his elected representative, regardless of the party allegiance of the latter, and of course he was technically correct in so believing. However, the political realities of the situation were somewhat different, and within a few days, Jim received a letter from the Coal Company, which was about to be subsumed into the new National Coal Board, enquiring whether he was, or intended to become, a member of the Communist party!

(In historical terms, the Communists had quickly supplanted the Nazis in the role of "the baddies," and the wartime alliance with the Soviet Union did not long outlive the war itself.) The letter made it very clear that if that were the case, his tenancy of Bogside would have to be reconsidered. Jim had no choice but to assure his landlords that he was no subversive, and as a result, he and Joey and all their neighbours had to wait their turn to be "switched on" at the convenience of the electricity board, an event which did not come about until the early fifties. This episode certainly made them aware of the existence of Big Brother, and the limits to which their franchise extended in reality, despite the finer points of political theory. This tended to confirm Joey in her left-of-centre instincts, but had the effect of encouraging Jim in his evenhanded, disinterested approach to conflicts, political or otherwise, or as Joey interpreted it, his determination to sit on the fence. "If your Dad was a country he would be Sweden or Switzerland!" A further very clear example of this was to occur when they first retired to Kirkcudbright thirty years later.

Joey and Jim started farming with very little in the way of equipment or livestock. They had one cow, which was in calf, and got two piglets from Broomfield. It was normal in those days for animals to be given names, especially when there were so few. So their solitary cow was called Mary, but in years to come, when farming became more technical and businesslike, such homely practices were lost. Of course, it would have been quite a task, thinking of names for all the individual cows in a dairy herd of more than one hundred animals, which was what they ended up with. The piglets were to be fattened for sale, usually quite a lucrative exercise, as pigs could be fed on kitchen scraps and meal, with no big outlay. Indeed, most farm workers would always have a pig "on the go" as one of their perquisites, along with milk, eggs, and potatoes from the farm. In the early weeks at Bogside, the pigs were going to do so much. "When we sell the pigs,…" became their talisman.

The buildings at Bogside were in a varying state of repair, but the byre was a pretty ramshackle affair, and a lot of time and energy was spent in making it windproof and watertight. There was a stable for the horse, a hay barn and loose boxes for the calves, a cartshed and a small dairy which housed the milk cooler, a boiler for heating the water, and two deep sinks for washing the milk cans. In addition, there were various small sheds and henhouses. One of Jim's first projects was to improve the byre, as he was intent on increasing the size of his "herd" of one as fast as he could. The main necessity to begin with was to lay concrete on the earth floor, so he had to invest in sand and cement, which could be procured at the local quarry, near Woodend on the Kinglassie road. His only obstacle was that he had no means of transporting the raw materials to Bogside, so he decided for the second and last time to ask his father for some help, in the form of his small pickup truck. This must have been their first winter at Bogside, and the arable demands of the land at their least, so Jim took the day off, leaving Joey to see to the milking and other chores.

Having no other means of transport, he took his bike and cycled down to Woodend. There, he left his bike with Dave Duncan the blacksmith, whom he knew from his horseshoeing services at the smiddy. In those days there was no direct bus to Markinch, the nearest bus stop to the Star, so you had to catch the Leven bus and change, either at Thornton or Coaltown of Balgonie, for Markinch. Jim reached there just as it started to snow, and he crossed the Cuinin Hill—a walk he had done almost every day of his young life—in a blizzard, arriving at the Star just as his father James, Nellie, Wullie, and Harry were finishing their midday meal. When he walked into the dairy kitchen, there was no display of pleasure from anyone there at this unexpected sight of their son and brother. Rather, the reaction was one of "What are you doing here?" Jim explained his planned byre improvement and ventured, "I wondered if I could get a len o' the pickup for the efternain to get some saund and cement tae Bogside?"

James never answered his son, but stood up from the table and pointing at Jim and speaking to Nellie, said, "See that he gets some denner afore he gets awa' hame." Without more ado, he left the kitchen and went outside, presumably to resume his day's work. This was not his normal routine, as he usually went and lay down on his bed for forty winks after his dinner, having been up since four in the morning for the milking, but perhaps he wanted to get out of the house in case Jim said any more to him. In the event, there was no likelihood of that happening, as Jim knew better than to counter his father's tacit refusal to accede to his request for help. So he ate the food Nellie gave him, no doubt thankful that at least he would be fortified for the long way home. Then he set out to repeat that morning's journey in reverse.

As he walked, bussed, and cycled his way home, he had a few hours to think over what had just happened, and I wonder what his thoughts were. He probably realised that he should have expected nothing else from his father, and that, having been warned to lie on the bed he was making, in a sense James was simply making good a promise he had made to his son. "Dinnae expect ony mair help frae me!" So, after collecting his bike, and before cycling back to Bogside, he went to see the local coal man, Saund Page, whom he had got to know and who, with his wife, would become longstanding friends of Joey and Jim. He arranged to hire his lorry to haul the sand and cement, and in due course the byre had a new floor. Jim vowed to himself that day that never again would he place himself in a situation where the humiliation and hurt he felt at the hands of his father could be repeated.

As that first year at Bogside passed, Jim and Joey worked all the hours there were, to improve their living and working conditions to the limits of what they could afford. They prepared the land and completed the first annual cycle through seedtime and harvest. They added gradually to their livestock and tended their animals with the knowledge that they represented the success or failure of their life together. Jim was constantly planning new developments even in those early days, and soon showed the business acumen that was to enable him to bring those plans to fruition. Meanwhile, Joey was learning new skills every day and relished the hard work this entailed.

By coincidence, at about the same time as Joey and Jim came to Bogside, the headmaster from Markinch, Mr Stevens, also moved to Cardenden and became headmaster of Auchterderran Junior Secondary School—no doubt a good career move to a bigger school. One day he took a walk from the schoolhouse at Auchterderran, and passed Bogside. The steading was right beside the road, and he stopped to chat to the young woman working there. They were both amazed when they recognised each other. It was irony indeed: here was the man who had pleaded with Hugh to allow his daughter Joey to transfer from Markinch to the high school and continue her education; and here was that same young girl, now grown up, and what was she doing? She was mixing and floating concrete on a new byre floor, apparently with consummate ease! He paid her the compliment of saying how impressed he was with her skill and that he always knew she would succeed in whatever task she set herself. But what mattered more to Joey was the knowledge that no matter what she had done, even if she had had the education he had wanted for her, she could not have been happier than she was that day. This says so much about my mother. She relished a challenge and loved learning new skills. Throughout her life she could turn her hand to anything, and would tackle tasks that may have appeared beyond her ability, almost always with success. Such was the love she had for work and learning new things, practical or otherwise. In this regard, Jim could not have been more fortunate in his choice of "an helpmeet for him" (Genesis 2:18). I wonder if Mr Stevens, as he went on his way, reflected that intelligence should be valued, not only in terms of academic achievement, but—to use another Biblical reference—in the way illustrated by the parable of the talents.

As a result of all their hard work, the days were long and leisure time an unknown concept, as for Joey there were all the usual domestic chores to be done in addition to the outside work. Added to that, she became pregnant with her first child, my sister Margaret, soon after coming to Bogside. She could remember the sheer exhaustion that would overtake her and how she would fall into bed at the end of each day. As the house fell quiet for the night, she would hear the mice scurrying around; even, (on occasion) being vaguely aware of them running over their bed. Had she been faced with that prospect in the days before her marriage, it would have been more than she could bear. Now she was so exhausted that the horror of it hardly even registered with her, and all the mice in the world could not have kept her from sleeping! She was always amazed that by the next morning they were refreshed and ready to start the hard work all over again.

When they ran into problems they had to find their own solutions, often by trial and error, no matter how much hard work or frustration this involved. In the absence of veterinary intervention, which they could not afford, they lost a young mare while she was foaling—a disaster of epic proportions. But they managed to save the foal and succeeded in hand-rearing it—a very unusual feat which amazed their neighbours. Even Jim's brother Wullie, a gifted horseman, must have been impressed, but (not surprisingly) he managed to refrain from saying so!

The orphaning of animals is, of course, a common occurrence, not least with sheep. A few years later, when they first kept sheep, and during one of their first lambing seasons, they lost a ewe, but hand-reared her offspring. In years to come, we would often have pet lambs at Bogside and Pitkinny. As children we loved them, but to Jim and, to a lesser extent, Joey they were a "damned nuisance," and represented hard, time-consuming work. It was not unusual for there to be one or two sickly or orphaned lambs being tended in a box by the kitchen fire, until, if they survived at all, they were well enough to return to the cold lambing shed outside. There they would be bottle-fed, but otherwise would have to take their chances. That first "orphan Annie," however, became a real pet and was named Sookey. Although I must have been very young, I do have a faint memory of her. She was a great novelty for us all, and certainly the female members of the family and I suspect Jim as well, although he would have denied it, became very fond of her. She was quite a character and probably suffered from an identity crisis as she was practically a member of the family and had no time for the other sheep. She would come into the kitchen and would be given titbits. She soon learned where the biscuit barrel was kept, on top of the high dresser, and she would stand on her hind legs and paw at the dresser until she was rewarded. From that time the dresser bore the scratches of her hooves as evidence of the indulgence she was shown.

Sookey was great friends with our old sheepdog Lassie, who also seemed to be rather confused about her identity and function in life, and they became inseparable. They began to "go walkabout" in the middle of the night, roaming the surrounding fields, ending their wanderings at Capeldrae Farm, where they would go to sleep together in the hay barn. Every morning, Lowry McFarlane would find them there when he went out to start the milking, and they would run off home to Bogside. One day when some residents of the DP camp were collecting their daily milk from the farm, they saw the two pals and noticed the bell that Sookey had round her neck. They explained that they were mightily relieved to discover the source of the strange tinkling sounds they had been hearing in the dead of night for weeks, as some of their number had convinced the others that they must have a supernatural origin! As it was, this was no ghostly apparition, just "a dug an'a yowe oot on the ran-dan."

Sookey was very friendly, but only with people she knew, and would frequently take exception to strangers and butt them at every opportunity. This meant that visitors had to be very wary not to present too easy a target for her; but after a few hours, she would become more tolerant of the strangers and leave them alone. As visitors were leaving, it was usual to walk with them to the bus stop at Woodend, and the dog and the lamb would come too. As time passed, Joey used to love to see the expressions on the faces of the passengers, as the bus stopped, when they saw a fully grown sheep standing at the bus stop!

Sadly the awful day came when Jim had to harden his heart and Sookey had to go off to market with the other sheep. There she was, as the door of the cattle float was raised, looking at us all and baa-ing frantically, having no interest in being with a load of sheep. "What are you thinking of? I don't belong here!" she seemed to be saying. I remember, young though I was, how dreadfully upset everyone was. It was a hard lesson for us that there is no time or space for sentiment where farm animals are concerned, and Dad swore that he would never allow us to become so attached to a pet lamb again. We never were, but where cats and dogs were concerned it was altogether a different matter!

A footnote to this story is that Jim kept this vow for nearly thirty years. In 1975 Margaret's three daughters, Pamela and Alison and Lynda, had spent Easter at Pitkinny. This would be Jim's last lambing time at Pitkinny before he and Joey retired, and they had a pet lamb, which the girls named Jamie. As their holiday drew to an end, they were very sad to be leaving Jamie, and Jim astounded everyone by suggesting that they take him home with them to Kirkcudbright. His three granddaughters jumped at the chance, and, although Margaret and John were not convinced it was a good idea, they were persuaded that there would be enough grass in their large garden for Jamie. In the event, after a few weeks, he had outgrown the food supply and Jim and Joey had to bring him back to Pitkinny. He had to travel in the boot of the car, a frightening experience, which had a disastrous effect on his digestive system. The result was that the boot had to undergo a major cleaning operation and it was tears all round again as a new generation of girls had to say farewell to their wee "sheepie-meh" pal!

In learning about the animals in her care, Joey had to become familiar with their minor, (and not so minor) ailments. In one case, she became more familiar with one than she would really have liked. Ringworm is endemic in cattle, and this skin complaint is very contagious, both to other cows and to humans as well, but can usually be treated quite successfully. It was not long until Joey noticed she had developed a small patch of ringworm on her thigh. When the Boots' agricultural travelling salesman paid one of his regular visits to Bogside, she asked him for something to treat ringworm. He obliged with a tin containing a paste which had to be applied daily. Joey proceeded to comply with the directions on the tin, but was surprised that after applying it to her leg, she suffered a painful, burning sensation. Never one to complain, however, she persisted with the treatment for a few days, only to find that the pain was getting worse, and that in fact, her leg was badly burned. Then, and only then, it dawned on her that the Boots' rep had assumed she wanted something to treat one of the cattle, and had never dreamed that she wanted it for herself! She had to admit defeat and go to see Doctor Brackenridge at his surgery at Auchterderran. Of course, he asked how she burned herself, and Joey had to own up to the fact that she had been using treatment that was actually designed for a cow, whose hide was a damn sight tougher than her fair skin!

The efforts of Joey and Jim to improve and add to their livestock were accompanied in time by continued work on the steading, with the erection of an entirely new byre and a lean-to extension to the old one, to house a petrol-driven engine which powered newly acquired milking machines. As these saw an end to hand-milking, so gradually the tractor began to take over from the faithful Clydesdale, whose draught strength had supplied power for all the arable work on the farm. In 1939 there were 1,233 horses on Fife farms. By less than twenty years later, in 1958, there were only 92. The number of tractors increased in inverse proportion, and by the 1960s horse ploughing was limited to a mere exhibitive or competitive activity in ploughing matches, for those with a nostalgic connection to the old farming ways.

For working farmers trying to maximise their living from the land, most of them embraced the labour saving advantages of the new technology in arable and pastoral farming methods with enthusiasm. Somewhere in between these two groups were those men like my grandfather and uncles who, although initially suspicious of the new ways, eventually had to submit to their attractions, albeit with reluctance to embark on the necessary capital investment, until the resulting benefits for their income proved obvious and irresistible. So it was that Jim led the way towards a radical change in agricultural techniques, which was amounting to a revolution in the work and life of the farming community, not only in Fife, but throughout the country. Where Jim led, his father followed, with reluctance, which only added to the existing antipathy he had for his middle son. I am sure James expected Jim to fail in his bid for independence and success and really never forgave him for being proved wrong. Their relationship, never a happy one, went from bad to worse and the limited contact we had with my grandfather was increasingly fraught with tension. Although we stayed on good terms with our aunts and uncles, Joey was always conscious of remaining an outsider in the family. However, she did her best to continue to make an effort to communicate with Nellie, as she had great sympathy for the hard life she had been subjected to.

In 1946, the Fife Coal Company was absorbed into the newly constituted National Coal Board. This was one example of the nationalisation of primary and strategically vital industries, embarked on by the first labour government, elected in 1945. Jim would later declare that from then onwards, farming would always do better under Labour than under Tory government. I imagine this was true for tenant farmers like my father, who mostly came from farm labourer stock, whereas the land-owning farmer class were probably more likely to continue to espouse the Conservative Party as their traditional sponsors. The man who was employed as factor for the Fife Coal Company to oversee this transition, and who continued in that role for the NCB, was Bob Edgar. The assets of the nationalised coal industry obviously far outstripped those of its predecessor, and there was capital to be invested in its farms. Jim immediately struck up a mutually profitable rapport with Edgar, and they developed great respect for each other. Edgar recognised Jim as a valued tenant whose innate business and farming ability couldn't fail to improve his land and steading. Jim saw Edgar as an approachable and empathetic representative of his landlord, who would always be willing to consider fairly any request for the investment necessary to support his plans to develop his holding in an imaginative and innovative way, to the mutual benefit of landlord and tenant alike. This symbiotic relationship has always reminded me of the one, on a global scale, between Churchill and Roosevelt in the days before the United States entered the Second World War, when that country supported materially the British war effort, as we stood alone against Hitler, with policies such as lend-lease. "Give us the tools and we will finish the job." Bob Edgar soon came to realise that Jim and Joey could be relied upon to more than keep their end of the bargain.

Similarly, from the early days, Jim was never afraid to borrow money for capital investment in his business. In this regard, he was certainly not his father's son. James was one of the old school, typical of the Scottish Calvinist tradition, which abhorred debt of any kind and would only contemplate spending money which had been assiduously saved. The idea of borrowing from a bank in order to invest in your business was anathema to Jim's father. Indeed, he didn't even trust banks to keep him money safe, far less to accrue interest on his behalf. It was many years before he could bring himself to have anything to do with any financial institution. Even in 1946, this gave rise to an amusing episode on the occasion of Wullie's wedding to Caroline Nicol, the daughter of the farmer at Lochty Farm near Thornton. As soon as the ceremony was over, James asked Jim to take him home. He could not be persuaded that he should stay on for the remainder of the wedding celebration. When pressed for a reason for his need to return home so early, he admitted that he had "hidden some money" before leaving for the wedding that afternoon, and was worried about its safety.

It was, of course, very rare for James and Nellie to leave the dairy at all, never mind together, and for the place to be left unattended, so he had concealed £1,500 in cash under the coal heap. He then feared that someone might steal the coal, so he moved the money and secreted it under a big pile of neeps (turnips) in the shed! At today's value this must have amounted to almost a six-figure sum, and represented his whole fortune! So James could be forgiven for being anxious, even at a time when theft and burglary were less common than now. It has to be said that a reluctance to pay income tax, as well as a mistrust of the banking system, no doubt accounted for James's decision to engage in such risky behaviour and entrust the results of his life's work to the neeps! Years later, in the 1970s, after Joey and Jim were retired, Harry and his wife Rina had their house burgled while they were having a very rare holiday and staying with them in Kirkcudbright for a few days. When they learned of the disaster, their biggest fear was that the robbers would have found a stash of cash they had hidden under the floorboards of one of the rooms. Some people never learn! Happily, their money was just as safe as Grandad's had been thirty years before.

STAMP
SIXPENCE

To -
The Fife Coal Company Limited,
L E V E N .

I, JAMES RUTHERFORD, Farmer, residing at Broomfold, Markinch, IN CONSIDERATION of your granting a Lease of the Farm of South Bogside in the Parish of Auchterderran and County of Fife, to my son James Rutherford Junior residing with me, for a period of fourteen years from Martinmas Nineteen hundred and forty one, with a mutual break at Martinmas Nineteen hundred and forty eight, at the annual rent of One hundred pounds sterling, Do Hereby GUARANTEE prompt payment of the rent for five years from the term of Martinmas Nineteen hundred and forty one, payable half yearly at the terms of Whitsunday and Martinmas in each year; And I bind myself and my heirs, executors and representatives whomsoever accordingly: IN WITNESS WHEREOF I have subscribed these presents at Markinch, on the ninth day of September Nineteen hundred and forty one, before these witnesses James Campbell Torrance, Bank Agent, and Jessie Shepherd Ballantine, Bank Clerkess, both of the Royal Bank of Scotland, Markinch.

(S I G N E D)

J. C. TORRANCE, Witness.
JESSIE S. BALLANTINE, Witness.

JAMES RUTHERFORD.

*Letter of guarantee*

All Communications to be addressed to the Company

Head Office:
Leven, Fife.

Telegrams "Carlow, Phone, Leven."
"Fifcol," Cowdenbeath

Telephone Nos 161 & 162 Leven
" Nos 3181 to 3185 Cowdenbeath.

Your Ref. ........................

Our Ref. WGC/MMc.

The Fife Coal Company (Limited)

Cowdenbeath 3rd June, 1941.
Fife.

Mr. James Rutherford, Jr.,
Broomfold,
MARKINCH.

Dear Sir,

South Bogside Farm.

We are favoured with yours of 8th May making offer of One Hundred Pounds Sterling for the above farm, including the cottage in Capledrae Row and we have pleasure in accepting same in terms of the conditions of let. A formal lease will be prepared and sent to you for approval at an early date. As a special condition to your offer, the proprietors will provide you with sufficient fencing material to repair the fences where necessary.

Yours faithfully,
For THE FIFE COAL COMPANY, LIMITED,

W.G. Cunningham.

*Conditional acceptance of offer for lease of South Bogside Farm*

ALL COMMUNICATIONS TO BE ADDRESSED TO THE COMPANY

HEAD OFFICE:
LEVEN, FIFE.

TELEGRAMS "CARLOW, PHONE, LEVEN."
"FIFCOL," COWDENBEATH

TELEPHONE Nos 161 & 162 LEVEN
" Nos 3181 TO 3185 COWDENBEATH.

YOUR REF. ........................

OUR REF. WGC/MMc.

The Fife Coal Company (Limited)

Cowdenbeath, Fife. 3rd June, 1941.

Mr. James Rutherford,
Broomfold Farm,
MARKINCH.

Dear Sir,

South Bogside Farm

With reference to your call here with your son James on 22nd May, we are now prepared to accept your son's offer for the above farm. You verbally undertook to finance your son by guaranteeing the payment of rent for a period of 5 years. A formal letter of guarantee will be sent to you for signature prior to the lease being signed.

Yours faithfully,
For THE FIFE COAL COMPANY, LIMITED,
W.G. Cunningham

*Final acceptance of offer for lease*

*South Bogside Farm, 1952*

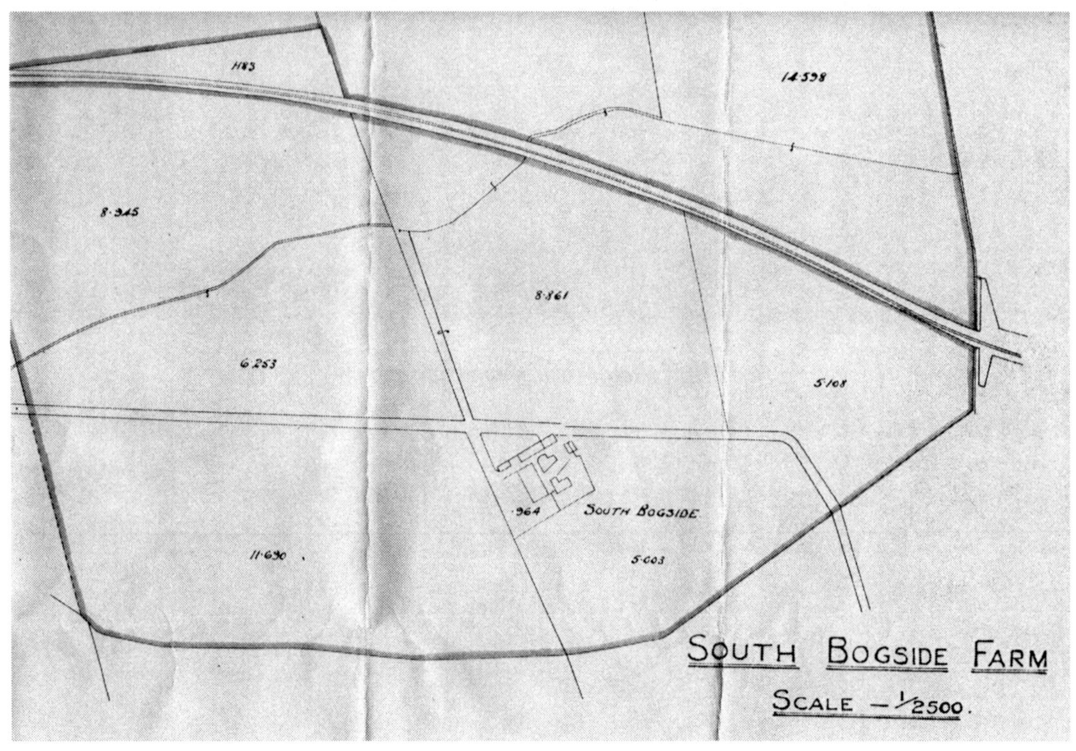


*Map of South Bogside Farm*

NUMBER

STKJ 1 : 2

SURNAME Rutherford

CHRISTIAN NAMES (First only in full) James

CLASS CODE A

FULL POSTAL ADDRESS PITKINNY. ~~[illegible]~~ FARM

CARDENDEN ~~[illegible]~~

HOLDER'S SIGNATURE James Rutherford.

NATIONAL REGISTRATION OFFICE · STA 15 MY 43

**CHANGES OF ADDRESS.** No entry except by National Registration Officer, to whom removal must be notified.

REMOVED TO (Full Postal Address) PITKINNY FARM BY ~~[illegible]~~ CARDENDEN.

REGISTRATION · STA AP 20 51

REMOVED TO (Full Postal Address)

REMOVED TO (Full Postal Address)

REMOVED TO (Full Postal Address)

REMOVED TO (Full Postal Address)

FOR OFFICIAL ENTRY ONLY (apart from Holder's Signature). ANY OTHER ENTRY OR ANY ALTERATION, MARKING OR ERASURE, IS PUNISHABLE BY A FINE OR IMPRISONMENT OR BOTH.

*Identity card for Jim*

NUMBER

STKF 94 : 3

SURNAME Rutherford

CHRISTIAN NAMES (First only in full) Johan

CLASS CODE A

FULL POSTAL ADDRESS South Boyside Glencraig

NATIONAL REGISTRATION OFFICE STA 15 MY 43

HOLDER'S SIGNATURE Johan Rutherford

**CHANGES OF ADDRESS. No entry except by National Registration Officer, to whom removal must be notified.**

REMOVED TO (Full Postal Address) PITKINNY FARM BY GLENCRAIG

REMOVED TO (Full Postal Address)

REMOVED TO (Full Postal Address)

REMOVED TO (Full Postal Address)

REMOVED TO (Full Postal Address)

**FOR OFFICIAL ENTRY ONLY (apart from Holder's Signature). ANY OTHER ENTRY OR ANY ALTERATION, MARKING OR ERASURE, IS PUNISHABLE BY A FINE OR IMPRISONMENT OR BOTH.**

*Identity card for Joey*

NUMBER

SHOS' 1946 : 88

SURNAME RUTHERFORD

CHRISTIAN NAMES (First only in full) Elizabeth A

FULL POSTAL ADDRESS South Bogside Farm, By Glencraig. STA.

THIS IDENTITY CARD IS VALID UNTIL 14th September 1962, ONLY

STA 27 SE 46

**CHANGES OF ADDRESS. No entry except by National Registration Officer, to whom removal must be notified.**

REMOVED TO (Full Postal Address) PITKINNY FARM BY GLENCRAIG

REMOVED TO (Full Postal Address)

REMOVED TO (Full Postal Address)

REMOVED TO (Full Postal Address)

**NOTICE. The parent, guardian or other person having charge of the person to whom this Card relates must sign his or her own name in the first vacant space on the back.**

**The person having charge is responsible for the custody and production, when required, of this Identity Card and for the notification of any change of address of the person to whom it relates.**

**Within seven days after the 16th birthday of the person to whom this Card relates that person must produce it at the local National Registration Office for the issue of a new Card.**

**FOR OFFICIAL ENTRY ONLY. ANY OTHER ENTRY OR ANY ALTERATION, MARKING OR ERASURE IS PUNISHABLE BY A FINE OR IMPRISONMENT OR BOTH.**

*Identity card for Elizabeth Anne Rutherford*

*Joey with Uncle Dave, Kingsmill Farm, Kennoway, 1946*

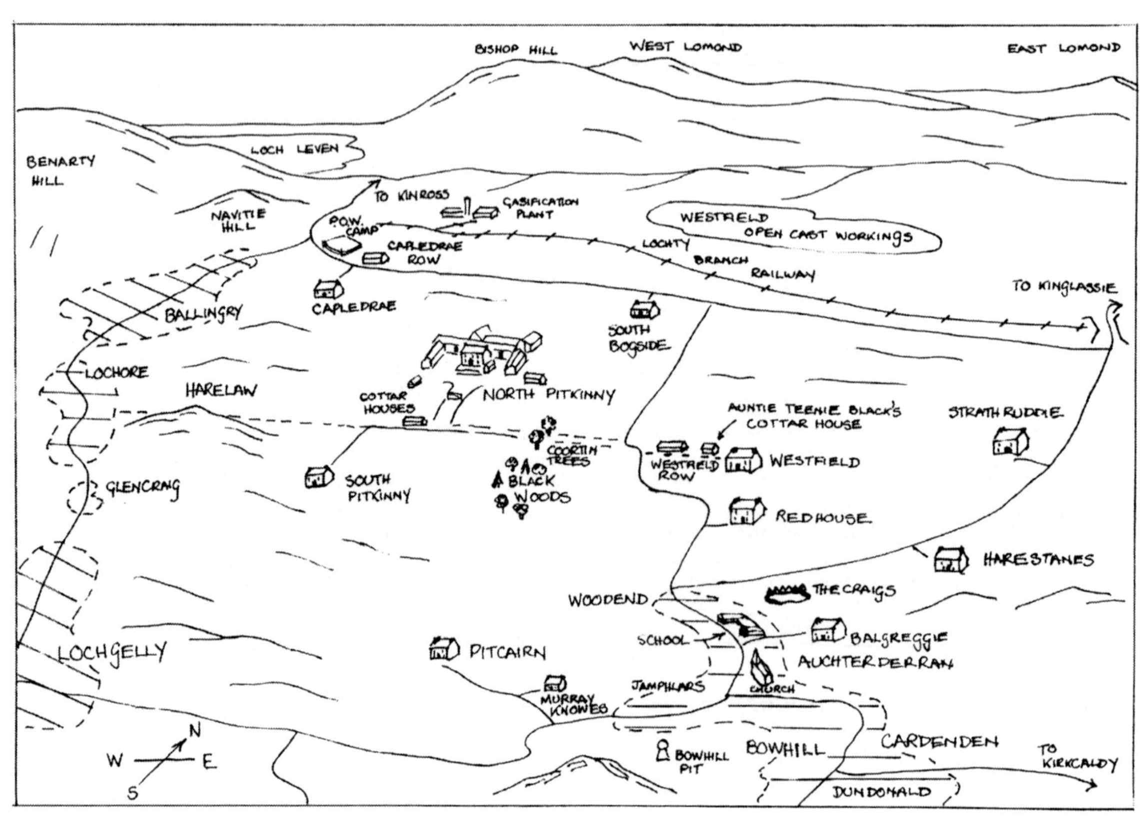


*Map of Pitkinny and the surrounding farms*

# PART 3

## SEED TIME

# Chapter 9

## "Newborn babies do not cough, Mrs Rutherford!"

Even in the early days of their marriage, the home Joey and Jim were building became a magnet for family and friends alike. Betsy and Hugh would often visit on a Sunday, taking the bus from Markinch to Woodend. They would often be accompanied by Joey's younger sister Doris, still a schoolgirl, and of course James, her wee brother and the baby of the family. Of course, Greta was in the ATS until her marriage later in the war. Hughie and then (later in the conflict) John were both in the RAF "for the duration." Betty, older than Doris by two years, was now working and having other interests, so visited less often. Later in the war, she would marry a Polish officer who, with many of his exiled compatriots, was stationed in Fife. They would have a daughter in 1946, but by then the marriage was already over and they were subsequently divorced.

Visiting the farm was, of course, a great novelty for Joey's family, but in times of rationing, visitors could not expect to be fed by their hosts. Although there was always a more plentiful supply of basic home-produced food on a farm than town-dwellers could count on, Betsy would always bring what food she could, and did her best to offer practical help to the newly-married couple in setting up home. Hugh was of great assistance to Jim, as he was to be in the years ahead, as he could turn his hand to anything mechanical, and would often manage to effect repairs, or devise additions or modifications to Jim's steadily increasing and developing machinery and buildings. Friends and cousins of the young couple would visit, some of them while on leave from the armed services, and I am sure they all had many happy times. Neither a certain degree of physical hardship nor a huge amount of hard toil could entirely dampen their young spirits or sap their youthful energy and enthusiasm.

There was to be one occasion, however, when a potential threat to their happiness presented itself, and it came in the form of an edict indirectly transmitted from James senior. Although he himself seldom came to Bogside, Wullie and Harry would often visit on a Sunday, sometimes on the same days as Joey's family. On one such day, in the evening after everyone had gone home, Jim seemed very subdued. When Joey expressed concern, he denied that there was anything wrong. However, Joey insisted on knowing the reason for his low spirits, and he described how his brothers had told him it was "unlucky" to have frequent visitors as they were still trying to get established and could not afford to feed extra mouths. Joey was furious and pointed out that

Wullie and Harry had never refused to eat any of the food she had given them! In addition, unlike Betsy and Hugh, they usually came empty-handed!

It was clear to Joey and Jim that Wullie and Harry had been induced to carry this message of bad luck by their father, but the next time they came to Bogside, it was Joey who sent them home with a flea in their ears. She insisted that her family and friends would always be welcome at Bogside, and pointed out that if any home is "unlucky" it is the one devoid of hospitality and, consequently, of visitors. She suggested that her brothers-in-law should take this message to their father and Nellie, assuring them that Bogside would never be that kind of "unlucky" place. She added that she hoped her two brothers would be frequent visitors in the future, if they survived the war, and that if either or both of them did not, she would never let Wulllie or Harry forget their sacrifice, especially since they were spending the war safe at home in a reserve occupation. Jim had tried to discourage Joey's outburst. "Wheesht, wheesht, dinna say anything," as he was always reluctant to confront an uncomfortable situation, preferring to let sleeping dogs lie, but that was never Joey's way, and she much preferred to clear the air. Certainly, neither the brothers nor their father could have been left in any doubt that the day they dared to confront Joey was not their lucky day!

A job in an occupation that carried exemption from military service was, of course, a coveted commodity for many young people. Jim's youngest uncle on his father's side, Thomas, also lived in the Star and had three children: Margaret, Bill, and Duncan. This youngest cousin of Jim had begun to serve his time as a painter but his mother urged his father to find him a job on a farm, to keep him out of the army. Tam asked his brother James to help, and he agreed to intervene on behalf of his nephew. So, one day, James unexpectedly turned up at Bogside with Dunc in tow. He told Joey and Jim that the young man would work for them "for his keep." He needed a job on the land and they needed his labour. He would not cost them anything but his bed and board. While Joey was dismayed by this intrusion into their home, Jim could see the sense in having another pair of hands about the place, and Joey realised that she had no choice but to agree to the proposed arrangement. Privately she feared that their new lodger would be a "spy-in-residence" for "the Star anes," as he would be party to daily life at Bogside. However, the visits from Harry and Wullie had slowed to a trickle after Joey's reaction to the edict they had previously tried to deliver from their father. While Joey had not exactly "shot the messenger," she hoped that James and Nellie realised that she would not tolerate any further interference from them.

Joey had a formidable workload to cope with at Bogside. The usual domestic chores of cooking, cleaning, and washing were supplemented by making and mending clothes and making as much necessary improvement to the comfort of the house as they could afford. In addition she worked outside, helping with the milking, where the cooling of the milk and the washing of the milk churns twice a day were her responsibility. She also kept hens and, in their season, fed calves and pet lambs. After my sister Margaret was born in September 1942, naturally her workload increased greatly. When the baby was very young, Joey's ability to work outside was severely curtailed. She had help from time to time from Jim's cousin, Teen Shepherd (née Wilson), who with her husband Jim and two daughters, Effie and Betty, lived at Capeldrae. However, Teen was sometimes needed to work outside, and Joey could not count on her help all the time. It was a few years later that Joey was to have more reliable live-in help. Her youngest sister Doris left school in 1944 and started work at Tullis Russell paper mill near Markinch. However, when the war ended, the consequent drop in demand for its produce resulted in the workforce being put on short-time work, and Doris asked if she could come and live at Bogside and work for Jim and

Joey. She had often visited with Betsy and Hugh and thought farm life would suit her. When Joey's health began to be a concern after I was born in 1946, it was clear that another fit young person would certainly make a huge impact on Joey's ability to fulfil all the demands made on her time and energy, and she and Jim agreed to Doris's request. She had to understand, however, that, as with Dunc, they could not afford to pay her a weekly wage, but she would get her board and lodging and a little pocket money. In addition, Joey and Jim opened savings accounts for their young helpers and paid money into them as and when their cash flow would allow, so that their labour would be rewarded in time, if not immediately or regularly.

This extended family arrangement worked well in those early days. Dunc proved to be very hard working, if somewhat dour and humourless. He had a little bedroom on the ground floor which, with the big room—a sitting room which was very damp and not much used—and the kitchen, scullery, and toilet completed the downstairs accommodation. At the top of the single steep flight of stairs, to the left was Joey and Jim's room and to the right the room where Doris, Margaret and, later, I slept. This in turn gave access to another bedroom, which was occasionally used by visitors. Doris, too, worked hard and was good company and a big help to Joey, both in the house and outside. In addition, she enjoyed the companionship of other young folk who did casual work at Bogside. The Imrie family, who also lived in one of the houses in Capeldrae Row, were to have a very long connection with Jim and Joey at Bogside, and later at Pitkinny. The father Jock was a miner, and he and his wife had six sons and a daughter. At least four of the boys worked with Joey and Jim at one time or another; John in the early days at Bogside, and Donald, Robbie, and Dougie at Pitkinny.

Dunc's normal working week on the farm usually ended after dinnertime (midday) on a Saturday, when he would go home to the Star on his motorbike, returning on a Sunday night. Sometimes, Doris would go with him on the pillion of his bike, and he would drop her off at her home in Markinch. So the two young people spent some time together, very much as brother and sister, as everyone thought. As time passed and the farm income could stand it, Dunc came to be paid a weekly wage, and he gradually eased into the position of foreman at Bogside and, later, Pitkinny. Doris, however, came to resent the fact that she was not being paid a wage for her work, and it came to Joey's notice that she was expressing her discontent to the other young workers on the farm. She challenged Doris about this and reminded her of the terms under which she had decided to work at Bogside. It was agreed that she should return home and resume work in the paper mill, at which point Joey and Jim gave her the little nest egg they had saved for her. Although this all involved some unpleasantness and Joey was confirmed in her reservations about the advisability of employing relatives, Doris and Joey remained on friendly terms, and she continued to visit the farm. With the benefit of hindsight, Joey and Jim should perhaps have seen the writing on the wall in terms of future working arrangements, as they were to turn out. Doris continued to visit the farm, but no one realised that she had any romantic attachment to Dunc. So Jim and Joey were, consequently, flabbergasted when he announced early in 1953 that they were to be married. So, in October of that year, Jim's cousin married Joey's sister, and they took up house in one of the cottages at Pitkinny. On the face of it, this arrangement was mutually acceptable, but as the years passed, it gradually became clear that there were strains and tensions in the relationship between the two families, which were to give rise to a parting of the ways in the 1960s.

When Joey discovered that she was pregnant towards the end of 1941, she was delighted that she would soon have a baby of her own. Being the oldest in her family, she had always been used to looking after wee ones; her own younger brothers and sisters, her cousins, or the babies and toddlers of friends and neighbours, and from a young age she had hoped she would be blessed with children of her own one day. She had virtually brought James up in his early years and saw him through a succession of childhood illnesses. By 1942 he was six years old and, hopefully, through the worst of his troubles. Joey naturally had tremendous patience with rearing infants and had developed great skill in home-nursing their ailments. Perhaps she had inherited and learned much of this from her granny Hann, but as she awaited the birth of her first baby, little did she realise how many of these assets she would need in the months and years ahead.

It was thought best for the baby to be born at Markinch, where Betsy and Hugh were now living at 83 Croft Crescent. They had enough room for Joey's confinement, and the services of a doctor, should they be needed, would be at hand more readily than at Bogside. James was by then at school, and Betsy learned that the twin daughters of a neighbour and friend of hers, a Mrs Fraser, who were in the same class as James, had come down with whooping cough. This was a very serious illness in those days, and, given his earlier delicate condition, Betsy worried that James might have been infected. Fortunately, he did not develop any symptoms, and there was no reason to worry that it was not safe for Joey to have her baby in the house. After a long and painful (but thankfully straightforward) labour, Margaret was born on 29 September 1942, an apparently healthy baby.

James was less than thrilled with this new addition to the family. He was, of course, very close to Joey and showed all the usual signs of sibling rivalry. Shortly after Margaret was born and he became aware of the fact that his place as the favoured baby of the family had been usurped, Hugh found him waiting at the corner as he returned home from work at the paper mill. "Joey's got a wee bairn an' it's a lassie. Go up and throw it oot o' the staircase windae, Dad!" Hugh, needless to say, did not comply, and he and Betsy tried to reassure him that they still wanted him as well as the new baby. He was not convinced, and in the coming months and years, it became clear that the relationship between James and Margaret would often be a stormy one. Happily, as they eventually grew up they would at last be good pals.

When the midwife called on the morning after Margaret's birth, Joey told her that the baby had coughed. The midwife smiled somewhat patronisingly and replied, "Newborn babies do not cough, Mrs Rutherford!" Joey felt rather foolish and tried to tell herself that she had imagined the cough, but within the next few days it became very clear that she had in fact been right and the baby was coughing regularly. The doctor was called and, although he found it hard to believe, had no choice but to diagnose whooping cough. He could only assume that James had been a carrier of the virus without showing signs of the illness himself, and had passed it, via her mother, to the baby before she was born. The doctor had no experience of whooping cough in such a young infant, and was rather at a loss as to what to do. He gave Margaret an injection of a recently developed drug—perhaps M&B, I can't be sure—but his only advice to Joey was to "keep her bowels open and lift and turn her every time she coughs." He would not attempt a prognosis, but was clearly not optimistic that the baby would survive, let alone thrive normally.

I really believe that, had she had anyone else for a mother, Margaret would never have come through this dangerous start to her life. Joey had to return to Bogside after a week or two, to resume her life there with the daunting prospect of rearing a very sick baby, in addition to all the other demands on her physical and emotional strength. That she succeeded is a testament to the patience and skill that came from her determination to be a good mother. Perhaps this defines mother love, what we glibly describe as the maternal instinct, but however we explain it, it carried

Joey and Margaret through. Although Joey did her best in the following weeks to follow the scant medical advice she had been given, Margaret failed to gain weight steadily, because, although Joey managed to feed her, the coughing fits induced vomiting, so the baby seldom got the benefit of her feeds. However, more importantly, she did not lose any weight, nor did she develop "the drawback" the whooping spasm that gives the illness its name, and which is so exhausting for the sufferer. This may have been due to the effects of the injection she had been given, but whatever the reason, Joey was able to nurse Margaret through that first winter, and the most critical phase of the illness, so that by the spring she was, if not much heavier, at least a little stronger.

In the course of the following two years, Margaret began to thrive and appeared to have thrown off the worst effects of her precarious start in life. Despite that, Joey always declared that throughout her childhood, she would find coughing as natural as breathing, as the aftermath of the whooping cough would surface whenever she had a cold or other minor ailment. Then, when she was only two and a half, Margaret developed infective hepatitis, more commonly known as jaundice. They never knew for sure how she caught this illness. Jim blamed her pet cat, while Joey suspected that the ever-present mice had carried an infection to her wee girl, because no matter how careful they were, it was never possible to rid the old house of the vermin completely. Joey remembered how one morning she noticed that something, probably a mouse, had chewed a hole in the cot sheet that Margaret was lying on. The illness made her so ill that although she had been walking for months, she went off her legs completely for some weeks. As she was recovering from the infection, Jim's Auntie Fame (Euphemia), his mother's sister and the mother of Teen Shepherd, called in one day while she was visiting her daughter at Capeldrae. She asked Joey how Margaret was, and when she replied that she was still not walking again, the old lady went over to the kitchen window and exclaimed, "My goodness! See what is coming down the road!" At that Margaret, who had been lying on the settee, got up and toddled over to the window to see what all the excitement was about! Of course, there was nothing to see, but Auntie Fame's ruse had worked and Margaret was on her feet again!.

She was to give Joey and Jim another major health scare some years later, after we had moved to Pitkinny, when she was about nine. We were being looked after by our Auntie Doris, while Mum was in hospital. Margaret had taken a very bad cold, which she was unable to throw off: what was then known as a "sittin' doon cauld." When Joey came home, she realised that Margaret was really ill, and the doctor sent her to hospital for tests. Joey realised with horror that he suspected that she had TB (tuberculosis), and all her worst fears came back to haunt her. She remembered all the young people she had known when she was a girl who had succumbed to this dread disease. She could not believe that despite all her best efforts, her wee girl had become so seriously ill. She could see nothing ahead but the prospect of Margaret having to go into a sanatorium to be treated for consumption. Although the discovery of M&B made the possibility of recovery much more likely than had previously been the case, she feared that Margaret might never enjoy full health and strength. Nurse MacMillan, the local district nurse, who had brought me into the world and had become a valued friend, advised Joey that she should rather keep Margaret at home, where she could have the best of food and excellent home nursing. The day came when Joey had to take Margaret to the Victoria Hospital in Kirkcaldy for the result of the medical tests. They saw the TB specialist, a Dr Cuba, who said, "Mrs Rutherford, I wish I could give every mother I see the news I am about to give you: Margaret does not have tuberculosis. She will soon be well. Take her home and look after her as only you can."

I can only imagine the enormous sense of relief that our parents must have felt at that news. Although this was little more than sixty ears ago, preventive medicine in the form of vaccination and inoculation was a relatively new phenomenon. In this as in so many other ways, I feel that my generation had the best of everything. We missed the war and the worst of the postwar austerity, while we benefited from revolutionary medical developments. Life and health were not the precarious prospects they had been for our parents' and their parents' generations. The Second World War was a huge watershed in political, economic, and social terms, and the changes that resulted meant that there were, for the first time, genuine educational opportunities for our generation which had been denied to earlier ones. Thanks to the policies of the postwar Labour governments, both on a national and local level, Margaret was able to attend a pre-nursing college for three years before starting her hospital training, while I was able to go to university and teachers' training college.

Both of these courses of action were open to us because there was funding available to assist our parents. Although they still had to make considerable financial and emotional commitment to us, to support us in gaining entry to our chosen occupations, there was nothing like the sacrifice involved that was the case a generation earlier. In that context both Margaret and I were able to gain qualifications which gave us the possibility of having good jobs, in secure professions, nursing and teaching respectively, which meant that we would always be able to earn our livings independently. I think that was important to Joey. She saw us achieve the ability to look after ourselves, because no longer was marriage the only route to security for girls. Access to health care would no longer depend on having the necessary financial resources, as had been the case when Joey was a girl and had to suffer the long-term effects of rheumatic fever, for want of having the money to call the doctor.

We were of the generation of children who benefited from the fact that government, for the first time, took great responsibility for the health and education of its citizens, whether it be in the provision of free cod liver oil and school milk, or the availability of university grants. This meant that for the first time, tertiary education ceased to be the exclusive province of the rich and privileged in society. It is difficult for me, therefore, to countenance the situation that now prevails in the early twenty-first century. It appears that neither health care nor education can be guaranteed for our young people: The National Health Service, despite a proud heritage, seems unable to bear the demands placed upon it, and prospective students and their families are faced with crippling financial disincentives to higher education. Whatever the political, economic, and social explanations for (and implications of) this situation, it seems to me that while things may not (thankfully) have come full circle since my parents were children, there is no doubt that progress in these areas during the last twenty years has been somewhat erratic. In addition, while our standard of living has improved immeasurably, our personal standards of behaviour and morality have in so many ways regressed. That is not to say that I would wish us to return to the "good old days," which were anything but good for the majority of people. As is usually the case, the answer lies not in either of the two positions but somewhere in between, and if only the best of all worlds could be combined, then perhaps we could really say that we have used what we have learned from our past to inform and enhance our future.

Returning to Margaret's early childhood at Bogside, another comparison with today strikes me: the issue of child care for working mothers. Nowadays, most mothers of families combine the roles of bringing up their children with paid employment. The provision of good child care, especially in the preschool years, is a problem in terms of availability and cost. When our children were born, I didn't work. This was the typical situation in our family and social circle. Every woman was married to the man she lived with, and those who had children stayed at home to look after them and their husbands as full-time mothers and housewives. This had tended to be the socioeconomic norm in previous generations, and, although there were, geographically and historically, places and times when women were the main breadwinners, these were usually the exceptions rather than the rule.

As mentioned previously, Joey had to fulfil a dual role, in her outside work on the farm and in her domestic responsibilities. From the time Margaret was a few months old, Joey would take her out with her whenever possible, bundled up against the cold in winter. When the weather made this inadvisable, she would leave her in the house. It is clear that this would now be viewed as neglect and would attract severe criticism, but there really was no alternative. Having said that, Joey's work was "all at the back door." In other words, she was always within a few yards of the kitchen. She could glance in the window every few minutes as she trudged back and forth between the byre and the dairy, lugging the milk cans, cooling the milk and washing the cans, walking to the henhouses, feeding the hens, and gathering the eggs. When Margaret was able to sit up, Joey would leave her playing on the floor with the few improvised toys she had. There was an apple basket, which contained some bits and pieces: a few wooden bricks, empty cotton reels and so on; in fact, any little things that a small child could handle and hold safely. Margaret would spend her time filling and emptying the basket, smiling happily at Joey each time she peeped in at the window. She was a very contented and placid child, and despite her poor health as a baby, she seldom cried. The temper tantrums of the "terrible twos" were unknown.

Nowadays, it might be suggested that she lacked stimulation, that it was wrong to leave her alone like that, but she was in fact quite safe and she learned to amuse herself. Of course as she grew older, there were many days where she was outside with her mother, following Joey around the place, listening and talking all the time as she watched her mother doing her work.

In general, as children we were expected to be "seen and not heard," the world did not revolve around us and we did not inhabit a child-centred environment. This is very different from the current ideal, which is aspired to in terms of our understanding of child development, but again, I believe that the best approach to child rearing is a combination of both methodologies. As the oldest of the cousins in our family, there were always younger children around and I remember my granny Betsy saying, "Whit that bairn needs is a guid dose o' healthy neglect!" Young as I was, I realised that this was a contradictory statement. How could neglect be healthy? But as I brought up my own sons, I began to understand what she meant. Children need to have some space and time to be themselves, to learn to be alone and develop their imaginations without the constant intervention of adults. In this way they begin to have a sense of themselves, and of where they fit into the family. Likewise, it is when they interact spontaneously with other children, their siblings and friends, that they develop their social skills and learn to negotiate with others in a way that they can control and direct without the imposition of grown-up rules of engagement. Having said that, I would not recommend going so far as Jim's child care suggestions. When our first Son Calum was a baby, and I was trying to do everything "by the book," he said, "When that bairn's sleeping, ye wake 'im up tae feed 'im, then ye want 'im tae gang tae sleep when 'es no tired! If Ah wis lookin' efter a bairn, I wid let 'im sleep when 'e's tired, feed 'im when 'e's hungry an' only wash 'im when 'e's awfy, awfy, dirty!"

In a similar way, often the most valuable communication between parent and child is in the context of the apparently mundane domestic routines, rather than in contrived "quality time" situations. Even young children can see through such strategies, and I always found that it was when they were relaxed and at ease in familiar routine situations that they would open up and tell you their fears and worries. So it was when you were bathing them, or they were sitting up by the kitchen sink watching you cooking or preparing the food, that you would have some of the most fun, listening and talking to each other.

Also, there are many educational opportunities, which present themselves in the most natural and uncontrived situations, when young children are spending time with their mothers or fathers at home. My mother never walked upstairs with us when we were small without counting out the steps with us. Nursery rhymes and other little poems, games, and stories would be repeated naturally, and there are many I recall from my earliest memories. All of these activities are known to be valuable learning strategies for the preschool child, but our parents never saw them as such. They were simply a spontaneous and natural way to interact with us, and when we became parents we repeated the same approach to rearing our boys. This was not part of a pre-determined attempt to educate them, or to give them a kick-start to their learning, but as an instinctive reaction to their needs.

In terms of child development, I realise that this kind of interaction is an ideal way to stimulate a child's intellectual and social development, but I was not aware that I was interacting with my children with this objective in mind. I think I was simply doing with them what my mother had done with me, and I really believe that as this is the only way we really learn to be effective parents, we have to be very grateful that we had such good role models. So I have serious concerns about the wisdom of mothers working outside the home in the first few precious years of their children's lives. While the benefits of nursery education are well documented and perhaps essential for children who lack good parenting at home, the intellectual and emotional development of young children is best served, I believe, by the consistency and security of spending their first months and years at home with their parents. This gives them the best foundation for a gradual introduction to the wider world: meeting and playing with little playmates, first in each other's homes, and then in toddler and playgroups, where they learn to interact with other children in new environments. So they gradually learn to be away from their mothers and their homes, but they still have the security of a strong sense of where their home is and what they can safely expect to happen there.

My sister and I and our respective families were fortunate in that we were able to have the best of both worlds. We were both able to return to the workplace gradually, finding part-time jobs in community nursing and supply teaching, until our children were old enough for us to return to full-time jobs in our chosen occupations, and so fulfilling our personal agendas while adding to the family income. It is in this way, as in so many others, that I feel we were a lucky generation. There were no conflicting possibilities for us when our children were small, no anxious decisions to be made about our relative priorities. Although we were much less well off in material terms, I really believe that we were more content, and just as fulfilled as modern parents. I am certainly glad that I did not miss those few short years, understanding as I do now, how short and precious they were, and how quickly our children grow up and start to make their own way in the world.

These conclusions are not in any way a prescription for child rearing. They are simply the result of my observations over the years, gleaned from my experience as a child and as a parent, and set against the less-than-ideal start in life which my parents had. On the one hand, Joey had been affected by a considerable degree of physical hardship, and Jim by a similarly damaging lack of emotional security, and both of these factors would tell on them later in their lives. My mother was determined to give us a good start in life, and although my father always found it harder to express his affection, I grew up knowing that they both always had our best interests at heart.

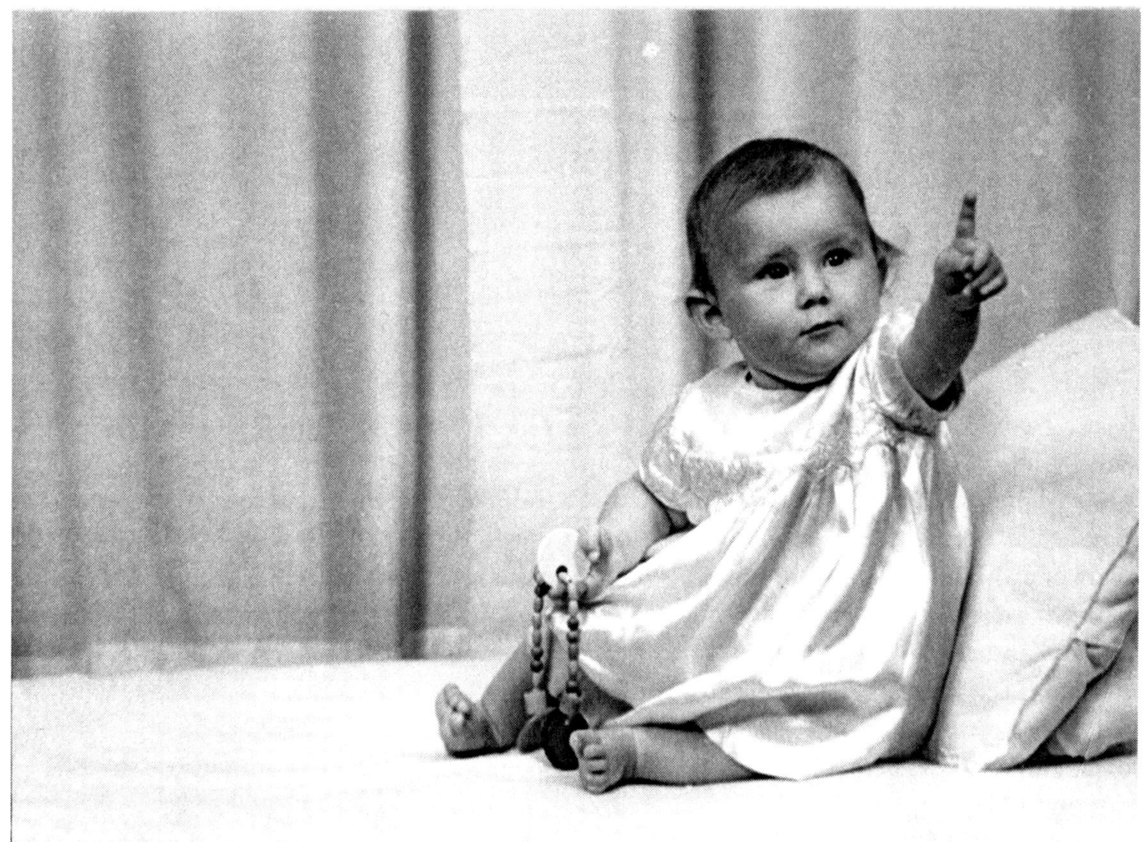

*Margaret as a baby, 7 months*

*Margaret at the back door of Bogside Farm, 3 years*

# Chapter 10

"She's maybe a lassie but she's a braw ane!"

While Margaret and, later, I were well cared for and had a happy if simple early childhood at Bogside, life there for Joey and Jim continued to be a regime of hard work, with little or no time for leisure or any kind of spare-time activity unrelated to the needs of the farm or family. My earliest memories were of them working outside, with me following Joey around as she went from one chore to another, or, when darkness or bad weather made outdoor activity impossible, Joey would be busy in the house. When she did sit down her hands were always active, sewing, knitting, mending, cleaning, and grading the eggs for private customers and, later, the egg-marketing board, a much more demanding customer. Even shoe mending was done at home, using a set of lasts and cobbler's tools.

I remember Dad kept diaries of his daily work, none of which survive, sadly, but I have some account and wage books, and some documentation of produce sold. He would have some time for reading his *Farmer's Weekly* and the *Scottish Farmer* while the daily paper, the *Dundee Courier and Advertiser*, was a necessary conduit of local and social news; the "hatches, matches, and dispatches" page an indispensable notice of births, marriages, and deaths in the Fife population. There was also a column that listed the estates of those recently deceased, the amount of money they had accrued in their lifetime to be commented on favourably or unfavourably by all and sundry! Joey could seldom indulge her passion for reading beyond this, as there were always more urgent chores to be attended to, and, in any case, she had no access to a library and could never have afforded to buy books. Although, as the years passed and she had more time and money, she would have the opportunity once again to enjoy the delights of books. She remembered enough of her granny's belief that reading was a sinful waste of time, to make a point of reading only when all her work was complete for the day. When Jim once complained about her reading late into the night, and suggested that she should take time during the day to read her book, she was quick to remind him that if he had caught her reading when there was work to be done, his reaction might have been not too dissimilar to that of Hann all those years before!

In common with many families in those days, outward physical demonstration of affection was alien to the naturally reticent, not to say dour, Scottish temperament, honed by centuries of Calvinist-inspired distrust of such flamboyance. Hugging and kissing between us and our parents, perhaps acceptable when we were small, gradually lessened as we grew up until it simply never happened, and it is one of my few regrets that we felt so discouraged from expressing our affection for each other in these ways. As a young adult, I would feel acute embarrassment when I witnessed families who would kiss or hug when meeting or parting, and it was only in later years that I began to feel comfortable with the custom. To some extent, this is probably because our society in general has become more demonstrative, and displays of physical affection have become more acceptable. I am happy that we have always been openly affectionate to our sons and took delight in their close physical contact with their grandparents, which continued into their adulthood. I can honestly say that while I remember being cuddled by my mother when I was small, I have few memories of even sitting on my father's lap, or having him hug me. This was because when we were young, child care was exclusively seen as women's work, and by and large most of my contemporaries would have had the same experience.

Thus I derived great surprise and even greater pleasure from the way my dad was always very close to his grandchildren, and took more interest in their well-being. When they had retired and were living in Kirkcudbright, I once said to him, when he took our boys out for a walk, Donald still in his pushchair, "You never did that for us, Dad." He replied that he wished he had and appreciated having a second chance with his grandchildren. I am sure that he found it wonderful having two grandsons after two daughters and three granddaughters, but he was just as fond of and involved with the girls as with our boys. Mum, of course, always inspired great affection in young children, who were instinctively drawn to her. She had great patience, combined with a firm but kind approach to discipline, which youngsters unfailingly responded to.

Jim and Joey first knew each other at school, and from the time they met again and were courting, and then were married, they were never apart for more than a day or two. Their first, and indeed only separation, was when Margaret was born in Markinch. They had no telephone in those days, and, having no car, Jim could visit only once or twice after the baby was born. Joey often used to tell us that during that time she received two letters from Jim. "Imagine! Only two love letters in all those years," I remember her laughing, "and one of them began 'Dear Sir'!" We were never quite sure whether to believe this story of such an unromantic "billet-doux," but after Mum died we found the letter in her "pansy box," the old biscuit tin where she kept all her important papers. Sure enough, the epistle began "Dear Sir," but it ended with great affection, "Love to you both from Pa. (Haw! Haw!)" The second letter began "Dear Joey," and ended even more affectionately, with twenty-one kisses and a PS: "You can count these and I'll get them next time."

Dad did, however, have a plausible explanation for his mistake in the first letter. When he sat down at the kitchen table at Bogside that evening to write the letter, his cousin Teen Shepherd, who was helping him while Joey was away, was in the kitchen. He was anxious that she might see what he was writing, so to put her off the scent, he wrote in pencil and began the letter "Dear Sir," intending to change it later. As it happened, he forgot and sent it off in its original form. These two letters give some insight into my parents' relationship, and remind me that, while they were always "Mum" and "Dad" to me, they were lovers and husband and wife to each other, still in their early days together, having had their first child and on the threshold of family life. Jim writes about his work on the farm, in the midst of the potato harvest at Bogside, but also helping at Westfield and Capeldrae. He mentions his first attempt to buy a car, from a man in Bowhill, part of Cardenden. He was asking £20 for it, which was more than Jim could afford at the time, and it also needed new tyres. Another prospective buyer was interested in it, a Mr Whyte from Kirkcaldy, so Jim wasn't too hopeful that he would be able to acquire this particular car, but clearly it was only going to be a matter of time until he had his own transport. This is a telling passage in the letter when contrasted with his purchase of his first Rover car less than ten years later.

It is a sad fact of history that wartime has always been a combination of disaster for many but opportunity for others. Joey and Jim would have been the first to admit that they were relatively untouched by the tragedy of war. Joey's two brothers survived the conflict, Hughie despite being in the thick of the action in the European theatre of war. John, being younger, was called up into the RAF only towards the end, and was posted to India where he was spared any engagement in hostilities. Ironically, however, he was the one who was to be injured. He was actually run over by an aeroplane! He failed to move fast enough when pulling away the chocks from under the wheel of a plane as it was taking off and the wheel went over his foot and broke it in several places. No doubt a painful injury, but acquired in a somewhat comical fashion, and it was enough to guarantee that he would sit out the remainder of the war. He returned home, to be married, still in uniform, to a girl from Leslie, Alice Wyse. Interestingly, her wedding gown was made out of parachute silk, a plentiful fabric as the war ended, when other dress materials were impossible to find.

The war in Europe ended with VE-Day on 9 May 1945. Our Aunt Greta was home on leave from the ATS, prior to her de-mobilisation, and about to be married. She and her intended husband, Bobby Drennan from Kinglassie, were at Bogside that day. The weather was warm and sunny, and the two young couples spontaneously marked the ending of hostilities by engaging in a water fight on a grand scale. It is a happy and heartening image, one of these four carefree young people having such innocent fun—throwing buckets of water and playing hoses on each other until they were all completely drenched—a small celebration of a historic occasion and a long-awaited release of the tension they had all lived under for six long years. This was but a tiny reflection of the joy felt throughout the entire country, and, indeed, the free world, that the threat to national and international survival had at last been overcome.

Country folk had profited from the war inasmuch as they had mostly been able to avoid active service, they had been spared the worst of the food shortages, and they had assured and profitable markets for their produce. Joey and Jim's hard work was beginning to pay off and they were "getting on." They would go on to do even better under the Labour government, elected immediately after the war.

One small cloud on Joey's horizon was her awareness that Margaret was now three years old and still an only child, so she was delighted to learn that she was pregnant again as 1945 gave way to a new year. I was born, two weeks overdue, on 14 September 1946; like Margaret, on a Saturday. ("Saturday's child works hard for a living.") That day as Joey realised that she was in labour, she was anxious that Dunc should leave for the Star so they would have the house to themselves. It would not have occurred to her or Jim to just ask him to go, because there was a reluctance, even within a family, to talk about things like childbirth. As it was, for once he did not seem to be in a hurry to leave, and sat down after his dinner to read the *Courier*. Joey thought he would never go, but at last he donned his motorbike gear and off he went. That allowed her the freedom to concentrate on her preparations for my arrival. In due course Jim, now a proud car owner, was despatched to take Margaret to Markinch and on the way to alert the midwife, Nurse MacMillan, who lived with her husband Alec and their son Alastair, in one of the roadmen's houses at Woodend. She asked Jim to go and tell Doctor Brackenridge to stand by in case he was needed, and she proceeded by bicycle to Bogside. She had understood that there was no urgency, but realised when she arrived that I was soon going to make an appearance. Fortunately, Joey had everything ready and, despite having kept everyone waiting for two weeks, I was born very quickly thereafter, at eight o'clock, nine pounds of healthy baby girl. Joey was overjoyed that her labour had been relatively short and easy, and vowed to herself that she would go on to have many more children. Jim admitted to some disappointment that I was not a boy, but on seeing me said, "Well she's maybe a lassie, but she's a braw ane—she kinda looks like masel, does she no?"

Within a short time, however, Joey was brought down to earth with a bump when Nurse MacMillan expressed some concern over her patient's alarmingly rapid pulse, and she decided to send for the doctor. He concurred that the new mother's heart condition was worrying, and he later insisted that she should see a heart specialist. She was not surprised, therefore, to be told in due course that her heart valves had been damaged by the rheumatic fever she had suffered as a child and, not for the first time, she was warned to take care of herself and advised against having any more children. While she was disappointed with this particular part of her prognosis, she very soon put it out of her mind. Instead of worrying about her health, she did as she always had in the past and got on with the business of living, which in her case involved looking after Margaret and me, working as hard as ever on the farm, and enjoying her role as wife and mother. She did, however, welcome the arrival of her young sister Doris, who would help both in the house and on the farm.

I was a healthy baby, and indeed gave Betsy a bit of a start when, at two days old, as she was bathing me, I appeared to be focusing on my granny's face and gooing and gurgling at her. She had never seen this in a baby so young. No doubt, the fact that I was more than two weeks late had something to do with this, but all in all Betsy found the whole experience somewhat unsettling, and declared that she believed Joey had kept me hidden under the bed for a few weeks. As my first winter proceeded, there was nothing unusual about the weather until the last day of January, when it began to snow and continued to do so, for the following six weeks! As the blizzard set in, in earnest, it soon became clear that this was no ordinary snowstorm and it was to become by far the worst winter Jim and Joey had ever known. The days were often clear, cold, and cloudless, but most nights would bring renewed snowfall to add to that already lying, so that by morning there would be a fresh white blanket covering the countryside and altering the contours of the familiar landscape. The greatest problem this posed for Joey and Jim was in finding a way to have their milk uplifted for sale, and in getting provisions. Jim managed to improvise a sledge for the milk cans, which was pulled by the horse to Woodend, the nearest pickup point, where he would collect their necessities from the little shop run by Mrs Watt.

The snow grew deeper and deeper, but most days the sun shone out of a clear blue sky, giving an almost alpine air to the scene. Joey and Doris would hang out the daily washing—my nappies and baby clothes, mostly, of course—and in the afternoon, Margaret, now nearly four and a half, would help by unpegging them. She could walk along the top of the snowdrift under the washing line, and easily reach the clothes hanging there. By that account, the snow must have been about four feet deep. Although it made life more difficult on the farm, Joey and Jim remembered this as a unique and special time in their lives. One night, the men from Capeldrae had to rescue the local fishmonger, who had gone missing. They found him stranded in his van, which had run into a snowdrift, and brought him to Bogside, obviously suffering from hypothermia. He had a bald head and it was covered in a thin film of ice! Joey thawed him out and looked after him until he was well enough to be helped home. This was certainly the worst winter they were to experience in their life on the farm. There would be many other times when we would be snowed in for short spells and other years when gales or very wet times would add to the difficulties in running the farm, but never again would we have such a long period of confinement due to the weather.

Young James continued to be a frequent visitor to the farm. He and Joey remained very close to each other, and he certainly hero-worshipped Jim. On one occasion, his father Hugh brought a relative of his to visit Bogside. I don't know who he was, but he had never been on a farm before, and he was very interested in everything Jim and Joey had to tell him about farming. By then their dairy herd had grown somewhat, and they had a few heifers, young cows that had not yet had their first calves. That evening, back at Markinch, their visitor asked Hugh to remind him of the name for these cows. "Heifers," replied Hugh. "Oh no, Dad," piped up James, "Jim cries them h****!"

Despite, or perhaps because, his father never used bad language, nor would tolerate it in anyone else, Jim, now he was his own boss, developed a very colourful vocabulary. As the years passed, he would employ many expletives, none of which were ever deleted. This would happen as a very natural part of his speech, not only at times of anger or stress, although at those times the variety and combinations of his utterances would become even more pronounced. The strange thing was that he never seemed to cause offence to anyone. It was so much part of his persona that it never seemed to strike people as objectionable, although I am sure that on first hearing it must have caused some considerable surprise. I don't know if Dad's choice of language would pass unnoticed these days, when previously unacceptable language is commonplace in the media, but as we grew up and became more sensitive to such situations, we would often urge him to "moderate his language" in advance of any social events where we would anticipate embarrassment. "Don't swear, Dad," we would plead, and to be fair to him, he would try, for all of a few minutes, but once he was in full flow, telling a story or describing a situation, he would forget, and let rip as usual. What I came to realise was more effective, was to warn anyone I suspected might take offence about Dad's tendency to forget himself, and I cannot remember any occasion where his affability and humour failed to disarm new acquaintances.

When young James would visit the farm after Jim had his first car, he went everywhere with him, greatly excited about riding in a car, in those days a rare experience for anyone, let alone a six year old boy. It was not surprising that he would choose to become a car mechanic when he left school. One day as they drove away from Bogside, James in the back of the car, Jim suddenly heard a noise and felt a draught of air on the back of his neck. He was horrified to realise that James had opened the back door of the car and had fallen out! By the time he stopped the car, he was mightily relieved to see James picking himself up and running towards the car, albeit with blood pouring from his face. The door handle had punctured his cheek, thankfully missing his eye. He was whisked down to Doctor Brackenridge, who stitched the gaping wound. James's face was terribly swollen and Joey was afraid to take him home to Markinch, fearing that Betsy and Hugh would never allow him back to the farm. It took a long time, but eventually his cheek healed, although he carries the scar to this day.

Another time, he came within a whisker of drowning. The DP camp near Capeldrae had closed down and there were two water storage tanks, which had been dangerously abandoned full of water. One summer evening, Jim, Joey, Doris, Dunc, Margaret, and James had taken a walk there. One of the farm dogs, Peeril, loved swimming and when Jim threw a stick in the water, he jumped in after it. When the dog climbed out, Joey warned, "Stand back, he's going to shake himself." James did as he was told, promptly stepped backwards into the second tank and disappeared under the water! There were a few moments of sheer panic as he bobbed up and disappeared again, but Jim managed to grab him when he next appeared, before he went down for the third time!

As James continued to live dangerously, causing Joey considerable anxiety each time he was at Bogside, his relationship with Margaret was not always harmonious. On a rare occasion when Jim decreed that they should all have a day out, the popular choice was a visit to Edinburgh Zoo. I was about a year old, and since neither Joey nor Jim relished the thought of carrying me around for the whole day, they stopped in Cowdenbeath on the way to catch the ferry, and bought a pushchair. Margaret commandeered my conveyance as soon as we arrived at the zoo. Throughout the day she resisted all attempts to persuade her to give James a chance to push me and resolutely refused to relinquish me for a second. If Joey tried to tempt her to look at any of the animals, she would reply, "I've seen them" and carry on pushing. James was basically a patient wee boy, and put up with this all day, but as time passed and the end of the visit came near, even he had had enough, as he saw his last chance of being in charge of the pushchair slip away. As we approached the exit, which was at the bottom of a long sloping path, he saw his opportunity, pushed Margaret out of the way and grabbed the pushchair, shouting at her, "Ye've had it a' day! Ah'm haen it noo!" With that he ran off at speed down the ramp, to the alarm of Joey who feared that he, the pushchair, and I would all come to grief, and to the disgust of Margaret who had lost out to her rival. The day out ended with tears and recriminations all round!

South Bog Side.
Kinneddar,
Thursday

Dear Sir.

It was a bit of a surprise to get those letters from Will Lyall, I have enclosed your [illegible] I hope you are up when you get this, and not feeling to bad. I have just got my dinner past, Jean was washing and it came a shower she ran out ~~[illegible]~~ to take down the clothes and fell all her length at the corner of the dairy I gave her a help in to the house, and I had to finish the dinner making myself she has been drinking whisky & Castor oil ~~[illegible]~~ and she seems to be pretty right again. I was at Bowhill this morning to tell Morris about the potatoes, and got my haircut. I seen the chap who had the car for sale on Saturday and I could of got it for £2. but I told him I could not gave him that just now, I had a wee drive in it and it seemed to be alright but its needing two new tyres as he said there was another man (White) of Kirkcaldy to come for it so I will maybe not hear any more about it.

*First letter to Joey after Margaret's birth*

South Bogoside
Glencraig.
12th Oct.

Dear Joey,

This is just a wee letter to say I might not manage along on Wednesday night as I will have so much to do, if we are at the potatoes all day.

I have been at West field today and we'll be at the potatoes at Capledrae to-morrow.

Well I hope you are up now and feeling better than you did on Monday night, but you will have to be carefull, and not go out to quick, I am looking forward to seeing you home again, and I was saying to Jean she will be better not to go to the potatoes, she can gave you a help in the house, and maybe go to the pits between times.

Well Joey I'm not writing much more at present, hoping this finds you both progressing fine, and getting past up for home, You will maybe write me a letter and let me know how you are getting on.

I might see you before the end of the week.

With Love to both from
Jim.

P.S. You can count these and I'll get them next time.

*Second letter to Joey*

**EXTRACT ENTRY OF BIRTH: 17 & 18 Victoriæ Cap. 80, § 37.**

| (1) Name and Surname. | (2) When and Where Born. | (3) Sex. | (4) Name, Surname, and Rank or Profession of Father. Name, and Maiden Surname of Mother. Date and Place of Marriage. | (5) Signature and Qualification of Informant, and Residence, if out of the House in which the Birth occurred. | (6) When and Where Registered, and Signature of Registrar. |
|---|---|---|---|---|---|
| Elizabeth Ann Rutherford | 1946. September Fourteenth 8h 30m P.m. South Bogside Farm, Parish of Auchterderran | F. | James Rutherford Farmer<br>Johan Barclay Rutherford m.s. Mitchell<br>1941, September 26th Markinch | (Signed) James Rutherford Father (Present) | 1946. September 21st At Auchterderran (Signed) William Cook Registrar. |

TED from the REGISTER BOOK OF BIRTHS, for the District of Auchterderran, in the County of Fife
Twenty first day of September Nineteen Hundred and Forty six. William Cook Registrar.

Anne Rutherford's birth certificate

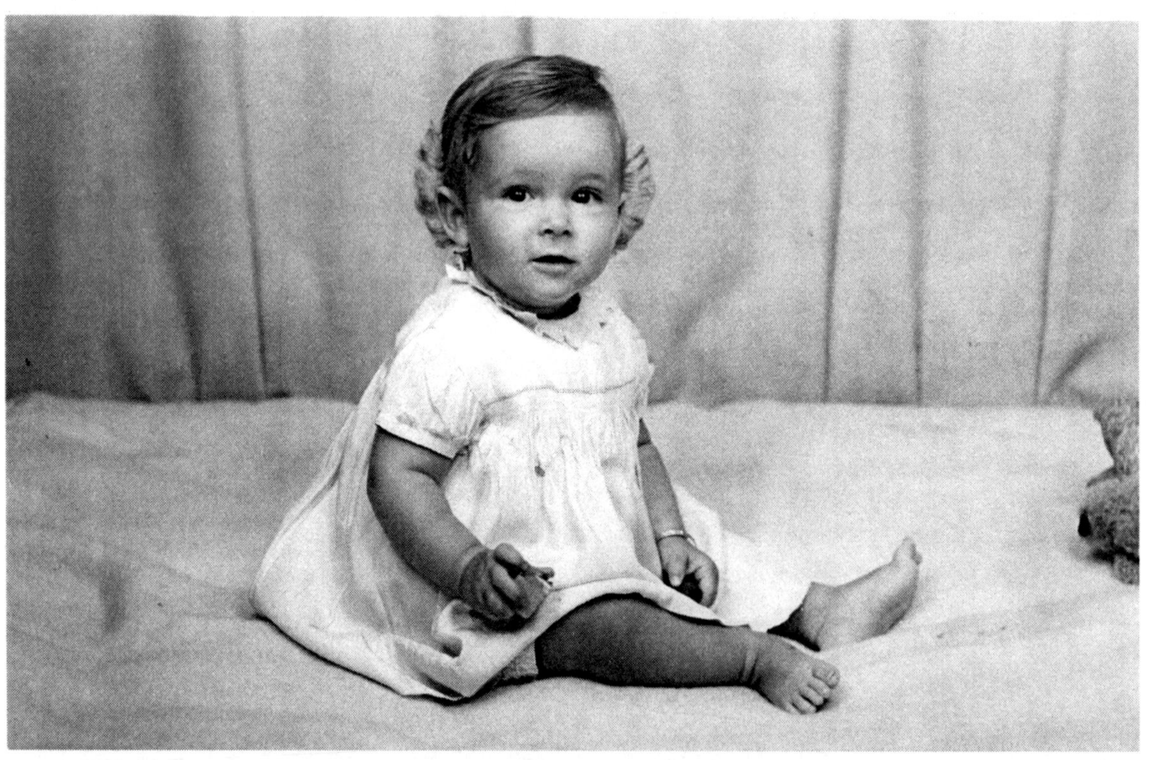

Anne Rutherford as a baby (7 months)

*Joey in the garden at South Bogside, Anne on her lap (1 year), Isabelle Imrie and Margaret at her feet (five years)*

# Chapter 11

## "Teeth sherpened an' ears preened back!"

Thirty years later I found myself once again in Edinburgh Zoo, for the second time in my life. This time, our younger son Donald was the one in the pushchair and the boys and I were with Mum and Dad. They had been spending a few days with us from Kirkcudbright, and Bill was at work. Dad surprised Mum and me when he suggested this outing, but as he was always anxious to do things that would please the boys, we went along with it. It was a very warm summer's day, and Calum, with the impatience typical of a four-year-old, decided that the only animals he was interested in seeing were the tigers. Their enclosure was at the furthest point from the entrance, at the top of the hill, so I had to keep up with his headlong rush to his objective, while Jim and Joey brought up the rear with Donald. As the afternoon wore on, we were all beginning to wilt. Calum was grumpy and Donald, who was in the throes of toilet training, had managed to "have an accident" on his Grandad's lap, so Mum and I decided on a tactical withdrawal to the tearoom and some much needed respite and refreshment. As we sat there, Dad said, "I've just remembered! Last time we were here, *you* were in the pushchair, and I've decided that once a generation at the zoo is too often!" As we made our way towards the exit revived, fed, and watered, and Donald with a dry pair of pants, I couldn't help but see in my mind's eye that other family group, one generation removed.

By the summer of 1947, Joey and Jim could look back on six years of marriage, and they had certainly come a long way. They were far from prosperous, but they were making a success of their farm. All of their acreage was in pasture or under productive cultivation of arable crops, including potatoes and oats, and the fodder crops of hay and turnips, which saw the animals through the winter months. They had developed the steading, their dairy herd was growing, they had started keeping sheep, and they had drained and improved the two bogs: the fields adjoining the Lochty Burn, which had previously been of little use. This reminds me of the passage in "Sunset Song," where Chae Strachan tells Chris Guthrie of the conversation he had with her young husband on the eve of his execution by firing squad during the First World War. "For he started to speak of Blawearie and the parks he would have drained." Like Jim and Joey, Ewan and Chris had been a young couple wedded to each other and to the land they worked, making plans for its future. But in their case they were cut tragically short by the intervention of external forces beyond their control, whereas Joey and Jim had the satisfaction of seeing their hopes begin to reach fruition.

Margaret started school in the late summer of that year when I was approaching my first birthday. She had to walk every day to Auchterderran School, a long stretch of the legs of more than two miles each way. The children from Capeldrae also went to Auchterderran, but they were all older than Margaret, some of them already in the secondary part of the school, and it was hard for her to keep up with them. However, she soon displayed great independence of character, and Joey would look back years later and realise that it was asking a lot of a wee girl to face that long walk twice a day in all weathers. Nowadays, fewer and fewer children are allowed to walk unaccompanied to school and the roads around schools are dangerously congested by parents' cars, while youngsters generally suffer from a lack of exercise and rates of obesity in children are soaring. Later, when I started school, after we had moved to Pitkinny, there was a school bus, which we caught at the end of the farm road, so our walk was then less than half a mile.

As the years passed, Joey and Jim got to know more local people. In addition to their close farming neighbours, they began to make friends of people in Cardenden. Mrs MacMillan, the district nurse and midwife, and her husband Alec, became valued friends. Their only son, Alastair, liked to spend time at the farm. He was an earnest and serious-minded young lad, who was always anxious to help, but he had one or two unhappy, not to say frightening experiences. One day he was helping Joey in the hayloft of the barn. There were two holes in the floor through which the hay was pushed down into the stable. Joey knew they were there and was always wary of them because they were often covered with loose hay, and she assumed that Alastair was also aware of their existence. She suddenly heard a whooshing noise and turned round to see that Alastair had disappeared! He had fallen through one of the holes, but fortunately was relatively unhurt. After they resumed their work in the loft, it was only a few minutes until exactly the same thing happened again, only this time it was the second hole he had fallen through! On another occasion, Jim asked for Alastair's help in delivering an old van he had to the garage in Cardenden. Jim would tow the van while Alastair sat in it and steered. What Jim did not tell the poor lad was that the van had no brakes! The road from Bogside to Robertson's garage was a series of right-angled bends and Jim was never known for his slow driving, even when towing another vehicle. When they arrived at the garage Alastair emerged from the van, ashen-faced and trembling. He recalled later that it was the most terrifying experience of his life, especially since he couldn't even drive. In those days the small matter of the lack of a driving licence didn't seem to register with Jim. He assumed that everyone was born able to drive and to cope with such a situation.

Another boy who spent a lot of time at Bogside was Bill Smith, the twin brother of Lena, who lived at South Pitkinny farm at that time. He was in the same class as Alastair, but was much more confident and worldly, and would tease him mercilessly. Joey was aware of how unkind Bill could be to Alastair, but felt it would make matters worse if she was seen to intervene on his behalf. However, one day Alastair's patience snapped and he went for Bill with a pitchfork! She had to disarm him and rescue Bill from the "worm that had turned," but from that day everyone treated Alastair with new respect, as he had clearly learned that attack is often the best means of defence. He would later do most of his National Service in Iraq, and his apprenticeship in the school of hard knocks at Bogside and Pitkinny probably stood him in good stead!

Mrs Blake, a regular customer for eggs, became a good friend to Joey. She and her husband Jarv had a daughter, May, who was exactly ten years older than me, and she would sometimes come with her mother during the school holidays. I was very much in awe of her, and would occasionally be overcome with shyness and once even refused to come out from under the table when she arrived. May left Auchterderran School the same summer as I started, and I remember

Mrs Blake saying that she was moving out of the school to make room for me. I really believed that I would be sitting in May's chair, not understanding that she was leaving the top end of the big school as I was starting the bottom end of the wee one!

Jock Allan was a miner who lived with his family at Capeldrae. He would often work a night shift in the pit, and then work during the day at Bogside or Pitkinny at the busy hay, grain, and tattie harvest times, presumably snatching a few hours sleep in between shifts. It was said that many miners would lie off their work and miss some shifts in the pit. As their wages were relatively high for those days, they could afford to do this, and there never seemed to be any possibility of them losing their jobs, but I have always felt that faced with the choice of going down the pit or working on the farm in the open air, I know what I would have chosen! Jim would often criticise the miners for their casual approach to life, but I used to feel annoyed with him for this. He took advantage of their willingness to work hard for him, and although I suppose they were well paid for their efforts, I felt it was hypocritical of him to have such a poor opinion of them in private, and yet be outwardly friendly towards them in public.

Although Cardenden was not a big place there were several different and distinct parts of the town. From the direction of Bogside, the nearest part was Woodend, followed by Auchterderran, the area around the school and the church. Then you turned in one direction to Balgreggie which nestled under the Craigs, a distinctive rocky outcrop. In the other direction the road to Lochgelly went through the Jamphlars, where Bowhill pit was situated. This name was a corruption of the French "champ de fleurs," a very attractive name for a less-than-pretty part of town, none of which could be remotely described as picturesque. The central part of the town was Bowhill, and beyond that was Dundonald, which gave its name to another pit, and further on Cardenden proper, the site of the other parish church, St. Fothad's, and a large area of newish council housing.

Young Jock Allan's father, naturally, Old Jock, a retired miner, lived in Woodend and came for eggs to Bogside every week. He had come to Cardenden as a young man, from the coal mines in the Lothians when the new Bowhill pit had opened. He had lodged with a woman in the Jamphlars. One day his landlady had asked him to meet her daughter off the train at Cardenden station. She was returning home from service and would need help with her suitcase. He said he knew as soon as he saw Maggie step off the train that she would be his wife, and so it was they came to be married. He was a really nice old man, and always had stories to tell. I would ask him each time if he would take his coat off, because I knew that if he did he would stay for a chat and a cup of tea. The old men at Woodend had a wee shelter, a little wooden shed where they would meet and play cards and smoke their pipes. Sometimes, we would see Jock there when we were on our way to the bus stop. He would say, "I see ye've got yer teeth sherpened an' yer ears peened back!" In other words, we were well turned out for our excursion to wherever we were going, almost always to Markinch, or sometimes to Kirkcaldy, the nearest shopping place of any consequence.

The coalman at Woodend, Saund (Sandy or Alec) Page and his wife, Jessie, became lifelong friends of Jim and Joey. They had two children: Elizabeth, who was a little younger than Margaret, and Frank, who was my age. Sadly, Elizabeth was born with only one hand and although this must have been a dreadful blow for her parents, she was brought up to be very resourceful, and there was nothing we did that she was not able to do. We took her disability for granted and it made no impact on us at all as we all played happily together. There was only one time when I remember becoming aware of her disability. One afternoon we had been playing at her house when the rain came on and we went inside. Her mother gave us some photograph albums to look at. There was a photo of Elizabeth as a baby in her christening robe. As I looked at it I suddenly noticed that one sleeve of her robe was empty and without thinking I blurted out "Oh Elizabeth! Where is your hand?" Young though I was, I remember being aware, perhaps for the first time, of a sense of acute social embarrassment, of having said something very hurtful and tactless, albeit unintentionally. I felt hot all over and couldn't think of a way to cover up for my unthinking outburst. It was only when I was older that I understood that this was a measure of how naturally we accepted Elizabeth's disability, and indeed a good example of how open and free from judgement children are, if left to their own devices. It is only as we grow older that we become affected by other peoples' stereotypes and prejudices. I see this episode now, in retrospect, as a compliment to the way we, and our playmates, were brought up.

We would have our second family holiday with the Page family, in Blackpool in 1950. We would often play with each other, either at the farm or at their home at Woodend. They had an uncle who lodged with them, a brother of Saund called Dave, but he was a very withdrawn and dour individual and we were always a little afraid of him. Their house was one of a pair of semi-detached cottages. The other half of the building had been occupied by their old Aunt Anne, who had died some years before, but for some reason her house had remained as it had been when she died. Perhaps there was a problem with her will or some other reason why nothing had been touched. Occasionally we would creep into the unoccupied house. It was forbidden, of course, but Elizabeth knew where the key was kept, and if there was no one around, we would unlock the door and ferret around, looking into cupboards, peering into wardrobes and drawers. There was the vicarious thrill of indulging in a wicked activity, but as the musty smells of old clothes assailed our senses, and the possibility of discovering some unspeakable evidence of this dead old woman suddenly occurred to us, we wouldn't be able to bear it another moment, and we would make a bolt for the door and the fresh air, as if the hounds of hell were behind us.

This was the time when the film *Annie Get Your Gun* was in the cinema, and Mrs Page would call Frank and me Frank Butler and Annie Oakley. Joey and Jim would remain on friendly terms with these people for the rest of their lives, but it was only after they had all retired, in the 1970s, that Joey and Jessie would call each other by their first names, and that never happened at all with Joey and Mrs MacMillan, Mrs Blake, Mrs Allan, or any of the other acquaintances they had made in the course of their married life at Bogside and Pitkinny. This was very much the norm when we were young—there was a degree of formality in social conventions that no longer pertains. I know my parents found it difficult to adjust to the fact that, latterly, their first names were used by many people in circumstances which to them seemed inappropriate, such as the bank manager or health professionals. It was not that Joey or Jim were in any way unfriendly or stuffy, it was simply that the younger generation now have a different understanding of what constitutes respect and good manners. We were always brought up to address older people as "Mr and Mrs," unless they were very close friends, when the courtesy title of "aunt " and "uncle" could be used, but never just their first names. It is a habit that dies hard, and I still prefer to use titles and surnames when addressing people who are much older than me, or people in a formal or work environment.

It was not in Joey's character to be anything but content with her lot, and in those early years of their long life together, she was more than happy to be a wife to Jim and a mother to Margaret and me. She derived great satisfaction from working hard and never looked for financial or material rewards for herself, as long as she could keep us all warm, well fed, and well clad. Her home and family were everything, and although she did have many friends, she never sought any kind of outside recreation. She was never a "joiner," although later she would occasionally go to evening classes for dressmaking, leather work, and other handcrafts. But she never joined the WRI or the Women's Guild at church. Many years later, after they had retired to Kirkcudbright, she was prevailed upon to join the WRI there. She disliked intensely the entire scenario, especially when it was her turn to provide the home baking for their supper. She was a very good baker and cook, but found that obligation quite distasteful. She had little patience for the company of women en masse because she always felt that such gatherings brought out the worst in some women who would give vent to petty disagreements and jealousies.

She was certainly not unsociable, and there was nothing she liked better than having a house full of visitors to cater for. However, she was always most comfortable in her own home and invariably welcomed friends, even when they were unexpected and she was up to her eyes in work, and she could always rustle up a meal and make her limited food supplies stretch miraculously with a cheerful and patient demeanour. This must have come from years of practice. Jim could be depended on to be "big-hearted Harry," and anyone working around the farm would be invited into the kitchen for dinner or tea and the kettle was always on the boil in between mealtimes. It was amazing how often commercial travellers of long acquaintance would just "happen to be" at Bogside or Pitkinny at these times. Having said that, unwelcome travellers or time-wasters would be given short shrift indeed!

If Joey did not seek outside distraction, the opposite was true of Jim. Despite, or perhaps because of, the sterile emotional and social environment of his young life, Jim in these years became increasingly gregarious. He was still working very hard, of course, and in the summer, work continued as long as the daylight lasted, but in the winter there were long dark evenings to be filled and he began to spend more and more time away from home. He craved the company of male friends, and increasingly this involved meeting them in the local pubs and hotels. Joey blamed herself later for being too naïve to see what was happening, and it was her sister Doris who first commented on how little time Jim was spending at home in the winter evenings.

As they built up their livestock, their dairy herd, and the sheep flock, Jim took to attending the cattle markets from time to time. There was a market in a different location every day of the week: Thornton on a Monday, Cupar and Dunfermline on a Tuesday, Milnathort on a Wednesday, Stirling on a Thursday, and Perth on a Friday. There was always a social dimension to market day, of course, and anyone who has heard or read *Tam O'Shanter* will be familiar with the scene. Bargains were sealed and deals celebrated in the market bar. As the farm prospered, so Jim could afford to pay more labour and could therefore delegate some of the practical work while he concentrated more on the business side of the farm. That was really his forte: he had an acute sense for proactive development and innovation, and a wonderful acumen for effective dealing in the buying and selling of livestock and produce. Allied to this was his very sociable temperament and likeable nature, which made him very successful in both practical farming and income generation. As much agricultural business is conducted in the bar of the cattle market, or of the ice rink after curling matches, as on the golf course in other business contexts.

The downside of all this progress was that Jim was sometimes, and increasingly, inclined to drink more than was good for him, and this came to be a source of friction at home, because the more Joey became aware of the problem, the more determined she became to save him from himself! While this did not make for a peaceful home life, had it not been for Joey's firm stand, it is not beyond the bounds of possibility that Jim could have gone off the rails completely. He would not have been the first farmer to drink away his business, and the fact that this fate did not befall him was entirely due to Joey's efforts.

When I began to write this chronicle, I said I did not wish to romanticise my parents or idealise the life they lived together. To do that would be a disservice to them and to their memory. I want to be honest about them, and about my memories of them, while having no wish to be in any way unkind or disloyal. So I hope I can present a balanced and fair impression of their relationship as I remember it. Neither of my parents was perfect. Jim had his weakness in his relationship with the bottle, but that was the one and only source of conflict between him and Joey. In later years I know that she often blamed herself for being too uncompromising in her attitude to his drinking, and she came to realise that this added to the impact that their difficulties had on us. I really hated the rows they would have and the worry they caused to me, especially as I became more aware of the problem as a young teenager.

This was a difficult time for me, as Margaret was by then living away from home for most of the time as she began her nursing career. I really came to dread the days when I knew that Dad would be at the market and would hope against hope that he would be home by the time I returned from school. If he wasn't, there was a good chance that he would come home the worse for drink and there would be a row. In retrospect, I came to understand that Mum had no choice but to stand firm against Dad's drinking, but at the time I would have given anything for a peaceful life. I suppose when we are young we tend to see things in black and white, and to believe that other people have perfect lives. I realise now that those rare individuals who grow up in a seemingly ideal world, where there is no conflict, are poorly equipped to face problems in their own lives and relationships. What I learned from Mum and Dad was that you do not give up on people you care for. There can never be a guarantee of happiness for any of us, and none of us is blameless in our dealings with each other. Even in the worst of times, Joey could always see the good in Jim and I know that he came to understand what he owed to Joey. The most important thing to me now is that, whatever happened in the past, I do not hold anything against my parents. They did the best they could in the circumstances they faced, and that is all any of us can ever do, and I know that they loved us and were proud of our achievements.

As the 1940s came to an end, Jim was intent on expanding his horizons. The tenancy of North Pitkinny fell vacant in 1948, when Montgomery retired. Jim and Joey had always looked from the Bogside kitchen window up to the fields and steading of Pitkinny, and it seemed a natural progression to extend their holding to the adjoining property. It would mean finding two rents every year, but the extra land would provide a greater income. Joey welcomed the chance to leave the dampness of Bogside and move up to the airier and, as she hoped, healthier location up on the brae. Thus Jim began negotiations with the Coal Board, and the stage was set for the next chapter of their life's story.

*Margaret (middle row, second from right) in Primary 1*

*Margaret, aged 4 years 4 months; and Anne in pram, aged 4 months*

*Margaret and dog Peeril in the stack yard at Bogside*

*Gran Betsy, Cousin Eunice, Jim, Anne, Margaret, and Aunt Doris*

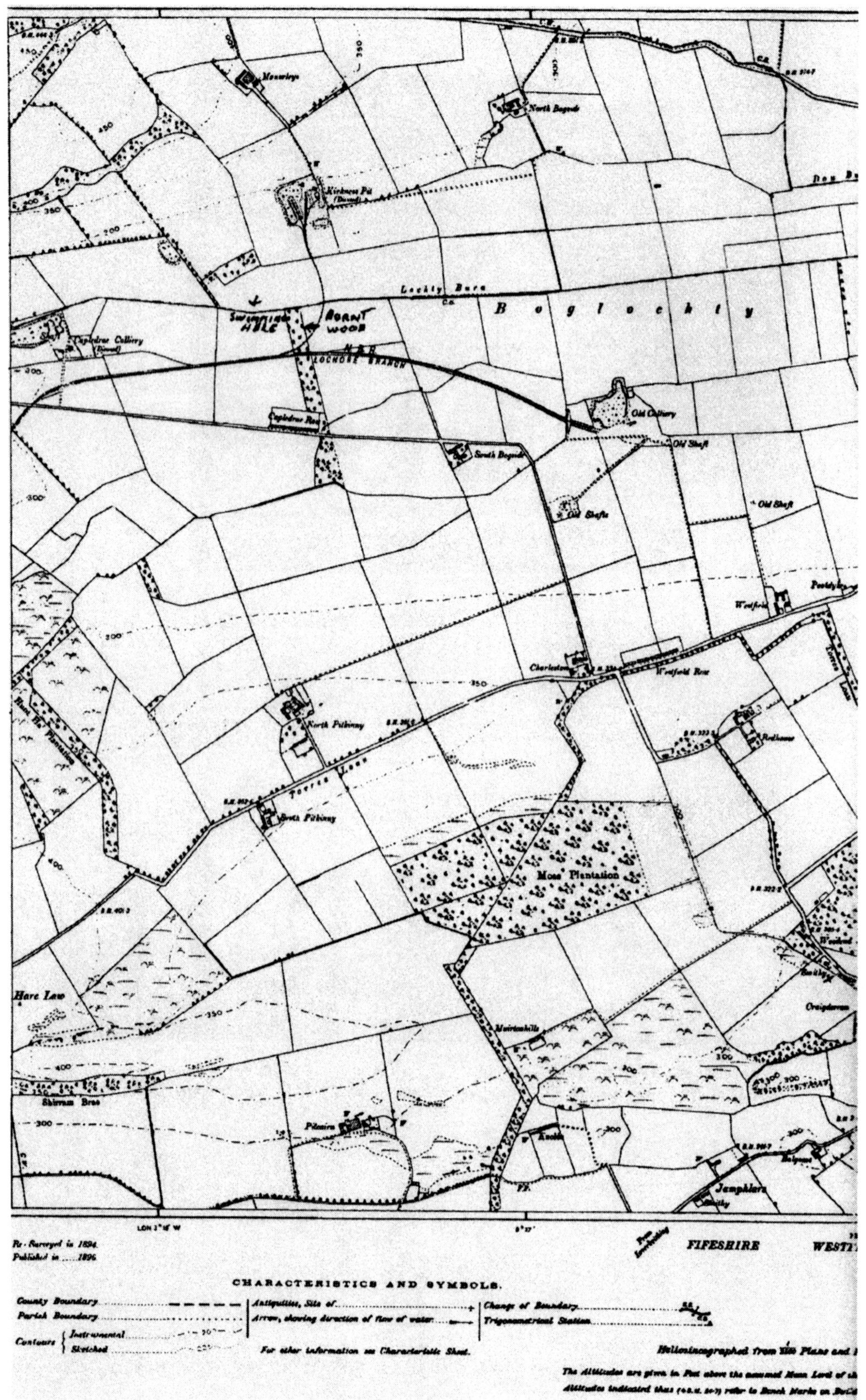


*Map showing South Bogside and Pitkinny Farms*

# PART 4

## GROWING TIME

# Chapter 12

## "Ye dinnae hae time fur a nervous brekdoon!"

When I was young, time seemed infinite. Looking forward to something even a few days ahead meant contemplating a seemingly endless length of time, which had somehow to be filled in order to reach the longed-for goal. Similarly, unpleasant experiences had to be tholed through creeping, crawling hours and days, which seemed to be neverending. One of the few lessons I can be completely certain of having learned, is that nothing—absolutely nothing—lasts forever, and one of the few accomplishments I have mastered is the ability to have patience. So now I no longer look forward with the same degree of desperation to exciting or happy events, because living has taught me that they will come in their own time, and be over almost before I can appreciate them. Likewise, the most painful, unsatisfying, or tedious experience must be endured until it comes to an end, and no amount of willing time to pass more quickly will bring that conclusion before its due time.

The year I spent in Sweden from 1969 to 1970 was my first experience of living in a foreign country rather than just having a holiday there. I was living and working in a small town on the west coast and initially, naturally felt homesick. Mum used to send me some of the local papers from time to time. One of them was *The People's Journal*, full of local news and homespun philosophy, which I seldom read when at home. However, when it arrived on my doormat in Varberg, I would eagerly devour it word for word and from beginning to end! A regular columnist was the Reverend J. L. Dow, who was a well-known Church of Scotland minister from Paisley. I had once heard a lecture of his when I attended the International Youth Camp in Aberfoyle, when I was sixteen and had been very impressed with his breadth of knowledge about Scottish history and culture. One week I was finding it particularly difficult to get to grips with my alien environment and was still in the early stages of making friends. Reverend Dow's homily was on the subject of tholing difficult times, something we all have to learn to do at various junctures in our lives. He reminded his readers that in the Bible it says, "It came to pass." It doesn't say, "It came to stay." I have never forgotten that piece of advice and it comes to mind whenever life is hard and I am longing for the passing of time to alleviate some worry or other.

Perhaps this acceptance of time's inexorable pace is simply a matter of growing up, but I have long been aware of a feeling that, as an absolute quantity, time shrinks as one grows older. A week is most certainly shorter than it used to be; a day flashes by, too often without enough to show for its passing. Each succeeding year seems to pass more quickly than its predecessor. I can understand that in relative terms, as one ages, this can be explained rationally: At the age of five, one year represents one-fifth of your life, while at fifty years of age, it represents only one-fiftieth of your conscious and subconscious memory and experience. However, while this may be explained by the laws of mathematics, it seems to me that, in addition, time as an absolute measurement diminishes with age! When my father signed the lease for Pitkinny, less than ten years had passed since he had done the same for Bogside. In less than a decade, he and Joey had made a success of their first tenancy, they had produced a family (Margaret was by then seven and I was already three years old), and that family had become an integral part of the social fabric of the farming community in our little northwest corner of Fife.

Now as I realise how short a time a decade actually is, it seems quite astonishing that so much had been accomplished by Jim and Joey in the time since their marriage, especially when I consider how little they started off with. The war was gradually receding in their consciousness, although postwar hardship would persist in the form of rationing of many commodities, but perhaps the fast-approaching half-century of 1950 heralded the promise of a more peaceful and prosperous future for them, their family, and the country in general. While Jim had been responsible for and had been working the three-hundred-odd acres of Pitkinny for more than a year, he did not move his family from Bogside until the autumn of 1950. The Pitkinny house had been occupied by the Stevenson family, who were due to take up the tenancy of Ballingry Farm. As a new house was being built there, and as Jim was in no hurry to move, the Coal Board had asked him if they could move into Pitkinny house as a temporary measure. During that time, Mr Stevenson senior had tragically died from injuries he received when his foot was caught in the power drive of a tractor, and it was his son, Wullie, who then succeeded to the tenancy of Ballingry. They had moved out some months before, since when the house had been standing empty, but the impending danger of frozen pipes as winter approached hastened our move up the hill from Bogside. My earliest memory of our new home, probably during our first visit, was of walking up the stairs by the light of a paraffin lamp, conscious of, above all else, an all-prevailing smell of dampness in this cold, strange, and empty shell of a home.

Jim had planned to keep Bogside as the dairy and concentrate the arable work at Pitkinny. In time to come, he would also centre his increasing involvement with the rearing and fattening of beef cattle there also. As we would be living at the new farm, he decided to employ a dairyman who would live at Bogside. This had the added attraction of freeing Jim from what he saw as the drudgery of twice-daily milking, and allowed him to develop the steading and the acreage of his new holding. He had advertised the position of dairyman and secured the services of Jock Steel, who by the summer of 1950 was already running the dairy and living in one of the "cottar hooses" at Capeldrae, until we could vacate the house at Bogside. Jock had been working at Annfield Farm, between Crossgates and Inverkeithing, and before that in Twechar, near Cumbernauld, but was originally from Ayrshire. He and his wife Helen, who was born in Kilsyth, had a family of three sons, Bob, John, and Tom; and three daughters, Margaret, Mary, and Joyce, the baby of the family, who was nearly three and would be a playmate for me as we grew up together.

Although the Pitkinny house needed considerable improvement, which the NCB, our landlord, had promised to arrange and finance, it was decided that would have to wait, and as the Steels were very overcrowded in the cottage at Capeldrae, the move up the brae could not be delayed any longer. Of course, the actual business of moving had to fit in with the demands of the farm work, so one Friday afternoon Jim announced that we would flit the next day! However, when he was reminded of the old saying, "A Setterday flittin's a short sittin'," and ever mindful of ominous and dire superstitions, Jim declared that, rather than take such a risk, they would flit there and then!

When I said that Jim moved his family, this is not really accurate. According to my mother, he had an acute aversion to flitting and always contrived to be conspicuous by his absence when it came to the hard work of packing, hauling, and unpacking the family's belongings. Despite that, the move was completed with the assistance of many strong, willing helpers, and, it has to be said, the quantity and complexity of our possessions was nothing in comparison with a modern household. My only memory of that day is that the kitchen of our new home seemed to be full of furniture and I remember sitting on top of a table, surrounded by other items of furniture incongruously arranged side by side, with the floor nowhere to be seen. Seen from the perspective of a four-year-old, the kitchen seemed huge and the tabletop on which I sat appeared to be immense and, young though I was, I was aware of a feeling of abandonment and some degree of alienation from my new environment.

In external appearance, our new house was not unlike Bogside, both being of a very traditional style for farmhouses in lowland Scotland. From the front there was, on the ground floor, a central porch and door, with one window of equal size on either side, and three equally spaced windows on the upper floor, the central one directly above the porch. The kitchen had been added to the back left side of the original structure at some time, and the back door into the kitchen was situated on the side of that extension and opened onto the close or farmyard. A small scullery and slightly larger kitchen occupied this addition, each with one small window. The original part of the house consisted of a small sitting room and walk-in pantry, both near the kitchen. A small bathroom and a larger sitting room completed the ground floor accommodation. The most striking feature of the house was its staircase, which had two sturdy newel posts at the bottom, each surmounted by a wooden sphere, while the wooden banisters and pillars were impressive and well-made, although the whole structure had been somewhat neglected. The stair comprised two flights of steps at right angles to each other, while the banisters and pillars continued round the top floor, connecting the three bedrooms: one very small one at the top of the stairs which Dunc had; the largest of the three, which was Jim and Joey's room; and the third, medium-sized one, where Margaret and I slept. The downstairs floors of the house were formed of huge flagstones which made the house feel very cold, and the roof was in grave need of renewal. The outside harled walls had been stuccoed at some time, but were extremely dingy and discoloured. Joey soon decided what was needed to improve the house, and within the first year we would decant into one of the two cottages that went with the farm to allow the renovations, agreed with the Coal Board, to be carried out.

Pitkinny house faced south down the loan, as we called the farm road, which led to two semi-detached cottar hooses, about two hundred yards from the farm, which had been built in the 1930s. There, the loan branched east and west; east to the main road which led south to Woodend and Cardenden, and north to Bogside and thereafter Capeldrae, Ballingry, Loch Leven, and ultimately, Kinross. The western branch of the loan led past South Pitkinny Farm, and over Harelaw to Lochore. Halfway between the farm and the cottages was an old barn and the original cottar hooses, one of which had been used as a bothy, where the single farmworkers lodged. It continued to be used in this way for a short time after we came to Pitkinny, but subsequently it would join its neighbour in becoming a henhouse. The old barn was used for grain storage, but has more recently been converted into a house, built and occupied by Sandy Black, once of Westfield and Jim and Joey's successor as tenant of Pitkinny from 1976.

The historic name of our road was Torres Loan, a very ancient right of way. When the monks from the monastery on St Serf's Island in Loch Leven made their way to the ecclesiastical settlement, later the site of Auchterderran Parish Kirk, they kept to the ridge of high ground on the eastern slopes of Benarty Hill, past the almost equally old religious site of Ballingry Church, through Lochore, over Harelaw, along past Pitkinny, and down to Auchterderran. From there, the ancient route, part of which was known as the "Bliddy Fits" (Bloody Feet), led along the Craigs, the rocky outcrop to the northeast of Auchterderran, to the ecclesiastical settlement at Kinglassie and beyond. The prefix "Pit" is of Pictish origin and means farm or settlement. As I grew up I became aware of the significance of its historic location in a region of great antiquity and historical importance: Auchterderran had been a religious site for nine hundred years; Castle Island in Loch Leven had been a place of imprisonment for Mary, Queen of Scots; the people of the district had always had, and always would have, an inalienable right to walk in the footsteps of the monks. I also became aware, in those early years at Pitkinny, of the mark that Joey and Jim were making on the land and settlement, which we very soon came to think of as our home and the source of our livelihood and happiness.

The farm buildings that comprised the steading were all in a similar state of disrepair to that of the house, and Jim had great plans to demolish and replace much of what could not be improved. This would involve an enormous amount of work and investment, only some of which would be undertaken by the landlord and, as Jim and Joey had little or no capital to hand, they looked to the bank to finance the rest. Bob Edgar, the NCB factor, had come to see Jim as a good risk and was, as always, very supportive of his endeavours, but the reality of borrowing money from the bank was not lost on Jim and Joey. With the additional rent to be found every year, Jim realised that he was taking a huge gamble, and once they were in residence at Pitkinny the full enormity of his venture began to sink in. One night when they went to bed, Joey noticed that Jim was shaking and seemed to be unable to sleep. He was clearly very anxious and when Joey asked what was wrong, Jim replied by asking a question of his own. "What does it feel like to hae a nervous brekdoon?"

Remembering what Nellie had said about Jim's youthful tendency to nervous debility, but having very little experience of or patience for emotional problems, Joey's practical and no-nonsense approach to real or imagined worries led her to reply firmly, "Well, I dinnae ken, but I'll tell you wan thing! Ye're no havin' wan! You made the decision to tak' on Pitkinny, and you've the girls and me to think of, so ye'll just hae to get on with it! Now get to sleep and get on with things tomorrow. Ye dinnae hae time fur a nervous brekdoon!" That was the end of the matter as far as she was concerned, and never again did Jim display any sign of having bitten off more than he could chew. As I have explained before, there was neither the time nor the energy to dwell on problems. This seemingly less-than-sympathetic response would be seen as somewhat harsh nowadays, when counselling and talking over problems is seen as the healthy means of dealing with emotional worries. However, something tells me that Joey's instinctive reaction was exactly what Jim needed at that time, whether he knew it or not. I would later be on the receiving end of a similarly brusque attempt at child psychology by my mother and I survived the experience emotionally intact, albeit with a sharp physical reminder of her advice!

The house renovations were begun in the summer of 1951, just as I was starting school. We lived for the duration in the western of the two cottar hooses. I do not recall how long the work took, but there were a few days when our home stood denuded of its roof and window frames. The flagstone floors had been lifted from the ground floor rooms, and the four exterior walls stood starkly outlined against the sky. Jim worried Joey by commenting, "I hope we dinnae get a high wind the nicht!" As Pitkinny was often buffeted by gales, standing as it did on the top of the ridge, she knew there was every chance there would be, but fortunately the Fates were kind and the skeleton of the old house remained in place long enough to be fleshed out and made secure again by new floors, roof, and window frames. The kitchen and scullery were combined, with a new large west-facing window, which allowed more light into the enlarged kitchen-cum-dining-and-living room. This also gave an outlook to the close and the back door, so it was now possible to witness the traffic and activity in the close from the kitchen. The later addition of a back porch onto the existing back door made the room cosier, sheltering it from the prevailing west wind.

Joey was always a wonderful homemaker, and she certainly had her work cut out, transforming what had been a cold, dark, and comfortless barn of a house into a warm, bright, and welcoming home, where we enjoyed the basic amenities of shelter, warmth, and sustenance, combined with the results of her ability to make much out of little. There was never much money for home improvement as any profit had to be ploughed back, usually literally, into the farm, but Joey's skills and her eye for design and colour in decorating and sewing created a degree of comfort which exceeded the norm in most farmhouses of the time. Much of the furniture and many of the rugs Joey acquired over the years came from Green's saleroom in Ladybank. Many a Friday evening was spent examining the lots to be sold the next day, and many Saturdays were passed happily bidding for items which were duly transported to the farm. The provenance of these household artefacts was often of great interest. On one occasion she bought a carver chair and four rugs which came from the staterooms of the great oceangoing liner, the *Mauretania*, which had ended her days in the breaker's yard in Inverkeithing.

Years later, just before Bill and I were married, further improvement was made to the house in the form of a new upstairs bathroom, which was made from part of my parents' bedroom. This was after they took down the wall between the kitchen and the small sitting room to create a larger open-plan living area. This was no mean feat, as it was an outside wall of the original house and was composed of at least a two-foot thickness of huge sandstones and lime-based mortar. Only the fact that they were beyond the point of no return sustained Joey through the resulting mess and chaos. She had many such experiences as she struggled to maintain and improve the old house. A sudden flood in the kitchen was explained by the discovery, under the floor, of a water pipe which must at one time have been connected to a hand pump in the yard of the original house, and had not been properly diverted or sealed many years earlier, presumably when the original kitchen extension was added.

Through the intervening years she had made gradual improvements to the decor and furnishings in the house, as time and money would permit. Linoleum floors gave way to carpets and rugs, while the walls were covered with light and airy wallpapers which helped to turn the dark old house into a much more pleasant place to live. As she became less able to tackle all the decorating herself, she started to employ a young man, John Smith, who would do her papering in the evenings as a supplement to his regular job. He was a very good decorator, but we realised that his eyesight might not be too good, or perhaps he was remarkably unobservant. On one occasion, Joey left him to start papering the kitchen one evening while she went to her sewing class. As she was out again on the evening he finished the job, he called a few days later for his payment. When she said how happy she was with his work and the finished result, he ventured to say that he thought the paper had been an unusual choice of pattern on her part. When she replied that she thought the yellow roses were a bright and cheerful touch, he said in amazement, "Roses? They're not roses, they're canaries, aren't they?" That became a standing joke and each time in the future when John was called upon to do some papering, he would ask questions like, "Golden eagles this time, is it, Mrs Rutherford, or maybe yellow finches instead?"

Just as Joey worked hard to transform our living conditions, Jim embarked on making changes to the ramshackle steading. Pitkinny was built in the traditional "fermtoun" style with some of the outbuildings connected, on the east, to the farmhouse, so enclosing one side of a hollow square, with the opening in the square, or the close, to the west of the house. As with all country dwellings and farms, vermin were an endemic problem, which Joey loathed almost as much as she hated the "gaiters" or mud, which was a constant accompaniment of farm life, and with which, as a diligent housewife, she did constant battle. Indeed, when the old flagstone floors were lifted, when the house was renovated during our first year there, the spaces between and under them were found to be transected by rat tunnels, smoothed and made shiny by untold generations of rodents that had over the years created their own underground transport system! So Joey was determined that the old byre which adjoined the east gable end of the house should be demolished, as she hoped this—with the new replaced floors—would help to make the house vermin-proof.

In the early months of his occupancy, Jim had begun to knock down the walls of the old buildings in the only way he knew—with manpower: picks, sledgehammers and shovels—very hard labour more akin to a chain gang than to farm work! There were various willing helpers involved in this process. Two of them were Jock Allen, the Bowhill miner who lived at Capeldrae; and Bobby Drennan, my Aunt Greta's husband, who was a miner at Kinglassie Pit. These two stalwarts would combine work for Jim with their regular jobs as shot-firers down the pits, and simultaneously came to the same conclusion: that there was a much faster and easier way to achieve the demolition of the old steading, namely: gelignite! "A wee spat o' jelly" was the obvious answer to their problem, and they weren't long in telling Jim of their plan. Always open to new ideas and labour, and moneysaving techniques, he was only too happy to concur with their strategy. So the jelly was duly "acquired" by his two accomplices and they set to with a will each weekend, to obliterate those parts of the steading which would not feature in Jim's future plans.

Joey was not at all happy about this highly illegal and dangerous venture and, given enough warning, would try to arrange not to be around when blasting was going on, by taking us off with her to Markinch. However, this was not always possible and there were times when we would cower in dread, ears covered and eyes shut, as we waited for the blast. Once, poor old Lassie the collie was so terrorised by the sound that she tried to get out of the window and ended up in the kitchen sink! Another time, one of the farm cats, who foolishly tried to cross the close just as the explosion happened, was bodily carried backwards, in *Tom and Jerry* fashion, across the close and into the tractor shed, fortunately without injury but with the loss of one of its nine lives! The worst misadventure occurred on the day the byre, adjoining the east gable end, was the object of Jock and Bobby's attention. They overestimated the amount of gelignite required and did not only succeed in demolishing the byre, but also made a huge crack which ran all the way up the gable end of the house and dislodged the keystone of the arch in the sitting room fireplace on the inside.

Joey really liked this fireplace, as it was made of tiles of emerald green, her favourite colour, and on hearing the ominous rumble of falling masonry and breaking tiles from the sitting room, she gingerly went in to find the remains of the fireplace meeting her in the middle of the floor and the room covered in soot from the chimney. This was the last straw. She redoubled her efforts to persuade Jim to call a halt to the activities of the demolition squad. As it happened, they had all but accomplished their work and Jim could now employ an architect to help him plan and build a new steading.

That summer that went with a bang stands out in my memory as an example of the way Jim would always favour direct action to achieve his objectives; for him, the end almost always justified the means. In retrospect it might seem foolhardy and irresponsible, but in those days, while it almost certainly involved breaking the law in several ways, no one seemed unduly concerned. Even Joey's worries about it probably derived more from her fear that someone would be hurt or worse by the blasting, than any intrinsic fear of retribution, despite her well-known healthy respect for the law. Certainly, Pitkinny was fairly remote from other habitation, but I can't believe that the frequent explosions went unnoticed or unremarked in the district.

It seems to me that Jim and Joey had an almost pioneering approach to their life at Pitkinny, and they imbued their friends and helpers with the same energetic and adventurous attitude. I know many others share my huge respect and admiration for their efforts and achievements. Now we live in a time when political correctness and accountability are everything, and I wonder to what extent this stifles initiative and self-reliance. Joey and Jim epitomised independence of thought and action in a way that is all but impossible now, when the strictures of health and safety regulations accompany and, perhaps, inhibit every enterprise. There would be other times in the years ahead where Jim's cavalier approach would cause Joey no little worry, but I am sure even the most stringently scrupulous couldn't fail to have a grudging appreciation, or perhaps even a sneaking envy, of their individualistic way of life.

Jim's new Pitkinny took the form of the "big shed," which would enclose about two-thirds of the original fermtoun. It was designed to accommodate the reids, or cattle courts where the stirks or bullocks would spend the winter, and their winter feeding: hay, barley, turnips, and draff, the byproduct of the whisky industry which was bought from the distilleries. Some of the larger machinery, like the combine harvester and later, the JCB, were kept in there too. There was space for indoor work such as potato dressing and neep-cutting, and of course, stock feeding in the winter. A further very large shed was erected behind this for silage storage, and yet another round the east end of the steading, for storage of potatoes. Some of the existing buildings, which were newer or in a better state of repair, were retained. The red shed on the east side of the farm, built of corrugated iron, housed many implements. The cart shed, which housed two trailers and the tractor and tool shed, were directly across the close from the kitchen window. A big new wooden henhouse was erected just outside the close on the southwest side, to accommodate Joey's increased hen stocks.

Thus, within six years of assuming the tenancy of Pitkinny, the house and steading had been transformed and Jim was well on the way to realising his ambition to develop the arable potential of their new land, while continuing the dairying operation at Bogside under the able management of Jock and Helen Steel and their family.

*The Rutherford family in the Pitkinny kitchen*

**PITKINNY** ADN S NT196967 2 115m
? *Pitrennis* 1445 × 1476 *Pitfirrane Writs* no. 728 [transumpt of Dec. 1476 of special service dated 5 Oct. 1445 of John of Kinninmonth (*Kynninmont*) to Sir James of Kinninmonth (*Kinninmont*), knight, his father, in the lands of Pitcairn (*Pitkarn*) ADN, Colquhally (*Coquhellis*) ADN, ? Pitkinny (*Pitrennis*) ADN and Urquhart (*Urquhard*) DFL, RHX]
*Petkenny* 1458 *RMS* ii no. 638 [to David Boswell of Balmuto, part of the barony of Glassmount KGH]
*Petkynny* 1476 *ADA* 52 [o.c.; see ADN Introduction above]
*Petkenny* 1476 *RMS* ii no. 1233
*Petkenny* 1493 *RMS* ii no. 2142
*Litill Petkenny* 1505 *RSS* i no. 1074
*Petcany* 1531 *RMS* iii no. 980
*Litill Petcanye* 1531 *RMS* iii no. 980
*Pitkenny* 1540 *RMS* iii no. 2106

*Explanation of the Pitkinny name taken from The Place Names of Fife*

# Chapter 13

"Ah'll pit a stop tae yer gairdnin'."

As a farmer's wife, Mum had a variety of outside occupations, one of which was the keeping of hens. This made a valuable monetary contribution to the running of the house, especially important to her because for the first half of her married life, she did not receive a weekly housekeeping allowance from Jim. This state of affairs derived from their early days at Bogside, when cash flow as a concept did not exist! They had no money to speak of at all, and in those days her egg production became part of a barter system, when she sometimes would pay for groceries with her eggs. What little cash there was, was husbanded carefully by Jim and as the years passed and more of their products were sold, and payments made either in cash or into the bank, Jim continued as he had done in those days. He would draw cash from the bank for wages and other expenses and give Joey a few pounds at a time as she needed it to purchase the essentials.

But at all times, he kept exclusive control of all financial matters, and was very clearly the Chancellor of the Exchequer. This did not worry Joey unduly, as she was the least mercenary of people, and had no interest in money for its own sake, as long as she had enough to feed and clothe her family. She became a wonderful manager of her limited financial resources. She had her egg money and her twice-yearly dividend from the local co-operative store where she did most of her shopping. In addition, "the store," as we knew it, had a variety of savings schemes which allowed her to save up for larger purchases over a period of time. She always managed also to give us a little money for the school savings bank, which we paid into every week. This, no doubt, was a service that the education authority had started to encourage youngsters to learn to save and to acquire good habits of financial probity. When it stopped during our primary school years, Joey transferred our savings to the post office and continued to pay into it. When we married, the money in our accounts was part of our bottom drawer and there was enough for me to buy a cooker and a fridge to help equip my first kitchen.

It was only when Margaret started her nursing training that she realised that Joey had no financial independence at all, and she suggested to Dad that he ought to give Mum a fixed weekly sum of money for keeping the house. He reluctantly acquiesced in this, and from then on Joey had more control over the domestic budget. She always reckoned, however, that this did not go down too well with Jim, and that he would often claim to need to pay extra wages or other unexpected expenses out of the money drawn from the bank, and would contrive to be late paying her allowance. She noticed that this would happen on several consecutive weeks, so at the end of a period of time, he had actually done her out of a whole week's money! Certainly I was aware that nothing pleased Dad more than getting the better of you, and if that saved him some money, then so much the better! At the same time he managed never to leave himself short of pocket money. Joey used to go to the bank for Jim on a Saturday morning and make up the wages for him. In time she also learned to take care of the PAYE and National Insurance contributions for the workers and later, the VAT returns as well. I am sure if she had had the same tendency to cheat as Jim did, she could have taken him to the cleaners'! It was only due to her scrupulous honesty that Jim would never have to worry that she might get her own back on him.

Jim was always pawky and this became more pronounced as he grew older. He was also very superstitious and would always try to avoid situations that might invite bad luck or tempt Providence into visiting him with some disaster. There was one occasion when he was going to a funeral and noticed that he had £13 in his wallet. "I cannae possibly go to a funeral with £13," he wailed. He asked Joey to give him a few pounds. On hearing this, I remonstrated with him for being so superstitious. When, having given it more thought, I asked him why he hadn't just removed some money from his wallet, he replied, "Look, I agreed that Ah'm superstitious, I didnae say Ah'm stupit!"

As Joey depended greatly on her income from the hens, she worked hard to make them a success. A short-lived venture into battery production at Bogside confirmed her in her belief that living creatures should never be treated as mere units of production, but ought to be kept as humanely as possible, and always after that she favoured free-range hens kept in deep-litter conditions. Of course, they were more vulnerable to the forces of nature, and she had occasional losses to the fox. For a time, she reared day-old chicks but gave that up after their incubator caught fire and she lost most of them. Thereafter she used to buy young pullets, which became layers and showed a financial return within a short time. She used to keep some young cockerels for the pot, and would wring their necks, pluck, and clean them for special occasions. (How things have changed! Now chicken is a basic, cheap food, whereas in those days it was for high days and holidays only. A chicken at Christmas and a steak pie at New Year were the culinary highlights of the year!) She was not too squeamish to manage that, or so she thought, until one day, as she turned this nearly plucked cockerel over on the table, ready to open and clean it, it let out a blood-curdling croak. It was probably just air leaving its lungs as she moved it, but she couldn't complete the job and never attempted the process again!

As her egg supply increased, in addition to her regular local customers, the egg marketing board was a regular, if very demanding, customer. They required that the eggs be graded and cleaned and this made for a lot of extra work. One of the perennial problems with egg production was trying to ensure a steady supply, as hens do "go off the lay" for various reasons and she would occasionally have to disappoint customers. Sometimes she and Aunt Nellie would help each other out with eggs to fill their gaps in supply. In addition to nature's refusal to co-operate, of course, there was the occasional accident due to human error! One day when Jim was more than usually impatient for his twelve o'clock dinner to be placed in front of him at the kitchen table (and that really *is* saying something! Joey used to say, "a hungry man's an angry man"), and Margaret was rushing to help Joey, she collided with a pail full of newly-gathered eggs and knocked it over. Her automatic reaction was, of course, to pick it up, despite Joey's frantic call of "Leave it alone!" As many eggs smashed as they tumbled back into the pail, as had broken when it fell in the first place, so it was scrambled eggs all round for the next few days!

A lifelong love of gardening saw Joey quickly get to grips with the small front garden at Pitkinny, but there was limited scope for her there, so her attention soon turned to the old, neglected walled garden behind the northeast corner of the steading. It had presumably been used as a kitchen garden in the past, and Joey soon had it reinstated to its former function. She grew all kinds of vegetables and soft fruits, and was never happier than when she was working there. Jim had little time for—and less interest in—gardening, which he may have viewed as a busman's holiday, and he felt that his wife spent too much of her time there. He used to say he could never understand the attraction for spending hours of your leisure time with "yer backside stickin' up in the air," tending a garden. In later life, once retired, he did develop an interest in their garden, but Joey was always the driving force in planning and designing their beautiful gardens. Having said that, he was happy to bask in her reflected glory and did help her greatly with the heavier work. His lifetime of farming could always be traced in the businesslike and large-scale approach he took to the tasks in hand, and in the early years of their retirement in Kirkcudbright, where they lived beside many other newly-retired and novice gardeners, he and Joey came to be regarded as local gardening gurus when, much to their amazement and considerable embarrassment, they won first prize in the best garden competition in the town three years running.

Sadly, in those early years at Pitkinny, she was not to know that the days of her wonderful vegetable garden were numbered. She had a fainting turn there one afternoon. Fortunately, or perhaps unfortunately for her as it turned out, her sister Doris was there at the time and insisted on telling Jim, who sent for Doctor Brackenridge. Joey's old nemesis came back to haunt her as she was warned that she should not be doing heavy gardening with her heart condition, especially alone and in such a lonely spot. When she showed no sign of taking his advice to heart, Jim was heard to mutter, "Ah'll pit a stop to yer gairdnin'." A few days later Joey went round to her garden to find a scene of utter devastation. 'Someone' had left the gate open and the sheep had got into Joey's pride and joy, and true to their nature, they had scoffed the lot! Only a few forlorn gooseberries were left hanging from the very top of the tallest gooseberry bush—only because the sheep couldn't reach them—as a sad remnant of the luxuriant bounty of the day before. Jim, of course, denied having left the gate open deliberately, but Joey always believed that he was the culprit, and in the deepest recesses of her heart I am sure she never forgave him. It brought back the painful memories of the time she was prevented from playing tennis and the other occasions she had been constrained from expressing herself in physical activity because of her health. What made her angry was that she had never been discouraged from working hard, only from playing hard! A much more tragic and heartbreaking example of this was still to come and would affect Joey for the rest of her life.

Thereafter her garden was used for keeping pigs during Jim's subsequent venture in pig-rearing. Farm workers who lived in the cottar hooses had, as one of their few perks, the opportunity to fatten a pig and sell it at market, so making a little extra money. Geordie Pryde, who lived with his family for a few years in the cottage we had briefly occupied, asked Jim if he could have a piglet to keep in the little stone-built pigsty at the top of his garden. So it was, Jim nearly came a cropper at the hands—or perhaps the trotters—of one of the sows in the old garden. We had all walked round with him to see him select a suitable piglet for Geordie. When he picked up the chosen one by the back legs, naturally it let out a series of frantic and ever louder squeals. Its mother, equally naturally, reacted by promptly giving chase to Jim, who had already taken to his heels in anticipation of this development. When he realised that the sow really meant business, he dropped the piglet, expecting the sow to then give up the hunt. However, she was not to be deterred so easily and obviously intended to teach Jim a lesson! As she gained on him, he had to change up a gear or two, and he just made it to the dyke, one step ahead of the slavering jaws of his pursuer, reaching safety only by leaping first into the water trough. So the chase ended with Jim rather shame-faced and very wet, but poor Geordie still without a pig! Needless to say, he was left in no doubt by Jim that he would have to get one for himself as, Jim's philosophy was certainly "Once (nearly) bitten, twice shy!" He was well aware of the fact that a bite from a pig is one of the most dangerous in the animal kingdom, owing to the way the jaws close and the teeth interlock, making it very hard for them to open again, and resulting in great tissue damage to the poor victim.

The loss of her beloved garden was a huge blow to Joey, and Jim's intervention, though perhaps a well-intentioned though drastic solution to what he saw as a possible threat to her health and well-being, much resented by her. A few years later, she would enlist his grudging cooperation in making a new vegetable garden by fencing off a wedge-shaped part of the yard near the red implement shed. The JCB came into its own in breaking up the ground and bringing in a large quantity of topsoil. Railway sleepers formed the retaining edges of the beds, where she proceeded to nurture a large variety of vegetable crops. I have two particular memories of that garden: of picking brussels sprouts with frozen fingers for Christmas dinners, and much illicit gathering of garden peas which we would consume in secret. We would then have to conceal the evidence of all the empty pods to avoid Mum's uncanny ability to detect our every misdemeanour, and really did suspect that she had eyes in the back of her head and, in fact, everywhere else as well! Having brought up our two sons, I now realise, of course, that what she had were very finely honed maternal instincts, which come to everyone with motherhood, and which she and, I hope I in my turn, put to very good use.

Joey continued to reclaim parts of the ground around the entrance to the steading, and turn them into lawns and flower beds. She planted bulbs around the henhouses and drying green, and every summer there would be more cascades of colour around the place as old discarded vessels, from chimney pots to old feeding troughs, were pressed into action as containers for bedding plants. There were occasions when her cherished flowers made tempting, tasty treats for any passing stray animal, and nothing made her quite so angry as finding her precious plants decapitated by hungry sheep or cattle who were carelessly herded or allowed to escape from the surrounding fields and sheds. One spring she was on a crusade to impress on Jim the need for his cooperation in this matter, after some stirks had made a quagmire of the lawns in the front garden. As I was hanging out the washing and was admiring the pretty crocuses flowering around the drying green, I suddenly remembered that it was April Fool's Day, or "Hunty Gowk" as it was traditionally known. I couldn't resist the opportunity to play a trick on Mum, and ran over to the kitchen window where she was at her usual place at the kitchen sink. "Mum, come and see! Something has chewed the heads off your crocuses!"

She came flying out of the back door drying her hands on her peeny, and charged over the close threatening all kinds of dire consequences for Jim—the least painful of which was divorce! Expecting to see what she had seen so often before, she peered down at the flowers, one bunch after another, still loudly proclaiming what she would do to him when she got her hands on him, as it slowly began to dawn on her that in fact they were all completely intact. She began to quieten down and look really puzzled, until she looked up at me and saw my beaming face. The awful truth began to dawn just as I called "Hunty Gowk" and took to my heels to run back to the house. Thankfully, I knew that my mother had a well-developed sense of humour, and she enjoyed the joke as much as I did. There were other times when she caught Jim out on that special day of the year, and for the most part his sense of humour helped him to see the funny side of his gullibility.

The front garden at Pitkinny was enclosed by a four-foot wall, and one year Joey decided it was too high! Her father Hugh helped her to lower it by half on the front part, on either side of the gate, and they used the resulting boulders and stones to make a lovely rockery, thus making the front aspect of the house much more attractive. Then she decided, with Jim's agreement, that there should be a lockable gate at the entrance to the steading. With the help again of Hugh and his grandson and namesake, my cousin Hughie Drennan, who was then about eleven years old, and staying at Pitkinny on his summer holidays, she set to and built two gateposts using stones, brick, and concrete. The pillars were finished and their tops decorated with some of the many lovely pebbles Joey had collected—sometimes reluctantly helped by us—over the years from the various beaches and shorelines we visited around the coasts of Scotland.

These projects of Joey's were further examples of her enterprise and imagination. In addition she was always able to inspire others to share her enthusiasm and join her in her ventures. My grandfather was often her right-hand man, while Jim rarely got directly involved beyond the level of a passive interest. Her last great effort at major improvement in the external appearance of the house came when she was in her mid-fifties, in the autumn of 1969. I was working in Sweden, and Margaret was married with two daughters and living in Ayrshire. As was her way, Joey always looked for distraction from the fact that we were no longer living at home and that her role as a mother no longer dominated her life. Having been whitened at some time in the past, before we lived there, the walls of the old house had become very discoloured and stained as the years passed. The cost of having it professionally painted was not something that Jim would consider, so Joey took her usual course of action. "Do you think we could do it ourselves?" Jim felt about painting very much as he did about gardening, so he didn't immediately follow her lead, but eventually, in the face of her persistence and enthusiasm, he gave way and agreed that he would buy the materials.

One of the workers at that time was Tony Barnes, a young man from Cardenden, and Jim said he could spare him to help Joey with painting the house. Hugh was on hand to lend moral support, although he was by then too old to get actively involved, and so the work began. There was no question of hiring scaffolding; the farm ladders had to suffice, as Tony did all the high work while Joey held his ladders and did a lot of the lower walls herself. They had to improvise when it came to the highest parts of the gable ends, by parking the lorry in the right place and fixing the ladders on top of its cattle float, so gaining the necessary extra height. When the work was completed, the result was wonderful. The old house, rejuvenated with a fresh white coat, set against the attractive gardens and neat entrance to the steading, was fitting testament to all Joey's efforts, and she had every right to be proud of her achievements. Even Jim must have been aware that the house and steading was a fitting setting for the successful business he had created in the twenty years that we had been at Pitkinny.

Photographs were taken and sent to me in Sweden. There was my family: Mum and Dad, Margaret and John, Pamela and Alison, standing in front of a gleaming house. No wonder I felt proud and not a little homesick when I saw how well they all looked and the transformation that had taken place in my old home. Perhaps it was a sign that I had at last grown up, or that when we live in another country, we see our old lives in a new and truer light. For the first time I was truly aware of just how important my family were to me, and of how much I owed to them all. Also, I began to appreciate fully the influence my parents had already had on me and to what extent I was the joint result of their undoubted abilities and talents.

I had always been aware of the strength of Joey's character. Indeed, if I am truthful, I suspect that in my teenage years, I probably felt unduly hard done by, when made to learn to share her high standards of honesty, hard work, and modesty. We were subject to very firm discipline in all aspects of our lives, almost all of which emanated from Mum, while Dad seemed to have a much more laissez-faire attitude. I now understand that he could afford to have a more relaxed approach in this matter, as he knew that our upbringing was in the capable hands of his wife. In addition, he of course always avoided any kind of confrontation, and would have hated us to think of him as a heavy-handed kind of father. By the same token, it probably never occurred to him to feel a responsibility to share with Joey any lingering resentment we may have felt on occasion, at what we saw as unduly firm treatment from our mother. The bringing up of daughters was very definitely a woman's business and I have sometimes wondered if he would have been different with a son.

By the mid 1950s the house, the steading, and the land had undergone radical change at the hands of Joey and Jim; a transformation which would continue to be a feature of their continued tenure there. Margaret and I were attending Auchterderran Junior Secondary School, Margaret already nearing the end of her primary education. Joey and Jim were working as hard as ever, but now had significant achievements to show for their efforts.

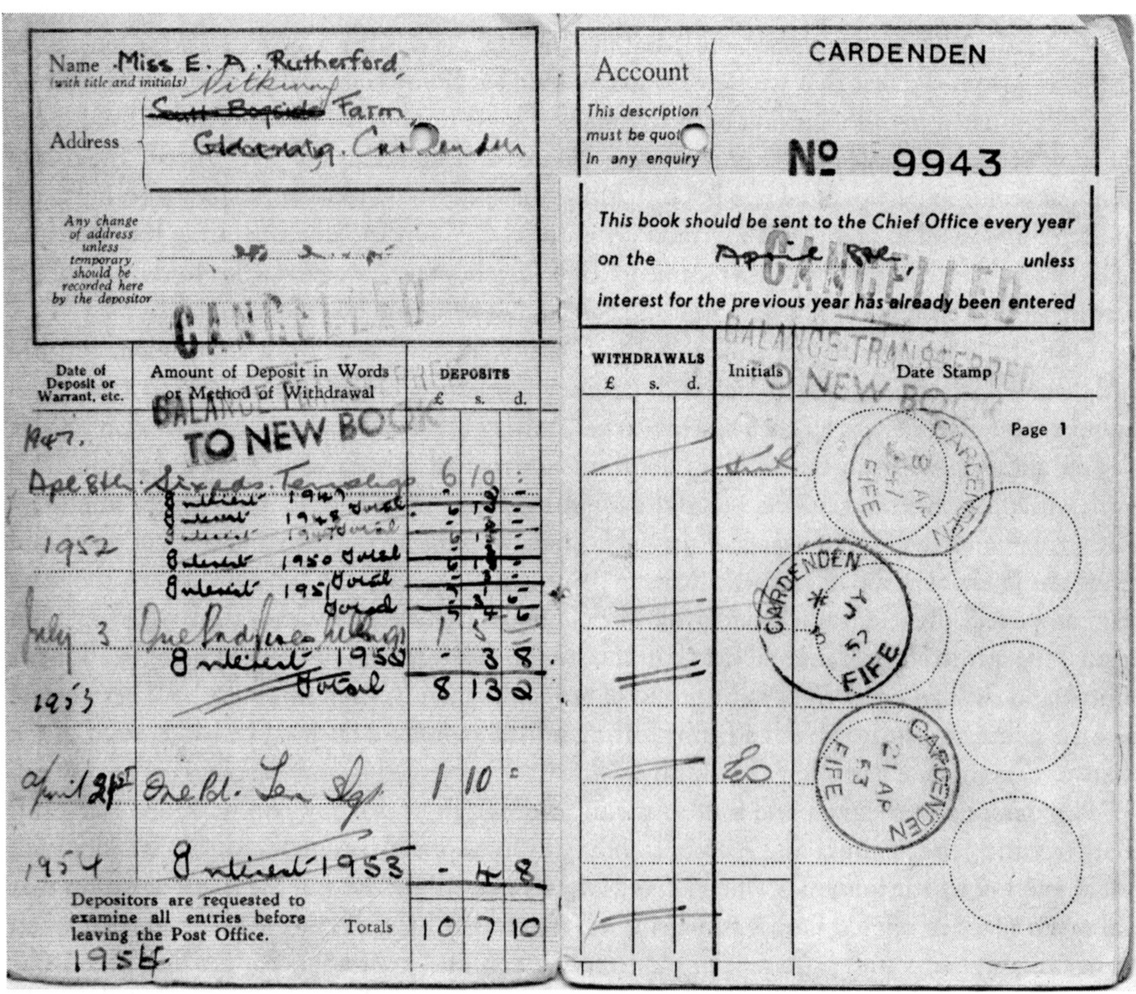

Name (with title and initials) Miss E. A. Rutherford

Address ... Farm

Any change of address unless temporary should be recorded here by the depositor

CANCELLED

TO NEW BOOK

| Date of Deposit or Warrant, etc. | Amount of Deposit in Words or Method of Withdrawal | DEPOSITS £ | s. | d. |
|---|---|---|---|---|
| 1947. Apr 8th | | 6 | 10 | |
| 1952 | Interest 1950 Total | | | |
| July 3 | | 1 | 5 | |
| | Interest 1952 | - | 3 | 8 |
| 1953 | Total | 8 | 13 | 2 |
| April 21st | | 1 | 10 | |
| 1954 | Interest 1953 | - | 4 | 8 |
| | Totals | 10 | 7 | 10 |

Depositors are requested to examine all entries before leaving the Post Office.

1955

Account

This description must be quoted in any enquiry

CARDENDEN

№ 9943

This book should be sent to the Chief Office every year on the ...... unless interest for the previous year has already been entered

| WITHDRAWALS £ | s. | d. | Initials | Date Stamp |
|---|---|---|---|---|

Page 1

CARDENDEN FIFE

BALANCE TRANSFERRED TO NEW BOOK

School savings bank book

*Artistic reminder of a typical scene at Pitkinny—Joey with Calum and Donald?*

*Joey's rockery in the front garden*

*Joey and Pamela before the repainting of the house*

*Jim, Alison, Margaret, Pamela, and Joey after the repainting of the house (1969)*

# Chapter 14

"Yer Dad's a fermer? Well, you'll be weel aff!"

I suspect to every little girl, her father is a hero, and I was no exception. Dad was certainly not one of the breed of "new men" we are becoming used to nowadays, inasmuch as he never involved himself in our day-to-day care or discipline, and remained, as many fathers of his generation, a rather remote parent, very much cast in the role of provider and protector, and perhaps for that reason I got used to seeing him as a strong and reassuring presence, always there, but usually just beyond our conscious awareness. On the other hand, it was Mum who looked after us and administered a strict discipline in bringing us up. She provided us with the security of a well-ordered and predictable routine in our physical well-being and a strong moral code from a very early age.

However, Dad was wonderful at saving us from the "creatures of the night"—especially moths and daddy longlegs which would often invade our bedroom on warm summer evenings, or spiders which made our downstairs bathroom a favourite habitat. We would call for him when the flying beasties scared us, and he would come upstairs and catch them and pretend to eat them! "That wis a real tasty/crunchy/salty ane!" he would declare, after chewing thoughtfully for a few moments. I remember relating proudly to my friends in infant school, "My Dad eats daddy longlegs!" and I really did believe it for a long time. If Margaret and I were having a carry-on instead of going to sleep, he would shout up the stairs, "Get yer e'en shut!" but would seldom scold us. That task was always left to Mum, who would occasionally preface a telling-off with the words, "Yer Dad's no pleased wi' ye..." I used to feel aggrieved, young though I was, that he wouldn't tell us directly the reason for his displeasure.

In retrospect, I am aware that I subconsciously assumed that Dad could always be counted on to provide us with anything we really needed. This is somewhat surprising in that he wasn't in the habit of giving us presents, and, as explained earlier, Mum had to manage the house on very little money. The few presents she received from him were all the more precious to her because of their rarity and the significance of the special occasions they recognised. The crystal candlesticks he bought her in Stirling on their honeymoon had pride of place on her dressing table throughout their married life. He once gave her a wooden, musical jewellery case which had a musical motif made of "emeralds" in one corner of the lid, and played the tune "Always." I remember thinking at the time that this was a romantic gesture, but as I grew older I had to admit that there was precious little evidence of romance in the day-to-day hard graft of life on the farm. When they celebrated twenty-five years of marriage, Dad gave us money to buy Mum a present from him, and we chose a dome clock and a brooch. When they retired, he gave her a gold watch and pearls, but Joey was never all that interested in jewellery. In fact, she hardly ever wore her pearls and was always afraid that she would lose them. Likewise, an old and valuable diamond ring she was given by her dear friend Teenie Black so worried her that she would hide it in a safe place; so successfully, sometimes, that she would forget where she had secreted it! Finally, when we were clearing their last home after Dad's death, we discovered Mum's pearl necklace, in its original box, hidden at the bottom of a box of dusters in one of the kitchen cupboards. It must have been put there by Mum for safekeeping at some time and forgotten about.

Joey's appreciation of a gift was never expressed in relation to its value, but she really exemplified the sentiment, "It's the thought that counts," and she set great store by the simplest tokens of affection she and Dad were given, especially when they came from one of their daughters or grandchildren. A garden trowel made by Calum in his craft, design, and technology class (or metalwork class, as it was more familiarly known), had pride of place amongst their garden tools. Joey and Jim were always meticulous in the care of their tools, each one being cleaned and oiled after use and hung up in its allotted space on the garage wall. Donald's gift of a bottle opener he had made was similarly cherished and proudly kept in their drinks cabinet.

Margaret and I were never showered with presents and had very little in the way of pocket money as we were growing up. We got threepence to spend on a Friday when the sweets finally came off the ration in 1953, and a sixpence piece on a Saturday, with twice that amount if we were going to the pictures at Markinch! As I grew older I would occasionally hear comments like, "Oh! Yer Dad's a fermer? Well, you'll be weel aff!" I could never understand what they meant, when I seemed to have less in a ready cash sense than anyone else I knew at school, whose fathers were not farmers! What I came to realise was that we were very well cared for, and according to Joey's priorities, and in relation to the deprivation she knew as a child, she always made sure that we were warm and well fed, and had a clean and comfortable home. As an old woman, she would say that perhaps we should have had more, but in retrospect I am sure that her approach instilled in us a sound sense of values that would serve us well.

Although we went without many of the extras that some of our friends enjoyed, we didn't miss out entirely. At Christmas we always had one main present from Santa and the ubiquitous orange and apple and a few little treats in our stockings, but birthdays were usually given short shrift. Only on one occasion did we have a real iced birthday cake (one between us as our birthdays were only two weeks apart), made by Joey's friend, Mrs Blake, and had a small birthday party attended by a few of our school friends. However, our twenty-first birthdays were each marked by the gift of an Omega gold watch, purchased from Greig the jewellers in Kirkcaldy. That was a handsome present indeed, and much cherished by us, but the idea of a coming-of-age party was never considered. There was generally much less celebration of these events in those days and we certainly were not alone in not having a public show of these rights of passage. It was somewhat different when it came to our marriages, however.

Mum and Dad were determined that Margaret and I would each have a lovely white wedding, and I would like to think that this was prompted by more than relief at having got us off their hands! Perhaps they wanted to make up for the necessarily austere wartime and relatively joyless wedding they, and many of their contemporaries, were forced to have. So they welcomed the chance to celebrate their daughters' marriages with more pride and joy than their parents were able to show on their wedding day in 1941. In addition, they saw it as an opportunity to reciprocate hospitality they had been shown over the years by some of their farming and business friends, who were used to entertaining in a more showy way than Joey and Jim had ever done. As in any business, there are accompanying social obligations which have to be fulfilled, and we accepted that many of the guests at our wedding were our parents' friends and associates, rather than ours. At the risk of seeming mercenary, it was not lost on us that we benefited in the shape of some very generous wedding presents!

So, in the memorable events of our lives, Mum and Dad were more than generous. We never missed out on educational or social opportunities which our parents, Mum particularly, believed would be to our benefit, but we were certainly never over-indulged or spoiled in the material sense. We did have, however, the advantage of having parents, particularly Dad, who enjoyed entertainment. While he would seldom take us out on his own, there was nothing he liked better than us all going to the pictures or to a variety show. We were never exposed to anything in the way of highbrow culture, but we did have the experience of seeing live entertainment at a young age. I have faint memories of going to the Dunfermline Opera House as a very young child, and I believe one of the variety shows we saw there included the famous Aberdeen comedian, Harry Gordon. Interestingly, many years later, in 2000, my mother-in-law, Enid Ewing, at the age of ninety, moved into an Abbeyfield Care Home in Aberdeen which occupied the house he had lived in, in the Mannofield district of the city.

We saw many of the well-known Scottish entertainers who were still treading the boards of variety theatres, artistes like Jimmy Logan and Robert Wilson. This encouraged Jim's love of Scottish storytelling and songs. We once saw a very young Andy Stewart in one of his early variety seasons in the theatre in Inverness, during one of our many summer holiday visits to the "capital of the Highlands," when Margaret and I waited at the stage door and got a signed photograph from him. Once a year we would have a day off school to attend the dairy show at the Kelvin Hall in Glasgow, and sometimes we would end the day by seeing a variety show at the Kings or the Empire theatre in the city. Such trips to Glasgow always seemed to be much more exciting and daring than any visit to the more familiar and mundane Edinburgh. It was further away, of course, and involved a much longer car journey. The city itself seemed imbued with an element of exoticism and even a hint of danger as we, as children, had overheard some reference to razor gangs and "keelies" in this "no mean city"! Dad used to sing a song "The Big Kilmarnock Bunnet," and one line went "stravaigin' through the muckle streets o' Glesca." These words to me summed up the strange vastness of a city, which I must have felt, subconsciously, to be culturally alien to us in a way that the more genteel and staid Edinburgh never was. Some of that feeling remained with me many years later when at the age of twenty-two I spent my post-graduate year studying at Jordanhill College. I never felt quite comfortable living there, and after the first term I stayed with my sister Margaret and her husband and two wee girls in Falkirk, and travelled in daily to Glasgow.

If Dad liked the theatre, he loved the cinema even more; provided, of course, that the films met with his approval. Westerns were his favourite and a very popular genre at that time. I remember days in the winter when bad weather prevented much outside work on the farm, and Mum and Dad would be waiting for us in the car as we came out of school. We would go to Kirkcaldy to the pictures, sometimes with a high tea in the Carlton tea room before the film, or a fish supper in Vissochi's chip shop in Dunnikier Road after it, or when Jim was particularly hungry, both! I remember a sign in the chip shop, which read "No Singing! No dancing! No spitting!" This used to fascinate me and I had to admit that I never saw anyone doing any of these things, so concluded that the populace of Kirkcaldy must be very obedient! Mum's taste in films was much more wide-ranging, but her favourite by far was *The Quiet Man* with John Wayne and Maureen O' Hara, which she saw at least six times!

As for most families in those days, the wireless was an essential adjunct to daily life. Saturday teatime was usually accompanied by the football results, followed by Scottish dance music, invariably introduced by the tune "Kate Dalrymple." (Many years later, again while I was living in Sweden, I happened by accident to pick up the Scottish Home Service on my radio one Saturday evening, and suffered an acute episode of homesickness as I heard that old familiar tune again. That was a mistake I was careful to avoid for the rest of my time there, as it made me so desperately sad with longing for home and my loved ones there). Work in the farmhouse kitchen on weekday mornings was to the sound of *Housewives' Choice* and *Music while You Work*, while Sunday morning was the time for *Two-Way Family Favourites*, which played requests for members of the forces serving overseas. *Mrs Dale's Diary* was an early example of soap opera based on the life of a middle-class English family, whereas *The McFlannels* and *Down at the Mearns* were somewhat more earthy and couthy Scottish examples of a similar genre. As the years passed Mum and Dad continued to enjoy listening to Scottish music programmes until latterly; in their last years at Cadham their favourites were Robbie Shepherd's *Take the Floor* and *The Reel Blend*, on which Dad once got a mention when he wrote to the programme asking for information about the song "Leaving Barra."

So it was no surprise that Jim took to the medium of television like a duck to water. It opened up the world for people in a completely revolutionary way, and as a means of entertainment and education its advent changed the patterns of family and social life forever. Although Joey appreciated television, she was always more discriminating in her choice of programme than Jim. Her preference was usually for the more edifying type of broadcast, while Jim loved the sport and variety shows. In the days when they had only one set, she would often have to watch his football matches and quiz shows, while he had no time for the costume dramas and documentaries that she liked. As a family in the early years of TV, we all enjoyed shows like *Café Continental* and later, *Sunday Night at the London Palladium*. When we were young we made the most of children's television, although by comparison with the menu available to youngsters today, it seems very innocent and tame in retrospect

The acquisition of television was determined, in our case, by the date of our connection to the mains electric supply, in October 1953. Having been promised connection earlier that year, Jim and Joey had everything ready for the big switch-on, and had bought a variety of electrical equipment: a cooker, washing machine and fridge, an electric fire, a standard lamp, a radiogram, and a television set. Unlike many families, we did not have TV in time for the coronation in June of that year, but saw the historic event at the cinema in Kirkcaldy. I seem to remember that Grandad Hugh took us all to the pictures that day, a very unusual venture for him, and perhaps in keeping with his reverence for the monarchy, something my mother did not share with her father. She had distinctly republican leanings, as I have myself, and always said she would not go the length of herself to see any of the royal family. This principle would be put to the test some years later when it could be said that the Queen came to see us! However, by the autumn of 1953 we were the proud owners of our first TV set. It was typical of the early versions of "the box": a small 12-inch-diameter screen enclosed in a very large wooden case, while the radiogram was an impressive piece of furniture. It stood about four feet high, the same width, and about two feet deep. The cabinet was made of walnut veneer with a six-inch-deep lid that gently and soundlessly closed automatically by hydraulic action. Inside it contained a radio and a record player, which was much more sophisticated than the old wind-up gramophone we had had before. It had been able to play only one record at a time, and used needles, which had to be changed very frequently, whereas the new machine had an auto-changer, which could play a stack of eight records in turn, and had a modern stylus. It could play not only 78 rpm, but 33 rpm long-playing records and the new 45 rpm discs, which became the new singles. The large solid cabinet gave wonderful sound quality, with a booming base tone.

As Dad gradually built up his collection of records of the Scottish songs and tunes he loved, Margaret and I began to be aware of the attractions of popular music. Sometimes, late on a Saturday afternoon, the three of us would visit Bob Beckett's electrical shop in Cardenden where he sold bicycles, radios, and records as well as the more mundane household items. Dad would buy the current Jimmy Shand and Robert Wilson offerings, while we would buy the latest hit parade records. Some of these were middle-of-the-road numbers, which would feature on the light programme of the BBC, but some of the more avant-garde music would be more likely to be heard on Radio Luxembourg, which we would sometimes listen to clandestinely. It was not exactly forbidden, but had a slightly naughty quality as it broadcast adverts, which was unknown in any other medium. As teenagers later we would tune in regularly and were rather fascinated by its advertising for things like "pro-plus" tablets, which were supposed to give you extra energy. We would never have dared to attempt to try them, of course, but the very idea gave us a vicarious thrill.

So our big sitting room echoed to the strains of a catholic variety of music from "Down in the Glen" by Robert Wilson and "The Bluebell Polka" by Jimmy Shand at one extreme, to the cutting edge of Bill Haley's "Rock Around the Clock" and Fats Domino's "Blueberry Hill" on the other; with singers like David Whitfield and his "Cara Mia Mine," "Oh Mein Papa" with Eddie Calvert on trumpet, and the sweet Irish tones of Ruby Murray singing "Softly, Softly," somewhere in the middle. This range of popular music was exemplified one New Year when I can remember watching Dad and Auntie Doris boogying to Guy Mitchell's "She Wears Red Feathers and a Hooley-Hooley Skirt" and then hearing him sing a duet of "The Crooked Bawbee" with Auntie Greta!

The hard work of the farm and the worries involved in running a business were certainly lightened by the ability to have fun and enjoy some degree of relaxation in the rare times of leisure. Joey and Jim's determined efforts to make their business a success were bearing fruit in the increasingly prosperous postwar world, and our life continued to be blessed by the warmth of friendships and family ties. There were difficulties too, of course, principally Jim's developing tendency to drink more than was good for him and Joey's continued health worries, but all in all, if they had stopped to take stock of their lives in the early fifties, they could have justifiably felt some satisfaction. Joey had succeeded in making a secure and comfortable environment for her family, which was, after all, her main ambition in life. Her concerns over Margaret's health were beginning to ease and, although she didn't know it then, her own life was about to take on a new and exciting dimension. Jim's business was going from strength to strength, he had many friends, and was very well liked as a man and highly respected as an innovative and increasingly successful farmer. Most of all, he was entirely different from his father, and in Jim's book that was the greatest accolade he could wish for. He had proved that he could make his way in life independently of his father, and had managed to shrug off the limiting and narrow outlook that would have been his legacy had he remained in his shadow.

*Harvest Home in Portmoak Church Hall*
*Left to right: Joey with Anne, Aunt Doris, Jim, and Margaret*

*Anne and Margaret at the Highland Show*

*Markinch Games*
*Back row left to right: Joey, Aunt Doris, Edith Hutchinson, Cathy Webster*
*Front row left to right: Eunice Mitchell, Anne, Margaret, Irene Webster*

# Chapter 15

"Come awa' in fur yer denner!"

In growing up I am sure for most people there is at least one aspect of their lives they would like to change if they could. In my case, I would have loved to live in the town. Of course now I realise that living on the farm gave us many advantages in terms of quality of life, but then, I wanted to be like everyone else and live within easy walking distance of the school or the bus stop. I thought my life would be perfect if I could walk to the shops and other amenities. So we loved staying with Gran and Grandad in Markinch and thoroughly appreciated the convenience of situations like walking down Croft Crescent to Mason's bakehouse for the warm, fragrant, morning rolls straight from the oven. If we missed the freedom to come and go on our own as children, as we grew older we found our social lives severely curtailed by living at Pitkinny. Unlike the myriad of leisure amenities available to teenagers today, our social activities were limited to what could be provided by the church and the school. Even then, the long walk home in the summer, or having to be picked up by Mum or Dad in the dark evenings, made it uncomfortable or impossible for any young man who offered to see us home. So any such possibility—from the badminton club, from the youth club or youth fellowship at the church, from the annual Christmas dance at school, or the more frequent sports or musical activities I was involved in there—was necessarily curtailed by the distance to Pitkinny.

For a year or two as a teenager, I attended the McAinsh Parish Church youth club in Lochgelly on a Friday evening. I would catch the bus home as far as the "Auld Hoose" bus stop at Auchterderran where I would be met by Mum or Dad. On one such evening an older boy, whom I knew and rather fancied, asked if he could see me to the bus stop. Naturally, I was pleased and not a little flattered (older boys were always much more attractive than boys of your own age!), but we had only gone a few steps when I heard my name called urgently. Looking around, I could see nothing but a big lorry parked by the church hall steps. To my horror, I recognised four beaming faces (five, if you count the collie dog, Nell!) crammed into the cab of the vehicle: Mum, Dad, Margaret, and her boyfriend John. Dad had taken delivery of a new lorry that day, and like a little boy with a new toy, just had to try it out. "Let's go up to Lochgelly and meet Anne, save her taking the bus," he said. Margaret and John were gleefully enjoying my embarrassment as I shamefacedly muttered to my somewhat surprised escort, "I'll have to go. That's my family," and proceeded to clamber up and squeeze into the already-overcrowded lorry cab, but Mum and Dad were blissfully unaware of my discomfiture and probably wondered why I seemed less than thrilled by their kind surprise. With the agonised self-consciousness of youth, I was never able to feel the same about that boy and, to my relief, he never again ventured to walk me to the bus stop.

Living in the country must always add a dimension of practical difficulty, and the necessity of forward planning, in accessing the services and exploiting the amenities of town or village. This was certainly the case for Joey when it came to food shopping. We did, however, have the advantage of the services of a variety of mobile shops and vans, which came regularly to the farm. The Lochgelly and District Co-operative Society operated fleets of vans: the grocer came once a week and the baker twice, while Christie the butcher from Kirkcaldy paid a weekly visit. Joey would never know from day to day how many mouths she would have to feed each mealtime. In those days, farming was a very labour-intensive business, especially at the busy times of the hay, grain, and potato harvests.

Jim was always very hospitable when it came to issuing general invitations to casual workers, visiting commercial travellers, or any other bodies who happened to be in the big shed or the close at mealtimes. "Come awa' in fur yer denner!" He insisted on regular times for meals: noon for dinner and five o'clock for tea. Of course, he allowed himself the privilege of being late, but pity help Joey, or us as we became old enough to help with the cooking and serving of the meals, if his food wasn't ready and he was there, hungry and impatient, on time! And Joey would never be quite sure how many cups of tea her teapot would have to dispense until she was ready to mask the tea, and counted the number of heads around the table.

Nor was he an easy taskmaster when it came to the quality of the food. He had very distinct likes and dislikes, and had become used to having what he liked when he liked it. Above everything he liked plain food, well-cooked. He distrusted anything he didn't immediately recognise, or anything in the least exotic or in the slightest way unusual. During one hay time, when Margaret was doing her nursing training at the Dunfermline and West Fife hospital, she invited a friend to come home with her for their day off. This was to be the first of many visits from Jean Sneddon (later Hume), who, over the years was to become a good friend and frequent visitor. One or two extra workers were also invited in for tea and, as she was very used to doing, Joey had to stretch the ingredients for a mixed grill to include all these extra appetites. She made some French toast, but as she put a piece on Jim's plate along with his chop, sausage, and fried egg, something told her she was making a mistake. Sure enough, as everyone else had been served and was settling down to enjoy their meal, and we were trying to be on our best behaviour in the presence of our new guest, Jim stuck his fork into the French toast and, regarding it with a suspicious and sceptical expression on his face, barked out the question, "What's this? Fish?" From that day onwards, whenever Jean was confronted by any dubious-looking item of food in the hospital canteen, she would also demand to know, "What's this? Fish?"

In the days of our childhood, food was generally plain and unadulterated. A major feature of the development of the food industry since then has been a huge increase in the degree to which food is processed and subjected to additives. One of the first examples of convenience foods I remember was the advent of sliced bread, and the day arrived when the store (the co-op) baker's van had only sliced loaves to offer. White bread came in plain and pan varieties, and not surprisingly, Jim preferred the plain type that had—up to now—always come unsliced. Now Joey would be spared the need to slice the bread herself, but Jim was having none of it! He declared the ready-sliced bread to be less fresh than its unsliced counterpart, and refused to accept that it was no longer possible to buy the latter. He telephoned the store manager in Lochgelly and demanded to know why he could no longer buy unsliced bread. The poor hapless manager had to admit that it was still possible to rescue some loaves of the unsliced bread before they went through the slicing machine, and he would see to it that two of them would be reserved for Mrs Rutherford each time the van called at Pitkinny. So is goes to prove that it always pays to complain! However, at busy times, when she knew there would be extra people to feed at teatime, Joey would buy one or two of the sliced loaves as well as the unsliced ones, and there would be a plate of each kind of bread on the table, Jim's favoured bread, sliced by Joey herself, nearest him. One day at teatime, there was a discussion about this at the table, and everyone except Jim agreed that there was no difference between the two, except, that is, in his imagination. "Well," said Jim, "if that's the case why are all you buggers eating *my* bread?" And he pointed to the plates. The one that had been full of the home-sliced bread was completely empty, while the shop-sliced one was almost untouched! He rested his case, but not until he had made the most of the results of this blind-testing experiment!

Many years later, during a telephone conversation with our son Calum, who was working in Hong Kong, he asked, "Have Gran and Grandad found the Holy Grail yet?" When asked to explain, he went on, "The perfect loaf of bread and the perfect tattie!" It was true that in their retirement they scoured the countryside for good old-fashioned bread and Jim's favourite potatoes. It was not unknown for them to drive up to Angus for potatoes if he saw an advertisement in the *Dundee Courier* newspaper for Keir's Pinks or Golden Wonders. Joey and Jim would sometimes reminisce about, and bewail the passing of, the old varieties of potatoes like Home Guard, Redskins, and Arran Pilot, and believed that plant breeding had adversely affected the quality of potatoes, often seeming to leave them subject to blight and spraing, the latter gravely affecting Golden Wonders. Suitability for processing and ease of preparation are most important in the marketing of potatoes, but, as a grower of the vegetable, Jim appreciated the different qualities of various varieties and preferred a dry, floury tattie like the Golden Wonder and the Keir's Pink. He felt that the latter was no longer demanded because it is fiddly to peel, with its awkward shape and many deep eyes. Also it needs very careful cooking because if boiled too long it will go to mush and should be steamed for the later part of its cooking. He believed that the modern housewife prefers smooth-skinned, regularly shaped potatoes, which are easily prepared and cooked, even if they lack flavour and texture. In his estimation, the ability to prepare his preferred type of potato was a measure of your expertise as a cook, and Margaret and I had to learn early from Mum the secrets of this culinary skill. Likewise, as a teenager, I was the only girl in my class at school who was able to cut a perfect slice of bread when we learned to make French toast in our cookery class at school, thanks to all the practice I had had in slicing bread at Pitkinny!

Joey did some of her food shopping at Fraser's—a licensed grocer's located on Jamphlars Road, near the Auld Hoose junction in Auchterderran. Mr Fraser would take an order over the phone and deliver the groceries in a box in his van. I sometimes shake my head in amazement when I think of this, as I am unloading a boot full of shopping from the supermarket for two of us, having already filled the trolley from the shelves in the shop, unloaded at the checkout, loaded it back into the trolley and then into the car! This is progress? And yet Joey could feed a family and any number of additional mouths without the necessity for this madness. Admittedly, we produced a lot of our own food: our milk, eggs, potatoes, and vegetables; Mum made lots of jam, and pickled and preserved beetroot in season, and there was always home baking to be enjoyed. We also had the services of mobile shops and ate a much simpler diet, but I really wonder whether the evils of living in a consumerist society do not vastly outweigh the benefits.

Fraser's, however, was to be the scene of one of Joey's most unpleasant shopping experiences. When fruit started to become available after the war, Mr Fraser told her one day that he was expecting a delivery of grapes. Would she like him to keep her some? He explained that the headmaster's wife, Mrs Inglis, had ordered some, as had Mrs Shearer the dentist's wife, the doctor's wife Mrs Brackenridge, and Mrs Blair the draper's wife. All these pillars of the local community had their businesses and homes around that part of Auchterderran and all patronised Fraser's shop. By the time he mentioned the Church manse as the last on his list of eminent customers, Joey felt rather cornered into agreeing to order some of his grapes. While she no doubt relished the prospect of giving her family a taste of a fruit which, having been for so long unattainable during the war, had an exotic allure, she was aghast when the promised one pound of grapes materialised the next time she was in Fraser's—at the horrendous price of one pound sterling! This was so far beyond the cost of any other food she had ever bought or dreamed of buying that she was scandalised at the thought of parting with so much of their hard-earned money for such a trivial reason. Nevertheless, she didn't see how she could lose face to the extent of refusing to buy the grapes, and had to cough up the £1 with as much grace as she could muster. She then spent the long walk back to Bogside trying to work out how to explain her blunder to Jim!

In retrospect, she blamed herself for being seduced by the idea that she could be included in the same economic or social bracket as the wives of the headmaster, doctor, dentist, draper, or minister, and vowed never again to be so taken in. Of all the people I have ever known, Mum was the least likely to be influenced by material or status symbols, and treated any display of pretension or ostentation with disdain, so I feel certain that this was a lesson she really took to heart.

I have a very faint memory of an ice-cream van coming into Pitkinny. It perhaps only happened the once, but I remember clearly the sheer joy of being bought a cone, complete with a dollop of raspberry syrup from the van in our very own close. Because we were quite a long way off the main road, we sadly never had the services of a lemonade lorry, unlike the Steel family at Bogside, who would buy bottles of the fizzy stuff every week. I well remember the unalloyed delight of being the recipient of a tumbler full of limeade or pineapple crush from Mrs Steel, when we were playing with her daughter Joyce at Bogside. At New Year we used to be similarly impressed by the fact that Mrs Steel made raspberry cordial, while we had to make do with the much less frivolous, boringly brown, ginger variety.

Other retail visitors would make less frequent but all the more exciting calls to Pitkinny. Jackson, the tailor from Glasgow, would come with his suitcases full of ladies' and men's clothes, and samples of suit material. Jim rarely bought clothes for himself, but when he did he made sure they were of the best quality, and was a "sucker for a label!" Even in his last years he had the occasional rush of blood to the head, and on one such occasion bought a Crombie overcoat in Jenner's in Edinburgh, which made Joey's costly grapes pale into insignificance by comparison! It did, however, last much longer, and after he died it was worn by his grandson Calum, who cut a dash in it in London. Wouldn't Dad have been proud if he had known!

Another twice-yearly salesman was the "Galashiels man," a Mr Redpath who represented the Borders wool and tweed mills. This was a chance for Joey to purchase her dressmaking materials and knitting wools which would be carefully stored, with mothballs in evidence, in her "kist": a wooden chest which had contained her "bottom drawer" when she first married. It was a treat when we were allowed to look in it; we would examine her store of lengths of cloth, skeins of wool, and still-to-be-used sheets, pillowcases, and table linen. Joey cherished these things as her stock-in-trade as a housewife and homemaker. We would sometimes go with her when she bought things from Wilkie's in Dunnikier Road in Kirkcaldy, a veritable cornucopia of haberdashery and dressmaking essentials. She was so glad that, while far from wealthy, she could manage to acquire the wherewithal to equip and clothe her home and family to a much greater extent than her mother could, or than she could ever have hoped for in her youth.

One of the most exotic travelling salesmen was undoubtedly the "Ingin Johnny" who would appear once a year, pedalling his old "sit up and beg" bicycle, weighed down by innumerable garlands of onions which festooned his person, his handlebars, and the frame of his bike. The turbaned Punjabi peddlers, with their heavy suitcases, would display a variety of multicoloured silks and satins. I don't remember Joey buying any of these flimsy and impractical materials from them very often, unlike the tinkers hawking their clothes pegs and offering to tell your fortune for some payment. Joey was always in the market for their pegs, but was far too rational to want to find out about her future. According to Auntie Nellie, you should never turn a tinkie away from your door without buying from them, in case they called down a curse on you!

The Betterware traveller would come occasionally, and he used to give me a little sample tin of polish, with which Mum would help me to polish my doll's pram. It was a lovely shiny brown colour, and I can remember Mum telling me to rub it hard so I could see my face in it. I think I believed that the little tin contained that elusive commodity that everyone talked about all the time: elbow grease! That pram was eventually given to some of our younger cousins after I outgrew it, and I remember the disappointment when I saw it lying in their garden minus its wheels. After all the care we had taken of it! As the oldest of the cousins in the family we were often prevailed upon to pass on our toys—not that we had that many—to the younger ones, but it was seldom done with good grace, especially after that! It was an experience that our younger son Donald was to repeat many years later. He had a little tricycle with the face of a lamb on it called, unsurprisingly, "little lamb," which he had grown too big for. We persuaded him to give it to the little boy across the street. He did so reluctantly, and I was surprised to find it back in our garden shed a few weeks later. When I asked him where it had come from, he declared, "Well, wee David left it out in the rain twice and so I took it back because he wasn't looking after it!" I understood how he felt and didn't insist, perhaps wrongly, that he should return it.

When Jim took to going to football matches, we were able to go shopping on a Saturday afternoon. In those days, he supported Raith Rovers, the Kirkcaldy team, and East Fife at Bayview in Methil, who played their home games on alternate Saturdays. As he enjoyed the matches, we became familiar with the shops in the high streets of Kirkcaldy and Leven. I remember the Kirkcaldy grocers' shops like Cooper's, The Buttercup, and Lipton's. There was a high-class hardware and china shop, Barnet Morton's, which had an agricultural department at the back, and another ironmonger's called Thomson Brothers, where Jim would also get things for the farm. There was a shop called Haxton's, which sold art and craft materials and stationery, always a weakness of mine. I was never happier than when I got a new notebook or colouring pencils and books. Perhaps I was programmed even then to become a teacher, and years later I used to love spending a few moments "having a fix" in the stationery cupboard at my base school, looking at and smelling the unique scent that emanated from the stacks of jotters, boxes of pencils and rubbers, and reams of lovely virgin white and coloured card and paper.

We always paid a visit to Burt's bookshop where Joey paid her subscription to the *National Geographic* magazine. Burt's either housed, or was next door to, May's travel agency, which in those days seemed to be something very esoteric and not a place I could ever imagine us needing to patronise!

Kirkcaldy Co-op was an imposing emporium, the nearest thing to a department store, consisting of various floors housing different departments accessed by a lift with an attendant. Its most impressive feature, to me, was its pneumatic cash system. The assistant would place the sales slip and the customer's payment into a little cylindrical container, open the flap on the end of the tube, which always made a satisfying sucking sound as it swallowed the projectile, and sent it whizzing through what seemed like miles of complicated piping to the cash office, where an unseen hand would remove the slip and money and return the cylinder containing the change and receipt through a different route to the counter, where it would be blown out of the tube with a loud plop into the receiving basket. This system always reminded me of a mouth organ with its alternative sucking and blowing, and the whole operation was the height of technical sophistication. In those days, assistants in such shops had to be very smartly dressed and well spoken, and seemed to me to be goddesses in their retail heaven. The limit of my ambition then was to work in a shoe shop, and many games were played in the empty byre at Bogside, where we showed imaginary customers into the cattle stalls to be served. We would climb up on to the manger, imagining it to be the little ladder the assistants used to use, to reach the invisible stacks of shoes. When our customer settled on a pair of shoes and paid for them, the milking machine pipework bore a tolerable resemblance to the cash transfer system of the Co-op.

Next door to the Co-op was Beveridge's: a draper's selling good quality clothing and household linens. We went there on the odd occasion when something special was called for. I remember Joey buying a green satin evening dress there, which she wore with a hand-knitted lemon fuzzy-wuzzy (angora) bolero on the very rare occasion when she and Jim went to a dance. This was a very exceptional kind of purchase, however, as for the most part her and our clothes were made at home by Joey.

Mum had a cousin, Grace Nicholson née Webster, who served in a sweetie shop near Woolworth's in Kirkcaldy, where we always had a warm welcome if we chose to spend some of our pennies there. It was much nicer than another small confectioner's in Leven, owned and run by two maiden ladies of indeterminate age who obviously hated children and served us very grudgingly and with ill-disguised bad temper. We were always much more at ease when patronising the sweet shops nearer home, and became authorities on their respective stocks and prices, especially after the auspicious day in 1953 when sweets finally came off the ration for the last time. I was seven years old and in primary three when we first became regular consumers of sweets, and in celebration of their new availability, Mum gave each of us threepence to spend on a Friday. The most convenient sweetie shop was Jenny West's, which I remember as a little hut in Balgreggie, a few minutes' walk from the school. We would hurry along there after school dinner and my threepence (the old octagonal "copper" coin) would find its way into Jenny's till in exchange, usually, for a stick of barley sugar. It was very good value, I discovered, as I could suck it for the rest of the lunch hour and keep the remainder in my schoolbag until it was time for home. Then the remnant could be enjoyed throughout the journey home on the school bus and the walk along the loan to Pitkinny.

Mrs Watt's was another wee shop between the school and Woodend. I don't particularly remember buying sweets there, but I must have gone in with Mum. The shop comprised a small front room of the cottage with a tiny little counter. There was an all-pervading smell of paraffin, and I could imagine anything consumable purchased there would taste of the same. I seem to recall an old man—probably Mr Watt—who could be glimpsed sitting in the back shop, no doubt their kitchen. Nearly fifty years later, when Bill and I visited our son Donald, who was teaching

English in Japan, we were surprised to learn that the classrooms in his high school were heated by paraffin. As soon as I entered that building, and was assailed by its smell, I was immediately transported back in time and many thousands of miles to Mrs Watt's shop. Although we must have used paraffin in the steading at Pitkinny, Joey was always distrustful of heaters fuelled by it, after the time her day-old chickens' paraffin incubator went up in flames, and I don't remember its smell being evident in our house.

A little shop even nearer to Pitkinny was Skinner's, also housed in a wee hut. It was the last building as you left Woodend on the way to Pitkinny, at the beginning of "the strip," that part of the road that led up to the corner at Redhouse Farm, later to become the site of the old men's shelter. Margaret remembers an occasion when she was very young, while we lived at Bogside and before I started school, and long before there was a school bus. She was with the older Capeldrae children, looking in the window of Skinner's shop. Bearing in mind that sweets were still in very short supply owing to rationing, they were staring longingly at the few items of confectionery on display. As the children fantasised about what they would choose if only they could, Margaret piped up and said to one of the older boys, "If you smash the window, I'll grab the sweeties!" Old Mr Skinner heard her and chased them away, threatening, "I know your names and I'll set the bobby on you all!" Margaret then spent a few very anxious days waiting for the police to arrive. As it happened, one of Jim's cows had recently been killed by a car at the corner of Bogside Brae, and a policeman came into the close to see Jim about the accident. When my sister saw him she assumed that he had been sent by old Skinner, and was in a state of terror! In Joey's case, her first brush with the law had been on account of an ice slide, and now it was Margaret's turn to develop a healthy respect for the police!

Apart from our trips to Kirkcaldy and Leven, the local Co-op or store was the mainstay of our shopping. The "top" store at Auchterderran had grocery, bakery, butchery, hardware, and drapery departments, while the "middle" store at Bowhill had a chemist's and a shoe shop. The "bottom" store at Cardenden itself had a grocery and a baker. In addition, Bowhill had two grocers' shops, Hay's and Low's; Wotherspoon's the baker's; and a private chemist, McLellan's; Hope's, which sold fancy goods, toys, tobacco, and cigarettes; which was next to Imrie's, the fruit shop. The more exotic and enticing establishments, as far as we were concerned, were the soda fountain and the Bijou sweet shop, both conveniently close to the Rex picture house. The chip shop was run by a corpulent man of Italian origin called Carati, who predictably was known by everyone as Fattycarati, a label which may have been unkind but had a satisfying alliterative ring to it. Some other retail establishments I remember were the D&E (Dundee Equitable) Shoe Service, one or two newsagents, the post office and the bank, two hairdressers (Nettie Lunan's and Torley's), a couple of barber shops, and drapers Tammie Nicholson and Blair's, later Ina Lunan's at Bowhill and Auchterdrerran respectively. Last but not least was Ginger Spence the bookie's, which bore the more pompous "turf accountant" on its frontage. For years, although I thought it sounded impressive, I had no idea whatsoever of what went on behind the mysterious and windowless face it presented to the world.

In the late forties and fifties, the thriving coal industry meant that the population of the mining areas could support such a large number and variety of businesses. There was prosperity both in material and cultural terms, but the day would come, as the mines in Fife began to close, when the spectre of economic recession hit hard, and many of these businesses went to the wall as an air of gloom and depression settled on the little towns and villages. The reality of this was that miners and their families either had to leave for other coal-producing parts of the country, usually down south, or had to retrain for jobs in other industries. The new alternative sources of employment promised in the new towns like Glenrothes were in the light industries such as electronics, and this did take up some of the slack, but unemployment became the inevitable fate of many. An anecdote related by our friend Alec Robertson is amusing but sadly and ironically telling. His brother was visiting his parents in Cardenden and his wee girls had some pocket money to spend. They had intended going to Hope's shop, but were disappointed when they were pre-empted by their granny, who said, "Oh no, girls, ye cannae dae that, there's nae Hope in Cardenden ony mair!" Out of the mouths of babes and sucklings—and grannies!

In my later years at primary school, Bono's café opened across from the store at Auchterderran, and we could buy one-penny ice lollies. They were no more than frozen coloured water, but how we loved them. When it came to sweets, my perennial favourites would always be aromatics: little brown and pink scented discs. A quarter-pound of these little delights, sweet and yet peppery too, sold in a wee white poke, represented sheer heaven to me. Along with many of my generation, my dental health certainly suffered due to the sudden onslaught of sugar it was subjected to after 1953. By comparison to what children consume nowadays, of course, our diet was actually quite healthy, and my sweet consumption was limited to threepence worth on a Friday, and that part of my Saturday sixpence that wasn't spent on stationery. Mum did have a green tin tea caddy which post-1953 she used as a sweetie box, and which she would sometimes open on a Saturday night. A great treat was a Mars bar which was shared, cut into four, for us to enjoy while watching television. Joy unconfined indeed! That sweetie box that was kept in the larder proved too much of a temptation for our cousin, Jim Drennan. One day Joey found him in the larder with some sweets in his hand. When she asked him where they had come from, he, despite looking very red-faced (and -handed!) and extremely guilty, claimed in a deceptively innocent voice, "They just fell into my hand!"

Looking back, I realise that as a generation we became hooked on sweets, but I think that there must always have been a great dependence on sugar in the Scots' diet. Joey remembered that seven bags—fourteen pounds—of sugar was always top of Betsy's fortnightly grocery list. That was seven pounds per week consumed by a family, at that time, before James was born, of two adults and six children. It seems a lot but we have to understand that sugar was the most instantly available (though short-term) source of energy, and that sugar refining was a staple industry in Scotland from the time of the industrial revolution. Raw sugar was imported from the West Indies into the west-coast ports and processed in the greater Glasgow industrial conurbation, so it is hardly surprising that it was an affordable and attractive commodity. Its rationing during the war did nothing to lessen its appeal, and its assured availability after the era of postwar austerity, combined with increasing prosperity, stimulated demand for, and supply of, a seemingly endless variety of confectionery: sweets, chocolates, biscuits, and cakes. The early days of McGowan's coo toffee and Lee's macaroon bars were only the beginning!

I used to feel that we were hard done by in having so little pocket money compared to many of our school pals. This was what probably tempted me into my only foray into stealing! The postie van came to Pitkinny every morning, and in addition to delivering the mail, he also brought our milk supply. His last call before Pitkinny was at Bogside, which of course was our dairy. He would bring up a big churn of milk, which Joey would then pour into a variety of milk jugs. These were covered with bead-edged round nets and kept in the cool larder in pre-electricity days and subsequently in the fridge. She would wash the milk can, which would then be collected by Jock Steel when he drove a trailer full of dung later in the day from the byres at Bogside, to be spread on the arable fields at Pitkinny.

The postie would have a quick cuppa and would uplift any letters for posting, and Joey would give him money for stamps. This was typical of the kind of informal arrangements that people would come to in those days. It was not part of the postman's job description to transport our milk from Bogside, nor to take away and post our letters, but he did it for the same reason that Joey always gave him a cup of tea and had time to listen to his chat. Nowadays such friendly and spontaneous relationships amongst people tend not to happen to the same extent, because we are so taken up with being accountable for everything we do and are reluctant to bend the rules. That is a pity, and the world is a poorer place for the loss of these human contacts.

For the purpose of paying for stamps, Joey would keep some coins in the lower of the two little drawers in the kitchen cabinet, the odd threepenny bit, sixpence, and a few coppers and ha'pennies. That was where temptation lay! I took to helping myself occasionally to a coin or two before school in the morning, when no one was looking. As I got away with it, I became bolder and greedier, and one day—lo and behold!—there was a shilling there in the drawer! That made two sixpences, or four theepennies, or twelve pennies! The temptation of such untold riches was simply too much, and I pocketed the shinily seductive silver shilling. I was amazed to discover that I actually had a problem when it came to spending my ill-gotten gains. Would Jenny West wonder where I had got all that money? Should I spend only part of it and save some for another day? What if Margaret saw me with sweets when it wasn't Friday? I worried all morning, trying to plan my trip to Jenny West's. I have no memory of what or how many sweets I bought, but I clearly remember the awful sick feeling of guilt, as I had to eat the booty before I got back to the school. It was added to, no doubt, by the overindulgence in sugar on top of my school dinner. Of course then I had to dispose of the evidence, in the form of the sweetie papers, before going home that afternoon. I was afraid to drop them in the wastepaper basket in the classroom. (Our teacher, Miss Christie, had eyes in the back of her head—and everywhere else—just like Mum!) So I had to surreptitiously deposit them in one of the dustbins the janitor kept at the top of the boiler-room steps, without anyone seeing me.

All in all I had a thoroughly miserable day, and returned home completely guilt-ridden. When I got into the kitchen, having trailed along the loan from the bus, Mum's first cheery words were, "Well how are you, Anne? Have you had a good day? Did you enjoy your sweets?" I couldn't believe it! As I crumpled into a tearful confession, I was aware of the confirmation of two facts: One: I was not cut out for a life of crime. Two: My mother was an all-seeing, all-knowing, supernaturally omnipotent being. She had carried out her sting operation to perfection. She had set and baited a trap with great skill and subtle timing, in which I was caught hook, line, and sinker. Her warnings of, "Don't smoke, don't tell lies, and don't steal," come back to me. The day would come when I would try the first, and I am not entirely blameless with regard to the second, but I can honestly say, hand on heart, that I have never been guilty of the third since that awful confrontation in the kitchen. In the event, I don't think Mum actually punished me for my fall from grace. I think she knew that the misery of the guilty conscience I had suffered, plus the shame of her disappointment in me, were retribution enough. It was not until I became a mother myself that I understood the uncanny intuition that connects you to your child. The only piece of advice I would ever dare give to any parent is that you should always trust your instincts when it comes to dealing with the myriad of problems associated with bringing up children. I found that I was seldom wrong when I sensed that something was amiss with either the physical or emotional well-being of our boys, but I did study at the feet of a master, or should I say, mistress!

*Street photographer snaps in Kirkcaldy—Joey and Anne*

*Street photographer snaps in Kirkcaldy—Cathy Webster, Margaret, Anne, Grace Webster, and Joey*

*Joey wearing her green satin evening dress and lemon bolero*
*Left to right: Tot Chrisp, Mrs Beckett, Mrs Chrisp, Bob Beckett, and Joey*

# Chapter 16

## "Thank goodness! Yer Dad's singin' again!"

When Joey and Jim began their farming life together at Bogside in November 1941, their entire livestock comprised one cow named Mary, who was in calf. From this modest beginning, they were to build up a dairy herd of Ayrshire cattle—attractive brown and white milking cows—by the end of the first decade of their married life. By 1951, when we moved to Pitkinny, Jim's dairy herd was big enough to justify the employment of a dairyman, Jock Steel, who moved with his family into the house at Bogside.

Grass will not grow when the temperature drops below 8°C, so the cattle have to be kept indoors in the coldest part of the year. The arable acreage at Bogside was devoted to the growing of vegetables for the family and fodder crops such as oats, turnips and hay, which supported the animals during the winter. Initially the cultivation of the ground was done by the two Clydesdale teams, Punch and Jolly, and Danny and Star, who pulled the necessary implements: ploughs, seed drills, harrows, rollers, and mowers. There was an extra or "orra" horse, whose name was Paddy. However, it was to be only a short time until Jim had the first of his many tractors, an early Ferguson. So the working days of the big, patient draught horses were numbered. Jim had no sentimental regrets about the passing of the Clydesdales into farming history. He had never been a horsey man like his brother Wullie, and held no brief for the idea that the animals represented some kind of rural idyll. He had only painful memories of the long, lonely hours spent as a young man thirled to the plough, and was only too eager to transfer his allegiance to his wee grey Fergie, which didn't need to be fed or groomed at the end of his working day, before he himself could eat or rest.

In the early days, Joey and Jim kept two pigs, which they looked forward to selling for cash, but in the main they operated a system of subsistence farming. So the bulk of their production of milk, potatoes, eggs, and oatmeal constituted most of their staple diet, only the surplus being sold. There was also some degree of barter, when Joey exchanged eggs with the local tradesmen as part payment for groceries and other essentials. As the years passed, the expanding proportion of their production that sold for cash was a measure of their increasing prosperity.

The most revolutionary of the changes in farming in the course of the twentieth century was the accelerating pace of mechanisation. When Jim retired at the age of fifty-nine, he was actually employing no more workers than he had at the beginning, when his acreage was less than a third, and his output infinitely smaller, than they would ultimately become. This was, of course, partly a function of the hugely increasing labour costs over the same period, and of the fact that he was working as hard as he ever had, but the impact that machines had made on the life and work of the farming community cannot be overstated.

With the acquisition of Pitkinny and its 300-odd acres, Jim launched into arable farming on a much bigger and more diverse scale than had been the case when he only had Bogside. In addition to the fodder crops he had always grown, he now grew barley and some wheat, as well as oats. As a child at primary school, I always had to fulfil a particular task come harvest time. My teacher would ask me to bring some stalks of oats, barley, and wheat from Pitkinny for our harvest display. I remember having to describe how to distinguish the three different ripe grains. It is now clear that few children have any real idea where food comes from, or of how we depend on the land for sustenance, when their only experience is of shopping in a supermarket. It is certainly true that children of my generation had the benefit of some connection, albeit a tenuous one in the case of those living in the town, to the soil and a more agrarian way of life.

The advent of the combine harvester in the 1960s meant that one man could single-handedly harvest a field of grain, completing an entire sequence of stages in the process that previously required many pairs of hands to accomplish. The sheaves, which had been cut and tied by the binder (in itself a huge innovation from the days of scything and hand-tying) would have to be stooked in groups of six or eight, to completely ripen, before being pitch-forked on to trailers and trundled into the stackyard. There they would be built into stacks to await the arrival of the travelling threshing mill, when the final process would be completed and the grain filled into jute bags, again only possible with the labour of a whole squad of workers.

The mill days were busy ones for all on the farm. The mill men, and other casual workers or neighbours and family who swelled the labour force, all had to be fed in the farm kitchen. Trestle tables and wooden forms would be set up to accommodate everyone, and every available piece of crockery and cutlery pressed into service. On one such day when Auntie Doris was helping, Joey found her with a "fit of the giggles." When she recovered enough to be able to talk, she indicated that one of the mill workers, a gentle giant of a man, was quietly eating his mince and tatties with my baby knife and fork—each complete with a little teddy bear on the end—almost hidden in his huge hands!

As a young man, Jim had on occasion been sent by his father to help at the mill, to the farms of friends and neighbours. An uncle of his had married into the Arnott family, who owned a threshing mill, and they would sometimes need extra help. Some farms were less popular than others with the mill men. Standards of food and hygiene in farm kitchens were at best variable and at worst a danger to health. One of the least salubrious was Myre End at Cairneyhill, and none of the men looked forward to their dinner there. The worst experience by far that Jim heard of, was when the old wife was heard to exclaim, as she pulled a roasting tin of beef from the range oven, "Oh! Is that whaur ye've been a' mornin', Pussy!" There lay a cat, which had probably crawled into the warming oven for a heat, and had been shut in with the joint and "done to a turn" alongside the beef. The old wife calmly proceeded to serve up the beef to the men, who no doubt had without exception lost what little appetite they had had, meanwhile remaining completely oblivious to the effect the perfectly roasted feline was having on her guests!

Towards the end of a mill day, as the stacks were being lowered and the last of the sheaves were fed into the mill, the vermin that had made it their habitat all gravitated to the bottom of the stack. As the final sheaves were lifted, the farm cats and dogs had a field day as they feasted on the resulting cascade of mice and rats. An abiding memory of Jim's was when, on such an afternoon, he lifted and put on his earlier discarded jacket, only to feel a rat run over his shoulders and down his back. It goes without saying that the jacket was removed more quickly the second time!

I can remember once watching Dad broadcasting seed by hand. He had a wide, shallow canvas bag slung around his neck, and I followed him as he walked along the drills, rhythmically scattering handfuls of grass seed to either side. Generally, however, by then all the processes involved in arable farming were increasingly subject to automation. At one time, the hay harvest was very labour intensive and I can recall squads of workers piling the mown hay into rucks in the field, each one secured by two ropes weighed down by stones or bricks. There it would remain until it was "led" into the farm and stored loose in the hay barn. Later, once mown, the hay would be left to dry, lying in rows and being turned mechanically by a hay tedder pulled by a tractor until it was dry enough to bale. Turning the hay was a vital and integral part of farm work in the hopefully dry and sunny weather in late June and July, and Jim would spend many hours on a tractor in the hay fields.

It is tempting to paint a picture of farm life and work in colours of bucolic contentment, but this would be inaccurate and misleading. There is no doubt in my mind that, while Jim and Joey were living the only life that their genetic inheritance and the social and economic conditions of the time had made possible, they were to be more successful in farming and business terms than they would ever have believed when they started off. I also believe that this is almost entirely due to their personal qualities of diligence and self-sacrifice, which made them quite exceptional, when compared to many of their contemporaries from the same background and faced with the same conditions. None of this came easily, of course, and there was a cost involved in terms of personal happiness, greater than many people of my generation would be prepared to pay. Our life at Pitkinny had more than its share of worry and hard times. The bottom line in farming must always be that you and your efforts are invariably at the mercy of conditions that are ultimately beyond your control. The most obvious of these is climatic. "The best-laid plans of mice and men gang aft aglae," and more often than not, that is due to the day-to-day vagaries of the weather.

An indication of how vital the weather is to farming is the myriad of folk sayings; the result, no doubt, of many generations of observation relating to the weather which are to be found in the vernacular of rural Scotland. Even now, when the connection to the land has become very tenuous or has ceased to exist at all, many people may well still be familiar with these old adages.

> "If Candlemas be fine an' fair, the hauf o' winter's tae come an' mair,
> If Candlemas be wet an' foul, the hauf o' winter's gaun at Yule."

This signifies that if 2 February is a good day, the remainder of the winter will be long and hard. Jim swore by the accuracy of this prediction. We were fascinated to discover, while our older son Calum was studying in the United States, that there 2 February is Groundhog Day. The saying there is, if there is enough sun for the groundhog to see his shadow when he emerges from hibernation, there will be forty more days of winter. The essence of both sayings is the same. I wonder if the early settlers from Scotland transplanted their Candlemas observations into the context of this new land?

Another favourite of Jim's, also explicable in meteorological terms is:

> "Mist on the hills, guid wither spills,
> Mist in the hullies (hollows), guid wither fullies (follows)."

"A green Yule maks a fat kirkyaird" suggests that hard early frosts are healthier than a too-mild Christmas.

"As the day lengthens, the cauld strengthens," reflects the probability of increasingly low temperatures after the winter solstice.

And, of course, "Cast nae a cloot till May's oot" has its counterpart in many other cultures, although there is some uncertainty whether "May" relates to the month or to the hawthorn blossom.

Farmers are notorious for complaining: The various elements of the climate are seldom in the right quantities at the right time and can make all the difference between success and disaster. As this has the effect of keeping their feet on the ground, they may not develop megalomaniac tendencies because they know that there is a very clear limit to the degree of control they can exercise. One might hope that this would result in the development of a degree of equanimity in accepting what one cannot control, and perhaps some farmers do achieve a fatalistic acceptance of troublesome weather conditions. But I suspect that more often it gives rise to serious depression or, as in Jim's case, a great deal of bad temper and the more than occasional outburst accompanied by exceedingly colourful language! Joey had a much more implacable and patient response to problematic weather, and could tolerate gracefully what couldn't be changed. What she did find increasingly difficult to put up with was Jim's ill temper and would only placate and humour him for so long before making it clear to him that she would not be a target for his frustration and annoyance. We grew used to judging Dad's mood, and learned at young age to avoid aggravating him when things were going badly. I've often heard Mum saying things like, "Thank goodness, yer Dad's singin' again, he must be feelin' better." He would very often sing to himself as he went about his work, or around the house. It was not always possible to discern the actual song, which was often an amalgam of many of his old favourite tunes, mostly with vague "tum ti tums" or "la de las," but it didn't matter. It was a relief to know that the dark mood had passed and he was again approachable.

Another source of trouble was the very machinery of which he was so proud and which was so indispensable to the work of the place. Often it seemed that even when the weather was cooperating, that was the very time mechanical breakdowns would hold up the progress of the work in hand. Jim and the men had become quite good mechanics over the years, but there were times when repairs would be beyond them, and spare parts and mechanical skills would have to be sought from firms like Farm Mechanisation (Farmec) at Ladybank and later at Cupar, or from Bowen's at Markinch. This eventuality involved financial outlay, of course, which only added to Jim's irritation.

If Jim and his workers became adept at fixing machinery, they also had to understand the health of the livestock. There was a limit to how much they could do in treating sick animals or in using preventive measures to keep them healthy, and sometimes he would have to call on the services of the local vets, Watson and Philp, at Milnathort. This also had a cost and would only be resorted to in times of absolute need. I well remember that when the vet came, he required a bucket of hot water, soap, disinfectant, and a towel at the back door. There he would roll up his sleeves and vigorously wash his hands and arms, before and after attending to the beasts. Jim Philp was a huge and, to me, intimidating man with red hair and freckles, and he always put me in mind of a Hereford bull. I much preferred Mr Watson, who was of much slighter build and had a refined and slightly scholarly air about him. Many years later when we watched the television programmes about the vet James Herriot, *All Creatures Great and Small,* I began to realise just what the vets got up to between the two bouts of hand washing that I used to see at the back door!

The need for manual labour persisted for a long time in the harvesting of potatoes. The technology involved in the design and operation of an effective and affordable harvesting machine took longer to perfect. Rather, squads of tattie pickers, mainly women, but including some men, would be organised in the small towns and villages around Fife. They would, in some cases, travel some distance, sometimes up to farms in Angus, Perthshire, and north and east Fife, areas which lacked the density of population to supply the necessary workforce for this kind of seasonal work. Jim's squad was usually one from Cardenden, and some of the women worked at Pitkinny year after year. The work was hard and dirty, and their pay very hard-earned. There had been a time when local schools in rural areas had "tattie holidays," two weeks in October when older school pupils would work at the tattie harvest, but this had begun to die out. As far as Jim was concerned, grown women were much harder-working and more dependable than youngsters. There was always a degree of negotiation involved between the squad leader and the farmer as to the length of the lifters' "bits" and the frequency with which the digger would come round to each "bit." Pitkinny soil was heavy and the lifting much harder work, especially in the wet weather which often accompanied the tattie harvest, than it would be in the farms with lighter, sandier soil in the Vale of Strathmore or the east of Fife.

Another feature of Pitkinny ground that caused much heartache for Jim and his helpers was its stoniness. Jim had a theory that the stones spent the winter breeding under the ground, and every year the ploughing would bring more to the surface! They could wreak havoc with machinery, and there was no alternative to the laborious work of lifting them by hand. As a teenager I would sometimes help, especially during the Easter holidays. It was a thankless and tedious business. A tractor and trailer drove very slowly over the field as you picked up stones "bigger than a man's fist," according to Jim's instructions. Sometimes, of course, there were really big stones, which would be lifted by rolling them on to a jute sack, then hoisted onto the trailer by two or three people. The real monsters of the stone world would have to be broken up by picks and sledgehammers before they could be lifted. The workers in the field, maybe three or four of us, would take turns sitting on and steering the tractor—a blissful relief which never seemed to come round fast enough, and then passed in a flash! I seem to remember the princely sum of three shillings and sixpence per hour (17½ pence in today's money) was the going rate of pay for me one year.

After the tatties were harvested and taken into the farm, they had to be "dressed" before they could be sold. This involved the dresser or grading machine, which shook the vegetables through a series of riddles, so that the smallest fell through. They were only supposed to be used for fodder, but can now be bought in the supermarket as "baby boilers." Meanwhile, workers standing on either side of the dresser had to pick out any damaged or diseased specimens, which would be thrown into the heap of "brock." In theory only the best potatoes, which would be sold as "ware," should make it all the way along, where they would be filled into the jute sacks which were fixed on hooks at the end of the dresser. Jim would "supervise," which meant that he would occasionally turn up and do a spot check. Pity help you if he found any substandard tatties in a sack or, even worse, any good ones in the brock! Sometimes the skin of a potato would look rough or discoloured, but underneath it might be perfect. You were supposed to scrape it with your nail to inspect it properly if you were in doubt, but if you did that too often, you would end up with very painful fingertips. This was a job that had to be done in the late autumn and winter, often when the weather prevented outside work. Although we worked in the big shed or the tattie shed and had the comfort of industrial heaters (similar to those sold now as patio heaters for barbecue parties), it could still be a cold and miserable business. You had to be warmly clad, and fingerless gloves were the order of the day.

Despite the physical discomfort and the pressure of working quickly to get a load ready in time for the arrival of a buyer's lorry, there was a camaraderie about the experience and it was still infinitely preferable to working outside on a cold, wet day. Once I was helping during my university holidays, and Dougie Imrie said to me at one point in the day, "You'll be wishing you were back at Dundee, Anne. Studying at the university must be better than this!" I tried to explain that there were times, perhaps when I was about to sit an exam or give a talk to a tutorial group, when the idea of dressing tatties at Pitkinny seemed a very attractive alternative. He looked extremely doubtful, as if he was having difficulty believing me, but it was true. Life at the farm seemed so simple and uncomplicated when I viewed it from afar, and although farm work was never easy and certainly not comfortable, I felt that its demands might be preferable to the academic and social pressures that beset me as a student.

I was always conscious of the fact that the two dimensions of my life were very, very different. I relished the intellectual challenges that I was faced with as an undergraduate and realised that I was lucky to be having the kind of education that had been denied to earlier generations of my family. This was true of many of my contemporaries who were, like me, the first in their family to go to university. But somehow it seemed even more pronounced in my case, given the fact that I already felt that my home experience was very different from that of most of my friends at school. This relates back to the yearning I had had in my childhood to escape from my country upbringing, and I suppose I felt a sense of guilt that I was in some way ashamed of my roots. The fact was that the older I grew, the more aware I was of the advantages they conferred on me, and the prouder I became of my family. The life of my parents and the people they worked with was so much more real and meaningful, and counted for much more in the greater scheme of things, than the shallow and seemingly trivial concerns of the lifestyle I had at university. My literary heroine has always been Chris Guthrie in "*Sunset Song*", and I am aware that in her, I saw a reflection of my own experience when she says:

> You saw their faces in firelight, father's and mother's, and the neighbours; before the lamps lit up, tired and kind, faces dear and close to you, you wanted the words they'd known and used, forgotten in the far-off youngness of their lives, Scots words to tell to your heart, how they wrung and held it, the toil of their days and unendingly their fight. And the next minute that passed from you, you were English, back to the English words so sharp and clean and true for a while, for a while, till they slid so smooth from your throat you knew they could never say anything that was worth the saying at all.

So those days, not many in number, remain dear to me in memory because I appreciate the worth of the people I was with. The funny incidents and amusing stories, and even more, the memories they cherish of their time spent working at Pitkinny, which they have shared with me since, are a testament to the fact that they look back on those days with affection and good humour. No matter how often they felt the sharp edge of Jim's tongue, or the fatigue of their days of unrelenting hard work and discomfort, or the many times they may have felt undervalued and taken for granted, on balance they have warm and gratifying recollections of their working life with Jim and Joey.

As paper sacks—which would be stitched closed mechanically—were only just coming into use, the final task in the harvesting and marketing of potatoes was the sewing up of the jute tattie bags. Dad once asked me to help him with this job, and my heart sank as he showed me the size of the task he was setting me. The enormous tattie shed was full of open, filled bags all waiting to be sewn shut in time for the arrival of a lorry to uplift them for sale in a few days. The job involved the use of binder twine and a long, lethal-looking curved "seck needle." Dad demonstrated the technique: having rolled up the top of the bag, you made three big stitches with two loops at either end forming "twa lugs" which would be grasped for moving and lifting the heavy bag. I thought I could just about manage to master the technique, but I dreaded the monotony of the job, all alone in this huge shed, perched on top of the sacks, inching my way along the rows. How would I survive the sheer tedium? Thankfully the transistor radio—a recent lightweight, portable version of the wireless—came to my rescue as did, unexpectedly, some advice Mum had once given me.

She said that whatever you have to do, no matter how mindless and boring it might seem, one way to make it bearable is to try to do the job as perfectly as you possibly can. She found this approach had helped her when she worked in the paper mill all those years ago, so I thought I might as well put it to the test. To my surprise, it really worked! By the end of that week I was certain there never had been such beautifully-sewn tattie bags. They stood there in perfectly symmetrical rows, like soldiers at attention, their lugs suitably cocked and alert as if they were waiting for orders: all of the same size, at identical angles to the body of the sack, all stitches uniform and, where possible, invisible to the naked eye! I half expected that they would jump up on the lorry all by themselves, given the right command! When Jim surveyed my completed task, and I asked him for his opinion on the quality of the work, he gave his usual ultimate compliment, "Aye, that's no' bad at a'." I had to be content with that, but secretly felt very proud of my efforts, and who knows? Maybe there was a lorry driver somewhere, who long remembered the meticulously sewn tattie bags that he once loaded onto a lorry at Pitkinny Farm!

## The Last o' the Clydesdales

Come a' ye young ploughboys that list tae my tale,
As ye sit roun the tables a' drinkin yer ale;
I'll tak ye a' back tae a far distant day,
When I drove the last Clydesdales tae work on Denbrae.

They were twa bonnie blacks wi' white faces and feet.
In the hale o' the roond they had never been beat,
An ye'd lookit gey far twixt the Forth and the Tay,
For tae match thae twa Clydesdales, the pride o' Denbrae.

They were matchless in power in the cairt or the ploo,
An' ma voice an' ma haund on the reins they well knew,
There was only ae thocht in their minds, tae obey,
My twa gallant Clydesdales, the pride o' Denbrae.

But the time it wears on, and the winters grow cauld,
An' horses, like men, can dae nocht but grow auld,
But I mind o' them still, as it were yesterday,
For I drove the last Clydesdales tae work on Denbrae.

A song composed in the 1950s by Archie Webster of Strathkinnes in praise of the last pair of Clydesdales he drove on the farm of Denbrae between Strathkinnes and St Andrews in Fife. (Source: East of Scotland Traditional Song Group 2003)

Potatoes 1962 Crop

David Kinnaird

| Date | Quanitity | Variety | Rate | £ | S. | D. |
|---|---|---|---|---|---|---|
| Dec 6th | 8 Tons 17 Cwts | RS Seed. | £20 | 177 | | |
| " " | 1 " 12 " | RS ware | £15 | 24 | | |
| 7th | 3 " 1 " | RS Seed | £20 | 61 | | |
| 11 | 7 " 12 " | RS Seed. | £20 | 152 | | |
| 12 | 5 - 12 " | RS Seed. | £20 | 112 | | |
| 12 | 2 - 10 " | RS ware. | £15 | 37 | 10 | |
| | | | | £563 | 10 | |

Paid 19th Jan 1963

*Potato crop, 1962*
*Part of the potato crop sale to David Kinnaird, late 1962 (in Jim's writing)*

Potatoes 1964. Wages 2nd Week

Started. Sept 28th

| NAMES. | MON 28th | TUE. 29th | WED 30th | THU. 1st | FRI. 2nd | | Sat 3rd Oct Forrester. | |
|---|---|---|---|---|---|---|---|---|
| Mrs Wilson | 1 | 1 | 1 | 1 | 1 | £7-10 | ½ day | 15/- |
| Mrs Cowser | 1 | 1 | 1 | 1 | 1 | £7-10 | ½ | 15/- |
| Mrs Renny | 1 | 1 | 1 | 1 | 1 | £7-10 | ½ | 15/- |
| Mrs Clark | 1 | 1 | 1 | 1 | 1 | £7-10 | ½ | 15/- |
| Mrs Fotheringham | 1 | [illegible] | 1 | 1 | 1 | £6. | ½ | 15/- |
| Mrs McCormack | 1 | 1 | 1 | 1 | 1 | £7-10 | ½ | 15/- |
| Mrs Tinney | 1 | 1 | 1 | 1 | 1 | £7-10 | ½ | 15/- |
| Mrs Young | 1 | 1 | 1 | 1 | 1 | £7-10 | ½ | 15/- |
| Mrs Dowie | 1 | 1 | 1 | 1 | 1 | £7-10 | ½ | 15/- |
| Mrs Clover | 1 | 1 | 1 | 1 | 1 | £7-10 | ½ | 15/- |
| Mrs Bell | 1 | 1 | 1 | 1 | 1 | £7-10 | ½ | 15/- |
| Mrs Stewart | 1 | 1 | 1 | 1 | 1 | £7-10 | ½ | 15/- |
| Mrs Howie | 1 | 1 | 1 | 1 | 1 | £7-10 | ½ | 15/- |
| Mrs Halleron | 1 | 1 | 1 | 1 | 1 | £7-10 | ½ | 15/- |
| Mrs Cowan | 1 | 1 | — | — | — | £3- | — | |
| Mrs Shaw | 1 | 1 | 1 | 1 | 1 | £7-10 | ½ | 15/- |
| Mrs Lightbody | 1 | 1 | 1 | 1 | 1 | £7-10 | ½ | 15/- |
| Mrs Rutherford | 1 | 1 | 1 | 1 | 1 | £7-10 | ½ | 15/- |
| Mrs Moffat | — | 1 | 1 | 1 | 1 | £6- | ½ | 15/- |
| Mrs McPherson | 1 | — | — | — | — | £1-10 | — | |
| F. Dickson | | | | 1 | 1 | £3 | ½ | 15/- |
| Mr Dickson | | | | 1 | 1 | £4 | ½ | £1 |
| | | | | £30-0 | £30-10 | £43"10 | | £15-5 |

Total for week beginning 28th - £103 - 10/-.

£61 for John Forrester

*Potato harvest wages 1964*
*List of wages to potato lifting squad, Sept–Oct 1964 (in Anne and Jim's writing)*

*Threshing mill; Jim's grandfather, William Rutherford, in the centre*

# Chapter 17

## "Mum! The string's broken!"

In the mid-fifties, as Joey passed her fortieth birthday, she was unaware that her life was about to change radically. We are told that life begins at forty and, although she was never consciously discontented, perhaps she had begun to feel subconsciously that she needed to assert herself more with Jim. Looking back, it would seem that he had the best of the bargain in their marriage. Joey was a wonderful wife and mother. She had become highly accomplished in all the skills demanded of a farmer's wife, despite not being born to the life. She had the grudging respect of Nellie, but knew that she would never be fully accepted by the rest of Jim's family. Jim was making a great success of his business with the indispensable assistance of his wife. He was his own boss, he answered to no one, and he had all the freedom that he had longed for as a young man. It seems only fair that Joey should also have been benefiting from their increasing prosperity, but it just wasn't in her nature to crave any kind of material recognition from Jim of her loyalty and hard work. She would have settled for seeing him take more interest in his family and spending more time at home. He was spending more and more of what little free time he had away from the house and Joey was understandably becoming increasingly worried about the direction he was taking and the risks he was running in terms of their business and their relationship. Whether she knew it or not, she was looking for something for herself, a new direction within the bounds of a life that she was, by nature, contented with. She was soon to find it.

Meanwhile Margaret and I, thirteen and nine years old respectively, wanted to make a special effort for Mum's fortieth birthday. We bought the ingredients on the quiet, and Margaret, who even then had learned to bake, made a cake in secret at Auntie Doris's house. Between us we managed to ice it and wanted to decorate it with candles. We had saved up our pocket money for a few weeks but when we went to a little stationer's shop in Kirkcaldy High Street to buy the candles and holders, we didn't have quite enough money for all forty. When the lady in the shop asked us what we wanted them for, and we told her it was for our Mum's birthday, she kindly let us have the rest for nothing. The relief was great and the cake duly finished. I think Dad gave us some money and we were able to buy Mum a pair of nylons as well. The day of her birthday was a school morning and we were up early to get everything ready. We somehow managed to light all forty candles and carry the blazing cake downstairs, at great danger to life and limb, but the look on Mum's face made the risk worthwhile!

Sometimes Jim was unable to go to the football due to pressure of work on the farm, and Mum, Margaret, and I would make our way to Kirkcaldy by bus. We would either walk down to the bus stop at Auchterderran or maybe get a lift from Dad, and we always got off the bus at the "cheenie shop" at the south end of the high street in the "lang toun." From there we would then work our way along the street, visiting all our usual haunts, until we finished off at "Woolies" and Grace's sweetie shop. One such day remains in my memory as "the day of the wellies." Dad needed new wellies and Mum bought them just before we made our way down to the bus station on the prom. As Joey was already laden with shopping, the size eleven boots were given to Margaret to carry, and although she was none too happy with the heavy, cumbersome load, she knew better than complain. When we got off the bus at the Auld Hoose in Auchterderran, she soon found the easiest way to carry them was to loop the string that joined them together around her neck. There was no sign of Jim, who had promised to pick us up, and although darkness was swiftly approaching, we had no option but to start walking. It was a wintry cold afternoon and although the main roads were clear, our loan was covered with the hard-packed snow that had fallen a few days earlier.

As Margaret struggled valiantly with her boot burden and I, never keen on walking at the best of times, trailed along behind her, Mum got further and further ahead of us. She was understandably furious at Dad for not keeping his promise to meet us. I remember calling, "Don't leave us Mum. It's nearly dark!" but her anger had the effect of making Joey walk ever faster. A few moments later, it was Margaret's turn to wail to a fast-disappearing Joey, "Mum, the string's broken!" as the two wellies went skittering across the frozen ground! Now it was even harder to carry the boots, and I was less than cooperative in helping to carry one of them for her. When Joey reached home and burst through the back door, it was to find Jim with Jock Allen in the kitchen, drinking tea and toasting their toes by the fire! When she remonstrated with Jim about the long, cold walk home, his lame excuse for not coming for us was that he had simply forgotten. That was the penultimate straw for Joey. In dumping her heavy bags on the floor, she bumped into the food safe that (in pre-electricity days) stood by the back door, and a jug of milk which had been on top of it went flying onto the floor. That was really the last straw, the less–than-perfect end to a less-than-perfect day for her. When she had cleaned up the mess, calmed down, and we were having tea, Jock declared that the jug had in fact jumped off the meat safe in fright at Joey's temper! To her credit, Mum was, as usual, able to laugh about a situation which only a short time before had caused her great annoyance. Her relationship with Jim was often volatile, and they would engage in shouting matches when Jim's sometimes selfish behaviour would drive her to distraction, and Joey would give as good as she got, and often better, in these exchanges.

There was a time when there were very casual laws relating to drink driving, and there must have been many times when Jim drove while "under the influence." One particular example was when we attended the Highland Show when it was held in Kelso. We were very young, but I can remember the journey home quite clearly. Margaret and Mum and I spent the day visiting the usual attractions at the show; features that we saw every year, like the flower show and the SWRI handicraft exhibition, while Dad went his own way. He always met many of his old friends and business contacts, and on this occasion he met up with our local blacksmith, Dave Duncan, who had been successful in one of the horseshoeing competitions. Jim had been only too happy to help him to celebrate his success, no doubt in "The Herdsman's Rest" tent or some other bar in the showground. By the time we met them they were three sheets to the wind and Jim had already offered Dave a run home to the smiddy at Woodend. Margaret and I had to share the back seat of the car with a very inebriated blacksmith. He was normally a very nice, kindly man who would often, in years to come, blow up the tyres of our bikes when we cycled to school and would call in at the smiddy on the way home, to watch him shoeing the horses. I can recall the warmth and the unique combined smell of horse and hot metal, and the glow of his fire as he pumped the bellows.

That evening, however, we were not so keen on him, but fortunately he soon fell asleep. The journey home was not a happy one. Joey had to do her best to navigate our way from Kelso, as Jim was of little help, and we got completely lost at one point. It was as much as Dad could do to steer the car and although it was June, dark was fast approaching before we got anywhere near Edinburgh. Then, as we came to some streetlights, Jim declared that he knew for sure that it was the west end of Edinburgh, but we were almost immediately out in the dark again as the small town of Dalkeith receded in the gloom behind us. Eventually we came to South Queensferry, in the pouring rain, only to discover, not surprisingly, that the last ferry had gone. As we sat in the car outside the Hawes Inn staring at the dark and deserted slipway, Mum could see a man watering the hanging baskets under the entrance door to the hotel. Dad suggested that she should "tell that stupit bugger that it's p****** doon wi' rain!" before he turned the car and we made our very slow and unsteady way to the Kincardine Bridge, a much longer route home. Dave Duncan snored on, blissfully unaware of the slow and tortuous journey we endured, until we deposited him, very bleary-eyed but grateful, outside the smiddy.

These were examples of the times in the first fifteen years of their marriage when Joey was made only too painfully aware of her dependence on Jim and of the lack of control she had over their life together. In general terms, hers was a generation of women who were expected to accept that, while marriage conferred financial security on women, they should be prepared, in return, always to defer to their husbands in matters of decision-making. Men, as a rule, had much more freedom of action than women, whose place was very definitely in the home. While "pregnant, barefoot, and in the kitchen" perhaps overstates the situation, in most families men most certainly wore the trousers! Joey accepted this scenario as the norm. She never complained about being financially dependent, or about having no access to or control over their assets. It was only in the early 1960s that Margaret persuaded Mum to insist on a weekly housekeeping allowance so that she could have more control over the financial management of the household.

What rankled more with Joey was the way she was dependent on Jim for transport. She loved living at Pitkinny but it completely curtailed her freedom of movement. Very few women could drive in those days. Indeed, only a very few families had a car, and where they did, driving was seen almost entirely as a male prerogative. Many years before at Bogside during the war, Joey had tried to learn to drive, and very briefly held a provisional licence. One of her few attempts behind the wheel in the stackyard had ended up with her colliding with a haystack, and she gave up almost before she had started to learn. However, in 1956, she made up her mind seriously to pass her driving test so that she would no longer have to wait for Jim to drive her or collect us from the bus stop, which she always wanted him to do on dark evenings. She applied for a provisional licence, to which Jim made no objection, but he showed no inclination to teach her to drive after the abortive attempt years before. So she asked her young brother James to teach her, but that didn't go too well either. James was a very good driver, but simply did not know how to explain to her something that he did instinctively, and he suggested that it would be better to have some lessons from an instructor.

After only one or two lessons, Joey discovered something that was to make all the difference to her attempt to pass her driving test. I can't explain it exactly, but for some reason, she was allowed to drive as a learner without the necessity of having a co-driver with her. The world had recently been plunged into the Suez Crisis and there was a threat of petrol rationing. Driving tests were suspended, and the fact that she had previously held a provisional licence, owing to some legal loophole, allowed her to drive unaccompanied. I don't think this applied to all learner drivers at that time, but whatever the reason, Joey suddenly found herself with the freedom of the Queen's highway, and she didn't waste any time in making the most of it. She decided that there is no better teacher than experience, and that the best way to learn was by doing! An example of serendipity if ever there was one! Jim had bought a Standard 8 pickup truck and it was the ideal vehicle for Joey, with the added advantage that she needn't go near Jim's prized possession, his Rover 75. Jim soon came to appreciate the benefits of having another driver around the farm, and one who was only too eager to be at his disposal for all kinds of errands. The tradeoff was that, in those early days behind the wheel, she did give him some anxious moments.

Joey's life was completely transformed. She was heady with the sheer excitement of a sense of freedom she had never had in her life before. She loved the physical experience of driving, and soon became very good at it. She was never nervous in the slightest, and was soon driving all over the place. She took Margaret in the pickup to Kirkcaldy, and from there to Markinch, and as they drove up St Clair Street she muttered, "I hope the traffic lichts are at green, because if we hae tae stop I'm no sure hoo tae start again on the hill!" A week or two later she went to Edinburgh with Auntie Greta. This meant driving on and off the ferry at Queensferry. Having completed their shopping, they decided to go on to visit an old school friend, Barbara More, who lived in Penicuik, returning on the ferry in the dark. Meanwhile, Jim and Uncle Bobby for once were sitting at home at Pitkinny, wondering where their wives had got to. It made a dramatic change from their wives waiting for them to come home from the pub in the early hours! Poetic justice, perhaps?

It has to be said that in those days traffic was very light and driving a much less testing business than today. There were only four sets of traffic lights in Fife: two in Kirkcaldy (in St Clair Street and Dunnikier Road), one in Dunfermline, and one at Windygates. Roundabouts were virtually unknown, and there was always plenty of room and time to make up your mind about necessary manoeuvres. Joey was not in any hurry to pass her test as she was already driving independently, but at last she got her full driving licence at the first attempt and she never looked back. Jim had always been a very fast but safe driver when sober, although very slow and probably very unsafe when drunk, but even he had to admit that Joey became a very competent driver indeed. She became his "gofor," and at busy times was a great help as she beetled around the countryside, fetching spare parts for machinery or picking up workers or delivering eggs. This suited her down to the ground and she loved being independent of Jim. As Margaret and I went on to nursing and high school, Mum was always able to pick us up or take us to the bus, so we also benefited from her new mobility.

Joey's newly-acquired autonomy acted as a catalyst, and she began to assert herself more and more in other areas of her life. She became much more confident in her dealings with other people and in particular in her relationship with Jim. She became ever more intolerant of his drinking, and refused to accept his increasing tendency to come home from markets or curling matches the worse for drink, and often not until the early hours. She worried, of course, that he might have an accident with the car, especially that he might end up being the cause of injury to other people.

Although she appreciated having a degree more financial independence once she had her weekly allowance, she often had to fight tooth and nail for it. For the first half of her life, she had been content to always yield to the men in her life, first as a daughter and then as a wife. But from the time she learned to drive, she refused to defer without question to the demands and dictates of her husband. Rather, she began to question his decisions and stood up for herself when she felt he was being unreasonable, and there were many such times at Pitkinny when life was tempestuous, and I would wonder why she didn't give in for the sake of peace. I came to realise that she was right and to admire her for the principled stand she took in her relationship with Dad, even if it often made life uncomfortable and even unhappy for me, especially after Margaret had left home and I felt unequal to coping with my warring parents alone.

When she was eighty years old and looking back on her life, I was aware that Mum herself could see that her life was one of two halves. She once said to me that, in retrospect, she was happier in the first half. "Asserting yourself doesn't make for happiness, Anne," she said one day. She also recognised that it had been hard on me, but in all conscience, she wouldn't have changed anything, if she had her life to live again. She knew she owed it to herself, and perhaps to women of earlier generations who had spent their lives at the beck and call of their menfolk, being denied control over even the smallest decisions, never mind the important ones, which would nevertheless have enormous bearing on their own lives. She wanted Margaret and me to have the ability to look after ourselves, with the possibility of some economic independence. Like many women of her generation, she helped to pave the way for opportunities in education and work. More important than that even, she wanted women to have more self-esteem in the domestic context. She still believed that there is nothing finer than being a wife and mother, and that the bringing up of children is a privilege. She never had the opportunity of, or felt the need for, a career outside the home, but was happy to devote herself to her home and family and to the business she built up with Jim. What she wanted for women was for them to have their efforts in the domestic context more recognised and valued, and for them to have the choice of a career if that was what they wanted.

Joey embodied the best traditions of thrift and skill in her homemaking and child care, and I value my childhood for the great example she set as a housewife and mother. I always tried to emulate her in the way I ran my home and looked after my husband and sons. Even now I am acutely aware of her influence as I go about my domestic routine. When I whisk an egg I always give it one hundred beats, as she did. When I wring out a dishcloth, I do it exactly as she taught me all those years ago. Every Christmas, I look at the stripped turkey carcass and am tempted to throw it out, but I just can't bring myself to contemplate such waste. So the bones are boiled up, the stock strained, and the vegetables prepared just as she did. As we enjoy our turkey broth on New Year's Day with our homemade steak pie and trifle, I can imagine Mum, smiling and content that all is well. As retired women, my sister and I have carried on her high standards in our domestic regime, but have also had the satisfaction of having had careers and contributed to the world in a wider context. For both of these achievements we have our mother to thank.

*Anne and Margaret at 64 Croft Crescent, Markinch*

*Joey, Margaret, and Anne at Pitkinny front door*

*Joey and James in the MG Magnette*

# Chapter 18

"Come on Ferdinand, ye stupit bugger."

Habits of good husbandry in arable farming and attention to the welfare of livestock are deeply ingrained principles in the psyche of good farmers. Of course, for Joey and Jim, their stock represented much of the value of their enterprise, but it was more than a matter of financial investment. It was bound up in a sense of the stewardship of both their land and their beasts. They had a deeply held belief, whether they were aware of it or not, that they had to leave their holding in a better state than when they found it—not just for the sake of their bank balance, but for the sake of something much more lasting and fundamental.

I believe in the concept of folk memory. In other words, I think it is possible that we inherit more than our physical and intellectual characteristics through our DNA. There may also be a legacy of cultural and emotional responses to our environment, which allows us to understand and even replicate those of our ancestors, even if our situation and lifestyle, for geographical and historical reasons, are very different from theirs. Neither my sister nor I made farming our lives, nor did we marry into the farming community, but we both certainly understood and respected the commitment our parents had to the land. We both feel a responsibility to improve and develop our physical surroundings, to maximise our potential, and to use the gifts we were born with, both in the jobs we chose to do and in our homes. In turn I am sure we inculcated the same desire and abilities in our children. We married men who had a very similar belief system and sense of values. We may none of us have worked on the land, but we have been aware of an imperative to add to the value of the area of society that we worked in: health, education, and other fields of public service. We not only learned the importance of hard work and self-respect from our parents, but I believe that we also inherited these qualities via the folk memory of untold, preceding generations.

Jim and Joey had an instinctive understanding of what their land and their livestock needed. They felt genuine outrage when they saw the Bluebell Farms of this world: places where the animals, land, and steadings were neglected and abused. This was certainly not just a sentimental response to animal welfare. It involved a genuine respect for living creatures and the place they occupied in the scheme of things as they saw it. Seen from a modern animal rights standpoint, this might be interpreted as a kind of hypocrisy, given that the ultimate destination of most farm animals is the abattoir and the butcher's shop. However, the raison d'etre of farming is the production of food for society, and Jim and Joey could take justifiable pride in the great reputation they acquired, not only for rearing the very best-quality livestock, but for doing so without compromising the highest standards of animal welfare. Pitkinny lambs may have had necessarily short lives, but when they arrived at market, they were well known to have had the very best of feeding and conditions.

Of course this was reflected in the prices they could command, which did no harm to the farm's income, but the outgoings in terms of feeding and effort were correspondingly higher. So it was clear to everyone that Jim and Joey's motivation was not only that of financial reward, and their good names were assured on that score. Jim foresaw the scourge of BSE when he witnessed the feeding of animal protein to cattle, sometimes in the form of processed sheep carcasses contaminated by the sheep disease scrapie. Cattle are naturally herbivores, and as a practitioner of sound stock-rearing principles, he shunned and abhorred this unnatural practice. I was so glad that his cattle-rearing days were over before the full gravity of the effects of this malpractice became fully appreciated, as it came to affect the reputation of all beef producers, even those who were not involved with a system so completely contrary to all the principles of good animal husbandry.

It was, of course, always satisfactory when measures taken to enhance the health of the livestock had the effect of adding to the value of the animals and of their produce. Joey and Jim's Ayrshires were one of the first TT dairy herds in Fife. Cows and their milk were notorious as carriers of tuberculosis, and as part of a public health drive to control the scourge of consumption, it became possible, on a regular basis, to test cattle for the TB bacillus. Once tested and found to be free of this infection, the herd and its milk, as acceptable to the recently formed Scottish Milk Marketing Board, became worth more. So the entire process, while enhancing the health of the cattle, made a valuable contribution to that of the nation as a whole.

Despite this wholehearted commitment to animal welfare, as a child I used to feel that there was less and less room for sentiment when it came to the rearing and treatment of the beasts. I remember in particular one incident that I found extremely harrowing. I had returned from school one cold, wet, miserable afternoon, and as Mum was working outside somewhere, I had to relay a telephone message to Dad. I could hear voices from one of the reids and went looking for him. There he was, with Jock Steel and Jim Philp, the vet. They were dehorning cattle. Horns on cows are dangerous, both for the animals and for the people working with them. Nowadays, they are destroyed electronically and painlessly while calves are very young, but in those days, before this was routinely done, horns on adult cows were simply sawn off! I don't know what attempt was made at analgesia, but the sight of those poor beasts undergoing such a tortuous and bloody procedure presented a horrifying and disturbing picture. I instantly recoiled from the image of the vet wearing a long rubber apron and big gum boots and wielding a huge bloody saw, and was barely able to give Dad the message before rushing out of the reid and back into the house. I found it very difficult to put the shock of that grisly scenario out of my mind, especially when I saw, in the gathering darkness, the newly de-horned cattle in the paddock near the house, stumbling around, shaking their poor bloodied heads from side to side, lowing mournfully and clearly in great pain.

As we had tea that evening, I remonstrated with Dad about the necessity for what seemed a barbaric and cruel business. While I had to accept his explanation that, on balance, this saved the cattle from possibly worse injury and made the handling of the beasts much safer for him and his helpers, the memory of this traumatic experience did nothing to endear Jim Philp to me, and he remained a figure of dread in my mind. Similarly painful procedures were the routine castration of the little male lambs and pigs, while the wee bull calves were summarily dispatched to the market as of no value for a dairy herd. Even worse, to me at least, although the small creatures might not have made that distinction, was when the wee lambs had their tails cut off. I was horrified to see a row of amputated tails lined up on the field wall beside the sheep buchts. These operations were no doubt necessary and justifiable in terms of the future growth and well-being of the beasts and of their future economic value, but I found them extremely distasteful and disturbing. As I grew older, I came to appreciate that the farm was our livelihood and that sentimental attachment to the animals was a luxury that Joey and Jim could not afford.

In the early years at Bogside, Joey and Jim became involved in exhibiting their livestock at the local agricultural shows. Dad had a cousin on his mother's side, Teen Shepherd, who lived at Capeldrae with her husband, Jim. Her brother Aund (Andrew) was a champion at making and exhibiting the elaborate show harness and tackle, and between them they would help Jim to prepare and show Punch and Jolly wearing their handiwork. They won many prizes with their combined efforts, and this encouraged Jim to go on and show some of his Ayrshire heifers and bulls. The rafters of one of the byres at Bogside were festooned with many prize tickets and rosettes from Leslie and Fife shows. As the years passed and Jim became more and more serious about farming as a business, he grudged the time that exhibiting demanded, and he gradually withdrew from the show element of his livestock operation.

Most people involved with livestock learn to be wary of some of the animals that can prove dangerous. This is especially true of bulls, and the Ayrshire breed was known to be particularly unpredictable and deserving of respect. Dad had one or two of this ilk, and both Margaret and I had frightening experiences with them. One Saturday afternoon I was playing with Joyce Steel and one of my cousins, Eunice Mitchell, at Bogside. We were involved in a serious game of hide-and-seek; of course, as there are innumerable nooks and crannies on a farm, we were experts! I had ventured into an empty loose box, one of two in the barn across from the back door of the house. I decided to coorie in among some hay bales—the perfect hiding place! What I failed to consider was the fact that the other loose box was occupied by the bull, a huge, rather morose beast who had always seemed fairly harmless. As I dodged through the entrance to the loose box, I dislodged an old wooden door, which had been propped up against the rails. It fell with a loud clatter, which startled the bull. He came to life to a terrifying degree, snorting, bellowing, and pawing the straw-strewn floor of his pen in an extremely threatening manner. I remember feeling trapped in the neighbouring pen, too scared to run past the bull, who was glaring at me with his huge red-rimmed eyes and becoming more agitated by the second. He seemed to fill the entire space between me and safety and suddenly the rails, which separated him from me, seemed much too frail and no match for his huge bulk. I let rip with some bloodcurdling screams, which in all probability did nothing to calm the beast. After what seemed like an age but was no doubt no more than a few seconds, Joyce and Eunice appeared, followed by a very alarmed Mrs Steel and her youngest son, Tam. I will never forget the sight of him. His face was covered with shaving soap, as he had been getting ready for his customary Saturday evening excursion to the greyhound racing at Thornton. Despite his somewhat comical appearance, he seemed like a knight in shining armour to me, as he quietened the bull and escorted me safely, but still rather hysterically, into the comforting embrace of Mrs Steel. She soon calmed me down—perhaps with some of her delicious limeade—and Joyce and Eunice commiserated with me about the dramatic way my hiding place had been discovered!

Margaret's misadventure with a bull happened a few years later at Pitkinny. She would have been about thirteen at the time and for some reason or other was coming home late from school one day, so she would have to miss the school bus and walk all the way up the road. Mum had asked her to buy a loaf of bread. This would be one of those extra loaves and consequently of the sliced and wrapped variety much despised by Jim. He was supposed to meet Margaret on his way back from some job that had taken him away for the afternoon. He had, however, been held up, so it was already starting to get dark as Margaret hurried up the road, schoolbag and bread in hand. She remembered as she came along the loan that the bull had just been moved into the last field before the farm. He was known to be rather frisky, and she suspected that he would give close attention to anyone walking alongside his territory. Bulls, and even cows, can be at best very curious creatures and at worst openly aggressive and dangerous towards people, especially at dusk, when they perhaps fail to recognise humans clearly. As Margaret approached the last field, the bull spotted her and came over to the fence that surmounted the lower dry-stane dyke. She crouched down below the level of the wall, but the bull was not going to be fooled and began to snort and bellow at her over the fence. As it was impossible for her to make any progress along the road in a crouching position anyway, and there was no sign of rescue in the shape of Dad in the car or pickup, she decided she had no other option but to run for her life! Of course, the bull kept pace with her on his side of the fence, still kicking up his heels and generally frightening the life out of her.

I was in the cottar hoose at the corner where our Aunt Doris and Uncle Dunc lived, and I can still remember the sudden sound of Margaret's frantic and desperately running footsteps as she pelted along their garden path and burst in the back door! She was by then hysterical with fright, and as Auntie Doris tried to find out what had happened, we heard the pickup passing as Jim drove up to the farmhouse. There he was met by Joey, who instantly became very concerned about Margaret's whereabouts as she realised she was not with her dad. He was summarily dispatched down the road to look for her, just as we came out of the cottage in time to see his rear lights disappear along the loan. Dunc had come in from work, and as he walked us up to the house, the bull was still up to his bullish nonsense and also escorted us up the road on his side of the fence. When Jim returned soon afterwards, by now worried about Margaret's disappearance, his relief at seeing us both safe and well was short-lived; Joey proceeded to berate him on several counts. He should not have been late; he should have had the sense to see if Margaret was in the cottar hoose with me; and finally, he would move the bull first thing in the morning to another field where he would not be able to terrorise us any more. Then, as things began to return to normal and she started to get the tea on the table, she asked Margaret for the bread. The bread? What bread? There, still grasped tightly in her hand, was the crumpled remains of the waxed-paper wrapper, but of the bread there was no sign whatsoever. Not a single crumb—never mind a slice of the loaf—was in evidence! Where was it? It was distributed, slice by forlorn slice, at regular intervals along the loan, reminiscent of the bread trail in *Hansel and Gretel*, only in this case it did not so much lead the way home, but marked the course of Margaret's frantic flight from the bull. If we were short of bread that night, nothing much was said; Jim kept a low profile in the doghouse. Margaret was just happy that her torment was over, and Joey relieved that nothing worse had befallen her elder daughter. Later on that evening, though, Jim could not resist having the last word. He was heard to point out to Joey that if that had been a loaf of his preferred unsliced bread, it would have survived the adventure, perhaps somewhat misshapen, but intact!

A much more serious—and not in the least humorous—incident with a bull involved Uncle Wullie, Jim's older brother. He was charged by his bull as he was climbing out of its loose box, having fed and bedded the animal. His leg was broken in several places, and it was fortunate that when he fell, it was out of rather than into the pen; otherwise, the enraged bull might well have gored and killed him. When Jim went along to the Star on hearing the news, he found his father and younger brother Harry starting to mend the shattered rails around the loose box. He advised them that it would not be necessary to rehouse that particular animal and that they should instead have it put down as, having once attacked, a rogue bull should never be trusted again. They took his advice, and the offending animal was duly dispatched. Jim privately also felt that Wullie was to some degree culpable for his accident, as he felt he had always been overconfident in his dealings with the beasts, whereas Jim would never turn his back on a bull when in close proximity to it.

Years later, however, Jim had a pedigree Hereford bull that was as docile and harmless as his Ayrshire predecessors had been wild and untrustworthy. His pedigree certificate gave his name as Ferdinand, and Ferdinand was what he was always called, in deference to his undoubted aristocratic background (although, no doubt, Jim would give him other monikers from time to time if he felt like it!). In those days Jim rented some extra pasture near Lochgelly, and the bull was there with his harem, earning his keep in doing what comes naturally to a bull. This particular weekend, John (Margaret's husband) had been helping at the farm, as he often did. He and Dad were planning to go to the football in Dunfermline, and after dinnertime Jim asked John and Robbie Imrie to do one more job before they left for the match. Would they take the Land Rover and trailer up to Lochgelly and bring Ferdinand back to Pitkinny?

When they arrived in the field, they found the bull and put a halter round his neck, but they could not get the beast to move. Naturally, he was unwilling to leave his female companions, and no amount of pushing, pulling, shouting, or cajoling could make the good-natured but intransigent beast cooperate. Time was passing, and John had just about given up all idea of making the football match when Jim arrived in his current car, a Jaguar 3.4. He bumped over the grass and slithered to a halt, shouting and cursing to John and Robbie, demanding to know what was holding them up, as he was as anxious as John not to miss the game. After they explained their problem, Jim walked over to the bull and said, quietly and reasonably, "Come on, Ferdinand, ye stupit bugger, get in the f****** trailer, will ye?" "His master's voice" had spoken. With one baleful glance in Jim's direction, the great beast lumbered up the ramp and into the trailer, while Jim skelped him benignly and affectionately on the rump.

Given our experiences with bulls, neither Margaret nor I have ever given much credence to the suggestion that the female of the species is more deadly than the male. Male sheep, or tups, as we knew them, could also be very aggressive and so unlike the harmless (if somewhat silly) ewes. They certainly display the rivalry typical of the male gender when it comes to competing for mates. Jim once bought a new tup and made the expensive mistake of putting it into the field with the ewes, next to the paddock where the old ram, redundant and soon to be time-expired, was confined. Not only did the old tup have a new and younger rival, but he was denied the company of the ewes in favour of this young upstart. The next morning, Jim was appalled to discover the old tup in the field with his harem and the young rival lying dead by the fence, clearly the loser in a battle between the generations! There was life in the old boy yet!

The other male creatures that really scared us around the farm were cockerels. They would fly at you when you approached to go into the henhouse to collect the eggs and feed the hens, and

I never ventured near a cockerel without a big stick to hand to defend myself from the flapping wings, stabbing beak, and sharp spurs.

When the days grew short in the autumn and the falling temperature stopped the grass from growing, the cattle were kept indoors in the reids and had to be fed twice a day. Hay, turnips, silage, draff, and bruised barley made up their varied and nutritious diet. We would help with the turnip cutting, lifting them one at a time into the cutting machine in the big shed, and the resulting chopped up neeps would fall into the waiting wheelbarrows, which would be wheeled down to the reids and shovelled into the mangers. In the cold, dark, early evenings of winter, the reids had a unique atmosphere. The warm, steamy breath of the beasts as they snuffled and munched at their feed mingled with the sweet scent of the hay and barley, and with the sour smell of the fermenting silage. The overall ambience was one of peace and contentment. It was very satisfying to see the cattle safely sheltered from the elements, well fed and comfortably bedded in the fresh straw that was regularly spread around them. The feeding completed, we would switch off the lights in the big shed and come in the back door to a warm kitchen, where Mum would be putting the tea on the table. But for Jim, the relentless regime of twice-daily feeding of the beasts represented very hard and trying work; Joey used to say, as the beasts grew fat and sleek through the winter, that Jim became thinner and more drawn. She was always glad to welcome the spring and the end to this gruelling aspect of stock rearing, when the beasts would be turned out into the newly growing pasture where nature could take care of their feeding for a few months. The cattle, too, loved their release into the fresh air and the green fields and would kick up their heels and positively frolic in their newfound freedom!

If the stock on the farm represented much of the capital invested and income generated on the farm, we were able to indulge in more sentimental and emotional relationships with our pets. Although there were many pet lambs over the years, the lesson of what had happened to Sookey, our pet sheep, had not been lost on any of us. We mostly confined ourselves to feeding the little orphan lambs, and they would all go off to market with the other lambs when they were big enough. However, when it came to cats and dogs, we were not prepared to compromise. We always had at least one border collie. These were working dogs, of course—in theory at least—who were expected to earn their keep by the gathering and driving of sheep and cattle, but we treated them as pets. Firm warnings about this from Dad did no good, and at every opportunity we sneaked them into the house.

The first dogs I remember were Bess, a lovely bitch, more snowy white than black, and Lassie, a big furry, black cross, as gentle as a lamb. Bess, on the other hand, had a significant measure of a personality trait common to all border collies. She was dependably good-natured with people she knew, but could be unpredictably treacherous with strangers or with visitors to whom she had taken a strong dislike. The latter would fall foul of her no matter how many times they came about the place. For example, Bob Beckett, the electrician from Cardenden, brought out the worst in her, and, no matter how careful he was, she always managed to sneak up on him and painfully nip his ankles. A more serious example of Bess's personality disorder happened one day when an unexpected visitor turned up at the back door. Every winter for a period in the fifties, an Irishman called John Boyle would come to work in the district for a few months. He lived in a cottage at the top of our loan on the way to Harelaw, which actually belonged to South Pitkinny farm. He would offer himself for work in the surrounding area, doing jobs like ditching, draining, and fencing. This particular year his sister, a Mrs Sharky, came with him to keep house. She had called to ask if they could have daily milk from us. As we got to know her, we found her a charming, quietly spoken, and totally inoffensive lady, who certainly did not deserve the introduction to Pitkinny she was about to have! As Joey opened the back door to her and started to chat, Bess was sleeping illicitly under the kitchen table. On hearing the strange voice, she leapt clean over Joey's shoulder and pinned poor Mrs Sharky to the wall, eyeball to eyeball with her, baring her teeth and snarling warningly. Maybe it was the unaccustomed Irish brogue that set her off, but whatever the reason, Bess meant business! Joey was almost as surprised as our poor visitor, but quickly pulled Bess off and brought the traumatised woman into the kitchen and sat her down. A cup of strong sweet tea and manifest apologies later, she was able to make her way home, but only after she was assured that "the hound from hell" was safely locked up in the coal house. Bess, of course, was soundly scolded and looked suitably tail-between-the-legs chastened, but we knew it would make no difference the next time she took exception to someone.

There was a time of great excitement when, having gone AWOL (absent without leave) for a few days, Bess was discovered with a litter of six puppies under the floor of the red implement shed. They were absolutely beautiful miniature versions of their mother. Margaret and I were in seventh heaven, and I can still recall that unique scent of warm, wriggling puppy flesh. Mum and Dad were less thrilled, as they had all to be weaned and found homes, but we made the most of the intervening weeks of fun as the puppies honed their inborn skills by chasing us and nipping our heels as if we were a couple of sheep! They lived with Bess in a little home in the hay bales in the big shed, and we were safe when we reached the back door, but as they grew they would learn to negotiate the back door steps. Eventually they would manage to follow us all the way up onto the settee in the kitchen, where we would feel their sharp little teeth nipping away as we cuddled them. The sad day came, of course, when the last one was claimed by its new owner, and the big shed, the close, and the kitchen returned to pre-puppy calm. Bess, unlike us, seemed somewhat relieved to be free of her boisterous brood!

Lassie was a very placid and gentle dog. Left to their own devices, she and Bess got on well together, but if Jim felt like having a bit of a diversion, he would soon get them riled up. They might be lying asleep together under the kitchen table—a favourite spot—and for sheer devilment he would say, quite quietly, "Scon 'em!" That was all it took for the twa dugs to start fighting, and skin and hair would fly as they knocked the chairs over and caused general mayhem in the kitchen. Joey would add to the noise by shouting at Jim, berating him for being so irresponsible, while he would slink away, a sly, naughty-schoolboy grin on his face, leaving her to try to separate the snarling, yelping canines at the great risk of being bitten herself!

Sadly, Lassie went missing on Bonfire Night in 1956. Everyone searched high and low for her, but she was never found. Perhaps she had been frightened by the sound of fireworks from Cardenden. (We certainly never aspired to such needless extravagance, the occasional sparkler the limit of our pyrotechnics.) Or perhaps, being very old and ailing by then, she went away alone to die somewhere, as dogs sometimes do. We really missed Lassie and would have been even sadder had we realised that this would not be the last time we would lose a much-loved pet in similar circumstances.

After Bess died we got Sweep, the only male collie we ever had, but he proved untrainable and would go walkabout all the time, so he had to be sold on. Then we acquired Nell, a lovely, good-natured collie bitch who had none of the suspect temperament of Bess. Jim saw her advertised by a shepherd in Glen Lyon who had developed arthritis and was no longer able to walk the hills. He wanted his dog to go to a good home, somewhere she could go on working. Jim and Joey went to collect her from the far end of Glen Lyon and brought her home. She had to be kept tied up for a few days until she got used to her new surroundings and owners. Of course, I made a great fuss of her, and she soon settled enough to be let loose. The next morning, Joey could hear her free-range hens making an alarmed din. She didn't think a fox could be the cause in daytime, but on investigating, she found a "wolf in collie's clothing!" There was Nell, intent on driving a hen back into the deep-litter henhouse. Each time she crept close enough, she would snap at the perplexed hen and relieve her of a few feathers. The poor creature's rear end was nearly plucked clean by the time Nell succeeded in getting her into the shed, whereupon she homed in on another wayward fowl and started stalking it. She had obviously never seen hens before, and was fascinated by them. It took a long time until she realised what a thankless task she had set herself and left them in peace to their scratching and pecking around the steading.

The only actual pet dog we ever had, one who didn't have to work for her living, was Trudy, our cairn terrier. When Margaret started at Fod House (the pre-nursing college in Dunfermline) in 1957, I really felt lonely. She was away from Sunday evening until Friday afternoon, and we all missed her, so Mum and Dad agreed that I could have a little dog. Later, Margaret would say, "Fancy! Replacing me with a dog!" But she was as delighted as the rest of us with the new addition to the family. Trudy got on well with Nell, and they became amiable companions. They loved travelling in the car, and while Trudy perched happily on the back parcel shelf, Nell was happiest in the boot or in the back of the pickup or land rover.

Sometimes Jim would forget that Nell was in the boot. After Margaret and John were married and living in a flat in George Street in Dunfermline, one Saturday Dad was giving me a lift to Dunfermline, as he was meeting John for the football match at East End Park. I was going shopping and then meeting Dad at Margaret's later after the match. On the way, we realised that Nell was still in the boot. She had been away with Dad earlier, and he had forgotten to let her out at the farm. As he was late for the match, I agreed that I would forgo my shopping and take Nell to Margaret's. I had no lead for the dog, but had to walk her through the public park to George Street. Coming from Glen Lyon to Pitkinny, she had probably never seen more than a dozen people together at any one time. Here she was now, confronted by hundreds of football fans, all making their way past us to the match. (Dunfermline Athletic was playing well in those days, and commanded big crowds.) The dog was frantic, and I had a really hard time keeping her with me, as I expected her to make a bolt for home any time as she scanned all the faces of the men passing us, looking for Jim. I am sure the passing crowd must have thought they were encountering a mad young woman, talking loudly and incessantly to her dog. I just managed to keep her with me until we reached George Street. She continued to be very agitated and when Dad and John arrived back from the match, she was delighted to jump into her familiar travelling place as soon as the boot was opened.

Another time, when Jim was heading through Dunfermline on his way to Glasgow, he realised again that he had a passenger in the boot. He decided to leave the dog with Margaret and collect her on his way home later. As she waved Dad off on his resumed journey with Nell beside her, the dog decided she didn't want to be left behind, and she suddenly took off and chased the car. When she caught up with it, she leapt on to the closed boot and clung frantically to the back of the car as Jim accelerated away. As he caught sight of Nell in the rearview mirror, he braked suddenly. The inevitable happened as Nell kept going and slithered off the roof of the car! Fortunately, she survived unscathed. Collies have an unerring homing instinct, and I am sure that had Nell been lost on either of these occasions, she would have found her way home to Pitkinny. If they went for a walk with you, they would stick close by you all the way. But, no matter how far you went, or how circuitous your route, the moment you turned for home, the dog would take off and would be patiently waiting for you on the doorstep on your return.

In 1964, little Trudy became ill and was diagnosed with kidney disease. Although she was being treated by the vet, she inexorably grew worse. I had started at university that October, and, although Jim and Joey knew that the kindest thing would be to have her put to sleep, neither of them wanted to take that step without my knowing. They agreed not to tell me until I came home for Christmas, when we could make a joint decision. Unfortunately, just before the end of term, Trudy simply disappeared. Just as Lassie had done, she went off alone to die, and despite extensive searches by everyone at the farm, she was never found. When I came home from Dundee, it was to discover that our little pet was no longer with us. The corner of the kitchen where her basket had always been was strangely empty, and Christmas that year was more than tinged with sadness. Yet again we had to accept that no matter how much our pets mean to us, we can only have a limited time with them. Ten years later, as Joey and Jim prepared to retire and leave Pitkinny, and as they cleared out the farm in preparation for the roup, Jim hoped he would come across the remains of Trudy. But he never did.

Every farm has its quota of cats, of course, and we were no exception. They were very necessary as a means of controlling vermin, and none of them was exclusively a pet. They were very happy to work their passage by catching as many of the ubiquitous mice and rats as they could. Nevertheless, there was a distinct hierarchy within the farm cat society. Some of them were house pets, while there were others who, though not exactly feral, would never come into the house and would keep to the fringes of the steading. They were all fed outside, but there again, you could see that feeding also obeyed a pecking order. The matriarch was "the mither cat," an imperious feline, almost entirely white with black nose, ears, and paws. She had an impressively patrician air about her and clearly ruled her extended feline family with a rod of iron. She was very much in charge of the house cats and underlined her privileged position by routinely accompanying Joey when she went, twice daily, to feed the hens and gather the eggs. One winter, the mither cat fell ill, perhaps with cat flu or some similar complaint, and Joey began to despair of her recovery. She would lie shivering under the fender of the grate, as close to the fire as she could get, would neither eat nor drink, and looked as if she was not long for this world. Notwithstanding her dire condition, as soon as Joey put on her coat to go to the hens, the poor cat would drag herself away from the comfort of the fire and follow her outside and down to the old henhouse. She did this faithfully for a week or two, until she spontaneously began to get better. An example of a fitting reward for exceptional feline loyalty!

We were quite young when we began to understand that Joey and Jim would not tolerate a constant increase in the cat population, which, to be fair, would have reached Malthusian proportions had nature been allowed a free hand. The number of consumers would eventually outstrip the food supply—in the form of vermin on the farm, if not in the shape of what could be supplied by their human landlords. So, when a litter of kittens was discovered, it was quietly disposed of. Mrs Steel at Bogside had a euphemism for this procedure. She said the kittens "joined the Royal Navy"! Eventually, as we realised this involved the use of a bag, a bucket of water, and a brick, we were able to put two and two together and understood what was really happening. Although Mum tried to explain that it was impossible to keep all the kittens that were born, and they had no choice but to take this course of action, which was carried out "as humanely as possible," we were having none of it! Today, of course, it is easy to see that a much more humane approach would be to have the cats spayed by the vet, but then the cost involved made such a solution a nonstarter.

As far as we could see, this was mass murder of poor innocent little kittens. We then discovered that this awful fate befell only those litters that were discovered soon after they were born. Once the kitlins' (as Dad called them) eyes had opened, they were safe, as disposing of them then was considered to be too cruel. Although we didn't completely appreciate the distinction, our course of action was clearly indicated. On finding newly born kittens, we would keep their existence a secret, and, if necessary, hide them from their would-be executioners, until their eyes opened and they were too old to be eligible for recruitment to Her Majesty's senior service! We once found two little fluffy kittens, one black and one grey, and kept quiet about them. We were horrified to discover, when their eyes opened, that they each had only one eye! We were very upset, and even more so when Smokey fell foul of the baker's van one day, but as Fluffy grew up we could see that she was in no way disadvantaged by her handicap. On the contrary, she became the best hunter of all the cats and was fearless in catching rats or even rabbits, in some cases bigger than herself! She was a firm favourite with us, but we suffered some terrible scratches from her until we realised that if we wanted to pick her up, we had to be sure not to approach her from her blind side.

I was in the business not only of saving our own kittens, but also of adopting the occasional stray. A family who lived at South Pitkinny left to go to another farm and either forgot or (more likely, deliberately abandoned) one of their cats. It was soon mooching hungrily around Pitkinny but was given short shrift by our sitting tenants. I was worried it might starve to death, so I started secretly feeding it. Joey was less than pleased when she found out and saw that she had yet another mouth to feed, but I would not be dissuaded; eventually Cheetah grew to be accepted by her host family and became one of the gang.

Gradually, after we had left home, our cats began to die off, and the population dwindled until Pitkinny virtually became a feline-free zone. Then one of the tenants of the cottar hooses came by two kittens, and Joey offered to take one of them. She was a pretty marmalade cat and she named her Topsy. She was "seen to" by the vet and soon settled into a life of ease in and around the house. She became a real personality who would occasionally deign to be petted but, as with all cats, completely on her terms, and she always retained a wild and independent streak, hunting successfully—but only when *she* could be bothered. She didn't seem to think it was part of her job description! Even Jim became very fond of her, although he would never have admitted to it. She was later joined by Tim, a black fluffy reminder of her earlier counterpart, who was given a home at Pitkinny when her owner, a friend of Auntie Caroline, had to move into residential care. The two cats became pals and, against all the stereotypes of animal behaviour, made friends with Jan, the last collie Jim and Joey had. In their last few years at Pitkinny, when Jim did his rounds of the cattle in the fields he was followed at a respectful distance first by Jan, and then in turn by Topsy, and finally Tim. I am certain that he was never more content than when, on a fine evening, he strolled, stick in hand, among his prized beasts with his three faithful companions.

*Jim with prize-winning Clydesdale (Punch or Jolly)*

*Jim's prize-winning Ayrshire bull*

*Margaret, cousin Lily Betsy, and Anne with Lassie and two kittens, Smokey and Fluffy*

*Jim with Trudy*

# Chapter 19

"Dae ye no ken, Ah wid trust this man wi' ma life?"

There were many, many people associated with Pitkinny over the years. There were workers, of course, some full time and some casual. Commercial travellers, some of whom became friends of the family in the fullness of time, would visit on a regular, if sometimes infrequent, basis. Family members and friends usually found a visit to Pitkinny an attractive proposition and were guaranteed a warm welcome and congenial and entertaining company.

Those who worked at Pitkinny no doubt had mixed feelings about their employment there. Farm work was usually hard, always at the mercy of the elements and often of Jim's uncertain temper. Which of these was the harder to bear would be for them to say, but I did often wonder how Jim retained the loyalty, respect, and in some cases, even the affection of his employees. I know from personal experience that he could be a hard taskmaster, but at the same time I am aware that he had an undeniable likeable and affable side to his personality and he was never, never dull company. Whether he left them laughing or crying or seething with frustration or fury, he made a great impression on all who came into contact with him. Joey was always a much more amenable boss and showed her appreciation much more, but she was not a soft touch either. She expected a high standard of work from others, as she demanded it from herself. But, unlike Jim, she realised that it was unreasonable to expect people to do something well that she couldn't do well herself and was much more patient with folk.

Historically, farm work had always been poorly paid, and traditionally agricultural workers had to move frequently from farm to farm to try to better their conditions, while some were little more than itinerant labourers who came and went, almost with the seasons and with little or no warning. On the other hand, by the middle of the twentieth century, there was some improvement in farm wages and terms. Increasingly, there were more workers of long standing who spent most of their working lives on one farm, especially if or when they found a farmer who paid a reasonable return for their labours. In the old days, the agricultural year was divided into four terms: Martinmas in November, Candlemas in February, Whitsun in May, and Lammas in August. The various skilled workers such as ploughmen, dairymen and dairymaids, orramen, foremen, or, on bigger farms, grieves and house servants, would present themselves for hire at the feeing markets held "at the term." In the old bothy ballad "The Barnyards o' Delgaty" we learn about such a man: "When I ga'ed doon tae Turra (Turriff) market, Turra market fur tae fee."

Another story about such a ploughman tells how he was interviewed by a farmer at the market. He asked his name and where he had previously worked, and said he would let him know if he wanted him later in the day after he had "spiered aboot yer character" from his previous employers, who were also at the market. When they met up later, the farmer grudgingly agreed to employ him, as his references had checked out all right. "Weel then," replied the ploughman, "*Ah've* been spierin' aboot *your* character, an' Ah'm no comin' tae wurk fur ye!"

By the time Jim and Joey were in a position to be able to hire labour, although there was some formal advertising of jobs, there was still a large degree of hiring and firing done on the strength of personal references and recommendations within the close farming communities. Increasingly in the course of the rest of the century, farming became more like other businesses, and wages and working conditions became subject to the same statutory regulations and personnel management as other areas of working life. Developments in mechanisation and automation have brought improvements in the conditions pertaining to farm work, but have been paralleled by a much greater need for workers to have formal qualifications and to continue to develop and upgrade their skills. I am sure that in farming, as in so many other fields of work, there in no substitute for good practical experience. But it is very often difficult for a young person to gain those practical skills without first having the paper qualifications to gain entry to the workplace and to get a foothold on the ladder of career advancement.

Pitkinny, to my knowledge, had its fair share of both permanent and irregular workers, some of the former spending years there, many of the latter simply "ships passing in the night." I am certain that the workplace in general is nowadays so much less colourful and interesting in the absence of some of the old worthies who added their own individual character and personality to the daily routine. This was equally true of Bogside and Pitkinny in the forties, fifties, and sixties. I personally remember many of these people, but for details of others who spent time at the farms in my early childhood, I have had to rely on the memories of people like Dougie and Chrissie Imrie, and Lena Imrie (née Smith), who worked there for much of their working lives.

Jim's cousin, Dunc Rutherford, worked at Bogside and later Pitkinny from the day in 1942 when he was foisted on Jim and Joey by James senior at the behest of his brother Tam. He married Joey's youngest sister Doris in 1953, and from then they lived in one of the Pitkinny cottar hooses; he assumed the role of foreman there. His predecessor in that position when we moved to Pitkinny had been Dave Thomson, who had been hired by Montgomery, the previous tenant of the farm. He lived in one of the cottages with his wife, Annie, and their three girls, Vida, Sheena, and Nanette; they moved on to Drumdreel farm near Cupar in 1953. The other cottar hoose was occupied by Math Morrison and his wife and family. He was an expert horseman, much devoted to the two pairs of Clydesdales Jim had, Punch and Star, and Danny and Jolly, with the orra (extra) horse Paddy. As it became clear that it was only a matter of time until tractors would entirely supplant the draught horse in the work of the farm, Math decided that his future lay elsewhere. His departure coincided with the horse roup (sale) in 1951 when the faithful Clydesdales were sold off with all the horse and stable equipment and accoutrements.

It was at this time that Dougie Imrie first started to work at Pitkinny. He was brought up at 13 Capeldrae Row with his five brothers—Donald, Dan, Dave, John, and Rob—and a sister, Isabelle. As a schoolboy, he would run home from Auchterderran School to Bogside, desperate to help his brother John, who was Jim's first dairyman there, with the afternoon milking. Dougie would deposit his schoolbag on the byre windowsill and "get yokit" with eager enthusiasm. So it seemed the natural thing for him to look for employment with Jim at Pitkinny when he left school. He had suspected that his new boss would be a hard taskmaster from what his brother had told him and from an earlier experience he had had at Bogside. His father, old Jock Imrie, happened to appear in the close just as Jim was berating Dougie in the cartshed in his usual colourful language for some misdemeanour or shortcoming. Dougie could not believe his ears when he heard his father apparently taking exception to Jim's form of discipline. "Dinna swear at 'im!" Dougie felt momentarily gratified that his usually very strict and authoritarian father was standing up for his son. He was soon deflated when old Jock continued, "Dinna waste yer braith; just kick 'im up the erse!" "Aye, that's mair like it!" Dougie thought to himself! Although Jim never resorted to corporal punishment, contrary to old Jock's advice, Dougie had no illusions that life at Pitkinny would be easy; still, farm work was all he had ever wanted to do, and he started his career at Pitkinny with relish.

During his first spring, while the sowing was well underway, he was dispatched by Jim to roll a barley field. He managed with a struggle to yoke Paddy to a roller and, having little or no experience with horses, plodded along to the field, which seemed discouragingly huge. His lack of experience seemed to carry no weight with Jim, and it never seemed to occur to him that Dougie would need training or help with this Herculean task. Perhaps he thought that the best way to learn was by being thrown in at the deep end and in any case may have felt that he could not spare the time to show the young man how to do the job. Having decided that quality of result was more important than speed, Dougie's work rate was painfully slow, as he kept having to go over bits that he had missed, especially at the end rigs where he had to turn the horse and the roller. Eventually he succeeded in achieving a reasonably flat surface on the field and returned worn out, but secretly quite pleased with his efforts. When he reported to Jim that the job was finished, his succinct and less-than-appreciative rejoinder was, "Finished? I should bloody well hope so! Ah could've clapped it quicker masel', wi' a shovel!"

Joey would often tell Jim that he was very lucky to have such good-natured and easy-going people as the Imries working for him, because they seemed able to tolerate his bad temper and impatience. Dougie was certainly remarkable in being able to withstand many such reprimands, perhaps because he was able to see the humour in the way Jim expressed himself, without feeling personally devalued by his comments. He remembers a very different reaction to an earlier occasion at Pitkinny at the hands of old Mr Stevenson. The Stevenson family were living there temporarily, by arrangement with Jim and Bob Edgar, the factor, while they waited for entry to Ballingry Farm, but Jim was already the tenant and therefore in charge of the workers there, although we were still living at Bogside. Dougie was helping Dave Thomson when Mr Stevenson senior came across him in the close. "Boy!" he imperiously commanded Dougie, "Fill my car radiator with water!" The old man had at one time farmed in Africa, and sounded as if he was giving orders to one of his African servants. He had been overheard by Dave Thomson, and while Dougie would just have done as he was told, the foreman quickly intervened on his behalf and pointed out to the old man that he and Dougie were not answerable to him, but to Mr Rutherford. It was the tone and manner of the directive that Dave objected to rather than the order itself, and Dougie realised that there was all the difference in the world between the two men: Jim, who had told Dougie off for the slowness of his work on the one hand; and Mr Stevenson, who had given him the imperious order on the other. The latter had no respect for Dougie and no wish to relate to him other than as master and servant, whereas Jim saw in him a young man who was capable of learning and with whom he could identify as he recalled his own youth. A day would come when, on another occasion, Dougie would have cause to be grateful to Jim for giving him evidence of the high regard and respect he was held in by his boss.

So Dougie worked with Jim from 1950 until 1976, when we left Pitkinny. He had two short breaks of service, one at the command of Her Majesty when he did his national service from 1953 to 1955. The second came in 1963, when he left Pitkinny, not on account of Jim but of his foreman and cousin, Dunc. As I have explained earlier, it is always difficult when family members try to work together. With the benefit of hindsight, it is easy to see that Dunc felt that his kinship to Jim and, through marriage, to Joey gave him a privileged position at Pitkinny, and he increasingly took advantage of that presumed situation. He and Doris had a son, Alan, born in 1956, and I am sure they came to hope that he would have a future at Pitkinny, and indeed might even be in line to inherit the tenancy, as Joey and Jim had no male heir to the farm, and neither Margaret nor I were making the farm our work. In terms of the day-to-day running of the business, Dunc saw himself as Jim's right-hand man, and hard worker though he undoubtedly was, he made Dougie's life increasingly difficult. He would never allow anyone else to drive the combine harvester or the JCB and left Dougie to do all the menial tasks around the place. He and his wife, Chrissie, had moved into the other cottage with their first baby son, William, who was the same age as little Alan, and she was finding it very hard having Doris as a neighbour.

When Jim began to contract out his big equipment in 1962, Dunc went with it as driver, and Dougie then had to cope with all the work on the farm. This he did willingly and well, but then when Dunc returned, he would take over again and criticise the work Dougie had been doing in his absence. In addition, he would try to discredit Dougie and his work to Jim and Joey. In 1963 Dougie and Chrissie felt they could no longer tolerate the situation, and he handed in his notice. Sorry as he was to lose Dougie, Jim was not fully aware of the effect Dunc had been having on the morale of the other workers. Meanwhile, Joey was finding relations with Doris ever more strained. She had always been a great help to her younger sister, and she would look after Alan to allow Doris to work outside. But increasingly, she saw that her help was being taken for granted, and Doris began to involve herself more and more in the running of the farm and in discussing business decisions with Jim. This all happened insidiously over a number of years, so that Joey and Jim were barely aware of the extent to which Doris and Dunc were setting themselves up as heirs apparent.

Matters came to a head in 1965 when Margaret and John had their first baby, a daughter, Pamela. Suddenly it became obvious that this development did not go down well with Doris and Dunc, as perhaps they saw that their hopes for the future of Pitkinny might not come to fruition. When Dunc refused to accept responsibility for his part in the failure of Pitkinny to secure the contract for a turnip harvester demonstration, it was almost the last straw, and Jim did not dissuade them from leaving the cottage and buying a house in Woodend. The final debacle came only a few months later, when Grandad Hugh at Markinch confided in Joey and Jim that Doris and Dunc had been giving vent to all the resentment they had been harbouring to anyone who would listen. They had been maligning Jim and Joey to many family members and acquaintances for a long time, all of which we had been blissfully (or naively) unaware. They clearly felt that they deserved more than the incomes and home that Jim and Joey had provided them with over the years, even bringing up the fact that when they worked at Bogside at the very beginning, when Jim and Joey had no cash flow, they were never paid. Of course they neglected to mention that money was saved for them and that they received nest eggs when Doris returned to work in the paper mill and also later when they got married. In addition to this, as Jim and

Joey got on their feet and could afford weekly wages, they were both handsomely rewarded not only in cash but in kind.

When Jim confronted Doris and Dunc about all this, they completely lost control and proceeded to berate all of us to such an extent that there was no way back. Dunc was dismissed with the words, "Get doon the road wi' yer kist!" It was a classic case of biting the hand that feeds you, and although he threatened to bring a case of unfair dismissal, Dunc was immediately forestalled by Jim's offer of maximum redundancy terms, a magnanimous gesture which they hardly deserved but which pre-empted any further unpleasantness. So came to an end a very unhappy episode for all concerned, which had repercussions in the wider family for many years; but in retrospect, I am certain that it had to happen. There could have been no other outcome, given the behaviour that Doris and Dunc had indulged in for years. Within a very short time Dougie and Chrissie returned, and in 1966 he resumed work at Pitkinny as foreman, where he would remain for the next decade.

There were various other occupants of the cottar hooses at different times during Jim and Joey's tenancy of Pitkinny, people whose names evoke a variety of memories. Geordie Pryde (whose request for a piglet to fatten had nearly cost Jim dearly) and his wife had one daughter, Margaret, who was older than me but younger than my sister. One Easter Sunday we planned to take a picnic up to Harelaw and asked her if she would like to join us. We each had the obligatory hard-boiled and painted egg, of course, and a few pieces (sandwiches). Our special treat was a chocolate egg we had each been given by Mum. When we realised that Margaret Pryde was not so lucky, we were faced with a terrible moral dilemma. How could we have her watch us enjoy this rare chocolate splurge when she couldn't join in? I am happy to report that we managed to do the decent thing and share our eggs with her, but with what degree of good grace, I can't actually recall! After the Prydes left, Jimmy Shand, who claimed to be a cousin of his illustrious namesake, lived there with his wife and two boys—Archie, who worked with his father, and Eddie, who was a mechanic at Rossleigh garage in Kirkcaldy. They moved on to other jobs in 1957, and Dougie and Chrissie Imrie moved into that cottage.

After Doris and Dunc left their cottage, Lena and Rob Imrie lived there for some years, but they had worked at Pitkinny previously for various lengths of time. Lena, whose maiden name was Smith, was brought up at South Pitkinny Farm with her sisters Mary and Jean and her twin brother Bill, (the same lad who nearly found himself on the wrong end of a hay fork wielded by Alistair MacMillan!). She worked with Joey and Jim when she left school, sometimes outside and sometimes in the house. One of my earliest memories, just after we moved to Pitkinny from Bogside, is of listening to Lena singing as I followed her round the house. "Can I watch you, Lena?" I would ask and I recall her singing, "Put another nickel in, in the nickelodeon," as she polished the wauxcloth (linoleum) in the front lobby at Pitkinny. She and Joey, years later, would reminisce about how she longed to be older and considered grown up. "I wish I was eighteen," she would sigh, and Joey would urge her not to wish her life away. Now, many years later, I am only too familiar with the wish to be eighteen—only now it is in a backward-looking direction!

When her family moved to Lochgelly, Lena would cycle the three or four miles to the farm. This took her down the steep Lisa Brae to Brigghills, then on past Murray Knowes farm and Annfield and into the Jamphlars and on down to Auchterderran. There she would turn left and cycle past the church, manse, and school, up to Woodend, and onwards to Pitkinny. A day came when Lena did not complete her daily journey. She crashed off her bike on the steepest part of the Lisa Brae and sustained very serious facial and dental injuries. When we duly visited her in

Bridge of Earn hospital, we walked past her bed because we simply did not recognise her! Only her muffled voice, calling "Hello, Mrs Rutherford," alerted Joey to the fact that this poor soul swathed in bandages was our dear friend. She was in hospital for many weeks, but thankfully made a good recovery, with only slight scarring to remind her of her accident.

She later married Dougie's brother, Rob Imrie, who worked as a miner at Kinglassie Pit, and they lived there. As the downturn in the fortunes of deep mining in the coal industry began to be felt in the Fife coalfield at the end of the 1950s, Kinglassie was selected as one of the first pits to be closed. This also affected my aunt and uncle, Greta and Bobby Drennan. Incentives were made available to the redundant miners to move their jobs and families to the Yorkshire coalfield, and Rob Imrie and Uncle Bobby were two of the first of the Kinglassie miners to take the plunge. They went to Doncaster to try out the jobs on offer there and, assuming they opted to stay, make preparations for their families to join them. In the event, Uncle Bobby decided that his future lay in England, and Auntie Greta and our three cousins had to give up their house in Kinglassie, while Rob Imrie chose to return home to Fife.

As economic recession bit deeply, not only in the mining industry, but in other areas of the economy later in the twentieth century, the Conservative government of the eighties and nineties advocated a "get on your bike" approach to finding work. I was reminded then of men like Bobby and Rob, who were in the vanguard of workers in the contracting primary and manufacturing industries like coal mining, steel, heavy engineering, and the car industry, and who had to make life-changing decisions to uproot their families and start new lives in the south. And of course this is still happening, even now in more recent industries like light engineering, electronics, and even tertiary service industries, where jobs and skilled workers are exported on a worrying scale to England and beyond.

I can remember how upset we all were the day we saw Auntie Greta and the three youngsters off on the train. Even Jim was moved by their plight. My aunt was heartbroken at having to leave all that was dear and familiar to her to undertake such disruption to her life. She later remarked that it brought back all the terror and homesickness her wartime service in the ATS had caused her. Jim said the sight of them boarding the train reminded him of newsreel film of refugees being forced to move. This might seem overly dramatic now, in an age when travelling—not only within our own country, but all over the world—seems commonplace and straightforward. But in the early 1960s many people still expected to be born, live, work, and die in their home area, and had a very restricted comfort zone in geographical, social, and emotional terms.

Uncle Bobby and Auntie Greta, despite the traumatic beginning, made a go of their life in Doncaster. They knew several other families who moved to the same area and in time made new friends among their new neighbours. Their children—Jim, Elizabeth, and Hughie—completed their education, found jobs, married, and settled in South Yorkshire. None of them would have chosen to live anywhere else, and when the time came for their parents to retire there was no question of them returning to Fife, because by then their roots had been well and truly transplanted. Meanwhile Rob Imrie found work in the opencast coal site at Westfield, and in the newly established and rapidly developing electronics industry in the new town of Glenrothes. He and Lena later returned with their family once more to live and work at Pitkinny, until they later moved back to Kinglassie. When Rob died in 1997, his wish was for his ashes to be scattered at Harelaw, within sight of the home where they felt they had spent their happiest years.

Another family who had a long association with us was the Steels. Various byremen had worked at Bogside, including John Imrie, but as Jim faced the prospect of running a second farm when the tenancy of Pitkinny became his, he realised that he would need a dairyman who would take full responsibility for the running of the dairy. Bogside house was available, and there could be work for other members of a prospective occupant's family. In the event, Jock and Mrs Steel were employed, and two of their sons, young Jock and Tam, also worked at Bogside, while their eldest son Bob found work with Sandy Black at Westfield Farm. Jock senior was a very hard-working man, who was as honest and conscientious as it was possible to be. In fact, it was almost impossible to get him to take any of the holiday time he was entitled to. As Jim would have to fill the breach and do the milking if Jock was away, his reluctance to take time off suited Jim down to the ground. Joey used to nag at her husband to encourage Jock to have a holiday, if not for his sake, for his wife's. But the only thing that interested Jock, apart from work, was his love of greyhound racing. He always kept one or two dogs, and Saturday night would see him and at least one of his sons at Thornton dog track.

Jock was not the most patient man in the world and must have been very hard to live with, as he demanded as single-minded an approach to life and work from his family as he had himself. He was very rough and ready in his dealings with his family, while Mrs Steel was the kindest and gentlest of women, who had her hands full running her home and seeing to the needs of the four men in her family and her little girl, Joyce, as well as helping Jock with the milking. By the time they settled at Bogside, their eldest daughter, Margaret, was married and had emigrated to Australia. Their second daughter, Mary, was married soon after. As she left the house that day, Jim and Joey were there to wish her all the best in her marriage, and in the absence of confetti or rice, Jim threw handfuls of barley over her. The symbolism was right, even if it represented a departure from the usual custom.

The running of the dairying side of his business was now in experienced hands, and this left Jim free to develop the arable operation at Pitkinny. Jock would frequently consult and advise Jim in decisions involving the dairy, and we would always know when the phone rang when it was Jock at the other end. The phone seemed to ring louder and vibrate with great urgency as it appeared to be about to leap off the windowsill in the lobby. So it was no surprise when we lifted the receiver to hear Jock's west-country accent barking, "Is the boss there?" We came to understand that his bark was worse than his bite, but he would brook no time-wasting or inefficiency. He was one of the old school, and if he had a fault, in Jim's estimation, it was that he had no time for, and little understanding of, the technology involved in the machinery which was becoming more and more a feature of dairying, as in all other aspects of farming. When a new electrically operated engine was installed at the dairy to power the milking machines, he found it hard to get used to. One day when it developed a fault, Jim was called to help and soon diagnosed that the belt needed lubricating with belt syrup. On hearing this, Jock shot out of the engine house and up the close, shouting at the top of his voice, "Helen! Helen, bring the 'seerap.'" Mrs Steel appeared at the back door with a tin of Tate and Lyle golden syrup in her hand, which Jock grabbed and proceeded to open, all before Jim could point out that belt syrup was not the same thing at all as the kind you would spread on your toast!

Joey was used to coping with Jim's short temper and volatility, and she wondered how Mrs Steel managed to put up with Jock with the patience and good humour that never seemed to desert her. She once told Mum about one of the few times she did lose her temper with her husband, when they lived and worked on another farm. Mrs Steel had been filling a bucket with water at the standpipe outside the dairy when the farmer's wife walked past. As they chatted for a few moments while the water filled the bucket, Jock appeared at the door of the dairy. "Come on, come on, woman, there's work tae be done. Dinnae just staund there, wastin' time!" As the farmer's wife walked away, the worm turned, and Mrs Steel lifted the now brimming bucket and threw its entire contents over Jock. There was a stunned silence as they looked at each other. Neither could quite believe what had just happened, and Mrs Steel waited for the storm to break. But all Jock did was to say, "Oh Helen, I'm soakin' weet! Gie's yer peenie tae dry masel'." Almost in a trance, she took off her peeny and handed it to him. He quietly dried himself with it as best he could and, handing it back to her, meekly turned round and went back into the dairy to resume his work.

I can remember two other episodes that showed evidence of a softer side to Jock's nature. As I have mentioned earlier, both Pitkinny and Bogside had large contingents of cats amongst their animal populations. Joyce Steel loved her pets and was very upset when one of the cats went missing. She was a year younger than I, so we were never in the same class at school but used to sometimes be together at playtime. One day during the school dinner break, she found her missing cat, which had somehow found its way down to Auchterderran, being fussed over by some of the other children. She was delighted to have found her, but what could we do with the cat until it was time to go home? We certainly couldn't keep it in the school, and she was worried that, if we left it in the playground, it would have disappeared again by the time school ended for the day. We decided that our only course of action was to phone home and have someone come and rescue the lost cat. So we walked up to the phone box at Woodend and somehow managed to phone Bogside and quickly explain our emergency to Mrs Steel. It is a measure of our despair about the welfare of the poor cat that we had the temerity to expect Jock or Tam to drop everything and drive down to Woodend to collect the lost pet. But that is exactly what they did; a short time later, Jock's green Standard 8 car came into sight, driven by Tam, who had recently passed his driving test. As it came to a halt, Jock leapt out, grabbed the cat from Joyce, unceremoniously threw the startled beast into the back of the car, got back in, and barked at Tam to get the car turned and head home. Not a look or a word passed between him and his wee lassie, but as Joyce and I walked hurriedly back to school, I understood that actions speak louder than words; I knew instinctively that, despite his fearsome manner, Jock's heart was in the right place after all.

Around the same time, in the autumn, Jock had gone to a livestock market with Jim and, in the course of the day's dealing, bought a turkey. It was a fine, big, pure white bubbly-jock, which would make a grand Christmas dinner. Jock's intention was to feed it up and then to pull its neck in time for the festive season. However, as the shopping (and butchering!) days to Christmas diminished, there was no sign of Jock doing the necessary deadly deed. None of the family could actually bring themselves to remind him about the turkey, and it survived that and many other Christmases unscathed. It could be seen for years happily living alongside Mrs Steel's hens, scratching and pecking contentedly with the rest of her flock. If it suffered from an identity crisis, it showed no sign of it. Perhaps it knew it owed its life to the unsuspected soft heart of an outwardly hard man.

A similar situation prevailed at Pitkinny later, this time with another white creature. Saund Page was the local coal man and haulage contractor at Woodend. He and his wife had become good friends of Joey and Jim, and they often helped each other out. It was Saund who years before had solved Jim's transport problem, when he drove bags of cement for him from the quarry to Bogside to make the first improvements to the byres there, after James senior at the Star had refused to lend Jim his pickup truck. Saund had bought part of a forest at Tigh-na Bruach and acquired a white Clydesdale stallion to haul the timber out for sale. When the job was complete, he had no more use for the horse and couldn't bring himself to send it to the knacker's yard, so he asked Jim if he could live out his days at Pitkinny. This he did, and for years he spent the winters with the stirks in the reid and went out to the fields with them in the summer. It was so amusing to see Punch's great long white head amongst those of the cattle as he reached into the manger to enjoy his winter feed. Like Jock's turkey, maybe he realised that living with a lot of strangers of a different species is infinitely preferable to not living at all!

Jim and Joey retained the loyalty and respect of these families who spent years working at Pitkinny, despite the many times when they must have felt undervalued and misused, owing to Jim's combination of impatience and uncertain temper. I am sure that in his heart he really did appreciate their hard work and commitment, but his gratitude was hardly ever displayed. The ambivalence of his attitude to his workers is well illustrated by two events, which were described to me by Dougie. Regularity of working hours was unknown in farming, and work went on all the time, weather permitting; but as a rule, unless it was a harvest time, the workers' regular week ended at lunchtime on a Saturday, and that was when the wages were paid. Joey would go to the bank, which opened on a Saturday morning in those days, and made up the wage packets, while Margaret and I were responsible for making the dinner. One such Saturday in the early sixties, Margaret's fiancé, John French, was also at Pitkinny; he and Jim were going to the football match in Dunfermline. Having picked up Saund Page at Woodend on the way, they were halfway to Dunfermline when Jim realised that he still had Dougie's pay packet in his pocket, having forgotten to hand it in on the way past his cottar hoose. "Oh well, he'll get it the morn, he'll no be needin' it the day," he dismissively said. John remonstrated with him, "Of course he'll need his money!" As he was driving, he promptly turned the car round and headed back to Pitkinny. Had it not been for John, Dougie and Chrissie would have been unable to go for their weekly shopping, this being long before the days of ATMs or credit cards. So Jim had to accept that being late for the football was less important than seeing that his foreman had the pay that was due to him; left to himself, he would not have taken that view.

Another incident served to prove that in fact Jim did value his foreman, although he usually appeared to take him for granted. Jim and Joey had been on holiday, and Dougie, as usual, had been in charge of the work while they were away. Unfortunately he had accidentally damaged a piece of equipment and was not looking forward to telling Jim about it when he came back. At the earliest opportunity he sought him out and found him in the big shed, talking to a traveller who was no doubt looking for an order from Jim. After Dougie explained what had happened, Jim, as expected, let rip with an angry outburst as he gave vent to his frustration that the necessary repair would hold up the work. The traveller sympathised with Jim, saying, "That's what happens when you leave your business to people you can't trust." At that Jim turned on him with fury, shouting, "And what's it got to dae wi' you? Trust? Ye're talkin' to me aboot trust? Dae ye no ken Ah wid trust this man with ma life!" And the hapless traveller got an order all right, but not the one he was hoping for. He was told in no uncertain terms that he was no longer welcome, and that if he knew what was good for him he would get the hell out of Pitkinny and never dare to come back! So it was in this roundabout way that Dougie had evidence, probably for the very first time, of something that he had probably instinctively always suspected: that his boss had implicit faith in him, and that their relationship was based on mutual respect and trust.

Years later, when Jim and Joey made the decision to retire and leave Pitkinny, Dougie was inconsolable that his working life there was over. He had no inclination to continue working for another boss there and chose instead to take the offer of a job with a potato contractor at Cluny, near Cardenden. He and Chrissie, like so many others, were genuinely sad to see the end of an era as the Rutherfords severed their ties with Pitkinny. Their working lives had been closely woven with those of Jim and Joey as their hard work left its mark on the farm, its land, and surroundings, but more even than that, on the memories of the many years they had shared.

| Wages Aug 12th 1961 | | Aug 19th |
|---|---|---|
| John Steel sen | £10-10 | £10-10 |
| Tom Steel | £8-10 | £8-10 |
| Mrs Steel | £3 | £3 |
| Dave Rutherford | £10- | £10 |
| Doug Imrie | £9-10 | £9-10 |
| John Steel jun | £9-10 | £9-10 |
| Self. | £44 | £15-10. |
| Casual | | £3-10 |
| | £95 | £70 |

| Aug 26th | | Sept 2nd |
|---|---|---|
| John Steel sen | £10-10 | 10-10 |
| Tom Steel | £8-10 | 8-10 |
| Mrs Steel | £3 | 3 |
| Dave Rutherford | £10 | 10 |
| Doug Imrie | £9-10 | 9-10 |
| John Steel jun | £9-10 | 9-10 |
| Casual | £8 | 3 |
| Self. | £19 | 11 |
| | £78 | £65 |

*Wages list, August 1961 (Jim's writing)*

Mr Hogg Berwick Redhouse Farm Cardenden

1965 Nov. To combining 8 ~~acres~~ hrs grain @ £5 per ~~acre~~ hr. £40.

Mr Sandy Black Westfield Farm, Cardenden Paid.

Sept & October 1965 To combining 17 acres @ £3 per acre £51

Mr Robin Baird Cardenbarns Farm Paid

Sept 1965 To combining 34 acres @ £3 per acre £102

Mr John Baird Urquart Farm Gateside

June 1965 14 hrs digging @ 30/- per hr. £21

Aug 1965 8 " " " " " £12

June 26th 1965 2 calves @ £15 each £30

1 calve £8 £8

£41

Mr William Hope Cardenden Paid

To 11 hrs digging @ 30/- per hr. £16"10.

Mr William Melville Kirkland Farm. Ballingry

To account rendered. Paid £24.10

Mr Alex Michie Plumber Cardenden Paid

To 10 hrs digging @ 30/- per hr £15

*List of contracts for combine and digger, 1965 (Joey's writing)*

*In the close at Pitkinny (L to R: Grandad Hugh, Alison, Pamela, Dougie Imrie, and Eddie Tinney)*

*The binder at South Bogside (L to R: Wull Beveridge, Teen Shepherd, and Dunc Rutherford) (© Dan Imrie)*

*Handling bales at Pitkinny Farm (Chrissie Imrie) (© Dan Imrie)*

*Baling at Pitkinny Farm (Robbie Imrie) (© Dan Imrie)*

*Horse and cart decorated for show (with Jim Shepherd) (© Dan Imrie)*

*Piecetime at Pitkinny (L to R: Dougie Imrie, Dave Thomson, and Dunc Rutherford) (© Dan Imrie)*

*Effie Shepherd (daughter of Jim and Teen Shepherd) with show horse (Punch or Jolly) (© Dan Imrie)*

# Chapter 20

"Naw, it's the wife's turn fur the froack the nicht!"

While families like the Steels and the Imries had longstanding connections with Bogside and Pitkinny, there were many other workers who came and went sporadically. They may not have been at the farm long, but their contribution to life there, not only in the work they did but in the colour and humour they added to everyday life, were long remembered by everyone who knew them.

One of the earliest of these characters was Wullie McKeeman, a byreman, who simply turned up one day looking for work. This was before the days of the Steel family and resident byre workers at Bogside, and Jim was in need of someone to relieve him of the milking there after John Imrie had moved on. It was agreed that, as a bachelor, Wullie could live in the bothy at Pitkinny. One of the old cottages there had traditionally served as accommodation for single men working on the farm, but it was in a very dilapidated state and had been completely neglected, so, although we were not yet living at Pitkinny, Joey decided to do what she could to improve it. She scrubbed and cleaned, but it needed more, so she found some wallpaper and, using her formidable decorating skills, she soon brightened up Wullie's new home. The only distemper she could lay her hands on was pink, but she assumed that it wouldn't matter to him that he would look up at a pink ceiling—at least it was much fresher and brighter than before—and Wullie was delighted with his new abode.

Wullie was a cheery soul and a hard worker, but he had two handicaps, the first of which was very unfortunate and beyond his control. He had a speech impediment, a very bad stammer of the type that made it very hard for him to begin to speak. Once he started he could keep going, but the first word was always very slow to come. "Eh ... ah ... eh ... ah ... eh ... ah ..." he would begin repeatedly, and sometimes he would get so frustrated that he would quickly finish by bursting out, "Ah'll tell ye the morn!" His second weakness, for which he was entirely to blame, was for the bottle! He would cycle down to Bowhill on a Saturday morning for his messages, and would as often as not end up in the pub. Doris worked as a dairymaid in those days, and would always get a lift home to Markinch with Dunc on his motorbike when the afternoon milking was done, as he was returning to his family in the Star for Saturday night. If Wullie was more than usually under the weather from his visit to the drinking establishments of Cardenden, he would be late back for the milking, and she would have to hurry him on so that her weekend could start.

Wullie was also a frequent patron of the picture houses, and cowboy films were his favourite genre, so it was perhaps inevitable that he should try to emulate some of his screen heroes. One particular Saturday he came weaving into the close on his bike very much the worse for wear, and urged on by Doris, proceeded to bring in the cattle from the field. What was different that day was that he had equipped himself with a cap gun, which he fired off with great gusto as he rounded up the beasts with much hooting and hollering, as if he was on a cattle drive in the American West!

On days such as this, he would sleep it off in the hay and straw bales in the barn, in preference to going back up to the bothy at Pitkinny. On occasion, he would be there all night and Joey, who helped him with the milking on Sunday mornings, would see him staggering groggily out of the barn, or sometimes would have to wake him in time for the early milking. One morning, when he had obviously overslept, he made the excuse, "Eh … ah … eh … ah … eh … ah … it's the hay mites, eh … ah … eh … ah … eh … ah … they've choaked ma alarm cloack!" Wullie never spoke about his family and for all anyone knew he was alone in the world. Joey felt sorry for him, and would often ask him to come in to the house for his dinner or tea, but he never would, so she would give him food to take up to the bothy. One day she offered him a bit of a cake she had baked. As she prepared to cut it, she asked him, "Dae ye eat a lot, Wullie?" "Eh … ah … eh … ah … eh … ah … naw," he managed. Then, as he watched the knife descend on the cake, he added quickly, "But, eh … ah … eh … ah … ah eat often!"

To everyone's surprise, a brother of Wullie's suddenly appeared at Pitkinny one day. He was very different from Wullie, and everyone suspected that he was not good news. In fact, he seemed to be a bad lot, and it was clear that Wullie was uncomfortable with him around. Joey and Jim were relieved when his brother left, but soon after that Wullie simply disappeared as suddenly as he had come. Although it wasn't unusual for itinerant workers to come and go spontaneously, Jim and Joey were worried about Wullie and reported him missing to the police at Lochore, the nearest police station. Word eventually came that he had been traced, and just after that his parents, who lived somewhere in West Lothian, visited Pitkinny. They were very decent, good-living folk, who thanked Jim and Joey for their concern and for looking after Wullie so well. Everyone at the farm had come to like their son and he was genuinely missed for a time, but it wasn't long before newcomers arrived who proved to be equally colourful and amusing.

These were Wull May and his wife, who moved from a farm in the Kirkcaldy area. Jim had moved their belongings for them to 5 Capeldrae Row, and was surprised at how little they had in the way of possessions. They turned out to be somewhat inadequate in their domestic arrangements, and lived a very chaotic life. After a few days, Dougie asked Wull what he had had for his dinner when they returned for the afternoon's work. The answer was, "Cornflakes and vimto!" As vimto was a fizzy drink, a forerunner to Coca-Cola in popularity in those days, it seemed an odd choice for the main meal of the day! Another day, Wull turned up for work black from head to toe. Their paraffin heater had developed a fault while they slept, and had belched out black oily reek all over their house. There did not seem to have been any attempt to wash off any of the sooty deposits, and Dougie remembered that Wull looked more like a chimney sweep than an orraman!

Both Wull and his wife were very regular cinema-goers. There were two picture houses in Cardenden in those days: the Rex, a smart, quite new art-deco building; and the Goth, an older establishment which had the reputation for being a bit of a flea-pit. (They used to spray Jeyes fluid from a flit-gun between performances, and I have heard it said that any particularly unkempt patrons amongst the children filing in at the door, of whom I am sure there were quite a few, would receive a direct hit of the stuff from the gun as they passed the watchful attendant!) As the programmes changed three times a week, it was possible to go to the pictures every night in the week and see something different each time. Most evenings would find the Mays walking down to one of the cinemas, but Dougie noticed they never went together, but took turn about. "Are ye gaun tae the picters the nicht, Wull?" Dougie asked one day. "Naw, it's the wife's turn fur the froack the nicht," was the reply. It then dawned on Dougie that "the frock" was a shirtwaister style of dress that Wull shared with his wife. No! He was not a cross dresser! He wore it as a shirt, tucked into his trousers, and she wore it, more conventionally, as a dress! They had nothing else to wear and in those days, even they had sufficient self-respect not to be seen out for the evening in their working clothes, so they could not go out together for the evening. Even allowing for the fact that farm workers' wages were always very poor, Wull and his wife were spectacularly feckless!

The social impact of the cinema on the population in the forties and fifties was of course immense, as was evident in the case of Wull May and his wife, whose expenditure on the pictures must have been considerable. Wullie McKeeman "rode the range with his six-gun" when bringing the cows in for milking. Another Hollywood aficionado who worked at Pitkinny was Wull Murdoch, who lived in a cottar hoose at Redhouse Farm with his brother, who was foreman to Huggy Buick there. Wull's favourite film genre was cartoon films and he could be heard before he was seen, imitating perfectly the call of Woody Woodpecker as he went about his work, and when lousing for the day would say, "That's all, folks!" These three men who all shared a love of the movies, as well as the same Christian name, did not stay long at Pitkinny and all moved on to other farms. Thereafter nothing was heard of Wull Murdoch or Wullie McKeeman, but sadly, Wull May was killed in an accident with a hay rake some years later.

Some other casual workers left less happy memories of themselves. A man by the name of McDonald, who briefly lived at South Pitkinny, was slightly hurt during the harvest. Unusually for those days, he threatened to sue Jim, despite the fact that he had only himself to blame for the accident; Jim left him in no doubt he didn't have an (expletive deleted) leg to stand on! Others who must have felt the rough edge of Jim's tongue and the blast of his temper were: a Jim Morgan from Kinglassie, who couped an entire load of barley off a trailer at the corner at Cluny; and Rab Bennet, who got the new Caterpillar tractor well and truly stuck in the one part of the bog fields that had resisted all Jim's attempts to improve its drainage.

One of the houses in Capeldrae Row was designated as a cottar hoose for Bogside and Pitkinny. The others were usually occupied by miners or other employees of the Fife Coal Company, later the NCB, many of whom did casual work at the farms, particularly during the busy times of the hay, grain, and potato harvests. Rab Gilmour lived at number 4; James Mitchell and his son Rab, who fought in (and fortunately survived) the Korean War, were in number 14. Dougie himself moved into number 5 with his new wife Chrissie after Wull May left, before moving up to one of the cottages at Pitkinny.

Another early resident at Capeldrae, Jock Allan, the miner who, with our uncle Bobby Drennan, formed the "demolition squad" in the early days at Pitkinny, later moved to Cardenden with his wife and four children, but continued to work at the farm in addition to his shifts in Bowhill pit. He was a larger-than-life character who worked hard and played hard too. He was known to "go walkabout" at New Year time, when for a few days he would wander from place to place, enjoying the hospitality of his many friends as long as his New Year bottle(s) would last. His poor wife would have to expect him when she saw him. Jock died a young man, at the age of forty-two, of a cerebral haemorrhage. It is tempting to draw the conclusion that this was due to his unhealthy lifestyle, or one could argue that he worked like a Trojan and ate, drank, and was merry because he somehow sensed that his time on this earth was destined to be so short. He was not alone in combining a regular job with extra work at Pitkinny. Brothers Jock and Dave Thomson were bakers with Mason's in the bakehouse near Robertson's garage. They would finish their early morning shift there and come up to Pitkinny, still seeming to be dusted with a fine patina of flour, and do a full day's work, before going home to snatch a few hours' sleep. Then they would rise at 4am, to start all over again.

Jim had never been keen on having youngsters working at the farm, after his less-than-happy experience with the squads of secondary school pupils who used to work at the potato harvest during the tattie holidays in the autumn. He did, however, employ two young men, Tam Wallace in the fifties, and Tony Barnes in the sixties. Tam was a very quiet, simple lad who tried hard to do his best, but needed more guidance and patience than Jim was capable of giving, and must often have been on the receiving end of Jim's anger when he didn't do exactly as required. Joey felt sorry for Tam and tried to make up for Jim's brusque manner in her dealings with him. There was to be one occasion when Tam came into his own and showed remarkable courage and fortitude, and another when he took great pleasure in a very difficult and stressful weekend. The first of these represented the biggest disaster to befall Pitkinny, and the second had the potential to be almost as serious. Tony was a much more able and confident lad who was less of a trial to Jim as he could be counted on to be more resourceful, but occasionally to the point of recklessness. This ability to show initiative represented a different but equally challenging demand on Jim's management skills. It was Tony who was to help Joey to paint the exterior of the house in 1969, a job he undertook with his typical energy and good nature.

In the last few years at Pitkinny, Dougie was helped by Eddie Tinney, and, occasionally, his wife Mary. Eddie was hard working and cheery and enjoyed the many and varied jobs he was set. By then Joey and Jim had five grandchildren: Margaret and John's three daughters, Pamela, Alison and Lynda; and our two sons, Calum and Donald, who were just a toddler and baby respectively. Eddie was fond of wee ones and always took an interest in them. One day at home in Cumnock, Alison was talking about Pitkinny, and she mentioned "the man who helps Dougie." She couldn't remember his name and did her best to describe him: "You know the man whose head is growing up through his hair!" Thus, Alison's childlike logic made sense of Eddie's tonsure-like hairstyle! When Calum was born, Eddie and Mary kindly gave him a black and white toy bear, which immediately became, and remained, Eddie the teddy! Eddie's culinary preference was for what became to us an "Eddie Tinney denner": namely, soup and pudding but no main course.

From time to time Jim would employ, on a casual basis, policemen who were stationed at Lochore. Police pay was relatively poor in those days and, although they were not supposed to have second jobs according to their conditions of service with the police, this did not deter them from taking on additional work on the farm, as it fitted in with their shift patterns. There was even a Sergeant Grey who was prepared to take the risk, and Jim certainly didn't worry about bending the rules. Chick Mitchell, a constable at Lochore, remembered his first experience of working with Jim during a potato harvest. He and his wife were about to have their first baby and they needed extra cash, but his moonlighting almost came to an end as soon as it started. The tattie field they were harvesting ran alongside the loan, and as Jim turned the digger at the end-rig he saw a police car driving in. He was horrified to recognise the inspector from Lochore getting out and walking towards the field gate. Jim didn't let on and proceeded back along the drills until he was within earshot of Chick. "Get doon under the trailer, Chick, yer boss is here," and kept going. The inspector stopped and spoke to the other lifters as Jim worked his way, apparently unaware of his presence, to the end of the drill, turned, and came back, feigning surprise to see the inspector, while Chick crouched under the trailer full of potatoes. His superior officer apologised to Jim for disturbing him, explaining that as he had been passing, he thought he would call in to check Jim's stock control book which had to be kept up to date. He said that it could wait until another day, which was probably a relief to Jim as paper work was never his strong point, and Jim blithely chatted away to him while the others welcomed this unscheduled break in the proceedings. They casually gathered round the trailer, ostensibly to have a breather, but in reality to make sure that Chick wouldn't be seen. Jim ended the encounter with the inspector by giving him a creel full of potatoes, reassuring him that he could return the empty creel when he came to check the stock book.

The working day came to a slightly premature end when the tattie digger broke down, and Chick got involved in the business of trying to repair it. When teatime arrived, he was asked in to the kitchen for his meal and then he and Jim worked well into the night, eventually succeeding in mending the digger, ready for the next day's work. Chick was on duty for the rest of that week, and came home on the Saturday afternoon to find that Jim had delivered his wage packet to his wife. When he opened it he found £45—much more than he had reckoned on. Thinking Jim had made a mistake, he phoned him, only to be told that the pay was correct. He had been paid not only for the hours he had spent lifting tatties, but for his work as a mechanic, which was "above and beyond the call of duty." Jim went on to suggest that the money might help to buy a pram, which was exactly what it was used for! Chick never forgot Jim's generosity, not only in terms of the wages he paid, but for the way he and Joey made Chick feel that, on the strength of a few days' work, he was "part of the team."

That team included many other casual but skilled workers in various capacities. There was John Boyle, the Irishman who drained, ditched, and fenced during his annual stay in the district; Bill Smith, and Aund Doig, who were steel erectors and blacksmiths, normally employed by Barnett Morton in Kirkcaldy. They were responsible for building the new grain drier and the new silage shed, along with Lowr Webster from Markinch, a consummate bricklayer. Charlie Butler was a mechanic from Milnathort. Adam Neilson and his son young Adam installed the new three-phase electricity required for the enlarged grain-drying operation and, incidentally, in the future helped Jim out with his electricity supply in other slightly less-official ways to be explained later! In earlier days, Bob Beckett the electrician, and Tammy Barbour the joiner and undertaker (happily in the former capacity!), both from Cardenden, would make their mark on the steading in their different ways. Jim once had a particularly grisly experience in Tammy's workshop when he arrived to pick up some lengths of timber from him. Never known for keeping to agreed deadlines, Tammy had promised faithfully to have the order ready for Jim by lunchtime that day. However, when Jim arrived to collect the wood, there was no sign of Tammy, except, that is, for two of his fingers lying in a pool of blood on the bench beside the circular saw. Poor Tammy was in the hospital, but these were the days before microsurgery, of course, so he had to do without those two digits for the rest of his life. Our Uncle James, Joey's youngest brother, who served his time as a mechanic with Farm Mechanisation at Ladybank and later Cupar, and Grandad Hugh, a paper mill engineer who could turn his hand to anything mechanical, also lent their skills and hard work from time to time.

Before and after his marriage to Margaret, my brother-in-law John French would spend many weekends and holiday times at Pitkinny. He had had no previous experience of farm work, but he threw himself into all the various jobs around the place with great enthusiasm. He soon came to realise that Jim's bark was worse than his bite, but initially was bemused and exasperated by his irascible nature and volatile temper, and by the colourful terms in which he gave vent to these aspects of his character. As with other workers, Jim assumed that John would be able to fulfil any role, and would consequently give him very daunting tasks. One day he told him to drive a lorry load of grain to Kilmarnock, warning him to be careful to check that the little trap door at the back of the lorry was kept locked. It had been known for the "street urchins" in Glasgow to deftly open one while a lorry was stopped at traffic lights. Once open, there was no way of closing it, and the full load of grain would pour onto the street!

Jim often drove grain to buyers in the west, but only once did he have to return by public transport, an unusual event for Jim, who for many years had never frequented buses, trains, or taxis. On this occasion, for some reason, it was impossible for his lorry to be unloaded and he had to leave it at the depot. Someone gave him a lift into the centre of Glasgow and, in the rush hour, he had to find his way to Queen Street Station and negotiate his way home by train. His account of that journey and the encounters with his fellow passengers would have made a cat laugh, and I am sure they must have found him a colourful and highly unusual addition to their homeward commute. When he at last got as far as Dunfermline station, he jumped into a waiting taxi and gave Margaret and John's address, but was scandalised when the ride lasted only two minutes and cost him ten shillings. They lived only a stone's throw from the station! His journey home to Pitkinny was later completed in the much more familiar and, to his mind, civilised mode of transport: John's car! Only many years later would Jim become familiar with bus and train travel, when he and Joey lived at Cadham from 1988, when they would make use of the pensioners' travel concessions.

John was always of great value to Jim as a driver after the breathalyser made it impossible to risk driving with more than a very little alcohol in your system. So journeys like the one home from Kelso Highland Show were no longer an option. Having said that, I am sure that Jim did take risks on many occasions, driving himself home from markets and curling matches, but was very fortunate to get away with it! During a visit to Stirling market, as he and John repaired to the bar at the end of the afternoon's business, John unusually succumbed to temptation and had a few drinks—too many, it soon became obvious, for him to be able to drive. Jim had bought cattle that day, and they were to be delivered to Pitkinny by one of Kinnear's floats. Fortunately, the driver was still around and a plan was hatched that one of his pals, who was returning to Fife with an empty float, would transport Jim and John—and Jim's car—safely home. So two floats arrived at the farm, one to the reid where the cattle were to be housed and the other round the back to the stackyard where the car and its two occupants were surreptitiously unloaded. Joey assumed that Jim had had a spending spree when she saw two floats driving into the close, and was even more surprised when he and John suddenly arrived at the back door when she hadn't heard the car drive up. Whether she suspected their ploy or remained in ignorance they would never know, but John did his best to appear completely sober, while Jim's condition was no different from what she had come to expect!

Weekends would often find family members and friends visiting, sometimes by invitation, but usually spontaneously. All were gladly welcomed by Joey, who subscribed to the adage, "the more the merrier," and was never fazed by having to cater for extra mouths. Work, at busy times especially, went on as long as the daylight and the weather lasted. I can remember summer days that would end with impromptu football games in the close as everyone loused for the day. "The highest the day!" I would hear Grandad Hugh call, as Jim belted the ball high up into the clear but rapidly fading light of a summer evening sky. Then it was into the kitchen, where Joey would happily and seemingly effortlessly feed and water everyone before Jim would run visitors home, almost certainly finding his way to the pub, while we were chased off to bed.

Another category of visitor to the farm was that of the commercial traveller. Over the years some became familiar and weel-kent faces, who were more of a welcome diversion than a nuisance. Others less well-known were at worst given short shrift by Jim and, to a lesser extent, Joey, or at best would be let down more or less gently as we became adept at telling (hopefully) white lies about Jim's whereabouts. "No, sorry, I don't know where Mr Rutherford is," as Dad sat at the table eating his dinner, or "Sorry, we haven't seen him since dinnertime," as he stood behind the door! It was easier to carry off these deceptions on the phone, of course, but then there were the times when you got rid of someone only to discover that Jim wanted to see them after all! This happened one day as there was a knock at the back door just as Jim was reading the *Courier* and enjoying his after-dinner cup of coffee. "I don't care who it is, just get rid of them," he commanded Joey. "No. I've no idea where he is. He could be anywhere," she rebuffed the hapless traveller. "Well, I'll just have a wee walk around and see if I can see him," came the reply, and he went off into the big shed. When Jim learned who the man was, he wailed, "But I really needed to see him!" As Joey pointed out that she was able to do most things, but reading minds wasn't one of them, he went skulking out of the front door, through the front garden, past the garage, into the end reid and, striding down into the big shed, came across the traveller who was greeted like a long-lost friend. "Oh, hello, 'So and so'," he began, "just the man I've been looking for," as if butter wouldn't melt in his mouth! Another time, as he was in the big shed, Jim heard the familiar litany from Joey at the back door, "You'll just have to look around the place, I don't know where he might be!" Having had a quick peek to establish that this was one of the unwelcome, nuisance-type of travellers, he nipped down into the grain pit, a seven–foot-deep hole in the floor, on this day shielded from view by a tractor and trailer. As he stood there on tiptoe, he could see the shoes of the unwanted caller as he walked past. Jim admitted later that he felt like a child playing hide-and-seek, and had great difficulty stopping himself from laughing out loud as he watched the to-ing and fro-ing of the disembodied feet and ankles! He stayed in hiding until he heard the disappointed salesman get in his car and drive off.

A friendlier reception awaited those travellers of long-standing acquaintance with whom Jim did business on a regular basis. Jim Torrance, a very refined and gentlemanly soul who represented Elder's the grain merchant, visited Pitkinny for many years. David Thomson of Bibby's feed merchants had the added attraction of being a director with Dunfermline Athletic Football team, and was always a good contact for match tickets. In 1961 when the "Pars" won the Scottish Cup, he brought it with him one day to show Jim, and I am sure they shared a dram from it in the kitchen. Adam Matthew, who (I think) may have been a representative of Kilgour, the maltsters in Kirkcaldy, also had a football connection as he lived not far from Stark's Park, the Raith Rovers' ground in Kirkcaldy, and Jim would park his car in his drive on big match days when the team (successful in those days) got big crowds. I, unwittingly, was the cause of some offence to Adam one day. As I was walking home from school, he stopped on his way to the farm and offered me a lift. "No thank you," I politely refused, and kept on walking. He caught up with me and again stopped. "Come on Anne, you know me. Let me take you home and save you the walk." "No thank you," I said, more loudly this time. "Well, let me take your schoolbag home for you." "No thank you," I repeated even more loudly, "I can carry my own bag." So he drove on and when he met Joey at Pitkinny, he told her what had happened. "Well, Adam, I have told Anne that she is never to get into a car with anyone at all." "But it's me!" he burst out, "Surely you know she would be perfectly safe with me." "Yes I know that, Adam, but she is doing the right thing." Joey sensed that Adam didn't understand her reasons for being so firm about her rule, but she stuck to her guns nevertheless, and that was the end of the matter. She felt more than vindicated some time later when another traveller, who had occasionally been to Pitkinny, but had transferred to a different area, was convicted of indecent exposure towards young girls. She wondered if Adam heard about that and made the connection!

These men who made their living doing business with farmers always seemed to be very well "suited and booted," unlike most of their potential customers, who were dressed in less elegant but very practical "wurkin' claes." They were also very personable and well spoken, typical of what was considered correct business dress and manners for those days. There was another man who was almost dapper in his appearance. I cannot recall his name or his firm, but he would come to Pitkinny less frequently, perhaps once a year or less. He lived in the Abbotshall Hotel in Kirkcaldy while he did business in Fife, but we had really no idea where he came from or, in fact, anything about him. He would arrive in time for a "fly cup" in the afternoon and conduct his business with Jim. Then Joey would invite him to stay for his tea. Thereafter he would spend much of the evening with us, before returning to the hotel later. Joey felt sorry for him, living in a hotel, and he seemed to enjoy spending time in a family atmosphere. He was a very polite, quietly spoken, and interesting man, and although on the face of it he was very different from Jim, they got on very well. The last time he appeared at the farm, probably around 1968, he told us he was retiring. He had brought a camera with him, and took photographs of the farm in the afternoon and asked if he might take a snap of us in the kitchen that evening. When he left later, we knew we would never see him again. He was definitely "a ship that passed in the night," but we never forgot him. It would be nice to think that he had some photographs of the people at Pitkinny where he always had a welcome, and some hospitality and company to warm and brighten what must have been a lonely life.

Life at Pitkinny was in no sense any kind of rural idyll. The farm was a business and a means of making a living. Jim had achieved what he had set out to do. He was his own boss within the terms of his tenancy. Joey had more than lived up to her decision to commit her life to her husband and family. Our way of life was very far removed from the stereotypical image of traditional farm life as imagined by those who have never lived it. As I grew up I was not always content with my lot, longing as I did to be like everyone else, to live in the town. I wished that Dad could be better tempered, that he didn't forget to come home from the pub or the market or the curling so often, or that when he did Mum could tolerate the situation better. I wished I didn't have to work so hard or that I could have more pocket money, and that I could have more attention. Later, as an adult I came to realise that much of this feeling was simply part of being a teenager, and that they were not just because I lived at Pitkinny. Had I been someone else, somewhere else, I would have had very similar complaints about other aspects of my life. At that time, there was no understanding that young people growing up are victims of their hormones as much as anything else, and even if there had been, I am certain that neither Joey nor Jim would have accepted that as in any way an excuse for laziness or self-indulgence. Looking back now, I can see that the contact we had with so many people of differing backgrounds, experience, and aspirations gave us the ability to appreciate the value of an individual. It helped us to be aware that not everyone starts off with the same advantages in life, and to become reasonably good judges of character.

This poem, written by my husband Bill on the occasion of Mum and Dad's retirement, sums up the way Bogside and Pitkinny were places of work and pleasure for so many different people over a period of thirty-five years. Workers, family, friends, and travellers all no doubt carried their own memories of the place and its people, and in turn all of them enriched our lives and took their place in our memories of those years.

## Pitkinny

The first time I came to Pitkinny, the finest sight I saw,
A sturdy farmhouse and buildings beneath the hill they call Harelaw,
The road was long and rough, beside fields of beast and corn,
The house was white and gleaming and the welcome there was warm.

Pitkinny's road has been travelled by monks from yesteryear,
By weary feet and by tractors and folk they held dear,
By farmer and by merchant, from far and near they came,
And when they left they never forgot the name of the Rutherfords' hame.

In the finest days of autumn, I remember the sunset nights,
Then the harvest moon shone over the barley fields full ripe,
The cattle at Bogside, the sheep up on the 'Law,
James Rutherford, his dog and twa cats lost among them a'.

As market days were wearing late, as Burns used to say,
And so it was at Thornton toun upon a Monday,
The bustle of the ringside as the cattle were quickly sold,
Then a dram or two or three or mair, and anither for the road!

My last days at Pitkinny were wet with the end of winter's cauld,
The fields were green and puddled grey, and their time was getting auld,
The roup, it was like a market day with folk from farms around,
And a lifetime's work then passed away as the auctioneer's stick came down.

The road was long and rough, beside fields of beasts and corn,
The house was white and gleaming and the welcome there was warm,
I'm proud to say that I've been there, with many I surely came,
And when we left we never forgot the name of the Rutherfords' hame.

Bill Ewing
May 1976

# Chapter 21

"Aye, you get a tawse, an' dinnae tak ony nonsense!"

In an earlier chapter, I described how Lena Smith, as a young woman, cycled daily from Lochgelly to Pitkinny and back, with a hard day's work in between. Similarly, I can recall the innumerable times I walked or cycled home. While Margaret and I were pupils at Auchterderran School, we caught the school bus, which dropped us off at the end of the loan, but after I went to Beath High School in Cowdenbeath at the age of twelve, the school bus from there only took me as far as Auchterderran. From there it was Shanks's pony to Pitkinny (a distance of about two miles) in the months of daylight, with a lift from Mum or Dad only in the darkest weeks of the winter. The route is imprinted on my memory: The first part took me past the church on the right, with its manse on the left, then past Auchterderran School to my right.

One day I had an early lesson in how socially divisive selective education was. I was the only pupil from my primary seven class who passed the qualifying (eleven-plus) exam in the top stream, which meant I went on to senior secondary education at Beath. Everyone else went to the secondary department at Auchterderran, although a few—namely Amilda Crichton, James Glancy, and David Chalmers—transferred to Beath at the end of their first year. I would like to think that this was, at best, a good example of flexibility in the system, but rather suspect it was, at worst, the result of poor teaching on the part of our primary seven teacher, who shall remain nameless. One day, shortly after the start of my first term at Beath, as I passed the gate of Auchterderran School, I met some of my former primary seven classmates as they were leaving the school. I was forestalled in my intention to stop and speak to them by their chanting this little ditty:

> "If you want to learn knowledge, go to Auchterderran College,
> If you want to learn cheek, go to Beath for a week."

It was clearly intended for me, and equally obvious that my erstwhile companions had no wish to talk to me. I was really upset about this and felt, perhaps for the first time, but certainly not the last, the impact of an awareness of social dislocation, which set me apart from my peers. As I walked on up Woodend Brae, I felt rather humiliated and not a little hurt by this hard lesson. I now realise that what had happened was that one of my corners had been firmly knocked off, an experience which was to be repeated many times as I grew up. I had left behind the safe and sheltered waters of primary school and was now cast adrift on the rougher seas of secondary education and beyond.

Walking up to Woodend took me past the Craigs on the right and the smiddy and Mrs Watt's wee shop on the left, to the top of the brae. There the main road turned sharp right to Kinglassie, but I continued on down to the last of the houses on the left and the old men's shelter on the site of grumpy old Skinner's shop. From here the road and footpath were sheltered from the elements by the trees of "the strip," until, on reaching the entrance to Red House Farm, I turned west into the sudden onslaught of the prevailing west wind. A couple of hundred yards further on, I turned right at the cottar hooses for Red House, and on up Westfield Brae. At its summit, a loan to the right led into Westfield Row, cottage, and farm. Turning left, it was only a hundred yards to the beginning of our loan, which continued west, while the main road took a right angle down Bogside Brae to our old home, the farm of the same name.

I once counted the steps it took me from this point to Pitkinny—1,457 in all—along the untarred surface of Torres Loan. It was dusty in summer and muddy in winter, dotted with potholes of varying size, shape, and depth, all filled with khaki-coloured rainwater in wet weather, and ice-covered on the coldest winter days, when they presented a welcome diversion as we cracked their hard, glassy surface with our heels. Sometimes, the loan would be covered with hard-packed snow and would form an almost continuous slide for most of its length. I remember on such days late in the winter when the air was filled with the sharp acrid smell of dung, as the byres and reids were mucked out and the resulting manure driven out to the fields in preparation for the ploughing and sowing which would come later.

Halfway along the loan there were two big sycamore trees, known locally as the "coortin' trees." It was only when I was much older that I understood the significance of this, but whether it was acquired because their stance, side by side, heads touching each other, resembled a courting couple, or because it was a favourite spot for local lovers, we will never know. Walking in the loan, as I looked to the left, to the southeast I could see the Black Woods and the moss—an inaccessible haunt, we always believed, of the foxes who occasionally wreaked havoc on Joey's hens. To the right, and on the distant ridge directly northwards, stood Kinninmonth Farm, while much nearer to the northwest, our white farmhouse, my ultimate objective, beckoned me on. While I turned right at the cottar hooses and up past the old barn and cottages (now in use as henhouses) to the farm, Torres Loan continued westwards over Harelaw and on to Lochore and Ballingry. This was the route taken in antiquity by the "bliddy-fitted" monks as they would wend their weary way home to their island monastery of St Serf's in Loch Leven.

I was a reluctant walker when I was very young, as Margaret would testify, and she would have to put up with my attempts at blackmail. "If you don't carry my schoolbag, I'm not going another step!" On hot, dusty afternoons, I would complain, "I wish a bottle of lemonade and a tumbler would drop from the sky!" Not content with the fizzy stuff, of which I was so fond, I had to get a glass as well! There was, however, some natural refreshment to be had. Roadside soorocks, or young shoots of wild sorrel, helped to quench our thirst a little, while in late summer and early autumn wild raspberries and brambles had the most wonderful sharp-sweet tongue-tingling effect. One autumn, when the two older Thomson girls were walking home from Sunday school, dressed in their Sunday best, Vida resplendent in a new off-white coat made of oatmeal tweed, they stopped to partake of some of the prolific bramble crop at the top of Westfield Brae. Mindful of her mother's warnings about looking after her new coat and not getting dirty, she declined to eat the brambles there and then, preferring to keep them for later. So, where else could she carry them, but in her coat pockets? She arrived home, perfectly clean, but with two rapidly spreading purple patches adorning her otherwise immaculate new coat. In due course, after her mother had recovered sufficiently from the shock, and Vida from the inevitable retribution, the coat in question was dyed navy-blue and relegated to duty as a school coat.

Other familiar plants had particular uses. Docken leaves were pressed into service for the relief of nettle stings. We would crush the dark green leaves and spit on them before rubbing them onto the painful raised white spots. You picked dandelions at your peril, as playmates would chant, "pee-the-bed, pee-the-bed," in case this would result in a "wee accident" in bed the following night. The diuretic property of these little yellow flowers was unknown to us, but presumably must have been the origin of the warning. The dandelion leaves were always a favourite snack for our pet rabbit, but obviously our failure to pick them often enough sealed his fate at Joey's hands. As so often happens with children, once the novelty of a pet begins to wear off, it is left to the mother of the family to see to its needs, and the feeding and cleaning out of the rabbit was becoming yet another task Mum had to find time for. She warned us that if we didn't pull our weight in that department, she would find a new home for the wee black and white creature. We should have known that Joey did not make idle threats, and sure enough one day he simply disappeared! When we reacted with dismay, she had no sympathy for us, but told us that our pet had been given away to some children who would really look after him. Frank and Elizabeth Page were his new owners, so we would see him in his hutch in their garden from time to time. Whether they were any more diligent in looking after him, I don't know, but he was a reminder that we should have known better than disregard our mother's warning.

A liking for butter was determined by holding a buttercup closely under the chin. The telltale yellow reflection on the skin was a sure sign, and it didn't seem to occur to us that there was never an occasion when the subject of the experiment was found not to like butter. The loan was punctuated by whin or gorse and dog-rose bushes, which bloomed bright yellow in spring and produced the palest of lilac and pink flowers in summer respectively. As a harbinger of autumn these would give way to the vibrant red of their hips which were actually harvested commercially by a company called Delrosa to produce rose-hip syrup, a valuable source of vitamin C. This was recommended and indeed supplied free along with cod liver oil and orange juice for young children by the recently-founded National Health Service from the late forties. For a time, schools co-operated in the collection of these little red berries, as school children were paid threepence (just over 1p of today's money!) per pound for the topped and tailed hips. It was hard-earned pocket money, as it took a long time to gather the hips in sufficient quantity, and we all suffered from painful fingertips after howking out their husks with our nails. Having carried our bounty to school, the shiny red hips, burgeoning (it seemed) with goodness, were weighed and poured into all the wastepaper baskets in the school to await collection, as Margaret and I divided up our meagre payment. The harvest was then transported to the processing plant, where it was turned into bottles of the delicious sweet, sticky dark red syrup we all loved. No doubt we benefited from the vitamin C, but probably at the expense of our dental health, as I am sure that a dangerous amount of sugar was added in the process.

Another infrequent and fleetingly tasted unique flavour was that of the wild strawberries that grew on the railway embankment in Markinch. Many years later I enjoyed a repeat of this sensation when my family gathered the same little fruits in the garden of our Swedish friends' summerhouse. There the custom is to thread the strawberries on to a grass stalk and nibble them from there. This unusual and charming way of eating them only added to my delight, as their incomparable taste transported me back in an instant to my childhood.

On another occasion, as had happened with poor Vida Thomson, it was our mother's turn to suffer at our hands, and we in turn at her chastisement of us. There had been heavy snowfalls for several days, and the deep snowdrifts on the loan verges were too much of a temptation. Having waded through the lovely deep snow most of the way in the loan, we arrived home with our wellies full of snow and our hand-knitted welly socks saturated. We were quite shocked by what we felt to be an unjustifiably violent reaction on Joey's part to what seemed to be the result of harmless fun on ours. What I failed to appreciate then, but did only too well years later when I became a mother myself, was the awful struggle she must have had in the absence of central heating or a clothes drier, and with a coal fire the only source of heat in the house, to dry out our footwear in time for the next morning.

Our primary school days at Auchterderran were, for the most part, happy ones. I remember my first day quite clearly. As the infant mistress, Miss Oliphant (or "Elephant," as some of her young charges would innocently call her!) was enrolling the new entrants, we were looked after that first day by Miss Christie, who normally had charge of primary three. She was extremely formidable, despite her very small stature, and when a wee boy sitting beside me started to wail, she, clearly fearing the start of an epidemic, fixed me with her steely glare and announced loudly, "Now, *you're* not going to cry too, *are* you Anne?" I wouldn't have dared as, young though I was, I realised she was not a woman to be contradicted. I was to live to regret forgetting that fact, as I suffered at her hands a couple of years later. However, after that first day, I was to find school an enjoyable and stimulating experience, except for an occasional trauma, which is unavoidable for most children.

An early one of these came at my first school Christmas party. As farm children, we could not go home for lunch, of course, so had to arrive dressed in our glad rags, such as they were, first thing in the morning, whereas the children who lived near enough the school got changed at lunch time. This was the first time I experienced the "oohing and aahing" in the playground as we inspected the party wear of each of the girls in my class as they returned to school for the afternoon party. Somehow I knew that, even if I had had the fanciest party dress in the world, I would never enjoy the opportunity to make an entrance like that. Arriving dressed for the party early in the morning in some way lacked the impact that was guaranteed by the anticipation that had built up by the middle of the day. This, added to the fact that Joey never bought us frivolous party frocks, favouring instead well-tailored, serviceable, homemade garments that could be worn for occasions other than school parties, perhaps helped to account for the fact that, apart from a brief period as a teenager, I never really developed much of an interest in fashion! There was one exception to our mother's general rule that I remember. She made us lovely lemon-colored organdie party dresses for the wedding of Dad's cousin, Peggy Leslie and, for the only time I remember, did our hair in ringlets instead of the customary, sensible plaits. Another memorable feature of that wedding was that Peggy's elder sister Joey had to wear a black armband on the sleeve of her bridesmaid's dress. This was a very old tradition, which I am happy to say has long since died out. I presume it was meant to convey the fact that if you had still not married by the time your younger sister became a bride, then you were well and truly considered to be on the shelf, and correspondingly should wear some indication of being in mourning! How cruel and insensitive!

Refreshments at the Christmas party included a cup of tea, and we were required to bring a cup and saucer from home. I insisted on having one from Joey's limited supply of china. While it was not her best, it was definitely "guid cheenie," and the worst possible disaster happened when I dropped and broke it. I was inconsolable and still sobbing incoherently when I arrived at Mrs (Nurse) McMillan's door. As she lived in one of the roadmen's houses near the school, and my infant class in the first term finished earlier than Margaret's age group, I used to go to her to wait until it was time for the school bus. She did her best to reassure me that one broken cup was not the end of the world, and that my mother would understand that accidents do happen from time to time, but I was not convinced. I somehow sensed that Mum did not have many special things, as gracious living was not something that was on the agenda of our busy farm life, and was worried that Joey would be bereft at the loss of her pretty cup. Needless to say, little was made of the episode and it was soon forgotten, but my reaction to the wee accident was symptomatic of my tendency to anticipate and over-react, because my imagination led me to attribute feelings and reactions to other people that, in the event, they never had. Mum would say I was "afraid of the snow that would never come on," and this hypersensitivity was to cause me some unhappiness in the future. Only much later did I begin to develop a protective layer of thicker skin, but it was a long time coming!

In those days, school discipline was very strict, even for young children. When I was seven, and in Miss Christie's primary three class, we had to do our sums every morning with chalk on little individual blackboards. One morning, she found me drawing a picture on mine, before I had finished my arithmetic tasks. I was made to stand in front of the class and was given one whack on the hand with the tawse. This instrument of corporal punishment was a leather strap, about eighteen inches in length, split into two or sometimes three tongues at the business end. While not quite in the cat-o'-nine-tails league, the principle was the same! I am sure that Miss Christie, a tiny little woman, was not all that much bigger than I was at that time, but she packed a mighty wallop, and I can clearly recall the physical pain that was the result. But the stinging and throbbing sensation in my hand was as nothing compared with the bitter humiliation and degradation of being punished like that in front of the class. It was an experience I would repeat only once or twice in my future school career, but never again would it cause me the same degree of hurt.

The tawse were manufactured exclusively by a firm in Lochgelly by the name of George W. Dick and Sons from the early part of the twentieth century. They were saddlers and leather workers who had this lucrative sideline which they exported all over Scotland and beyond, so much so that their belts were known as "Lochgellies" in some parts of the country. Two thousand of them were produced by John Dick, the grandson of the founder of the firm, in 1950. No self-respecting Scottish teacher who claimed to be any kind of disciplinarian would have been without their tawse, and although corporal punishment in Scottish schools would be abolished in the early eighties, it was still in vogue when I qualified as a teacher. When I returned from Sweden and began teaching in Auchmuty High School in Glenrothes in 1970, I was recommended to equip myself with one. As I was living at Pitkinny for that year just before my marriage, and I had not passed my driving test, Jim or Joey would pick me up at the bus stop at Woodend. One afternoon we went straight up to Lochgelly, as Jim had to collect a new belt for the tattie dresser from Dick's. I took the opportunity to buy a tawse at the same time, encouraged by Jim, "Aye, you get a tawse and dinnae tak ony nonsense aff thae Glenrothes bairns!" The belt, stamped with a large "H" to denote its weight, was duly purchased, and later that evening my niece Pamela, who was only about five, was playing with it. "Come on, Grandad, put your hand out!" she commanded. Jim indulgently agreed and held out his hand. Pamela was a sturdy wee girl, and she hit him surprisingly hard. The room echoed to the sharp smack of leather as the tawse made contact and Jim yelped with pain. As he muttered a few oaths and tucked his reddened palm under his oxter, he warned me, "Ye canna dae that tae thae bairns, ye'll hurt them!" I had to conclude that, either he had forgotten how painful a stroke of the tawse could be, or he was becoming soft in his middle years!

It is to my shame that I have to admit to using the belt once or twice on the most recalcitrant of the big boys at Auchmuty, as I struggled to establish my authority with some of the most difficult third-year classes. It was not an experience that I enjoyed, and in our much more liberal and politically correct educational environment nearly forty years later, I feel it is necessary to apologise for resorting to the use of the belt. However, in a time that has seen evidence of serious indiscipline in many of our schools, it would seem that something needs to be done to redress the balance and introduce some kind of meaningful and effective strategy to prevent this general trend from impeding the education of the children who *do* know how to behave. I am reminded of how the threat of the belt was usually enough of a deterrent for most youngsters. One boy in a second-year class at Auchmuty was proving to be a "wee pest," so I kept him behind one afternoon. I produced the tawse and laid it on the desk. I asked him if he knew what it was, and he replied, "Aye Miss," with a touch of bravado that belied the shake in his voice. I pointed to the 'H' and asked him what he thought it stood for. After a moment's consideration, he ventured, "'Hurts', Miss?" I told him he was quite right, and that if I ever had to use it, it certainly would. That was enough. He was never any more trouble after that

While my attitude to physical punishment was somewhat equivocal as a teacher, and the memories of my first acquaintance with the tawse remained painfully with me, my worst experience of chastisement at school was undoubtedly one that came towards the end of my time in primary school. The top junior classes at Auchterderran benefited from some specialist subject teachers in the secondary department. So, twice a week, we would be marched through the gap in the wall that separated us from the "big school" to have music and art lessons. While Mrs Agnew the music teacher was a genial, if flamboyantly dramatic soul, Mr Pryde the art teacher was altogether more intimidating, and seemed to have very little time for younger pupils. It was only rarely that I found myself in the same class as Joyce Steel, as she was a year younger than I, but on this occasion our classes were together in Mr Pryde's room. Looking back, I realise that he may have been prevailed upon to have two classes at the same time, and this may have made him even more than usually annoyed. For some reason, he left us unattended for a time, and while he was out of the room, some of the boys had been capering and throwing wet paint rags around the room. When Mr Pryde returned, he read the riot act with the class, and the remainder of the art lesson passed in stony silence. As usual, Joyce and I had to ask out of class early to return to our own room to collect our things in time for the school bus, and I was aware of being very nervous of the teacher's reaction to this request. He reluctantly let us go, but instructed us to return to see him first thing the next morning.

I didn't say a thing about this situation at home that evening, but spent a very uncomfortable night. I was dreading what I suspected would be an unpleasant interview, as Joyce and I made our way, almost visibly shaking in our shoes, over to the big school and knocked on the door of the art room. What followed was certainly the most frightening experience I ever had at school. Mr Pryde towered over us in a very threatening posture as he bellowed, "If you ever misbehave in my class again," he promised, "I will horsewhip you to within an inch of your lives!" After much further shouting and waving his arms about, none of which registered with me, he dismissed us, and we made our way back to our class. I was literally trembling with fear, and spent the rest of the day in a state of terror. I didn't actually know what a horse whip was, but had enough imagination to understand that it would make the tawse look like a liquorice lace. I was too terrified even to feel the injustice of the situation: that we had not been involved in the misbehaviour that went on in the class that day. Still, not a word of this passed my lips at home. I am not quite sure why I did not want my parents to know anything about it, but it was Mrs Steel who let the cat out of the bag. Joyce had told her what had happened, and she sought Joey's opinion on the matter. Then the floodgates opened, and I remember the tremendous relief I felt at being able to share my fears, the greatest of which was that I would have to go into that art class again soon.

The general feeling amongst parents in those days was that education was the business of the teachers, and by and large schools did not encourage parental involvement in their children's education beyond the occasional parents' day. This was therefore the one and only time I knew of my parents making spontaneous contact with the school. The head teacher Mr Fraser took their complaint seriously, and Mr Pryde had to apologise to my parents for his intemperate use of language. Then I felt a real sense of injustice: the apology, when it came, was not made to Joyce and me, the innocent victims of his needlessly cruel treatment. This was a clear case of using a "sledgehammer to crack a nut." An old-fashioned look from the art teacher, or any other authority figure was enough to discipline me if I needed it in those days. I am sure that was true also of the majority of the children at school then. Most of us were brought up to respect authority, and there was a general standard of behaviour that was adhered to by most people, and a code of discipline in most homes, which guaranteed good conduct by children at school. So the fraught issue of poor discipline in our educational establishments today, which leads many people to bemoan the passing of the tawse, has more to do with the lack of such a standard in the family context, than with the absence of the sanction of corporal punishment in schools.

Thankfully, these unhappy incidents were very much the exception, and generally my years at Auchterderran School were happy and fulfilling ones. I was very lucky to have an older sister like Margaret, whom I could always count on to come to my aid if I landed in hot water. She was more than able to stick up for me, and no bully would risk tangling with her. I loved school and relished all the learning I did during my seven years there. I have many pleasing memories of that time, but one particular day stands out as an example of the general sense of contentment I had for most of my school days. It had become the custom for the National Coal Board, our landlords, to distribute Christmas trees to their various tenants. One day just before the Christmas holidays, when I was about nine years old, I remember seeing, as I stood by the playground railings at lunch time, an NCB lorry drive up past the school, laden with Christmas trees. I couldn't wait to get home, hoping against hope that one of those trees had been destined for Pitkinny. And there it was! Propped up against the back porch, the realisation of my dearest wish. Margaret and I soon had it firmly planted in a pail of sand, which was duly covered in red crêpe paper, festooned in turn by its customary red bow! After tea we set to and decorated it with our carefully-garnered collection of glass baubles, paper chains, and little Chinese paper lanterns. As the tree took on its festive dress in the window of the big room, we enjoyed the first BBC television adaptation of *David Copperfield*. Then it suddenly came to me that it was a Friday night, and the realisation that we could stay up later than usual was the icing on the cake. The sense of utter and complete contentment that I felt at that moment is as clear to me now as then. It was the perfect end to the perfect day!

When I left primary school alone out of my class, to transfer to Beath High School, I was made very much aware of the fact that I would now become a "wee fish in a big pool." I was cautioned by my parents that while I had always been clever in primary school, I could not necessarily expect the same to be true at the high school. I would now be one of many clever pupils, many of whom would be better than I was. It certainly signified an enormous change in my life, and I can remember how nervous I was on that first day. Resplendent in a brand new school uniform, every item too big for me (bought for my growth, of course, in typical thrifty fashion), I felt a huge lump in my throat, made worse by the constricting effect of the unfamiliar school tie. I stood with what seemed like hundreds of other new girls and boys in the hall of the high school as we were allocated to our new class and given a timetable for the first time, with so many subjects, each one with a new teacher. They all seemed so fierce and forbidding in their voluminous black gowns, and it was all so different from the couthy comfort of my old school peopled with familiar and friendly weel-kent faces. But within a few days, I had begun to make friends, some, but sadly not all of whom I still have to this day, and soon started to enjoy my new environment.

I found the challenge of all the new subjects stimulating, and soon found that most of the teachers became less formidable with closer acquaintance. As I found my feet socially in my new surroundings, I gradually got over the fear that everyone would be cleverer than me and was gratified to discover that I could more than hold by own academically. That unfortunate encounter with my former classmates outside Auchterderran that afternoon confirmed for me that I had undergone a rite of passage, and that I could never really go back to my old situation. This was a valuable lesson in the need for accepting and welcoming change—hopefully ever onwards and upwards! I have earlier referred to the fact that I always felt rather different from my peers inasmuch as I lived in the country. The old adage, "You can take the girl out of the farm, but you can never take the farm out of the girl," has always rankled with me, because I have too often been oversensitive to any suggestion that country people are in any way inferior to townies. I understand now that I grew up feeling torn between pride in my family and my home on the one hand, and a longing to be just the same as everyone else and live in the town on the other.

I consider that I had a successful school career, coming first in my class in the first two years of senior school and getting seven passes in "O" grades. I achieved enough higher grades of sufficient merit to secure a place at St Andrews University in my fifth year. I had been made a prefect at the end of fourth year, and represented my school at hockey, tennis, and netball, and took part in a variety of musical and other extracurricular activities. So it would be disingenuous of me to say that I did not privately entertain some hope of being chosen as head girl at the end of fifth year, and dishonest not to admit to some disappointment when that did not happen, although I would never have admitted to either of these private feelings. Consequently, I was flabbergasted when Mr Watson, my music teacher, took me aside and expressed his regrets that I had not been chosen. He declared that I was the obvious front runner, and that he was not alone in this belief. He wanted me to know that "had your father been a miner rather than a farmer, you would certainly have been head girl." From this I was able to work out that the school had to be seen to make the correct "political" choice. The head boy's father was a town councillor representing the Labour party, and the head girl chosen in preference to me was the daughter of a miner who was a stalwart of the Miners' Welfare Institute. So I chalked up another important lesson on sociopolitical reality!

Fortunately none of this led me to develop a jaundiced view of the world. "Oh! So yer faither's a fermer, is he?" had often been said to me, usually with raised eyebrows and an arch expression, but through time this troubled me less and less. At university, I mixed with all social classes, from "chinless" young men of aristocratic origins, to sons and daughters of unashamedly working-class homes; my mixed pedigree as a farmer's daughter from an area steeped in coal-mining, and the mixed blessings that endowed me with, equipped me suitably to bridge that social divide. That, together with the legacy of feet firmly fixed on the ground, or rather more aptly, planted in the good soil, that I had inherited from my parents, stood me in good stead as I strove to treat all people the same, and to see beneath the superficial veneer to the real person and his or her values.

My association with education in Fife, first as a pupil and then as a teacher, began and ended in Auchterderran School, and spanned a period of fifty years. I retired in 2001, after sixteen years as a bilingual support teacher, based for most of that time in the same building, albeit much altered and enlarged, where I had acquired my primary schooling. Our office actually looked out onto what had been the infant playground, and I could see the doorway where I had taken my first steps into school in August 1951. As I stood there on that June day nearly fifty years later, I could see, in my mind's eye, that little girl taking her first tentative steps on a road that would eventually bring her back to her starting point. In writing this, I hope I am making it possible to understand something of the people, places, and events that shaped and influenced the person she was to become in the course of that journey.

*Auchterderran School photograph—Margaret aged 9 years, Anne aged 5 years*

*Auchterderran School photograph—Margaret aged 12 years, Anne aged 8 years*

*Auchterderran School photograph—pantomine (Anne back row, second from right, aged 7 years)*

*Margaret aged 16 years, Fod House Pre-Nursing College*

*Anne aged 12 years, Beath High School*

# Chapter 22

"Get lost, there's nae wavies the day!"

Although as children and young adults, there were far fewer recreational activities than exist today, there were some possibilities for us to extend our educational and social life beyond our school attendance and life on the farm. However, the distance from the town would always limit the degree and number in which we could participate. Our parents, especially Joey, encouraged us to make the most of every educational and social amenity available to us, within the limits of the time and money they could afford.

We had acquired a piano from Uncle Hughie in part payment for Jim's help in moving his belongings down to Liverpool. I must have been about six and Margaret ten when Joey arranged for us to have piano lessons from a lady called Mrs Split, who lived in Balgreggie Park, not far from the school. When we went for our first lesson, I took fright! I was clean terrified of this formidable old lady with her halo of pure white hair and her very prominent false teeth, which frequently slipped alarmingly out of place whenever she opened her mouth to speak. So I chickened out of piano tuition and left Margaret on her own. She persisted with lessons for a few years until she was able to persuade Joey that she would never make a pianist, and Joey allowed her to stop. I did eventually begin to learn to play when I was about eleven, and went for lessons to a much younger, prettier, and less intimidating teacher, Mary Fernie, who lived in Kinglassie. She was a hairdresser to trade, but studied piano in her free time and gained an LRAM. I also studied music at high school and sang in the school choirs there. While at primary school, I attended a choir run by the Lochgelly and District Cooperative Society. Margaret and I joined a Scottish country dance class run by a Mrs Maggie Lennie, who had a shop in the Jamphlars. We wore kilts, white blouses and tartan ties, and black dancing pumps. It took a lot of practice (with help from Mum and Dad in the kitchen at Pitkinny) for me to master the pas-de-bas, the skip change of step, and the slower strathspey step that were the main features of this dancing. I remember I even went to an elocution class one winter, which met in the Lochgelly East School.

The Co-op Society and the Miners' Welfare Institute sponsored many cultural and educational opportunities for children and adults alike. Bowhill Colliery Pipe Band were world champions in the 1950s, so there was a great demand for piping and drumming tuition. There were clubs and classes for a myriad of skills and interests: choirs, drama, boxing, dressmaking, first aid, and athletics, amongst many others. Cardenden even had its own swimming club, very many years before it had a swimming pool. Its members campaigned and raised funds for years to build their own pool while they travelled to pools in other towns like Dunfermline, which, thanks to Andrew Carnegie, had swimming baths long before any other place in Fife.

Added to this plethora of social and recreational activities were the facilities offered by the school and the church. Margaret and I never attended the Sunday school, mainly because neither Joey nor Jim was a churchgoer in those days. Jim was a communicant member of the church since he had joined as a young man, but Joey only joined the church in 1957. We became regular attendees at church thereafter, and by then we were old enough to join the Bible class. In addition to the Sunday meeting, there was a badminton club in the church hall once a week in winter. When we were younger, Margaret had joined the Girl Guides and became a very enthusiastic patrol leader. She encouraged me to join the Brownies, but, as in many other things, I did not live up to my sister's good example. On a Wednesday at teatime, Joey would be ironing and folding my tie and Margaret would be polishing my badge with Brasso, as I single-mindedly finished my tea. No amount of urging would get me excited about the prospect of assembling round the toadstool. I tolerated it for a few weeks because I was a member of the Kelpie six. The other Brownies in it were all good at games, and we usually had a fair degree of success in our competitions. But then, the Fairy six lost one or two of its members, and Brown Owl made Morag Bell, a classmate of mine, transfer to even up the numbers. The following week Morag brought a note from her mother, complaining that if she had to move, then so should I as we started on the same night. So Brown Owl decided (somewhat precipitously, in my opinion) to accede to this directive, and made me move as well. That was the last straw. My new six was a "proper bunch of fairies" and I could see no hope of us ever winning anything again, so I dug my heels in and refused to continue attending the Brownies. I think my dislike of this experience had something to do with wearing a pseudo-military uniform and having to salute and march. I never did feel comfortable with uniformed organisations, and even baulked at having to wear our high school uniform, although there were ways that we made it more appealing and attractive. As fashion dictated, we would hitch up the skirt and started wearing nylons as soon as we could persuade our mothers to buy us them for school!

In Cardenden in the summer, children enjoyed three special Saturdays: the school treat (or gala), the miners' treat, organised by the Miners' Welfare Institute, and the store (co-op) treat. We would parade with our class, waving flags behind the pipe band, to the park where a bag of buns and a wee bottle of lemonade represented the height of enjoyment. We would run races and take part in games for the afternoon. These were simple and unsophisticated pleasures by today's standards, of course, but I feel blessed to have had the benefit of growing up in an area and a time where true community spirit thrived. Working people, by combining together in the workplace and in their free time, endeavoured to create opportunities for social cohesion and educational advancement for themselves and their families. An adult country-dancing group would travel every other year to Czechoslovakia, and then would host a return visit from dancers from that country in alternate years. A well-known Scottish actress, Jan Wilson, was a protégée of the Cardenden Drama Club and longed to become a professional actress. Her parents, who owned a fruit shop in the village, agreed to her going to drama school on condition that she also qualified in an occupation that would be more likely to give her regular employment. So she trained as a hairdresser, and her parents sold their fruit shop and bought a hairdresser's business. Jan worked there in her college holidays and in between acting jobs, but it was not long until she was able to give up her day job. After she became a successful actress, we would see her on television from time to time and I would remember when she used to cut my hair.

This was a time of relative prosperity, as the coal mining industry thrived in the immediate postwar political economy of gradually lessening austerity and increasing consumerism. The "never had it so good" years of the second half of the twentieth century were just around the corner. The working life of a miner was still hard, and the legacy of occupational disease and its resulting disability was to be the fate of many. So Uncle Bobby Drennan's years as a shot-firer led to profound deafness in later life, and many miners' lungs were devastated by pneumoconiosis. But in their economically active years miners could make a good living, and those who were prudent and who had the right priorities could provide well for their families, and encourage them to benefit from the wealth of educational opportunities opening up for them. There were some, inevitably, whose wages went the way of the pub, the social club, and the bookie's, but even in these areas there had been some attempt at self-regulation.

Every mining community had at least one "Goth." These drinking establishments were products of the Gothenburg system of "reformed" public houses, a philanthropic approach to licensing, inspired by developments in the Swedish city of the same name at the end of the nineteenth century. They were to be run "solely in the interests of temperance and morality." Licensees or their managers derived no profit from encouraging alcohol consumption, but instead provided food and meeting rooms, and the money made was ploughed back into the community. So, as they relieved the drouth of miners and other workers, they funded social, educational, cultural, and health amenities, ranging from street lighting to libraries, from silver bands to ambulances. Such was the edifying foundation of the Gothenburg movement, but just as the grandiose and imposing buildings through time decayed into faded grandeur, so the high-flown idealistic principles underpinning these enterprises often degenerated into purely commercial licensed premises. One or two notable exceptions in Midlothian have been restored and are being run on principles akin to their original concepts; a local arts festival is the recipient of the profits in the case of the Prestongrange Goth. Many years later, when I worked for the British Centre in Sweden and lived in Varberg, a seaside town on the west coast about one hour south of Gothenburg, I was reminded of the connection that city had with the public houses in the mining towns of eastern Scotland. Interestingly, the suite of classrooms where I taught my evening classes was owned by IOGT, a temperance society of long standing, which had been built on similar principles to the Gothenburg system. By the 1960s it was mostly involved in administering the property it had accrued over the years. Its social and philanthropic functions had diminished after the Swedish state took over responsibility for the regulation of alcohol production and retailing.

As a young girl, Joey had been good at sports. She and her sister Greta used to "clean up" at the races run at Markinch Highland Games, and Jim always enjoyed football and other games, so they were happy for us to participate in a variety of sports. Margaret and I both played netball and tennis, and I was usually in the tennis, netball, and hockey teams at high school. I was fortunate that Beath was not a big school, so the competition for places was not too great. We both had the chance to go on school trips abroad. Margaret went to Holland and we both visited Paris with Auchterderran Shool, then I went on a school excursion to Rome, Sorrento, Capri, and Florence when I was in fourth year—a tremendous highlight of my young life and a never-to-be-forgotten experience.

Our access to the many organised activities depended on our ability to reach the village and its nearest bus stop to travel further afield. This all became much easier after Joey learned to drive, of course, and we certainly benefited from her enterprise. Prior to that, much of our free time was of necessity spent at the farm. Being four years older than I, Margaret's interests were not often the same as mine, and this grew increasingly the case the older we became. Consequently, I spent a lot of time in solitary pursuits and play. Perhaps I was always destined to become a teacher, as my favourite indoor pastime was "schoolies." Joey was always amused at how, having spent all day at school, I would start to re-enact my day as soon as I came home. But now I was the teacher, in charge of my imaginary pupils. I loved books, notebooks, and all kinds of stationery. I would arrange the little sitting room next to the kitchen into an approximation of a classroom, and I can never remember Joey becoming irritated with us if we disrupted her housekeeping routine. Rather she was always extremely tolerant of our need to play and to exercise our imaginations. We didn't have many toys by today's standards, and much of our play was improvised. One toy we loved and played with a great deal was a post office set. We would prop up Joey's cooling rack on the back of a chair to simulate the post office grill and counter. We loved the rubber franking stamp and ink pads, the play postage stamps and postal orders. Another Christmas present, our little blue cash register, held the cardboard coins.

There was a time when the height of my ambition was to be a bus conductress! One year when I was very young, a much-longed-for and loved Christmas present was a bus conductress's set, complete with cardboard hat, money bag, and ticket-punch. Everyone we knew was prevailed upon to save their used tickets. The staircase at Pitkinny became the bus and we would happily spend hours conducting our invisible passengers all over Fife. Our Gran had a cousin whose son Addie Grant was engaged to a bus conductress, a lovely young woman named Christian Cowan, who came from Cardenden. Very occasionally, she would be on our school bus, and we felt so excited that we were able to impress our friends that we were actually on friendly terms with such an exalted being! We thought she was really wonderful, and even more so when she gave us a whole stack of unused tickets, in the customary green (for inward journeys), yellow (outward), and purple (return journeys). Tragically, Addie was killed in a motor-bike accident as he drove to work one morning, and the loss of such a fine young man was keenly felt by everyone in the family. Through time we lost contact with Christian, our tragic heroine and benefactor.

I was to learn a salutary lesson courtesy of another bus conductress one morning some years later. On the school bus to Cowdenbeath, I and some friends were helping each other to memorise Portia's speech from *The Merchant of Venice*, our homework for the English lesson that day. We were making heavy weather of it, and to our surprise, the conductress, who was sitting near us in her customary place by the door, suddenly launched into the speech and delivered it word perfect. I am sure we stared at her open-mouthed as we all thought the same thing: "How could a bus conductress know a passage from Shakespeare?" I am ashamed now when I remember our youthful conceit and arrogance. Reaching the end of her recitation, she casually remarked, "That was one of my favourite bits of Shakespeare when I was a student," and I for one understood properly for the first time in my life the old saying about a book and its cover.

We had plenty of space for outdoor play, of course. When our cousins or some school friends came to play, kick-the-can and hide-and-seek took full advantage of all the many nooks and crannies around the steading. We would play in the hay and straw bales, which were stacked as high as the roof in the big shed at the end of harvest and would gradually lower as the winter feeding was used up. One of the men around the place would help us to rig up rope swings from the rafters, and hours would be happily spent on Tarzan-like manoeuvres. In retrospect, I realise now that a farm can be a very dangerous place, but we were fortunate in not having any serious accidents, with the exception of one potentially fatal mishap from which Joey rescued me.

Male cousins, "the three Jims" (namely Jim Drennan, Jim Rutherford, and Jimmy Rutherford) occasionally persuaded us to take part in their games of cowboys and Indians or Japs and commandos, both of which I loved. Maybe because of this, I became a bit of a tomboy in preferring these pursuits to more girlie pastimes. Most of the time, however, I had to make do with my own company.

There was lots of space for cycling, and I always had a bike of sorts which had been handed on to me from my sister. Our one and only new bike was bought for us when I had grown tall enough to share it with Margaret. It was a smasher! Red and white with lights and a dynamo, and three gears, it made the Woodend and Westfield braes easier propositions. The fact that there was only one bike and there were two of us made for many arguments, and Joey had to act as umpire to ensure fair play—or, rather, fair cycling! Later, when I discovered tennis, the big gable end of the house that bordered the east end of the close was ideal for belting the ball against. We could play a form of netball, with two hoops Dad fixed for us, one on the shed and the other on the telegraph pole by the garden wall.

Of our quieter outdoor pursuits, a favourite was "shoppies." In the summer the byres and the cattle courts were empty as the beasts were out in the fields. A cattle stall would be turned into a shop. A plank of wood on top of a couple of piles of bricks simulated a counter, while Mum would be asked to open all her tins and packets upside down, so we could display the empties as new. We would improvise all manner of accessories and products, with the cash register having pride of place on the counter.

A perennial favourite which came into vogue regularly was the game of hopscotch, or as we knew it, "paldies." Beds would be chalked on the cement floor of the big shed, and a shoe polish tin filled with earth or sand. We would throw the tin into the numbered beds in turn, each time hopping into the bed and, by sliding the tin with the side of our foot, get it out through the beds in order. This required a lot of stamina and skill and a very good sense of balance.

Skipping ropes also had their turn, both at home and in the playground at school. We would skip alone with a short rope. Ropes bought for the purpose would have handles at either end, but more often we would beg, borrow, or steal ropes, especially if we wanted to have a number of friends join in. This was when mothers' washing lines were most in danger! In that case two people would ca' either end of a long rope; the longer the rope, the more people could be "in" at the same time. Again, this required a lot of skill and a good sense of rhythm. Rhymes were chanted and songs sung as we skipped in and out of the rope.

"On yonder hill there stands a lady,
Who she is I do not know,
All she wants is gold and silver,
All she wants is a nice young man.
Call in my sister _______."

Then one would leave and a new one would join the rope.

Sometimes at school, there might be a dozen or more girls skipping in one rope. I remember watching Margaret and her friends at this pursuit and longed to join in, but we younger children were a pain in the neck, because we had not mastered the art of jumping into the turning rope. If the owner of the rope could be persuaded to allow you a turn, they would do a "wavy" for you.

You would have to stand close beside the rope as the ca'ers started it moving back and forward slowly, so that you could manage to get going as they turned it all the way round. I remember hearing the dreaded words. "Get lost! There's nae wavies the day!" I was always happiest when Margaret managed to equip herself with a rope from the farm, because as the controller of the game, she would sometimes let me have a shot with her and her friends.

Ball games were also very popular, and the purchase of new rubber balls would account for some of our pocket money. We played for hours with one, or sometimes two, either throwing them in the air or, more often, up against a wall. We had many different rhymes that we chanted as we played, and the games were sometimes very complicated and demanded a lot of practice to achieve a high degree of skill.

"Charlie Chaplin went to France,
To teach the ladies how to dance,
First the heel and then the toe,
And then you do big birlie O."

If Uncle James was around, you could count on our quiet and absorbing pastimes giving way to more boisterous and noisy nonsense. One summer's day we were innocuously cleaning our bikes at the back door when he turned up. Only six years older than Margaret, he was more like a big brother than an uncle, and in typical fashion, it wasn't long till the fun started. James playfully squirted some water at us, using the bicycle pump as a water pistol. Before long it had developed into a full-scale water fight, with even Mum and Dad joining in by the end, with buckets and hoses pressed into action as weapons of war. Just as well it was a warm day, as we all ended up soaking wet.

I don't remember ever feeling lonely or yearning for playmates when, as was usually the case, I had to amuse myself. I was content with my own company and if all else failed I could always lose myself in books. My earliest titles I recall are books like *Mr Blossom's Shop*, *The Red Umbrella*, *Ameliaranne Goes Motoring* (an early school prize), and *The Water Babies*. If I could bestow any gift on a child, it would be a love of reading. I have always found it to be a wonderful companion and solace when you have to spend time alone. The year I was in Sweden, when I lived alone, I would read seven or eight books a week, borrowed from the town library, which had a very good English section and a helpful librarian.

Far from longing for friends to play with, I remember one occasion when we were saddled with playmates we could have well done without! Jim and Joey had re-established contact with a couple they had known before they were married. They lived in Kennoway and by then had two boys and a girl. When we visited them there, my parents could see that the youngsters were "wild as the heather," so when the time came to invite them to the farm, they took some basic precautions. Since these children seemed out of control in their own home, they dreaded to think what they could do on a farm, so Jim made sure that the starting keys were removed from all the machinery, and that the more obvious dangers were pointed out to them and their parents when they first arrived. Needless to say, the boys ran riot right from the first moment, but it was the girl who caused us the most anguish. At one point we saw her holding Margaret's favourite kitten up by the neck. When Margaret told her off, she threatened to throttle the poor thing. Then my sister managed to impress on her, thankfully while no adults were looking on, that an even worse fate would befall her if she didn't put the cat down. At one point, Joey suggested we should all go for a walk, in the hope of tiring out her irrepressible guests. As the evening wore on and we hoped that they would soon decide to go home, Joey could hardly believe her ears when she heard Jim invite them to stay the night! To be fair, he and Joey were enjoying the company of the adults, but Joey believed that Jim's motivation for making the invitation was that he couldn't be bothered driving them all the way back to Kennoway that night! Before we knew where we were, the three kids were upstairs choosing which beds they wanted to sleep in, while their hapless parents looked on helplessly, and Joey struggled with difficulty to remain every inch the perfect and patient hostess. Privately, she said she felt like subjecting her dear husband to the same treatment that Margaret's kitten had so narrowly avoided earlier. Not surprisingly, regular contact was not maintained with that family, since Joey said she could never go through another day like that!

During my teenage years there were times when, as most young people do, I longed for more freedom. Even for those days, Joey was very strict when it came to us spreading our wings, especially when it came to going out with boys. As long as we were going to be under some degree of supervision it was usually allowed, so we had to make the most of the opportunities to meet boys at school and church functions. Of course, as I grew older, I began more and more to resent the restrictions that living at Pitkinny inevitably imposed, but as I neared the time to leave school and go on to university, I think Joey remembered how her father had tried to dictate his daughters' every move. Also she probably realised that I would soon be living away from home entirely when she would have no control, and I did begin to be allowed more freedom. In later years Joey and Jim came to realise that they were spared the worst of teenage rebellion, because on most days, once I was home from school I was home to stay. I could only go out as and when they were prepared to drive me where I wanted to go. Most teenagers try to kick against the traces, and in that respect we were probably no different, but Margaret and I were very much aware that there was a limit to Joey's patience, and we knew better than try to cross that line.

*Maggie Lennie's Scottish country dancing group (Margaret, top and Anne, bottom, both circled)*

*Anne, Sheena, and Vida Thomson in the garden of the Thomson's cottar house*

*Margaret, Cousin Jim Rutherford, and Anne at Peggy Leslie's wedding*

*Anne and Margaret on the ferry to Dundee*

# Chapter 23

"Thae lassies hae a long road tae walk tae the skail bus."

Neither of my parents had an easy or comfortable childhood. Jim's major deprivation was a lack of affection, particularly on the part of his father, while his mother's ill health and early death cast a shadow over their family life. Hard work was the order of the day, and his father's demands in that direction left precious little time or energy for familial bonding. Nevertheless, while his mother lived, he never knew serious physical hardship. A class photograph taken when he had just started the advanced division, or secondary department, of Markinch school shows him wearing a white shirt, tie, and smart jacket, well-turned-out by comparison with some of his contemporaries. Joey, on the other hand, knew only too well as a child and young woman what it meant to be cold and hungry. This had the effect of making her determinedly single-minded when it came to the care of her own children. She would see to it that we would always have enough to eat and be warmly clad. Winters in those days were longer and colder and we were exposed to the elements, not only on our way to and from school, but (especially in the years before Joey could drive) on any excursion that took us away from Pitkinny. Farm work, of course, involved a constant battle with the weather, and working clothes had to be warm and waterproof.

Central heating was unknown in any form. We had open coal fires in the kitchen and the two sitting rooms. The latter were hardly used in our early years at Pitkinny, and usually only when we had visitors thereafter. Later, after 1953, when we were connected to the electricity supply, heating from electric fires and a convector heater in the hall made life more comfortable. But this only took the cold air off the rooms and we still had to wear significantly more clothing indoors than is the norm nowadays, when short-sleeved lightweight garments are sufficient in our centrally heated and well-insulated homes. So the primary requirement for clothing was that it had to keep you warm. Style and colour certainly took second place to functionality!

There was a generally held belief that warm underwear was essential to present and future health and well-being. Also, we had the feeling that our mother was obsessed with keeping our feet dry and warm at all costs. So as young children, we always wore vests: woolly with sleeves in winter, sleeveless cotton interlock in summer. The ubiquitous navy blue knickers, with optional pocket for your handkerchief, only gave way to white cotton ones on high days and holidays. Atop the winter vests, we wore a "liberty" bodice. This strange and misnamed garment was made of heavy woven cotton. Its worst features were the detachable rubber buttons front and back, to which could be attached suspenders, designed to hold up long stockings. Joey knitted these stockings for us from brown and fawn marl "purple heather" wool, the source of which was Miss Cutland's wool and haberdashery shop in Whyte's Causeway in Kirkcaldy. These stockings were the bane of our lives for some winters. We hated their appearance, especially as we were the only wearers of such old-fashioned hosiery in our school. They were unbearably itchy next to your skin, and when the inevitable happened, and you fell and made holes in the knees, they were assiduously darned and then looked even worse!

When the very worst of the cold weather was over, the only concession was that we could then wear "tappit stockins"—knee-length hose, also made by Joey. (She must have spent a large proportion of her life wielding the four pins that gave rise to all these stockings, as she also kept Jim supplied with his favourite knee-length hand-knitted woollen socks!) Our tappit stockins were held up by elastic garters, which, although marginally preferable to suspenders, left red itchy weals around your legs, which I am sure must have been bad for the circulation—a possible cause of varicose veins in later life, perhaps? Extra hand-knitted tappit stockins were fashioned for wearing inside our wellies, and even loose-fitting and particularly unglamorous bed socks were de rigeur to guard against chilblains. These were red, itchy, and sore bumps on the feet, the result of inhibited circulation due to the cold, aggravated by the use of hot water bottles in bed.

Only when spring gave way to the first signs of summer did the length of our socks descend completely. The first summer morning we went to school in our ankle socks was a highlight in our calendar. How lovely it was to feel the air around my legs as I felt the sense of freedom that the arrival of summer always seemed to bring. I only have to think of the hymn, "Summer Suns Are Glowing Over Land and Sea," which we always sang in our end-of-summer-term service in the church, to be reminded again of that heady seasonal feeling of excitement. Little did Joey know that Margaret usually anticipated this red-letter day by at least a week or two, by smuggling ankle socks out of the house in her schoolbag in the morning and changing into them as we waited for the bus. According to the usual custom, the discarding of warm clothes could never happen until the first day in June at the earliest, as the old adage, "Dinnae cast a cloot till May's oot!" was religiously adhered to.

May must have been viewed as a dangerous month, a time when you might be tempted to assume that summer had arrived, only to be caught out by the weather's occasional sudden reversion to days of cold and wet. This was evidenced by the superstitions that accompanied the washing of bed blankets. These were made of wool, and in the absence of washing machines, this was a mammoth undertaking, only to be attempted on a really dry, sunny, and drouthy day. One May in the early years of her marriage, Joey boasted to Nellie that she had accomplished this feat. The reaction of Jim's sister immediately took the wind out of her sails. She pronounced the dire warning that if you washed blankets in May "you would lie in them thereafter." Sure enough, within a few days, Joey came down with a very bad bout of bronchitis and had to take to her bed for a few days. She needed no further convincing of the truth of the warning. (An even more ominous rhyme on the subject, as intoned by a friend's grandmother, was "Wash blankets in May, wash someone away!") When I was seven, I reinforced Joey's distrust of the month of May. While staying with Gran Betsy and Grandad Hugh in Markinch during the Miners' Gala school holiday at the beginning of May, my cousin and I took advantage of the nice sunny weather to indulge in a spot of sunbathing on the back green. Within a day, I had developed a terrible pain in my side and a high temperature and was promptly carted off to hospital with pneumonia!

Free time at the farm was at a premium, and even in the evenings, when Joey did manage to sit down, her hands were still busy: knitting, sewing, mending, and darning, or grading and cleaning eggs. All our jumpers and cardigans were regular products of her busy knitting needles. In the school photograph in an earlier chapter we are wearing twin-sets made of fawn wool with a pattern around the neck picked out in lemon "fuzzy-wuzzy" or angora yarn. She was a skilled dressmaker, regularly turning out frocks and skirts. We were often dressed alike. I well remember the black and white gingham dresses with white lace trimming, which we are wearing in a photograph taken of us on one of the few holidays that we spent outside Scotland, in London in 1955. Mum once made us lovely suits, grey skirt and jacket, with white satin blouses. Our accessories were cherry red shoes and handbags. These, with the lemon organdie dresses, were the most elaborate outfits we aspired to. There is no doubt that we were well and warmly clad. Outdoor wear in winter usually included knitted pixie hoods: hats which tied under the chin and came to a point on the crown, in the manner of the headgear favoured by the elves in illustrated fairy stories! Boys and girls were often seen sporting long woollen scarves that were crossed uncompromisingly over the chest in front and then firmly pinned at the back with a safety pin. Woolly pawkies or mitts were secured against loss by being linked by a long crocheted cord, which was then threaded through the sleeves of your coat.

Wet weather walks along the loan made waterproofs indispensable. We had outgrown our raincoats as winter approached one year, and with this in mind, Joey had been saving up her Co-op dividend. Someone had told her that it was possible to buy raincoats at cost price from the waterproof factory in Cellardyke, near Anstruther. Presumably, this manufacturing enterprise had developed in response to the demand for oilskins and the like from the local fishing industry in the East Neuk of Fife. Factory shops were quite a novelty in those days, and Joey was intent on equipping us to withstand the wet weather at a discount! She persuaded Dad to drive her, and they picked us up from school on a very wet afternoon. It was certainly appropriate weather for the task in hand, and Jim's temper was in danger of giving out by the time we found our objective. After eventually dropping us off and promising to return later, I suspect he beetled off to check out one of Enster's hostelries, while Mum proceeded to find us the perfect raincoats.

This was no simple matter! They had to be long enough to come down over the top of our wellies, otherwise the rain would run off into our boots, and roomy enough to accommodate our school coats underneath. "Thae lassies hae a long road tae walk tae the skail bus," she would keep reminding the sales girl. In the end the one she chose for me was fairly tolerable—pale green with a fixed hood, and anyway I was too young to really care how I looked. Sadly, the same could not be said for Margaret, who was reaching the age when she was becoming self-conscious about her appearance. Joey insisted on a voluminous, bright cerise pink creation that came with a separate but matching rain hat. Effective as a means of keeping her dry it undoubtedly was, but "cool," in today's terminology, it certainly was not!

Despite Margaret's desperate protestations, the raincoats were duly purchased with Joey's precious, carefully saved divi, and it was decided that we should wear the new additions to our wardrobes right away, since it was still pouring with rain, and we couldn't wait inside, as the shop was closing for the day. As we stood in the lashing rain, waiting for Jim as we so often did in those days before Joey could drive, Margaret made the tactical mistake of voicing her displeasure about the coat: "I didn't want this stupid coat anyway." Joey's normally formidable patience snapped, and her open palm made loud contact with Margaret's cheek just as Jim pulled up, all smiles now that his thirst had been quenched. Driving home, steaming damply, and in total silence, our senses assailed by the pungent aroma of linseed oil from our newly christened raincoats, experience may have led Jim to suspect that his lateness was the reason for Joey's silence and our sulks. He was not to know that she was feeling, not for the first time, just like King Lear: "How sharper than a serpent's tooth it is, to have an ungrateful child." As in the matter of the snow-filled wellies, it was not until we became parents ourselves that we could understand Mum's frustrated response to our failure to appreciate her efforts on our behalf.

There must have been other times when Joey felt that her attempts to clad us well were doomed to failure through no fault of her own. She once made us lovely cosy nightgowns of pretty floral patterned wincyette. When she had finished them off by trimming the neck, yoke, and sleeves with lace, and was completely satisfied with the result, she hand washed them and carefully hung them out to dry. I have described elsewhere how she had threatened terrible retribution on Jim when carelessness allowed wayward animals to damage her precious gardens. On this occasion the vandals were some pigs, which escaped from the paddock and strayed onto the drying green to wreak havoc on her handiwork. Pigs will eat absolutely anything, and our new nightdresses constituted a tempting snack. When Joey returned to the scene of their crime a few hours later, the offending animals had been quietly and guiltily rounded up by Jim and returned to their quarters, but the evidence of their destructive appetites was all too obvious. All that remained of her painstaking efforts was the top nine inches of our nightgowns, still firmly but forlornly pegged to the washing line! So she was never to have the pleasure of seeing us wear what she had so skilfully and lovingly made for us.

Joey's dressmaking had to be fitted in around a myriad of other more pressing tasks, but on another occasion, her desire to complete some dresses she was making for our holidays distracted her at a crucial time. The Royal Highland Show had no permanent site until about 1960, when it became situated at Ingliston near Edinburgh. Before then it was located in a different place each year, and we would usually visit for a day, as we did on that famous occasion at Kelso, when we made that epic journey home in the company of a very drunk but happy, prize-winning blacksmith. In 1956 the show was to be in Dumfries, and Jim decided to make a holiday of the occasion. As some other farming friends did, he hired a caravan so we could stay for the week of the show. The Thomson Almond caravan was to be towed to Dumfries, and when Dad collected it and brought it to the farm, there was great excitement as Margaret and I, with the help of Grandad Hugh Mitchell, took it upon ourselves to pack all the things we thought we would need, while Joey put the finishing touches to her dressmaking. This was to be our first of many caravan holidays, and we really did not know what was appropriate. It was not until we stopped for the first night in a car park in the centre of Lanark that Joey discovered that our fixation on "guid cheenie" had caused us to take some of her few but valued china dishes. There were never more badly organised gypsies as we were, as we spent the first night on wheels. Jim went out, in the pouring rain, of course, to forage for food, as Joey valiantly attempted to get us settled while trying to safeguard her precious crockery. By the time Dad returned, somewhat cheered by a visit, no doubt, to a suitable watering hole, bringing very welcome sustenance in the shape of fish and chips, there was a semblance of order in our mobile home. We were soon fed, watered, and happily bedded down for what was to be the first night of many happy, and sometimes very eventful, caravan holidays.

As we grew older, Margaret and I experienced much angst in the matter of footwear. Joey always insisted on sensible shoes—sturdy, well-fitted, Start-Rite, brown leather, lacing shoes in winter and Clarks' sandals (also brown) in the summer. Of course, the day came when we longed for more glamourous and fashionable footwear. I became fixated on "slip-ons" and we fantasised about "toeless and heel-less" sandals. The year the Highland Show was in Alloa, we spent a day there touring the various attractions. There were usually one or two stalls selling shoes, and we found ourselves looking longingly at some beautiful scanty, strappy sandals. Unusually, Dad was with us at that point, while Joey was away looking at something else on her own. He had probably been enjoying the hospitality of the Herdman's Bar by then and was in a mellow and accommodating frame of mind. We had almost got him to agree we could each have some of the coveted sandals when Joey appeared and put the kybosh on our plan. Our disappointment was acute—foiled again as usual, as Mum displayed that uncanny intuition she had for knowing exactly what we were up to, even when she was nowhere near us. However, within the hour, we did get some new footwear, but certainly not what we had hoped for. A sudden thunderstorm and torrential downpour enveloped the showground, rendering our newish Clarks' sandals unequal to the task of negotiating the resulting sea of mud, and Dad was firmly instructed to take us back to the shoe stall and buy us new wellies!

We once went to Baird's shoe shop on The Bridges in Edinburgh for new school shoes, accompanied by Grandad. By then, Margaret's feet had reached adult proportions, while I still had to go to the children's department. To save time, Mum asked Grandad to take me to look for my shoes, while she dealt with Margaret's needs. She was undoubtedly dreading the argument that always ensued over our conflicting ideas of what constituted suitable footwear, but for once I saw a golden opportunity. I really thought I could put one over on Grandad, and I enjoyed a few minutes of heady anticipation as I tried on a pair of my longed for slip-ons. But it was to no avail, as I saw Grandad's doubtful shake of the head. "I don't think that's quite what your mother had in mind, Anne," he announced in his usual well-spoken and lofty tones. He then proceeded to explain to the salesgirl that we would need to see some sensible lacing school shoes. Was I never to have my heart's desire? Of course I did in the fullness of time. As a young woman I would gladly suffer agonies in the name of fashion. Stiletto heels, winkle-picker toes, platform soles, skintight vinyl shiny white boots; they would all be mine one day! My great-grandmother Hann Barclay was well-known in her day for declaring, "If ye're no in the faushin' ye micht as weel be daid!" and for a few years I did my best to live up to her dictate. But as a child, my growing feet remained sensibly and oh-so-boringly shod, courtesy of Messrs Start-Rite and Clark.

For the most part, clothing in my young day was made from natural fibres, generally wool in winter and cotton in summer. Man-made material was still unknown, until the first nylon, terylene, and tricel fabrics began to be produced in the fifties. As these improved in quality and variety life became much easier, as they were much lighter and easier to launder and care for. Even Jim in the fullness of time would abandon his hand-knitted socks in favour of Damart, and Joey would be liberated from the tyranny of sock-knitting. But, as children, I remember wash day meant an entire day devoted to laundry. Double sinks, scrubbing boards, boilers, wringers, and mangles demanded hard manual labour, and housewives were judged by the appearance of the resulting drying green full of carefully pegged-out clothes: "She pits oot a luvly washin'!" the ultimate accolade for the diligent laundress. Although Joey welcomed the easing of the wash-day burden with the new materials and the advent of the washing machine, I clearly remember her teaching us how to hang everything the right way round and in the correct order, so that the resulting clothes line would have a symmetrical and well-planned appearance. Our grandmother Betsy never owned a washing machine, refusing to believe that it could possibly clean the clothes as well as she did by hand! In this day and age of automatic washers and tumble dryers, many people would scoff at this distrust of labour-saving devices and attention to detail in the matter of laundry. Nevertheless, I still enjoy hanging out washing and have to admit to taking a pride in its appearance as it blows in the wind, albeit on a "whirly" rotary clothes line rather than the straight washing lines strung between clothes poles, supported at intervals by wooden props or stretchers. It was, and still is, for me, a matter of achieving the best standard possible in even the most mundane task, which raises it to a higher and altogether more satisfying level. This involved the same motivation, which Joey recommended to me and I first discovered to be successful, when I sewed up that shed full of potato sacks for Jim all those years ago!

As Joey was the oldest sister in her family, we always had younger cousins, and I remember how different things were then in the realm of child care, particularly in the matter of how babies were dressed. There were no disposable nappies, for a start. Rather, white towelling, with muslin ones inside, were used. These had to be rinsed, soaked, and then boil-washed on a daily basis. A great improvement was effected with the advent of waterproof pants, which covered the terry nappy. Previously, no good mother would have resorted to rubber pants, which were known to encourage nappy rash, so the outer covering had been made of flannel, which must have taken forever to dry! Under the baby's vest went a binder, a wide belt-like strip of material, which was designed to compress the navel, in order to ensure a neat belly button. Sometimes a penny was held in place by the binder to help achieve the same result! For the first six weeks, an infant was dressed first in a vest, then in a barrowcott—a sleeveless gown tied in the front with ribbons—over which went a long white flannelette gown with long sleeves, which completely covered the baby's legs. Hand-knitted garments completed the baby's clothing: a matinee coat, or little cardigan, a bonnet for wee girls, and a helmet for wee boys, woolly little bootees, and finally a shawl, usually knitted by the baby's grandmother. This last, made of pure wool, was wrapped tightly around the baby, reminiscent of the idea of swaddling clothes mentioned in the story of the Nativity. My own Gran used to wrap the baby up really tightly—almost like a parcel, believing this had the effect not only of keeping the baby warm, but of making it feel secure, perhaps simulating the snugness of the womb. The last baby she so swaddled was our son Calum, who was born only three months before she died of a sudden stroke.

When my young cousin Hughie Drennan was about four years old and saw a new infant cousin for the first time, he commented worriedly later, "What a shame for the baby." When his mother asked him to explain what he meant, he added, "He hasnae got ony legs!" I remember being similarly alarmed when I heard one of my aunts comment to my mother, "It will be time to shorten the bairn next week." Naturally, I was horrified to think that this involved something awful, perhaps of a surgical nature, and was correspondingly thoroughly relieved when Mum reassured me that it just meant that, having reached six weeks of age, the baby would begin to wear short dresses or romper suits instead of the long gown and barrowcott!

It is clear that much thought, energy, time, and some expense went in to the clothing of babies and children when we were young, and Joey was especially preoccupied in seeing that we were always warmly clad. Her other major concern was to make sure that we were well nourished. There is no doubt that our food was plain, but plentiful and unadulterated. It is well-known that under the restrictions of wartime rationing, most people generally had a better diet than we do today, when we have access to the world's markets, and have an almost limitless choice of all kinds of convenience foods. I can remember when we had porridge twice a day—at breakfast and at teatime. Our main meal—dinner—was always in the middle of the day, and would almost always consist of homemade soup and a main course of meat or fish with potatoes and another vegetable. Instead of soup, sometimes a milk pudding like rice or semolina would complete the meal. School dinners followed a similar pattern, cooked in a central kitchen and transported to the various educational establishments. There was no choice on the menu and everyone was expected to clean their plates!

As time and money became a little more plentiful, porridge at teatime gave way to something like cheese or sardines on toast, eggs boiled or scrambled, and later still, a "knife and fork" or high tea, with bacon and eggs or fish. Very often, Mum would reserve some of the dinnertime mince and tatties for us, and we would tuck into shepherd's pie for our tea. The food, though plain, was far more plentiful and nourishing than what Joey had known in her childhood. Compared with today, we enjoyed home-produced meals, freshly cooked from scratch every day. Virtually nothing was processed, and additives were unknown. On balance we had a healthy diet, which may have been quite high in cholesterol with its dependence on milk, cream, home-produced butter, and eggs, but Joey felt justifiable pride that she was feeding her family on the fat of the land. The high fat content of the food was less of a concern then, because people generally did much more hard physical work and could not avoid daily exercise, unlike today when sedentary occupations, labour-saving devices, and car ownership conspire against an active lifestyle.

Traditionally, home baking was a regular source of the fancier items on the table, but in our case, Joey preferred scones, of the girdle, oven, and dropped varieties, and sponge and fruit cakes, to more frivolous cakes and pastries. Most Sunday mornings of her married life would see her up early in the kitchen baking girdle scones, which went wonderfully with the sausage, bacon, and eggs of our one cooked breakfast of the week. From the mid-fifties this would be accomplished—in addition to the partial preparation of the dinner—before we all went to church. We always enjoyed home-grown garden vegetables and stored leeks, carrots, and onions, along with field potatoes and turnips, would sustain the constant preparation of homemade soup throughout the year. Joey made a wonderful variety of soups: kale; scotch broth from beef and bone stock; potato soup from a mutton shank; lentil, using ham bones and chicken broth. Only after many years of practice can I honestly say that I have begun to approach her very high standard. Jam-making was a regular, if seasonal activity. Strawberry came first, then raspberry, followed by rhubarb and ginger and finally, bramble and apple jelly, the result of foraging from the many bramble patches around the farm. To be at their best the brambles needed a touch of frost, so for a week or two every autumn, the jelly bag full of brambles and sliced apple, suspended from a pole supported between two chairs, would occupy part of the wee sitting room near the kitchen, as the precious juice dripped into the jelly pan. There is nothing like the wonderful aroma of bubbling jam or jelly, and the greatest treat was the first taste of the new preserves as we were allowed to wipe a slice of bread around the sides and bottom of the newly emptied jam pan. I will never forget the exquisite sensation of the still-warm jam, with little bits of crystalline, partially dissolved sugar crunching on the soft, fresh bread. Joey would sometimes make lemon curd for special occasions, but only a few jars at a time, as it couldn't be stored for long, unlike the vast quantities of filled jam jars that lined the shelves of the pantry, part of the sweet bounty of garden and hedgerow that would see us through the long months of winter.

As hungry children, the usual between-meals snack we had was a "jeely piece," a sandwich of bread, butter, and jam. This was seen by older generations as extravagance, as they frowned on having both butter and jam at the same time. Grandad Hugh would always have only one or the other, but never both on the same slice of bread. There was nothing tastier or more satisfying, nor more fondly remembered by generations of Scottish children! The lyrics to a Glasgow folk song, written by Adam McNaughton, "Ye cannae throw pieces oot o' twenty storey flats," encompasses a wealth of meaning in terms of social, economic, and dietary changes that were wrought in the second half of the twentieth century. Now in the opening years of the new millennium, serious concerns over childhood obesity, fast food, and ready-made meals make the nutritional standards we grew up with seem ideal by comparison. As awareness grows of how far we have gone wrong in the way we feed ourselves and our children, I wonder how or even if we can reverse the trend and return to a healthier dietary regime.

We are caught up in a spiral of increasing prosperity which, together with more awareness of international cuisine, creates a demand for an ever more exotic and hugely varied food supply, available twenty-four hours a day, seven days a week, from our increasingly powerful supermarkets. We live in a society where we expect instant gratification of our every whim, and where fewer and fewer people have any connection with those who produce the food we eat. But can tasteless, hard, out-of-season strawberries, available the year round, or anaemic, plastic-wrapped, uniformly sized brussels sprouts ever be any substitute for the sublime experience of tasting a sun-warmed, newly-picked summer strawberry, or the experience of plucking a deep-green frost-speckled sprout with freezing fingers on Christmas morning? While this chore was much less pleasurable to me as a child than the illicit enjoyment of pilfered garden peas scooped out of their crackling, scrunchy pods, I consider myself to have been fortunate in experiencing both.

It saddens me to think that future generations of children will not share in any of these delights. Our own sons did have that privilege, as they can remember the times they spent with Jim and Joey after they retired to Kirkcudbright and established a wonderful vegetable garden in their new home there. One year during our early summer visit, the boys were desperate to taste the new crop of peas, and kept asking Gran when they would be ready to eat. She advised them that when they could feel peas inside a pod, they could eat them, and so each time they passed the end of the first row of peas outside the kitchen door, they would give the nearest pod a squeeze. Sadly, we had to return home before the peas were ready to harvest, and Joey was subsequently amused to notice that that particular pod never did produce any peas, but withered on the vine, having had all the life squeezed out of it by anxious little fingers!

I can trace in memory how at Pitkinny increasing prosperity, coupled with a growing awareness of how other people lived, affected changes in our daily lives. Compared with the previous generations, we were increasingly influenced by formerly unknown factors. Television opened up the world to everyone. The box in the corner of the living room showed us more and more of what other more affluent lifestyles were like as the "hidden persuaders" of advertising began to insinuate their power over us. As we began to travel further and further afield, and higher education allowed us to meet and mix with people from other social, geographical, and cultural groups, so we aspired to change our situation in life. It is part of human nature, given sufficient intelligence, motivation, and opportunity, to strive to improve our standard of living. So our parents wanted us to be better off than they had been. Joey, particularly, hoped we would have opportunities to ensure our material well-being, but more than that, to enjoy a degree of education and cultural attainment that would allow us to reach our full potential in a way that had been denied to her. Although Mum was the least pretentious person I have ever known, and always kept her feet—and ours—very firmly on the ground, as they became more prosperous, she did aspire to improve our living conditions. She worked very hard to make our home as comfortable and as aesthetically pleasing as time and money allowed.

In the early days, our table setting was very basic: a wooden table which had to be scrubbed gave way to the much easier and more hygienic formica. I remember when we had only a cup, knife, fork, and spoon, and when our main course was served in our used soup bowl. Gradually we began to have saucers under our cups and glasses to drink our milk or water out of, side plates, and separate dishes for soup and main course. Joey began to acquire more nice crockery and china, and even occasionally would put on a tablecloth, although we never bothered with napkins. All these changes were not only signs of growing affluence, but of Joey having a bit more time to concentrate on the appearance and presentation of our table. She just wanted things to be a little nicer, but Jim never saw the need for these details and didn't really appreciate her efforts in this direction. As we grew older, Margaret and I would encourage Mum to try out different ways of doing things in the house, probably because we saw what happened in other homes or on TV and, as youngsters naturally feel, longed to be like everyone else.

At the end of 1954, Joey decided that we would have a proper Christmas dinner. It was the first time we had a turkey, rather than just chicken, and she worked hard to make all the trimmings to go with it. We helped her to make the table look as festive as we could. Unlikely as it seems, Christmas Day was not the sacrosanct holiday that it has now become. In those days in Scotland, New Year was still the major winter festival and most people still worked on Christmas Day. (Even ten years later, in 1964, as a student auxiliary postie I delivered letters on the morning of Christmas Day!) At that time, Jim was in the throes of planning the new big shed, the first major new building to replace those that had been demolished by high explosive, and he had engaged an architect from Kirkcaldy, Jim Hutcheon, to draw up the plans. He had arrived that day and was outside with Jim as he finished feeding the beasts, and they walked around the steading, discussing the proposed new building. We assumed that the architect's wife would be expecting him home for his Christmas dinner, and when Mum called Dad to come in for his dinner the first time, we thought Jim Hutcheon would take the hint and leave. They clearly hadn't finished their discussion, and when Dad didn't appear after about ten minutes, I was sent out again to tell him his dinner was waiting. I can remember the sinking feeling I had as I heard "big-hearted Harry" say, "Come awa' in fur yer denner, Jim!"

The architect didn't decline as we might have hoped, but instead another place had to be set, and the two men made absolutely no reference to the fact that this was Christmas Day as they continued to talk business throughout the meal! As we helped Joey to serve the food, Jim ate his with no comment at all about the turkey and its accompaniments, or about the nice table setting. Although she stoically said nothing, I could sense Joey's disappointment as everything she had done was completely lost on her husband, so preoccupied was he in his guest and their business. This was a typical example of how selfish Jim could often be, and of how he took her efforts entirely for granted. He would never have dreamed of joining in her wish to give us all a nice Christmas. As in most families in those days, domestic arrangements were seen as exclusively the woman's business. It was not the lack of involvement on Jim's part, nor even his failure to show appreciation of Joey's huge contribution to our comfort and welfare, but his seeming inability to even notice that hurt her. Young though I was at eight years old, I remember feeling outrage on her behalf, and for myself, that our attempts to make that one day in our life more special and meaningful had to be shared with an almost complete stranger—and a chain-smoking one at that—with not even a token gesture on his or Jim's part to enter into the spirit of the occasion. It would later become clear that some of Jim Hutcheon's lack of social graces could be accounted for by his own domestic arrangements, and that there was probably no question of a delicious Christmas dinner awaiting him at home that day!

The fact that Joey worked very hard all her life to support his efforts in developing the farm did not seen to be appreciated by Jim, nor did he see his wife as an equal partner in their venture, no matter how much she put into the business. He would eventually, many years later, come to realise how much he owed to her, but by then, sadly, it was too late to tell her, and more than once he confided to some old friends, "I wish I could have ten minutes with Joey, ten minutes would be enough." In the years after that first unsatisfactory Christmas dinner, there were many more festive occasions in which we would support Mum's efforts, and I know, as he grew older, Jim came to value his family more and appreciate the times we spent together.

Throughout my childhood and youth, Joey more than achieved her ambition to ensure that we were all well fed and warm. In so doing, she took great satisfaction from knowing that neither my sister nor I had to endure any of the physical hardship she had known in her young life. For that I am enormously grateful to her. In our turn, Margaret and I would also take pleasure from following our mother's example in homemaking and bringing up our own children.

*Margaret aged 11 years, Anne aged 7 years, in dresses made and cardigans knitted by Joey*

*Margaret aged 10 years, Anne aged 6 years, in blouses and skirts made by Joey*

# Chapter 24

"That's the dearest sair heid ye'll ever hae!"

The diligent attention that Joey gave to looking after her family amounted to a form of preventive health care. This was largely based on a regime of good nutrition, warm clothing, and hygienic living conditions, backed up by a working knowledge of home nursing which she inherited from her granny. We did, of course, sometimes have to resort to professional health care in the person of our family doctor who, for the most of our time at Bogside and Pitkinny, was Dr Brackenridge, who lived and ran his surgery in Auchterderran. Mrs MacMillan, district nurse and midwife, brought me into the world in September 1946, and went on to be a reliable source of advice and comfort for Joey. When the spectre of TB briefly but terrifyingly threatened our family, she it was who urged Joey to keep Margaret at home rather than have her admitted to a sanatorium. With her help, good food, plenty of fresh air, and careful nursing, she promised that Margaret would recover and that all would be well. Happily, none of this was to prove necessary, as Dr Cuba the TB specialist gave Joey and Jim the good news that my sister did not after all have the dreaded disease.

The school nurse and health visitor was a Miss Dempster, a tiny little woman who had a fierce reputation as a stickler for good child care, and who would stand no nonsense from any of her patients who did not do as they were told. She it was who would summon us regularly from our classrooms to be inspected in the medical room. These careful observations, combined with the postwar welfare system which supplied free orange juice, rose-hip syrup, and cod liver oil for babies and young children, and a comprehensive inoculation programme, ensured swift remedial attention for childhood ailments and prevention of the most serious diseases that had previously threatened the well-being or indeed the very survival of infants and older children. Smallpox, diphtheria, whooping cough, tetanus, polio (or as it was then known, infantile paralysis), and of course the scourge of TB were all subject to the panacea of immunisation.

Some treatments were, of course, very much less sophisticated. Who can fail to remember the plight of the poor souls who would appear at school with faces disfigured by vivid purple patches of gentian violet, the cure for impetigo or scabies? How I dreaded ever having to face the world so violetly, not to say violently, adorned! Head lice were kept at bay by frequent inspections from Nurse Dempster, and even more regular torture sessions administered by Joey, as, bone comb in hand, she would painstakingly search our heads by the light of the gas or paraffin lamp, as we leant over a sheet of newspaper to catch the lice. Seldom did she find anything, but on the odd occasion when some nits or "beasts" dared to appear, our heads were immediately shampooed with some foul-smelling substance that effectively destroyed the infestation, and very nearly rendered the entire household insensible in the process!

Margaret had started life already in the throes of whooping cough, and it was only thanks to Joey's skill as a nurse and mother that she survived and eventually began to thrive, albeit with a perennial cough. Once the threat of TB passed, her health improved greatly, especially after she had a tonsillectomy at the age of nine in 1951. Many children underwent this operation for the removal of the tonsils, and it was seen almost as a rite of passage at some stage in childhood. Modern medical opinion is less convinced of its efficacy; indeed, it is believed that the tonsils are the protective barrier to other more vital organs in the respiratory tract. Infected tonsils, in other words, are Nature's way of preventing more serious potential infections elsewhere. But, on the other hand, repeated bouts of tonsillitis in children could in themselves be dangerous and were often implicated in a failure of children to thrive, and so this procedure was then viewed as being absolutely necessary. I was spared this ordeal, but felt somehow deprived when I heard prospective tonsillectomy patients promised nothing but ice cream to eat in the immediate post-operative phase. I was disabused of the notion that there was something attractive about such a prospect after Margaret's admission to hospital.

We were living for some weeks in one of the cottages, during the major refurbishment of the farmhouse. The postie delivered the mail—along with our churn of milk from Bogside—as usual, but somehow some letters had been left in error at the big house, and subsequently mislaid. When Jim came across them and gave them to Joey, she found one addressed to Margaret. It was the notification of her tonsillectomy, and she was to be admitted that very afternoon! Of course, she was at school, and there was an almighty rush on Joey's part to get her things together, and we were collected unexpectedly from school by Mum and Dad and driven to Cameron Bridge Hospital. It was all so sudden that there was no time to prepare Margaret for her stay in hospital or to explain what was to happen there. The last straw was when the ward sister refused to let her keep her dolly—which Joey had made sure to pack—and only eventually relented after much coaxing by Mum. I remember leaving Margaret at the hospital, and making up my mind that I never wanted to have my tonsils out, no matter how much ice cream there might be on offer! This unfortunate episode is probably what made Joey determined that when I later had to be taken by ambulance to the same hospital, she would do her best to prepare me for my ordeal in advance.

The last time that Margaret's health gave Joey and Jim serious concern was when she suffered a very severe nosebleed. Joey had to call Dr Brackenridge out late that night, but before he arrived, Margaret passed out from loss of blood. In retrospect, this frightening occurrence was not treated with the degree of seriousness or urgency that would now be expected. There was no investigation as to the cause of the haemorrhage, and no question of a blood test to determine whether it had left Margaret anaemic, although it almost certainly did. Our expectations then of the Health Service were far fewer than they are now, and people took much more responsibility for treatment of minor ailments. There is no doubt that we understand much more about medical matters than we did in those days, thanks to the media in general and television in particular. We shouldn't die of ignorance these days, which makes the inability of many people to act on medical advice regarding lifestyle choices such as diet, smoking, and alcohol all the harder to understand.

Our general practitioner was a nice, rather gruff but kindly man who would always open his consultation or visit by asking Joey, "So what do you think the trouble is, Mrs Rutherford?" While no doubt tempted to reply that she thought that was what he was there for, nine times out of ten, she would be able to make a rational and very often accurate stab at a diagnosis. So it was when I developed scarlet fever at four years old. I had an extremely high temperature and very sore throat, but it was only when she asked me to show her my tongue that she suspected it was scarlet fever. It was for all the world like a ripe strawberry—a sure sign of the illness. Public health measures had put a stop to the days when most children fell victim to "the fever" and were incarcerated in one of the fever hospitals that were to be found in every area. But scarlet fever, or scarletina as it is now known, was a notifiable disease, and may well still be, and because we had a dairy, I had to be removed from the farm until the infectious phase of the illness was past. When Dr Brackenridge was called and concurred with Joey's diagnosis, he whispered behind his hand that he would call an ambulance. His advice was to say nothing to me about my imminent departure, but Joey would not countenance such a deception. So she explained to me exactly where and why I would be hospitalised, so that, while not exactly overjoyed at the prospect, I was at least prepared for the arrival of a nurse and an ambulance driver, and went with them without too much fuss. I remember noting with interest that the blanket they wrapped me in really was red in colour, as I had once been told that this was the case, so that the blood didn't show up against it!

Now when young children are in hospital, their parents can stay with them or at least visit as much as they want. Then, I was not allowed visitors for the duration of my stay, and when I came home everything belonging to me that could not be sterilised sufficiently had to be left behind. A subsequent hospital stay when I was seven and contracted pneumonia as a result of unwisely sunbathing on Gran's back green in early May 1954 was much more traumatic inasmuch as I had to endure injections four times daily. I remember being very disappointed and hurt when I realised that the nurse would still give me my injection even when my parents were there visiting me, and even more so when they helped her by holding me down while she gave me the jag! The finer feelings of children were seldom considered in those days. While I am sure that my parents were worried about me and missed me, their major feeling was probably one of relief that I was being looked after and that I would recover, and if that meant some temporary emotional upset for me and them, then so be it. In common with most people in those days, they expected children to be seen and not heard, and the possibility of stressful experiences causing us psychological harm never occurred to them.

At school, I learned to read quite quickly, and the day soon came when I realised that I could read things other than my reading book. I quickly developed a voracious appetite for the written word, and this, coupled with an insatiable curiosity, led me to consume everything I could lay my hands on. This was to cause me much grief, as my fluency in reading greatly outmatched my understanding. Joey once noticed that I was always opening and closing my hands and flexing my fingers, and when she at last got me to explain the reason, I confided that I was worried in case I caught polio. The disease was very much in the news, and on reading about it, I assumed that it must be like musical statues—you would be quite normal one minute and the next would be instantaneously afflicted with a sudden and complete paralysis. So I was continually reassuring myself that I had not become smitten by constantly moving my limbs. Remembering how a reasoned and patient approach had worked to good effect with me when I was hospitalised with scarlet fever, Joey took great trouble to convince me that I would not catch polio. She reminded me that I had been immunised against it, and explained that, at any rate, it wouldn't manifest itself in such a dramatic way. She was confident I was reassured that I would not get polio by her rational explanation, but sadly this was not the case. A few evenings later, after we were in bed, she was summoned upstairs by Margaret because I was crying. When she arrived by my bedside and asked me what was wrong, she was understandably perplexed when I wailed, "I've got polio in my tongue!"

No doubt she was tired at the end of a busy day, and completely exasperated by the evidence that I was still allowing my imagination to get the better of me. So, without further ado, she whipped down the blankets, and with one swift movement, turned me over, lifted my nightie and applied another rational explanation to my bare bottom! Her accompanying words were, "There! Now ye've got polio in yer erse!" I was so surprised by her actions and her words that I stopped crying immediately. Many years later, we talked about this episode and Joey confessed to feelings of guilt. By then people were becoming more aware of child psychology, and she said that she had come to realise that what she did and said was wrong, and could have been damaging. But I had to disagree with her. The smacking caused me no particular distress, because I think I understood, even on a subconscious level, that if there had been the slightest chance of me having polio—in my tongue or any other part of my anatomy—my mother would never have reacted in the way she did.

Even at that age I knew that she loved me, and sensed that above all else she cared about my welfare, so the only conclusion had to be that she was right! I did not—nor ever would have—polio! I decided that was one worry I could put firmly out of my mind. That is not to say that I didn't worry myself silly about many other equally unlikely hypotheses throughout the rest of my childhood, but polio would never again be one of them. Joey had acted spontaneously and instinctively, and most of all with utter honesty. I believe that I was far more able to respond to that than to a hypocritical declamation of some politically correct response, based on some incompletely understood theoretical explanation of my behaviour, of the sort to which parents are inclined to resort these days. Joey's response to my imaginary fears was similar to the one she had to Jim when he was under great stress after taking on the lease of Pitkinny. She told him in no uncertain terms that a nervous breakdown was a luxury they couldn't afford, and that he had better pull himself together and get on with the job in hand. I am sure this reaction was a reflection of her own fears and anxieties, just as much as it was evidence of her common sense and realism, but it served Jim and his situation better than all the tea and sympathy in the world.

Jim, in common with other workers at Pitkinny, was not immune to the occasional accident. Early in their time at Bogside, he caught his thumb in some machinery and had to have his nail removed under a general anaesthetic at the general hospital in Kirkcaldy. As he began to lose consciousness, he suffered an adverse—and violent—reaction to the gas and lashed out at the doctors. As he came to, he was aware of one doctor sitting on the floor holding his jaw while his colleague was in the process of removing his white coat and suggesting that Jim should keep his **** nail! In the end, after Jim had apologised, the nail was removed, but only under a local anaesthetic at Jim's insistence and to the doctors' obvious relief!

Some years later, in 1954, he suddenly developed a very painful swelling on one side of his face. He went to see Dr Brackenridge, who initially suspected that he had mumps. But as the pain and the swelling became worse, he changed his mind and thought the source of the trouble was more likely to be his teeth, so Jim went to see Mr Rennie, our dentist in Markinch. He was at a loss to explain his symptoms, but clearly saw the seriousness of the situation and arranged for him to see an oral surgeon, a Mr Middleton, at Edinburgh Royal Infirmary the next day. His diagnosis, having seen Jim's X-rays, was at once as definitive as it was alarming. He said there was a growth of some kind in Jim's jaw which required urgent investigation, and he insisted on his immediate admission to the infirmary. He warned that there was a strong possibility that the tumour was malignant, and intended carrying out a biopsy to determine whether it would be possible to remove it. Meanwhile, he prescribed a course of penicillin. As they prepared Jim for surgery the next day, one of the nurses noticed that the swelling around his jaw had begun to subside slightly. Mr Middleton interpreted this as a sign that the antibiotics were beginning to have an effect on the growth, which suggested that it was more likely to be benign, so he announced that he would go ahead and operate to remove the tumour. So as Jim was wheeled away to the theatre, his main fear was not of the surgical procedure he was about to undergo, but that his pugilistic instincts would manifest themselves as they had before! However, he needn't have worried, as the general anaesthetic he received this time resulted in instant unconsciousness, so that he was completely unaware of the sensation of passing out he had had the time before. "That stuff's deadly!" was his comment when Joey saw him after his operation.

Fortunately, it turned out that the operation was a complete success, and as far as he knew, Jim had not assaulted anyone in the process. He remained in hospital for a week or two as he gradually recovered the use of his jaw. However, in excising the benign cyst, the surgeon had no choice but to also remove a part of his jaw bone, and, as a result Jim was never again able to open his mouth fully. He underwent rigorous physiotherapy, during which his therapist suggested the objective of being able to fit an old ha'penny coin between his upper and lower teeth. This he was never able to accomplish, and this restriction would give rise to difficulties in the future every time he had dental treatment, when his dentist would struggle to find room for manoeuvre. In 1975, a routine local anaesthetic injection had the effect of paralysing his jaw, and for a number of weeks, he had to exist on a semi-liquid diet until he regained full use of the joint. It was noted by Joey that his idea of what constituted a liquid diet differed significantly from hers in terms of its alcoholic content and nutritional value!

The cause of Jim's tumour was never determined, but there were two possibilities. As a young lad, Jim had sustained a blow to his jaw from one of the plough shafts, which sprung up unexpectedly as he unyoked the horse. From that time he was aware of a clicking sensation in his jaw when he yawned, perhaps a sign of some damage. He never mentioned it at home because he knew that no notice would have been taken. Likewise, little or no attention was paid to dental health, other than the very occasional visit to the dentist when toothache demanded the extraction of a tooth. It may have been an impacted wisdom tooth that gave rise to his cyst. Our younger son Donald is built exactly like his Grandad, and at the age of thirteen our dentist noticed that he was unlikely to have room in his jaw for his wisdom teeth to come through, so she recommended that four of his premolars be removed to prevent the danger of impaction. It may be that he had inherited this tendency from his grandfather. Had the same vigilance been exercised on Jim's behalf as a young man, he might have been spared much pain, and Joey much needless worry when she feared that her husband had a malignant tumour.

She had to shoulder the responsibility and work of running the farm while he was ill, and as he was recovering in hospital, I remember her pointing out how white and smooth his hands had become. Normally, they would be rough and reddened from constantly working outside in all weathers. I have a vivid memory of how he would use Snowfire in winter to take care of his hands. This was a medicinal preparation, which came in the form of solid emollient in a little cube wrapped in paper on all sides but one, resembling the chalk used by snooker players. In the evenings Dad would often sit rubbing this little cube on to his fingers to soothe and heal the hacks which were an occupational hazard for outdoor workers. Protective clothing and safety equipment was virtually unknown in those days. I never remember any of the workers at Pitkinny ever wearing gloves, goggles, or ear defenders. In his later years Jim had a slight degree of farmer's lung caused by inhaling the fine dust off the grain while working in the grain drier. Now, such a possibility is prevented by the wearing of masks, an unthinkable precaution in the old days.

The most potentially serious accident Jim had at the farm was when his head came into sudden, hard contact with the moving arm and bucket of the JCB digger as it swung round unexpectedly towards him while Dunc was parking it in the potato shed. One of the nuts on the digger literally made a neat round hole in his temple. It was a Friday at teatime, and Mum and I found him sitting by the fire holding a towel over the wound when we came in after Mum had done her messages and picked me up from the school bus. She knew the injury was serious and that he should be seen in hospital, but he made light of it and said she shouldn't make such a fuss. We ate our tea in silence as Dad grew paler and paler. Margaret was due home for the weekend from the hospital, and Jim was determined to collect her from the bus stop. Joey refused to let him drive, and she knew perfectly well that his intention would be to nip into The Auld Hoose for a quick one or three while waiting for the bus, and she was sure that alcohol consumption was not advisable in these circumstances. She insisted on going instead while I stayed with Dad. When Margaret, primed in the car by Joey of course, came into the kitchen, she took one look at Jim's head and ordered him straight to hospital. He responded, much to our surprise, by meekly saying, "I'll get ma coat then," and allowed himself to be escorted by his elder daughter and his wife to the A&E department at Kirkcaldy, where he had several stitches inserted in his head wound, and a couple of injections of antibiotics and anti-tetanus in his arm. Despite the pain and shock he was in, he was able later that evening to chuckle, as he related how Dougie had remarked (bearing in mind the considerable capital investment the JCB represented), "That's the dearest sair heid ye'll ever hae!"

Another mishap with some expensive machinery was less serious but correspondingly more amusing in retrospect. Jim had been looking for something just inside the door of the big shed, across the close from the back door of the house. As he moved around the front of the parked combine harvester, he lost his footing and slowly fell backwards onto the protruding tines of the machine. He felt the sharp spikes penetrate the seat of his trousers and stick into his rear end! He managed to extricate himself and came stumbling out of the shed gingerly feeling the holes in his trousers to see, much to his amazement, Dr Brackenridge parking his car in the close. He had decided to call in for eggs as he frequently did, but realised as soon as he saw Jim that he was required in his professional capacity. Ascertaining the cause of Jim's pain, he ushered him into the kitchen and wasted no time in ordering him to drop his trousers and underpants, and bend over the table so he could examine the wounds in his buttocks. "I'll have to make them bleed, Jim," he announced as he began to squeeze the holes, and Jim began to moan with the pain this caused. Joey chose this exact moment to appear from the hall. She had been upstairs and was quite unaware of the unfolding drama, so the scene she was confronted with was totally unexpected, and, had it involved anyone other than her husband and the doctor, might have been open to misinterpretation! As it was, all three of the participants in a scene that would not have been out of place in a French farce saw the humour in the situation, and agreed that it was indeed serendipitous that the arrival of the doctor had been so perfectly timed. Some time later he went on his way, fortified no doubt by a fly cup and a scone or two, supplied as always with a dozen of Joey's free-range eggs, having in return applied a suitable dressing to Jim's punctured dignity!

Accidents and serious illness apart, people in those days only resorted to the services of the doctor when their home nursing skills failed to achieve a remedy for illness or injury. Joey had a host of curative, palliative, and preventive strategies, none of which we welcomed and some of which we positively dreaded. The application of heat was generally seen as beneficial in the healing process. This would take various forms, the most drastic one of which was poulticing. Joey favoured the kaolin variety of this particular torture, but mustard and bread were other forms. The tin of kaolin—an innocuous-looking grey paste—was placed in a pan of boiling water on the stove. As it heated up it gave off a very pungent, tear-provoking smell. When she judged it to be hot enough, Joey spread some of it thickly on to a piece of pink lint, and covered it with white gauze. The resulting "sandwich" was then slapped firmly on to the affected area of the anatomy; most often, in my experience, the chest. If you had a really bad chest cold, a second would be applied to your back as well. Then the whole lot would be held in place by a bandage superimposed in turn by a piece of felt pinned either to your vest in the daytime or your pyjamas at bedtime. Looking back, I am amazed that we never sustained first-degree burns or shock, as the heat from the poultice was terrific. It retained its heat for a long time, and combined with the very strong smell, the whole palaver made the business of being ill a thoroughly miserable one. Perhaps the entire exercise was designed to discourage the malingerer! I certainly couldn't imagine anyone being stupid enough to pretend to be ill when you had to endure such agonies!

Sometimes the injury to your dignity was even worse than the physical discomfort you were subjected to. Another remedy I had to thole was the "saut sock" treatment for a sore throat. Coarse cooking salt was heated (in industrial quantities, it seemed) on a shovel over the fire, and when really hot, poured into one of Jim's long hand-knitted woollen socks. The open end was firmly tied with string and, despite my protestations, the resulting "sausage" tied firmly round my neck at bedtime. The salt retained the heat for a long time and, mortified though I was at having to undergo what I saw as a thoroughly undignified ordeal, when I awoke the next morning, I had to admit that it was no longer painful for me to swallow. Vicks vapour rub was an unavoidable part of Joey's treatment for colds. The strongly smelling, greasy substance was rubbed well into your chest, throat, and back, and you went to bed muffled up in a woolly scarf. Even worse were the vapours of friar's balsam, camphorated oil, or menthol crystals, which would have to be inhaled at bedtime.

In addition to these cures, Joey had a whole range of preventive measures she used routinely to ward off illness. As well as warm clothing and good food, in the winter we would be given malt or virol, both extracts from the barley distilling process and Uncle John, who worked at Haig's of Markinch, would procure these health tonics. I disliked them, but Margaret was not averse to the occasional spoonful of the sweet sticky goo. We both hated with a vengeance the Angier's Emulsion Joey would insist on, on winter mornings before setting out for school. The white chalky tonic had to be accompanied, if not by a spoonful of sugar, at least with a wee sweetie to help the medicine go down. (If it was good enough for Mary Poppins's charges, it was good enough for us!) If Joey suspected that you might be constipated, the California syrup of figs would appear. Thankfully we were spared sulphur and treacle, which some of our friends had to endure, and only once did I have to take castor oil, and then only in freshly squeezed orange juice. (Even Joey did have her limits!) An occasional (much nicer) treat were butter balls: little bits of butter rolled in sugar, which were a remedy for croup. Our older son, Calum, suffered bouts of this alarming and distressing condition—a genetic inheritance from me and, in turn, from his grandfather—serious enough in his case to require several stays in hospital. His Gran would make him butter balls, the only nice part of his memory of these times.

I remember a cough mixture that Joey would keep as a standby for use when we were croupy. I was very impressed whenever I heard her coming out with her authoritative demand to the chemist, "A bottle of ipececuanha wine, syrup of squills, and glycerine, please." How could she remember all that, never mind pronounce it so clearly? There was also a slight sense of unease on my part as I assumed that there was a connection between the "squills" part of the name and porcupines. I didn't allow myself to think too much about what this might mean, and was retrospectively relieved to understand some years later that the prefix of the's' to the word that I thought I had heard, rendered it merely the name of a plant extract, namely that of the sea-onion from the genus scilla, which has both a diuretic and expectorant effect—quite innocuous and harmless in comparison with the prickly creature I had imagined to be the source of this exotic medicine. I actually quite liked the taste of it, so didn't really ever believe that it could contain anything dangerous. I was somewhat disappointed to discover years later, when I wanted to buy some for Calum, that the only available approximation to it was labelled simply "lemon and glycerine." Whatever happened to the wine of the ipecacuanha (from the root of the Brazilian uragoga plant) and the syrup of the squills?

These treatments and medicines, some weird and wonderful, others homely and couthy, were often accompanied by a host of folk sayings—or, to be less charitable, old wives' tales—relating to health and welfare. Never sit on hot or cold surfaces, or you'll get haemorrhoids. Years later I was amused to hear our younger son Donald admonishing one of his wee pals, "Ryan, don't sit on that big stone, you'll get heaps!" Joey was always wary of sudden changes in temperature. On venturing outside from a warm house or car, she would insist on us putting on a jumper or cardigan, warning, "The cauld'll flee tae ye!" You should never sit indoors with your coat on, otherwise you won't feel the benefit of it when you go out. Don't eat cheese late at night, or you'll get nightmares. These warnings and omens may seem mere superstitions when viewed from our modern and well-informed stance, but there was usually at least a grain of truth in most of them, and a sound basis for much of the home nursing and its remedies. They were often based on the experience and observations of earlier generations, when the unavailability or expense of professional medical advice was beyond their means. While not suggesting for one minute that we should eschew the benefits of modern medicine and health care, if we had persevered a little more with other, less sophisticated treatments before, or instead of, resorting too readily to antibiotics, we might have avoided developing resistance to them and the problems that has brought in its wake.

One aspect of health care which has unequivocally improved is that of dental treatment. In my childhood, you only ever visited a dentist when you had toothache, and the only outcome was extraction of the troublesome tooth. The dentist at Auchterderran was a Mr Shearer. I remember only one visit to him to have my first tooth extracted. Joey warned me that he would ask me to "smell some nice scent" and I should breathe it in deeply. I would have a nice sleep and when I woke up the pain would be gone and the sore tooth would be out. I must have done exactly as I was told, to the extent that the dentist had difficulty in getting me to wake up. Joey panicked as she saw him slapping my face and forcing me to my feet. I did eventually come to—obviously—but continued to cry with pain. "That man made a hole in ma mooth," I complained as we went home. To distract me as she prepared the dinner, she let me sit up on a cushion on the windowsill beside her at the kitchen sink. She told me to watch Lena and Dougie as they worked in the close.

But even their waving and laughing at me didn't pacify me, and I continued to cry until, all of a sudden, I said, smiling, "Ma mooth's a' better noo," and then, "There's somethin' in ma mooth." With that I spat into the sink, and there was a big abscess that must have been left in the tooth socket, but still connected to my gum. All my crying must have dislodged it and when it came away the pain disappeared. Joey was horrified at the carelessness of the dentist, and thereafter we began to go to Jim's dentist in Markinch. Although it was less convenient, Joey was determined that never again would we suffer at the hands of Mr Shearer.

Margaret and I did not anticipate any great improvement, however, and both dreaded the visits to Mr Rennie's dental surgery. He was a huge man who wore an elaborate white coat which buttoned right up to his chin, and he seemed enormous as he loomed over us in the chair! The upstairs waiting room contained the ubiquitous fish tank, and from the window you could see the passengers on the top deck of the passing double-decker buses. I used to say longingly to myself, "Why can't I be one of those people instead of me?" Preventive dentistry didn't really feature in our visits to Mr Rennie; only painful fillings and scary extractions, where gas was administered without the presence of a doctor or any kind of resuscitation equipment, a dangerous practice which would never be permitted now. Many young people faced adulthood with few if any of their own teeth remaining. Indeed, it was said that a common twenty-first birthday present was their first set of dentures. Joey had lost all her teeth because of untreated gum disease as a young woman, and although our dental care was much better than hers had been, it still left much to be desired.

We always had toothbrushes, certainly, but cleaning our teeth was at best a perfunctory token gesture. In contrast, my husband Bill cleaned our sons' teeth for them at night almost until they were too tall for him to reach and they could be trusted to do it properly for themselves! Toothpaste as I remember it came in little tins made by Gibbs, and had a gritty texture and none too pleasing taste. Later, toothpaste became available in tubes, Gibbs SR or McLeans, with gradually improving and varying flavours. When we first had commercial television at the end of the 1950s, one of the early exciting and amusing adverts was for a toothpaste: "You'll wonder where the yellow went, when you brush your teeth with Pepsodent." Our national addiction to sweets, which resulted from the combination of the end of rationing and the burgeoning confectionery industry, wreaked havoc on our fragile dental health, and most people of my generation have had to spend much time and money on remedial dental treatment. Not so our children; in common with many of our friends and family, we have brought up sons with perfect teeth—the result of good dental hygiene, healthy diets, and a control on the amount of sugar they consumed. These factors, together with the addition of fluoride to toothpaste, if not to the drinking water supply, and regular visits to the dentist for timely preventive measures such as fluoride coating of their molars, have ensured that they have never suffered the agonies in the dentists' chair that we did. When they were young, our boys always found a visit to the hairdresser much more traumatic than one to the dentist!

Soon after her marriage, Joey found herself the victim of an occupational hazard of living on a farm which was to cause her a lot of discomfort over the years: hay fever! She could hardly avoid coming into contact with pollen, but the main cause of her allergic reaction were the hay mites that infested hay stored in the barn for cattle fodder. These were tiny little pests that could sometimes be seen like drifts of pink dust around the floor of the big shed. She gradually developed a degree of tolerance to them, but I remember her at her worst with streaming eyes and nose and a chesty wheezing and coughing. As with all the other health issues she had to deal with—and there were many—she was able to thole discomfort or pain with remarkable equanimity. She was prone to serious ear trouble, which may have been related to the chronic hay fever, and was twice hospitalised in Edinburgh Royal Infirmary with mastoid infections that required surgery. She was in Ward 38 of the ear, nose, and throat department there, and described how depressing the old Victorian nightingale ward was. The windows were so high it was impossible to see outside. Only by standing on the pipes in the bathroom could you catch sight of the outside world. The sister ruled the ward with a rod of iron, and when the matron did her round of the wards each evening, the staff virtually stood to attention while she surveyed every detail. The patients had to be in bed, and not a thing was allowed to be out of place.

Joey noticed that every evening at about seven she could hear the sound of marching feet, almost as if a column of soldiers was marching outside. When she investigated from her vantage point on the bathroom pipes, she could see a large group of men hurrying down to the Simpson Memorial Maternity Hospital, which was the next building. These were the proud new fathers rushing to visit their wives and new babies. They were kept waiting at the gate on Lauriston Place until seven o'clock exactly, when the gate was opened and the strictly controlled hour's visiting began. I was to experience Ward 38 myself when I also suffered a mastoid infection in 1960, and realised that absolutely nothing had changed in the intervening years. Now, in a new century, we are very aware of the dangers of hospital-acquired infection from so-called super-bugs. When I hear of a move to bring back the hospital matrons to clean up our dirty hospitals, I recall those days when hospital wards were run with military precision, but I doubt very much whether people would accept the level of discipline it required of staff and patients alike. The media would soon be bleating about the infringement of our human rights and personal freedom this would entail.

Joey's later years were affected by spondylitis and osteoarthritis which emanated from wear and tear in her spine, which gave rise to great pain in her neck and arms. It all began in the late 1940s, when she was diagnosed with torn ligaments in her neck. She thought the damage was caused by either painting a ceiling or dancing strip-the-willow, both of which activities she had recently been indulging in, albeit not at the same time! The treatment involved wearing a rigid plaster, or stookie cast, on her neck. This was put on in the general hospital in Kirkcaldy, and the method used was literally hair-raising. She had to sit on a chair with a nurse on either side of her. Each nurse gathered handfuls of her hair and held her head up as the doctor took away the chair! With her neck at full stretch the plaster bandages were wound around with little splints inserted at regular intervals. She was left completely unable to move her head in any direction, but she was very resourceful, and found ways round this great restriction in order to cope with her daily life at Pitkinny. She learned to sleep sitting up, and the only way she found she could eat with any comfort was to stand up with her plate on top of the old-fashioned wireless, which sat on the kitchen dresser. She struggled to continue to do as much as she could, and longed for the day when the plaster could come off.

On a visit to the hospital for a checkup, accompanied by her cousin Grace, she was walking along a corridor with seats on either side when, out of the corner of her eye, she could see a man waving to her. Grace was walking behind and, assuming this was someone who knew her, Joey had to stop and turn round fully to ask her if she recognised him. When Grace looked at the man, it was immediately obvious why he was waving at Joey. He was sitting with his two legs encased in plaster and sticking straight out in front of him. Realising that there was no way Joey could see this potential hazard, and fearing she would fall over his legs, he was trying to attract her attention. It was only then that Joey realised that to be any good as a guide and helper, Grace should have been walking in front of her, not behind! When the longed-for day came and the plaster cast was due to come off, Joey was horrified when the doctor simply cut it off and told Joey to go home. She felt as if her head was going to fall off! The muscles of her neck had, of course, atrophied and she should have continued to wear some kind of support for her neck, and to have physiotherapy to build up her neck muscles. She suffered great pain for a few months, and periodically from that time on.

As the years passed this became steadily worse, and she began to experience loss of sensation in her hands and fingers, until she eventually underwent major surgery at the Western General Hospital in Edinburgh in 1976, when bone grafts were taken from her hip and used to fuse vertebrae in her neck. It was successful insofar as it prevented further paralysis, but did not relieve her chronic pain. Her last years were spent trying various palliative treatments, such as relaxation and exercise therapy and TENS ultrasonic treatment. All in all, Joey's stoicism and sense of humour, which never left her, helped her to carry on an active and satisfying quality of life despite her worsening condition. She forced herself to continue to do all the things that were important to her: running her home, cooking and cleaning, and of course, tending her beloved garden. Jim did his best to help her around the house and did all the heavy outdoor work, and only her closest family knew the degree of pain she put up with, although she seldom complained even to us, while she always presented a cheerful and positive front to the world.

Joey had been plagued throughout her youth by the spectre of heart trouble, thanks to the bouts of rheumatic fever she had suffered as a girl, but it was the extent to which this limited her leisure pursuits—playing tennis when she was young, or restoring and tending that wonderful walled garden at Pitkinny—rather than the fact of the condition itself that irked her so much. She had always wanted to have a big family, and after I was born so quickly and easily, she was confirmed in this ambition. However, within a very short time of my birth, her erratic heartbeat alarmed the midwife, Nurse MacMillan, who consulted with Dr Brackenridge. He in turn insisted on her seeing a heart specialist, whose advice was that Joey should limit her physical exertions and that she should reconcile herself to having no more babies.

It was the greatest sorrow of her life that she eventually had to accept their advice, but it was only after much heart searching on her part. The doctors tried to impress upon her the danger another pregnancy and birth would expose her to, and warned Jim that at best this could jeopardise, if not her life, then certainly her future health. Joey was utterly convinced that none of these dire consequences would prevail. How could she work as hard as she did if there was anything seriously wrong with her heart? But, on the other hand, shouldn't she put her future ability to look after the family she already had before her determination to have another baby? No wonder she felt caught between the devil and the deep blue sea. She was being asked to make an impossible choice, but as Jim was convinced that the doctors knew best, in the end she had to resign herself to the fact that her family was complete.

When she understood the depth of Joey's disappointment about this, her mother Betsy declared that had she known the pain and sadnesss that was in front of Joey, she would have looked after her better when she was young. Joey's reaction to this was one of resignation: It was too late to have regrets, and she supposed that Betsy and Hugh had done the best they could in the circumstances they were faced with. However, it is a measure of my mother's courage and selflessness that she was able to rise above her sorrow and carry on as a devoted wife and mother. It was not until I was a young woman that she shared this experience with me. I am ashamed to say that at the time, I felt this knowledge to be a burden. It represented a degree of pain that

I was unable to really appreciate, and would probably have preferred not to know about. Only later, as the mother of two sons, did I fully understand the depth of anguish that she must have felt, made even worse by the fact that she suffered it alone. Jim was never able to talk about this painful time, and there was no way he could in any way assuage her sorrow, even if he had been emotionally capable of doing so. His early life had failed to equip him to deal with another's intense personal feelings, and he was always ill at ease in emotional situations.

Generally speaking, women of my mother's generation subscribed to the belief that what doesn't kill you makes you stronger, and this was certainly exemplified by Joey's ability to accept and move on. She was brokenhearted never to have another child, but it was to her credit that it didn't make her bitter. When I saw the sheer delight she took in her three granddaughters and two grandsons, I knew they were a priceless comfort and a soothing balm on that place in her heart that had been left empty and aching for the want of that other wee boy or girl she would have cherished and nurtured, and that wee brother or sister we should have known and loved.

*Kirkcaldy General Hospital children's ward Christmas party.*
*Sister MacMillan invited us. It was the day Margaret decided to become a nurse.*
*Margaret aged 14 years, top; and Anne aged 10 years, centre; both circled.*

# Chapter 25

## "It's the bliddy Opencast tae blame!"

By the beginning of the 1960s, it became clear to Joey and Jim that they had reached a watershed in their farming life. Despite the alterations and improvements they had made to Bogside in the early days, innovations in the dairying industry were fast rendering their setup there old-fashioned and inefficient. New, automated machinery and more specialised buildings were now the norm. The system of bringing the cows in from the fields for milking twice a day, or keeping them in the byre throughout the winter, was being supplanted by the use of milking parlours and cattle courts. Such a change would call for huge capital investment and, in Jim's opinion, the future for dairy farming did not look bright enough to justify such a risk. In fact, the future existence of Bogside as a physical entity could not be guaranteed at all, owing to far-reaching developments that were completely out of his control. These were related to trends in another industry altogether: that of coal mining.

As Pitkinny and Bogside lay on the junction between the coalfield, with its urban and industrial character to the south, and the entirely different geology and land use of Kinross-shire, with its rural and agricultural landscape to the north, so the future direction of Jim and Joey's farming enterprise was closely bound up with the parallel developments in the coal industry. The incontrovertible fact of the matter was that the NCB was their landlord, and their fate was inextricably linked with that of coal mining. There was an irony in that, of course, because while Jim lived cheek by jowl with the pits and counted some of his best friends (and not a few relatives) amongst the mining community, he had an equivocal attitude to many of its features. Maybe it was simply the old antipathy between town and country (something Joey felt keenly when she first married Jim), but I suspect that it ran more deeply than that, and actually came down to a fundamental difference in their understanding of the economic and social systems in which they operated. In other words: Politics. While Jim would never see himself as a political animal, he instinctively inclined more to the right; while Joey, given her harsh experience as a child, was definitely more left-wing in her beliefs.

Jim had accepted when he first became a tenant of the Coal Board that he would never be entirely free in determining his future, but had made the best of his situation. It was still infinitely preferable to working for his father, with all the frustrations and inhibitions that engendered. He had become valued as a good tenant who had vastly improved his holding, to the mutual benefit of both himself and his landlord. This was facilitated to a large degree by his excellent working relationship with the factor Bob Edgar, but now he had to deal with the Opencast Executive, a new branch of the NCB, which had a much harder-nosed approach to its relationship with tenant farmers. Nevertheless, it is to Jim's credit that the negotiations which he engaged in at regular intervals, as their mining operations impinged more and more on his farm, were accompanied by a high degree of mutual respect and fairness on both sides. Although there were times when Jim would explode with fury at some unacceptable intrusion into his business, he always managed to steer a course that ultimately resulted in a beneficial conclusion for him, the farm, and his family.

Historically, mining had first started as open-adit, or "in-gaun een" mines where horizontal or gently graded shafts gave access to the coal measures as they approached the surface at an angle. Only much later, in the late nineteenth and early twentieth centuries, did industrial progress allow for the development of deep mining with vertical shafts and all the accompanying technology. Then, before the Second World War and long before nationalisation had seen the inception of the NCB, its predecessor, the Fife Coal Company, had had a brief venture into opencast mining. They had dug some coal out of the area between the Lochty Burn and the road linking Auchmuir Bridge and Loch Leven. In retrospect, this might have been seen as a harbinger of things to come, in the postwar development of the coal industry. The move away from deep mining, and all the angst and socioeconomic hardship this caused, was paralleled by a huge expansion of opencast operations by the NCB in the fifties, sixties, seventies, and beyond. As the idea of nationalised industries became incompatible with changes in economic and political theory and practice, this even saw a return to private enterprise in coal mining.

The Opencast Executive had already made it clear to Jim that an extension of their mining south of the Lochty would lay claim to the steading and some of the fields around Bogside, so Jim knew that any replacement for the dairy would have to be at Pitkinny. That would mean the loss of a significant part of his arable land to pasture, and his profitable grain production would have to be proportionally cut. Added to the fears that the future for dairying was less than rosy in terms of markets and profitability, this meant that Jim and Joey had to conclude that they should change direction away from milk production and into the rearing and fattening of beef cattle. Barley beef was a current and attractive proposition, which would exploit their arable production of grain to support a new livestock venture.

In the late fifties the NCB began the large-scale expansion of its Westfield site, which encompassed massive coal excavation combined with a new method of extracting gas from the resulting low-grade coal. Thus was built the Lurgi gasification plant on the site of the old POW and DP camp. Capeldrae Row (which had been gradually emptied of tenants) was demolished, and a large new electricity substation built across the road in one of Bogside's fields. The expanding mine would in time become the "biggest hole in Europe" as huge excavators removed the surface of the land to expose the coal measures underneath. At the same time, a new road was built from the bottom of Bogside Brae eastwards towards Kinglassie. Parallel to this on the north, the old Lochty branch railway line was improved and reopened. Wagons filled with the coal that was not used at the Lurgi plant would transport it eastwards to Thornton Junction, from where it went south and west to the coal-fired power stations at Kincardine and later Longannet on the River Forth.

As is always the case with mining, the waste material had to go somewhere. In this case the overburden produced thousands of tons of topsoil, which was mounded for future re-instatement of the landscape, and subsoil, which had to be disposed of constructively. A German-designed and built conveyor belt system was devised to move this vast quantity of material from the mine. This belt was built parallel to the road to the west of Bogside Brae, crossing the end of our loan via a high bridge, then west along the south side of the loan up towards Hare Law, where it culminated in an enormous spreading machine which disgorged the overburden into the hollow between our loan and Pitcairn Farm to the southwest. This obliterated South Pitkinny Farm and extended all the way eastwards to the Black Woods and the moss around there nearly as far as Woodend. Apart from a narrow band to the west of Bogside Brae, this did not impinge on any of the Pitkinny acreage, none of which extended south of the loan. Huge earth-moving machines helped to spread and grade this new mantle over the entire area. The plan was to eventually reinstate the land to productive agricultural use, and this was in fact achieved by the early 1970s, when this phase of the opencast operation was more or less completed. Although the contours of the land were forever altered, this new area was returned to grass fields separated by shelter belts of trees. A stranger to the area would be hard put to see any evidence of the tremendous upheaval the land had been subjected to. One negative outcome in the longer term, sadly, was that Pitkinny lost its outlook to the south, as the new land was much higher than the previous aspect, and eventually Pitkinny would no longer be approached from the south. On the other hand, one of the few fringe benefits was that we were never again snowed in in winter, as the mining contractors had to keep the road open and in a reasonable state of repair, as they had to use it for access to their site.

As tenants of the NCB, there were few alternatives available to Jim and Joey when faced with this prospect. Although the outcome was ultimately satisfactory, they were not to know that as they decided to stick with their tenancy and ride out the storm. At least they had security of tenure and, although there was some consideration of the possibility of making a move to another farm, it never came to that. I do remember that we went to look at the vacant Coal Board farm at East Baldridge to the northwest of Dunfermline, but the thought of starting again with a house and steading little better than Pitkinny had been ten years before did not appeal. It was, of course, far from ideal as the expanded opencast mine gave rise to noise, dust, smell, and general inconvenience all round for years, but with hindsight it is possible to see that in many ways it was a blessing in disguise. Likewise, although the final phase of the mining at Westfield in the seventies was to prove to be a step too far for Jim and Joey, as it brought an end to their farming life, it was to prove to be of benefit to them in the long run. Overall, the farm and the opencast site managed, albeit often with a great struggle, to maintain a state of reasonably peaceful coexistence.

So in the early 1960s, as it became obvious that neither Bogside nor the dairying portion of their business had any future, their greatest immediate concern was for the Steel family, who would be left without jobs or a home. Although Jock and Tam received redundancy payments, and Jim would have helped them to find new employment and accommodation, they pre-empted the need for the latter by making a decision that took everyone's breath away! Their eldest daughter, Margaret, had emigrated to Australia when she married in the early 1950s and they decided to join her, along with their other daughter Mary and her family, their son John and his wife and children, their youngest son Tam, and my playmate Joyce, their youngest daughter. Altogether, in 1967 thirteen of the family took assisted passages and travelled by ship to Australia and settled in the greater Melbourne area. Only Bob, their oldest and unmarried son, remained. He had worked for Sandy Black at Westfield and later joined Costain, the main Coal Board contractor at the opencast site. Bogside was never lived in again and the house and steading were later demolished when the expected expansion of the site to the south of the Lochty Burn took place.

From that time, Jim's involvement with pastoral farming changed to the buying and rearing, fattening and selling of stirks for beef. He fed them on grass pasture in the summer, and silage, draff, hay, turnips, and bruised barley in winter. He invested heavily in silage production when he built a big, new self-feed shed, and acquired forage harvesters and silage trailers. The use of draff, a by-product from the whisky industry in the form of the spent mash from the malting process, had always been bought from Cameron Bridge, maintaining a connection with the distillery there, which went back to the days when Jim's father worked there and later supplied it with milk. As the best of Jim's barley was sold to Robert Kilgour, the maltsters, and from there to Ballantine's, the distillers, this was a fine example of recycling, as was that of Jim's consumption of the finished article: whisky! He always said the reason he drank whisky was that he felt duty bound to support the industry that supported him; not because he liked the stuff!

So the pattern of farming at Pitkinny as it evolved in the early to mid-sixties was to continue until they retired from the farm in 1976: the rearing of beef cattle and lambs; the growing of barley and potatoes as cash crops; the production of hay silage and turnips, along with barley, as fodder. Joey continued with her egg production, but on a gradually smaller scale than formerly. Jim began to offset the capital expenditure on the expensive items of machinery by contracting out the combine harvester and the JCB digger, and the considerable investment in an improved three-phase electric-powered grain drier, by drying grain for other farmers. So he continued to think big and to innovate in the development of his business, and excelled as a dealer in livestock and commodities. While the business evolved and prospered, Joey continued to maintain and improve the house and to make its immediate surroundings ever more attractive with her additions and improvements to the gardens and around the steading.

I find it hard to believe now that this phase of their lives lasted for only a little over a decade, perhaps because, in retrospect, those years after I left home constitute a very significant part of my memory. It covers the period from when I left school until our second son was born—only twelve years—but they were years of great change and richness for me personally. Also, these were the years when I saw my home from a distance and fully began to understand and appreciate just how much my parents had achieved in their working lives. It may be that it is only when we become parents ourselves that we really develop a true perspective on our own childhood and on our relationship with our own parents. Also, of course, these years represented the climax of the growing time in Jim and Joey's working lives. They represented the fulfilment of their hopes and ambitions and when they saw their efforts come to fruition. They could look back on thirty years of hard work, years of much joy but also of heartache and regrets. There were so many different facets to our life at Pitkinny. Each one reflects a different impression of that life and the years of my childhood and youth, just as each one will be seen from a different perspective by all the people who shared them with me. Now I can look back from as great a distance again and hope that hindsight allows me a reasonably objective view. My youth and childhood were not perfect, and I am aware that as I was growing up there were things I ached to change, but I realise that, on balance, my overwhelming feelings are of gratitude and pride, not only in my family, but in all the other people who feature in my memory of those years, who, in touching our lives enriched them, and who hopefully were enriched in turn by the contact they had with Pitkinny and its tenants, the Rutherfords.

AUSTRALIA BOUND ON 13th, THE UNSUPERSTITIOUS STEELS

They're off with a smile –all 13 of them!

Express Staff Reporter

SUPERSTITION didn't daunt the 13-strong Steel family heading for a new life in Australia.

Hopes high, eyes shining, their luggage piled on to two railway trollies, they set out at the weekend undeterred by their sailing date ... November 13 ...

Dad, [illegible] dairyman John Steel, decided to emigrate with [illegible] wife Helen after he became redundant at South [illegible] Farm, Carden-[illegible]

Thirteen smiles from the Steel family at Waverley Station, Edinburgh, before setting off on the first leg [illegible] heir journey.

*Newspaper report on the departure of the Steel family to Australia*

*Jim with Nell and his last dairy herd at Pitkinny*

*Jim and his last dairy herd in front of Pitkinny farmhouse*

*Anne, Gran Betsy, Joey, Grandad Hugh, and Jim in Anstruther*

70 FIFE – THE MINING KINGDOM

The Star Coal Company worked a small basin of coal near the hamlet of Star in the 1920s. The ramshackle-looking mine employed only a handful of men. The six here are, from left to right, William Annandale, William Paton, James Gourlay, Alex Wishart, John Grierson and Thomas Rutherford. Little mines that worked isolated pockets of coal were a useful source of employment and fuel for local communities. But the local community had reason to curse the little mine when it was pumped clear of water and drained the village supply as well.

Mine openings, like this entrance to the Star Mine, were known by Scottish miners as 'in-gaun een' – in-going eyes.

*Fife, The Mining Kingdom*
*(Source: Fife, The Mining Kingdom, Guthrie Hutton, Stenlake)*

# Chapter 26

## "A gey decent chap, fur a meenister!"

When we were young children, our parents were not churchgoers. Having been baptised in May 1917 at the age of three months, Jim had later joined the Church in October 1938 along with his brothers, presumably in reaction to the death of their mother Maggie two months earlier. As far as I am aware, he did not attend church regularly thereafter. Joey, like Jim, had been baptised by the Rev James Bryden, but not until June 1930 when she was fourteen years old. In her case the sacrament was sought because when her baby sister Eunice was dying of meningitis, she and all her siblings were baptised at the same time in the house by the local minister. When Joey and Jim were married in her parents' home at 83 Croft Crescent in September 1941, the simple service was conducted by the Rev Edwin Davidson. After their marriage they seldom if ever attended church, but Margaret was christened at Markinch soon after her birth, as she was so ill with whooping cough, and I was baptised at Bogside by the Rev Borrowman, the then incumbent of Auchterderran Parish, in 1946. A commonly held belief among the religious and non-religious alike was that unbaptised souls would be denied the kingdom of heaven after death, so the decision to have babies or older children christened was prompted as much by superstition as by faith. For past generations, in an uncertain world where infant mortality was a fact of life, having a child was always giving a hostage to fortune, so it was as well to hedge your bets!

It was not until 1956 that Joey decided to be confirmed and join the Church. Her younger sister Doris, who had married Jim's cousin Dunc Rutherford in 1953, had a little boy in September 1956, and Joey was invited to be godmother to her new nephew. It was typical of Joey that she did not take this important obligation lightly, and, aware of the vows she would have to make and the duty she would subsequently have to the child, she announced her intention to join the first communicants' class at the parish church, under the current incumbent, the Rev Watt. From that time, Joey became a diligent church member, attending very regularly and encouraging us to go with her. She more than lived up to her duties as godmother to wee Alan, who became very much part of our family, as he lived with his parents in one of the cottar hooses down the road. Indeed Joey helped to bring him up, as he would often be with her while his mother worked outside on the farm.

A new minister arrived in 1959: the Rev Kenneth Ogilvie, who moved from the parish of New Deer in Buchan, Aberdeenshire. The Kirk Session appealed for help from the congregation to tidy up the manse garden in preparation for his arrival. As was traditional, the manse at Auchterderran was a huge barn of a house surrounded by an enormous overgrown garden, and beyond that the glebe. This was a field of considerable size, which would historically have been for the use of the minister. As time passed, however, the parish incumbents had no direct use for the land, so as a major landowner, the Church of Scotland would rent out these pockets of agricultural land, so adding to its income. Joey prevailed upon Jim to respond to the request for help at the manse, and he was working there when he met the new minister for the first time. He described him to Joey as "a gey decent chap, fur a meenister!" He seemed very affable and appreciative of Jim's work in the garden. Now Jim could look somewhat rough and ready when in his workin' claes, and almost always in dire need of a shave, but even he noticed that the minister was extremely scruffy in appearance. The most noticeably inelegant aspect of his dress was the great big safety pin (of the nappy variety!) that was holding his trousers together. At least when Jim was dressed to go out, he always looked very clean and smart. (Joey at any rate would never have allowed anything else, as she rightly felt that people would see such an oversight as a fault on her part: "Fancy her lettin' 'er man oot like that!") The minister, on the other hand, always looked rather grubby and unkempt, even when on duty in the pulpit.

Despite his (or his wife's) shortcomings in the sartorial department, we grew to quite like Mr Ogilvie, and he seemed to take to Jim and Joey. Within a short time of his arrival, he approached Jim to become an elder in the church. The only other farmer on the Kirk Session was Tot (Thomas) Chrisp from Balgreggie Farm, and the minister was keen to add another. Jim, much to Joey's surprise, agreed almost at once. She was quick to point out that this would place him under an obligation to attend church and Kirk Session meetings, but to an extent, I think Jim felt flattered by the invitation and, given his natural wish always to please, saw no reason to be churlish enough to decline. So it was in the late fifties, while not exactly becoming pillars of the Church, both Jim and Joey assumed responsibilities. Joey was a church member with a serious intention to be a good Christian, but she never joined the Women's Guild or any other ancillary organisation. She always hated meetings of women en masse and fought shy of being inviegled into what she saw as the purely social aspects of "gaun tae the kirk!" Meanwhile, Jim had a more public church profile, and would have to take his turn on duty at the church door, in carrying the sacraments at Communion or laying the weekly offering on the communion table. He found it hard to refuse any request, and on a few occasions he would be prevailed upon to do a reading at the watch-night service on Christmas Eve. In truth, Jim was no shrinking violet and given the chance, was a natural performer who relished a bit of the limelight now and again. The problem was that, each time this happened, Jim could not resist partaking of some Christmas spirit in its liquid form during the earlier part of the evening, and we once even had to ply him with strong black coffee in an attempt to make sure that he would not slur his words or in some other way betray the fact that he was anything but stone cold sober! A fringe benefit of his connection to the church was that Jim managed to secure the lease of the glebe land at a time when he needed more grazing for his beasts!

Although Margaret and I had never attended Sunday school, by the time our parents became more involved in the Church we were old enough for the Bible class, and I later became a Sunday school teacher for a short time before I went off to university. At the age of seventeen I joined the Church, as Margaret had before me. What I most remember about that confirmation service was that I had to shake hands with Dad as one of the assembled elders. My first Communion as a full member of the Church of Scotland was a very memorable occasion. The restoration of the ancient abbey of Iona had been underway for many years under the direction of the Iona Community led by the Rev McLeod, later Lord McLeod of Fuinary. As it reached a climax with the completion of the west door, our church at Auchterderran was one of many that had been involved in the sponsorship of the work. A group visit was organised to attend the service of thanksgiving and dedication that was to take place on the island. Our bus left in the early hours of the morning for Oban, where we caught the steamer that stopped off at Iona. As there was no roll-on, roll-off facility at the pier on the island in those days, we had to transfer to little boats, which ferried us to the quayside. We were familiar with this procedure, as we had visited Iona on a family holiday some years before. So I partook of my first official Communion in an open-air service on a beautiful summer's day on the hillside overlooking the historic abbey, the site of the dawning of Christianity in Scotland. I found the experience very moving, as the history and symbolism of the event was not lost on me.

Despite this auspicious start, I still remain to be convinced that there is anything more to religion than history and tradition. I went on to be married in church and we had our sons christened, but I would be the first to admit that I was paying lip service to a belief system that I found impossible to rationalise. Ultimately, I stopped going to church, as did both my parents. Joey, I think, came to the same conclusion as I did: that religion as embodied in church attendance has a value in terms of social cohesion but, while Christianity provides a moral framework that few would argue with, we found it increasingly hard to accept the doctrinal and ideological precepts that underpin the moral and ethical structure it undeniably has. I felt that it was wrong to cherry-pick the parts that appealed to me, and that I couldn't justify continuing what amounted to a cynical exploitation of the services of the church.

Joey found it ever harder to equate the principles of Christianity with the small-minded, hypocritical attitudes so often engaged in by the very people who considered themselves to be good Christians. When the church needed emergency repairs to the roof, she volunteered to help in a door-to-door collection round the parish. I went with her, and we were embarrassed to find that these were often the people who either refused to contribute or who made the most facile of excuses not to help. Conversely, generous donations were sometimes made by residents of the parish who had little or no connection to the church, but clearly valued its history and social function. Joey also felt that a religious faith is easy to sustain when all is well with you and yours. Hers came into question in the sixties when her relationship with her sister Doris broke down under the strain of her and her husband Dunc's unreasonable and jealous behaviour. Then when one of her other sisters, Betty, died from cancer at the age of forty-seven, leaving six children, in 1971, she began to drift away from the Church. Jim also attended less and less, especially after Mr Ogilvie left Auchterderran and the new minister, a much younger man, Alastair Younger, took over the charge. I suspect he seemed still wet behind the ears to many of his older parishioners!

It was he who married Bill and me, but just before our wedding I had unexpectedly met up with Mr Ogilvie. He and his wife, like us, were guests at the wedding of an old friend of Bill's in Banchory. I was genuinely pleased to meet him again, and in the course of our conversation that day, gratified to realise that he had fond memories of his years at Auchterderran, and that he held Joey and Jim in great respect and affection. It was very touching, therefore, to receive a wedding gift of a New Testament from him on the occasion of our wedding a few weeks later. He had not had an easy time as minister at Auchterderran, and had many a run-in with the Kirk Session, who found him too progressive and intellectual for their liking. So I think he always appreciated the warm welcome and honest reactions he could count on from Jim and Joey on his occasional visits to Pitkinny. We never met again, and I noted with some sadness the death notices of both Mr and Mrs Ogilvie in *The Scotsman* in the opening years of the millennium.

Notwithstanding my drifting away from regular church attendance, I do value in retrospect the positive aspects of the moral guidance we received from our contact with the Church during a very formative period of my childhood and youth. Religious education and observance was an integral part of the school curriculum and activities. We became familiar with Bible stories of both the Old and New Testaments: Joseph and his coat of many colours, Daniel in the lions' den, Jacob's ladder, the miracles of Jesus and, most of all, the stories of his Nativity and Passion. Many well-loved and word-perfect hymns and psalms remind me even now of school days and Sunday mornings in church. "Summer suns are glowing," redolent of the impending summer holiday freedom as we sang it at the end of session service. "There is a green hill far away, without a city wall," would always puzzle me. What did a green hill need a city wall for, anyway? We were subjected to the rote learning of many topics with a religious theme: the books of the Bible (Genesis, Exodus, Leviticus, Numbers…); passages from the Bible ("Though I speak with the tongues of men and of angels…"). Learning by heart a new metrical psalm each weekend was part of the homework set by our primary seven teacher ("I to the hills will lift mine eyes, from whence doth come mine aid.") Mum and Dad would help me to memorise these words, which seemed to me on the one hand incomprehensible yet on the other impressive and beautiful in their mystery. Jim would sometimes interject with less edifying snippets from his memory of his school days:

Matthew, Mark, Luke and John,
Haud the cuddy till Ah get on!

Or, rather more seriously, he told us this epitaph that appealed to him:

Remember, Man as thou goes by,
As thou art now, so once was I.
As I am now so must thou be,
Prepare for Death and follow me.

And its answer:

To follow thee I won't consent
Until I know which way you went!

The thought of death and dying was something I preferred not to think about, as I assumed when I was very young that you had to be really old before you could die. So it came as a real shock when I realised one day that young people could and sometimes did die. As I grew older and became increasingly aware of the complexity of the human condition, I would sometimes frighten myself by trying to wrest with concepts that are beyond my understanding even now. How big is the universe? Why am I me, and not someone else? What happens to you after you die? Did the tinkies really leave me on the doorstep, as John Imrie used to tease me? So the mystical and ethereal aspects of religion, natural science, and philosophy seemed almost credible and, if not an answer to my questions, at least a comforting crutch. There was another world and a Supreme Being who would make everything all right ultimately. It is a measure of the impact that early exposure to religious experience (both through the church and the school) must have had on me, that I was recently moved to tears on hearing, unexpectedly, the strains of "By Cool Shiloam's Shady Rill" sung by the Glasgow Orpheus Choir on the radio one day. I was immediately transported back in time to those occasions when we would sing that beautiful old hymn, full of the mystery of barely understood words and mystical imagery, most significantly at our children's christenings. It was also sung at the funeral of Auntie Teenie Black, as it had always been her favourite hymn. Such is the power of words and music to evoke memories of childhood and youth.

At a distance of half a century it seems to me now that in addition to this emphasis on Christian knowledge, albeit mostly barely understood, much of our early education was archaic in both content and method. Rote learning has great limitations in pedagogic terms, but I do think there is some value in training the memory to retain essential facts. Our grasp of numerical and multiplication tables became entrenched in our memory banks, where it remains to this day. We chanted them on a daily basis, to the benefit of our mental arithmetic skills. Our teacher would draw a clock on the blackboard, with a number from one to twelve in the centre. Everyone had to stand and she went round the class pointing to a different number on the clock face each time, which had to be multiplied by the number in the centre. Only when you got the right answer in a few seconds were you allowed to sit down. No one wanted to be the last one left standing, which was great motivation to know your tables. Then the teacher would change the number in the centre and the whole process would start all over again.

This methodology is perfectly valid, but some of the content of the maths curriculum was less easily justifiable. Why were we still, in the fifties, learning about and doing calculations with bushels and pecks in weight; rods, chains, and poles in length; and gills in capacity? No wonder much of the maths language sounded biblical! The intricacies of the pre-decimal imperial currency system, or LSD as it was abbreviated, made huge demands on our numeracy! Many wearisome hours were spent on calculations like: "Change £1,382.17.6½d. into halfpennies" or "Change 436 threepennies into pounds shillings and pence!" The names of our notes and coins sound so old-fashioned and quaint in retrospect: shillings, florins, sixpences, half-crowns, and even guineas—while, of course, one generation later, nothing pertaining to the imperial system was ever learned by our children. The old conundrums like "If a herring and a half cost a penny and a half, how much do you pay for a dozen?" were regularly trawled out to test our understanding of our monetary system, but that one defeated my grasp of a priori logic for a very long time! I was told that the answer was twelve, but I could never see why!

Much of our early introduction to, and later immersion in literature comprised learning by heart reams of poetry and prose. This began in infant school, through the primary, and on up to higher English and beyond. When I was very young my parents would recite rhymes and sing songs as they went about their work or interacted with us in the house:

> Anne-Pan, toorly-ann
> Washed her face in the frying pan
> Kaimed 'er hair wi' the leg o' the chair
> Anne-pan toorly-ann.

Little rhymes accompanied by actions amused us:

> Round and round the garden, like a teddy bear
> (Running fingers over my outstretched palm),
> one step
> (tickled the front of my wrist),

two step
(tickled the front of my elbow),
an' tickle you under thair!"
(tickled me under the oxter—to much giggling!)

No matter how often we heard these rhymes and knew exactly what was coming, we always found it fun, but as we grew older other games, while similar, were more puzzling. Gran Betsy would hold our open palm and trace circles on it with her finger saying:

Roond and roond the radical road,
the radical rascal ran,
hoo mony 'Rs' are in that,
tell me if ye can!

Brought up, as she was, in the shadow of Arthur's Seat in Edinburgh, she was familiar with this track that wound its way round the distinctive hill, as she was with the Bonnie Wells o' Wearie nearby, the natural spring which featured in her favourite song. When we managed to count the seven letters, she would always shake her head until we realised that the question actually referred to the word 'that'.

Another riddle of that type was:

'Constantinople' is a very big word,
If you can't spell it ye're a dunce!

We would chant the spelling of M-I-S-S-I-S-S-I-P-P-I and then do it backwards, I-P-P-I-S-S-I-S-S-I-M. This came to have some relevance for us when our primary six teacher would read us instalments of *Tom Sawyer* and *Huckleberry Finn* on a Friday afternoon, always stopping on a cliffhanger, just as the heroes were about to be caught by Indian Joe in the cave, or some other disaster was about to befall them, and we would have to wait till the next week to learn their fate. Little did I know then that our elder son Calum would spend his gap year of 1991–1992 in a small town in Mississippi state and would sail on that famous river, and walk or drive along its levées.

I was reminded of Tom Sawyer on another occasion in 1990, just after Jim and Joey returned to Fife for the second phase of their retirement. They had had a new wooden boundary fence erected, and I arrived one sunny spring day to find Dad painting it with preservative at Joey's behest. He never liked that kind of chore and was doing the work with a rather bad grace. "You remind me of Tom Sawyer, Dad," I said. "Is that right?" he replied, "Well I've never met the chap, but I bet he disnae hae a boss like your Mum." I tried to reassure him that Tom's Aunt Polly was probably just as formidable as Joey, but he took no consolation from that suggestion!

Other counting rhymes I remember Joey saying were:

One, two, three, four,
Mary at the cottage door,
Eating cherries off a plate,
Five, six, seven, eight.

and

One, two, three, four, five,
Once I caught a fish alive,
Six, seven, eight, nine, ten,
Then I let it go again.
Why did you let it go?
Because it bit my finger so.
Which finger did it bite?
This little finger on the right.

On reflection, it is clear that these little poems and rhymes were effective means of beginning to establish early concepts like number, colour, left and right, and so on, in our preschool learning, although neither of my parents was consciously educating us, just doing what came naturally in a family context. Most importantly, we were spoken to all the time and encouraged (again, totally unconsciously) to communicate effectively, as we were exposed to a wide variety of linguistic devices, which in pedagogic terms are so vital in the early establishment of speech. It is very sad that nowadays, in an era when we are bombarded by an infinite variety of communication, and technology has brought huge advancement in mass media, there are still children starting school lacking the most basic communication skills.

More romantic and lyrical examples were learned and chanted in our skipping or ball games. Some may have had a historical origin, and in this case seemed to have a particular resonance for us, but as to whether the third line was true in our case, we could only imagine!

Queen Mary, Queen Mary, my age is sixteen,
Ma faither's a fairmer on yonder green,
He's plenty o' siller to dress me fu' braw,
But nae bonnie laddie'll tak me awa'.

The last line of this ditty seemed to echo the dire warnings Joey would give us when we failed to come up to scratch in the domestic skills area: "Nae man'll ever mairry ye if ye cannae dae better than that!" or "Ye'll be nae guid tae onybody if ye dinnae pu' yer socks up!" This might sound as if Joey was concerned that we would be left on the shelf if we lacked the necessary marriageable accomplishments, but I don't really think she thought that way at all. She was more concerned that we should have the necessary education to be able to earn our own living rather than have to depend on a man for security.

One poem with a rural theme that we learned at school was instantly recognised and remembered word for word by both Jim and Joey:

John Smith, fallow fine,
Can ye shae this horse o' mine?
Yes, indeed, an' that Ah can
Jist as weel as ony man.
Ca' a nail intae the tae
Tae gar the pownie speel the brae;
Ca' a nail intae the heel,
Tae gar the pownie pace weel;
There's a nail an' there's a brod

There's a pownie weel-shod,
Weel-shod, weel-shod, weel-shod pownie.
(Unattributed traditional)

Recollecting the incident when I had to walk Nell the collie through the football crowds in Dunfermline brought to mind the poem "The Lost Collie" by W.D. Cocker:

Cockin' ma anxious lugs,
Hidin' ma fears doon deep,
Speirin at daft-like dugs,
That hae na the smell o' sheep;
Tryin' tae fin some trace
In a' the streets Ah've crossed.
Keekin' in ilka face
Does naeboby ken, Ah'm lost?

We were fortunate in having access to those aspects of the Scots heritage examined and illustrated by the work of our national poet. The Burns Federation encouraged the study of his song and poetry in schools, and rewarded with certificates of merit successful recitations and recitals of learned poems and songs. I have a clear recollection of standing in the kitchen practising "Scots Wha Hae" with the help of my parents, and still sometimes sing, "Ye Banks and Braes o' Bonnie Doon." Stories, songs, and poems in the Scots vernacular certainly developed in me a pride in our musical and literary heritage, although there were times when Jim could introduce a note of levity and irreverence into the most stirring of historic events. Even the famous skirmish between Robert the Bruce and a Norman knight on the eve of Bannockburn was subjected to Jim's treatment:

Bruce and de Bohun were fechtin' fur the croon,
Bruce took 'is battle-axe and ca'd the bugger doon!

A factually correct, if somewhat prosaic and comical description of a seminal moment in Scottish history!

Jim could recite from memory many songs and poems learned in his childhood and youth. His rendition of "The Burial of Sir John Moore" and its pornographic version, which he would occasionally launch into when he was in his cups, had its counterpart in "The Boy Stood on the Burning Deck." Jim and his friends had bowdlerised this famous poem to take into account the warnings they had been given about a local man in the Star who had paedophilic tendencies:

The Boy Stood on the burning deck,
His back against the mast.
He darena' move a bloody inch
Till So-and-So had past!

At high school we had to learn tracts of poetry: "The curfew tolls the knell of parting day" from Gray's *Elegy*; "Water, water, everywhere, nor any drop to drink," from *The Rime of the Ancient Mariner*. A favourite was, and still is, *Tam O'Shanter*, one of Burns' comic Scots verses:

Whaur sits his sulky sullen dame,
Gatherin' her brows like gathering storm,
Nursing her wrath tae keep it warm.

And the more reflective stanzas, some of the most beautiful ever written in Standard English:

But pleasures are like poppies spread,
You seize the flow'r, its bloom is shed.

Much of this rote learning had the effect of firmly lodging such poems and songs in the memory bank, and where there are gaps, I can turn to a well-used copy of *The English Parnassus*, or a slightly less tattered Palgrave's *Golden Treasury.*

Jim had a large repertoire of mostly Scottish songs, which he would gladly sing when he had an audience, particularly when he was sufficiently lubricated by some "bold John Barleycorn." Some were humorous and light-hearted, like "Ma Big Kilmarnock Bunnet" or "The Soor Milk Cairt," while others more seriously gave voice to sentiments of love of country, like "Bonnie Gallowa'," "Bonnie Strathyre" or "Rothesay Bay," or of romantic love, such as "The Lea Rig" or "The Road and the Miles to Dundee." Joey would sometimes be prevailed upon to sing in company, her favourites being "Teddy O'Neal" and "Bonnie Mary o' Argyll." Both of them would often sing as they went about their work. Indeed this was always a reliable indicator of Jim's mood. "Things are no sae bad efter a', ye're faither's singin' again!" Joey would sometimes say with relief in her voice. They would also sing songs that were popular in the days of their youth and courtship. "When you were Sweet Sixteen," "When They Begin the Beguine," "South of the Border, Down Mexico Way," or "A Nightingale Sang in Berkley Square." Jim enjoyed some songs from popular music and films in the early fifties like Guy Mitchell's "She Wears Red Feathers and a Hooly-hooly Skirt," "The Yellow Rose of Texas," or "The Man from Laramie."

Neither of my parents was able to benefit from any kind of further education, and both left school at the first opportunity, aged fourteen. However, it seems that despite this relatively short formal education, they must have had a very sound basic training in the three Rs. They could both read fluently, and had an excellent grasp of grammar and vocabulary. Their numerical skills were also very well-founded and they could both do mental calculations very quickly and accurately. Every month, the milk book would have to be completed and the top copy sent off to the Scottish Milk Marketing Board creamery. This involved counting up the number of gallons of milk produced by the dairy herd each day for a month. So a column of 28, 29, 30, or 31 three-digit numbers had to be added together. This was always Joey's job, and she would quickly run up each of the three columns of units tens and hundreds to arrive at the monthly total. Sometimes she would ask me to check it, which I did, but much more slowly than she did, and there was never a mistake in her calculation. I remember Dad talking about the capacity of the new grain drier. He had to work out the volume of grain in the storage tanks, and I remember being so impressed that he had the formula for the volume of a cylinder in his head and was able to work it out with no trouble at all from the measurements of the tanks.

Joey was a voracious reader and became a regular borrower of books from the library. In 1954, she began to subscribe to the *National Geographic* magazine, which was sent to her every month. These publications were such a window on the world, not only for her, but for all of us. The articles about the restoration of Thomas Jefferson's home at Monticello near Charlottesville in Virginia really captured my imagination, with their photographs of the grand antebellum mansion and ladies dressed in beautiful crinoline gowns. I vowed to myself that one day I would visit it, an ambition I had little or no hope then of realising, but it did come to fruition in 1998. Later, Joey also joined the Dunfermline branch of the Scottish Geographical Society and attended their monthly lectures in the Carnegie Hall. She also bought *The Scots Magazine* every month, the oldest published magazine in the world, dating back to 1739. Many winters would see her joining an evening class, usually for dressmaking or some other handwork activity. She had a spell of learning to make lampshades, and another when she did leatherwork. Brodie's, a shop in Link Street, Kirkcaldy, was the source of her materials and tools. The first thing she made was a purse for herself, and she was so pleased with it that she replicated it as Christmas presents for her sisters and her mother Betsy. Unfortunately, as they were all identical they were forever getting them mixed up, and there were times when Mum would come home from Markinch with Gran's purse, or one of her sisters would mistakenly pick up Joey's and take it home. Although her spare time was of necessity very limited, Joey used what she had in a constructive and positive way. She never lost the love of learning and of mastering new skills.

Jim enjoyed watching football and was a regular supporter of East Fife at Bayview in Methil and of Raith Rovers at Stark's Park in Kirkcaldy. Later, as East Fife hit lean times, he would alternate between the Kirkcaldy team and the swiftly improving and ultimately very successful Dunfermline Athletic (the Pars) at East End Park. He never played football for a team, other than the impromptu games at Pitkinny, but he was a participant in curling. He played for the Bishopshire and Thornton clubs, but Joey always suspected that he was more interested in the social (or more accurately, drinking) aspects of the the apres-curling features of the sport! His one more intellectual activity was membership for some years of a discussion group at Auchterderran, which would feature visiting speakers who could be very entertaining. He would sometimes relate stories to us, one of which was told by Chief Constable Merrilees, who had retired from Edinburgh and Lothian police. He was being driven to a meeting by his chauffeur in an unmarked car one day, and as they were late he had told his driver to "step on the gas." They were stopped by an officious young constable, who was on point duty at a busy junction. As he began to question the chauffeur, the chief constable was about to intervene from the back seat to explain who he was, and that there was no need to take the matter any further. Before he could say more than a few words he was waved back imperiously by the young officer with the words, "When I've finished with the organ-grinder, then I might talk to his monkey!" I don't know what fate befell the young constable, but I am sure he would live to regret his less-than-courteous language and manner.

*Burns Federation certificate for singing*

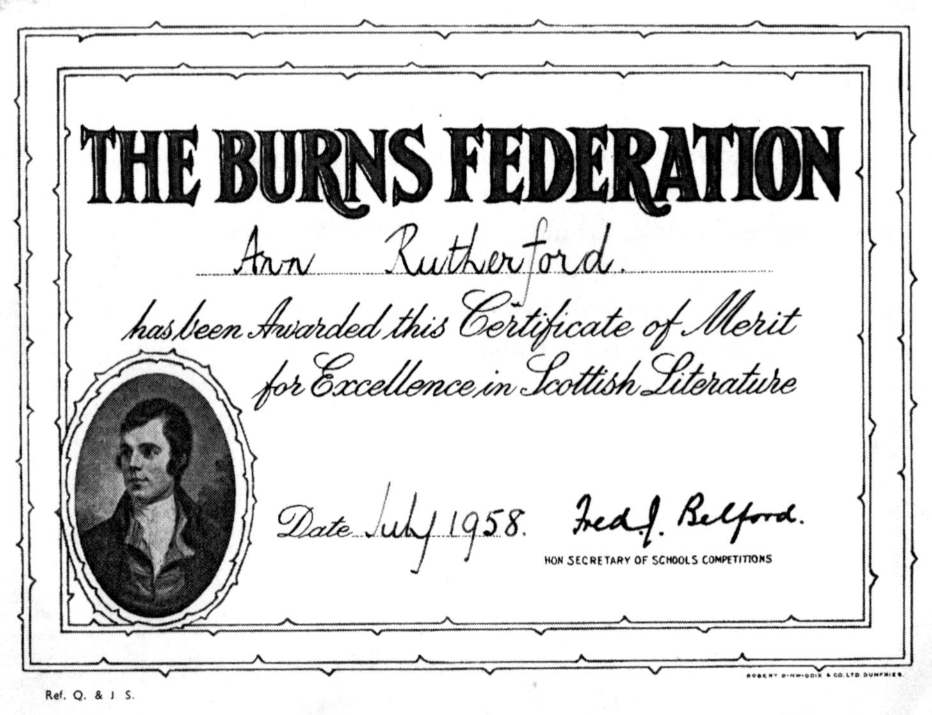


*Burns Federation certificate for recitation*

I am the bread of life:
he that cometh unto Me
shall never hunger, and
he that believeth on Me
shall never thirst.

Be thou faithful unto death and I
will give thee a Crown of Life

This do in remembrance of Me

ELIZABETH ANN RUTHERFORD

did this day confirm the vows
of her Baptism by professing
her faith in Christ and was
admitted to

THE LORD'S TABLE

and to the full Communion of
the Church

Kenneth G. Ogilvie

Minister of
The Church of Scotland

Date ~~31st October~~ 1965

*Anne's confirmation certificate*

To
Ann Rutherford
With every good wish
from Kenneth and Joan
Ogilvie
3rd April, 1971

Old Manse of Auchterderran
Fife 1959 - 1968.

*Inscription on New Testament wedding gift from the Reverend Kenneth and Mrs Joan Ogilvie (3 April 1971), who lived at the old manse of Auchterderran from 1959 to 1968*

# Chapter 27

## "There'll be nae hunkerslidin' here!"

The nearest that Cardenden came to a posh area or a "west end" was Auchterderran, where the triumvirate of institutions was located: the junior secondary school, the parish church and its manse, and the doctor's surgery, headed respectively by the headmaster, the minister, and the doctor. In the absence of a lawyer, who would have given us a full set of establishment figures, we had to make do with a dentist in the other big house. As far as these men represented their respective organisations or professions, they were accorded a degree of respect by most people, but there was very little of the forelock-tugging variety of deference. They were viewed with a healthy realism by most of their pupils, parents, parishioners, and patients, and regarded as being just as likely to have human frailties and foibles as themselves. An example of this is when Moffat's, the local petrol station on Woodend Brae, lost patience with their account holders who were constantly in arrears with their fuel bills, and posted a list of their names at the petrol pumps. The minister's name was there with all the others! This combination of respect and scepticism in dealing with one's "betters" is, in my experience, peculiar to the Scottish character, as exemplified in Burns's poem "A Man's a Man for A' That":

> The man o' independent mind,
> He looks an' laughs at a' that.

A much coarser, but no less eloquent response to shows of ostentation or pretentiousness that I heard from my father from time to time was, "They're jist a bunch o' hoors an' comic singers!"

We were brought up to show respect to our elders, no matter what their social position. Joey particularly had an extremely egalitarian view of society, and did not see why someone in a privileged position should automatically be deserving of respect. Rather, she believed that respect had to be earned. She encouraged us to believe that we could achieve anything if we put our minds to it, but at the same time she would not tolerate us becoming too big for our boots. One summer day, Margaret was looking forward to going for a cycle run, but discovered that she had a flat tyre and, worse, that the valve was missing and she couldn't blow up the tyre. Jock Steel happened to pass by and asked what the trouble was. He sympathised with Margaret's problem and promised to look for a valve for her as soon as he returned to Bogside. As he left, impatient for a resolution to her problem, Margaret (overheard by Joey) called after him, "Hurry up then,

Jock!" Joey wasted no time in taking Margaret severely to task for daring to tell a hard-working man like Jock to hurry up. She berated the crestfallen "young madam" for being so impudent and told her she could forget all about the cycle run. The only place she would be going was to walk to Bogside and apologise to Jock for her cheek. When Margaret very reluctantly did as she was directed, Jock reacted by phoning Joey to assure her that Margaret had done nothing wrong. Joey then proceeded to ask Jock how he would have felt if one of his sons or daughters had had the temerity to tell him to hurry up! He was forced to see her point. What Joey really meant was that the fact that he worked for her and Jim did not mean that we could treat him any differently from any other adult we came into contact with. We had to learn that good manners as drilled into us by Joey amounted to more than "Yes, please" and "No, thank you." It was the imperative of having true consideration for other people and their needs and feelings.

Equally, Joey and Jim were determined that we should share their work ethic. "There'll be nae hunkerslidin' here!" Towards the end of the fifties, Joey had some help in the house. Mrs Smith, a lady who lived in the prefabs in Cardenden, came every Friday to clean the house. She was a bundle of energy and industry as she dusted, swept, scrubbed, and polished her way round the house. During school holidays we dreaded a Friday, as we had to be up just as early as on a school day, and ready to work as soon as Mrs Smith arrived. Joey would allocate us jobs, as she would not allow us to be idle while Mrs Smith was working. So we would have to help in the kitchen, tidying cupboards, polishing the linoleum tiles, ironing, and finally ending up with cleaning Joey's many brass ornaments. Mrs Smith talked as hard as she worked, so Jim found Friday dinnertime a trying ordeal, as our guest gave a comprehensive account of everything that had happened in the past week. Each comment or observation would be prefixed by: "I just turned round and said...," or "As I always turn round and say...." I am sure that Jim wished fervently that she would go and turn round somewhere else, but Joey found Mrs Smith's help such a boon that she would hear nothing against her.

Joey saw to it that we learned the basics, not only of housework, but also of cooking. Jim was no easy taskmaster as a consumer of Joey's culinary efforts, and he was very fussy about the quality and consistency of the potatoes on his plate, and indeed of most other things as well. His preference was for a "mealy tattie," particularly Keir's Pinks or Golden Wonders, neither of which was easy to cook. They could easily disintegrate completely if boiled in water for more than ten minutes, and rather had to be steamed slowly in a little water only, so that they cooked without actually falling apart. In those days, before the advent of the five-day week, banks opened and the farm workers worked on Saturday mornings. Joey would go to the bank for the wages and to the post office for the National Insurance stamps. Then she would make up the wage envelopes. (At one time Margaret would help by writing the names on the envelopes and would write one for herself, in the vain hope that she might get some money too, but it never happened!) We were left to make the dinner on a Saturday, but after Margaret started a Saturday job in Low's the grocer's in 1958 or 1959, when I was twelve or thirteen, that left me in sole charge of the kitchen and the dinner. One Saturday after her errands to the bank and post office, Joey had to drive up to Dundonald House where the Edgar family lived, to deliver a wedding present for their eldest daughter, Valerie. Bob Edgar, as NCB factor, had been a good friend and great support to Jim and Joey, but we realised that the Edgars had a lifestyle very different from ours. The girls were mad about horses, and Bob Edgar indulged their passion to the full. They took part in show jumping and dressage events at the local agricultural shows, and we would see them dressed up to the nines or, as Joey would say, "like flee-hooks," in their top hats, jodhpurs, riding jackets, and boots, resplendent with immaculate hairdos and buttonholes perfectly colour-matched to their cravats. Bob Edgar would urge Jim, "Get yer lassies a couple o' pownies, Jim!" but we never had the slightest interest in horses, and certainly didn't aspire to the horsey set.

As Joey left Dundonald that morning, Mrs Edgar said, "Of course you'll have to be back for Jim's dinner." "Oh no, not at all," replied Joey, "Anne makes the dinner on a Saturday." "Anne makes the dinner? Really? How horrid for her," said Valerie in disgust. Needless to say, domestic duties did not feature at all on the agenda of the Edgar girls. A few years later, when Irene, one of the twins, was about to be married to a gentleman farmer from Angus, she was asked by Mr Ogilvie the minister how she felt about being a farmer's wife and helping on the farm. She exclaimed in horror, "But Mr Ogilvie, I'll only be arranging the flowers!" Mrs Edgar confided to Joey at the wedding that she had had a terrible time trying to entertain and cater for her daughter's prospective in-laws. Of course she had to cope single-handed as there was no help forthcoming from her girls. She declared in an exasperated tone, "I realise that I have brought up three useless daughters!" Joey privately felt like replying with another question, "And whose fault is that?" However, she really felt sorry for Mrs Edgar, whom she had always liked, despite her shortcomings as a housewife. She remembered visiting the Edgars some years earlier when Bob complained that he had often to get into an unmade bed. "Well," rejoined his wife, "I spent all day yesterday weeding the drive, so why don't you go and sleep there!"

I have explained before how, as I grew up, I had a rather equivocal attitude to living in the country and to life at Pitkinny. I suppose it is natural to feel that the grass is greener on the other side of the fence, but one particular event served to underscore how vastly different lifestyles can be. One of my best friends at high school (and in the years since) was Elizabeth Ritchie, who lived in Haggis Ha' in Lochgelly. (I refused to believe that was really her address until I saw it for my own eyes!) Her father was an engineer with the NCB and her mother was a full-time housewife, as were most of my contemporaries' mothers, who devoted herself entirely to her three children, Elizabeth and her older siblings Peter and Gus (Georgina). They were a very talented and gifted family, the girls especially—both were very fine singers who would go on to study at the Royal Academy of Music and Drama in Glasgow—while Peter became a dentist. Mrs Ritchie was a tiny little lady, not much over five feet, who was always terribly well spoken and invariably beautifully dressed and made up. She usually wore very dramatic hats, which impressed me no end. It was obvious that her daughters had inherited their artistic flair and temperament from her rather than from their father, who was a very quiet man.

Elizabeth and I both played hockey for the school and were involved in various musical activities. The first time I went home with her for tea was an utter revelation to me. As we walked up the garden path, the door opened to reveal Mrs Ritchie, who had obviously been watching for us. "Come in, come in, girls. You must be tired after your long day at school." I couldn't believe it as she took the schoolbags from us and helped us out of our blazers. "Now through you go to the fire. The kettle's on and I'll bring your tea straightaway." There was the tea table all set ready, complete with dainty napkins, and as Mrs Ritchie fussed over us, plying us with food and drink, I felt myself reeling from delighted surprise. How different from my usual homecoming at Pitkinny! Joey was always busy inside or out, indeed sometimes in the years after she had learned to drive, absent altogether, away from the farm on some errand for Jim. On days such as that, having walked up from the school bus, I would come in to the kitchen to find the dinner dishes still on the table, along with a hastily scrawled note from Joey: "Away to Coupar Angus for a spare part for the digger. Do the dishes and start the tea. Mum." Although I was used to this scenario, after my visit to Elizabeth's house, I couldn't help feeling some aggrieved resentment that the typical situation at Pitkinny was one of "all hands to the pump" and, "Aye, an' that means you too, young lady," as Joey would say. It was only some years later that I learned that Elizabeth envied me my life at Pitkinny and that she loved the boisterous and earthy atmosphere at the farm, which contrasted so vividly with the air of refinement and gentility of her home. Experiences like feeding the pet lambs, or relishing Joey's scrambled eggs made from eggs she had bravely gathered herself (usually with much squealing, shrieking, and giggling, leaving some very startled hens in her wake!). Elizabeth appreciated Joey and Jim's down-to-earth approach, and Jim's "colourful" language appealed to her wicked sense of humour, just as much as the gracious living and tender loving care she enjoyed from her mother impressed me. This was a valuable lesson for me, in becoming aware that there is room for an infinite variety of ways of living and that we must have respect for all of them, whether or not we share or understand them.

I also came to understand that real, assumed, or perceived social position and professional status did not guarantee correspondingly high standards of personal integrity, probity, or industry. So an architect could live in conditions of domestic chaos, not to say squalor; a minister could neglect to pay his way with local businesses; and a land factor could have daughters who looked down disdainfully—usually from the back of a horse—on the lesser mortals around them. Nevertheless, these same men and their wives were in themselves often likeable and successful individuals who had many other good qualities. I later grew to recognise people who were examples either of impoverished gentry or of the gentrified "nouveau riches," and people from working-class backgrounds who had to struggle gracelessly with the weight of huge chips on their shoulders. The most fortunate people were those who never lost sight of—or felt that they had to apologise for—their origins, but whose personalities allowed them gracefully and unselfconsciously to feel comfortable and be accepted in all manner of social or professional situations. Perhaps the greatest influence my parents and the experiences of my young life had on me was to help me to always try to see the real worth of the person beneath the outward veneer of class, wealth (or lack of it!), creed, or colour, and on the basis of that evidence, decide what to make of them.

So we were brought up to work hard and to respect the efforts of other people. We were encouraged to believe that you only get out of life what you put into it, and that the world does not owe any of us a living. In later life Joey came to feel that she had been too hard on us when we were young, but her own experience of life made her determined that we should learn to be self-reliant and, more than anything, be capable of looking after ourselves and our families. Compared to youngsters today, we had to grow up quickly in the sense that we were expected to assume responsibilities at home at quite an early age. After Margaret started her nursing training at seventeen years of age, she would come home from the hospital on her days off, but she really just changed one job for another. As a teenager during the school holidays, I was expected to do my share of work in the house and sometimes on the farm. On one of the rare occasions when Joey was ill in bed, with a bout of bronchitis, Margaret had worked very hard on her days off. As she was leaving to return to the hospital in Dunfermline, Joey gave her ten shillings for all her help. Then when she was getting out of the car at Auchterderran to catch the bus, Jim also gave her ten shillings. She was faced with one of those awful moral dilemmas for which we are never prepared. She had to make an instant decision as to whether she should tell him that she had already had some money from Joey. What to do? In the event, the moment passed and Margaret was left at the bus stop, delighted on the one hand to be richer to the tune of £1, a not inconsiderable bonus in those days, but consumed by an uneasy feeling of guilt that she had profited unduly by her parents' unaccustomed generosity with hard cash, all the more since it had been prompted by Joey's misfortune to be ill.

I always knew that money was tight for Joey, and that cash flow on a farm, or in any other business, is a perennial problem. When I started high school in 1958, I had a season ticket for my bus journeys to and from Cowdenbeath, and Joey gave me money every week to pay for my school dinners. In addition, on the very first day at high school she gave me a shilling, which was intended for use in an emergency only, in case I missed the school bus or needed to phone home for some reason. That shilling was to burn a hole in my pocket for the next six years. Most weeks, I would give in to the temptation to spend part of it in the wee shop near the school on Friday lunchtime, with the intention of paying in back out of my weekend pocket money of a few shillings. I would then pass the rest of a Friday afternoon in fear and dread that I would miss the bus, then have to pay for the service bus fare, and have to phone home, and would not have the wherewithal to do both! Joey's oft-repeated warnings about smoking, stealing, and telling lies did not include anything about embezzlement, but the chronic and insidious guilt associated with this misuse of the emergency funds was almost as bad as the acute shame of the incident when I stole the money intended for the postage stamps out of the dresser drawer years before.

As children, we were made to have good manners and show respect to adults, but equally important to Joey was that we should learn to develop self-respect. Her strict code of conduct stressed to me that if I did wrong, I might not be found out, but I would still have to answer to my conscience. My experience of dishonesty with money had certainly reinforced this lesson. The old poem "Conscience" by Walter Wingate ends with the verse:

Conscience, thou Justice cauld and stern,
Aften thy sairest word I earn:
But this is a thing I'll ne'er forgie,
It wasna fair wi'a bairn like me.

Later verses of the same poem prompt recollection, not only of my own battles with my conscience, but of the miserable and lonely day that Jim spent when he played truant from school for the one and only time:

I wanert awa ayont the knowes,
Whaur the bluebell blaws and the arnut grows;
The bee on the thistle, the bird on the tree,
Athing I saw was blithe— but me.
Weary and wae at last I sank
'Mang the gowan beds on the railway bank,
But never a train cam whistlin by,
And, oh! but a lanely bairn was I.

As we approached puberty, Joey's moral imperative extended, of course, to the question of boys, and we were left in no doubt that she expected us to be and to remain "good girls." Dire warnings of what would happen if we strayed from the straight and narrow were accompanied by the promise that once lost, our reputations could never be retrieved. Grandad Hugh used to say, "You're known by the company you keep," and if we complained that So-and-So was allowed more freedom than we were, Joey would say, "If So-and-So jumped in the Ore, wid ye jump in efter 'er?"

The only contact we had with boys was at church or school activities. Bible class, youth club and fellowship, badminton club at our own and other churches in the area, and the sports activities at school provided plenty of opportunity for social interaction involving both girl and boy friends. The occasional invitation to Boys' Brigade and Scout parties, were greeted with varying degrees of pleasure and anticipation, depending on how fanciable the source of the invitation was! It was a relief to be spared the annual ordeal of having to accompany my cousin Jim Drennan to his BB party (where he refused to allow me to dance with anyone but him) after he got over his early shyness and could invite girls he really liked instead of his cousin.

Certain locations and activities, however, remained taboo where Joey was concerned. She had an absolute abhorrence of cafés and coffee bars. "Don't ever let me catch ye sittin' in a café," she would warn. She, as most parents in those days, subscribed to the belief that "The deil maks work fur idle haunds." And there was no worse way to be idle, in her opinion, than to sit in a café. She clearly believed that we would be in danger of succumbing to temptation in the flesh-pots of Lochgelly and Cowdenbeath, which the cafés there represented to her. When I saw pupils who lived in Cowdenbeath adjourning after school to the Central Café in the High Street, as I passed on the way home in the school bus, I knew that its hedonistic delights would be forever denied to me. On the frequent occasions when I would be returning home on a service bus from sports or choir practice, and had to wait for a Kirkcaldy bus at the top of Auchterderran Road in Lochgelly, a desperately cold and exposed location, I longed to be able to go into the café there for a hot drink. But I knew better than to risk Joey's wrath should she find out I had blown some of my precious emergency shilling on a pyrex cup of frothee coffee!

Another completely forbidden temptation was to accept an invitation from a boy to go to the pictures. Perhaps Joey's memories of her and Greta's frantic struggle to retain their crêpe de chine–clad virtue on that well-remembered date with two young men in the cinema in Kirkcaldy had something to do with her absolute refusal to allow me to accept such an invitation. Only once did I go against her wishes. When I was nearly sixteen, I was staying for the weekend in Kelty with my best friend Sandra McGregor, whose mother was slightly less strict than mine, and she raised no objection to Sandra and me going to the Regal with two boys from school. Sadly, I found the experience less than enjoyable, thanks again to my overactive conscience. I was on heckle-pins for the whole evening, convinced that someone would see me and tell Mum, or that Mrs McGregor would spill the beans. The fact that Joey knew no one in Kelty except Sandra and her family, and that she seldom met Mrs McGregor, did nothing to lessen my fears. The discovery that the back row in the Regal consisted of double seats or "chummies" only heightened my misgivings about the whole enterprise, ensuring that the extremely innocent kisses between my date and me were the chastest of the chaste! It was days, if not weeks, until I could relax enough to believe that my duplicity would remain undiscovered.

Joey had a great disregard for good looks and social popularity. She firmly believed that beauty is only skin deep, and had a profound distrust of flattery or compliments of any kind. When I was in fifth year at high school in 1963, an incident brought this into sharp focus for me. Joey usually dropped me off at Woodend, where I caught the school bus from Kinglassie, but one morning, as she needed some messages at the top store, she took me to Auchterderran, where I crossed the road to get the Cardenden school bus. As she went into the Co-op, she met Mrs Miller, the art teacher at Auchterderran, who remembered Margaret but didn't know me. Mrs Miller asked Mum, "Who was that young girl, Mrs Rutherford?" "That's our Anne, our younger lassie," Joey replied. "Really? She's certainly growing up to be a pretty girl," said Mrs

Miller. "Oh, do you think so? Well I only hope that she never has to rely on her looks to get on in the world, Mrs Miller," came Joey's distinctly reproving reply. "Well there's a young woman in London whose looks are making her very famous indeed!" With horror, Joey realised that the art mistress was referring to Christine Keeler, whose role in the notorious Profumo affair was in all the headlines that summer. "And I hope ye're no' suggestin' that Anne should follow her example!" Despite the teacher's immediate and apologetic reassurance that nothing was further from her mind, Joey was scandalised at what she interpreted as tacit approval of such a wayward and immoral lifestyle. "The cheek of that woman!"

Two years later, as a first-year student at Queen's College, Dundee, I was chosen to be a finalist in the Charities' Queen competition. My photograph with the three other finalists was in the *Courier* under a fatuous heading about "beauty and brains." I personally was pretty doubtful about the whole thing, but was interested to note the contrast in reactions from Mum and Dad. Jim was very pleased about it and carried the newspaper cutting around in his pocket for weeks, showing it proudly to everyone he met. Joey, on the other hand, made absolutely no reference to it whatsoever. She studiously avoided the subject entirely, and her silence spoke volumes! She was clearly unhappy about it, and probably feared that it would distract me from my studies, bring me into contact with undesirable people, and encourage me to have an unhealthy pre-occupation with my looks. Maybe she was concerned that Mrs Miller might see the photo and draw the wrong conclusions about me! It was with some relief on my part, and undoubtedly on Joey's, that I came second in the competition and could turn my back on the limelight.

I could understand Joey's misgivings, but her reaction to some other more important success of mine hurt much more. The next year, I won the university award for best student in second year history. I came home that weekend, looking forward to telling my parents about the prize. When I got into the car with Mum at Cardenden station and burst out with the good news, I was really deflated and disappointed by Joey's cool response: "Oh good, lass, that's fine. Now I have some eggs to deliver before we go home." My news was received with no more enthusiasm by Jim who, it seemed, like Joey, was too preoccupied with their work and the farm to get excited about my news. Perhaps they took my success for granted, and expected nothing less from me, or perhaps they lacked the emotional response that I longed for because they didn't appreciate exactly what I had achieved and the hard work it represented. It may be that this was a reflection of the Scots dour and puritanical attitude to pride and pleasure. Was it an attempt to keep me in my place, so that I wouldn't become over-confident? All I know is that I wanted to shout at them, "Look! I'm in a very big pool now, and I'm not just a wee, wee fish any more. I'm swimming with the big ones, and I'm leaving most of them behind!" This experience made me determined that, when I had a family of my own, I would try to make the most of their successes. So with our sons Bill and I have always made a point of showing how much joy and delight they have brought us and how much pleasure and pride we have taken in their achievements.

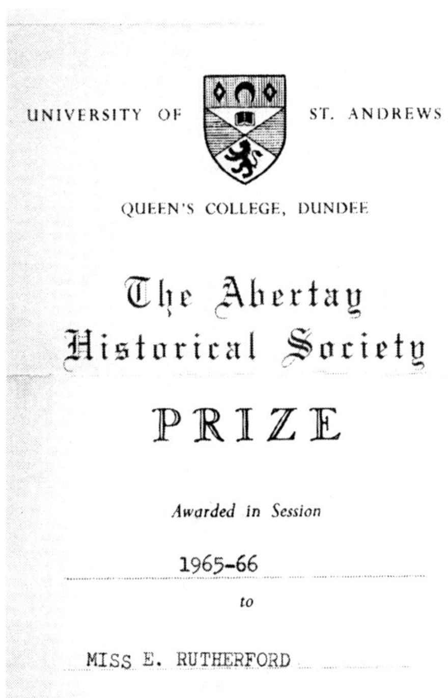
UNIVERSITY OF ST. ANDREWS

QUEEN'S COLLEGE, DUNDEE

The Abertay Historical Society

PRIZE

Awarded in Session

1965-66

to

MISS E. RUTHERFORD

*Prize for second year history at St Andrews University, 1966*

**Brains and beauty**

All the finalists for the title of Dundee Charities Queen study at Queen's College. From left—Susan Dye (19), Cobham, Surrey (social science); Anne Rutherford (18), Pitkinnie Farm, Cardenden (social science); Angela Olsen (19), 40 Elizabeth Crescent, East Newport (medicine); and Margaret Stewart (21), 12 Arnhall Drive, Dundee (accountancy, law).

*Charities Queen competition, Dundee 1965*

# Chapter 28

## "We'll hae tae sleep in the car the nicht, lassies!"

Looking back over the years of my childhood and youth, I appreciate that I am fortunate in retaining many vivid memories of our day-to-day life at Pitkinny. Some are happy or funny and pleasing to recall, others less so. Living on a farm is not the pastoral idyll that many imagine it to be. The tyranny of the weather and the seasons constituted a backdrop to a lifestyle of hard work and systematic routine, interspersed with frequent crises, as Jim and Joey strove to make a success of their business. Thankfully, the inevitable tedium this involved and the sheer physical hardship that sometimes accompanied their efforts were relieved by the warmth and pleasure of contact with family and friends, whose visits to the farm provided a welcome and spontaneous contrast to what was otherwise usually a serious and sometimes lonely life.

We were also fortunate and, it seemed, rather unusual when compared to many of our contemporaries, in having the pleasure of an annual family holiday. From the late forties we would go away for at least a few days once or twice in the course of the summer for a break from the routine of the farm and its demands. Compared with the possibilities for travel enjoyed by most people nowadays, we didn't go very far and did not do anything particularly adventurous. Jim and Joey never ventured abroad, nor did they ever have the experience of flying, but over the years they travelled extensively within Scotland, and occasionally south of the border. They particularly loved getting off the beaten track, and got to know most of the northwest Highlands really well, exploring the Inner and Outer Hebrides, and northwards to Orkney. They got to know many of the nooks and crannies of their own country that most people never see, and in the process they met many people and made life-long friends in the course of these journeys.

Of course, it was never possible to plan ahead for these holidays. Their timing depended entirely on the work and the weather. It was usually possible to manage a few days away between the sowing and planting time, and that of the hay harvest, so the end of June would see us spending a day or two (or later, the best part of a week) at the Royal Highland Show. Then, again depending on the co-operation of the weather and the completion of hay reaping accomplished by the end of July, this left a window of a week or two before the onset of the grain harvest for the main summer holiday. This would usually be presaged by a casual remark from Jim along the lines of, "We micht manage a wee brek sometime next week," or "We'll mibbe get awa' fur twa or three days gin the end o' next week." Joey would then have to be ready to go at a few hours' notice or even sooner. So we would have to wear our oldest clothes, as she kept everything clean and ready for the off. Sometimes, after he had retired, Grandad Hugh and Gran Betsy would come and stay at Pitkinny while we were away, otherwise things would be left in the more than capable hands of Dunc, and later, Dougie. Joey's forbearance was far greater than ours as we all waited impatiently for Jim's decision that we could in fact go, but at last he would fire the starting pistol and, our hastily-packed motley bags and cases safely stowed in the boot, we would at last set off. Even at this late stage, there would be no plan, at least not that Margaret and I were aware of, but on reaching the end of the loan, Jim would hesitate briefly. Which way? Left and north, or right and south?

Nine times out of ten we turned left, and we would begin a follow-your-nose tour northwards, stopping at hotels or bed and breakfast houses, usually for only one night at a time. We often found accommodation only at the eleventh hour (sometimes literally!), always with the worrying, but at the same time, thrilling possibility that "We'll hae tae sleep in the car the nicht, lassies!" This fate never actually befell us, but we had a few close calls as catering establishments in the Scottish Highlands were much fewer and further between then than they are now, and it was never possible to book ahead. Joey would always be a little tearful as we left Pitkinny behind. We could never understand why when we were young, but she explained it later, when we were older. She had a fear that in some indefinable way, everything would have changed by the time we returned home. Perhaps this illustrates an almost superstitious distrust on her part. She never lost sight of the fact that her early life and upbringing had led her to expect very little of life, and she had never thought she would be fortunate enough to have a family of her own, far less to be a farmer's wife. She was supremely contented with her lot, and perhaps feared that the fickle finger of fate was waiting in the wings to burst her bubble of happiness. Meanwhile, Margaret and I would be beside ourselves with excitement in the back of the car, often with notebooks and pencils at the ready to make a record of our trip. Of course, these journals usually petered out as the first day's journey wore on and the first bout of incipient car sickness threatened, brought on by trying to write in the car, especially since Jim was never known for his slow and careful driving!

Although Jim and Joey came to prefer touring holidays, our first two family holidays when we were very young each consisted of a stay in one place. The first was at the Windmill Hotel in Arbroath, in the summer of 1950, just before my fourth birthday. I have a hazy recollection of a big house set in lovely gardens and sweeping lawns, which included my first experience of a putting green. Many years later, as an undergraduate in Dundeee, I looked in at the Windmill during a visit to Arbroath. It sadly did not live up to my memory. Either it had fallen on hard times, or my childish mind had innocently embellished its charms, but it had, by then, an air of faded grandeur. Of course, in the intervening years, increasing affluence and accompanying changes in expectations and fashion had made it possible for Scots to holiday abroad. No longer did special trains deliver thousands of holidaymakers from Glasgow, Edinburgh, and Fife to spend their fair fortnight in the holiday towns of the east coast, such as Aberdeen, Montrose, Stonehaven, and Arbroath. Genteel establishments like the Windmill Hotel deteriorated as they lost the major part of their clientele, or closed down entirely.

Much of my recollection of that holiday came from listening to Joey's fond memories of it, although her pleasure in the experience was tinged with a sense of unease, because for the first time in her life, someone else was responsible for housing and feeding her family. Sheer leisure time was a concept Jim and Joey were completely unfamiliar with, and I think they felt a little like fish out of water, without the normal demands of the farm and our home on their time and energy. Photographs show us in the hotel garden, putting sticks in hand, and on the miniature railway at the beach. Interestingly, as in most family snapshots of those days, our parents were dressed quite formally, Joey in a smart day dress and Jim in a jacket, shirt, and tie. Now, in a similar family summer holiday photograph, everyone would be dressed much more casually, perhaps in shorts, vest, and flip-flops, and even that would seem overdressed to some of our most assiduous sun-worshippers!

While I am sure we had a happy time, the holiday had, in my childish perception, overtones of horror and terror, the reasons for which remain very fresh in my memory. One of the other guests at the hotel was a friendly old man, a retired doctor who usually chatted to us in the dining room. One day as Joey was looking out of our bedroom window, she saw him carrying a deck chair onto the lawn. As she watched, she was aware of a sudden ominous premonition as he adjusted it and began to sit down, his fingers gripping the frame of the seat. In that instant, she knew that he hadn't secured the backrest properly, and even as she frantically banged on the window, she knew it was too late. The deck chair collapsed, trapping the man's fingers between the two wooden edges of the frame beneath his full weight. Joey ran down to alert the hotel staff to the emergency and an ambulance was called, and amidst the ensuing melee, it was clear that the poor man had lost at least one of his fingers. From that day onwards, Joey had a great distrust of deck chairs. We had two at Pitkinny, one green and white and the other orange and blue, and we were never allowed to have anything to do with them. Whenever an adult went to sit on one, Joey would anxiously warn, "Keep your fingers out of the way!" I am sure the particular danger these seats represented to Joey for the rest of her life had the effect of reinforcing her general tendency to avoid at all costs spending time sitting down and relaxing anywhere, but particularly in the garden. When Joey was there, and that was for a great deal of time, she was either working or harvesting vegetables for the table; the idea of sitting down and enjoying the results of all her hard work did not occur to her, and she didn't see why anyone else would want to do it either!

The horrific nature of the injury sustained by the old man in the garden was equalled in my young imagination by another experience we had at the harbour in Arbroath. I clearly remember walking with Dad, clinging tightly to his hand, on the long stone jetty that jutted out into the North Sea, and looking down into the deep water on either side. As I grew up and heard the expression "between the devil and the deep blue sea," my fertile imagination failed to conjure up a vision of the devil, so I would mentally change the saying to "between the deep blue sea and the deep blue sea!" I remembered vividly the feeling of having no way to turn during that nightmarish walk along the sea wall. Yet I am sure Dad thought nothing of it at the time, and had no way of knowing how this gentle stroll with his wee girl assumed terrifying proportions in her eyes, or that the memory of it would remain with her for years. As adults we should be aware that situations and sights we know from experience to be safe and harmless may seem entirely different viewed through the innocent and inexperienced eyes of a child.

A further memory of that holiday is of going on a boat trip to see the caves near Arbroath, and this time it was Jim's turn to be afraid and, unlike me on the sea wall, he wasn't long in communicating the fact to everyone else in the boat. It was the first time Joey realised that he had absolutely no sea legs and was genuinely terrified as the wee motor boat puttered in and out of the caves on a glassy-green, calm sea. On the other hand I remember loving the whole thing, unable to understand Dad's worries. A year or two after that trauma, Jim was persuaded to accompany his friend Jock Allen and some other keen fishermen on an angling trip on Loch Leven. As he should have expected, he hated the whole experience and took no part in the fishing, spending the entire time holding on tightly to the sides of the boat. He only let go long enough to devour most of the sandwiches, his share and almost all of everyone else's as well, so he was never invited to repeat the experience—a great relief all round, I am sure!

Our second holiday was the following year, 1951, just before I started school, when we went with the Page family to Blackpool for a week. We stayed first in the Chequers, then in the Cliffs, hotels. As I remember them, they were on a much grander scale altogether than the Windmill in Arbroath, which seemed homely and couthy by comparison. Seemingly endless carpeted corridors and grandly sweeping and mirrored staircases were very much the order of the day, and I am sure that Joey and Jim must have felt completely out of their element in such grandiose surroundings. Similarly, the dining room was on a grand scale, and the food offered there seemed strange and unappealing to my (not quite) five-year-old palate. According to Mum and Dad, I quite innocently entertained a couple at the next table by my horrified reaction to the taste of fresh grapefruit one morning. "It's soor!" I exclaimed, utterly unimpressed by this strange fruit masquerading as a pale imitation of an orange. Even Joey's placatory sprinkling of sugar on it provoked the even more appalled rejoinder, "It's even soorer noo!"

As with the previous holiday, what stands out most clearly in my memory of the stay in Blackpool were two negative experiences. I have a vague recollection of going to "the shows," in other words, the Pleasure Beach. At one point Margaret and I had our photograph taken in a little car against a backdrop of a painted cardboard representation of the sea, and I remember feeling that it was silly to have to pretend when the real thing was so close. I have a vague memory of watching apparently terrorised people screaming on the Big Dipper and being carried, similarly frightened, by Dad over the cakewalk and between huge rotating barrels that seemed about to crash into us in the Fun House—definitely, I remember deciding, a misnomer of the first order. But at some point, from a sideshow I acquired a little ring with a pretty green stone. I was thrilled with the look of it on my finger for the rest of the day. That little ring made up for all the unpleasant noise and trauma of the rest of the day, and I refused to take it off as Mum bathed me that evening. But disaster struck as the bath was emptying and the ring slipped off my soapy finger and promptly disappeared down the plug hole. I howled with fury and disappointment as I visualised my precious jewel hurtling through what I envisaged as miles of pipes through the hotel, down under the ground and out to the sea. No amount of promising to buy me another ring would console me. Somehow I sensed that no replacement would ever give the same unique delight as that first treasure, now lost forever.

The next day was spent on the beach, along with hundreds of other holidaymakers. I remember our bathing suits were made of a stretchy material with complicated folds and ruching, designed (it seemed) to trap the wet, abrasive sand very effectively and most uncomfortably. As the adults sat (very gingerly) on deck chairs, and after much warning and checking by Joey, Margaret and I, with Elizabeth and Frank Page, busied ourselves with the obligatory buckets and spades and paddled in the sea. Jim and Saund, like most men on the beach, wore shirts, trousers, and jackets, their only concession to their holiday status being that they had sandals on and dispensed with ties, while Mrs Page and Joey wore nice summer dresses. Mum's was made of a green and white striped material, which Jim disliked intensely, joking (much to her annoyance) that it made her look like a walking tyke (mattress)! But they were to bless her choice later in the day. At some point as I paddled in the water, I must have strayed some distance along the sand. Suddenly Joey realised that she had lost sight of me, and mayhem ensued as she panicked and the adults began a frantic search for me. Meanwhile I had realised, as I turned from the waves, that I recognised no one and that I was lost. Of course I started to cry, and a kind lady tried to calm me down and asked me what my mother was wearing. A green and white striped frock? No problem! There was no one else so attired on that entire beach and very soon she had reunited me with my very relieved parents. So, as with that first holiday at Arbroath, our second one in Blackpool stands out in memory for all the wrong reasons. I wonder if other peoples' memories of childhood are like mine? Much of the normal, happy time I know I had, while not exactly forgotten, exists as an amorphous, monochromatic timeless span, punctuated by fearful, desperate, inexplicable episodes in brilliant unforgettable technicolour!

Almost all of our subsequent holidays were peripatetic ones. The first of these I recall, probably in 1952, was when we were joined by Gran and Grandad Betsy and Hugh, and Uncle James. It must have been the summer before my sixth birthday, when Margaret was nearly ten and James fifteen or so. I don't recall our precise route, but the tour ranged from Ayr and the Clyde coast in the southwest to Oban and Inverary, and then northeast to Aberdeen. We were four adults, a teenager, and two kids in one car—Jim's first Rover 75, his pride and joy. Finding bed and breakfast accommodation for us all each night was often difficult, as the tourist industry was in its infancy and of course nothing had been pre-booked. Sometimes Jim would stop the car to ask passersby for information, and it fell to Grandad in the front passenger seat to enquire if they knew of a likely hotel, guesthouse, or B&B establishment. Very often they would be unable to help because they were also on holiday there. After this happened a few times, presumably in order to save time, Hugh would start with a preliminary question delivered in his usual patrician and sonorous tones, "Are you a resident here?" Only when the startled and understandably suspicious recipient of this inquisition answered, often reluctantly, in the affirmative, did Hugh cut to the chase and ask for information and directions to possible accommodation. Sometimes to make the number of rooms required fewer, sleeping arrangements had to be amended and we would have to share a room with Gran, while James and Grandad had a room together. Much as we loved our Gran, we hated the loud snoring she would often indulge in, and one night, desperate to stop her without actually waking her, we resorted to a remedy for snoring that Margaret had heard of. This involved blowing in the ear of the offending sleeper. Kneeling by Gran's bed, Margaret gave it a go, but each time she was ready to blow, she would catch my eye and would burst into a fit of the giggles. Needless to say, it wasn't long until Gran woke with a start. "What's goin' on here?" she demanded. "You twa get tae sleep and stop yer damnt nonsense!" At least our immediate objective had been achieved and we were able to get to sleep before the inevitable resumption of Gran's wood sawing!

I remember we crossed the Clyde on the Erskine Ferry, long since superseded by the bridge of the same name. It was worked by a chain mechanism, a system I was never to see again until recently on a river in British Columbia. We then stayed in the Queen's Hotel in Helensburgh before driving up the "Rest and be Thankful" road towards Dunoon. This was a steep mountain route, and on the way the car began to overheat. Water was needed to top up the radiator and the only possible supply was to be found in the tumbling waterfalls cascading down the hillside on the north side of the road. There was only one problem: How could we carry the water? As it happened, Mum and Gran had each bought half a dozen tumblers in a china shop in Helensburgh. They were a pale golden shade of very fine glass, and were pressed into service as the only possible means of transferring the water from the waterfall to the radiator. "Fancy hansellin' ma bonnie new tummlers like this!" wailed Gran, "Noo watch an'no brek them!" We spent a night in Oban when it rained as it can only on the west coast of Scotland. "It's jist a nicht fur the picters," declared Jim, and so we all went to the local cinema. I remember nothing at all about the film, not surprising, you might think at a distance of more than fifty years, but perhaps it was as much to do with the fact that the building had a corrugated tin roof and the noise of the hammering rain made it impossible to hear a bit of the soundtrack and so to make any sense of the film! Later on in our tour we had a struggle to find somewhere to stay the night in Royal Deeside. Eventually we had to split up, Mum and Gran with Margaret and me in a house in Maryculter, while Dad, Grandad, and James stayed in Peterculter on the other side of the river. I was fascinated by the fact that the two little towns had been so named, and thought that they must be brother and sister, Peter and Mary. It also seemed fitting to my childlike logic that the boys stayed with Peter while we girls were with Mary!

Another tour a few years later, this time with just the four of us, took us up to Forres via Tomintoul and Grantown-on-Spey. We stayed the first night in a hotel in the centre of the Morayshire town, where we were very impressed and felt very much at home when we saw that the twin-bedded room that Margaret and I shared had exactly the same rose pink candlewick bedspreads as we had in our room at Pitkinny. Next day we visited the Culbin Sands near Findhorn, where I remember being fascinated and horrified in equal measure by the image of a village being swallowed by the shifting sands, failing to understand that the process had not happened all at once in a cataclysmic disaster, but over a period of time. From there we turned west to Inverness before negotiating the long and convoluted route round all the firths (Moray, Beauly, Cromarty, and Dornoch) and then heading northeast along the coast of Sutherland and into the county of Caithness over the impressive Berriedale summit.

Our objective was the town of Thurso, which held sheep sales every August, when all the sheep from Caithness, north Sutherland, and the Northern Isles were auctioned. The little Caithness town was bursting at the seams with people as well as sheep, and we had great difficulty finding accommodation. Eventually, one of the hotels directed us to a B&B house down near the harbour in Soutar Square. This was a newish housing estate just at the back of the newly-opened Woolies (F.W. Woolworth) store, the recent opening of which had really put Thurso on the map! Mrs McKay, the lady who opened the door and showed us the two guest bedrooms in her immaculate and comfortable home (whose stair carpet was, to no great surprise, identical to ours!), seemed extremely shy. Having agreed to take the rooms, we went out to look around the town. The normal convention when staying in a bed and breakfast establishment in those days was that that is exactly what you were getting, and you were not welcome to have the run of the place in the evenings. Given the apparently introverted nature of our hostess, Joey and Jim's intention was to return only in time for bed; so Mum, Margaret, and I strolled round the harbour in the "simmer dim" of a Caithness summer evening while Dad checked out one of the local hostelries. When we eventually returned to the house, Mrs McKay was anxiously waiting for us and urged us to "come away in for your supper!" in the soft, lilting cadences we were to come to know so well. There, set out by the fire in her living room, was a lovely selection of sandwiches and mouthwatering home baking, with what we soon learned was a bottomless teapot. That evening saw the start of a great friendship with a wonderful lady, and the first of many August visits to Thurso for us.

Bella McIntosh had been born and brought up in Kinlochbervie in the far northwest corner of Scotland, just south of Cape Wrath. Her family were fisherfolk and stalwarts of the lifeboat service. Her mother had died young, and Bella became the mainstay of her family as her father went with the fishing fleet as it moved from there round the north coast and down the east in the course of the season. The barrel of salt herring, with their home-produced oatmeal, potatoes, and mutton, comprised a staple diet which was common throughout Scotland in those days. Life was hard, and some years their food supply barely kept pace with the needs of a hungry, hard-working family. Bella would share these worries with her father, but his answer was always the same: "God will provide, Bella, God will provide." "And you know, he always did!" she would tell us.

She married a Thurso man before the war. He became coxswain of the Scrabster lifeboat, a position later filled by her brother Angie. Sadly her husband, who had joined the Coastguard Service for the duration of the war, was drowned during an air raid in Grimsby. His body was recovered and he was buried in the ancient churchyard near their home in Thurso. "I am so glad that he was found," she told us, "otherwise I could never have looked at the sea in the same way, and I love the sea." When her daughter Jenny was born just before the war, the midwife, in trying to phone for the doctor, mistakenly set off the lifeboat maroon instead and the lifeboat crew arrived just in time to welcome Jenny into the world. "So they all stayed and we just had a wee ceilidh!" Knowing Bella's "wee ceilidhs," it probably went on well into the next day! On a later visit, Joey was treated to a trip on the lifeboat with Bella and Angie out into the Pentland Firth, not a treat for the faint-hearted as Jim had wisely suspected, and was glad he had opted for a day at the sheep sale ring instead. Bella had a nephew, Hamish Henderson, who had a farm just outside Thurso, and he and his wife became friends of Jim and Joey, as did Margaret and Donnie Mcleod, Bella's neighbours. The Premuim Bonds had recently begun and Bella would say to me, "When Ernie comes up, Anne will you come with me to America?" Very early one morning during one of our visits, she took our little terrier Trudy for a walk down to the harbour. When she returned, she had a newspaper-wrapped parcel under her arm. Later, as Joey helped her to wash up the breakfast dishes, she unwrapped her mysterious bundle to reveal a lovely big salmon. It was illegal for the fishing boats to land salmon at sea, but Bella believed that "God put the wee salmon in the sea for the fishermen who are brave and clever enough to catch them, so who is to say they can't?" She was very well known and liked, and had her connections amongst the fishermen in the town, so we all tucked into delicious salmon steaks that evening.

Bella once visited us at Pitkinny when her friend, Miss Kennedy, brought her for a visit. She also had a very interesting background. Her father had been a general practitioner in Thurso during the war, and was called out one night to attend to those involved in a plane crash in Caithness. He was very surprised when he learned that one of those killed in the crash was the Duke of Kent, the brother of the then King George VI. In recognition of the work he did and the help he was to the family, he (and later, his daughter) was always sent a Christmas card by Princess Marina, the widowed Duchess, and Miss Kennedy was invited to the weddings of her children, Princess Alexandria and the young Duke of Kent. So what had begun as a tentative request for a night's accommodation developed into a lifelong friendship with Bella and her friends in Thurso. She was one of the kindest, most hospitable, and generous people I have ever met. She would promise that one day she would take us to "God's own country," Kinlochbervie, but sadly neither that nor the promised trip to America ever happened, as Bella died quite suddenly in 1965.

It was during the first of our stays in Thurso that we went for the first time to John o' Groats. Mum, Margaret, and I made the short journey along the north coast, while Dad spent the day at the sales. We found the location somewhat disappointing. While technically the furthest-north point on the Scottish mainland, it lacked the dramatic coastal scenery of other nearby features that we got to know later, such as Dunnet Head, which had some of the highest cliffs in the country; or Duncansby Head and its Muckle Stack, which had witnessed many shipwrecks, even after its lighthouse was built. These seemed much more in keeping with the end of the world than the tame, rather featureless shoreline at John o' Groats. That day, however, it was the need for some nourishment rather than scenic satisfaction that began to make itself felt, despite the hearty breakfast Bella had given us. Eschewing the rather grand and forbidding John o' Groats Hotel in favour of the only other obvious catering establishment, a small house with a discreet advertisement outside, we were rather surprised to find the door firmly locked. We had no choice but to ring the doorbell, and after some time the door opened a few inches and a voice whispered suspiciously, "What do you want?" "We would like some lunch please," Joey answered tentatively. "Wait here and I'll go and see," came the reply.

We did as we were told and sat and waited in the tiny little porch, where we were joined some time later by three rather dishevelled and tired-looking young men who were as surprised as we had been when they realised that they had to ring the bell. Their welcome was no more enthusiastic than ours had been and as we all waited, by now overflowing the accommodation of the porch to the yard outside, they explained that they were on a midge-tormented camping trip. They were all sleep-deprived and ravenously hungry after a few very uncomfortable nights in their tent. Just then, we three were ushered in to a very small room with only one or two tables by the owner of the disembodied voice that had greeted us so grudgingly. She never made eye contact with any of us as she struggled through an agony of embarrassment to serve us a meal which, although of acceptable quality, was unlikely to make much impact on a huge appetite. The rule of the house seemed to be that only one table could be occupied at any one time, because as we left, the three young men, by now clearly nearly dying for lack of nourishment, were only then being very reluctantly shown to their table. As we left, we hoped they would feel that their long wait had been justified, and that they would be suitably fortified to face another night of torture as they continued with their camping trip.

On a later visit to Thurso, Joey persuaded Jim that it would be a good idea to take the ferry over to Orkney. Margaret had by then started her nursing training, and could not come with us on our holiday that year. So the three of us set out one morning, well fortified by one of Bella's gargantuan breakfasts, to the little harbour of Scrabster to embark on the steamer for the two-and-a-half-hour voyage to Stromness. This was before the advent of roll-off, roll-on ferries and our car, the 2.4 Jaguar, had to be hoisted on board with the use of slings. It was to Jim's credit that, while he loved his cars and was especially proud of his Jag, he was never afraid to take chances with them and was always happy to let Joey and, later us, drive his cars. On reflection, he was to have more fear for his own health and welfare by the time that sea journey was over! As we waited to board the venerable old lady, the St Ola, we witnessed what we might (in retrospect) have seen as a bad portent for the imminent voyage. After a flurry of activity involving the ship's officers and the local constabulary, a shrouded stretcher was hurriedly carried down the gangway and loaded foot first into a waiting ambulance. Word soon filtered through the waiting prospective passengers that a man had died on the crossing to Scrabster that morning. Jim and Joey had got into conversation with a couple from Kirkwall, who were making their way home after a holiday on the mainland. We didn't know it then, but this was to mark the beginning of a firm friendship with Mina and Tom Sclater which was to last for many years. Mina confided in Joey that she was dreading the voyage as, despite making the journey many times over her lifetime, she was a terrible sailor and was always seasick. Joey found this hard to understand. After all, it was a perfect day in the middle of summer, with bright sunshine and a benevolent breeze, as we strolled on the quayside. Nevertheless, as soon as we boarded the St Ola, Mina retired to the ladies' restroom to lie down for the duration of the crossing while we three, with her husband, excitedly explored the ship.

Now it has to be said that Jim was never at ease on the water, as we had discovered on our trip to the Arbroath caves, and as his friends had found out to their chagrin when his only contribution to the trout fishing on Loch Leven was to eat all their sandwiches. But this was a very different situation. The St Ola seemed so big and sturdy, stable, and safe as she sedately made her way out of the sheltering embrace of the harbour at Scrabster and we sat on the top deck watching the coast of Caithness recede into the distance. It was only minutes later that Dad and I began to experience the beginnings of doubt. We had gone to the cafeteria for tea and cakes, and found to our surprise that we had to hold on to our cups and plates as the ship began to pitch and roll. Soon after this, Jim made for the gents' restroom and I found my very unsteady way to the ladies' one, where I encountered Mina Sclater flat out on one of the couches. My most vivid memory of the next two hours was of gingerly raising my head from a prone position to see, through the porthole, the Old Man of Hoy, that famous sandstone pinnacle, his head soaring majestically into a sky of unbroken blue with his feet lost in a churning froth of foam and spray, similar to the turbulence going on in my insides at the time. As the St Ola continued to cleave its way through the deceptively calm, glassy, bottle-green water, any fleeting appreciation on my part of the unique geological feature I had just seen was immediately overwhelmed by a wave of the awful agony and misery of mal de mer, and I had to make a hasty dash into the adjoining ladies' convenience!

Meanwhile Dad was suffering just as badly in the gents' rest room. When the purser called in there to check passengers' tickets, he helpfully reassured Jim, "I understand that your daughter is in the ladies' room, but I have no idea where you wife is." "I don't give a damn where she is, it's a' her faut that we're on this bloody ship in the first place!" came the muffled but heartfelt reply from the prostrate figure on the couch. As it happened, Joey had continued to occupy her seat on the top deck, determined to make the most of the whole experience and confident that she would not be sick. However, it wasn't long until, to her genuine surprise, she began to feel suddenly and alarmingly squeamish, to the extent that she had to make a tactical withdrawal to the deck rail. She was vaguely aware at that moment of a man saying, "Look at yer wee dug, missus," but the words failed to register with her as the inevitable happened and she succumbed to her seasickness. It was only later that we realised that poor little Trudy must also have been sick. We began to notice that she would react violently whenever she was anywhere near white railings of any kind. She would slam on the anchors and refuse to budge if she was on the lead, or would bolt rapidly in the opposite direction if free to do so. She must have associated the deck rails of the ship with her feeling of nausea and never forgot the experience.

The remainder of that sea crossing was spent in mute misery by all three of us, each feeling abandoned by the other members of the family, unaware that they were similarly afflicted, until the ship reached Stromness and we shakily and groggily met up with each other. We then began to understand that the Pentland Firth had always been notorious as one of the worst sea passages in the world, and has been the nemesis of all but the hardiest of sailors and the strongest of stomachs. On our return to Thurso, Bella told us that she had made the voyage many times over the years, as she had a sister who lived in Stromness. She was well known to the crew of the St Ola, and on one occasion the sea was so rough and the crossing so hazardous that she was the only passenger the captain would agree to having on the ship. Jim (indeed all of us) wished that she had told us this story before we embarked on our ill-advised adventure, but we all agreed that in failing to visit Orkney we would have missed out on a great experience, and that it was almost worth the pain and anguish we had suffered on the Pentland Firth. In addition, we would never have met Tom and Mina Sclater, and that would have been a great pity.

In the event, as we disembarked from the ship and waited for the cars to be unloaded, they invited us to visit them the following evening. They occupied a flat above the town hall in Kirkwall. Tom was the council officer, and he and Mina looked after the town hall. He had an important ceremonial role on official occasions, when he would wear his official robes and carry the mace, escorting local and visiting dignitaries. He also ran a haulage and taxi business with his son, while Mina helped her daughter to run a knitwear business which specialised in Fair Isle garments. They were extremely generous in their hospitality, and wonderful company as they regaled us with stories of Orcadian culture and local characters and historical events. As a young man, in common with many islanders of his generation, Tom had circumnavigated the globe more than once, working his passage across the oceans and in various occupations ranging from lumberjack in the wilds of Canada to jackaroo on Australian sheep stations. During the war he had been a special constable in Orkney, and the most moving of his stories was of the sinking of the Royal Oak battleship in Scapa Flow early in the war. We were so impressed by the fact that despite its seemingly remote location and its wealth of prehistoric sites of interest, Orkney played a pivotal role in twentieth century naval and air operations. The German fleet had been scuttled in Scapa Flow at the end of the First World War, while the later conflict gave rise to such features as the Churchill Barriers and the Italian chapel. This had been transformed from an old Nissan hut into a lovely place of worship and work of art by the consummate skill and artistic vision of some of the Italian POWs who were incarcerated in those islands.

From the very first evening of our first time in Thurso, we realised that Bella Mckay was the epitome of highland hospitality, but otherwise the welcome we received at most of the other places we ate and stayed during that tour was at best lukewarm and at worst positively hostile. Admittedly, the tourist industry was in its infancy in those days. The well-established hotels were almost exclusively of the "hunting, shooting, and fishing" variety and notoriously uninterested in families with children. Guesthouses or bed and breakfast establishments, where they existed, with the notable exception of Bella, tended to be run by very inexperienced and often very shy people with no awareness of the need for customer care. So that first visit to John o' Groats was certainly not the first or last time that we felt unwelcome and unsatisfied as we continued on our tour, but we didn't always show our disappointment in the way that Jim did when we reached Durness and stopped at the hotel there about lunchtime!

The notion of catering for nonresidents was obviously unknown to its proprietors, because the dining room was barred to us. When pressed by Jim and Joey, they very grudgingly agreed to give us tea and sandwiches in the residents' lounge, a dark and dismal room made even more so by the hunting trophies and glass-encased, equally long-dead fish. It was made clear that this was a huge concession on their part, because not only were we nonresidents, we were clearly not of the calibre of their usual clientele, being uninterested in hunting, shooting, or catching anything that moved! I am sure, however, that by the time we left, Jim would happily have had a go at the proprietors if they had been unwise enough to let him near one of their guns! When the sandwiches eventually arrived, they would have done British Rail proud. They looked as if they had been made days earlier of stale bread curling up at the edges and containing some very doubtful-looking ham. They were simply inedible, and Jim (remember Joey's maxim, "A hungry man's an angry man"?), by now absolutely furious, slung them one after the other with deadly accurate aim under the big oak dresser which stood against one wall, as we and the various mournful stags' heads and foosty fish that adorned the room looked on. When he had thus given vent to his anger, we quickly wolfed down the few uninspiring custard creams and drank the pot of tea, its weak and watery nature a final insult added to Jim's injury, before paying and leaving. We often wondered when—or if—they ever found the decaying remains of their sandwiches, and if they could possibly work out how they came to be under the dresser.

Driving south from Durness that day, we began to look for somewhere to stay. Joey dismissed the Cape Wrath hotel as another austere and unwelcoming fishers' retreat, and at any rate it was still too early to stop for the night. We then passed (unawares) the road to Kinlochbervie at Rhiconich, but it would be some years before Jim and Joey would take that route. We must have eaten at some point in the journey, in addition to those few biscuits at Durness, but I don't remember what or where. As we approached Ledmore junction without finding anywhere to stay, we stopped and asked for advice at the petrol station there. It was suggested that we might find beds at Altnacealgach Hotel a few miles to the southeast towards Strath Oykel. While he had intended to go southwest, Joey persuaded Jim to take the detour of a few miles rather than risk having nowhere to stay. So it was getting dark as we arrived at the hotel across the road from the loch at Althacealgach. Thankfully, they could accommodate us, but had only one twin-bedded room in the main building, with two singles in their fishing annexe, a sombre-looking timber extension to the hotel. Margaret and I took one look at the single rooms, which were dark, wood-panelled and -floored, their only decoration the ubiquitous glassy-eyed fishing trophies, and immediately decided that we didn't fancy sleeping alone. So it was agreed that we would have the bedroom in the main part of the hotel, which was much homelier, even if it lacked any identical soft furnishings to those at home, for a change!

As Joey settled us for the night, Jim checked out the bar, and shared a nightcap or two with the night porter, who probably assumed (as he was staying in the annexe) that Jim was a lone fisherman. When Joey went to bed alone in her dark, dismal room redolent of tobacco and surrounded by those glassy-eyed fish, the noise of the generator outside which supplied electricity to the annexe explained the significance of the candle and matches which she had found on her bedside table. As she tried to make the best of her depressing abode, the room was suddenly plunged into inky blackness as the generator was switched off at midnight. For once, even the comforting gleam of the simmer dim outside failed to penetrate the very high small window to mitigate the darkness. Unable to sleep, she lit the candle and tried to read by its feeble light. As she adjusted her pillows, she was horrified to see a neat little pile of pipe tobacco lying on the dingy sheet. That did it! She had had enough! She leapt out of bed, opened the door, and beetled across the corridor to Jim's room and crept in beside him.

Single bed or no single bed, she knew nothing would persuade her to return to her now-abandoned bedroom and the unmistakable evidence of its pipe-smoking and fishing-mad former occupant, whose sheets she had unwittingly been sharing. What she couldn't know was that the night porter had decided to bring Jim, his erstwhile "trusty drouthy cronie," an early morning cup of tea to fortify him for the dawn rise he assumed he would be making to start his day's fishing! The slow, sly, conspiratorial wink he gave Jim as he put the tea tray down and nodded in the direction of Joey spoke volumes. How was he to know who she was and how she came to be in Jim's bed? Of course, Jim enjoyed the whole episode, but his amusement did nothing to temper poor Joey's acute embarrassment. She was somewhat relieved, therefore, when she saw the night porter pass through the dining room as we were having breakfast. She hoped that the sight of the four of us, obviously a decent and respectable family, would correct any misapprehension he had had about her relationship with Jim, even if it did dent Jim's image as some sort of angling Don Juan!

It was with a sense of relief, and weariness on Joey's part, that we left Altnacealgach and retraced the few miles to Ledmore before resuming our journey to the southwest. Since leaving Thurso, all the miles we had driven had been on very narrow, single-track roads with passing places. Fortunately, the low volume of traffic meant that this did not constitute a great problem, but on some stretches the condition of the road surface left a lot to be desired. I remember some scary times as Jim, happily a very competent driver, had to negotiate some very precipitous slopes and dizzying hairpin bends. Gruinard Bay was one such location, made all the more unsettling by Joey's description of the status of the brooding island of the same name out in the bay as a poisoned and therefore forbidden place, having been used as a testing ground for the use of anthrax as an agent of biological warfare during the war.

We made our way along the spectacular west coast and enjoyed, for the first of many times, the dramatic and beautiful landscapes of Sutherland and Wester Ross. We stopped in Ullapool, the bustling fishing village on Loch Broom, and were amused to see the sheep grazing right up to the doors of the houses, none of which had fences, walls, or front gardens. We were interested to witness the unloading and marketing of the newly landed fish from the myriad of fishing boats. Some of the boxes contained dogfish, and in my ignorance I called to Mum, "Look at the wee sharks!" A fisherman overheard me and said with feeling, "They're no sharks, my dear. All the sharks on this pier have two legs!" We reckoned that he was a skipper off one of the boats and that he was more than a little disappointed with the price he was getting for his catch! Just south of Ullapool, we stopped at the Corrieshalloch Gorge, where Jim made us all scream in terror as he mischievously shook the handrails while we stood on the spindly suspension bridge which spans the seemingly fathomless depths of the gorge.

We spent a night in Poolewe and watched the most spectacular of all the west coast sunsets I have ever seen, before driving on along beautiful Loch Maree, through Glen Torridon, Shieldaig, and Kishorn, to Strathcarron where we checked into the hotel there, situated beside the railway station of the same name, one of the stops on the West Highland line from Inverness to Kyle of Lochalsh. For some reason I have forgotten, we had no way of telling the time. Perhaps Jim's watch had broken or he had lost it, but the only timepiece we had was the car clock. When Joey woke up the next morning it was clear and bright, and she could hear vehicles arriving outside and many voices as people milled around. Jim was always very reluctant to get up early when on holiday, naturally, since he normally had to be up so early, and welcomed the chance to have a long lie. Consequently, when staying in hotels we were often late for breakfast and we were used to being the recipients of some old-fashioned looks from waitresses anxious to clear the tables. Fearing we had slept in far beyond breakfast time, judging by all the activity outside, Joey quickly dressed. Unable to locate the car keys, and unwilling to waken Jim yet, she crept downstairs in search of a clock, but without success. She decided to walk the short distance to the station, where there was sure to be a clock. The reason for all the hubbub soon became obvious. The east-bound platform was full of people waiting for the Inverness train. Clearly, much of the dispersed population of the entire area was bound for the highland capital. Sure enough, Joey heard the first sounds of the approaching locomotive, in the same instant as she caught sight of the station clock. She could hardly believe her eyes! Four o'clock! Yes, it was only four in the morning! Within a few short minutes the passengers had boarded the train, some remaining vehicles that had delivered them to the station had gone, and the train departed for Inverness. As Joey stood and watched it receding into the distance, she was aware that a deathly hush had fallen on the now-deserted scene, and she walked slowly back to the still-sleeping hotel and up the stairs, creeping back into bed with the happy sense of having caught a fleeting sight of one aspect of local life, with the added luxury of the delicious anticipation of a few hours' more rest.

Towards the end of that holiday, our last night was spent in the Ballachulish Hotel, south of Fort William at the western end of Glencoe. I had been learning all about the Massacre of Glencoe at school, and we had read *Kidnapped*, the story by Robert Louis Stevenson, which referred to the Appin murder of the Red Fox, and the subsequent unjust trial and conviction of James of the Glens. We were all interested to be in the location of these famous historical events. During his customary visit to the hotel bar that evening, Jim got into conversation with a gamekeeper. When Jim mentioned this to him, the gumpy offered to meet us the next morning to show us a memorial to James Stewart, which was situated on the hillside behind the hotel. This monument was not well-publicised, and we otherwise would not have known of its existence. In addition, Jim's new acquaintance was himself a McDonald of Glencoe, and had recently been at a family funeral at a graveyard on one of the islands in Loch Leven. So the next morning we waited, as arranged, outside the hotel. Because the heavens had opened and it was raining west highland cats and dogs, we sheltered in the car. True to his word, the gamekeeper soon arrived, pedalling his trusty old bike, dressed in the obligatory Harris-tweed jacket and plus fours, with a battered old ghillie's hat vividly festooned with a variety of flee-hooks. In addition, he wore thick socks and very sturdy brogues and had a pack on his back, with the muzzle of his gun protruding from its top. He alighted from his bike as Jim got out of the car and shook his hand, introducing him to Joey, who was still sitting in the front passenger seat.

As the gamekeeper briskly leaned in the driver's door to greet her and shake her vigorously by the hand, his bag swung round and the sights on the end of his gun muzzle hit Jim on the head, just behind his right ear. Within seconds the blood started to pour from the resulting wound. As Jim tried valiantly to staunch the flow with his hankie, the gumpy, completely unaware of what had happened, urged us out of the car. "Come away! Follow me!" He took off up the hillside in the pouring rain like a startled rabbit, leaving us to follow in his wake, first Margaret, then me, then Jim and Joey. He was still bleeding like a stuck pig, and she was trying to help him as the blood, diluted with rainwater, dripped pitifully down his neck. By the time they reached the memorial, the gamekeeper was coming to the end of his lecture on James of the Glens, and Margaret and I were trying to keep our faces straight and to avoid looking at the sorry state Jim was in. Having said all that he had to say, our guide bade us all good morning, turned on his heel and scurried off back down the hill, still blithely oblivious to the damage he had done, as we all trailed behind him, soaking wet and (in Jim's case) bloodied but not so unbowed.

We knew we should feel grateful to our tour guide, as he added significantly to our knowledge of some aspects of Scottish history. He had vividly described how James's body was left to hang there on the gibbet until it was just a "rickle o' banes," his kinsmen having been warned not to remove it on pain of a similar fate befalling them, and "pour encourager les autres." Eventually, one of his cousins could stand it no longer and, one dark night, cut down his remains and threw them into Loch Leven. Jim had heard enough of the lecture to be able to identify with his namesake: "Jist think, they cam and took him awa' when he was workin' in his fields an he never got hame again!" In retrospect, perhaps Joey felt secretly gratified that Jim's painful experience might encourage him to be more circumspect in his conversations with new acquaintances in hotel bars late at night. And maybe Jim, while happily suffering a fate much less serious than James of the Glens, had the scars to prove that sometimes it pays to keep your mouth shut!

*Margaret, Anne, Jim, and Joey on the miniature railway in Arbroath, 1950*

*(L to R) Saund Page, Jim, Joey, Anne, Elizabeth Page, and Frank Page in Blackpool, 1951*

*Anne and Margaret in Blackpool, 1951*

*Jim, Hugh, Betsy, and James in Helensburgh, 1953*

*Margaret and Anne in Thurso, 1958*

*Joey with Bella McKay and Trudy in Thurso, 1958*

*Joey and Anne in Ullapool, 1958*

*Tom and Mina Sclater on the occasion of their golden wedding, Kirkwall, Orkney*

*Leaving Scrabster on the St Ola in August 1962*

# Chapter 29

## "Wha the bliddy hell is Eros?"

There were to be many more touring holidays in the north and west highlands and islands, but more and more of them saw Jim and Joey on their own, as Margaret began her nursing career in 1960 and I went off to university in 1964, just after she was married. It was on one of these holidays that they first visited Kinlochbervie, and found the "God's own country" that Bella had so loved and longed for. They got to know her cousin Lachie McIntosh and his wife, who would welcome them to their home at Sheigra several times, and soon became firm friends. Bella was right. Assynt is a very special part of Scotland. The little house she was born and grew up in still stands—a tiny wee roadside cottage, long unoccupied and now becoming steadily more derelict as the years pass. Each time we visit, we half expect to see it gone, or completely refurbished and occasionally lived in as a holiday home. As I think of that wee lassie growing up there all those years ago, I can't help but wonder which of these equally sad outcomes she would prefer for her old home.

During that and subsequent visits to Kinlochbervie, they stayed in the Rhiconich Hotel, which stands at the junction of the main road north to Durness and the winding coastal route out to Sheigra, Kinlochbervie itself, and on to Oldshoremore and beyond. The hotel was owned and run in those days by John McLeod, and he was one of a kind. He did not encourage anglers, as they always hoped for wet weather (it being more conducive to good fishing); he believed that most people have only short holidays and deserved to enjoy some sunshine. He also did not suffer fools gladly, and had very limited patience for any guests who were in any way pretentious, rude, or plain stupid. He had a dry, sardonic sense of humour and would say, as guests arrived, "Oh, it's always good to see you're back!" It seemed that he ran his hotel less as a serious business and more because he enjoyed the way of life and was happy to provide employment for many of the local people. His barman was Murdo McLeod, also a cousin of Bella's and a very friendly soul, who ran the wee shop and the petrol pumps at the hotel.

He had a second job at Kinlochbervie pier, where he mended fish boxes and looked after the fish market used by the fishing fleet, which grew steadily through the years of the sixties, seventies, and eighties, although it is now in sad decline. The Scottish fishing industry oversaw much investment in Kinlochbervie with the enlargement and deepening of the inner harbour. The building of new roads, sheds, and a fishermen's mission facilitated the landing and transport of the ever-increasing catches, and served the crews of the trawlers, most of which were owned and manned by men from the east coast. Most weekends would see them return there in a fleet of minibuses as the huge fish lorries left for markets in the east and south.

When Murdo was not on duty and "the boss" not around, the lounge bar operated an honesty system. You helped yourself to your drinks and put the money in the till. Mr McLeod was a genial and easygoing host, but Jim and Joey suspected that underneath, he was an astute observer of human nature and would not tolerate dishonesty or improper behaviour. They witnessed an example of this one summer, when Mr McLeod had employed a couple of students from Glasgow. The girl, who worked as a waitress in the dining room, had a room in the main part of the hotel; while her boyfriend, who helped in the kitchen, stayed in a caravan at the back of the hotel. In conversation with the girl, Joey discovered that she was a music student at the Royal Academy of Music and Drama, and was in the same class as my old school friend, Elizabeth Ritchie. The next day, Mr Mcleod told Jim and Joey that he had had to undertake an unpleasant task: he had fired the couple when he discovered that they were cohabiting in the caravan. He believed that he owed it to their parents to put a stop to their misbehaviour under his roof. This will be seen nowadays as an over-reaction, but the moral climate has changed so much in the intervening years; seen in the light of the social mores of the time, his actions appeared to be quite reasonable. The last they saw of the chastened young people was as they waited by the roadside at Rhiconich to thumb a lift from one of the fish lorries that evening.

Mr McLeod kept a family of donkeys at the hotel. They had the run of a wee paddock, but most days he let them out and they grazed the roadside verges and the grassy banks by the burnside. Sometimes they would wander a long way from the hotel in the course of the long summer days, and he would go and find them and bring them home in the gloaming. One evening he was strolling along, two donkeys on either side, occupying the entire width of the narrow road, as a large powerful car driven by an impatient driver came up behind him, imperiously honking his horn. Eventually, Mr McLeod moved very slowly to the side and as the car inched past, he preempted an imminent outburst from the by now red-faced and furious driver by asking innocently and politely, "Could you tell me? Am I on the right road for Jerusalem?" This put the driver's gas at a peep, and no mistake, and with an exasperated shrug, he drove on at speed. When the proprietor reached his hotel, he allowed himself a wry smile as he saw the offending car parked, and he timed his arrival in the lounge bar perfectly, just in time to hear the driver declaiming about the mad old guy with the donkeys. Mr McLeod had gleeful pleasure in watching the face of his embarrassed guest drop almost to the floor as he marched behind the bar in "mine host" fashion, heartily enquiring, "And what will you be having to drink, my fine friend?" On another occasion, Jim and Joey overheard a guest ask pompously, "So, do you breed the donkeys yourself, Mr McLeod?" "No, I generally leave that to the donkeys. I've found that they're much better at it," came the deadpan reply!

Bill and I stayed at the Rhiconich for one night of our honeymoon, and then for a weekend with Jim and Joey during the first year of our marriage. That was the last time we met Mr McLeod. He died not long after that, and the hotel went through some sad years as it passed into the ownership of proprietors who allowed it to deteriorate into little more than a pub, and a poorly run and not very pleasant one at that. Joey and Jim called in once during that time and were shocked at the state it was in, so much so that they found B&B accommodation elsewhere. Happily, in the 1990s it was bought and completely refurbished by people from the northeast of

England, who ran it very well. Once again it became a focal point of the area, catering for visitors in an exemplary way, while retaining its character and employing able, young, local people.

Now that his beloved hotel is thriving in safe hands, I think we can safely assume that Mr McLeod is no longer birling in his grave in the lovely but lonely little cemetery within the sound of the sea at Oldshoremore. The bay of the same name is one of the most beautiful and tranquil beaches in the northwest, usually a totally deserted sweep of pristine sand, with a backdrop of little crofts. Further along the road is the beginning of the pathway to Sandwood Bay, five miles away and reachable only on foot. This is an even more spectacular beach, possessed of such an ethereal and unearthly atmosphere that it isn't hard to believe the old tales that it is the haunt of mermaids and selkies. The remote and utterly untouched landscape shows no imprint of human activity whatever. Hopefully, it will always remain so.

On one visit to Kinlochbervie with Jim and Joey when I was still a teenager, we were accompanied by our cousin Hughie Drennan, twelve years old, the youngest child of Auntie Greta and Uncle Bobby. One evening we went to see the unloading of the fishing boats. This was in the days before the inner harbour had been deepened; after unloading, the boats had to move round the headland to the old outer pier to get deep water for sailing out the next morning. Dad came to us and said he had been talking to one of the skippers, and that he told him he was going straight back to sea, but he was short-handed. He wondered if we would go with him and give him a hand? We all fell for it and Mum immediately began to fuss. "I dinnae think we'll be muckle yaise tae him, Jim. We've nae waterproofs or warm enough claes." "Oh, he'll gie us oilskins and sou'westers, dinnae worry." Hughie's face was a mixture of terror and delight at the thought of a night in a fishing boat. I should have realised that there was no way Jim would volunteer for what to him would be a terrible ordeal, given his record as a sailor. But sure enough, the skipper was waiting for us as Jim ushered us towards the trawler. "Come away on board now, and we'll see what you're made of!" bellowed the old sea-dog, who looked as if he had salt water flowing in his veins. As we cast off and made our way out of the harbour, we were still taken in by Jim's subterfuge. Of course, the skipper was in on the joke, and it was only after we were moving into a berth at the old pier that the truth—and immense relief—began to set in. So our career as trawler-men was short-lived, but that short exhilarating voyage was memorable—another wonderful memory to store away. I wonder if Hughie remembers that happy occasion as fondly as I do.

If the visits we made to Thurso were occasioned by the August sheep sales there, it was also livestock that prompted a visit Jim and Joey made to London in the winter of 1962. They set off on a very snowy December day to drive all the way to Bletchley in Buckinghamshire to stay with Uncle Hughie and Auntie Ellen. From there they took the train and underground into the city to the world-famous Smithfield livestock show and sales. Of course the annual agricultural outing was to the Royal Highland Show, and in the 1950s we took a caravan and stayed for a few days at the show in Dumfries in 1955, Inverness in 1956, Dundee in 1957, and Ayr in 1958. This involved towing the caravan to the show and back, which we managed quite satisfactorily.

Perhaps this lulled us into a fall sense of security, for in 1959 Jim hired a caravan from the Regent Garage in Cowdenbeath for our summer tour up north. This represented a significant improvement on the Thomson Almond vans we had had before, which were very compact. This new one was a Lundale super deluxe model, the Rolls Royce of towing vans, much bigger and more elaborate in every way. It had leaded windows, beautiful fitted furniture and elaborate fittings, all of which made it very heavy. But Jim was confident that he would manage to tow it successfully with his long-wheel-base land rover, and did not foresee any problems. The caravan even had a toilet cubicle! There was a chemical toilet at the farm, which was annually pressed into service for the squad of pickers at the potato harvest, and this would fit in the caravan perfectly. Only when we were ready to go did Jim discover that there was none of the chemical liquid to use in the loo, but he didn't see that as a problem. We could use sheep dip instead! After all, it was a disinfectant, and would surely do the same job. If you have ever smelled sheep dip, you will understand that, in the confined space of a caravan, it was absolutely overpowering and in danger of rendering us all insensible, and was dispensed with after the first night. So it was agreed that the toilet was to be used only in dire emergencies in the middle of the night, otherwise we would have to make do with the facilities the caravan sites had to offer.

Apart from this disappointment, we revelled in the luxury afforded by our mobile home. Jim found the land rover the ideal vehicle for towing the caravan, and all went well for the first few days. One incident, amusing in the retelling if not at the time, was embarrassing for Joey, but fortunate that it happened miles from any human habitation, and as always, she was soon able to see the funny side of her discomfiture! We were approaching Bonar Bridge from the northwest, when war broke out in the back of the car! Margaret and I had an imaginary line of demarcation that bisected the back seat into our respective territories, but a disagreement arose about who had jurisdiction over a tin of sweets. Joey turned in her seat to sort out the dispute at the exact same moment as Jim asked her for directions at a road junction. You might think that the choice of road would be obvious in an area where there are so few routes, but between our continued squabbling and Jim's barked "Whit road, Joey?" she made a mistake. Knowing how he hated to stop while she consulted the AA book, she chose at random, "Turn richt." He did as she said, but it soon became clear that we were on the wrong road and heading alarmingly into the hills on a rapidly narrowing and deteriorating road. Of course, there was nowhere to turn the land rover and caravan, and as the tortuous miles passed we were berated by both parents as the cause of the debacle. "This was a' your faut! That's the last time we bring you two on holiday. Ye'll bide at hame frae noo on!" Margaret and I cowered in the back seat, each of us thinking that we would love to have been at home at that particular time. At long last, we came to the rocky opening to an old quarry at the side of the road, where Jim estimated there might just be enough room for him to turn. But he needed Joey's help to accomplish the difficult manoeuvre. "Git oot an' direct me," he commanded as he began to nose into the overgrown and rock-strewn space. Unfortunately, Joey forgot that she had loosened the zip of her skirt as she had felt uncomfortably full after breakfast, and as she stood waving him on, her skirt began to slip slowly but inexorably to the ground. The look of shocked horror on her face, accompanied by Dad's "***** ******* ******! Look at yer mither!" induced a state of complete, but suppressed, hysteria in Margaret and me. We dared not laugh out loud, and hoped that the tears running down our faces would be interpreted as the result of the row we had just had, rather than amusement at our mother's predicament. Jim's raucous laughter added to her annoyance as she hitched up her skirt while looking all around to make sure that there were no witnesses to the unintended exposure of her petticoat to the surrounding implacable hills, heather, and highland glen other than a few startled sheep!

However, this was but a precursor to a real disaster, as we made our way from Bonar Bridge along the south side of the Dornoch Firth. With no warning there was a loud crash, and the land rover began to lurch from side to side until Jim managed to regain control and steered into the side of the road, where we came to rest at an alarming angle. The reason soon became abundantly clear. The nearside wheel of the caravan had come off and had disappeared completely. A passing motorist stopped and helped to search for the missing wheel, which was eventually spotted at the bottom of the banking that led down to the railway line. The air was a vivid shade of blue by the time Jim had wrestled it back up to the road. It was of no use, of course, because the wheel nuts had sheared. The only thing was to find a new wheel, and a mechanic to fit it. But where? Jim managed, with a struggle, to unhitch the land rover, and off he went in the direction of Tain, leaving us stranded in a lopsided caravan miles from anywhere. A search of Tain proved fruitless, and he had to carry on to Invergordon. He succeeded in locating a scrap yard which, after much searching, yielded up a wheel (albeit a very rusty one) of the correct specification. When Jim arrived back at the caravan in the early evening he was tired, hungry, and verging on the desperate. But after an improvised meal eaten at our inclining table, some measure of composure was regained in time to welcome the arrival of a mechanic from Invergordon, and in due course the replacement wheel was fitted and we gingerly limped into Tain for the night.

The next day or two passed comparatively uneventfully as we continued our tour to Inverness and then on to Aberdeen. We spent a couple of nights at Stonehaven, where we stayed in the beachside caravan park, and Margaret and I made the most of the outdoor swimming pool and the tennis courts. Dad ventured to play tennis for the first—and last—time in his life. He mistakenly assumed that the point of the game was to hit the ball as hard as humanly possible. We were aghast as we watched, one by one, the tennis balls we had hired, fly not just over the net, but hopelessly high above the fences surrounding the courts and, for all we knew, out over the North Sea itself. A very shame-faced Jim had to pay the attendant for the lost balls and admit that "It's a bliddy sicht harder than it looks!"

We left for home the following day, and as we neared Laurencekirk, Margaret asked, "Dad, do you think the wheel could come off again?" "No, no it'll be a' richt noo, till we get hame." No sooner were the words out of his mouth than (with a dreadful sense of déjà vu) there was that familiar crash, and we skidded and skittered all over the road before shuddering to a halt, this time inclined into the near-side ditch. The replacement wheel had come off in an identical fashion to its predecessor, but this one was easier to find, nestled into the bottom of a nettle-infested hedgerow. The usual oaths and expletives accompanied its retrieval, some of them occasioned by the unavoidable nettle stings he had to endure, but most of them directed at the Fates who had visited such a repetition of this torture on him. His fury was only slightly mollified by the serendipitous intervention of a passing AA patrolman who, lacking the necessary equipment to help, kindly promised to send out a mechanic from the garage in Laurencekirk. As Jim sat disconsolately and still bemoaning his bad luck by the disabled caravan, Mum, Margaret, and I (who were standing) could see a second Good Samaritan pull up on the other side of the road, in the form of the driver of a very small car and an even smaller caravan. As he crossed the road he anxiously enquired if he could be of any help. "Help? Help?" Jim reiterated. "No. Naebody can help me! Here Ah am wi' a fancy big caravan an a tap o' the range long-wheel-base land rover, an' see whit happens? An' yet ye'll get some bugger wi' a wee matchbox car an' a stupit wee caravan tourin' the length and breadth o' this country an' nuthin' ever happens tae him!" To be fair to Dad, he genuinely could not see our would-be helper's vehicles, and I am sure if he had, he would never have said what he did. Even Jim had some sense of fair play, but he gave vent to his frustration on this poor innocent and helpful but hapless passerby. Having been so rudely rebuffed, he paradoxically apologised to Jim before making a tactical withdrawal from what probably seemed to him to be a dangerously deranged and wild-eyed maniac, with two apparently deaf-mute daughters and a red-faced and acutely embarrassed wife.

When the mechanic arrived, he managed to effect a temporary repair to the wheel, but suggested that it would last only a very short distance, so Jim proposed to tow the caravan into Laurencekirk and leave it at the garage there to be collected by its owners. So we were ordered to empty the van of all our belongings, which we piled into the back of the land rover. Then we all watched as Jim began to tow the now-empty caravan, but he had only gone a few yards when, with a huge crack, it slumped to the ground as its axle broke. That did it! He had had enough! "Get in the land rover," he yelled, as he began to unhitch it from its mortally wounded trailer. "The **** thing is stayin' here. Ah never want tae see anither **** caravan as long as Ah live!" So we piled unceremoniously into the land rover with all our worldly goods, including the less–than-fragrant (non)-chemical toilet, which we realised, now that we were in such close proximity to it, must have been surreptitiously used in a very recent "dire emergency," but no one would own up! We headed for home, stopping only for much-needed sustenance at the chip shop in Milnathort. The next morning, Jim took vicarious pleasure in phoning the Regent Garage to tell them where their super deluxe Lundale caravan was, and suggesting what they could do with it if and when they succeeded in finding it.

It would be no great surprise if this had been Jim and Joey's last caravan holiday, and that was the case for many years. But much later, in 1967, they were joined by Margaret and John and their first little girl, Pamela, when she was two years old. Also accompanying them was our would-be Kinlochbervie trawlerman cousin, Hughie Drennan. Once again they toured to the northwest with a hired caravan towed by Jim's land rover, which doubled as sleeping accommodation for Margaret and John. The only problem with that was, as soon as the sun shone on the metal roof in the mornings, the resulting heat buildup was so much that they simply had to get up; so as long as the weather was sunny, there were no long lies for them and they were always on breakfast duty. They were not alone, of course, as their little alarm clock Pamela had already woken Jim, and they would be having their first cup of tea together in the caravan. As tradition demanded, this tour was not without mechanical mishap, but this time it was the land rover that broke down. Fortunately, they could still get around while it was being repaired, as they had decided they would need to have the car with them too, to accommodate all their gear. Another little problem came in the form of some kind of twenty-four-hour viral infection which visited each one of the party in turn, starting with Pamela and ending with Jim. All of the others had suffered a sudden onset of lethargy, slight fever, and aching limbs, symptoms which fortunately did not last longer than a few hours, but when Jim succumbed, he seemed to be much worse than everyone else. He was lying down in the caravan and Joey covered him with a travelling rug, telling him to rest and he would soon feel better. When he called her within a few minutes, she was flabbergasted to hear him ask weakly, "Joey, move the rug, the fringes are tickling my nose!" Naturally, she wasn't long in telling him that she didn't mean him to rest to that extent, and that he was perfectly capable of moving the blanket himself. So Joey and Jim's last caravan holiday, spent with three generations of the family, had the usual quota of humorous incident; although, as always, it may not have been so easy to see the funny side of these as they were happening.

The decision to turn left at the end of the loan at the start of our holidays almost invariably led us to the north and west—almost, but not quite. The first time we turned right and headed south, we were in convoy with another car: a Ford Consul driven by our Uncle Wullie. The two cars actually contained three families: the four of us; Auntie Caroline and Uncle Wullie with their son Jim, who was six months younger than me; and Caroline's sister Betty Nicol (her maiden name, by which she was always known for some reason), her husband Jim Henderson, and their wee boy Charlie, who was only about four years old. We toured through the Borders and into Northumberland where we stopped for a night in Whitley Bay, in the Rex Hotel on the promenade. I can remember the novelty of all sitting down together at a big table in the dining room, having dinner in the evening—a strange concept for us, being used to our main meal in the middle of the day.

I can't remember if there was any confusion, there being three Jims in our party, but some highlights of the tour remain quite vividly in my memory. We sometimes found it hard to find accommodation for six adults and four children, and also to secure sufficient table space in eating-places. I remember we were in a restaurant in Barnard Castle, County Durham. It was housed in a very old and historic inn that was showing its age and in great need of refurbishment and repair. Added to that was the fact that the food was barely passable and the service dreadful. We were seated in twos and threes at various tables which were otherwise occupied by complete strangers. On the way into the dining room, I read a plaque on the wall which claimed that Oliver Cromwell had once slept in the old inn. I was keen to pass on this information and called out to Dad at another table, "Dad, Oliver Cromwell once slept here!" "Is that right?" he answered. "Ah'm no surprised, and Ah'll tell ye something. He'll be back here afore Ah am!" There was a deathly hush as everyone digested the fact that Jim was not altogether pleased with his lunch, the place, or its historical associations.

I seem to remember that Uncle Wullie had only just passed his driving test. Why he had to sit a test at all is beyond me, as Dad never did, and I imagine that Wullie, like him, must always have driven vehicles on the farm. Whatever the cause, it was evident, even to us children, that he was a very slow and cautious driver. When we were in his car, we were always miles behind Jim and his passengers. We were crossing the north Yorkshire moors in driving, almost horizontal rain, with visibility practically zero. Auntie Caroline was sitting in the front (although she was a back seat driver!), keeping a watchful eye on the speedometer. As it edged towards forty miles per hour, she snapped at her husband, "Slow doon Wullie, we cannae see the craps." She seemed unaware of the fact that crops tend not to grow on moorland, or that even if they did they would hardly be visible through the rain and murk, or that Wullie's speed would hardly prevent her from admiring them!

We crossed the Pennines and stayed in Lancaster. The hotel there had the first self-service lift that we had ever been in, and it soon became obvious that Jim had a tendency to claustrophobia, as he panicked when the doors didn't open right away. Perhaps it was a response to his spending most of his life in the open air, but there were to be later instances in his life where he had an adverse reaction to small rooms and confined spaces. Auntie Caroline bought herself a tea set, but most of it never made it home intact, as she dropped it on the pavement and most of the dishes were smashed. A visit to Morecambe included a frightening ride on the scenic railway there with Mum, Margaret, and Betty, which recalled the terror of the Pleasure Beach in Blackpool. I am happy to say that this fear of "the shows" did not last throughout my young life, and that by the time I was a teenager, I had grown to love all the atmosphere and thrills of the fun fair. The higher and faster the better!

The most notable journey we ever made southwards was a year or two later, in 1955, one of the hottest summers of my childhood, when I was nearly nine and Margaret almost thirteen. I can't be sure if Joey and Jim had a destination in mind when we headed south, but our first night was spent in the hotel at Scotch Corner, a misnomer in my book, as we were by then most definitely in England. The next day was very hot as we continued our journey, and the traffic was becoming noticeably heavier as we reached Yorkshire. There were no motorways in those days, and our route followed the Great North Road or the A1, which led straight through Doncaster. Little did we realise then that a few years later, Auntie Greta and Uncle Bobby would move from Kinglassie to make their home very near there in a village suburb of Doncaster called Woodlands. At some point on the congested A1 through the south Yorkshire town we came to a busy junction where a policeman was on point duty. It had been in the news that owing to the very hot weather that summer, for the first time ever, policemen were allowed to dispense with their uniform jackets. That, and the distinctively different style of helmet worn by the English bobbies, made this particular constable very conspicuous to us. Not conspicuous enough, however, as it turned out. As the policeman waved Jim on, Dad noticed throngs of people on either side of the road and hesitated. That was enough to open the floodgates, and the pedestrians streamed across the road in both directions in front of us. Jim was by now at a complete standstill, and that was clearly not what the policeman had intended. He marched furiously up to our car, opened Jim's door and let fly with a stream of invective that left Jim in no doubt what the policeman thought of his driving skills, his intelligence, and his parentage. For once Jim was on the receiving end of language every bit as colourful and imaginative as he himself could have come up with on a good day! All delivered in a thick Yorkshire accent from a very red-faced and sweating bobby in shirtsleeves. Jim's reaction, much to Joey's surprise and relief, was to meekly apologise, and nothing more was said as we continued to crawl our way through the traffic jam until we reached the open road south again.

At some point it must have become obvious that we were nearing London, as the rush hour traffic became heavier and heavier, and suddenly Joey announced, "We're in London richt enough! This is Piccadilly Circus!" In recalling this, I have a mental image of the opening credits of the old television programme *In Town Tonight*, which showed vehicles circulating round this famous landmark. "Hoo dae ye kain that?" asked Jim sceptically, as he concentrated on his driving. "Because there's Eros," she replied. "Wha the bliddy hell is Eros?" he demanded to know as he continued in the whirlpool of cars, taxis, and red buses around the winged statue. Deciding that was hardly the time to explain her classical reference, she answered, "Never mind whoa he is, jist try to get us oot o' here!" Although it seemed to us that we had never seen traffic so heavy, in relative terms—compared to the congestion in London nowadays—it was nothing, and Jim was soon able to get into a side street, where he parked right outside the Piccadilly Hotel. We sat in the car while he went in to see if he could find B&B accommodation there. "Well girls, we're really in London," said Mum with a mixture of excitement and trepidation in her voice.

When Dad returned, it was with the news that despite the enormous size of the hotel—"It's like a ******* railway station in there!"—it was full up. That was the first of many refusals that evening, as we repeatedly tried and failed to find somewhere to stay. As time passed we moved further and further away from the centre and lower and lower down the star ratings, until very late at night we succeeded in getting a room in a very run-down guesthouse in Pimlico. It was in a typical Georgian terrace of once very grand houses, which now had an air of faded grandeur. This general dilapidation became increasingly evident in our lodgings with each floor we went up, and we were at the very top of the house, but at least we had somewhere to sleep—a huge family room containing several beds and not much else.

We were in London for no more than three full days, but in that time, we saw most of the famous landmarks. We were the archetypal country cousins come to town, but one way or another managed to navigate our way around the city. We started off watching the changing of the guard at Buckingham Palace. Jim and Joey had a camera and we have a few snaps of our holidays, but generally much fewer people had cameras than nowadays, and they were used much more selectively. So we were fascinated by one tourist (perhaps an American) at Buckingham Palace, who was snapping away at everything that moved, and blocking the view for most other people. One frustrated Cockney voice in the crowd at the gates called out after some time, "Hoi, mate! Give it a rest, you've enough film in there to fill the bleedin' Odeon in Leicester Square!" We fed the pigeons in Trafalgar Square, and Margaret and I had our photograph taken sitting on the paws of one of Landseer's lions there, a repeat of which we took of our boys thirty-two years later in 1987. We had a sail down the Thames from Tower Pier to Greenwich and were lucky enough to sneak under the open arms of Tower Bridge on the way back, as they made way for a big ship to pass up the river.

We visited Madame Tussaud's and scared ourselves witless in the Chamber of Horrors. There was one exhibit covered by a black curtain with an "Adults Only" sign, but Margaret and I sneaked a look and wished we hadn't. I couldn't sleep that night in our creepy bedroom for thinking of all those horrors, and seem to remember sneaking into Mum and Dad's bed for comfort during the night. We went to the London Casino cinema one evening to see a Cinerama show. It was one of the first examples of a wrap-around screen and stereophonic sound format in a spectacular travelogue film. One of the items shown was the Edinburgh military tattoo, and it seemed as if the pipers were marching not only in front of you, but on either side as well. You felt as if you were in the centre of the action and the sound, colour, and movement completely enveloped your senses. As we moved along the Grand Canal in Venice, and the gondolier ducked his head to pass under the Bridge of Sighs, everyone in the audience followed suit. Likewise as we flew over the Grand Canyon, we all leaned to one side as the plane banked. It was a wonderful show, very much a forerunner of the current IMAX-style cinemas, and ahead of its time in 1955.

I realise now that, although Jim and Joey must have felt very much like fish out of water in this big, cosmopolitan city, it was Jim who embraced the local culture the more readily, adopting a "When in London, do as the Londoners do" approach. So he soon learned to ask for "mineral waters for the kiddies, please, love," while Joey persisted with "some lemonade for the bairns, please, hen," reluctant to compromise her own dialect and accent. We had lunch one day in the restaurant at Regent's Park. It was quite posh, and the waitress was making heavy weather of the silver service with the French fries on a paper-doyley-lined silver salver. Taking pity on the lassie, Joey urged her, "Never mind that, hen. Jist coup the chips on!" The look of utter incomprehension on the girl's face spoke volumes. What foreign language could this be? Jim would hail a taxi and happily pay what seemed to Joey like an exorbitant sum of money to the cheeky chappy cabbies, who seemed altogether too familiar for her liking.

It is not only linguistic differences that can inhibit communication. Misunderstandings can arise from subtle cultural differences in the simplest of situations. Jim and Joey soon realised that in London, licensed restaurants did not always welcome children. One day at lunchtime Jim went to investigate a particular eating place (and no doubt, have a swift half or two at the same time!). As we waited for him, Margaret and I were amusing ourselves playing a game as we sat on a bench, so Joey strolled a few yards down a typical side street of Edwardian houses, most of them divided up into office accommodation with stairs up to the front door and down to the basements. All of a sudden a man came running up the basement steps just as Joey approached. He was dressed in the formal business suit of that time: black jacket, striped trousers, and bowler hat with a rolled umbrella and briefcase in hand. He stopped and looked at Joey, then, to her surprise, immediately tapped her on the shoulder. "I'll be with you in a few minutes my dear, just you wait here," he urged with a smile, before running on up the steps to the front door. Joey's genuine bewilderment very soon gave way to an understanding of her situation, and she called after him, "Ah'm no yer dear, and whit's mair, Ah'll no be waitin' fur you!" I remember her rushing back to us, and as she shepherded us away in search of Jim, we knew she was upset but couldn't understand why. As we were having our lunch, she couldn't eat for asking Jim repeatedly, "Ah dinnae look like a wummin like that dae Ah?" "Dinnae be daft Joey," he reassured her, "but ye cannae go trailin' along the street, swingin' yer haundbag here, yer in London noo!"

The significance of this event only became clear to me when I was older, and I can understand why Mum was so upset. It was a sobering lesson in the need to be aware of how actions can so easily be misconstrued. As usual, Joey's sense of humour came to her rescue and she was able to laugh it off. She wondered if the man in the "strippit troosers" had heard her and if he had, did he understand that his hastily arranged assignation was very definitely not going to take place, and if so, how disappointed was he?

The London we visited in 1955 still bore many of the scars of the Blitz. It was less than ten years after the end of the war, and there were many cleared bomb sites still awaiting redevelopment. Viewed from my perspective now, understanding how short a time a decade really is, it is easy to appreciate how raw the city's wartime experience must still have felt for the citizens of London at that time.

An interesting footnote to our London holiday relates to a milestone in Scottish legal and criminal history which was reached three years later. The last man ever to be hanged in Scotland was Peter Manuel, who was convicted of several murders in 1958. In the course of our few days in London, Jim (as was his custom) visited one or two of the local hostelries close to our guesthouse in Pimlico. In one of them one evening, he noticed a young couple sitting together. As Jim sipped his pint and had a short chat to the barman, he could hear that the man had a strong Glasgow accent and that the girl was obviously Irish. As he made to leave, Jim exchanged a brief nod and "Aye there" with the young man—tacit recognition between two Scots meeting, however fleetingly, far from home—as London undoubtedly seemed in those days. Jim thought no more of this encounter until the morning after Manuel's execution in Barlinnie prison. His photograph, published for the first time, was on the front page of all the newspapers, and Jim was certain it was the face of that young man in the pub that night. The accompanying article made reference to the fact that Manuel was suspected of being implicated in the murder of a young Irish prostitute—in Pimlico in the summer of 1955! He was never charged with that crime due to a lack of evidence, but it made Jim shudder to think that in the course of our happy few days in London, he may have rubbed shoulders with a notorious murderer and his unfortunate victim.

We drove home from London via Stoke-on-Trent, where Joey bought a dinner service: white china with a pink and blue floral border. Thankfully those dishes, unlike Auntie Caroline's, survived the journey home. Then we detoured into Wales, stopping briefly in Wrexham. We were in a sweet shop there, buying some goodies for the onward journey, when another customer remarked on our Scottish accents. He said that he had met a Scots girl during the war, who came from Fife. When Joey said that was where we were from, he asked if she knew a little village by the name of Star! It was a typical "Isn't the world a small place!" moment, made even more so by the fact that the girl's name, Effie Thomson, was well known to Joey. She had been a few years older than Jim at Star school. The man explained that he had lost touch with her after the war, but would like to make contact again. Would Joey mind passing on his name and address to Effie?

She agreed to do what she could. It was only a short time after returning home that yet another coincidence intervened before Joey could carry out his request. She was visiting Mrs McMillan, our erstwhile district nurse and midwife, who had brought me into the world and had become a lifelong friend, who was a patient in Bridge of Earn hospital. During the visit, Mrs McMillan told Joey that one of the other ladies in the ward was from Star and knew Jim and his family there. Of course, she turned out to be Effie Thomson, and Joey, having his name and address still in her handbag, was able there and then to fulfil the promise she had made to that stranger in Wrexham. Sadly, we were never to know the outcome of that contact, if indeed there was any, because Effie died soon afterwards. But Joey would often wonder about those two people, ships who had passed in the night, brought together briefly by the fortunes—or misfortunes—of war, but destined never to meet again, despite that tentative possibility of renewed contact.

When I think of us in the great city of London, my mind returns to the day when Jim, a wee boy then, reported to his scandalised father that they were "only" four hundred miles from London and, in so doing, put paid to any more car rides in the old model T. What did old James think when he knew, more than thirty years later, that his son and his family were "stravaigin' through the muckle streets" of London? I can imagine him shaking his head, not in wonder or delight that his son had spread his wings and was seeing something of the world, but in grave foreboding that nothing good would come of such foolhardy adventuring! What he made of my year spent in Sweden, I can only imagine. Years after his death our two sons Calum and Donald lived and worked for some years in America, Hong Kong, and Japan. Two of his granddaughters, Margaret and I ("What are they?"), with our husbands John and Bill, met up in New Zealand during our round-the-world tours in 2002. To some extent, of course, this has become possible because of increasing prosperity and the advances in technology and communication generally. But also I believe that our parents, Joey and Jim, encouraged us to look outwards at the world and its people, not inwards at only our own little part of it. After all, to motor to London and stay there for those few days in 1955 required a sense of adventure and a degree of self-confidence that were alien to my grandfather, not only because of the generation he belonged to, but because of the narrow confines of his mind and the coldness of his heart.

*Hughie Drennan, Joey, and Jim on Kinlochbervie pier, 1962*

*Joey and Jim with caravan at the Highland Show in Dumfries, 1955*

*Joey, Jim, Margaret, and Anne in Trafalgar Square, London, 1955*

*With the Edgar Family at the Highland Show in Dumfries, 1955*

# PART 5

## HARVEST

# Chapter 30

"Run, lawdie, run. The ferm's on fire!"

Our annual summer holiday tours might seem to be unadventurous by today's standards, but to Joey and Jim they represented a break from the hard daily grind of work at Pitkinny. More importantly, it gave us an opportunity to spend time as a family and to explore new areas of Scotland and, more occasionally, England. Making contact, and in some cases, lifelong friends with people along the way was a great and lasting pleasure for all of us. The monotony of day-to-day life was also relieved, less happily, by occasional disasters, which varied from mere inconvenience and expense to real danger to life and limb, and in one case to the possible loss of the farm itself.

Over the years, the increasing reliance on machinery brought with it the frustration of mechanical breakdowns that always seemed to happen at the most inconvenient times. The first dry spell after days of rain would be interrupted by the failure of the combine harvester, or the baler would let Jim down at a crucial stage of the hay harvest. Working long into the night, as he and Chick Mitchell did to get the tattie digger going for the next day, was not unusual, and everyone at the farm had to become adept at mechanical repairs if costly bills from Farmec or Bowen's were to be avoided. These efforts were usually accompanied by much "swearing and tearing" on Jim's part, and in fact I am sure that many of the helpers were relieved if and when Jim left them to it, and we knew to keep our heads down at such times.

The vagaries of the weather were a perennial problem, of course, and it seemed that it was always too wet or too dry, too cold or too windy. Bad weather held up the outside work, of course, but there were always jobs to do in and around the steading. Winters were much more extreme in those days, and sometimes hours would have to be spent thawing frozen pipes with blowtorches to get water flowing to the cattle in the reids. There were those wonderful mornings when we would be told by Joey, "Just stay in bed and coorie in, lassies, we're snowed in. Ye'll no get tae the skail the day!" These must have been trying times for Joey and Jim, even more so after we had electricity and were almost totally dependent on it for light, heating, and cooking in the house, and of course for light and power in the steading. The blizzard would bring down the power lines, so we always had to keep a coal supply. On these occasions, it was back to lighting the coal fire for heat and cooking, and to looking out the old paraffin lamps for light. With the carelessness of childhood, we found the whole business exciting, and enjoyed the novelty of going to bed by candlelight and to watching Joey carry the last few embers of the kitchen fire in a shovel up to the fireplaces in the bedrooms. Then we loved falling asleep with the flickering flames casting shadows on the walls after blowing out the candle, but now I can understand the extra work and mess all of this involved. Looking back over the years, I can see that distance and time lends an enchantment to a view that Joey could hardly have appreciated then.

Draff is a byproduct of the malting process in the making of whisky, and represents a good example of recycling. The brown mash is used as a very nutritious and apparently delicious supplement to the winter feed for cattle. One Saturday morning in early February 1958, Jim left at seven to go for a load of draff to Cameron Bridge. This was the same distillery where his father had worked as a young man and to which Nellie had driven milk in the pony and trap as a young woman. I don't know whether the memories of his family's links with the place occurred to Jim that morning as he kept a weather eye on the conditions, but the direction of the wind that brought some light snow flurries alerted him to the possibility of a blizzard. An east wind and snow was a worrying combination, and sure enough the further east he went, the heavier the snow became, so after collecting his load of draff, he decided to return along the "Staunin' Stane" road to Kirkcaldy rather than risk the narrower and more winding route through Windygates and Kinglassie. Nevertheless, he found the road blocked near Chapel Farm west of Kirkcaldy, and he had to abandon the laden lorry at the end of the farm road. As he realised that he had no choice but to start to walk home, another stranded motorist asked him where he was making for. When he said Cardenden, this helpful chap suggested that he should walk to Kirkcaldy station, as the trains would still be running.

So he took this advice and trudged the two miles back into the town, only to find that there were no trains at all, and he had to retrace his steps to Chapel. Faced for the second time with the six mile trek to Pitkinny in rapidly deteriorating conditions, he stopped to fortify himself with tea (and no doubt some of a stronger beverage) and sandwiches at the pub in Chapel village. Meanwhile, "back at the ranch," both the power and phone lines had come down and Joey set to with the coal, candles, and paraffin to provide us with heat and light. Jim had left the morning feeding of the cattle in the hands of Tam Wallace, the young lad from Cardenden who, although very willing, could not be relied upon to use his initiative and would often bear the brunt of Jim's uncertain temper. That day, however, everything seemed to have gone well and he finished the feeding by lunchtime. By then the snowstorm was closing in, and he told Joey he was going to leave his bike and walk home to Cardenden. However, she persuaded him to stay, as she was worried he might come to harm in the blizzard. As it happened, he had to attend to the afternoon feeding as well, as Jim did not appear with the lorry. She was by now getting extremely worried about his whereabouts, and hoped that he had taken shelter somewhere.

We had some food, and as the snow continued to fall and the blizzard howled outside, an early darkness began to fall. Joey had some soup keeping warm on the coals in the fireplace in case it was needed. Suddenly we heard a scuffling in the back porch, accompanied by a familiar and very welcome voice giving vent to some well-chosen adjectives to describe the journey he had just endured. It was Dad! He resembled a snowman as he shuffled into the kitchen. His face was bright red except for the tip of his nose, which was dead white, probably in the early stages of frostbite. We couldn't believe that he had walked all the way home, but the stream of colourful and vituperative descriptions of his trek soon convinced us. As we helped him out of his soaking clothes, his greatest ire was reserved for the "stupit bugger" who had caused him to suffer four more miles of agony than necessary. It is probably just as well that he would never know who his unwitting torturer was. In her urgency to get Jim as near to the fire as possible, Joey knocked over the soup, and in one movement lost the restorative hot broth and put the fire out!

It wasn't long, however, until Joey—with her usual resourcefulness and patience—had Jim fed, and as he warmed up he began to mellow, and some good humour returned. We were all relieved that he had survived his ordeal unscathed, and even more that he was even quite nice to Tam, who was obviously enjoying the whole adventure of having to spend the night at the farm. "Well, Tam," I remember him saying, "what are we goin' to see on the television the nicht?" "We cannae watch the television, Mr Rutherford, 'cause there's nae electric," came the timorous reminder. Thankfully, Jim realised that he couldn't very well shoot the messenger, and contented himself with the consolation of a candle-lit reading of the *Courier*, which (happily) had been delivered that morning before the snow intervened. It was when he glanced at the front of the paper that he let out a cry of disbelief: "I dinnae believe it! Di ye kain whit day it is? It's the aichth o' Febury! It's ma bliddy birthday!"

His sudden outburst was met with stunned silence. He was quite right. None of his family had remembered his forty-first birthday. He had spent the best part of his special day trudging through the snow to make it home to us. He could have been forgiven for wishing that he had stayed in Kirkcaldy and enjoyed himself, but such a course of action would never have occurred to him. As mentioned in an earlier chapter, birthdays in our family were never considered that important, and beyond a brief "Many happy returns" nothing much would have been made of it, even if he had not had such a misadventure. We all hurriedly wished Dad a belated happy birthday, which was received with a grunt from him as he returned to his perusal of the newspaper, and silence descended on the snow-shrouded farmhouse.

The longest-lasting period of confinement due to snow was the six weeks in the winter of 1947 when I was a baby, and there were many other times when we were snowed in for a few days at a time, but that 1958 storm was to be the last. One of the few benefits of the coming of the opencast developments was that its operators, Costain, kept the road open for us, as it was essential for their work. However, there were other headaches caused by adverse weather. There was the summer when the weather was so wet that the gaiters in the close never dried up. Joey fought a constant battle with the mud, and worked hard to improve the ground around the house to try to achieve "clean fittin'" with concrete and slabs, to minimise the amount of mud that would encroach on the house. It was useless expecting Jim to take the time and trouble to take off his claurty boots before coming inside, especially when shortage of time or temper propelled him to the phone in a hurry.

The exposed situation of Pitkinny on the top of the brae left us open to the full fury of the wind in whatever direction it came, so we were used to severe buffeting. The worst gale we ever had, however, came in January 1968, when the whole country was affected. John and Margaret had lived for about eighteen months in Warwickshire, but John had changed his job to Bonnybridge and they had bought a house in Falkirk. This had happened just before their second daughter Alison was born, just before Christmas 1967. While John had lodgings near his work, Margaret stayed with the new baby and Pamela, who was two and a half, at Pitkinny until they could move into their new home. It was a Sunday evening as the wind grew stronger and stronger, and by midnight it was howling like a banshee. Margaret had to feed the baby and Joey got up to help her, bringing little Pamela downstairs. Baby Alison finished her bottle, and as Margaret lifted her to her shoulder and started to pat her back to wind her, the baby was sick, bringing up her entire feed, and at that precise moment, on cue, the lights went out. The storm had brought down the electricity lines and they had a power cut to add to the pleasures of the stormy night.

They could hear all manner of banging and rattling from outside. Jim also got up with the intention of going outside to see what damage was being done, but when they looked out from the porch they could see the big sheets of corrugated asbestos that formed the roof of the big shed floating around in the wind like pieces of tissue paper. They knew that it was too dangerous to attempt to go outside, so they had to sit out the storm and hope for the best. It was considered too risky to go back upstairs in case the chimneys came down on the roof, and they slept as best as they could in the kitchen and the sitting rooms. By the time daylight began to filter in the wind had begun to die down, and they were able to see the havoc the gale had wreaked. The two smaller henhouses beside the drying green had disappeared—all but one of their floors, a solid twelve-foot timber square. It had been turned upside down and was impaled on one of the clothes poles as if it was a sheet of paper that some giant hand had placed neatly on a spike, as Betsy used to do with her Co-op receipts. A cast-iron sheep feeder, which must have weighed many hundredweight, had been blown three field widths away, over three dry stane dykes and across the road, and was found with its wheels buried a good few inches into the ground in one of Westfield Farm's fields. The big shed had lost many of its roofing sheets, and many loose items of equipment were missing, some never to be located.

I was in Dundee at university at that time and lived in a flat on the Perth Road, which ran west to east. Fortunately my building was end-on to the gale and my windows somewhat sheltered, but all night I could hear loud clanging and rumbling from the main road outside. The reason was clear when I went to the bus stop in the morning. Monday morning was the time the dustbins were emptied on the Perth Road and most of the bins, which had been left ready for collection the next morning, had been blown like tumbleweed the length of the road. They were all piled up against the railings at the Sinderins junction where the road direction veered to the southeast, and their contents strewn far and wide. Whether or how they were all returned to their respective owners I never knew, but it was quite a sight. Sadly, it must have been less than amusing for the car owners whose vehicles had taken direct hits from the passing bins or from some of the chimney stacks on the tall buildings which had succumbed to the wind.

Farms can be very dangerous places, especially for children and the unwary. I suppose we must have been lucky to avoid anything too serious. The nearest I ever came to disaster was when we were playing hide-and-seek in the in the big shed. There were great hiding places amongst the hay bales, which occupied one entire end of the shed, stacked to the roof. Followed by Elizabeth Page, I had burrowed in further than usual between the bales, and suddenly came to a vertical gap. I fell a long way down to where the hay was very old and had remained undisturbed for a long time. It was extremely dusty and I can remember the feeling of airlessness. As I began to choke, I panicked and didn't have room to start climbing up the gap. It was just as well that Elizabeth had seen me disappear and, realising that I was stuck, she ran for help to Joey. Fortunately, as I fell my arms remained above my head, and Mum was just able to reach my hands and somehow managed to pull me clear. Her reaction was a typical one for a parent who has just had a bad fright. She cuddled me and then smacked me and told me to be more careful and not ever to scare her like that again. I think I realised that I had had a narrow escape, but it didn't deter us from playing in the bales for long.

Maybe it is just as well that when we are young, our memories of such near-disasters are short, otherwise we would lose our fearlessness and miss out on a lot of harmless fun and, more importantly, fail to develop essential survival skills. Nowadays children are shielded from every conceivable danger, and have less freedom to learn from personal experience the lessons that are so necessary to negotiate life's potential hazards. If you always have a stair gate, your toddler never learns to climb the stairs safely. If you never let your children out of your sight, they never learn how to deal with the sinister stranger if they ever meet him, or to cross the busy road if you happen to be late picking them up from school. Warn them and prepare them, but don't stop them learning for themselves. So I was more careful in the bales after that accident, but I still took the risk of playing there, and Joey had the common sense to let me.

Pitkinny was prone to wind damage, whereas flooding would never have affected us up on the brae, but the greatest catastrophe that befell the farm came in the form of fire. In October 1956, Jim and Joey had good reason to feel a sense of satisfaction. Within eight years of acquiring the lease of the farm, they had accomplished a great deal. The house was in a much better state, thanks in some part to the NCB landlord, but even more due to Joey's unceasing efforts at homemaking. Much of the steading had been rebuilt, and the centrepiece of this enterprise was the big shed, which housed under one roof much of the day-to-day operation of the business. To the east it accommodated the cattle reids, linking into a pre-existing one and leading into what would become the silage shed. The central area contained space for activities like potato dressing, neep-cutting, and some machinery storage. What had been the barn to the north of this area now housed the first-generation grain drier. The large section to the west was always filled to the rafters after harvest time with hay and straw bales. In the middle of October that year, they had all been safely brought in from the fields; the fruition of a successful harvest and testament to several weeks of hard graft on the part of everyone at the farm, and there they waited, ready to provide the cattle with their winter fodder and bedding.

In those days, Dougie, not long married, lived with his wife Chrissie at Capeldrae. He cycled to the farm each day, and on this particular morning the sight that greeted him as he pedalled up the loan from the cottar hooses was of smoke spiralling up from the roof of the big shed. It was before seven o'clock and Joey and Jim were in the kitchen having breakfast when they heard Dougie's bike clattering down at the back door, and his shouts of "Fire! Fire in the big shed!" as he ran past the window, made a grab for a fire extinguisher, and rushed into the shed. Joey heard Jim's muttered but anguished, "Aw no. No ma big shed!" as she passed him on his way to the back door, and ran to the phone. Margaret and I were still in bed directly upstairs, and I have a vague memory of hearing Mum making unusually frantic noises into the phone as she summoned the fire brigade. Then she shouted to us, "Girls, get up and bring your clothes, the big shed's on fire!" Margaret, a sensible fourteen-year-old, quite calmly dressed herself, but I, only ten and much less sensible, to my shame, completely panicked and lost control. I assumed, for some reason, that Joey wanted us to bring *all* our clothes, not just the ones we would be wearing that day. Perhaps I thought that was because absolutely everything was going to be destroyed, and I gathered every article of clothing I could find and came staggering downstairs with this big bundle, yelling at the top of my voice and no doubt adding to the general sense of panic and dread that Joey was already feeling. Fortunately, Mrs Shand, who lived in one of the cottages, happened to have arrived and Joey despatched her, I am sure with a great sense of relief, to escort me down to Auntie Doris who lived in the other cottar hoose with Dunc and her recently born seven-week-old son, Alan.

Meanwhile Jim's first job was to let all the livestock out of the reids and into the safety of the nearest field, before joining Dougie up on ladders with the fire extinguishers, but by then the fire was beyond their control. The fire-fighting equipment they had was totally unequal to the task, like fighting a tank with a peashooter, he described it later, and Joey was worried that they would get hurt, not so much by the fire at that stage, but by falling off their precarious perches.

As Mrs Shand and I approached the cottages, Dunc came out of his garden gate, totally unaware of the unfolding drama up the road. "Run, lawdie, run, the ferm's on fire!" As he took to his heels up the loan, Doris came out of the house and Mrs Shand passed me over to her, returning to see how she could help Joey. She found Dunc driving, pushing, or pulling the machinery that could be moved out of the big shed. It wasn't long until the first fire engine arrived, and the firemaster assessed the situation. He went immediately to the phone, and Joey heard him say urgently, "Send everything we've got, this is a bad one." He then told Joey that owing to the strong west wind the house was in danger, so he was going to hose down its entire north and west sides, those parts nearest the fire. It was at that point that Joey went into shock, and a few minutes later Margaret saw her walking across the close.

She was holding on grimly to her crystal candlesticks, those precious mementoes of her honeymoon. Over her arm she had her and Jim's dressing gowns, (ironic in that she despised the wearing of such garments, which she thought barely acceptable only when you were really ill, and then only when you wouldn't be seen so attired!), their two toilet bags containing the usual toothbrushes and toothpaste, soap and face-cloths, together with a few pounds that she had saved up. When Margaret asked her what she was doing, she explained, "Ah'm looking for some place to pit thae things that'll no burn doon," she explained, making for one of the wee henhouses. Margaret managed to persuade her to bring them back to the farmhouse, but then Joey grabbed a tea towel and made for the stairs. She had remembered that there was a tiny wee hole in one of the window panes in the little bedroom at the top of the stairs which faced the big shed, and she tried to block it with the tea towel to stop the fire from getting in. Of course, these actions were prompted by the same irrational response that had caused me to empty the wardrobe earlier on, and after a few minutes, Joey came to her senses and started to function normally, her habitual common sense and practicality reasserting themselves.

As more fire engines started to arrive, and helpers came from the surrounding farms as the word spread, she realised that all these people would need to be fed and watered. With Margaret's help, she lifted the rugs in the kitchen, leaving the tiled floor bare, and phoned Fraser's the grocer and the Co-op bakery for extra supplies. She decided the quickest and easiest way to steadily feed hungry and tired workers was to make a continuous supply of jeely pieces and a neverending stream of strong tea. As huge quantities of bread, tea, and butter were delivered, Mrs Shand, Mum, and Margaret set to and embarked on a mammoth effort to produce vast quantities of sandwiches of good (ready-sliced!) bread, thick with butter and Joey's delicious homemade jam. Almost her entire supply of strawberry, raspberry, and blackcurrant jam, along with her bramble and apple jelly and rhubarb and ginger preserve was used in that one day. All the teapots and crockery were pressed into service, but I think we managed to avoid using the "guid cheenie" for once! The firemen and workers from Pitkinny and elsewhere came into the kitchen in relays to have a rest. Meanwhile, I spent the first part of the day with Doris and the baby in the relative calm of the cottar hoose, until we too came up later and Doris got involved with the catering while I helped by minding the baby.

There were seven fire engines and crews from various fire stations in attendance that day, and many helpers from around the neighbouring farms. These numbers were swelled even more after the rain came on and their tattie harvesting was abandoned for the day. All were under the control of the firemaster, who directed operations. The first necessity was to make big holes in the roof of the big shed to let the fire travel upwards rather than along to other parts of the steading. This was achieved by the firemen crawling along the roof wielding their big fire axes. Then, as the hoses were applied to the fiercely burning hay and straw, it had to be pulled down by pitchforks and loaded on to trailers, which were then driven out to the nearest grass field and dumped in smouldering desolate heaps in the rain. Some of the older trailers were made of wood, and from time to time they would catch fire and have to be hosed down. This process went on for the whole day, until most of the burning material had been removed, by which time the roof of the big shed had all but been destroyed, although the bulk of the steel structure and the brick walls remained standing.

Throughout the entire operation, Jim remained silent. For once he did not give vent to his anguish by letting rip with any choice language. Instead, he directed his workers and helpers in consultation with the fire chief, ashen-faced and with the minimum of words. The other notable aspect of his behaviour that day was that he chain-smoked his way through several packets of cigarettes, unusual for Dad, who was very much a social and occasional smoker who only indulged in the company of other smokers, and hardly ever when he was on his own. Tam Wallace was in the thick of the action, and obviously found the whole experience very exciting and enjoyable. Sometimes he would get carried away with the whole experience and had to be prevented from risking his life by getting too close to the burning bales in his exuberance and anxiety to help, and had to be forced to come into the house for food and rest from time to time. "This has been the best day o' ma life, Mrs Rutherford," he said on one of these occasions, when Joey remarked that he seemed to be enjoying himself. "Jist dinnae let the boss hear ye sayin' that, Tam," she wryly replied, knowing that it was certainly one of the worst days of *his* life.

I have heard it suggested that when you read a report of a fire, and it says "the fire was brought under control," what that really means is that there is nothing left to burn. And in a way, that was probably true of the fire at Pitkinny that day. By late in the evening, most of the burning hay and straw had been removed out to the field, and in turn each of the fire crews was stood down. However, the firemaster left two of his men on duty overnight, just in case of the possibility that there were some unseen, smouldering pockets of fire. As the workers and helpers drifted away, Joey's kitchen was left in a complete shambles. The green and yellow tiled floor was obliterated with a thick coating of mud and burnt straw and hay from the countless pairs of filthy boots that had trodden in and out. I was sent to bed, but Margaret continued to help Joey until she too was told to get upstairs. She remembers that that was the first time she was aware of being really exhausted, but was afraid to go to sleep in case the fire started again, despite the reassuring presence of the firemen outside. Joey simply could not bear the thought of facing the kitchen in the morning, so despite her weariness, she decided she had to clean the floor. Jim helped her and as he swept the tiles, she got down on her hands and knees and scrubbed and washed until she could see the pattern of the tiles again.

As my parents tried to rest after what was undoubtedly one of the most harrowing days of their lives, they consoled each other that no one had been hurt in the fire, and that the house had been saved, the fire being confined to the big shed. Also, the heartwarming response of their many friends and neighbours who rallied round to help, and the tireless efforts of the firemen, took the edge off the trauma of the day. But nothing could help to assuage for Jim the desolation he felt at the loss and damage to his new steading. All the hopes and dreams that he had invested in his big shed now seemed to be in peril. He was always a great believer in insurance, and was initially confident that he was fully covered for the cost of the fire, but in the event, once the loss adjusters had their say, the final insurance settlement fell far short of his losses. The building had lost its roof, but fortunately the new brick walls and their adjoining stone counterparts in the older part of the building, though blackened, had withstood the worst ravages of the fire, as had the new steel framework, but the roof had to be completely replaced. Another major cost was that he had to buy in all the hay for fodder and straw for bedding to see him through to the next harvest.

The cause of the fire was never determined for sure. Initially there was some wild speculation that a tramp might have crawled into the shed to sleep and had dropped a cigarette or a lighted match. Or maybe it was maliciously started by someone with a grudge against Pitkinny. In fact, the less dramatic and more mundane reason for the fire was eventually put down to either an electrical fault or to spontaneous combustion. There was a broken glass light cover, but that may have been the result rather than the cause of the fire. It was well known that hay and straw in storage can generate a substantial amount of heat, which may with the right conditions cause it to burst into flames spontaneously. I can remember how in the immediate aftermath of the fire, the entire farm was pervaded by the awful acrid stench of the burnt hay and straw. The clear perspex skylight panels in the roof had exploded and melted with the heat, and their remains were left hanging down like forlorn curtains, the colour and consistency of honeycomb toffee.

Jim's plans for the future of Pitkinny suffered a great setback, and there were many evenings when he and Joey sat at the kitchen table dealing with the paperwork and juggling the figures involved in their insurance claim. But gradually they began to regain their confidence and put the disaster behind them. As always, it was Joey who kept their spirits up with her practical and patient forbearance which helped to balance Jim's understandable disappointment, which initially bordered on despair. I remember how when we returned to school after a day or two, I rather enjoyed the attention the fire received, (there was even a bit about it in the *Courier*!), but at the same time, I did realise how worried Jim and Joey were. But with the resilience and carelessness typical of childhood, I soon forgot all about the fire and its aftermath. One amusing postscript to the disaster came when the fire extinguisher salesman called at Pitkinny, to try to interest Jim in reconditioning or upgrading his equipment. He left very quickly with a flea in his ear, but could have considered himself fortunate that he didn't also have a fire extinguisher lodged in another part of his anatomy!

Another potential disaster which threatened, but fortunately bypassed Pitkinny, was the foot and mouth disease outbreak in 1960. When the first case was reported, it turned out that Jim had bought cattle at Stirling cattle market in the same sale ring on the same day that some of the infected beasts had gone through. Thankfully, none of Jim's developed the disease. Several other farms in the area were affected: East Bowhill, Inchgall, and New Carden. The location of Bogside right beside the road made the dairy herd there more vulnerable than the livestock at Pitkinny, and a close watch was kept on the cows by Jock Steel. He phoned early one morning to say that he didn't like the look of one of them, as it seemed to have a sore mouth! Some hours of great anxiety passed before the vet gave it the all clear, and there were a few other false alarms during the weeks of the epidemic, but happily we survived unscathed. Vehicular and pedestrian traffic in and out of the farm had to be kept to a minimum, and strict precautions observed. A bed of disinfected straw was laid at the end of the loan and at the entrance to Bogside, which all vehicles had to run over. We had to dip the soles of our shoes in a bucket of the same liquid disinfectant every time we left or returned to the farm. Even our little terrier, Trudy, had to have her wee paws dipped one at a time in a little cup of disinfectant—an ordeal she hated—and we had to keep our collies confined to barracks! No livestock could be moved off the place, nor could we visit any other farm. The public were barred from encroaching onto farmland, of course, but, as always, there were those who did not think that the rules applied to them. When the New Carden herd was being destroyed and the carcasses burned in a deep trench in one of the fields there, one of the local bobbies came across a man from Cardenden who had decided to take a stroll over the fields to watch the grisly operation. He was collared by the policeman and taken to task. Then he was made to undress and watch as his outer clothes and shoes were added to the pyre. He was sent off with his tail between his legs, a condition that was no doubt visible to all who saw him skulking homewards!

As those farms that were hit by the disease had all their livestock culled, a heartbreaking event for farmers who had spent years building up their herds, the fear of God crept into our hearts when we learned that their farm cats had also to be put down, as they could be carriers of the disease to other livestock. Even wild birds were sometimes implicated in the spread of the disease, but of course there was no way of controlling their movements. The current worries over the possibility of an epidemic, or even pandemic, of bird or swine flu carries echoes of that foot and mouth outbreak and others since. As the emergency gradually eased, there were some jaundiced reactions on the part of some farmers like Jim, who had been spared the loss of their herds and felt that they had come off worse than those who had actually been hit by the disease. Compensation agreements with the government meant that the latter received generous recompense, and were able to restock their farms completely in due course. The former, on the other hand, who had been unable to sell their livestock or their dairy products due to the restrictions imposed by the government, were severely out of pocket and had no compensation. Some went as far as to say that they wished they had had foot and mouth, but Jim could never have countenanced seeing the destruction of his livestock, even if it might have made financial sense in the long term.

The fire and the foot and mouth outbreak were very serious problems, either or both of which could have seen the end of Jim and Joey's business, but fortunately they were able to rise above them. Other less critical but still very frustrating problems came along from time to time, but some of them had amusing or even profitable sides to them in the long run. We had been connected to the main electricity supply since 1953, and Jim particularly enjoyed the relative comfort and ease it brought to our living and working conditions in the house, and even more so in the steading. He was never in the least miserly in his use of electricity, and was not in the habit of nagging us to switch off lights. He said he had lived the first half of his life in the cold and the dark, and he was determined to make up for that in the second half! Margaret and John had become engaged to be married, and the Christmas before their wedding, in 1963, John's parents Flo and George French and his aunt and uncle Mary and Eck Forrest were invited to join us for Boxing Day dinner. A boy friend of mine, Nick Chalmers, was also at the farm. Joey timed the meal to be ready about four o'clock, just as Jim finished the afternoon feeding of the cattle. Everything was almost ready and the nine of us were about to sit down at the table when we had a sudden power cut. Jim phoned up and reported the loss of supply to the South of Scotland Electricity Board, who promised to send a breakdown team, but could give no estimated time of arrival.

Jim soon discovered that the problem was in the supply from the steading to the house, as the outdoor power was still on. He managed to run a long trailing cable with a single large light bulb from the big shed which, when it was hooked over the clothes pulley in the kitchen, at least gave us light. But by then all the food had grown cold and had to be reheated. Joey had by then invested in a portable gas camping cooker with two burners, run off calor gas, so we managed with a struggle to warm up the dinner. As usual in such circumstances, everyone mucked in and we were all in good spirits despite the inconvenience. I can remember George was delegated to warm up the sprouts by holding the pot above four candles, and it wasn't too long until we were able to tuck into a delicious meal. Some time later the SSEB linesmen arrived, and reassured Jim and Joey that they would do their best to effect a temporary repair, and so rescue the remainder of our party. They were all very jolly and good-natured, and we had the definite impression that they had been partaking of some liquid Christmas spirit during the course of their shift. Remember, this was in the days before the breathalyser test to detect drunk driving, and no doubt some grateful customers had plied them with some "thank you" drinks during their earlier calls.

A year or two before this, Jim had installed his second-generation grain drier, which had necessitated the upgrading of the farm supply from one-phase to three-phase electrical power, and from that time the entire supply was metered in the steading, including that for the house. As they didn't have the time or the means to diagnose what had caused the break in supply from the steading, they decided to rig up a temporary line from the main supply cable outside the house and connect it into the house's ring mains. They assured Jim that they would report this to their office, which would then arrange a permanent repair after the festive break. Having restored us to full power, the linesmen went on their merry way, fortified a little more for their subsequent jobs by some of Jim's festive cheer in the shape of a few nips. We resumed our Boxing Day celebrations, and as far as we were aware, that was the end of the matter.

The effect of that "temporary" repair was that the electricity supply to the house at Pitkinny bypassed the metre in the steading and meant that as long as it was in place, all the electricity consumed in the house was free of charge. The SSEB never got back to Jim to arrange a permanent repair and he conveniently "forgot" all about the matter. Joey was aware of the situation, and every so often she would remind Jim and nag him about it, but his attitude was, "Ah'm jist a fermer, I dinnae kain onythin' aboot electricity." He wasn't about to look a gift horse in the mouth, but at the same time he was canny enough to know that if his electricity bills suddenly plummeted, this might alert the electricity board to the situation. So he made sure that he used plenty of power in the steading, to keep his consumption at a level that would not raise too much suspicion! As you drove along the loan on winter evenings, Pitkinny would often resemble a scene from Blackpool Illuminations, there were so many lights on. Comments were sometimes passed, but only Jim and Joey knew the real reason for his profligacy.

Although there was no central heating, thanks to storage heaters, electric fires, and a gradually increasing number of electrical appliances in the house, and effective lighting and power for the machines in the steading, we enjoyed a degree of comfort that was unknown in Jim's youth, and he revelled in it. Margaret, John (who worked for SSEB!), and I were unaware that the temporary repair had never been changed, and it was some years later that Margaret found out. She had fed the hens for Joey and had accidentally spilled a little of the grain outside the henhouse. Jim may not have been miserly in most ways, but he hated to see any feeding wasted, so when he happened to spot Margaret's mistake, he came into the kitchen demanding to know, "Whoa fed the hens last?" When Margaret was duly told off about wasting the corn, she remonstrated with Jim: "Dad, why di ye get in such a state aboot a wee drap corn when ye burn electric as if it gaun oot o' faushion?" Jim looked at Joey and said, "Will we tell 'er?" So they explained the situation to Margaret and then to me, and in a sense we all became accessories after the fact!

Unlike Jim, Joey was really worried about it, and expected that one day their situation would be discovered. She feared that Jim would at best have to pay all the estimated costs of the electricity we had used, or at worst be accused of doing something illegal. Each time there was a problem of any kind to do with the electricity supply (a regular occurrence as our exposure to the vagaries of the weather often led to power cuts), Joey would get in a state of anxiety in case the SSEB had to be called. The one that happened the night of the gale in 1968 when lightning had hit the transformer between the farm house and the cottar hooses was one example. Then not long after that, the cable from the main line into the house, installed by those inebriated linesmen that famous night in 1963, began to smoulder. It had not been meant to last all that time, of course, and Joey feared it would cause a fire, so something had to be done urgently. Adam Neilson, the electrical contractor who had installed the three-phase electricity for the new grain drier, was called. His son, young Adam, inspected the "temporary" cable and, knowing there was no metre in the house, asked Jim about it. When Jim "remembered" what had happened in 1963, he agreed with Adam that the linesmen must have neglected to report the need for a permanent solution to the failure of the supply from the farm to the house. So young Adam and his father managed to both rectify the original fault and remove the evidence of the metre bypass.

So Joey's peace of mind was restored, and Jim saved from any possible retribution, as the era of free electricity came to an end. While Jim was no doubt sorry that he would have to stump up for every unit of power he used from then on, it really did not make him any more careful about their electricity consumption. I am sure that what he enjoyed more than the money saving involved in his subterfuge was the fact that he had managed to get the better of the electricity board. It was a feature of his character that he took gleeful pleasure in outwitting people, especially those he perceived to be in a position of authority of any kind. Perhaps it was the result of the authoritarian regime his father had always subjected him to when he was young. It still rankled with Jim and inflamed his basic dislike of being told what to do, or being subject to any limitation on his freedom of action, whether that came from his own family or from the powers that be, electrical or otherwise!

There was a second brush with fire at Pitkinny, and this time it involved Grandad Hugh Mitchell. The original grain drier was still in use during the harvest of 1960. The system was operated by a diesel-powered engine that blew hot air under the floor of the grain drier, which was punctuated by open grills on which the filled bags of grain lay to be dried. The engine was lit by an asbestos torch, and on this occasion, as Grandad started to light it, a piece of glowing asbestos dropped unseen onto the floor of the engine house. By the time Hugh noticed, it had set fire to the oily dust on the floor, and he was not fast enough to stamp out the rapidly spreading flames. Jim was having the new silage shed built and Lour Webster, the brickie from Markinch and Bill Smith, the steel erector, were working that day. Fortunately they heard Hugh's shouts of alarm and were able, and quick-thinking enough, to use the sand they had for mixing their mortar to douse the flames. By the time the fire brigade arrived, the fire was out and the damage limited to the engine house only. It was just as well, because on the other side of the wall there was a large tank of diesel, which could well have exploded if the fire had reached it. Grandad was in a state of shock, but happily not hurt, and Joey was at pains to reassure him that it was not his fault. She also told Jim off in no uncertain terms that it was wrong of him to leave Hugh, who was by then getting well on in years, to do such a potentially dangerous task. But of course, as usual, Jim assumed that everyone would just do what he required of them, able, trained, or not, and Hugh was invariably ready and willing to help in any capacity.

After Bogside was demolished in the extension of the opencast towards the end of the sixties, the Dutch barn that Jim had built near the steading there was left intact and was used for extra fodder storage. It was open on one side and one day as he drove past, Jim could see some boys in the barn, wreaking havoc on the carefully stacked bales of hay and straw. They had pushed them over and cut their strings, tossing the loose fodder all over the place. Jim was naturally furious at this wanton damage and the waste of all the work and effort that the contents of the barn represented, so he stopped and shouted at the lads. They wouldn't give him their names, only that they came from Ballingry. So he quickly lifted their bikes which were lying on the ground and told the boys to walk home and tell their fathers that they could collect their bikes any time from Pitkinny Farm. He knew this meant that he would have the opportunity of confronting the parents of the vandals and impressing on them what their boys had done, although he knew better than to hope that he would get any recompense.

However, later that day it was not the parents who arrived at Pitkinny, but a police car from Lochore. The constable was a newcomer to the Lochore station, the policemen who had been there and had worked at Pitkinny years before having long gone. He told Jim officiously that he had had a report that Jim had unlawfully taken bikes belonging to some lads. Their fathers had complained and he would have to return the bikes. The sergeant had some sympathy with Jim's reasons for removing the bikes, but he doubted whether anything would come of attempting to have the boys charged with causing malicious damage. So Jim had to give up the bikes, with no hope of even an apology for the loss he had suffered. This came as no great surprise to him, but what made him really mad was when the policeman warned him that he had noticed one or two pitchforks in the Dutch barn when he was "investigating" the incident. Jim should not have left them there, as they could have injured the boys! He was tempted to point out that the boys shouldn't have been in the barn anyway, but realised that he would be wasting even more of his time. This was an early example of a scenario that we have become increasingly familiar with in recent years. Injury or death results when youngsters put themselves in danger, but it is then considered to be the fault of someone else. It reminds me of the rhyme we used to say when we were young if such a situation arose:

> Paddy on the railway, pickin' up stanes,
> Along came an engine an' broke Paddy's banes.
> 'Aw', said Paddy, 'that's no fair',
> 'Well', said the engine-driver, 'ye shouldnae hae been there!'

The last straw for Jim in the saga of the Dutch barn at Bogside came only a few months later, when he had a phone call late one Saturday night from Saund and Jessie Page. They had just driven past the barn and saw that it was on fire. They had alerted the fire brigade before calling Jim and Joey, but of course by the time they arrived it had been completely destroyed. This was the last time fire affected Jim and Joey in their time at Pitkinny, but sadly, not the last time it played a part in their lives. The old adage that things, good or bad, come in threes was not to be true in their case.

After their retirement, Joey and Jim lived in two modern houses. Jim would claim, "An auld hoose is like an auld car, nae bliddy guid tae onybody." They certainly had plenty of experience of dealing with the problems that the maintenance of an old house brings. One of the last was in 1972 when Bill and I lived in Cumbernauld. They were visiting Margaret and John in Kirkcudbright when Dougie phoned to say he had discovered that the sitting room ceiling in the house at Pitkinny had fallen in. He had been in the house using the phone when he glanced along the hall and saw that the room was in an uproar. Thinking to begin with that it had been vandalised, he then realised that the old lathe and plaster ceiling had collapsed. The mess was horrendous, but none of the furnishings seemed to be too badly damaged. The dome clock that Joey had been given by Jim for their silver wedding had been knocked sideways and was balancing precariously on the very edge of the mantelpiece. Dougie tip-toed over and rescued it, but decided that everything else would have to wait until Jim and Joey returned. I passed the buck to Margaret and phoned and asked her to tell Mum and Dad, so when they called in to see us on their way home, Joey was dreading the job of refurbishing the sitting room that was waiting for her. The next day Sandy, the husband of Nurse McMillan and the father of Alistair, happened to call at Pitkinny. When Joey showed him the sitting room, he said "Aye, it's a terrible mess, Mrs Rutherford, but it could be worse!" "Hoo the hell could it be worse, Sandy?" she exclaimed. "Well, it could be ma ceilin'!" he retorted. It was to Joey's credit that she could laugh at Sandy's joke and that her sense of humour would always come to her aid in times of undoubted stress and frustration.

There were other emergencies at Pitkinny over the years, happily none of them too serious, and again usually with a funny side. Joey was never nervous of being alone with us at the farm, not even on the darkest of nights, and there were many when Jim was out by himself well into the early hours. It was only towards the end of their time there that one or two things happened to dent her confidence. One Sunday evening in July 1971, just after Bill and I were married, we were all at Pitkinny for the weekend. It was during the school holidays, and the start of the Fife fair fortnight, so the next day was a public holiday. Margaret and John had gone to visit old friends in Edinburgh, and their three girls were all asleep upstairs. Jim, Bill, and I had gone to bed, while Joey decided to stay up until Margaret and John came in. It had been a very hot day and the doors and windows had been open. Joey was sitting in the sitting room reading the *Sunday Post*, and as usual none of the curtains were drawn. She heard the handle of the front door being turned. Now it was seldom used and always locked, so she thought it must be me checking it. I was still not asleep and also heard the door handle, and assumed it was Mum doing the same, but the next moment she tapped on our door and asked, "Was that you at the door, Anne?"

I got up and we went into the kitchen to find the back and porch doors wide open. Somehow I got across the floor to the back door and closed and locked it. Then Joey went to check on the girls and to waken Jim as I roused Bill. Jim, typically, replied to Joey's frantic, "Jim, get up, somebody tried to get in the front door!" with "Well? Get Bill." She insisted that he get up, and within a few minutes the two men were standing sleepily in the kitchen trying to decide what to do. Then they sallied forth, Jim armed with the (unloaded!) shotgun and Bill with the poker from the fireplace, while Joey and I cowered in the kitchen behind belatedly firmly locked doors. The glennie blink of a July night allowed them to see quite well, but when a quick look round did not reveal anyone, Jim suggested that a prowler would probably have headed up the loan in the direction of Lochore, so they jumped in the land rover and set off in pursuit. They did not find anyone on the loan, and turned round at Harelaw. As they were driving down the loan towards the cottar hooses, Margaret and John were coming in from the main road. They saw the lights of the land rover and thought it was visitors leaving the farm, but then the lights disappeared as the land rover turned up to the farm, and as John and Margaret arrived in the close, it was to witness a scene from the Wild West as Bill and Jim, brandishing their weapons, continued their search of the steading. "What on earth's going on? Are the girls all right?" Margaret frantically enquired as she rushed into the house. We never did discover who our late-night visitor was. It might have been an opportunist sneak thief, walking home along the loan to Lochore, and needing some easy holiday money.

The summer before that, before we were married, Bill was staying one Friday night at Pitkinny, as we were due to leave early the next morning to go to Aberdeen. Jim woke at about four in the morning to hear someone trying to start a vehicle. He thought it must be Bill and me leaving, but then thought it was too early. As he got out of bed, he saw his nearly new pickup being driven at great speed down the loan. He quickly checked to see that it wasn't one of us who was driving and then went straight to the phone to report it stolen to the police. Of course, he had no idea of the registration number, and couldn't locate the log book, but in the meantime, Bill had got up, dressed hastily, and set off in pursuit in his own car. By good luck, he made the correct choices of direction at each junction he came to, and within a short time had located the stolen vehicle, crashed into a gate post between Kirkness Farm and Righead, where the Baird family lived. The pickup was empty, but there was some blood on the steering wheel. The gate of the field had swung open and the cattle had got out on to the road, which had alerted the Bairds to the problem. Bill had a scout around, but could not find anyone. Presumably, the thief had been slightly hurt but had been able to flee the scene. Bill then made his way to the bungalow at Righead, the nearest house, and asked Margaret Baird to phone Pitkinny. Of course, she didn't know Bill from Adam, and I answered the phone to hear her say doubtfully, "There's a young man here who claims to know you and has some story about a stolen pickup." She obviously thought Bill was likely to be the culprit, but once I reassured her that he was in fact my "intended," she relaxed and invited him to stay for his breakfast! Within a few weeks, the same car thief was arrested for another heist and asked for previous misdemeanours to be taken into account, including one of having stolen a pickup from Pitkinny Farm. His justification for the theft was that he was walking home from a dance and was really tired, so he thought he would "borrow" the pickup!

The incident that Joey and Jim found the most unsettling in retrospect, and genuinely frightening at the time, was during their last winter, that of 1975–76, at the farm. Joey had had to give up driving after her spinal operation, and early one evening Jim was getting the car out of the garage to run Joey to Glenrothes for her dressmaking class. This was the transitional period just before they were to relinquish the lease and retire, so there was no one living in the cottar hooses. From down the loan there came a sudden outburst of shouting and swearing, obviously from more than one person, and they went on to make threats to Jim, referring to him as a "******* big fermer." In the lights from the farm, they could presumably see Jim moving around, but he couldn't see them. He was furious and about to walk down towards them, but Joey stopped him. She insisted that they should get in the house, and then she phoned the police. They sent a car, but by the time it arrived the culprits had vanished. She found this episode very upsetting, and from then until they left Pitkinny, she wouldn't stay on her own at the farm after dark, and would always make sure that the house was properly secured. It was a great pity that, having never been afraid of anything or anyone throughout her life, these last few months of their life at Pitkinny should have been spoiled by these few events. Whether this was a measure of Joey's growing older, or of the increasing likelihood of her and Jim being the victims of burglary, vandalism, or worse, given the isolated nature of the farm and the mounting crime rates in those days, is difficult to say, but it certainly was a feature of their final year or two at Pitkinny.

# Harvest in—then 150 tons are destroyed

**Last week-end farmer James Rutherford saw the last of his harvest safely in.**

Yesterday he watched about 150 tons of hay and straw go up in smoke at North Pitkinny Farm, Cardenden.

Fire in a barn he built less than two years ago caused damage estimated at over £6000.

All day Mr Rutherford and his workers toiled to clear the building of the baled hay and straw.

Neighbouring farms rallied round with labour and tractors and trailers. The Coal Board, who own the farm, sent helpers from the West Fife area estates department.

Late last night smouldering hay and straw was still being carried to nearby fields to be hosed down by firemen.

The outbreak was spotted by a farm worker shortly before 8 a.m.

Before firemen arrived from Kirkcaldy, Lochgelly and Cowdenbeath, Mr Rutherford and his men tackled the flames with buckets of water and extinguishers.

A gale-force wind placed the farmhouse, only a few yards away, and adjoining buildings and a stackyard in grave danger.

But thanks to the laying of a new water main in the area recently, firemen were able to get three jets on the blaze quickly. They confined the flames to one end of the barn.

The roof of the building, which is 130 feet long and 40 feet wide, was damaged and the contents destroyed.

Said Mr Rutherford: "We were just congratulating ourselves on having got the harvest in last week-end. Some of the hay had been in storage in the barn since 1954."

Dundee Courier *report on Pitkinny Farm fire, 1956*

# Chapter 31

"Weel, ye never ken, the Queen micht come along the loan!"

If there were times of crisis and catastrophe at Pitkinny, on balance they were outweighed by occasions celebrating some degree of success and achievement. These represented good reason for pride and satisfaction, but given Jim's (and especially Joey's) natural reticence and modesty, were always understated and occasionally accompanied in my memory by an element of embarrassment. In retrospect, I can remember a trace of irony and humour in the responses these situations invoked in my parents.

The sentiment implied in the ironic statement, "Ah've never seen a fermer on a bike," pokes fun at those in the farming community who constantly complain about the hardship of their lot in life. Jim was not immune from that tendency, but when he and Joey started out in their farming enterprise, that was the only mode of transport they could aspire to. Jim's abortive attempt to borrow his father's pickup reinforced his overwhelming natural desire to be independent of his family, indeed of anyone, and resulted in his decision to acquire a vehicle at the earliest opportunity.

In one of the two letters he wrote to Joey on the occasion of Margaret's birth in Markinch, he refers to an early unsuccessful attempt to buy a car, but this failure was soon followed by the realisation of his ambition. In the years thereafter at Bogside, he owned a series of second-hand cars, each one better than the one before, and soon added a small lorry and a tractor to his fleet of vehicles. This period marked the beginning of Jim's lifelong affection for cars that deserted him only in the last few years of his life. I firmly believe that his cars were not only concrete symbols of his material success, but the embodiment of his independent and individualistic approach to life in general and his business in particular.

As it grew, he invested increasingly in an array of mechanical systems and implements, which increased in cost and sophistication as the technology of farming developed apace in the postwar years. His first milking machines that superseded hand milking, and the first tractor which took over from the faithful draught horses, inspired much head-shaking and dire warnings of disaster from "the Star anes," especially since much of the capital investment was financed with money borrowed from the bank—a cardinal sin in their eyes. Each new acquisition, from ploughs, sowing machines, binders, balers, or tattie diggers and eventually to combine harvesters and grain driers, failed to convince old James that his middle son's adventurous and innovative spirit in the forefront of these developments was making his business a success. This, even as he himself was forced, grudgingly and reluctantly, to trail along in Jim's wake as the benefits to be gained from the mechanical innovations that were transforming farming became undeniable and irresistible. But he never gave his son any credit for his enterprise or imagination, both qualities that my grandfather at best distrusted and at worst despised.

Although Jim was to own a number of lorries and land rovers, vans and pickups in the course of his life, it was his cars that were the focus of his ambition and brought him the greatest pleasure. His first purchase of a brand new car came as something of a shock to Joey, and was the cause of much soul searching and anxiety on her part. One Saturday afternoon in 1952, Dad dropped us off at the shops in Kirkcaldy, but instead of going to the football as he usually did, he headed off to the Fidelity Garage. As we waited later for him to pick us up at the appointed place, Joey was astounded to see him drive up in an unfamiliar vehicle. The car was a spanking new Rover 75, and the driver was grinning from ear to ear as he enjoyed his wife's astonishment. He had kept his plans a secret and had concluded the deal that day without Joey knowing anything about it, but as he struggled to convince her that this was indeed their new car, he realised that she was less than thrilled with the surprise.

The car was a beautiful shade of turquoise, almost unheard of in an era when you "could have any colour as long as it's black." In addition, as it was a demonstration model, it had an inordinate amount of flashy chrome styling. Joey felt extremely conspicuous as we drove home, and as we neared Cardenden, she urged us to crouch down in the back seat, as she herself slid as low down in the passenger seat as she could, so we wouldn't be recognised. She felt very uncomfortable in such unaccustomed (and what she thought of as unnecessary) luxury. Her egalitarian principles, honed in the harsh years of her childhood and youth, could not sit comfortably with the evidence of affluence that Jim's new acquisition represented to her and, she was sure, to everyone in Cardenden. That car, HSP 222, was the first of a series of Rovers. The second one, NFG 100, was powder blue; thereafter there was a two-tone chocolate brown and cream one, and much later peacock blue and fawn ones. In between, he had a green and cream Riley Pathfinder and a black MG Magnette. In the early sixties, he bought two Jaguars, a 2.4 followed by a 3.4. I remember the day he bought the first of these. He picked me up from the school bus and said he had to go to Dunfermline. We arrived at Ben Armit's Garage in Halbeath Road, and much to my surprise we left in this Jaguar. "Let's see what it can do," he said with relish as he drove through Crossgates and down the Inverkeithing straight, the first time I was aware of "doing the ton."

After the Jags, he had three Triumph 2000s. I had heard him mention this new car that he fancied the look of, but had no idea he was thinking of getting one. It was a Saturday lunchtime in the early autumn of 1963, and I was walking home from an early season school hockey match. As I came along the loan, I saw a car approaching. I could see it was an unfamiliar shape, and as it drew nearer I realised it was Dad in a taupe-coloured 2000. He was off to the football and as he drew near, he blew the horn with great gusto. Then, as he passed me I could see he was "laughing like a pooch," clearly delighted with his new toy as he waved and accelerated away in a cloud of dust. As I stood and watched him, I was conscious of a feeling of swelling pride, almost as if he was the little boy and I was the indulgent parent. Somehow I knew that he was reaping the rewards of much hard work and risk-taking in his business, and I was genuinely happy for him and proud that he was my Dad.

I suspect that many people thought he was unduly extravagant in indulging his passion for cars, but looking back over the years, I am so glad that he was able to experience such joy in the fruits of his labours. It must have helped to make up for the hardship—both physical and emotional—he had experienced as a young man at the hands of his father, and the pain that the loss of his mother must have caused him. I am sure that Joey did not begrudge him the pleasure that he got from his cars. She probably didn't understand it, as she was the least materialistic of people, and she never tried or desired to fulfil the image of a prosperous farmer's wife, but I am sure she was proud of his achievements for his sake, if not her own. Although eventually, after he retired, he bought a number of BMWs, which had great status in the 1980s, out of all the cars he owned I suspect that none of them gave him the pleasure and delight, nor Joey the angst and unease, as the purchase of that first Rover in 1952. Jim's love of cars and the pleasure he took in driving only began to desert him in the last few years of his life, when he began to enjoy being driven by his daughters, two sons-in-law and, even more, by his grandchildren. He got a real kick out of seeing the youngsters behind the wheel of his car, and he was happy to pay higher insurance premiums to make that possible. After Mum died, his increasing emotional and physical frailty combined with ever-growing traffic congestion, made driving less and less of a pleasure for him. But even before that, the debacle which led to the loss of his last "real" car (the third of his BMWs in 1997) marked the end of his lifelong love affair with the car and foreshadowed the end of his driving.

As we grew up at Pitkinny, each year brought the usual annual red-letter days. As explained earlier, birthdays received only the most cursory attention. Our twenty-first birthdays were marked by a gift to each of us in turn, from Mum and Dad, of a beautiful Omega wristwatch. This acknowledged the right of passage to adulthood, as we attained voting age and "the key of the door," but there was no question of any public display in the form of a twenty-first birthday party for either of us. Other milestones in our lives were, by comparison with nowadays, similarly low-key. I know that Jim and Joey were very proud of us and of our achievements, but they seldom made any open show of their feelings in this regard. They attended school prize-giving ceremonies when Margaret and I would feature regularly. When Margaret started her nurses' training at Fod House they would attend functions there, and as she completed her training at West Fife Hospital in Dunfermline, they were gratified with her success, but again in a measured and private way. My university graduation evoked much the same response, and it would be dishonest of me not to admit that I was often disappointed with the lack of fuss that attended these occasions. The effect was to make me determined that if and when I had a family, I would take more obvious pleasure and pride in their achievements. But I understand that our parents' attitudes were typical of the dour Scottish character that abhorred too much public show and discouraged young people from getting above their station in any way.

The one occasion in our lives where Jim and Joey made something of an exception to this rule was when we were married. They gave us both a lovely white wedding, the ceremony in Auchterderran Parish Church followed by a reception in the Station Hotel in Kirkcaldy. They saw this as an opportunity to entertain their friends and family on a scale they could never aspire to normally, but more than that, it was perhaps a way of making up for the terribly meagre and austere nature of their own wartime wedding day. When Bill and I returned from our honeymoon, Dad presented me with the bill for our wedding reception as a souvenir. I was suitably aghast at the cost of the celebration, but he assured me that he had had a wonderful day and didn't grudge a penny of the expense. However, he left me in no doubt that if he hadn't enjoyed himself so much, it would have been a very different matter! In return Margaret and I did our best to mark the occasion of Mum and Dad's silver, ruby, and golden weddings (in 1967, 1982, and 1992 respectively) and their eightieth birthdays with family gatherings each time. They also enjoyed the christenings of their five grandchildren, and lived long enough to attend the weddings of their three granddaughters and four of their great-grandchildren's christenings. The graduations of their grandsons and their granddaughters gave them great pleasure, as did the successful careers they embarked upon. The happiest times of their lives in later years were those they spent with their family, and I know in my heart that we all meant everything to them and they considered themselves blessed in this regard.

In common with most children in Fife, we used to look forward to the yearly fun to be enjoyed at the Links Market in Kirkcaldy. The fact that this fair—held on the promenade of the seaside town—was of great antiquity, stretching back hundreds of years, was lost on us. All we were interested in was the mesmerising variety of sideshows and rides. These ranged from the "habby horses," roundabouts, and swing boats (which satisfied us when we were small) to the more adventurous waltzer, speedway, and dodgem cars as we grew older and braver, and to the delights of the positively hair-raising rotor, steamboats, dive bombers, and ferris wheel that we indulged in as teenagers. Now that I no longer have the head—or the stomach—for such pursuits, the very thought of the dizzying and disorientating effects of these rides is enough to make me feel physically sick. I believe we are born with a certain capacity for such fun and when that is used up, never again can you contemplate engaging in such activity. I doubt if I could even sit on a swing for more than a few minutes, and yet we spent hours on the swings in the John Dixon Park in Markinch. We also made the most of the handful of shows that came to the Highland Games every year, but they paled into insignificance when compared with the scale of the Links Market.

We would save up every penny as Gran and Grandad, our aunts and uncles, and friends of my parents would add to our carefully garnered hoard, which we would usually manage to blow completely as we made our enthralled way along the prom on that cold spring Saturday every April. I remember one year having nearly a pound to spend, and when most sideshows cost threepence a go and the most expensive of rides a mere sixpence, that went a long way. Remember, the pre-decimal pound had 240 pennies, so that meant that there were eighty threepennies or forty sixpennnies in a pound, as we well knew from the sums we did at school! (Jim would reminisce as an old man that Scotch pies from a real pie shop like Pillan's in Kirkcaldy cost tuppence when he was a boy, so you could have bought one hundred and twenty of them for a pound. By the end of the century you could not even buy two for that amount!) Our parents, of course, took a much less frantic delight in the Market than we did. Joey could take it or leave it, but she probably enjoyed watching us having fun. The thing she most liked was listening to the competing barkers at their china stalls, haranguing the crowds, mainly mums and grannies, to buy their wares. They were funny men, and there was a lot of leg pulling and laughter to be enjoyed by their potential customers, but how much actual buying went on, I don't remember. Jim could always be counted on to win us a coconut at one of the sideshows by throwing darts or balls or by target-shooting with an air gun. He also invariably had a go at swinging the mallet and making the bell ring. I remember having a sense of pride that he never missed once, while there were always some other more puny fathers who struggled even to lift the mallet. I suppose this was testament to the hours he must have spent knocking in pailing stabs when fencing the fields at Pitkinny.

A less enjoyable and quite scary aspect of the Links Market for me was the boxing booth, where spectators were enticed to win money by having a go at fighting the resident champ. I was terrified that Jim would take up the challenge, and very relieved that he never did. I should have realised that he had a very well-developed sense of self-preservation, and much preferred to watch other foolhardy spectators take the risk of a bloody nose! In those days there were always a few attractions which would be seen as rather unsavoury now. In effect, they were nothing more or less than freak shows. I remember in particular, The World's Fattest Lady, Siamese Twins, and The Smallest Couple in the World, to be viewed at a cost behind the discreetly curtained entrance to these stalls. In any case we much preferred the Hall of Mirrors, where we could laugh at ourselves and at each other freakishly but harmlessly distorted! As the fresh air and activity made us hungry, we would taste the culinary delights of greasy sausage and onion rolls followed by a toffee apple, or the pink and sticky treat of candy floss. Watching it being made and wondering at the magic way it appeared on the end of the stick as it was flicked around the mysterious turning drum, and the smell of the hot sugar, were almost as good as the taste of it.

I have described something of the Christmases we had as we grew up, but of course, traditionally in Scotland, it occupied a subordinate position to that of Hogmanay and the New Year in the pecking order of midwinter festivals. However, as the second half of the twentieth century passed, their relative positions began to change. As affluence grew, Christmas began to assume the higher profile, and present giving, decorations, and Yuletide food and drink and customs have become ever more elaborate and costly, until the festive season has become a marketing frenzy. The religious significance of Christmas has diminished almost out of sight for most people, as the celebrations have become almost entirely a commercial exercise. Correspondingly, the old customs associated with Hogmanay have gradually faded in most households until it has degenerated into yet another excuse for excess bingeing on food and drink. When we were children the changing of the year was imbued with much symbolism and as the old year waned, frantic activity ensued as families prepared for this annual highlight.

Midnight on 31 December was seen as a highly significant watershed as everyone strove to start the New Year with a clean sheet, in every sense of the expression. The remnants of this can be seen in a halfhearted attempt to observe New Year resolutions, most of which do not survive the first week of the year. Then, bills had to be paid, houses had to be cleaned from top to bottom, and great efforts were made to complete unfinished tasks. Joey never liked to have anything "on the pins" on Hogmanay, so she worked hard to finish all the sewing and knitting she had on the go. There would be no unwashed or unmended clothes in the house. The coal fire was cleaned out and set ready to be lit at twelve o'clock. On the stroke of midnight, the New Year was welcomed in as the front door was ceremoniously opened, and the Auld Ane was ushered out the back door. Jim would by then have had his ritual Hogmanay bath, and we all met the New Year well-scrubbed and polished! I am sure that housewives must have been too exhausted to enjoy the celebrations by the time the midnight hour came. In the days leading up to Hogmanay the house was redolent of festive baking. In addition to the Christmas cake, some of which would still be intact, Dundee cake, black bun, and shortbread were baked and ready to be offered to guests. For sandwiches and quick meals, bowls of tasty potted heid were made by Joey—another seasonal addition to the bill of fare.

In a time when people hardly ever kept or consumed alcohol at home, the main exception was when the man of the house would buy his New Year bottle or, more often, half bottle. Whisky was the drink of choice for most men, and very occasionally women might indulge in a glass of port or sherry, but generally, women did not drink alcohol, preferring instead to have a glass of the ubiquitous ginger cordial. This was made from a small bottle of ginger essence, obtained from the Co-op chemist's of all places, almost as if it was a potentially hazardous liquid to be treated with great respect. Mixed with sugar and water and boiled in the jam pan, it produced a dark brown syrupy concoction which could be taken neat if you didn't mind the burning sensation it produced at the back of the throat, or diluted with water or preferably, in our opinion, some fizzy lemonade. An alternative to ginger cordial was the raspberry equivalent, a much prettier and sweeter drink altogether, but for some reason, Joey could never be persuaded to make it. We could rely on having some from Mrs Steel when we went down to first-foot at Bogside. This reinforced her reputation as the source of a wonderful variety of drinks, such as limeade, pineapple crush, or American cream soda, all of which came off the lemonade lorry that called at Bogside, but hardly ever ventured in the bumpy loan to Pitkinny. A time came, however, when Joey started to make homemade lemonade, wholesomely produced from oranges and lemons, as an alternative to ginger cordial.

Throughout the first hours and days of January, first-footing was the social norm in those days. Our relative remoteness from the town might have curtailed the number of guests who made it to Pitkinny, but in the days before the breathalyser, there was nothing to deter drivers from making the journey. We would exchange visits with the Steel family and the Pages at Woodend, and the families in the cottar hooses, and of course our grandparents, aunts and uncles, and cousins. There would be a duty visit to and from "the Star anes." This was always a great opportunity to share Christmas toys and games with our cousins, and sometimes the adults would join in the fun. In the first days of the year, there was a certain solemnity in the offering and partaking of hospitality, "Ye'll hae yer New Year," and even those men who did not normally indulge in "the cratur" would make an exception. One such man was Jock Steel, who was normally quite abstemious. Unused as he was to drinking, and generous to a fault, he would fill a shot glass to the brim with neat whisky and offer it to Jim. His preference was for some water in his whisky, but of course there was no room for it; since good manners demanded that he should grin and bear it, he managed valiantly to knock it back! Others of less sober persuasion than Jock made the most of their opportunities, and there were some who managed to stretch the celebrations several days into the new year. Jock Allan would actually "go walkabout" for a few days as he exploited the hospitality of his many friends and acquaintances to (and sometimes beyond) the limit. He once turned up at Pitkinny on the second of January at half past six in the morning, before any of us was awake. He was in the company of Jock Thamson the baker, and Joey and Jim heard them singing at the top of their voices as they made their unsteady way along the loan. It was as well they had that much warning, as they were able to get dressed and downstairs before the happy twosome arrived at the house, otherwise they would probably have joined them in the bedroom. Jock was very affectionate when drunk and kept promising Joey, "If that big bugger dees, Joey, Ah'll mairry ye masel'!" Joey tactfully distracted him by asking him when he was last home, in the hope that he would remember he already had a wife of his own! Needless to say, Mrs Allan was a quiet and long-suffering wife and Jock a normally hard-working and good husband, but normal rules were suspended for the duration of the New Year celebrations.

In the early days at Pitkinny, chicken was comparatively expensive to buy but, in the years before we aspired to having turkey, would usually be the centrepiece of our Christmas dinner. Joey kept some young poulets for the occasional special meal, but the traditional New Year dinner was homemade soup, followed by steak pie, mashed tatties, and sprouts (at their best in the frosty garden), with trifle as an unaccustomed treat for pudding. This is still a favourite celebratory meal on New Year's Day, and in the days leading up to the end of the year, butchers' shop windows are full of steak pies; although, of course, Joey would never have dreamed of buying a ready-made one. So, in loving deference to her, my sister and I have tried to maintain her high standards when it comes to our catering arrangements at that time of year. The bones of the Christmas turkey are boiled to make stock for the New Year's Day broth, and the steak cooked and the pastry rolled out for the pie just as she did it. Although many of the rigid and demanding rituals of New Year have fallen by the wayside, there remain vestiges of the old customs in women of our generation. Margaret and I often remark that, having been brought up as we were, and trained in all aspects of cooking and housewifery as thoroughly as we were by our mother, I have a sense that she is sitting on my shoulder, making sure I do everything correctly. "There's a richt wye an' a wrang wye tae dae everythin', so ye micht jist as weel dae it the richt wye!"

As is typical with children everywhere, we would protest when Joey called us in from playing to get ready for bed, and even more when we had to have a bath or have our hair washed. The universal wail of "But, why?" sometimes evoked the response, "Weel ye never ken, the Queen micht come along the loan!" In retrospect this seemed a strange thing for Joey to say, as she had very definite republican leanings and never had any time for the royal family or their aristocratic hangers-on. Little did she realise, then, that her prediction would actually come true and that the day would come when the Queen really did that very thing! The reason for that unlikely turn of events, in June 1961, was the official opening of the Lurgi Gas Plant and the extension to the opencast coal site. As explained earlier, the late fifties and early sixties saw the beginning of the downturn in deep shaft mining in favour of opencast excavation, and this occasioned a major expansion of the existing small-scale operations around Pitkinny.

As NCB tenants, Jim and Joey had no choice but to learn to live with the close proximity of these developments. The conveyor belt and huge spreading machine to distribute the overburden from the mine was accessed from our loan, and we learned that the Queen would drive along the loan to perform the opening ceremony. The Lurgi opening ceremony would be held earlier the same day down at the gas plant, and Jim and Joey were invited with all the other tenant farmers and local dignitaries. Joey refused to be impressed by the very grand-looking invitation, and was convinced they would just be part of "rent-a-crowd," and refused to buy a new outfit for the occasion as some of the other farmers' wives were doing. We, however, saw this as an excuse for a party, and I managed to secure a day off school. Margaret arranged her days off from the hospital accordingly and plans were laid! Our grandparents, John's mother, and some of our aunties were invited along with some of our pals. As it was midsummer, Margaret, a great baker from an early age, set to and made lots of goodies, including strawberry tarts.

We had discovered that no members of the public would be allowed along the loan, but they couldn't keep us out since we lived there. There was an old trailer that Jim had parked at the top of the loan which made a great vantage point, and we took up station there in time for the arrival of the royal party. We were rather surprised when we saw that the Queen was dressed in a white boiler suit with a hard hat and wellies! Despite our disappointment with her fashion statement, we waved and cheered as she alighted from her very shiny land rover. I think we got a bit of a wave from her as she strolled round the enormous spreading machine and viewed the huge excavators before declaring it open and then departing. There were press photographers and a TV camera, but we were very disappointed not to feature in the evening news or in any of the local papers. Nevertheless we had a good time, and when Joey and Jim returned from their junket they wished they had stayed at Pitkinny instead. Joey's suspicions had been confirmed, as she said they had been herded like sheep and kept waiting for hours. To add insult to injury, the refreshments had been very poor, with not a strawberry tart in sight!

At a distance of more than forty years, it is hard to believe that less than ten years before that royal visit, the country had celebrated the coronation of that same queen. I have hazy memories of a wee party at Pitkinny attended by the children from the cottar hooses, surprising given Joey's lack of interest in anything royal. A bonfire had been built for that June day, but due to the incessant rain that afflicted the whole country, it wasn't lit until evening when, as the torrential downpour persisted, we watched from the car as Dad struggled to set fire to the pile of old wood and junk. There was always plenty of rubbish for burning in those days, thanks to the ongoing renovations he was carrying out in the steading. I also seem to remember an occasional Bonfire Night and once, I think we actually made and burned a Guy Fawkes on 5 November, although we never aspired to fireworks, having to be content with a few sparklers.

There was always a member of the royal family in attendance on one of the days of the Highland Show. In 1965 we were at the show at Ingliston, and Pamela was a wee girl in her pushchair. Again, it was a very wet day and as the showground, although now a permanent site, still had very limited hard standing, mostly it was a case of walking along greasy duckboards at best, or ploughing through puddles of muddy water at worst. Princess Margaret, the sister of the Queen, was there that day, and at one point her land rover passed us and the word spread that she was about to get out. It may have been a case of mass hysteria, as people began to run after the vehicle in the hope of seeing the princess, and within seconds I found myself, with Margaret, joining in the pursuit, splashing through the dubs and slithering amongst the mire, to arrive breathless and dishevelled as her vehicle glided to a halt.

Now I am certain that I have inherited Joey's republican instincts, so I feel a degree of shame that I should have been so manipulated by a spontaneous desire to look at this young woman. She alighted daintily from her very shiny and completely mud-free land rover, with the help of a lady-in-waiting, to much bowing and scraping from the others in attendance. I know a cat can look at a king, but that day I never felt more like a peasant as I watched this rather insignificant and very tiny princess as she was escorted past us, sheltered solicitously by an umbrella-toting toady. She was of course beautifully dressed, and what I was most conscious of were her dainty feet, spotlessly shod in peep-toe high-heeled shoes, stepping along the red carpet. By comparison, Margaret and I by then looked like mud-spattered scarecrows as we turned and sloshed our way back to find Joey, who was waiting with Pamela, highly amused by our rather shamefaced and thoroughly bedraggled appearance. "Whit did ye expect? I telt ye I widnae gang the length o' masel tae see ony o' them. Ah aince saw 'er mither. She had a bonny hat on, richt enough, bit she was wearin' corsets just like the rest o' us!"

We had a close encounter with another member of the royal family ten years later, again at the Highland Show. This time it was our elder son Calum who was in a pushchair, and it was a couple of months before his wee brother Donald was born. Margaret and her girls Pamela, Alison, and Lynda, and Mum and I were making our way round the outside of the arena where the show-jumping was going on. I felt Margaret tapping me on the shoulder, and as I turned round while still pushing Calum, I realised my sister was discreetly pointing to someone ahead of me. I looked back just in time to see this young man in riding gear making frantic efforts to avoid the wheels of the push chair, as I almost rammed it into his legs. "Oh! Sorry," I hastily apologised. By now Margaret was urgently whispering to me, "Look, it's Mark Phillips!" She was right. It was the first husband of Princess Anne, who by now was beating a hasty retreat away from the mad and dangerous-looking pregnant woman with the pushchair. In the years since, we have once or twice been in close proximity to royal personages, and nothing I have seen or heard in any way made me feel that Joey had the wrong idea. They are, of course, not just like everyone else, as some people would like to suggest. Rather, they are incredibly privileged individuals who just happen to have inherited their birthright from the robber barons of old. They may well have bonny hats, but they still need held in, in certain places!

In the days after the Second World War, there were few leisure facilities available to people other than the cinema, the only really affordable regular entertainment outside the home. Families, in the limited spare time they had, would devise their own means of recreation. Making music had been part of Jim's young life with his brothers in the bothy at Broomfield. He would sing while Wullie played the pipes and Harry the melodion. Board games would feature in most homes. Jim had a board with ludo on one side and snakes and ladders on the other, which we still have in the family. Playing cards was frowned on by Grandad Hugh, but Auntie Kate and Uncle Jock Webster and their family at Woodside were enthusiastic card players, and I well remember evenings in their house when everyone—adults and children alike—would also play other games like "hunt the thimble" or "I spy." Joey was always fond of jigsaws, and often when our cousins would visit there would be a combined effort at completing one of her many puzzles.

Paid holidays became the norm in the course of the fifties and sixties, but for many families, a day's outing would be the limit of their travelling. For those on the west coast of Scotland a trip "doon the watter" was a traditional summer treat, whereas in Fife a turn to the seaside meant a journey to Ravenscraig Sands, Kinghorn, or Burntisland at the nearest, or to Elie or Lundin Links, much further away. There were various occasions as we were growing up when Jim and Joey organised extended family picnics. The first of these, in 1950, was to Shell Bay, along the Fife coast towards the East Neuk. There was no public transport to that beach, and as few families had cars, a means had to be found of getting everyone there. Jim realised that the only vehicle on the farm that could carry everyone at one time was the cattle float. So it was scrubbed out to Joey's satisfaction and we all piled in. All the accoutrements of a picnic went with us: buckets and spades, deck chairs (horror of horrors!), food and drink, beach balls and cricket bats, umbrellas and raincoats (this was a Scottish summer's day after all!), and the primus stoves, without which no picnic in those days was complete. We collected various family members and friends with all their gear en route as we made our way from Woodend through Kinglassie, Woodside, and Markinch and on through the various villages to Leven and beyond. All the ventilators in the side of the float were open, of course, and within a few minutes of leaving the farm, the passengers had begun a sing-song, in time-honoured tradition. The raucous noise of singing and laughing grew in volume as the number of passengers increased. As Jim drove with Grandad Hugh beside him, they were very amused at the reactions of pedestrians as they passed. Without exception, each of them would look around for the source of the racket and would become very puzzled when the only thing they could see was the passing lorry and float. As they stared open-mouthed, Jim would wave and shout out of the window, "Aye, they're guid singers fur beasts, eh?"

We duly arrived and were unloaded at the beach, where the usual fun and games proceeded. As the afternoon wore on Gran Betsy, who was sitting beside all the picnic things, suddenly felt very thirsty. She had noticed a lemonade bottle, and couldn't resist having a swig of its contents. What she didn't realise until it was too late, was that the bottle was filled not with lemonade but with paraffin for the primus stoves. As she gagged and spat out the offending liquid, someone casually enquired what was wrong. "Oh! Ma Goad, ah've jist drank paraffin!" she gasped. There was a brief flurry of interest, but no one got too concerned. "Jist dinnae hae a fag fur a while, Betsy," came advice from Uncle Bobby Drennan, and at that everyone returned to their games, their snoozing, or their paddling, and the emergency was over almost before it began. I can't help but wonder how differently such an event would be dealt with today. I am fairly certain that at the very least, Gran would be hauled off to Accident and Emergency, or that some health and safety investigation would soon be underway. The coast guard might be called and the whole episode reported on some TV disaster documentary. "Tsk! Tsk! Paraffin in a soft-drink container? How irresponsible!" "What? No risk assessment had been carried out?" "Human beings transported like animals!" "What about their human rights?" As it was, Betsy was none the worse for the experience, and I am sure she was soon puffing happily away at her beloved cigarettes as she watched her family and friends having the time of their lives on the beach that day.

A few summers later there was another picnic "en famille," but on this occasion an increase in affluence and/or enterprise allowed for a rather less original means of transport, and a bus was hired. This time the destination was further afield and in the opposite direction. The location of the picnic was Balloch on Loch Lomond side. For some reason my recollection of that day is somewhat more hazy than the earlier excursion, but I assume the usual games, races, and activities were indulged in. The part of the day I do remember quite vividly was that on the way home we called at Alva Glen for a comfort stop. There was a paddling pool, but it was decided that it was too late in the day to make use of its obvious attractions. Never one to be disappointed, though, I managed to run down the steps fully clothed and straight into the water! I spent the remainder of the journey home dressed in a motley assortment of clothes acquired from various sources. As often seemed to be the case, it was the comparatively dramatic, not to say traumatic, features of the occasion that stand out in stark relief against the backdrop of what was undoubtedly a happy and eventful adventure in my young life.

A later mass drive and picnic, probably around 1960, also came to a watery end, though on this occasion I was not the victim. This time we went in a convoy of cars, but our Uncle Dunc, who was a motorbike enthusiast, decided to tag along on his Norton. This was his pride and joy, but had only an occasional airing now that (like everyone else in the family) he had a car. We headed for Aberfoyle and the Trossachs, where we had our picnic on a lovely afternoon. There was a stop at Loch Achray where some horseplay ensued, as we splashed each other and pushed each other into the shallow water at the edge of the loch. One or two of the younger cousins had fishing nets with them, their hope of catching minnens (minnows) becoming increasingly desperate and unlikely as the day wore on. At every juncture of the day out, Dunc was there, resplendent in his full motorbike leathers, in contrast to the rest of us who were dressed rather more suitably for the hot sunny weather. In the early evening, as we made our way back towards Callander, Uncle Bobby suggested a final stop at the Falls of Leny to have a last attempt at fishing for the elusive wee tiddlers so that the kids would have something to put in their still-empty jam jars.

We parked the cars in a parking area and walked down the steep riverside path to the Leny, which was very full and running fast. Dad, never one for messing about in or beside the water, elected to stay in the land rover and read the *Sunday Post*. His only contribution to this last activity was to warn everyone, "Watch whit ye're daen, and dinnae fa' in the watter." As the men in the party started to look for the most likely place to find their quarry, reckoned to be the deeper pools where the water eddied at the side of the rapids, and the women watched the kids and admonished everyone to be careful, there was a sudden loud splash. Margaret and John were standing further up the path and John, pointing downstream, called out, "Look! Look! A seal!" Sure enough, there, floundering from a deep pool, came a black shiny head, followed by flailing limbs. But it was no aquatic creature that emerged from the foamy waters of the Leny. Rather, it was the crash helmet, leather suit, boots, and gauntlets of our motorcycling uncle. His wife Doris was the first to react: "Oh ma Goad! Dunc's fa'in in the watter!" He had stepped on an unstable rock at the river's edge and tumbled in head first, and despite his protective clothing, was completely soaked to the skin by the time he struggled out on to the bank.

Fishing for minnens was abandoned as everyone tried to help to deal with this rather bigger catch. There were no dry clothes for him to change into. I remember Auntie Greta and Joey trying to wring out his sopping wet garments, and Uncle Bobby slapping them against the rocks to remove the excess water. There was a barely suppressed incipient hysteria as everyone sympathised with Dunc's plight and at the same time tried not to start laughing. The very idea that there could be a seal in the Leny, miles and miles from the sea, was funny enough, but that it should turn out to be Dunc was unthinkable. He always took himself so seriously, and had no time for nonsense or fun at the best of times, so there was no way that he could be expected to see anything amusing in his situation. Joey thought she had a solution which would allow him some dry clothing. She went up to the land rover and suggested to Jim that he should give Dunc his trousers and drive home in his underpants. "Ye could pit a traivilin' rug roond yer legs," she helpfully ventured, as if that would make it acceptable to him. "Aye, shairly!" he spluttered. "It wis 'is ain stupit faut if 'e fell in the watter. I warned yiz a' to watch whit ye wir daen. 'es no gettin' ma troosers!"

So poor Dunc had to get dressed again in his cold and wet clothes and leathers. No one else could drive his motorbike or be persuaded to give up any dry clothes for him, so he had no choice but to set off for home, looking much less full of himself than he had been on the outward journey. Still minnen-less, but able at last to give way to much mirth at the whole episode at Dunc's expense, we followed him home, but not before we had the last stop of the day, for fish and chips at Alari's in Dunfermline. Jim and Bobby, by now starving, were first to reach the shop, but were disappointed to be told that the sitting room was about to close. They appealed to the waitress to let them in, and taking pity on them, but unaware that there was a hungry horde behind them, she relented and opened up. She lived to regret her kindness as we all piled in behind them, adding substantially to their takings, but extending their working day by many fish-tea orders from a crowd that must have resembled *The Broons* on a day out.

So these high days and holidays lent a counterweight for Joey and Jim to the workaday life of running the farm. They must have come as light relief, especially for Mum, when there were so many times when problems would set light to Jim's simmering temper. The result would sometimes be shouting matches as and when—and this happened increasingly as she asserted herself more and more—she refused to kowtow to his uncertain disposition. However, over the piece, there were probably as many happy and amusing episodes as unhappy and depressing ones. I remember the laughter as vividly as I remember the rows, and one thing life at Pitkinny never was, was boring or humdrum. As the sixties gave way to the seventies and Margaret and I in turn had our own growing families to care for, there were many weekends and holiday times when we would all be together at Pitkinny. These were the happiest of times for Jim and Joey, but the burdens of running the farm were not getting easier, especially as Mum's health began to be an issue. The chronic but severe pain in her arms, accompanied by loss of sensation in her hands, was diagnosed as spondylosis, the result perhaps of the neck injury she had suffered early in her marriage.

She and Jim were working as hard as ever, but it never occurred to us that they would do anything but struggle on as best they could, as farmers had always had to do. The difficulty was that there was no one to pass the tenancy on to, as neither Bill nor John envisaged a career change. The solution was to come out of the blue, and when it did it was due to the most fundamental of reasons. The geographical location of Pitkinny, and its underlying geology, which meant that the coal measures approached the surface there, had given rise to the existing opencast coal workings, and they were about to also call in question the continued existence of the farm and Jim and Joey's future way of life. While not entirely subscribing to a determinist philosophy, it seems to me now, in retrospect, that the fate that had led them, in 1941, to farm in west Fife had also set in motion a chain of events that would, by the mid-seventies, influence the remaining twenty-five years of their lives.

*Joey and Jim's wedding, 26 September 1941*

*Joey and Jim's golden wedding, 26 September 1991*

*Margaret and John's wedding, 26 September 1964*

*Anne and Bill's wedding, 3 April 1971*

*Joey and Jim's ruby wedding, with their five grandchildren, 26 September 1981*
*(L to R: Alison 14 years, Donald 6 years, Pamela 16 years, Lynda 11 years, Calum 8 years)*

# Chapter 32

"An' whit is it worth? It's no worth tuppence!"

As the sixties gave way to the seventies, both Joey and Jim began to find it harder to maintain their accustomed intensity of work. They had passed their half-century, and although their enthusiasm never waned, the high costs of labour meant that they themselves had to put in as much, if not more, effort than ever. Joey's health, always a worry to others if not to herself, became ever more precarious, and each winter she could see that the relentless and long hours of feeding the beasts was taking more and more out of Jim. They could still rely on the ever-dependable Dougie and Chrissie, and Rob and Lena Imrie, but as their families grew, although they still worked for Jim and Joey, they would move in turn, to live in Cardenden and Kinglassie respectively. Then Rob got a job in one of the factories in the fast-developing electronics industry in the New Town. For a time, Rob and Mary Bennett worked at Pitkinny and lived in one of the cottar hooses, but they moved to Glenrothes, and eventually both houses would be rented out to people who had no connection to the farm. Eddie Tinney and his wife Mary worked part-time at the farm, and there were some other casual workers at the busiest times, but the days were long gone when there was a real community working and living alongside Jim and Joey, and Pitkinny became a quieter and lonelier place to be.

Margaret and I both had our own families, of course and, although we would spend many weekends and some holiday time at the farm, our lives were centred elsewhere. Both Joey and Jim were delighted with their growing family, and were loving and indulgent grandparents to Pamela (born in 1965), Alison (in 1967), and Lynda (in 1970). During their frequent visits with Margaret and John, Jim enjoyed spoiling them and would take them down to the swings in Cardenden and buy them ice lollies and sweets, while Joey had endless patience for their child-like ploys and games. One day they came across a wee, low henhouse that had been long unused in the stackyard at the back of the farm, and they had great fun playing in it. This gave Joey the idea of turning it into a Wendy house for the girls. Murray Knowes was a small holding on the road to Lochgelly, tenanted by Geordie West. Jim sublet its grazing when Geordie was no longer able to work the land, so that he and his wife could stay on in the house, and Jim would give him bits of work from time to time. He was a good carpenter, so Jim asked him if he would heighten the walls of the henhouse and recondition it. Then it was moved into position in the close, across from the back door of the house, and Joey set to and finished the transformation with wallpaper, paint, flooring, and curtains. She found small bits and pieces of furniture and some toy dishes and soon had it kitted out as a perfect playhouse for the girls.

While my three nieces have some memories of these happy days at Pitkinny, our two boys were too young to be able to recollect much about the farm. Calum was two when his little brother was born in the summer of 1975, and it had become clear that we were fast approaching a watershed in all our lives. Jim had been aware for some time that moves were afoot in the NCB Opencast Executive and Costain, their principal contractor, to bring about a major expansion of their coal-excavating operations centred on the Westfield site. The last extension in their working had been in the late fifties and early sixties, when it had involved the demolition of Bogside and the building of the conveyor belt and spreader which transported and distributed the overburden from the "biggest hole in Europe." This phase was approaching completion, and the newly contoured resulting landscape to the south of Pitkinny was already reinstated. Its shelter belts and the interspaced, reseeded fields belied the tremendous wastage and upheaval that had been visited on the land in the intervening years, as the trees and grass grew vigorously. Whereas this phase had not encroached on Pitkinny's arable acreage, the latest developments threatened to engulf most of its productive fields to the east of the steading, leaving intact that part of the farm which consisted of the poorer, rougher land leading up to Harelaw.

This was a step too far for Jim and Joey. It would see the disruption of the better half of their land for the foreseeable future, to the extent that they would find it very hard to make the remainder pay. Ever the businessman and negotiator, Jim saw an opportunity to turn these events to their advantage. It would mean the end of their lives as farmers, indeed the end of their working lives, but would give them a greater element of control over their future than they might otherwise have had. The farm to the east of Pitkinny was Westfield, which gave its name to the entire opencast site, and it was going to be obliterated completely, as all of it—steading and house as well as its fields—would disappear in the onslaught of the new mining operations. The NCB would have to find an alternative farm, or in other ways compensate Sandy Black and his family. Knowing that, at ten years younger than himself, Sandy wanted to continue his farming life, Jim presented his landlords with the obvious solution to their problem: If they could make it worth his while to retire and leave the scene, they could then offer the occupancy of Pitkinny to the Blacks. Of course, Jim would retain the tenancy of the area that was being excavated, and he would have to be compensated for its use as long as coal was being mined from it. Only after that would he finally relinquish his tenancy of those acres. It was against this scenario that his negotiations with the NCB were carried out. On the basis of land valuations, and with the advice of a land agent, he embarked on a period of arbitration and negotiation.

The end result of all this wheeling and dealing was that Jim and Joey would retire and leave Pitkinny. By early in 1975, they had more or less reconciled themselves to this fact. Quite where they would go, and how they would adapt to such a radical change in their lifestyle, were matters to be decided. One thing Jim was determined on was that he could not bear to live nearby and see the devastation that was inevitable as the land they had poured their hearts and souls into was torn asunder. It came to them that they should consider a move to Kirkcudbright in southwest Scotland. Margaret, John, and their girls had lived there since 1971 and both Jim and Joey had developed a liking for the wee town, so with Margaret's help they found a suitable house, and made an offer to buy it in June 1975. Although the negotiations with the NCB were not complete, Jim decided that if they fell through, he would sell the house on. As it happened, the actual purchase of the house was not complete until late September, by which time the settlement with the Coal Board had been finalised.

Jim had been involved in these negotiations at what was a difficult time for us all. Joey's diagnosis of spondylosis was made in the spring of 1975, and she was to undergo major neurological surgery that summer. This involved taking bone grafts from her hip to fuse some of the vertebrae in the cervical section of her spine. It was a delicate and dangerous procedure, but it was hoped it would cure at least some of the pain she was suffering and halt the loss of sensation in her hands. While Jim was never one to willingly share his business decisionmaking, even with his wife, he was even more reluctant to worry her about the progress of the protracted negotiations he was engaged in while she was in the throes of several hospital stays that summer. It was only when she was recuperating from her operation in hospital in Edinburgh at the beginning of September that he told her that everything was settled. We were with Dad visiting Mum that day when he spelled out the details of the settlement he had arrived at. I can see her now, holding Donald, only two weeks old, for the first time and listening to what he had to tell us.

He would get a one-off cash compensation payment if he agreed to leave the farm, giving up his tenancy of the steading and house. But he would retain the rights of a sitting tenant over that proportion of his acreage that was involved in the excavations, and for that, he would receive an annual index-linked cash settlement as long as that land was out of agricultural production, and until it was reinstated. He would then have the right to dispose of his tenancy of that proportion of the original holding as he saw fit at the end of that period. Sandy Black would move his operation to Pitkinny and would continue to farm there, albeit on a smaller acreage than Jim had had, but this suited him as he had a dairy and needed fewer arable acres to make a living. Of course the Coal Board would have to pay for alterations to the steading to accommodate his dairy premises, but as Jim saw it, that was their problem and they were welcome to it! In the event, this arrangement was to last sixteen years in all, until in 1992 Jim would renounce the remaining part of his lease: sixteen years of an inflation-proof annual income. This was a great deal, in anyone's book; the result of Jim's insight and tenacity and of fair dealing by the NCB.

I can't be sure whether the full implications of the situation were really clear to Joey, or indeed to any of us at that stage, but there was an element of relief that the uncertainty was over. Margaret and I were most definitely pleased that our parents were going to have the opportunity of a retirement with a degree of financial security they would never have had without the unforeseen benefit of the opencast developments. They would no longer have to work so hard, and they would have time for the things they enjoyed doing. There was a brief time of speculation, when it was mooted that Bill and John could perhaps take on the tenancy and continue to run Pitkinny, with Jim on hand to advise and consult, but neither Margaret nor I were keen on the idea and in fact, I don't believe that our parents ever really saw that as a workable possibility. We had all seen what can happen when families have to work in close proximity to each other, and with the best will in the world, petty jealousies and clash of ideas or personalities can ruin the best of intentions and relationships. Added to that, neither Bill nor John had been born to farming, and the hardships and sheer drudgery that it often involves are not things that are easy to learn to tolerate. There would be no question of the regular holidays, or indeed, regular salaries, that we had all become used to. Joey certainly did not want us to sacrifice everything we had worked for in our education and careers to give it all up for the vagaries of farm life and work, however strong the emotional pull in that direction might be, and the idea was discounted almost before it had time to take root.

The fact that we did not speculate on the full impact the impending change would have on us all was partly because we were in the midst of a rather fraught period in our lives. In addition to looking after our new baby son and his big brother Calum who had just turned two, we were visiting Joey in hospital and supporting Jim, who was having to manage on his own at Pitkinny. He was never very adept at domestic things, and was having his meals with us most days on his way to or from the hospital. That was complicated by the fact that he had to be on a virtual liquid diet, as a routine visit to the dentist had resulted in some damage to the nerves in his jaw, the latest repercussion of the surgery he had had when he was forty. Then Calum had a serious attack of croup on his second birthday, when his wee brother was only ten days old, and had to be hospitalised for a few days. I was torn between worrying about leaving the baby with Bill's mother, and spending time with Calum so that he didn't feel that he was being abandoned in the hospital in favour of the new arrival at home. I was trying to visit Mum in hospital and then stayed at Pitkinny to help her and Dad when she came home, all the while seeing to the children and all that involved, so the whole issue of the future of our parents and the farm was put on the back burner for the next few weeks.

But as the autumn passed and Joey, recovered from her surgery, took up the reins fully at Pitkinny again, we began to realise that what would have seemed unthinkable a few months before was really going to happen. Jim and Joey were leaving the land, leaving the home we had grown up in. They were about to embark on an enormous change of direction. Could it really be true that their connection with the land would be severed forever? Would other people live in this old farmhouse and walk around those so-familiar rooms; would other hands, bodies, and minds bend to the work in the steading and in the fields that Jim and Joey had made so irreplaceably their own? It seemed to me that Pitkinny was populated with ghosts and memories that could belong nowhere else. How could they be transported to another place? I could imagine the echoes of voices reverberating round the old and new buildings and in the house, the laughter and angry outbursts that would go unheard when there were none there that remembered them, and the sounds that measured the passing years and the changes they brought: the blasts of gelignite that downed the old walls; the noise of each new piece of equipment and machinery as it took its place in the work of the farm; the sounds of the beasts, from the sonorous bellowing of the stirks to the bleating of the new born lambs; the barking of our beloved dogs and the feeble mewing of the newly born and carefully secreted kitlins, as we longed for them to open their eyes and be saved!

Every corner of the steading and each part of the house evoked its own memories. I only had to stand at the kitchen window and look out into the close to find images, like old film archives, flashing through my mind's eye. The hot, sunny harvest day—and there were probably as many like that as there were wet and hopeless ones—as Jim was driving grain from the combine into the grain drier. As he passed down the close on one of his many journeys, I heard Joey exclaim, "Jist look at yer faither! The stupit', silly man!" I was just in time to catch sight of Dad as he drove into the big shed, and could immediately see what had prompted Mum's outburst. He was, for the first—and last—time I could recall, stripped to the waist, his lily-white torso contrasting with the farmer's tan of his arms and neck. Joey wasted no time in going out and remonstrating with her husband for his foolishness, but he would not be warned about the dangers of sunburn or heatstroke. Of course, he regretted his failure to take heed of her that night as he lay in bed feeling very unwell, shaking with the rigour of a high temperature, brought on by the sudden unaccustomed exposure of his milky white skin after a lifetime of being hidden from the sun!

When things were going badly on the farm, often we would hear Jim before we saw him, as he would call down all manner of curses on the Fates that brought bad weather or mechanical breakdowns to thwart his plans. The first sight we would get of Dad would be as he came storming in the back door, either heading for the phone or looking for Joey to vent his spleen. One day she both heard and saw him tearing in through the kitchen and into the hall. Unusually for him, he had taken to wearing dungarees a few days earlier, and it was that particular garment that he was cursing about as he disappeared into the bathroom. When he reappeared some time later, he was looking very shame-faced and much less furious than before. As Joey encouraged him to explain what all the fuss was about, she was unable to keep a straight face, and in a very few minutes both she and Jim were roaring with laughter as he described the disaster he had just had.

In common with many of his generation, Jim tended to be unhealthily pre-occupied with the workings of his digestive tract. He had bought some laxative chocolate he had seen advertised, thinking it would satisfy his sweet tooth and keep him regular at the same time. As was his habit, he always used more than instructed. This applied to everything: fertiliser on the fields, veterinary medicine for the beasts, painkillers on those infrequent but dreadful times when he was assailed by toothache, and of course his whisky measures were also extremely generous when he was pouring his own! His intake of laxative chocolate was no exception, and within a very short time, the inevitable happened as he realised that it was having a quite dramatic effect on his insides. Unfortunately, he was driving up from Woodend and, as it was clear that he had no hope of making it home in time, he had to stop the pickup and make a beeline for the scrubby trees on the steep banking near the end of Redhouse Farm road. All might have been well but for the fact that he had to deal with the unfamiliar bib and straps of the dungarees. As he tossed the straps back over his shoulders, they snagged in the branches of the trees, and he found himself firmly trussed up and unable to divest himself of the dungarees. I will draw a veil over the remainder of his misadventure, but suffice it to say that not since he was a very wee boy had he returned home in "shitty breeks!" This entire incident convinced him of something he had always felt: dungarees were in no way suitable dress for a grown man anyway, and somehow he seemed to come to the conclusion that they, rather than his overdosing on laxative chocolate, were the cause of the undignified and childlike predicament he had—just—survived!

When I think of that day when he had to make a hasty entrance to the sanctuary of the bathroom at Pitkinny, I am reminded of another occasion when he had a mishap there. It was the end of another long day of driving grain from the harvest field, and as he came in to the kitchen he complained to Joey that he had "A richt sair scadded erse." She advised him to use some talcum powder after his bath. Now the very concept of male toiletries was still decades away, and I am certain that Dad had not had even a passing acquaintance with baby powder since he had been an infant, so to be fair, he probably didn't know what to look for or where to find it in the bathroom. It so happened that at that time an early example of diversity in the packaging of household cleaners had been pioneered by the makers of Vim scouring powder, and it was available in small plastic tubs, either blue or pink, with perforated tops, presumably to match the décor of the bathroom. There was one of these on the shelf under the wash basin, and Jim made the understandable mistake of thinking it was the aforementioned talcum powder. As (with his usual hearty and liberal approach to the use of any remedy) he applied what should have been a soothing balm to the part of his anatomy in question, the ensuing howls of anguish, punctuated by many colourful expletives to describe both the powder, and the suggestion that it would help ease his discomfort, were drowned in the sound of rushing water as he filled the bath again to soak away his now doubled agony! I am fairly certain that this would have been the one and only time that Jim strayed away from his normal reliance on plain soap and water for his ablutions. In this regard it may have been as well that Joey used to say, "Yer Dad has 'is fauts, but there's wan shair thing, 'es no a smelly man!"

Another occasion when I remember Dad in a fix in that bathroom was in the week before Margaret's wedding. Again it was harvest time and the work had to go on as usual, despite the fact that we were having a show of the wedding presents. Jim and Joey's bedroom was used to display the presents, and so was set up with trestle tables, and every available surface was festooned with the usual variety of gifts. Usually, it was only the ladies who would come to a show of presents, but because many women then did not drive, their menfolk came along as well. The typical scenario was that while the women were in the house "oohing" and "aahing" at the presents and having a glass of sherry and partaking of some of Margaret's and Joey's delicious home baking and endless cups of tea (definitely an occasion for the "guid cheenie"!), the men would congregate outside as Jim and the other workers completed the day's work. Then Jim would quickly have to wash and change before entertaining the male visitors in the kitchen with, in their case, a nip or two before their tea and goodies. However, the first evening this happened, we hadn't foreseen that Mum and Dad's bedroom was out of bounds to Jim. As I came through the hall, I heard an urgent "Psst, psst!" and saw Dad's head poking out from the bathroom door. "Get me some claes to wear, will ye!" So I had to go upstairs and discreetly gather some clothes out of the wardrobe and tallboy for him, as Margaret continued to detail to the ladies the nature and donors of her wedding gifts. So for the remaining evenings, we had to make sure that Dad had a change of clothes ready in our bedroom. His other problem was that before he could get to bed, he had to help Joey to clear it of all the presents of table and bed linen that was displayed there. "It's like gaun tae yer bed in a shop windae every nicht!" A few days later, as we arrived at the church for Margaret's wedding to John, we were greeted by the minister, Mr Ogilvie, in the broad Doric he had acquired in his previous parish in Buchan: "This wid be a braw day fur the hairst!" Jim's proud reply was, "Aye but there's mair important business than that the day!" Surely it was the greatest compliment he could have paid his lassie.

The close at Pitkinny was the scene of many dramas, not to say the occasional farce and the (thankfully) even more occasional trauma. It will have become crystal clear that Jim could never be counted on to have much in the way of patience or understanding for others' inability or unwillingness to do what he asked of them, and that was no less true of his dealings with his family than with anyone else. One afternoon, I had just come home from school when Dad called me outside to help him to cape some stirks. The float had come to collect them for the sale ring the next day, and the driver Sam Stewart was well known to us. He and Dad needed one more body to help drive the beasts into the float. They were very frisky and disinclined to go where they were herded, and each time we got them near the lorry, one of them would kick up its heels and take off in the opposite direction, closely followed by its pals. Jim was getting inexorably more furious each time this happened, and his shouting and cursing only made the poor animals even more agitated. I couldn't help having sympathy with the bullocks, knowing as I did their imminent fate, and perhaps they sensed that this would be their last journey.

Joey always maintained that Jim did all the shouting and none of the running in situations like this, and sure enough it was Sam and I who were having all the chasing to do while Jim directed operations. When they broke away from us yet again, Jim's fury reached a climax as he yelled and swore at me to run after them. When we eventually succeeded in getting the stirks into the float and Sam was closing the gates and the big door on the back of the vehicle, he spoke in a very measured but determined tone to Jim: "Ye kain somethin' Jim? If ah had a braw lassie like Anne, I widnae be swearin' and shoutin' at 'er like that. That's an awfy wye tae cairry on!" It was the only time I had ever heard anyone other than Joey gainsay Jim, and while Sam didn't raise his voice or get excited, his message was very clear. I might have expected Dad to retaliate in some way, but he had the grace to look rather shame-faced and, clapping Sam on the shoulder, just said, "Come on Sam, come awa' intae the kitchen fur yer tea." The event was never referred to and the matter made no difference to the good working relationship they had with each other, but I never forgot how grateful I felt to Sam, my champion that day. I could have hugged him and might have done, had I not suspected that he would have been dreadfully embarrassed, but the day came when I reminded him of the time he came to my rescue, and of the way he lifted my spirits and soothed my battered ego by sticking up for me with Dad.

An amusing incident that occurred in the close another day saw Joey get the better of Jim. He owned two guns, one a shotgun and the other a .22 rifle. They were seldom used, of course, except on the very infrequent occasion when rogue dogs would worry the sheep, or the hoodie craws would peck at the eyes of the newborn lambs in the paddock. On this day, the guns had been out of their hiding place because the local police had called, as they did once in a while, to check over the guns and inspect the licences for them. As Jim was about to put them away, Joey said that she didn't see the point of keeping them as he couldn't hit the barn door holding on to the handle. He immediately denied that he was a poor shot and said he would prove it to her. Away over in the paddock where the yowes were kept at lambing time, he had erected a floodlight on the top of a high pole to assist with the nighttime lambing. "See thon licht, Joey? I bet ye I kid hit it!" "Never in a month o' Sundays," came her convinced reply. So he blithely took aim, fired—and blew the floodlight to smithereens! No one was more amazed than Jim, but the unexpected skill he inadvertently displayed in no way compensated for the expense and trouble he would have in replacing the light fitting. "Whey kin Ah no learn tae keep ma mooth shut," he was heard to mutter as, shaking his head, he made his way into the big shed, while Joey went back into the house with a satisfied smile on her face, "Ah've often wondered that masel'," her parting shot!

The front door of the house was seldom used, but was the scene of one or two incidents that I remember in addition to the night the potential intruder tried to get in the locked front door. Joey and Jim went to the Smithfield Show in London in December 1962. They had left in the Jaguar 2.4 in a blizzard and I remember Dunc—always a Job's comforter—speculating on the possibility that they would be stranded in a snow drift somewhere by now, as he picked me up from the bus stop that late freezing, dark afternoon. Margaret was off work and home from the hospital with a badly infected hand, and after we had tea we battened down the hatches as the wind picked up and the snow continued to fall. We wondered about Mum and Dad on their journey, but as there were no mobile phones then to help you keep in touch, we just had to hope for the best. Margaret was always more nervous than I was when we were alone in the house at night; knowing this, Doris said she might come up and see that we were all right. As we sat watching television in the big sitting room, there was a sudden bang on the window. Initially, we thought it might be Doris, but were too afraid to look out of the window. When the noise came again, louder this time, and we called out, "Is that you, Auntie Doris?" the only answer we got was another even louder clatter against the window.

By now Margaret was terrified and I was beginning to feel almost as bad. We eventually reasoned that we had to look outside to discover the source of the noise, so we put out the lights and very gingerly peered out of the side of the curtain. Our first impression was that there was someone there, and we both squealed in fright, until we realised with huge relief that what was banging against the window was nothing more sinister than a pair of Dad's "wurkin' troosers." Joey had a short clothesline outside the sitting room window that she used for the occasional few items of laundry. She had taken the chance to wash Jim's working clothes at the last minute that day, knowing they wouldn't be needed for a few days, and had forgotten about them. Of course, given the low temperatures, they had frozen and were stiff as a board. The problem was that no amount of persuasion would make Margaret let me go out into the garden for the trousers, and we had to listen to them rattling against the window for the rest of the night!

Years before this, Margaret had unconsciously terrified our parents when it was feared she might have TB. Fortunately, it was confirmed that she did not in fact have the dreaded illness, but she was off school for some time, and Joey, skilled in home nursing, did everything she could to promote her recuperation. One autumn day, she thought Margaret would benefit from some fresh air, so she sat her in a chair wrapped in a blanket at the open front door, where she was in the sun but sheltered from the wind. As Joey returned to the kitchen to get on with her work, she was suddenly aware of the most dreadful noise, getting louder and louder by the second. She couldn't identify the sound but knew it was right on top of the house. As she ran to the front door she could see Margaret frantically trying to get in to the porch, the chair crashing against the open door. As she tried to calm Margaret, who was really terrified, she suddenly recognised the sound as it receded in the distance. It had been caused by a low-flying aeroplane, which must have skimmed the chimneys of the house.

Within a very few minutes Lena Smith arrived at the back door, white-faced and shaking. She had been working in the stackyard, on a ladder propped up against the side of a stack, as she pulled the loose straws from the sheaves to neaten the edges of the stack and leave it looking as it should, when, like Joey, she was aware only of a tremendous noise and vibration. She clung to the ladder and pushed herself as flat against the straw as she could. The ground shook and the air pressure seemed to increase as the plane passed only a few feet from the top of the stack. As they all came to themselves and calmed down, and Joey got Margaret back to the front door, she could see a deep scratch on its paint-work, caused by the chair as Margaret had fought her way past it in her panic. When she pointed it out to Margaret, she immediately assumed it had been caused by the wing of the plane, and Joey didn't have the heart to disagree! So, for the next twenty-five years that scratch remained there, a reminder of that terrifying moment when it seemed that, as in the story of Chicken Licken, the sky really was falling down. Also, never once in the intervening years would Lena be persuaded to go in an aeroplane, as she recalled her terror that day.

The years at Pitkinny had been full of incidents like these, and I have recorded those I remember and those that have been recounted to me by family and friends. I am certain that many other people have good reason to remember time spent with Joey and Jim. Not all of these will be happy recollections, of course, as there were many times when there was nothing funny or pleasing about the difficult and trying aspects of farm life. Inevitably, by 1975 some of the characters who peopled these stories had, in the course of the thirty-five years of my parents' farming life, passed on. Many of the older generation had died: Gran Betsy in Markinch in 1973 and Grandad James at the Star the year before, while Joey lost her younger sister Betty in 1971. Uncle Hughie and his family emigrated to the United States in 1966, and Auntie Greta and Uncle Bobby and their three children Jim, Elizabeth, and Hughie had lived in Doncaster since the early sixties. Bobby's partner in the demolition business, Jock Allan, had sadly died a young man in the fifties. Many others who had made their mark on our lives and on the farm were long gone, not all as far away as the Steel family in Australia, but by then just as surely with us only in memory.

So the harvest of 1975 was the last for Joey and Jim. Ironically, and just as well, given the preoccupation Jim was subject to in terms of Joey's health and his marathon negotiations with the NCB, it went completely smoothly. The weather, for once, co-operated and the combine and baler never once broke down. There were no crises at all involved in garnering the last barley Jim ever grew, and the high prices he got from Robert Kilgour, the maltster in Kirkcaldy, were testament to the high quality of his last harvest, and undoubtedly of the Ballantine's whisky it would make. As each field was left stubble-bare and the straw bales hauled into the farm for their last winter's cattle bedding, and the hay bales and some of the barley stored for bruising for their winter fodder, Jim could feel highly satisfied that he had ended his tenure of the farm with a flourish. But as the days passed into autumn, the full understanding of what was about to happen began to dawn on him and Joey, and on everyone associated with Pitkinny. It was when it was Sandy Black's plough that started to cultivate the stubble fields for next year's crops, and when, apart from the winter routine of cattle feeding and dealing, there were no plans to be made for the next year's work, that the full significance of this scenario began to sink in.

What had to be planned was the winding up of Jim and Joey's life's work. The die was cast, and the stage set for the final act of their life together that had started thirty-five years before, on that day they first came to Bogside. The renunciation of part of their lease on Pitkinny was, in fact, the beginning of the next phase of their lives, but I think it was very hard for them and us to envisage a future they had never, until recently, thought would be theirs. If they looked forward at all, I am sure they had probably expected life to carry on unchanged indefinitely. The closer they came to the end of their tenure of the land in general and of their home and steading in particular, the harder the prospect appeared for all of us. The fact was that there would have to be a roup, when all the livestock, implements, and equipment would be sold at auction. Traditionally, a farm roup is as much a social occasion as a commercial undertaking. It amounts to a weighing up, not only of the financial worth of the farmers, but of the standing and reputation they have acquired over the years of their occupancy of steading and ground. It is when they give an account of themselves to their peers. In a sense they are weighed in the balance and the monetary result is only part of the accounting. "Aye, it wis a guid roup," could be seen as the ultimate accolade for a retiring farmer, and it was with this awareness that Jim and Joey approached the final hurdle of their race. Had the young upstarts who arrived from an alien part of the county in 1941 made a go of things, after all?

There was much to be done in preparation for this momentous day. "Everything must go!" was certainly the custom at a roup, down to the last rusty nail and the last stoory, foosty bale of hay, maybe well past its sell-by date. A huge redding up of the steading occupied Jim and Dougie, and other helpers, for many weeks during that last winter. Anything worth selling had to be cleaned and tidied up to be shown at its best, from the most sophisticated and costly machinery to the occasional example of the more archaic and homely artefacts which had survived from an earlier age. Every nook and cranny that had long been ignored had to be cleared out, and decisions made as to the saleability of whatever it held. None of the contents of the house were included in the roup, but during the few weeks after it, and before they left for Kirkcudbright, Joey would invite visitors to choose a keepsake from amongst the many and varied items in her pantry, whose shelves were occupied by a range of some weird and wonderful curiosities long since fallen out of use and fashion. As the first few weeks of 1976 passed, the farm became uncannily tidy and, increasingly, strangely unfamiliar to us each time we visited. In the last week or two, Margaret and I and our families were all at the farm, and there was increasingly frenetic activity as the day approached. The auctioneers from McDonald and Fraser were there every day helping to prepare the livestock for sale, and the kitchen never seemed to empty or the teapot to cool down, as helpers came and went.

Margaret and I helped Joey as she planned the feeding and watering of the crowds who would attend the roup. Meanwhile Margaret's girls kept Calum amused as they played in their Wendy house, seeming a little bemused by all the unfamiliar faces and comings and goings. Donald, only seven months old, was often in his pram in the corner of the kitchen, and was naturally the centre of attention from many of the visitors. He once took fright and nearly brought the place down when assailed by the loud and boisterous tones of Bob Doig, one of the auctioneers, more used perhaps to addressing potential buyers in the sale ring than a baby, as he bellowed at him, "An' whit's your name, wee lad?"

The other auctioneer, Jimmy Garland, did not exactly endear himself to John either. The washbed at the back of the house was in constant use as the machinery was steam-hosed and smartened up with the application of much spit and polish and elbow grease. John had spent the whole morning preparing the land rover for the roup. He had it spotless inside and out when he came into the house for his lunch break. As he glanced out of the back window of the kitchen to admire his handiwork, he was horrified to see Jimmy open the door of the newly cleaned vehicle and urge his very muddy labrador to jump up onto the driver's seat. "Ah've jist left ma dug in the land rover, Mrs Rutherford, 'es ower mucky tae bring in the hoose," he explained as he joined John in the kitchen. I don't know whether John said anything to the auctioneer, but he knew that part of his afternoon would have to be spent repeating some of his morning's efforts. The biggest cleaning job was of course the combine harvester, and a photograph shows Calum and Lynda sitting together on the driver's seat of the gleaming monster, well bundled up by Joey in coats and hats against the "coorse Mairch wither."

All of this activity and anticipation perhaps had the effect of diverting us from the emotional impact of the occasion, but there was inevitably a sense of sadness as we knew that the climax of the exercise we were engaged in would spell the ending of a way of life for us all. The strain showed most on Jim, as he became ever more quiet and tense as the days to the roup dwindled. The hardest time I recall was a week or two before, as we all assembled at the farm. Jim had been for a final meeting at the NCB offices in Cowdenbeath, and arrived home just as we were sitting in at the table to have tea. I remember we were having haddock and chips—one of Jim's favourites—and as he sat down, he announced to us all that he had received the written notification of the lump-sum cash settlement, dated 18 March. He produced the letter and as he read it out to us, his voice broke and he ended with his own words, "An' whit is it worth? It's no worth tuppence!" With that he got up from the table and went outside to the big shed. None of us could speak, far less attempt to eat our meal, as we realised how hard this was all proving to be, especially for Jim and Joey, as they faced the greatest watershed in their lives so far. The anguish of that moment passed, as Jim came back into the kitchen and we did our best to continue with our meal, although I felt as if I was trying to eat cardboard!

But the children were there, and their chatter and Joey's unfailing ability to get things on an even keel helped us to regain our equilibrium. Nevertheless, in the course of the following days, and as 31 March dawned blustery and wet, we all faced it with a mixture of excitement and trepidation. I tried to see the positive aspects of the situation, as I knew Jim and Joey were pragmatic enough to appreciate them. This settlement was the best outcome they could hope for, given the circumstances that had been forced on them. The alternative would have meant struggling on, all the time getting older and weaker and finding it increasingly difficult to cope with the demands of the farm. A smaller acreage and relatively shrinking income, with the eventual worry of trying to retire only on the proceeds of their roup, were not prospects any of us could have contemplated with equanimity. But still the lump in my throat resolutely refused to disappear as we embarked on the last of many memorable days at Pitkinny.

*Alison and Pamela at the stackyard gate with the Lurgi Plant and Bishop Hill behind*

*Lynda, Alison, Pamela, Donald, and Calum on the front gate at Pitkinny*

*Margaret, Alison, Donald, Pamela, Lynda, Joey, and Calum in the kitchen at Pitkinny*

*Lynda and Calum on the combine harvester on the roup day, 1976*

JAMES RUTHERFORD, CARDENDEN.

TRADING ACCOUNTS
YEAR ENDED 30th JUNE 1976.

LIVESTOCK

| | | OUTPUT | Valuation at 30/ 6/75 | Valuation at 30/ 6/76 | | |
|---|---|---|---|---|---|---|
| CATTLE | | | | | | |
| Sales | £48757 | | | | | |
| Purchases | 28855 | | | | | |
| | | £19902 | £13793 | £ 9915 | | £16024 |
| SHEEP | | | | | | |
| Sales | £ 3678 | 3678 | 1727 | - | | 1951 |
| | | £23580 | £15520 | £ 9915 | | |
| | | | GROSS OUTPUT - LIVESTOCK | | | £17975 |
| LIVESTOCK EXPENSES | | | | | | |
| Feeding | | | | | £ 1189 | |
| Carriage | | | | | 858 | |
| Vet and Medicine | | | | | 56 | |
| | | | | | | 2103 |
| | | | NET OUTPUT - LIVESTOCK | | | £15872 |

CROPS

| | OUTPUT | Valuation at 30/ 6/75 | Valuation at 30/ 6/76 | | |
|---|---|---|---|---|---|
| Barley | £23526 | £11704 | £ - | | £11822 |
| Hay and Straw | 3509 | - | - | | 3509 |
| Manures | 1120 | | | | 1120 |
| Cultivated Land | - | - | 650 | | 650 |
| Grass | - | - | 640 | | 640 |
| | £28155 | £11704 | £ 1290 | | |
| | | GROSS OUTPUT - CROPS | | | £17741 |
| CROP EXPENSES | | | | | |
| Casual Labour | | | | £ 915 | |
| Seeds | | | | 164 | |
| Other Crop Expenses | | | | 94 | |
| | | | | | 1173 |
| | | NET OUTPUT - CROPS | | | £16568 |

*Pitkinny's last trading account*

1st.

NATIONAL COAL BOARD
**Legal Department**
EDINBURGH OFFICE

**W.S.R. MOWBRAY.**
Solicitor

39, LAURISTON STREET,
EDINBURGH, EH3 9DH

Telephone: 031-229-4243

Our Ref: RM/GA1925

Ext. No. 31

Your Ref:

18th March, 1976

Messrs. Johnston & Herron,
Solicitors,
Bank House,
22 Station Road,
LOCHGELLY,
Fife, KY5 9QW.

Dear Sirs,

Westfield Extension - 010042
Mr. James Rutherford
North Pitkinny

Further to my letter of 15th March I now enclose a cheque for £35,827.95 in payment of the compensation plus interest due under the renunciation. The amount of the cheque is calculated as follows:-

| | | |
|---|---|---|
| Consideration ........................................................ | | £35,000.00 |
| Interest from 28/11/75 to 18/3/76 (111 days).......... | £1,273.77 | |
| Less tax at 35% ........................................ | 445.82 | |
| | | 827.95 |
| | | £35,827.95 |

I may say that our Opencast Executive in calculating the amount of the interest have done so on a 366 day basis to take account of the leap-year. In exchange for this cheque I shall be glad if you will let me have the duly executed Renunciation together with particulars of signing and the draft Renunciation.

In case your client requires it for his tax returns I enclose a Certificate of the tax deducted from the interest.

Yours faithfully,

Solicitor (Scotland)

*Letter of compensation for renunciation of Pitkinny lease ("no worth tuppence")*

Date 25/9 1975 83-25-30

The Royal Bank of Scotland Limited

COMMERCIAL STREET BRANCH COMMERCIAL STREET MARKINCH KY7 6DE

Pay Messrs Williamson & Henry, Solicitors or order

Fifteen Thousand and three Hundred & eighty five Pds 19 P Stg

£15385·19.

JAMES RUTHERFORD JR.

Jas Rutherford Jr

PAID OCT 1975 COMMERCIAL ST. BRANCH MARKINCH

⑈935554⑈ 83⑆2530⑆ 00245147⑈ 11 ⑈00001538519⑈

*Cheque in payment for the new house in Kirkcudbright*

# Chapter 33

"Well, that's the last time Ah'll hae tae dae this, hen!"

We had been a big family in the days leading up to the roup. In addition to us six adults and five children, Hughie Drennan, our cousin from Doncaster, had asked if he could come to help. He had often spent his summer holidays at Pitkinny in the years since his family, Auntie Greta, Uncle Bobby, sister Elizabeth, and big brother Jim had moved to Yorkshire. He sometimes came on holiday with us, once when he was convinced by Jim that we were going to spend the night fishing on a trawler in The Minch, and again with Jim and Joey when they had a caravan holiday touring the northwest with Margaret, John, and Pamela as a toddler. He had many happy memories of these times, and now that he was doing an apprenticeship in the railway engineering workshops in Doncaster, he was a valuable assistant in preparing the machinery for sale. In addition, he was well used to the sharp edge of Jim's tongue, and could hold his own in a quiet way amongst the rough and tumble of farm work. His namesake and grandfather Hugh, although no longer able to contribute his valuable practical assistance as he had in the past, was nevertheless keen to be around the action too.

Evidence of the preceding weeks of preparation was everywhere you looked. A makeshift sale ring had been erected in the big shed for the auctioning of the livestock. Eighty crossbred Hereford and Fresian bullocks would pass through the ring that day. Sixty ewes with lambs at foot, and two pedigree Suffolk tups would be sold from the sheep buchts down the loan beside the old cottar, long since turned henhouses. The field nearest the steading contained all the machinery and vehicles, arranged in serried, gleaming ranks, testament to the steam-cleaning and smartening up of the past days and weeks. These ranged from the least significant to the most impressive such as the lorry and float, the combine harvester, the JCB digger, and the land rover with its cattle trailer. Along with the five huge, red Massey Ferguson tractors—bigger and infinitely grander than their original wee grey Fergie counterpart that had represented Jim's first tractor purchase all those years before—were already the object of interested inspection by early-arriving potential bidders. The tractor shed held all the hand implements, tools, and myriad flotsam and jetsam of farm work, while at the far end of the big shed, the unconsumed remains of the baled hay and straw for fodder and bedding was stacked. The barley feed was housed in the grain drier near the bruiser, and the draff and silage were in the most recently built shed at the back of the reids.

"An important and extensive displenishing sale," widely advertised by Macdonald, Fraser & Co Ltd, listed and described all the lots to be auctioned in the *Courier* and the *Scottish Farmer* publications. "Terms cash" meant that everything sold had to be paid for there and then. The auctioneers set up their office in the big wooden henhouse, now unnaturally clean and quiet, as the cashier and his clerks sat at their trestle tables where once the busily fussing, clucking, pecking, laying hens had thronged.

"Refreshments at sale" promised an essential element of any farm roup, and the necessary catering arrangements were in place and operational by the starting time of 10:45 a.m. The tattie shed, empty and swept cleaner than it had ever been since the day it was built, now housed a fully stocked bar, provided and run by Alec Torley, whose pub in Lochgelly had been Jim's favourite watering hole in the later years at Pitkinny. Trestle tables covered in white cloths fronted the beer barrels and optics which would soon see action, while further from the door, Neilson the "baker, confectioner, and caterer," also from Lochgelly, who had been contracted to provide the food, was preparing to dispense his wares. While liquid nourishment was the responsibility of the punters themselves (traditionally a welcome opportunity to partake of at least a few legitimate bevvies as business and social obligation demanded, and many more which extended far beyond the call of duty), Jim and Joey paid for the food available. Tickets were handed out, which could be exchanged for snack lunches at 50 pence per head. Three hundred fifty-two of those tickets were distributed, a figure which gives some indication of the numbers attending the roup.

In addition to these feeding and watering arrangements, the custom was to invite family, friends, helpers, and the auctioneers and their staff to have their dinner in the kitchen. That, of course, was traditionally the responsibility of the farmer's wife, and in the days leading up to the roup Mum, Margaret, and I had cooked and prepared as much as we could in advance, while Auntie Rina from the Star and Margaret's friend Jean Hume (née Sneddon) helped on the day itself. We knew the menu had to be sustaining and manageable, so vast quantities of soup were made. The obvious choice of main course was mince an' tatties, and while the mince was cooked the day before, the tatties—seemingly hundreds of them—were peeled on the eve of the big day. Every available pot and pan had to be pressed into service, and eventually the deep second tub of the sink unit was also filled to the brim with peeled tatties covered in water. Then later, when Jim eventually came in from the steading, he complained that there was no soap for him to wash his hands at the kitchen sink. "Nae soap? Whaur is the soap? It was there earlier when I was finishin' peelin' the tatties," fretted Joey. Then, fearing the worst—that the soap had fallen into the tub and all those laboriously peeled spuds would be tainted by its taste—the tub had to be emptied and searched for the offending soap. Fortunately it was never found, and once again the sink was full of tatties covered safely in unadulterated aqua pura.

Tables and chairs were set and arranged around the kitchen so that we could have sixteen people at a sitting. We would have to discourage our diners from lingering over their cheese and biscuits and cups of tea and coffee at the end of the meal, to make way for the next sitting of hungry folk. All of these preparations had to be accomplished while also feeding the family and helpers during the days before the roup, and making endless fly cups and offering sandwiches and home-baked goodies to the constant stream of droppers-in: helpers, well-wishers, or downright nosey parkers who made their way into the kitchen. Looking back now, I wonder how we also managed to look after the five children, ranging in age from Pamela at ten years to Donald at eight months. I think plenty of Gran Betsy's "healthy neglect" must have been involved, but in addition, Margaret and John's three girls Pamela, Alison, and Lynda were always wonderful at amusing and caring for their two little boy cousins, so much so that "Pam, Dan, or Din do it" was Calum's war cry in those days, as he always preferred that one of his much-loved cousins should attend to his and Donald's needs.On the eve of the roup, as the children from the youngest to the oldest had been put to bed, we had begun to relax a little, knowing that we had done all we could in preparation for the big day, but still anxious about the daunting challenge that awaited us.

The morning of Wednesday 31 March dawned wild and blustery with sudden heavy, squally showers of sleety rain. March must have come in like a lamb that year, because it was certainly leaving like a lion. Despite the lengthening day, spring seemed a long way off, and the snell wind fought a losing battle with the rain, as it strove to dry the gaiters in the close. Joey's war with her perennial enemy, the mud, was to continue almost to the end of her time at the farm. Mornings always started early at Pitkinny, but even more so on this momentous day, when everyone was up "at sparrowfart." Even without our dependable alarm clock of young children, we would have wakened early with the knowledge that this day would be like no other.

I faced the day with a physical awareness of the sense of anticipation, that lump in my throat that was a hybrid of excitement and dread. It had been with me since that awful teatime two weeks earlier when Dad untypically betrayed his fragile emotional state with his outburst: "What's it all worth? It's no worth tuppence," as he looked at the letter confirming the cash settlement from the NCB. I understood exactly what he meant. A monetary figure, no matter how essential and satisfactory, could in no way represent the worth of the investment, which transcended mere money: the time, work, worry, and hopes Jim and Joey had expended on Pitkinny. It was their life's work, and it was drawing to a close, culminating in this last mammoth effort in the weeks and months that had led up to this much-anticipated, but grudgingly welcomed March morning.

As the usual rush and hurry of washing, dressing, and feeding our two children ensued, Calum, two years and eight months old, protested, "But why?" just as I had as a child. Joey's promise of a visit from the Queen, having been fulfilled, could not be repeated, so I made do with, "Because lots and lots of people are coming to Pitkinny today." Donald, at eight months old, sat in his pram in the corner of the kitchen, fascinated by the endless stream of passing faces, none of whom failed to stop and make a fuss of him, as they hurried to and fro on their urgent business. I found time to slip out to the big shed where Dad, having finished the morning feeding of the beasts, was sweeping up the last vestiges of bruised barley and draff from the gangways alongside the reids. The cattle breakfasted contentedly, blissfully unaware of the day's significance. "Well, that's the last time Ah'll hae tae dae this, hen," he said. I couldn't immediately answer him, as a surge of emotion, close to panic, came over me, not for the last time that day. As we turned to leave the big shed, I managed, "The beasts are looking great, Dad." "Aye, well, they'll hae tae dae the wye they are noo. Is ma parritch ready?" and he followed me into the kitchen for breakfast

As we all finished our breakfasts and cleared the decks for action in the kitchen, people were already arriving for the business of the day. The auctioneers were standing by as the loan rapidly filled up with cars, vans, and lorries, most preferring to park on its hard surface rather than risk the field. Experience had taught them the dangers of becoming stuck in a muddy field if the rain persisted all day, and no one wanted to be pulled out of the mire by one of the tractors, especially since by the end of the day all of them would have been sold and not one of them would belong any longer to Pitkinny! By half past ten the close was full of people—mostly men and only the occasional woman—most of them suitably garbed in wellies, rain jackets, and bunnets. There were many weel-kent faces of family, friends, neighbours, and other members of the wider farming community, but there were numerous strangers attracted by the advertisements from further afield in east-central Scotland and perhaps even beyond. For each serious prospective bidder, there were others who came out of curiosity or to show support for Joey and Jim, or perhaps some even just for a complimentary food ticket. Who said there was no such thing as a free lunch? A roup is as much a social occasion as a commercial enterprise, and to see and be seen was motivation enough for many, especially since the day had started wet and windy with little prospect of outside work on the still "winter-cauld grund." So a day off, meeting up with old friends and acquaintances while witnessing the climax of the Rutherford tenure at Pitkinny, was a welcome alternative to finding some tedious indoor work for farmer and farmhand alike. And, of course, there was always the tempting refuge of the bar, where they could continue to chew the fat in relative comfort, conversation suitably lubricated and thus all the more stimulating and entertaining.

At 10:45 exactly Jimmy Garland, from his vantage point on the back of a trailer outside the tractor shed, began the roup with its miscellaneous contents. Soon, the staccato rhythms of his auctioneer's patois rapidly disposed of lot after lot, as clerks ran to and from the henhouse with sale dockets, and successful bidders followed somewhat less eagerly to pay their dues. Mostly, portable items would be removed and stowed in vehicles, while bulkier purchases would await collection later. There was method in starting the roup with the smaller items in the catalogue; the marketing maxim "Everything must go" certainly applied to this situation. The crowd grew a little restive as all the bits and pieces came under the hammer, and there was a collective sigh of relief when the last wee item was sold: a bag of nails for 10 pence! But nobody had left, and when this first—and least interesting—phase of the roup ended, the crowd eagerly followed the auctioneer out to the field where the larger items were to be sold off.

As the bidding started, it soon became apparent (when it came to the big equipment and vehicles) that most of them had been targeted by a dealer—a stranger to everyone at the roup—who successfully outbid them all. He was a relatively young man, rather flamboyantly dressed in a light tan leather coat, who had arrived in a big Mercedes of the same colour. He certainly stood out from the crowd, and caused even more of a stir when he let it be known that the destination for most of his acquisitions was somewhere in the Middle East. This somewhat exotic young man and his determined and single-minded approach generated great interest. Was he a front man for some shady organisation? What possible use could there be for a combine harvester in Saudi Arabia, or a cattle float in Egypt? The crowd was buzzing with speculation and rumour, but at the end of the day his money, in the form of hard cash, was as good—and as reliable—as anyone else's, and his presence may have stimulated the bidding to the ultimate benefit of Jim and Joey, so no one had reason to feel aggrieved that they had lost out. All is fair in love and war—and farm roups, it seemed!

In the house, as dinnertime approached, the first of our invited guests arrived. We were soon into our stride as the soup was ladled out, the mince an' tatties and peas dished up, and the first of countless pots of tea and coffee, to go with the biscuits and cheese, were brewed. We served more than fifty lunches over the next few hours, and everything went smoothly and everyone declared themselves well satisfied with their meal. Joey couldn't help but think back to the early pre-combine days of their farming life, when she would feed the gang of mill men and other workers when the threshing mill paid its annual visit to the farm. But the occasion that was uppermost in her mind was that other hectic and infinitely more stressful one, when the kitchen was full of hungry and exhausted firemen and neighbouring helpers, and the air full of the acrid stench of disaster, the day of the fire in October 1956, nearly twenty years earlier. By contrast, while the day of the roup brought a degree of anxiety and not a little sadness, it marked the successful culmination of thirty-five years of hard work, and proved that they had overcome that earlier catastrophe and other struggles that had punctuated their lifetime of ups and downs, highs and lows, successes and failures.

Jim was one of the last to have his dinner that day. While he was still at the table, I took the chance to slip out to the big shed to see what was happening. It was obvious that the auctioneers were about to start to sell the cattle, as spectators and potential bidders were crowding round the improvised sale ring. "Whaur's Jimmy?" shouted Bob Doig, as it was customary for the owner of the beasts to come into the ring and officiate over the sale of the first of the livestock, but when I told Bob that Dad was still having his dinner, he said, "You come an' dae it, Anne. You'll dae fine!" For the second time that day I felt myself assailed by an overwhelming wave of emotion. With welling eyes and through trembling lips I replied, "No, no, I'll get Dad," and I rushed into the kitchen to find him. For once he did not react angrily to being disturbed at his dinner, and I watched him as he hurried out to take his rightful place and sell the last contingent of Pitkinny beasts that would ever pass through the sale ring.

I regained a degree of emotional equilibrium as we cleared the dinner tables, and restored the kitchen to receive the onslaught of visitors who would descend there for the traditional apres-roup celebrations that would surely ensue later that day. One of our lunch guests had remained in the kitchen. David Nimmo was a cattle dealer Jim had dealt with for years. Although he had recently been very ill with bleeding stomach ulcers, he had been determined not to miss the roup, but Joey persuaded him not to go back out into the cold after his lunch, as it was obvious that he was far from well. "Have you two girls had a drink at the bar the day yet?" he enquired of Margaret and me. "No, they've never had a minute, Davy. We've been that busy," replied Joey on our behalf. He went into his pocket and thrust some money at Margaret. "Awa' ye go roond tae the tattie shed and get yersels a drink on me," he urged. "Ah wish Ah could come wi' ye, but Ah've been telt tae avoid the booze fur a whilie yet." So Margaret and I did as we were told, and saw the outside catering arrangements for ourselves for the first time. We were very impressed by the transformation that had been wrought on the shed where years before I had toiled for days, sewing up all those jute tattie bags. I seem to remember that we had a vodka and orange each, followed by one or two others, bought for us by some familiar faces who, now that the business part of the roup was drawing to a close, were intent on patronising the bar and continuing the social element of the day.

With some difficulty, Margaret and I managed to extricate ourselves and, as we left the now heaving tattie shed, we could see that the sun had come out and the wind, while still strong, was much less cold. We decided to hang out the big basket of washing that had been done the previous evening. As we pegged out all the clothes and Donald's nappies, we became increasingly conscious of the effect the sudden intake of alcohol was having on us. Margaret reacted by moving at the speed of light, while I seemed to be incapable of coordinating the action of hand and eye and felt able to operate only in slow motion! Between us, however, we succeeded in achieving a full drying green of laundry merrily blowing in the strong west wind that almost always blew over the fields to the steading at Pitkinny, and in no time at all the clothes were dry.

By then the kitchen was rapidly filling up with well-wishers and old friends and neighbours, with a few newly made acquaintances who had figured prominently as clients of the auctioneers. In particular, the dealer in the leather coat, who was the principal buyer, had been only too ready to take up the invitation to join in the party. He had brought his flashy Merc up from its earlier parking place along the loan and it now had pride of place right in front of the garden gate. He was obviously aware of the social conventions which accompany the business of farm sales, one of which is that of the luck-penny tradition—the offering of some money in recognition of the respect you have for your customer. Perhaps he was unclear as to who should pay whom, because although he was assured by Jim that a gratuity was not necessary, he persisted in giving money to each of the children, some of them more than once. Our usual warnings of "never take money or sweets from a stranger" would have seemed churlish in the circumstances, and as the girls and Calum passed us the banknotes, Margaret took charge of them, promising we would have a divi-up later on! We even found money in Donald's pram, presumably left there by the same generous benefactor, who did another kind and thoughtful thing that day. He had seen our cousin Hughie looking longingly at his car and, handing him his car keys, urged him to take it for a spin. Hughie did not need a second invitation, and was thrilled to be able to report to his family and friends in Doncaster that he had driven a Merc—and a particularly flashy one at that! The man with no name made a young lad very happy that day!

As the party got into full swing and the ubiquitous tea, sandwiches, and cakes appeared, while the whisky bottles circulated steadily, there was a definite air of relief and a sense that the day had been a success. Jimmy Garland and Bob Doig declared themselves well satisfied, on behalf of Macdonald, Fraser & Co. Although Jim remained rather subdued, he and Joey clearly appreciated the good-natured and sincere congratulations heaped on them. Bill continued to make a photographic record of the day; thanks to his efforts, these snaps show groups of smiling friends, family, and helpers, and constitute a wonderful record of what must rank as one of the most successful moments of my parents' lives. Andy Hume, Jean's husband, is seen listening attentively to Willie Stevenson, the farmer at Ballingry Farm, who was at the roup as he had been at all the other important events in Jim and Joey's time at Pitkinny. Jock Lyall, the old neighbour of the Rutherfords at the Star, is pictured having a snooze during the party, cigarette in hand, while Alison looks on. I remember the times we would hear Jock from Gran and Grandad's house in Croft Crescent as he did his round of Markinch with his fruit and vegetable van, and would alert his customers with his loud "Fruiter-are-are-are!" call. Grandad Hugh (a widower since Betsy's death in November 1973) is caught on camera, sitting beside Jimmy Dall from Balgedie and my brother-in-law John and wee Lynda, taking a lead in the predictable sing-song. Sandy Black from Westfield—the future tenant of Pitkinny—and Bob Harley from Redhouse are in another photograph. Alec Torley (the licensee of the bar in the tattie shed) is part of a group with Joey, Jean, Auntie Rina, and myself at the other end of the kitchen, all enjoying the banter and music, while appreciating the fact that this day of days had passed off successfully and we could begin to relax.

However, as the party continued in the house, I was unaware that, outside, the final stages of the roup were being played out. Vehicles were coming and going as buyers collected their purchases. But it was only later that the real impact of this struck home when we went out to the big shed after the children were in bed and the last stragglers from the party were leaving. (Willie Stevenson always prided himself on being the last to leave any party, and this was no exception!) The cattle floats had been and gone, and there was an all-pervading silence. Not a sound could be heard in the oddly eerie emptiness of the reids. During the winter months there was a subdued but continuous sense of movement and sound, as the beasts jostled each other or ruminated contentedly, broken by sporadic, gentle lowing or the occasional startling bellow. The sweet, organic, somehow comforting warm smell of their steamy breath and the dungy bedding mingled in the cold air with the sour-sweet scent of the silage and draff, barley, hay, and turnips as they were fed twice a day. A day came every spring, of course, when the beasts were turned out into the fields once the grass was growing sufficiently, and they would frolic happily in their freedom and literally kick up their heels. Then its corollary came in the autumn when they would again inhabit their winter quarters, but this time we knew it was different.

We were all only too aware of the fact that Joey and Jim would be long gone by the next time beasts occupied the steading. Indeed, Sandy Black would by then have made great changes to accommodate his milking cows. Down the loan, the deserted sheep buchts stood forlorn and empty, where only hours before they had been full of bleating ewes, tups, and lambs. It seemed that with the departure of the livestock the life had gone out of the farm, and it now stood as an empty shell, devoid of almost all of its animate and inanimate elements. Indeed, the sheep dog Jan and the two cats were the only living creatures remaining. Within a short time Jan would go to her new home with our cousin Jimmy Rutherford and his family at Purin Farm, Falkland, leaving only Tim and Topsy as feline custodians, who would remain to oversee the arrival of the new tenants, their new owners. Fond though Jim and Joey were of their pets, they knew it would be unfair to subject their country cats to the ordeal of adapting to life as town moggies. That was going to be a hard enough adjustment for Joey and Jim to contemplate for themselves.

For now, it was enough to reflect on the day and, tired out with all the excitement and work, we went to bed. As usual, Jim and Joey were the last to come upstairs, and as I drifted off to sleep, I was aware of Mum coming into our room. In a whisper, she told me the monetary total that had been realised by the roup, and while I was gratified that it was clearly a very satisfactory outcome, I couldn't help but feel that, as with the NCB compensation, the significance of the figure paled in comparison with the wealth of friendship and goodwill that had been shown to our parents that day. The next few days were filled, understandably, with a sense of anticlimax. We had all been focussed for so long on the roup itself that, now it had been accomplished, there seemed to be a degree of uncertainty: "What happens now?" In some ways, the normal structure of Jim and Joey's life had been removed from them. Essentially, there was no farm work to be done any more. Even the garden and its usual springtime demands no longer mattered, and that was a huge gap for Joey. There were still decisions to be made about the move to Kirkcudbright, of course, and many loose ends to be tied up with the auctioneers and the accountants, and final details to be completed with the NCB. These early days and weeks after the roup marked, in fact, the beginnings of their transition into retirement, and were merely the precursor to that huge adjustment that awaited them when they moved.

Jim and Joey must have felt that they were living in a kind of limbo during the last few weeks at Pitkinny. They would often visit us in Cairneyhill, and one such afternoon they left me and the boys to go into Dunfermline for a final meeting with the valuation firm who had dealt with the final settlement of their compensation. An hour or so later, I had a phone call from Mum to say they had locked themselves out of their car in the town, and to make matters worse, their house key was in the car. I had just started to bath Calum and Donald, so I had to call a friend to come and look after them while I went and picked up Jim and Joey. After Bill came home and we had our dinner, Jim borrowed our car and drove home to the farm. He knew that their bedroom window was unlocked, so he had to get a long ladder and climb up to the window to get the spare car key from the bedroom. Jim hated heights and was never comfortable about climbing ladders, so was dreading the whole enterprise. Much later, after he had retrieved his car and we were having some supper before they left for home, I asked him how he had managed the climb. "Well it wisnae sae bad gaun up the ladder an' in the windae, but efter Ah goat the key, Ah hid an awfy joab gettin' back oot the windae an' on tae the ladder again!" There was a stunned silence as we all looked incredulously at each other, until the awful truth dawned on Jim. He had been so fixated on the ladder and his fear of heights, that it never dawned on him that all he had to do was walk down the stairs and let himself out the back door, pulling it locked behind him. I'll draw a veil over the actual words he used to describe what a fool he had been! Suffice it to say that they consisted of an interesting and original combination of nouns and adjectives, none of which were deleted!

Margaret and John had lived in Kirkcudbright for five years, in a house that went with John's job with the SSEB, near his work at Tongland power station just outside the town. They had decided to build a house in the town, not far from the one Jim and Joey had bought in June 1975. As their new house would not be ready until the spring of 1976, Margaret and John agreed to move into our parents' new house in the interim, rather than have it sit empty all winter. The date of the move from Pitkinny was fixed for the end of May, by which time John and Margaret would be in their new home. So preparations had to be made for furnishing the new house, and decisions about what to take and what to leave behind, which occupied some of the time left at the farm. Margaret and I, with John and Bill, decided that while the roup had taken care of the climax of their working life, we should make plans for a final get-together with all their family and friends before they moved away. It was agreed to hold a party at Torley's function suite in Lochgelly, on Saturday 22 May, two days before their flitting to Kirkcudbright, and to that end, catering was arranged and a band booked.

The farming fraternity decided they wanted to give Jim and Joey a presentation, and Margaret and I were consulted about what they would like. We suggested that some crystal would be very acceptable, and on the evening of the party that was just one of the many gifts they were given. In addition, their local farming friends had a scroll made to honour the occasion, and it put into words the high regard and genuine affection in which they were held by their many friends and acquaintances. The evening was a great success, and for the most part represented not just a celebration of their working lives but, in a spirit of happy anticipation, the beginning of their retirement to come. However, towards the end of the party, I was reminded of how much of a watershed this really was, not just for us as a family but for other people who had been connected for so long with the farm. Dougie Imrie and his wife Chrissie were sitting with his brother Rob and his wife Lena. They had all worked for Joey and Jim for much of their working lives and expressed how much they would miss Pitkinny. Dougie had found a new job with Kinnaird the tattie merchants at Cluny, so he would still be in a similar working environment to the farm, but I will never forget his words to me that evening: "Yer dad'll never kain whit 'e's done tae me the nicht, Anne. Ma life'll never be the same again." So despite the happy time we all shared, emotions were running high by the time we sang "Auld Lang Syne," and the words of the old song were never more sincerely meant.

Many of our family who were at the party that night paid their last visit to Pitkinny the next day. It was like so many other Sundays that I remember throughout my life, when visitors would arrive, usually quite unexpectedly, and as she had done for years, Joey stood in the kitchen calmly making sandwiches and pouring cups of tea as if this *was* just another Sunday. I kept reminding myself that the removers would be arriving first thing in the morning to uplift their belongings to a new life entirely, but either this had not really sunk in with Joey and Jim or they were determined to enjoy their last day to the very end. It seemed very fitting too that some of the last photographs taken that day were of all the children, the next generation. As I look at Jim and

Joey's grandchildren and the sons and daughters of Jim and Joey's nieces and nephews standing in front of the old house at Pitkinny, with Joey's garden in its full spring beauty, I see them as representing the future, as symbols of the years and generations to come. Most of those children are now parents themselves, and as we all grow older, there is great comfort to be had from knowing that we were all together that last day at the farm. Jim and Joey were indeed fortunate to have had that assurance, as they spent their last day surrounded by the youngsters who meant so much to them and to the future of the family.

As Bill and John had work the next day, we left for home in Cairneyhill and Kirkcudbright respectively. I couldn't see for tears as we waved goodbye and drove out the loan for the last time, but along with the sadness there was a feeling of contentment that Jim and Joey were going to have a comfortable retirement and reap the rewards of all their hard work. There was also relief that Auntie Greta, Uncle Bobby, and Elizabeth were spending the night with them and would be there to help the next day, and to be with them when they closed the door for the last time. I thought back to the happy time those two young couples had shared together on VE-Day when they had celebrated the end of the war in the youthful exuberance and joy of a water fight at Bogside. It was also good to know that Margaret and John would be waiting for them at their new home, and the presence of their three granddaughters would help to take the edge off the strangeness and stress of their first night in their new surroundings.

We later learned that as soon as we all left the farm that night, Uncle Bobby equipped himself with a screwdriver and began to dismantle the kitchen fittings that Joey had decided she would take with her the next day, while Jim did his usual disappearing act when a flitting was in the offing, and went off to bed! I had privately entertained grave doubts as to whether Pickford's, the removal firm, would be able to cope with moving a household that had really done very little in the way of packing, but I shouldn't have worried. When I phoned the farm at twelve noon, I was amazed to discover that the first removal van was already full, and the second one partly filled. There was one potential disaster when Auntie Greta's handbag disappeared, and she realised that it had gone into the van along with the chair that it had been sitting on! Thankfully, it was quickly recovered, and the last item of furniture to go into the van was the carver chair that Grandad Hugh was sitting on; that same chair that had come off the *Mauritania* oceangoing liner, and had been bought by Joey years before at Green's saleroom in Ladybank. So it and its owners set off on another chapter in their lives that day as they left for Kirkcudbright.

Indeed this was to be a major change in the life of Grandad Hugh as well. Widowed less than three years before, he had continued to live on in his home in Markinch, but found it very hard to manage on his own, despite great support from Joey and frequent stays at Pitkinny. Clearly, Joey was unhappy about leaving him behind in Fife, and after some discussion it was decided that he would go and live with them in their new home. In retrospect, perhaps we all should have given this move more thought, but in all the years Grandad had come to Pitkinny, he had been very easy to get on with. While he had few domestic accomplishments, he had many other practical skills and could turn his hand to anything mechanical, so the house and steading bore many traces of his handiwork. We assumed that the same situation would prevail in his new environment and that, as his general health was very good for his age, he would continue to be as active and interested in participating in the life around him as his age would allow. Sadly, this was not to be the case, but as they left Pitkinny, there seemed to be no reason to anticipate any problems where Hugh was concerned.

I never really asked about the feelings my parents had on that last drive out the loan, partly because I was so relieved that the first part of the removal had gone so smoothly, but mostly because I really couldn't bear to dwell on the painful scenario my imagination could only too easily conjure up. Remembering how Joey would shed tears whenever we left the farm to go on holiday, I could well understand how hard it must have been for her, to know that she would never come home to Pitkinny again. As the removal vans headed for Kirkcudbright, Joey, Jim, and Grandad Hugh joined Uncle Bobby, Auntie Greta, and Elizabeth for a late lunch in the Burnside Hotel in their old home village of Kinglassie. Then they said their goodbyes, and the two cars parted company at Halbeath as the Doncaster contingent headed for the A1 and Jim, Joey, and Grandad went west through Dunfermline towards the Kincardine Bridge, the A74, and their new home in the southwest. So they left Fife, the home area where they had been born, Joey sixty-one years, and Jim fifty-nine years before.

They couldn't guess what lay ahead, but they were only too aware of what they were leaving. Joey later confessed to feelings of apprehension, and even dread, as she contemplated a completely new way of life. What Jim's thoughts were I have no way of knowing, but I am certain that he, like Joey, felt entirely bereft and aimless after a lifetime of being firmly rooted in the land they had made their own, first at Bogside and then at Pitkinny. The words of Eric Bogle's song "Leaving the Land" vividly echo the emotions that I am sure accompanied Joey and Jim on that fateful journey to their new home. They arrived in Kirkcudbright, where Margaret and John and the girls were waiting to help them to begin life in their new surroundings. As they waited next day in the empty house for the removal vans to arrive and Margaret was showing Joey all the preparations they had made to get the house ready for them, Joey's general uncertainty and fears surfaced as she said, "I'd have been as weel stottin' roond the empty hoose at Pitkinny, as stottin' roond here!" However, she was never one to complain openly about her feelings, and within a short time she found herself distracted from her understandable doubts. Grandad's chair was the first item of furniture to come off the removal van, so he had somewhere to sit as Joey "got wired in" and started to make this new house truly their home, as she had always done. No doubt Jim made himself as scarce as possible while everyone else set to with the unpacking and arranging of the household that had last seen the light of day in the close at Pitkinny.

Had Joey looked back to the first time she was faced with settling in an alien environment, she would have been transported back to the bleak, unwelcoming Bogside house three months after her marriage to Jim in 1941. This time she didn't have the consolation of a friendly hen laying her daily egg on the armchair, but she had the comfort of some of her family just up the road; Margaret, John, Pamela, Alison, and Lynda soon helped Joey and Jim to feel at home. Also, of course, the living conditions they were able to enjoy in their retirement were a world away from the cold and comfortless old house they made into their first home, and they were to enjoy twelve happy years in Kirkcudbright. They would make some very good friends and have many wonderful and, of course, some difficult times during those years. They were central to the growing up of our two sons and their three granddaughters, and we all have wonderful memories of the happy days that lay ahead in Kirkcudbright.

# Leaving the Land

It's time to go Jenny, no need to close the door,
What if the dust gets in the house, it doesn't matter anymore,
You and that dust have been at war for far too many years,
Well now the war is over, Jenny dear.

Chorus
Leaving the Land, Leaving the Land,
Leaving all I've ever been and everything I am,
Leaving the Land.

Remember when I brought you here, those long bright years ago,
For all that time you've been my heart, but this land has been my soul,
The long bright days are over now, though still the heart beats on,
But Jenny dear, the soul is gone.

And all I see around me, seems to me of the past,
For generations have loved this land, never thought I'd be the last,
All that toiling, all that dreary birth and death and joy and pain,
Was all for nothing, all in vain.

Its time to go, Jenny, drive quickly down the track,
We'll never see what lies ahead, if we keep on looking back,
Behind us just an empty house, old memories and ghosts,
And our small dreams gathering dust.

Eric Bogle

# THORNTON AUCTION MARKET.

**IMPORTANT and EXTENSIVE DISPLENISHING SALE of LIVE-STOCK, CROP and IMPLEMENTS at NORTH PITKINNY, CARDEN-DEN, on WEDNESDAY, March 31, 1976.**

Macdonald, Fraser & Co. Limited, Thornton, favoured with instructions from Mr J. Rutherford will submit to Public Auction the following:

CATTLE.

**40** Cross Hereford and Friesian Bullocks (in forward condition).
**40** Cross Hereford and B.P. Grazing Bullocks.

SHEEP

**60** Cross Ewes (3 crop) with Lambs at Foot.
**2** Suffolk Rams.

CROP.

Quantity Baled Hay.
Quantity Baled Barley Straw.
Approximately 6 Tons Shellstar No. 2.

IMPLEMENTS.

New Holland Clayson 133 Combine Harvester (1967); 2 M.-F. 165 Tractors (1968 and 1970), Multi Power and Power Steering; M.-F. 135 Tractor (1972) with M.-F. 40 Loader and Buckets; M.-F. 135 Tractor (1967), Multi Power; M.-F. 203 Tractor with 702 Loader and 710 Digger (1963); International B47 Baler; Petrol Land-Rover (1975, s.w.b., hard top, 6000 miles); Laurie Livestock Trailer (as new); Denis D100 Grain Dresser on Wheels (as new); International 3F Tripleg Plough (as new); M.-F. 794 12 in. 3F Plough; M.-F. 10 in. 3F Plough; Sellar 12 in. 2F Plough; M.-F. 34 Combine Grain Drill; Set M.-F. Semi-Mounted Discs; M.-F. Flexi Harrows (29 Tine); 2 M.-F. S.T. Cultivators (9 and 11 Tine); 2 M.-F. Ridgers; 2 Sets Parmiter Harrows; 3 Sets Diamond Harrows; 2 Weeks 22 Trailers (One with Grain and Silage Sides); Kay 3-Ton Trailer; Kay Dumper Trailer; Flat Trailer; M.-F. 3-Ton Trailer with Grain and Silage Sides; M.-F. 2-Row Potato Planter and Fertiliser Attachment; Stanhay 4-Row Precision Seeder; Bean Steerage Hoe; Cambridge 3-Gang Roller; 9 ft. Mounted Roller; Set 12 ft. Gang Roller; Bamford Manure Distributor; Allman 8/80 Sprayer; M.-F. Dung Spreader; M.-F. Hay Mower; Gemini Hay Turner; Bale Slave; 2 Bale Sledges; Bale Carrier (21 bales); Tractor Hay Rake; Lister Multi-Level Elevator and Electric Motor; 3 Grain Augers and Electric Motors (18 ft. x 4 in. 3 phase, 18 ft. x 3 in. 12 ft. x 3 in. single phase); 2 Turnip Cutters with Electric Motors (3 phase and 1 phase); Steelyard and Weights; Turnip Shawer; 2 Newlands Potato Diggers; 2 Aluminium Extending Ladders; 4 Aluminium Ladders; 2 Galvanised and 5 Wooden Cattle Troughs; Silage Barriers; Sheep Feeding and Turnip Troughs; Sheep Nets; Rylock Nets; 2 Sheep Hacks; Lamb Feeder on Wheels; Sheep Sprayer and Foot Rot Bath; Sheep Foster Mother Pens; Tubular Cattle Catching Crate; Set Wolseley Cattle Clippers; Sheep Turning Crate; M.-F. Transport Box; 2-Ton Grain Hopper; Field Gates; Stobs; Plain and Barbed Wire; Galvanised Feed Bins; Metal Hay Haiks; Quantity Asbestos Pipes; Quantity Sleepers; Galvanised Water Troughs; Set Rear Wheels for M.-F. 165 (11 x 36); Set Rowcrop Wheels; 3-Phase Electric Welding Plant; Oxy-Acetylene Welder; 3-Phase Compressor; Oil Cabinet; 2 Diesel Tanks (600 and 250 galls.); 100 gall. Paraffin Tank; Lister Engine; Electric Drill and Stand; Electric Grinder; Forge; Anvil; Vices; Electric Silage Cutter; Buck Rake; Garden Shed; 12 Wheelbarrows; Sack Barrows; Potato Baskets; Electric Motors (1 and 3 phase); 2 Moisture Meters; Water Tank with Drinking Bowl; Trolley Jack; Electric Water Pressure Pump; 2 Meat Coolers; M.-F. Earth Leveller; Usual Barn and Stable Utensils.

**Refreshments at Sale.** Terms—Cash. **Sale at 10.45 a.m.**

Dundee Courier *advertisement of the roup*

*The Courier and Advertiser, Thursday, April 1, 1976.*

## FARMING NEWS

# Fife farmer retires to Borders

**BY OUR FARMING REPORTER**

**For the second time in his life Mr James Rutherford has had his farming plans upset by opencast coal production.**

He started farming 35 years ago at Bogside, Cardenden, and six years later he had to move from there to allow coal to be worked.

He moved to North Pitkinny's 370 acres in 1947 and made a grand job of the farm.

Two years ago the National Coal Board intimated their intention to extend their open-cast operations and would require the 200 acres which lie to the ~~west~~ east of the farmhouse.

He considered continuing farming on the remaining acres, but decided he would be better off retiring.

He and Mrs Rutherford will shortly move to a house they have bought in Kirkcudbright, where they have a married daughter and grandchildren.

Yesterday a displenishing sale was held at the farm which has been their home for almost 30 years and the stock and implements met a very good trade.

Buyers paid £17,878 for the 78 head of cattle all in forward store condition.

Cross Hereford bullocks sold to a top of £274; cross Friesians to £259; and outwintered black Hereford bullocks to £231.

Cross ewes with 1¼ lambs at foot went to £40.

Top prices for machinery and implements included £2600 for a Claeson M133 combine harvester, £2700 for a Massey Ferguson 135 tractor and loader, £1500 and £1200 for two Massey Ferguson 165 tractors, and £1200 for a M.F. 203 tractor and digger.

A Land-Rover went for £2100.

Auctioneers were MacDonald, Fraser & Co., Ltd., Thornton.

Matthew Black & Son, Westfield, whose farm is being taken over for open-cast coal production, are to move to the North Pitkinny farmhouse and steading and work the remaining acres.

## Store cattle and sheep in demand

LIVE STOCK MARTS, Ltd., had forward 1346 store cattle and 364 sheep

Dundee Courier *article about Jim and Joey's retirement, 1 April 1976*

R. & J. Neilson

Shop:
Main Street, Lochgelly

Bakers, Confectioners, Caterers

V.A.T. Reg. No. 271 0048 95

Parkview Bakery,
Plantation Street,
LOCHGELLY.
Tel.: 780347

J Rutherford
per Messrs Macdonal , Fraser & Co., Ltd., Thorton, Fife.

| | | | |
|---|---|---|---|
| 76 | | | |
| March 31st. | To 352 Lunches @ 50p each. | £ 176 | 00 |

Deducted from Sales
31/3/76

R & J Neilson's account for catering at the roup

*Johnny McFarlane, Dougie Imrie, and Jan the collie on the day before the roup*

*Dougie moving the combine harvester to the wash-bed for steam cleaning*

*John French, Pamela, and Alison washing the cattle trailer*

*Jim and Jimmy Garland preparing a beast for sale*

*Some of the beasts and tractors in the big shed*

*The large machinery displayed in the field, with customers' and visitors' cars parked in the field and loan*

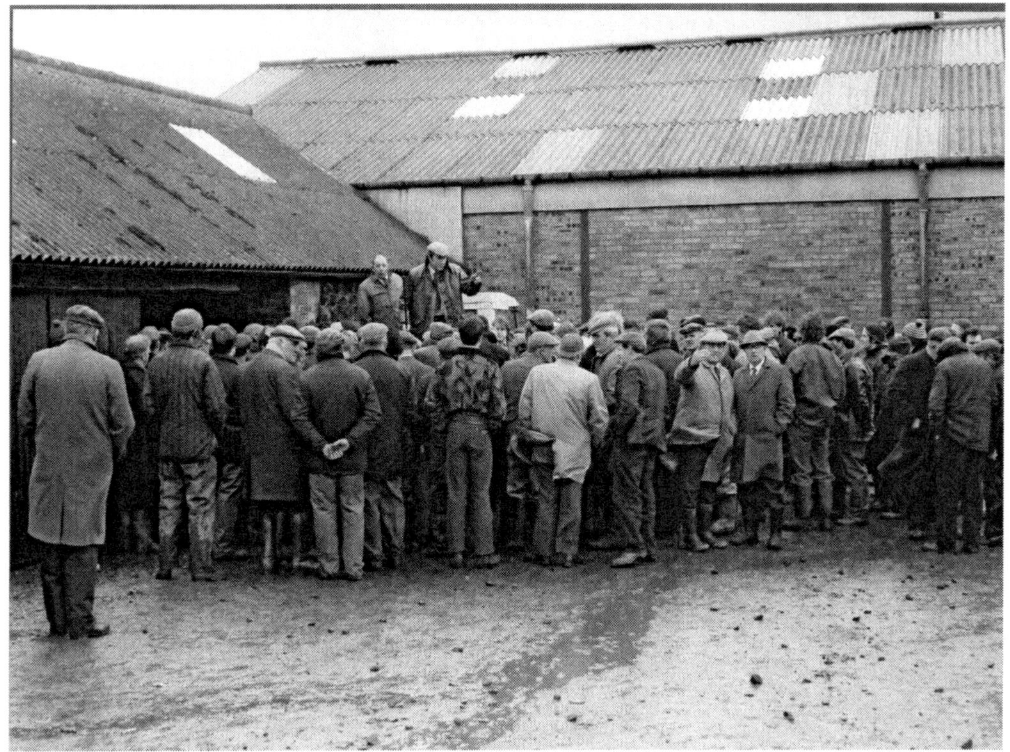

*The sale begins*

*The first of the cattle go under the hammer*

*The sheep await their fate with Calum in attendance*

*Jimmy Garland selling the tractors*

*Hughie Drennan has just parked "the drive of his young life"*

*Celebration drams—Jim and Andy Hume. With back to the camera is the "man with no name": the mystery man whose coat matched the colour of his Merc!*

*The party begins in the kitchen.*
*Back L to R: Auntie Rina and Anne; Front L to R: Alec Torley, Jean Hume, and Joey*

*The sing-song gets going. L to R: Grandad Hugh, Jimmie Dall, John, and Lynda*

*Jock Lyall (asleep) with Donald behind, Willie Stevenson, Pamela (crouching), Andy Hume, and Alison*

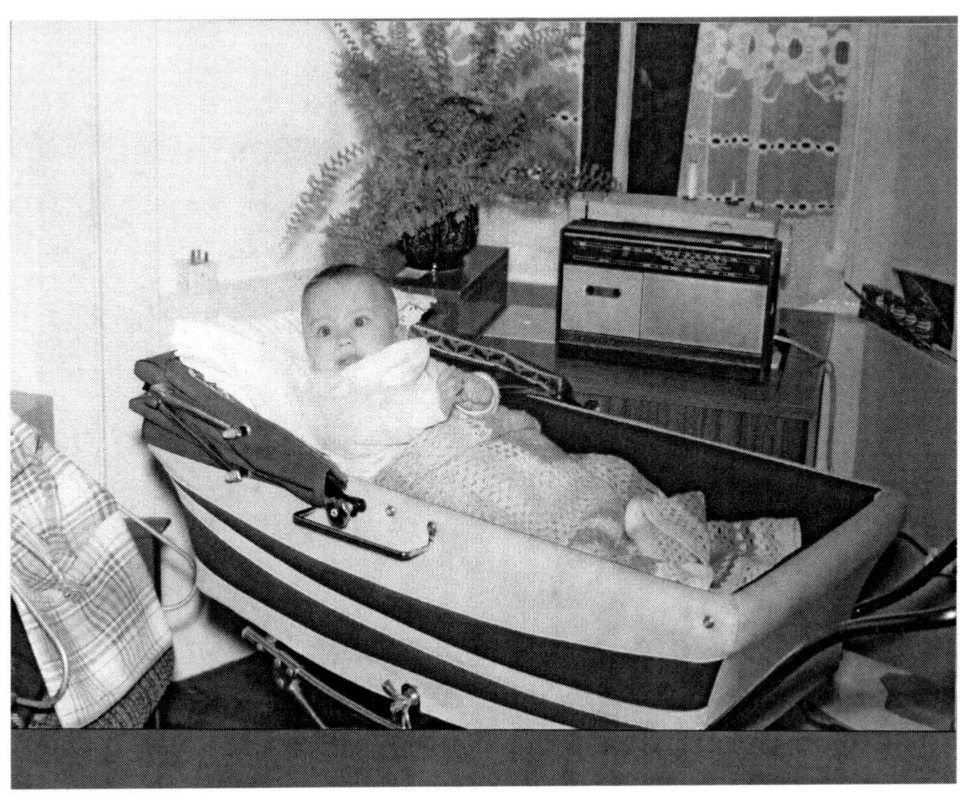

*Donald looks on at all the fun and games*

*The last spring garden at Pitkinny*

*The last day at Pitkinny*
*Back Row, L to R: Elizabeth Drennan, John, Margaret Anne, Calum. and Bill*
*Front Row, L to R: Alison, Lynda, Pamela holding Donald, Pauline Drennan, Bruce Drennan, and Gordon Mitchell*

54/ 4151

HEAD OFFICE: PICKFORDS LTD., 102 BLACKSTOCK ROAD, FINSBURY PARK, N.4.

**PICKFORDS**

**REMOVAL AND STORAGE SERVICE**

2/4 Kirkgat~~95/97 CHALMERS STREET~~, DUNFERMLINE, FIFE

DUNFERMLINE 21615 24 05 1976

Mrs Rutherford

Pitkenny Farm Cardenden

| | | |
|---|---|---|
| Removal | 140 | 00 |
| V.A.T. | 11 | 20 |
| Insurance | £ 7 | 00 |
| | £168 | 20 |

Paid with thanks £158-20 25.5.76 J.K. Pearson

CHEQUES ACT 1957, UNLESS SPECIALLY REQUESTED RECEIPTS ARE NOT ISSUED FOR CHEQUES

*Pickford's account for removal to Kirkcudbright*

Best Wishes

on your

Retirement

To: Mr & Mrs James Rutherford

We, the undersigned ask you to accept this expression of our very best wishes on the occasion of your Retirement

It is our hope that you may enjoy many years of Health and Happiness and the Friendships you have made among your colleagues and associates may be an enduring source of Pleasure and Happy Memories

Signed: Your Many Friends and Neighbours

*Scroll from the farming community*

*Jim and Joey Rutherford on their last day at Pitkinny*

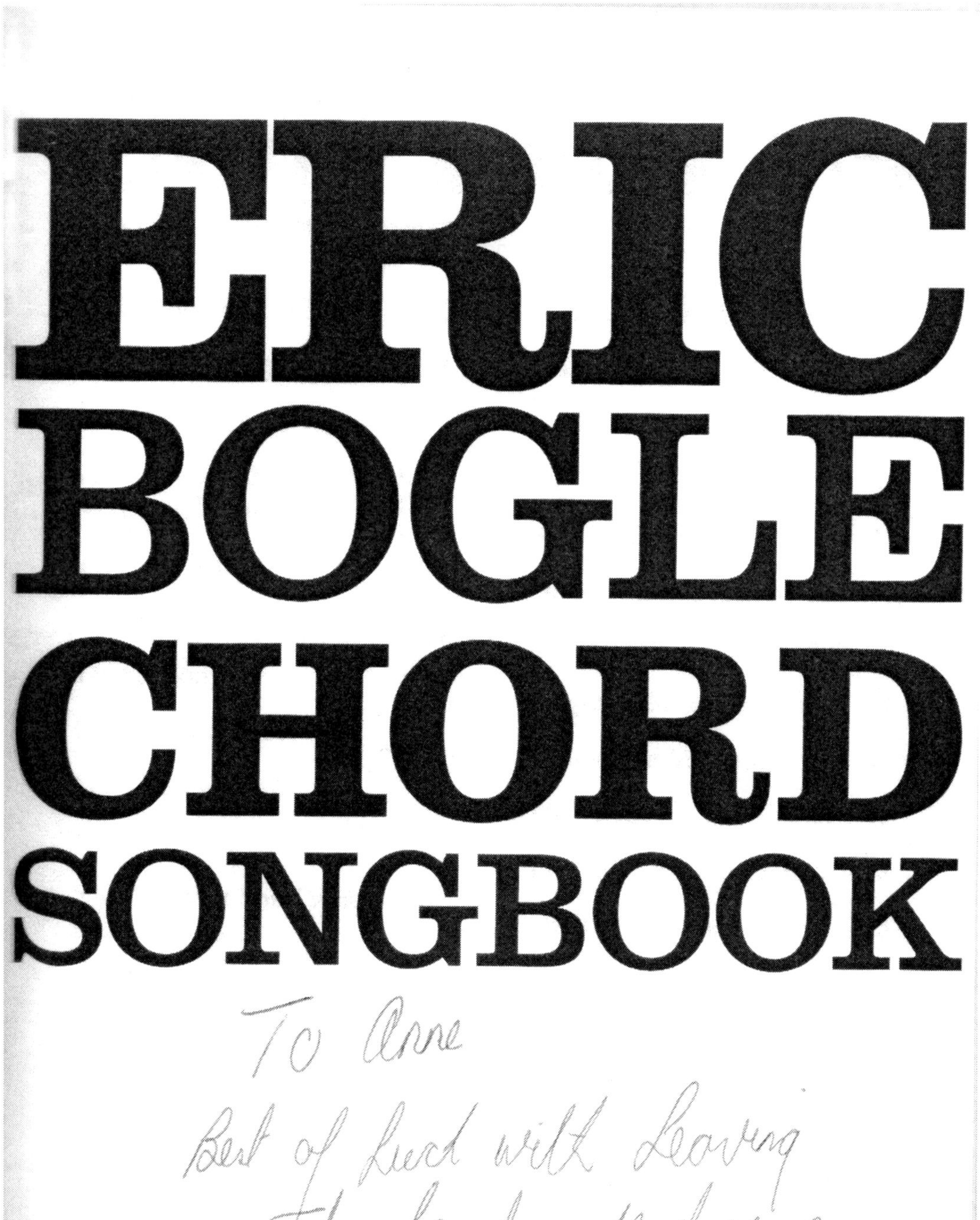

ERIC
BOGLE
CHORD
SONGBOOK

To Anne
Best of luck with Leaving
The Land - send me a
copy. Eric Bogle

*Eric Bogle approval*

Dear Eric,

In 2006, at Glenfarg Folk Club, you were kind enough to grant me permission to use the title and words of your wonderful song, "Leaving the Land" as the name of the forthcoming account of my parents' lives.
This is now - at last- in the final stages of preparation, and I enclose Chapter 33, which describes the end of my parents' farming life, as they left the land. As promised, I will send you a copy of the full version of the story when it is complete.
Thank you for all the beautiful words and music over the years - your gift to the world! I wish you every success and happiness in your farewell tour and in the future.

Anne Ewing

*Letter to Eric Bogle, 1 June 2009*

*Anne with Eric Bogle, 1 June 2009 at Glenfarg Folk Club*

# Chapter 34

"The wither can dae whit it likes!"

Their decision to retire to Kirkcudbright was arrived at by Joey and Jim almost by default. They were both acutely aware that they couldn't bear to face the thought of living within daily sight or regular knowledge of Pitkinny and its future without them. They had come to like the wee town in the Stewartry during their visits to Margaret and John and the girls, and thought it was the kind of place where they could feel, if not at home entirely to begin with, at least comfortable in their new surroundings. Having some of the family near at hand would also ease the process of adjusting to a completely new way of life. My enthusiasm for their move helped to remove Joey's initial worry about leaving us behind in Fife, as we looked forward to seeing them settled in their new home.

Kirkcudbright was in some respects similar in character to many of the little towns that they had visited in their travels around Scotland. On the estuary of the River Dee, and close to the Solway coast, it had a picturesque but still working fishing harbour, with an agricultural hinterland that made sense to Jim and Joey. The other small towns nearby were attractive: Castle Douglas, Newton Stewart and Gatehouse-of-Fleet, each with their satellite villages and farm settlements, held interest for them; the wee coastal villages like Kippford and Rockcliffe had a charm reminiscent of their many counterparts in the north and west of the country that they had got to know well; while Dumfries was near enough when the amenities of a large town were called for. This corner of Scotland—now known as Dumfries and Galloway—traditionally comprised the counties of Dumfries-shire, Kirkcudbright-shire (or otherwise, the Stewartry), Wigtownshire, and South Ayrshire. It is for many people a forgotten corner of Scotland, but it contains many historic, scenic, and literary gems: the Solway coast at Dundrennan near Kirkcudbright was where Mary, Queen of Scots left her kingdom of Scotland for the last time, while the hills and rivers of the region give rise to landscapes ranging from the dramatic to the couthy, and the life and times of our national poet Rabbie Burns are recorded in the farms and towns of the area. Little did Jim think when he was a young man and learning to sing "Bonnie Gallowa'" that he would one day choose to live in that area of the country and get to know the "Solway's foaming sea," the "darkly rolling Dee" and the "silvery winding Cree" so well.

Kirkcudbright's reputation as an artists' colony was probably lost on Jim and Joey, but what drew painters to the town was surely the same as what made the town an attractive proposition as a retirement destination. Most of all, its location and distance from Pitkinny meant that there was at least a semblance of being protected from constant reminders of the home they had left. To begin with at least, as is probably true for most people when they first retire or first leave a home they have lived in for many years, they felt as if they were on a protracted holiday and. perhaps subconsciously, they expected that some day they would return to their old home and revert to their former lifestyle. For, there was no mistake, the demands of the necessary adjustment they faced were huge, and would take time to make themselves felt and even longer to overcome.

Typically, however, they realised that they just had to get on with it, and little would be gained by bemoaning their situation or talking about it. It wasn't the first time they had to get accustomed to a new bed of their own making, and they had no choice but to lie in it long enough to get used to it! It was only in retrospect that I realised just how hard it must have been for them. As with the leaving of Pitkinny, my genuine relief and gratitude that they had the opportunity to enjoy an easier life, free of the strain and worry of the farm, outweighed any misgivings I might have had, which were pushed to the back of my mind as we anticipated the first of many visits to 6 Mount Pleasant Avenue in the early summer of 1976.

We were all justifiably delighted with their new home, which they suitably decided to name Pitkinny, with the name plate above the door. It was a detached two-storey house in a good-sized garden. The ground floor consisted of a lounge/dining room, a second sitting room, a small bedroom for Grandad Hugh, and a bathroom. The kitchen was spacious and was soon made more so by incorporating into it the small back porch. A breakfast bar was dispensed with in favour of a table and chairs, which made it into a real dining kitchen. Well provided with cupboards and appliances, Joey was very satisfied with her new principal domain. There was a storeroom/workshop at the back of the garage, linked to the kitchen door by a covered, sheltered patio. The dining room, on the other side of the kitchen, had glass doors which opened onto another patio and the back garden, while the open-plan staircase with a large window on the landing gave the hall a bright and airy feel. The front door was slightly recessed and sheltered, a welcome change from the windy exposed back door on to the close at the farm!

Upstairs, Jim and Joey's room was a good size with built-in wardrobes, while the other room was large enough to take three single beds, ideal for Pamela, Alison, and Lynda or (with the addition of a cot) for Donald, Bill, Calum, and me when we visited. The house was well furnished with some items from Pitkinny, such as their bedroom suite, of postwar "utility" provenance, but nevertheless walnut veneered and of a quality which would make modern furniture look flimsy by comparison. In addition they had bought new lounge and dining room suites and carpets, and it gave me great satisfaction that they had the unaccustomed luxury of choosing new things. Having said that, Joey's lifetime habit of "making do and mending" would never leave her, and I am certain that she got no greater pleasure from her new furniture than she had enjoyed from everything she had bid for at Green's sale room all those years before!

As always Jim and Joey did not waste any time in making changes. In addition to the alterations to the kitchen, they had soon added a shower to the upstairs toilet and wash basin, and a large built-in cupboard in the spare room. While these changes indoors were soon accomplished, they were much less dramatic than those planned by Joey and Jim to the external function and appearance of their new home; a transformation that would be a source of interest for their neighbours and would inadvertently (but in the nicest of ways) make them the "talk o' the place!"

It soon became clear to them that they were not alone in choosing Kirkcudbright as a retirement location. Most of their neighbours were of a similar age to themselves, but there were one or two younger families as well. At number eight, their immediate neighbour was a Mrs Van Hagen, a widow. She had lived in the East Indian colonies with her Dutch husband, although she herself was from a wealthy family who had made their money in industry in Manchester and had owned a country estate in the Stewartry. So she was very different from her new neighbours and must have found them something of a culture shock. She had a reputation in the town as a bit of a martinet, and had not made herself popular with the local tradesmen, service providers, and her neighbours in the years since she had moved to Kirkcudbright. However, Jim and Joey, in their usual way, approached their new neighbours (including her) with an open mind. They treated her in the same down-to-earth and friendly way as they did everyone else, and never had any problem with her at all.

Having neighbours of whatever kind was a new experience for them. They found it quite hard to adjust to living in close proximity to other people, compared to the situation at Pitkinny where the nearest habitation were the two cottar hooses a couple of hundred yards away. The house at the back of theirs was occupied by a Mrs Lunn and her daughter and, initially (before the cypress hedge they planted had time to grow and shield them) they were very conscious of their exposure to her kitchen window, which was directly in line with theirs. In the morning as she filled the kettle, Joey could see Mrs Lunn doing exactly the same thing. "Dae ye think I should wave to the woman?" she asked me. "It seems a wee bit stuck-up jist tae ignore her!" I reassured Mum that an acknowledgement of her neighbour in this way was not really necessary. But in many other ways, Joey and Jim never really got used to town living, and in some respects made no concession to the fact that there were other people around. We always noticed this whenever they visited us. After the move to Kirkcudbright, they would often come and stay with us for a few days and take the chance to visit family and friends in Fife. We were used to them arriving home in the early hours and as they got out of the car, they would slam the doors as if they were still at the farm, not surrounded by houses with sleeping residents. We would cringe as they chatted away to each other at the top of their voices as they came up the drive to the house. "Aye, it's a braw nicht, Joey, an' it'll be a guid day the morn," would be followed by Dad's habitual "tum-ti tum-ti tum" tuneless singing. The front door would be closed loudly and their audible conversation would continue as they got ready for bed. Sometimes we would hear them laughing about some amusing (or arguing about some disputed) aspect of their evening out, just as I could remember listening to them as a child, long after we were in bed and should have been sound asleep.

While Joey's daily life did not change that much in many respects, with her typically rigorous attention to her housework, cleaning, and homemaking as she made their new abode as homely and personal as Pitkinny house had been, Jim at first felt rather aimless and ill at ease without the demands of the farm. His work had been his whole life, and he had never developed any hobbies or pastimes. He was never interested in reading, beyond the daily *Courier*, the *Scottish Farmer*, and the *Farmer's Weekly*. He had to make special arrangements to have the Dundee newspaper sent to him by post, an extra expense he was willing to bear, even if it meant that he had to read it a day late. He would have felt bereft if he couldn't keep abreast of the events if Fife; an early morning scrutiny of the "hatches, matches, and dispatches" always had been—and would continue to be—a vital part of his routine. He soon became familiar with his new surroundings as he walked around the district, and, always ready to stop and chat, he began to get to know not only his neighbours but various people in the town.

He infuriated Joey on several occasions when he returned to the house with items that had been left on the kerbside to await collection by the dustmen. He was perplexed that people could throw away what seemed to him to be perfectly good things, like a nearly new suitcase and an occasional table, but Joey made sure that they were promptly recycled on to their bit of pavement and hoped that their original owners did not spot them and wonder how they came to be there! There were days when they luxuriated in the freedom and leisure that their new status as retired folk had conferred on them. Early one morning when Joey commented on the particularly bad weather of heavy rain and strong wind, Jim replied with a heartfelt "The wither can dae whit it likes, we dinnae hae tae gang oot in it, if we dinnae feel like it," and turned over in bed to enjoy a long lie. As a way of keeping his hand in, Jim decided to rent some grass parks in the area, and bought and sold cattle to graze on them. He would go to the market in Castle Douglas and bid for Irish store cattle, and in so doing got to know some of the farming fraternity in the Stewartry. He had also kept the sublet of the Murray Knowes fields and the church glebe grazing (which Geordie West looked after for him), and he would come up from Kirkcudbright regularly to buy and sell cattle at his old haunts. There was also some residual business involved in the final winding up of his deal with the NCB and with his accountants and lawyer in Fife, which made regular visits necessary.

It was in this regard that the first hint of a problem with Grandad Hugh began to surface. Grandad made it clear that he did not want to be left on his own at Kirkcudbright, even for a night or two, although he was quite capable of looking after himself. Indeed, he had been living in his own house in Markinch until very recently. It seemed, however, that he had made his mind up it was time for him to be looked after much more closely now, and it was clear that he expected Joey to attend to his every need. Despite being quite able to help in little ways around the house and garden, he was very reluctant to do anything at all. This was so different from the willing and active participant he had always been at Pitkinny. Even as his physical abilities had begun to wane, he had continued to try to involve himself in some way with what was going on, despite increasing deafness, and it was a shock for us all to see how he had changed, becoming increasingly demanding and querulous. So he would either have to accompany Jim and Joey on visits to Fife, which made accommodation a problem, or stay behind in Kirkcudbright and make his displeasure obvious. The way he always sat in the front of the car with Jim while Joey was relegated to the back seat demonstrated the chauvinistic attitude to women he had always had, (and which was common for his generation). It was this male selfishness that had begun to rankle with Joey and had made her begin to assert herself with Jim in her middle years, and here she was faced with it all over again. Jim had had to learn just how far he could take advantage of Joey's inherent good nature before she would resist his sometimes unreasonable behaviour, but Grandad was oblivious to the way he was affecting his eldest daughter. He had been retired for more than fifteen years, while Joey and Jim were only starting on their retirement, and their freedom of action was already being limited. This affected Joey much more than Jim, of course, as Grandad looked to her for care and attention, and was not equipped to consider her needs or the fact that her health was in many ways more precarious than his, despite the difference in their ages. He would take no responsibility for himself and it was becoming all too obvious that the hasty decision to take Hugh with them when they left Fife may not, in retrospect, have been a wise one.

Although this difficulty did not manifest itself to begin with, I could see that the adjustment to retired life was not going smoothly for Joey and Jim in other ways, when we paid our first visits to them in the early summer of 1976. With no work to get up for, Jim was never in a hurry to rise in the mornings, and never felt like eating right away. At Pitkinny, he had always had a cup of tea and gone out to see the day's work started before coming back in for his porridge, but now he wasn't hungry in time for the midday dinner that he had always insisted on before. Joey had offered to give the three girls their dinner as a change from school lunch, and as Margaret was now sometimes working as a relief district nurse, felt it would help her too. But Jim wasn't ready to eat by the time of their lunch break from the Johnston primary school, and for a time Joey was making two dinners, one for the girls and one for her and Jim and Grandad. It seemed to me that instead of having an easier life, Joey was tied to an even more demanding routine than previously and Jim, of course, was blissfully unaware of this.

He was less than pleased when I pointed it out to him and suggested that he should be more considerate. He was in fact (I now realise) grieving for his old life at Pitkinny, and had not yet found a new purpose to his days. As the weeks passed he began to start his day earlier, and as the novelty of having their Gran and Grandad up the road from school began to wear off and the girls reverted to their old routine of school dinner and time to play with their school friends, the situation began to resolve itself. There were still times, though, when Jim expected Joey to drop everything to fit in with his plans. One day he suggested they go for a run in the car and have lunch out somewhere, but Joey was in the midst of making soup, and said she couldn't go until later. He was none too pleased. "Ye're never oot that bliddy sink, Joey!" "Aye, ye're richt Jim!"came her swift rejoinder, "Ane dae ye kain whit Ah'm gaun tae tell ye? Ah've been in the bliddy sink fur the last thirty-five years, only ye never noticed afore!"

While there were tense and fractious days when Jim's uncertain temper could still boil over and Joey would give as good as she got, as the summer progressed they began to work together with a common purpose. Once the house itself was the way they wanted it, they turned their attention to the garden. While it hadn't been neglected exactly, it was crying out for some tender loving care. Now Jim had never been keen on gardening (too much of a busman's holiday, perhaps), and Joey was the undisputed expert and director of operations. Jim deferred to her in most decisions in that area, but he took a very professional approach and tackled the refurbishment on a grand scale. On the basis of a soil analysis, he ordered huge quantities of topsoil, fertiliser, and lime for a new vegetable garden at the back of the house. This would raise the level of that part of the back garden behind a low retaining wall, while a new lawn was laid on the rest of the back garden, with a green house at the other end. The topsoil was delivered while Jim and Joey were out one day, and they were faced with an enormous pile covering their drive when they returned. So they set to: as Joey filled the wheelbarrows, Jim trundled them round the back and began to spread their precious new soil. After some time, their neighbour Mrs Van Hagen came out to protest to Jim, "Mr Rutherford, do you think you should be allowing your wife to do such rough, heavy work?" "Och, Ah think she'll manage, Mrs Van Hagen," he reassured her. Not satisfied, she then spoke to Joey in much the same terms. "Ah'm only daen whit ah've aye done, Mrs Van Hagen, an' ah'm fair enjoyin' masel!" For the first of many times, her neighbour expressed admiration for Joey's fortitude and love of hard work. "You're a remarkable woman, Mrs Rutherford!" Their backgrounds were at opposite ends of the social spectrum and their lives had followed totally different paths—one a product of a privileged colonial lifestyle where she no doubt had everything done for her, the other the result of a hard young life of social and economic disadvantage, which had led her to have quite left-wing opinions—but there was a mutual respect between the two women. Joey always felt an empathy with the older woman, who had long been a widow with a grown-up family far away, of whom she saw little or nothing. Wealth can be measured in many currencies, and Joey had no doubt which of the two was the richer.

As I have explained, many of the people living around Jim and Joey were recent retirees like them, such as Mr and Mrs McNee at number four, Mr and Mrs Winning at number two, and Mr and Mrs Moore across the road from them. Directly across from number six lived the Smallwood family, a young couple with a wee girl, but they would soon emigrate to Western Australia, and another younger family came in their place with three wee girls, so there was some balance of age and youth in the street. Some of these people had little or no experience of, or had had little opportunity for gardening before. As Jim and Joey's garden developed, with new flower beds and shrubs at the front and side in addition to the transformation at the back, they began to acquire the status of gardening gurus, and given their friendly and approachable demeanour, were soon dispensing advice and encouragement in equal measure to their new neighbours. Even Mrs Van Hagen was not averse to seeking their help when her gardener was unavailable or unequal to the tasks she set him. I heard Jim one day reply to such a request in these terms: "Aye, certainly, Mrs Van Hagen. Ah'll shift that bush fur ye. Jist you tell me whaur ye want it, an' it'll be nae sinner said than din!"

What she or other folk in the street made of his colourful language at times, which must have reverberated over garden hedges and walls, especially when he (and Joey, it has to be said!) gave vent to their occasional volatile reactions to intractable gardening problems, I can only guess, but without exception they got on well with all their new acquaintances, many of whom would soon be counted as friends. They made few if any concessions to the fact that they were no longer living in comparative isolation as they had done at Pitkinny, and refused to change the way they behaved or spoke with their new neighbours, and I think those new acquaintances respected them for their honesty and genuinely liked them for their amiable and easy-going attitudes. The kitchen at number six soon became the scene of occasional get-togethers for fly cups and blethers as Joey's tea or coffee and home baking were once again dispensed in welcome measure. There were no posh coffee mornings or afternoon tea parties, for that was not and never would be their style, but the warmth of the welcome, the good sense of their advice, and their fund of stories, all washed down with liberal doses of their good humour and genuine interest in other people, in a short time had made them new friends.

Interest in and appreciation for their efforts in the garden were not limited to their immediate neighbours, and one day Joey noticed a few strangers looking over the garden wall and writing on clipboards. She told Jim, but by the time he came to the window they had moved on, and they forgot all about them. It was a week or two later that they received a letter informing them that they had been granted the award of the best garden in the town. Their reactions to this unexpected recognition were typically different. Jim was rightly proud and pleased, while Joey was quietly gratified but in no small way embarrassed by the attention. Never one to seek the limelight, she much preferred to get on with things in a private way, and would have been just as content to make do with compliments on her garden from friends and family. Public recognition was not wasted on Jim, however, and he basked in the warmth and light of his fifteen minutes of fame.

He was similarly very proud, of course, when his family enjoyed a degree of public attention. I remember how he had carried around a *Courier* newspaper cutting of a photograph of me when I was entered in the Charities Queen competition at university, while Mum did her best to ignore what (to her way of thinking) was an unpalatable business, and not what I was at university for! As they settled down in retirement, there was a Saturday evening television programme called

*Songs of Scotland* featuring Alastair McDonald and Peter Morrison. With its mixture of Scottish songs, music, and humour, it was a great favourite with all of us, especially Jim and Joey. Some of the songs were recorded in their particular locations, and the parents of the Johnston school were notified that the BBC had requested the participation of some of the children in the filming of Alastair McDonald signing "The Wee Kirkcudbright Centipede." Alison's class accompanied him, dressed up and dancing to represent the antics of the wee creature. The town had often been the location for film and television work, and as usual, everyone was excited by the attention this focussed on the place. Jim was not averse to a bit of limelight, and was determined that he would manage to "accidentally" happen to stray onto the film set and perhaps see himself on the screen. But each time he was getting close to the action, he would be politely but firmly ushered away by one of the film crew, so he had to content himself with waiting to see fleeting glimpses of Alison and her classmates in the finished version of the programme when it was eventually shown, many weeks later, minus a guest appearance by Jimmy Rutherford! In recent years, Bill and I have met Alastair McDonald on the occasions he has appeared at our folk music club. It was lovely to hear that he fondly remembered that time in Kirkcudbright.

Likewise, when Bill came first in the veterans' section of the Kirkcudbright half-marathon in 1986 and 1987, Jim basked in his reflected glory and made a point of alerting everyone to his relationship to one of the winners of the race, particularly as it was a good pretext for a few celebratory drams or even a free drink or two in the Selkirk Arms! Although never a royalist at heart, and not normally all that interested in growing flowers, he also had the nerve to claim a tenuous relationship to Queen Victoria in the matter of some polyanthus plants. His cousin Margaret (the daughter of his Uncle Wull, who had sent the young Jim a copy of "The Howe o' the Mearns" from his home in Yorkshire) had married a man called Bill Thomson. He had started his career as a municipal gardener in Duthie Park in Aberdeen and eventually became head gardener at Osborne House on the Isle of Wight, the former home of the venerable old queen-empress. When he retired from there, he and Margaret made their home in Glenrothes, where he once gave Joey some polyanthus, which he declared had been propagated from plants originally grown during Victoria's reign. She in turn had carefully nurtured their offspring, and was able to give some of their descendents to their new neighbours. "Aye, only the best polyanthus here, ye ken, only the wans wi' a royal pedigree!" Jim would joke.

In fact, much to his—and Joey's—surprise, Jim did begin to develop a real interest in growing and showing wonderful begonia plants. They had magnificent blooms of dinner-plate dimensions in a stunning range of colours. He would lift the corms in the autumn and preserve them all winter in the greenhouse, replanting them early each summer. In addition, he tended his lawns with lavish loving care, and they and his begonias became a focal part of the garden. The vegetables and tomatoes and other salad crops produced in the greenhouse and garden were of the highest quality, many finding their way into the grateful hands of visitors and neighbours alike. We would return from our frequent stays during the summer with our share of the fruits of the labour of our parents, much as we had from Pitkinny, but in those previous days the volume and range of booty emanating from the farm were that much greater. Margaret used to declare that she was sure their neighbours would watch as they returned from trips to the farm and emptied the car. Bags of potatoes, trays of farm-fresh eggs, huge turnips of a size never seen in the shops, were just some examples of the bounty that would emerge from the car, and of course there was that famous occasion when a live pet lamb by the name of Jamie appeared when they lived at Fannich, outside Kirkcudbright, before they moved into the town! Ambulant Sunday lunch, perhaps!

But appreciated by us even more were the many wonderful memories of those happy times, which we cherish to this day. We were lucky that some of those twelve years were blessed with very warm—indeed, hot—summers. The first one in 1976 was especially memorable, and we enjoyed two weeks of unbroken hot sunshine. The evenings were so delightful that we didn't want to go to bed, and one night Dad and Bill were drinking tea on the patio at one in the morning, in a temperature of 22°C! With Margaret and John and the girls as guides, we began to know the joys of the Stewartry and Galloway countryside and shores. During that and subsequent summers, we established a pattern of excursions to increasingly familiar and well-loved places, and no stay with Jim and Joey was complete until we had managed a visit to them all. We spent one glorious hot day on the beach at Sandgreen, but Donald (who was approaching his first birthday) decided he did not like the feeling of the sand on his toes, and was taken off home early by his Gran and Grandad while the rest of us made the most of the sun and the waves, for once without the shivers and blue-tinged skin that usually accompanies sea bathing in Scotland. The Doon, an attractive beach near Kirkcudbright, was a favourite place for a sausage sizzle when Joey's frying pan and some bangers from Haining's the butcher were fried and enjoyed. Other times Joey would take some of her delicious soup and we would light a fire to heat it up. Jim's favourite on these occasions were pies bought from the baker's in Kirkcudbright, and sometimes he would be unable to wait until the picnic was ready before starting on them. There was a nice grassy playground just behind the beach where I remember games of rounders and football.

Sometimes we would be joined for her school holidays by Wendy Mitchell, the daughter of Uncle James and his wife May. Wendy, the same age as Lynda, was their youngest child and only daughter after two sons, Kenneth and Gordon, so she was much loved and always beautifully dressed, with lovely long wavy hair. When she arrived at Kirkcudbright at the start of the holiday, she was like Alice in Wonderland, but when the time came for her to go home, after all the adventures and fun and games with the our nieces and two boys, I always felt that she more closely resembled Huckleberry Finn! Joey would do her best with Wendy's hair before May saw her, saying, "Your Mum won't let you come back, Wendy, when she sees the state of you after your holiday here!" But we knew that Wendy always had the time of her life and enjoyed all the rough and tumble with the five other youngsters. Indeed, they could have been brothers and sisters, as they all shared a definite family resemblance; there was more than one occasion when people assumed that we were the parents of all six! "How lovely to see a big family!" We were quick to put the record straight and claim responsibility for only two of the six!

Carrick Shore was a lovely beach and had the added fascination of a little offshore island that became accessible at low tide, so we once managed to catch the tides right and walked over to the island. Although we knew we had plenty of time to explore the island and still get back safely, it didn't stop us all feeling the thrill of the prospect of perhaps being marooned. Of course we made it back all right, albeit with the water lapping ever deeper around our ankles for the latter part of the return to the mainland. Close to Carrick Shore was the country estate that had once been owned by Mrs Van Hagen's family, whose fortunes had been made in the textile industry in Manchester. We noticed that huge expense must have been lavished on the building of very elaborate stone walls around every part of their land. The most impressive part of this venture was the magnificent "cow palace," a huge and beautifully built and decorated steading to house the dairy premises of the home farm, on a scale and with a degree of substance and comfort for the cattle far exceeding those of the very basic cottages provided for the workers on the estate and the farm! We became aware of other examples of the existence and influence of the gentry in Joey and Jim's new home area, and of the land they owned and the homes they lived in. This was no different from any other part of Scotland. Indeed Jim, during all his young life, and Joey, in the three months she and Jim had lived at Broomfield when they were first married, were subject to the dictates of the Balfours of Balbirnie, who were their landlords.

This situation did not sit easy with Joey as a young woman, nor when she was older. One of the many books she read just after they moved to Kirkcudbright was the autobiography of Gavin Maxwell, naturalist and author of *Ring of Bright Water* and other accounts of his work with wild otters. He had been brought up a son of the laird near Monreith Bay on the Solway coast. We paid a visit there one day and found a memorial to him in the sand dunes, in the shape of a bronze otter. Much as Joey loved his books and admired his expertise as a naturalist, she realised that it was his lifestyle of leisured ease that made his accomplishments possible—this in the same years as she and Jim were working themselves into the ground to make an honest living. So she had mixed feelings when she read the inscription: "The place he loved as a boy and made famous as a man." When one of Jim's cousins, Bella Wilson, by then widowed, came to visit them, she remembered coming to the Stewartry when she was young and employed in service as a housemaid. She accompanied the family she worked for when they "took a house" in Kirkcudbrightshire for the summer. She remembered the name of the house, and Jim and Joey turned detectives to find it. So Bella was able to look on the place she had lived for one of her girlhood summers. She remembered the thrill of being able to travel so far from home, despite the fact that she had to work just as hard there as she normally did in the family's usual residence. So a holiday it was not, but an adventure of a sort it undoubtedly was.

Inland from these beautiful coastal locations were other delights for us to enjoy. The Raiders' Road runs through the Galloway Forest Park, following the course of the Black Water of Dee, the upper reaches of the river where it tumbles over a series of large flat rocks, with deep swimming holes located in the calmer sections. Great times were to be had paddling in the pools and sliding down the natural water chutes, while Joey presided over the cookout or the picnic and Jim—ever distrustful of the delights to be had in or on the water—enjoyed watching the fun and frolics from his deck chair. Glen Gap, also in the Galloway Forest Park, was a favourite place for playing hide-and-seek, and for building dams across the little stream that flowed from the forest under a little bridge and on into the trees again. A game of nonstop cricket was a great success on one of our outings there. On the way home from Glen Gap, the boys always reminded their grandad to go past Bluebell Farm. Despite the picturesque name of the place, it was without doubt the worst farm steading any of us had ever seen. Long before you reached the buildings, both sides of the road were festooned with every type of flotsam and jetsam associated with farming that you could imagine, ranging from old bits of machinery to discarded feed and fertiliser bags, old timber, and straw and hay bales. The concentration of rubbish and junk gradually increased as you neared the farm, which itself was in an advanced state of dereliction. The saddest and most worrying aspect to this were the forlorn and dejected-looking beasts that could be seen, knee-deep in mud in the fields and paddocks. This was an affront to Jim and Joey, whose overriding priority had always been the welfare of their animals.

Often, the homeward journey from our various haunts would culminate in a visit to Paterson's café in Kirkcudbright for a delicious cone or slider of their wonderful ice cream. Then we would arrive back at Pitkinny, where the kettle would soon be boiling and cups of tea would appear as Joey began to prepare the meal. Sometimes we would insist on her having a break from cooking, and we would enjoy a fish supper from the local chip shop, another holiday treat which the children always loved. On one occasion we decided to have something more exotic. Kirkcudbright's first Chinese takeaway had recently opened, and we suggested a change from the usual fish and chips. We knew that Jim was very conservative in his culinary tastes, whereas Joey liked to try different things, so we couldn't wait to see their reaction to this new experience. When we returned to the house with our cartons of rice, noodles, and their various sweet-and-sour, chow mein, yong chow, or chop suey dishes, it was to find the table set with the usual toast, butter and jam, homemade scones, and cakes that would usually accompany a fish tea! As expected, Joey enthusiastically tried most of the dishes, while Jim gingerly tried only one or two before saying, "Aye, they mak guid gravy." This was his only grudging admission that Oriental cuisine had anything at all to recommend it, but he quickly added that despite this, he would in future stick to his tried and tested preference for a fish supper, as he thankfully filled up on the more familiar toast, scones, and cakes.

So, many happy days in our Easter or summer holidays were passed in this way in the first phase of Joey and Jim's retirement, and the recall of those halcyon days is firmly etched in our memories. These were the years of childhood for our boys and their cousins, and we know how much pleasure they all gave to their grandparents as they grew up. They now had the time and the leisure to enjoy those wonderful times with their family, and the experience of those years soothed the ache they must have felt for their old life. On one occasion when we were all together playing on the grass at the Doon, Joey noticed an elderly lady who stopped to watch us as she walked with her dog. They began to chat, and Joey soon surmised that the old lady was very well off and well educated, as she commented on how lovely it was to see three generations of a family spending time together. She confided that she and her husband had always taken their children abroad and wanted them to see as much of the rest of the world as they could show them. But now she was a widow and her children and grandchildren were all living far away, in Australia, South Africa, and America. As with Mrs Van Hagen, Joey felt that though these ladies may have been very well off in one way, they were infinitely poorer than she was in the things that really matter.

## Bonnie Gallowa'

Wha but lo'es the bonnie hills
Wha but lo'es the shining rills
Aye for thee my bosom fills,
Bonnie Gallowa'.

Wha 'mang Scotia's chiefs can shine,
Heroes o' the Douglas line,
Maxwells, Gordons, a' are thine,
Bonnie Gallowa'.

Land o' birk and rowan tree,
Land o' fell and forest free,
Land that's aye sae dear tae me,
Bonnie Gallowa'.

Traditional

G. Garden Davidson, A.R.I.A.S.
Registered Architect
Telephone No: 241

22 Castle Street,
Kirkcudbright DG6 4GA.

Messrs. Williamson and Henry,
Solicitors,
13, St. Mary Street,
Kirkcudbright.

10th. July, 1975.

Dear Sirs,

Mr. and Mrs. I.A. Howie.
6, Mount Pleasant Avenue,
Kirkcudbright.

As instructed by your letter of the 30th. ult. I have made a survey of the above property and am able to advise you on it's accommodation, condition etc. and value as follows viz :-

Accommodation.

| Ground Floor. | Ceiling height - 2440mm.(8'-0"). |
|---|---|
| Entrance Vestibule. | Tiled floor. |
| Hall & Staircase. | Storage cupboard. |
| Sitting Room. | Tiled fireplace. |
| Dinning Annexe. | Glass door to rear exterior. Hatch to kitchen. |
| Bedroom. (west). | Built-in wardrobe. |
| Bedroom. (east). | Built-in wardrobe. |
| Bathroom. | W.C., Wash basin, Bath with shower attachment. |
| Kitchen. | Stainless steel sink unit, Floor and wall units. Electric cooker. Breakfast bench. |
| Back Porch. | |
| Garage. (attached). | Concrete floor. Up and over door. |
| Boiler Room. (off garage). | Concrete floor. Danesmore heating boiler. Oil storage tank. (600 gal. capacity). |
| First Floor. | Ceiling height - 2300mm.(7'-6"). |
| Staircase and Landing. | Cupboard. Linen cupboard containing calorifier and cold water header tank. |
| Bedroom. | Built-in wardrobe. |
| Bedroom. | Built-in fitting having centre dressing table with flanking wardrobes. |
| Lavatory. | W.C. and wash basin. |

Construction.

The house is built in cavity walling with inner leaf probably in insulation blocks. The outer surfaces of walls are finished in

*Description of the new house at 6 Mount Pleasant Avenue, Kirkcudbright (Page 1)*

G. GARDEN DAVIDSON, A.R.I.A.S.
REGISTERED ARCHITECT
Telephone No: 241

22 Castle Street,
Kirkcudbright, DG6 46A.

10th. July, 1975.

Page 2.

Continued.

roughcast while the inner surfaces are in normal plaster work. The floors are of timber except where otherwise stated. The doors are flush panelled and the windows are picture type having casement opening parts. The roof of garage is of corrugated asbestos.

Services.

The cold water supply is from the Water Boards' mains and the drains which are satisfactory are connected to the Burgh sewage system. The electrical installation is fed from the Electricity Boards' grid supply and the lighting, switch and 13 amp. plug points are according to regulation. Space heating is by small bore piping with radiators throught. The oil fed boiler caters for both space heating and domestic hot water which is run to all the appropriate sanitary fittings.

Condition.

The house which is of recent construction, probably around three old is in first class condition both inside and out and there are no visible signs of dry rot or woodworm.

General.

The house is situated in a private housing development on the northern outskirts of Kirkcudbright with front and back garden having clothes drying area. It stands in approximately one sixth of an acre and has a western exposure.

Value.

From my inspection I would assess the present day value of the subjects as they stand at say :-

£ 16.300.00.

Yours faithfully,

G Garden Davidson

*Description of the new house (Page 2)*

WILLIAMSON & HENRY,
SOLICITORS.
ALEX. HENRY.
W. D. HENRY, LL.B., N.P.
TELEPHONE Nº 692.

13 St. Mary Street,
Kirkcudbright.
DG6 4AB

ACH/SMG

4th June 1975

James Rutherfurd, Esq.,
Pitkinnie Farm,
CARDONDEN, Fife.

Dear Mr. Rutherfurd,

Mr. & Mrs. I.A. Howie
Subjects: Allanbank, 6 Mount Pleasant Avenue,
Kirkcudbright

We understand from both your daughter,and from Mr. & Mrs. Howie, that you have arranged to purchase the above subjects at the price of £15,000.00.

In that connection, we confirm that we are preparing a form of offer for signature by you, and shall forward same to you in early course. We understand that various carpets, etc., are included in the purchase price. Inaddition, we understand that you are interested in acquiring the lounge and dining room carpet, the electric log-effect fire in the lounge, and the dining room curtains. Mr. and Mrs. Howie have placed a value of £200.00 on those items, and we shall be pleased to learn if that value is acceptable to you.

With regard to the whole purchase price, Mr. and Mrs. Howie have expressed the view that they would prefer if the purchase price could be split in the proportion of £14,500 for the heritable subjects, and £500 for the various items which are included in the sale. We shall be pleased to learn if you are agreeable to that proposal.

Yours faithfully,

Williamson & Henry

*Letter about Jim and Joey's offer to buy the house*

No. 74

CASH ACCOUNT

between

MR. and MRS. JAMES RUTHERFORD, Pitkinny Farm, Cardenden, Fife.

and

MESSRS. WILLIAMSON & HENRY, Solicitors, 13 St. Mary Street, Kirkcudbright,

re

Purchase of 6 Mount Pleasant Avenue, Kirkcudbright.

V.A.T. Reg. No. 263 9270 44

| | | | | | | | | |
|---|---|---|---|---|---|---|---|---|
| 1975. | | | Purchase price of heritable subjects | £14,500.00 | | | | |
| | | | Purchase price of various fittings | £ 500.00 | | | | |
| | | | Purchase price of electric fire, lounge and dining room carpets and dining room curtains | £ 200.00 | £ 15,200 | 00 | | |
| | July | 14 | To G. Garden Davidson, Architect, Kirkcudbright, fee for survey | | £ 10 | 00 | | |
| | | | To Keeper of the Registers of Scotland, recording dues on Disposition in your favour | | £ 18 | 75 | | |
| | | | To Williamson & Henry, fees, taking your instructions, preparing offer and going over same with you, and completing Missives, examining title deeds and advising thereon, drafting Disposition in your favour, engrossing same and having same executed, and finalising transaction, | £ 160.00 | | | | |
| | | | restricted to | £ 120.00 | | | | |
| | | | posts and incidents | £ 3.00 | | | | |
| | | | | £ 123.00 | | | | |
| | | | V.A.T. thereon @ 8% | £ 9.84 | £ 132 | 84 | | |
| | | | By balance due by you | | | | £ 15361 | 59 |
| | | | | | £ 15361 | 59 | £ 15361 | 59 |

*Cash account from solicitors*

6 MOUNT PLEASANT AVENUE
KIRKCUDBRIGHT

5th Sept 1979.

ALAN. W. COWIE, M.A. LL.B.
Secratary & Clark.

PARISH OF AUCHTERDERRAN
GLEBE RENT REVISAL,

Dear Sir.
With reference to your letter of the 20th July 1979. and our telephone coversation regarding Rent of above. I here by agree to pay the Rent of Two Handred & Fifty Pounds (£250) per annum

I am Yours Sincerly
Jas Rutherford.

*Letter from Jim agreeing to rent the glebe*

# The Church of Scotland General Trustees

SECRETARY'S DEPARTMENT

ALAN W. COWE, M.A., LL.B.,
*Secretary and Clerk*

Telegraphic Address "Teinds, Edinburgh"
Telephone: 031-225 5722
Extn. No: 50

121 George Street,
Edinburgh.
EH2 4YR.

10th September 1979

JT/DN

James Rutherford Esq
6 Mount Pleasant Avenue
Kirkcudbright

Dear Mr Rutherford

Parish of Auchterderran
Glebe - Rent Revisal

Thank you for your letter of 5th September confirming your agreement to the new Rent being £250 per annum with effect from after Martinmas 1979. This is inclusive of the Shooting Rights. I have conveyed the appropriate instructions to my Treasurer and on behalf of the General Trustees wish to thank you for your co-operation in this matter.

Yours sincerely

If telephoning or calling, please ask for Mr Tudhope

*Reply from Church of Scotland*

*Joey and Jim's new house at 6 Mount Pleasant Avenue, Kirkcudbright. L to R: Jim, Joey, Calum, Anne, and Donald*

*Back garden, L to R: Bill, Joey, Jim, Anne, Donald, and Calum*

*Margaret and John's new house at 22 Mount Pleasant Avenue*

*L to R: Margaret, Donald, Lynda, Pamela, Anne, Alison, Calum, and Joey*

*Jim and Joey at the Doon (Donald in the background)*

*Paddling at the Doon, Easter 1981. L to R: Calum, Lynda, Bill, Wendy Mitchell, Donald*

*Making a dam at Glen Gap. L to R: Calum, Lynda, and Joey*

*Carrick Shore: heading for the island! L to R: Donald, Wendy, Lynda, Anne, Calum, and Joey*

*Twa fermers at Monreith Bay, 1982*

*Calum and Donald with Gavin Maxwell's otter*

*At Monreith Bay. L to R: Jim, Calum, Anne, Joey, Donald, and Bill*

*At Laurieston forest, 1983*

*Raiders' Road: paddling in the "darkly rolling Dee"*

*Natural water flumes on the Dee (Calum and Bill)*

*On the island at Carrickshore Summer 1984*

*Time for tea in the kitchen at Pitkinny, Mark 2*

*Carrick Shore in winter, February 1985*

*Another otter (in a bunnet!) at the Raiders' Road, August 1985*

*Bill's first veterans' win at the Kirkcudbright Half Marathon, May 1986*

*Bill's second win in May 1987. L to R: Bill, Joey, Jim, Jock Paterson (sponsor of the trophy), Anne, Aunt Ellen, Donald, and Uncle Hughie*

*Celebration drinks on the patio following the 1987 Half Marathon*

*Jim in the vegetable garden at Kirkcudbright*

*Part of the prize-winning garden at Kirkcudbright*

# Chapter 35

"Aye, but ye get a second chance wi' yer grandbairns!"

While we all had wonderful times with Joey and Jim in Kirkcudbright, it became clear, with hindsight, that it wasn't all fun and games for them when they were on their own. In between the high days and holidays, when they enjoyed our visits or their excursions up to Fife, they had to work hard to build a day-to-day life in their new surroundings, and I know there were times when Joey felt lonely and longed for her old life, and when Jim missed the old routines and challenges that went with running the farm. But as the months and years passed, they began to feel more and more at home, and some of the people they got to know would become friends in time. Others, whom they were on good terms with (like Mrs Van Hagen), were people whose lives until that point had been entirely different from theirs, either because of the vagaries of social class, or of economic and geographical disparity in their working lives. Other immediate neighbours, like Mr and Mrs McNee or Mr and Mrs Moore, had spent their lives in urban and business environments. They became friendly, however, with one particular couple whose lives had followed a pattern quite similar to their own. Although some years older than Jim and Joey, Mr and Mrs Watson had worked on farms in the Stewartry and Ayrshire, and all four spent many happy, couthy times together, sharing experiences and stories of their younger, harder, but in many ways happier, years as they had all wrought their living from the land. Sadly, Mrs Watson died quite suddenly, and thereafter Joey would often ask the old man to have a meal with her and Jim. He was lost and sad on his own, but his homespun philosophy and happy memories sustained him until he too died. Joey remembered how he described the time their only son left home to join the army and he felt that it was his duty to offer him some advice. The only thing that he could think of to say to the young man was, "Aye mind, son, that ye had a guid mither!" On first hearing, it seemed a strange thing to say, but on further reflection, I could see that those few words embody a world of sense in terms of holding on to the principles we are brought up with, and that we all continue to live by, if we have been fortunate enough to have good parents.

As well as getting to know new people in their retirement, Joey and Jim also became increasingly familiar with, and knowledgeable about, their new location. Initially they would walk together around their immediate area, but as Joey became physically less able to do that, Jim would set out on his own, trusty stick in hand. One day he announced his intention to walk into the town and out again along the opposite bank of the Dee estuary, which they could see from their staircase window. He pointed to a white cottage, and told Joey to watch for him through the binoculars and wave to him when she saw him. She did as she was told, and when she spotted him she waved a white tablecloth from the open window, in the hope that he would be able to see her signal. It occurred to her only later that the neighbours might well have wondered at her strange behaviour, but as always Joey never wasted time on such speculation. She was just pleased that Jim had been able to locate their home from across the river. They made many journeys by car around the Stewartry and into Ayrshire and Galloway, often stopping to have their lunch or to buy some of the fruits of the rich farming region. For a time they used to go to Creetown to buy the delicious bread produced from a little bakery there, and of course they were always on the lookout for the perfect tattie, the Holy Grail that Calum spoke of!

In the course of those first years in Kirkcudbright, the pain of leaving Pitkinny began to recede, and Jim gradually eased himself away from those farming activities that he had clung on to. He gave up leasing grass parks in the Stewartry and in time relinquished the lease on the glebe and Murray Knowes ground back in Cardenden. These represented a responsibility that he realised he could well do without, and he was happy to draw a line under that part of his business, although he was to have one more venture into buying, grazing, and selling cattle in the years ahead. His remaining tenure of the land at Pitkinny (from which coal was still being extracted) would not be relinquished until much later, but it did not involve him in any responsibility or involvement beyond accepting his yearly compensation cheque. According to his agreement with the Coal Board this was index-linked and, as such, without doubt helped to make their retirement that much more comfortable. Joey and Jim continued to develop their garden in Kirkcudbright, and went on to win the award for the best garden in the town two more times. They enjoyed having the company of their three granddaughters on a daily basis, and their proximity to Margaret and John and the girls undoubtedly helped to ease their way as they settled into their new life. There was only one family problem that gave them concern, and that was the increasingly difficult worry about Grandad Hugh.

The first summer at Kirkcudbright was extremely hot, one of the best summers we could remember. Grandad refused to make any concessions to the heat in terms of his clothing, and would sit on his chair (the same one that had seen service on board the *Mauritania*) at the back door dressed in his customary cavalry twill trousers (under which he had his long johns!), a vyella shirt, tie, cardigan, sports jacket, the whole outfit topped off by his bunnet! No amount of persuasion would get him to divest himself of some of his clothes, and looking at him made us all feel hotter than ever. He began to complain of feeling unwell, and in due course the doctor was called. Dr Malone immediately diagnosed dehydration and prescribed only one thing: water—and lots of it! He ordered Hugh to fill a large jug with cool water, add a pinch of salt and sugar, and drink it steadily until it was finished, when he should refill the jug and repeat the treatment until he began to feel better. He also suggested it might be a good idea to wear cooler clothes, given the high temperature. "All right, Doctor!" said Hugh in his usual patrician manner. When he added, "Joey and the girls will see to that," Doctor Malone quickly replied in no uncertain terms, "No, Mr Mitchell, you are perfectly able to see to that yourself, and if you don't, I'll have you admitted to hospital where you'll be put on a drip!" Hugh was not at all pleased to be spoken to like that, and was thereafter very downcast each time Joey reminded him to fill the jug and take his medicine!

This was one symptom of Hugh's determination not to contribute to his own welfare: expecting Joey to see to his every need. The following year, Jim and Joey decided they would like to have a short holiday up north, but the problem of course was what to do with Grandad. It was suggested that he could have respite care in one of the retirement homes in Fife while they were away, and arrangements were made for him to go into South Parks Home in Glenrothes for the time Joey and Jim would be away. He was not very happy with this but accepted the situation. We visited him there, and he seemed to be quite content as he had met a number of elderly people he had known in Markinch whose company he was enjoying. However, when Joey and Jim arrived to pick him up they were astounded to learn that he had requested, and had been allocated, a permanent place in the home. It appeared that he had been visited a few times by his granddaughter Eunice, whom he had helped to bring up, and she had encouraged him to stay on in Fife. She had not been happy when he had decided to move with Jim and Joey to Kirkcudbright because for a long time she had had nothing to do with the rest of the family.

The die was cast; although Joey was upset initially, she had to agree with the rest of us that it was for the best. And to be fair to Hugh, he held no grudge against Joey or Jim. They would always visit him when they came up to Fife, and between times we would go to see him with the children. We never met Eunice, who had exerted an undue influence on the old man at a time when he was probably feeling rather fragile and abandoned, but from then on she was listed as his next of kin and had ultimate responsibility for his well-being. It made sense inasmuch as she was living locally, and it liberated Joey from what had become a burden of care that she was struggling to fulfil. Although Joey continued to feel a degree of guilt that she might have let her father down, she and Jim certainly appreciated the added freedom they now had. They could come and go without the constant worry about Hugh. After all, he had already enjoyed nearly twenty years of retirement, while Jim and Joey were only starting theirs. As it turned out, Grandad was to live for only one more year, and in 1978 he had a recurrence of the cancer he had had eight years before. He was told that he was to have radiotherapy for a tumour, but the next day he suffered a heart attack and died quickly and peacefully in Victoria Hospital in Kirkcaldy. Inevitably, Joey and Jim felt some regret that he had not stayed on with them, but no one could foretell the future, and we reassured them that they had nothing to reproach themselves about. So they became the oldest generation in the family, and we were ever more grateful that they had by then established themselves in their new surroundings and were increasingly contented there.

Margaret's three girls were a great joy to Jim and Joey, and they spent a lot of time with them. Sometimes they would stay the night if Margaret and John were going out. On a Saturday evening, the Scottish country dance music programme was on the radio, and as the girls were learning some of the steps and dances at school, so the settee and chairs would be pushed back and the girls and their Gran and Grandad would "pas-de-bas" and "skip change of step" around the lounge. Having lived at the farm all those years, Jim and Joey were not in the habit of drawing the blinds and curtains, and now they were not really overlooked, their house being slightly higher than those on the other side of Mount Pleasant Avenue. Nevertheless, their neighbours across the road must have noticed something going on. It was only when Mrs Woodburn said one day to Joey, "I hope you don't mind me asking, Mrs Rutherford, but what do you and the family do every Saturday evening?" She was delighted to hear about the dancing, and as she and her husband Wyllie had three daughters too, Joey recommended that they follow suit!

So it came as something of a shock when Joey and Jim learned that Margaret, John, and the girls would have to leave Kirkcudbright. John worked for the South of Scotland Electricity Board at the power station at Tongland, part of the Galloway Hydro Scheme on the River Dee. Plans were afoot to automate the stations and his job might well cease to exist, so he knew he had to make a move before that happened. He secured a job at the National Grid Control centre at Kirkintilloch, and they found a house in Falkirk. They moved in 1979, very much with mixed feelings, of course, as they had lived in Kirkcudbright for some years. It meant new schools for the girls and a complete change of scene, from the couthy peace of the small town in the Stewartry to the bigger, busier town of Falkirk. They had actually lived there before in the late sixties, so they were familiar with the town, but it was still a wrench to make the move. Of course, Jim and Joey missed them all dreadfully, but never ones to complain, they made the best of things, and fortunately they had already made their own friends and had established a good life for themselves since they retired. They would still see a lot of the girls in their school holidays, and they would visit them often, but it must have been hard for them initially, every time they passed Margaret and John's old house, knowing that strangers now lived there.

Shortly before this, a new family had come to live near Margaret and John: Mary and Jimmy Dewar and their children Gary and Corinne. They moved from Lochgelly, so they had quite a lot in common with Joey and Jim and Margaret and John. Jimmy also worked at the power station, and Mary was in due course to find a job as a school secretary at Kirkcudbright Academy. They soon became good friends, and when Mary lost her mother shortly afterwards, Joey became something of a mother figure to her. Then their son Gary became very ill with a suspected brain tumour, but after a desperately worrying time, it happily turned out that he had been wrongly diagnosed, and he gradually made a full recovery. They were to be a good practical support to Joey and Jim and were able in a small way to make up for them missing Margaret, John, and the girls living just up the road.

They continued to have regular visits to Falkirk and Cairneyhill, where they would stay with Margaret and me and our families and take the opportunity to visit their many friends and relatives in Fife. Most of these folk visited them in Kirkcudbright from time to time, and there was nothing they liked better than to welcome them to their home. As always, Joey would happily cater for any number of guests whether she had warning or not, and they loved showing their friends around their new neck of the woods. Many of their friends and relatives had never been in that part of Scotland, and they all came to like it just as much as Jim and Joey did. They would tour around their favourite spots and stop for lunches or teas when they felt like it, although it was never a chore for Joey to feed and look after her visitors. They were delighted to have a visit from their dear old friends from Orkney, Mina and Tom Sclater. It so happened that a retired bank manager who had once worked in one of the branches in Kirkwall lived not far from Jim and Joey, and they told Tom where he lived. That evening, the former bank manager noticed a tall man walking down the road just outside his house, and said to himself, "If I didn't know that Tom Sclater lives in Orkney, I would swear that is him!" He couldn't believe his eyes when the tall man turned into his garden path, and he saw that he was indeed that very man.

A postscript to Joey and Jim's friendship with the Sclaters came as recently as 2008 when Bill and I went on an organised tour of Orkney, his first ever visit and my second. Although some years had passed since we had heard of the deaths of Tom and Mina, I felt an urge to make some kind of contact with their family. Our tour guide knew their youngest son, Bob, who had recently retired as a councillor and chairman of the local tourist board, and she contacted him on our behalf. He was kind enough to pick us up and take us to the cemetery that overlooks Scapa Flow, where his parents are buried. I laid some flowers as a token of the long friendship they had enjoyed with my parents, and of the happy memories I had of the times we had met them. As we left the little graveyard and met Bob's wife Anna at his home for a wee dram of Scapa whisky, it was with a sense of a circle closed, and recognition of a long friendship shared by our respective families.

Bill and I and our boys have so many happy memories of times shared in Kirkcudbright with other friends and family too. Donald remembers the time he and Calum were with Gran in the kitchen as she prepared dinner for some newly arrived unexpected guests. She had cooked a lovely steak pie, but as she lifted it out of the oven it slipped from her hands and landed upside down on the floor. Quick as a flash, she retrieved it even before any of the gravy could escape. Donald and Calum looked aghast at her as she quickly said, "I didnae see onythin' wrang the noo. Did you boys?" "Not a thing, Gran!" they agreed, and she blithely continued to serve up the meal. The boys shared a fit of the giggles with their Gran as everyone heartily tucked into the delicious steak pie. "What the eye doesn't see…"! Joey loved having her family around her, and nothing was too much trouble for her where they were concerned. They would enjoy all their favourite things, like her homemade ice cream, French toast, her wonderful mince and doughballs, and her even more scrumptious haddock in batter and homemade chips. The highlight, though, had to be her fantastic Sunday morning breakfasts, complete with freshly made girdle scones (even more delicious when fried in the bacon fat!). Calum would say, as he tucked into bacon, eggs, sausages, mushrooms, and fried scone, "We haven't had a breakfast like this since the last time we were here, Gran!" And he was right! Such a treat is now looked on as unhealthy, but our occasional enjoyment of it was complete and made Joey the happiest of grannies.

After all, for her generation of women, to feed her family was to show her love for them. In many other ways Joey was generous, especially in giving her time, and she was always very tolerant of children's messes around the house and garden and loved watching the wee ones enjoying themselves. She would often set out a big jigsaw puzzle at the dining room table, and everyone would get involved. She had endless patience with children or with tiresome and tedious jobs and was never too busy to put the kettle on and enjoy a blether with whoever happened to be around, or to drop in. She and Jim looked after our boys in 1978 when they were four and two years old respectively, as we went on holiday to Sweden. One night Calum and Donald were having highjinks after they had been put to bed, and as their bedroom was immediately above the sitting room, their Gran and Grandad could hear them leaping from bed to bed and generally "gettin' their horns oot." Joey showed great forbearance for her grandchildren, much more than she had had for us when we were naughty, but when she had to go upstairs for the third time and tell them that they really should be going to sleep now, she spoke to them more sharply than usual. As she started down the stairs she could hear Donald start to cry and Calum say, "Don't cry Donald, Mum and Dad will be home tomorrow and Gran is just a silly old woman." "What was that, Calum?" Joey called out. Caught out being cheeky, Calum, no doubt shamefaced, replied sweetly, "Nothing Gran. Good night, see you in the morning!" It speaks volumes about Joey's good nature that she continued on her way downstairs with a chuckle, and both she and Jim had a laugh as she related the story and Jim said he was in complete agreement with Calum! "Out of the mouths of babes and sucklings…"

Although very gregarious and sociable with people she knew, one thing Joey had always hated was finding herself in a big group of women. She had never been a joiner of organisations, and had for years studiously avoided the Women's Guild at the church or the WRI ("the Rural" as it was known in Fife). However, when she arrived in Kirckcudbright she was persuaded, against her better judgement, that it would be a good way to get to know people, so she reluctantly attended the meetings for a couple of winters. But she confided in me that she really hated the entire scenario, and the worst thing of all was when it was her turn to help provide the home baking for the tea that was an integral part of the meeting. Although she was a good baker, she never went in for really fancy cakes, and she found that most of the members of the Rural were very competitive when it came to showing off their baking skills. Indeed there were actually baking competitions from time to time, which Joey avoided like the plague. (Auntie Caroline at the Star had always been a great one for these.) Never a good sleeper at the best of times, Joey would lie awake night after night as the dreaded evening approached when she would be "doing the teas." "A lot o'clackin' wimmen, passing judgement on my baking. I cannae bear it!" she said with feeling. "Well don't go, if it worries you that much," I advised. And she never did again!

If Joey was an indulgent granny, Jim was an attentive and involved grandad with all his five grandchildren. I was always so surprised and delighted to see him attending to their needs in a hands-on way that he never had with us when we were young. I pointed this out to him one day and he said, "Aye, but ye get a second chance wi' yer grandbairns!" He would take them anywhere they wanted to go, swing parks or seaside, and could usually be counted on for ice creams, ice lollies, or sweets. He always kept a bunnet on the back window of his car, and Calum and Donald would take turns to wear it. This of course often led to arguments, so he soon bought another one so they could have one each, and we have photographs of them proudly wearing their Grandad's headgear! He managed to find two short walking sticks for them, and they would invariably use them whenever we were out walking with their Gran and Grandad, trying to match him stride for stride. Jim, like Joey, never worried about keeping up appearances, and always acted spontaneously even when others might see his behaviour as somewhat eccentric. Alison certainly felt that one summer's day when she and her sisters were in Johnston Primary School, and one of her classmates said, "Alison, is that your grandad?" When she looked out of the window, there was Jim strolling across the playground, wheeling Donald in his pushchair, singing to him and wearing his slippers! He had decided to take Donald for a wee walk but ended up going further than he intended, so decided they would have a tour of the school grounds.

Jim had always had a singular approach to fashion. In the early days of their marriage, money, of course, was tight and there was certainly little or none to be spent on clothes, but sometimes Jim would have a hankering for some new items in his wardrobe. He once decided he would like a cardigan, so he cut up the front of one of his jumpers and asked Joey if she would hem the edges and make it into a cardigan! Then one day she found him cutting the heels off a pair of shoes because he fancied a pair of wedge-heeled shoes! That first very hot summer of their retirement in 1976 saw his most adventurous fashion foray to date. He came downstairs wearing an improvised pair of shorts: he had cut the legs off an old pair of trousers. Never before, according to Joey, had his lily-white legs seen the light of day, and she tried to persuade him that the sight was too much for us, never mind for public view. She reminded him of the time he had had sunstroke when he divested himself of his shirt while driving grain from the combine at Pitkinny on a hot day. But nothing would deter him from "gettin' the air roond ma legs!" as we had our picnic at the Doon, although he would not, as usual, be persuaded into the water for a paddle. This far and no further! In his later life, Jim became a "sucker for a label," and although he didn't buy many clothes, when he did he bought expensive ones. There was one gents' outfitter's in Castle Douglas that he frequented, and he would occasionally treat himself to some really good quality clothes. A few years before he died, he splashed out on a Crombie overcoat one day when he was in Jenner's in Edinburgh with Margaret. Joey was in another part of the shop, and he cautioned Margaret not to let on what his coat had cost. (It seems to me that it is usually the wife in a marriage who tries to hide the cost of her clothes shopping from her husband, not the other way around!)

Jim's idiosyncratic behaviour got him noticed in Kirkcudbright in other ways too. Joey's cousin and his wife, Jack and Mary Webster, were once staying with Jim and Joey for a few days, and they all went shopping to the supermarket in the town. It was a lovely sunny day and the men opted to wait by the car while Mary and Joey went in to the shop. As she was starting to select what she needed, Joey was suddenly aware that she could hear Jim shouting at the door of the shop. "Wha's dug is this oot here in this Range Rover?" A big man, one of the green-welly brigade, of whom there were many in Kirkcudbright, came striding towards the door. "Would that be my dog you're referring to?" "Oh it's yours, is it?" barked Jim, "Well, ye'd better see whit ye can dae aboot it, because it's just bitten a man!" The dog that had been sitting on the driver's seat had leaned out of the open window and bit a passing man on the arm. Jim was incensed when he saw this offence against natural justice, and determined that the owner of the dog should be called to account. Meanwhile, Joey was doing her best to pretend that she had nothing to do with Jim, as everyone in the shop made their way to the door to see what all the hullabaloo was about! Jim and Jack left "the biter and the bit" to sort out their altercation, and no more was heard about the incident; but a few days later, as Joey followed Jim into the paper shop, she heard a woman passing by say to her companion, "See, there's the man who was doing all the shouting about the dog!"

Jim was always anxious not to knowingly offend anyone. Joey would accuse him of sitting on the fence, waiting to see how the land lay before deciding which way to jump. "Ye must have a great big crease across yer erse, Jim!" she would declare. One day they were working in the front garden when a prospective Conservative candidate in a forthcoming election turned up and started to canvass for their vote. Joey was always much more left-leaning in her political opinions than Jim, so she was horrified when Jim asked him into the house for a cup of tea. But she made the best of things as she poured the tea and offered the man a piece of her homemade sponge cake, but even worse was to come when Jim gave him a subscription for party funds as he left. Joey was furious with Jim and said as much. "Well, Jim, when the red revolution comes, ye'll be the first up against the wa', ye ken." "No, Ah'll no, because the Labour man was here the ither day, an' he got the same!" This was typical of the way Jim hedged his bets, and so different from Joey's very forthright and unequivocal attitude to things.

Joey was always very contented with her lot and seldom aspired to acquire material possessions. So it was surprising to hear her say, "I'd like a dishwasher an' a microwave afore Ah dee!" She managed to realise this ambition in the eighties, and they were suitably fitted into her kitchen. When we saw them for the first time and was admiring them, she said (with a wry grin), "Aye, noo Ah've got them, Ah'm startin' to get a wee bit worried!" Jim had indulged his passion for cars since they retired. The yellow Triumph 2000 was traded in for a BMW, the first of three he would have. He loved them, of course, and his enjoyment of the third one was made all the greater because when he bought it, Calum happened to be staying with his gran and grandad, so he had the thrill of driving in it for the very first time. We have all been lucky enough to have that wonderful sensory experience of the look, smell, and feel of a new car many times, but for Jim I am sure that it always reminded him of his first new Rover, the one that caused Joey such angst as we drove home from Kirkcaldy in it that far-off Saturday many years before.

So the eighties passed, with all of us making frequent visits and enjoying holidays with Joey and Jim in Kirkcudbright. We were all getting older, but obviously the years made most difference to our parents, and Joey's health continued to be a worry as she developed diabetes and continued to suffer great pain and deteriorating mobility due to her spondylosis. As with her heart condition, she refused to give in to these problems, and on the face of things all seemed to be well with them, but looking back now I realise that there must have been lonely times for her and Jim, the kind of loneliness that only close family can remedy. What they missed most was the spontaneous visit, the chance that some of us, or old friends might drop in to see them unexpectedly. It may have been for these reasons that they began to think of returning to Fife, but it was a totally unexpected and traumatic event in November 1986 that would hasten that decision: yet again it was a fire that intervened in their lives, this time to a much more potentially serious extent than the other previous disasters. This time it was not only their livelihood that was threatened, but potentially their lives, health, and well-being.

As explained, Jim had very definite likes and dislikes where his food was concerned, and he loved his fish battered and deep fried, chip-shop style, which Joey did to perfection as we all knew. One day, after they had had haddock for lunch, Joey did not have time to strain the oil after cooking the fish, as she was going to the hairdresser; she left it to cool, intending to see to it later. When she came home, the oil had solidified, so she set it on the cooker to melt. (She was using polyunsaturated oil, and was careful about straining it after each use, for health reasons.) As she waited by the cooker she noticed that Jim was in the workshop, opposite the outside glass back door. He was making a coffee table from the base and castors of an old television table, and she popped out to see how it was coming along. Once there, Jim, never very patient with tedious little jobs, asked her to search through a box of screws for something he needed. This distracted Joey, and of course she forgot about the melting cooking oil. When she turned round a few minutes later, it was to see flames shooting out of the pan and black smoke filling the kitchen. Naturally, she panicked and ran inside, completely forgetting all she knew about the correct procedure for such an emergency. So she did the very thing you are not supposed to do: she carried the flaming pan outside, burning her hands in the process. When she reached the patio, the smoke obscured the fact that Jim was coming towards her. Unable to hold the pan any longer, she dropped it on the ground. Some of the burning oil splashed on Jim's leg and set his trousers on fire!

Fortunately, the garden hose was lying nearby, connected to the outside tap, and Joey had the presence of mind to turn on the water and direct the hose onto his leg. She ordered him to hold it in place as she ran through the house opening all the windows. Of course the smoke had reached every room, as the door from the kitchen into the hall had been open. Afterwards she remarked that her panic had enabled her to run upstairs, a feat that normally would have been impossible for her with her limited mobility, and when she returned downstairs, it was to be confronted by a fireman wearing a breathing apparatus! A neighbour had seen the smoke and called the fire brigade, but by then there was little they could do, other than to arrange for Jim and Joey to be taken to Kirkcudbright Cottage Hospital, where they had their burns dressed. It was obvious that Jim's leg was quite seriously burned, while Joey's hands were more superficially affected, but they refused to stay in hospital and were home again by the evening. Mary and Jimmy Dewar phoned us at teatime to tell us the news; I arranged a few days off work and drove down the next day with Pamela to see what we could do to help.

Both Joey and Jim were in a state of shock when we arrived, and the house significantly smoke-damaged, the lingering smell reminding me of that fire at Pitkinny years before. It was clear that most of the rooms would need to be redecorated, as there was a fine greasy black film on all the surfaces, but that would have to wait until the insurance claim was sorted out. Meanwhile, Pamela and I started to wash all the movable ornaments, and either wash or have cleaned the curtains, soft bedding, and soft furnishings. Even clothes in the wardrobes upstairs had been affected by the smell of the smoke, and we were only able to do some of the work before we had to return home. We were more worried about the emotional impact of the fire on Jim and Joey although, as usual, they tried to make light of it. "I ken yer Mum was bound to want rid o' me often," said Jim, "but Ah never thoct she wid set me on fire!" Dad quipped, but I could see that Mum found it hard to see a funny side to their predicament. She obviously felt awful that she had been the cause of the disaster, and no amount of reassurance would help to assuage her feelings of guilt. Worse was to come when Jim's burned ankle became infected, and he had to be admitted to the burns unit in Dumfries Hospital for a skin graft. This posed many problems for Joey and for us. It meant that Jim would be in hospital over Christmas, but Joey would not hear of us going down to her, as the house was in no fit state for visitors. Anyway, we felt that she could not cope with all the extra work, as she was by then having the redecorating done. As it turned out, heavy snow made the roads treacherous, and she forbade us to risk driving more than necessary.

She herself had had to give up driving after her spinal operation, so visiting Jim in Dumfries posed another problem. However, a retired policeman who lived near them offered to drive Joey to the hospital as often as she needed; she insisted that he use Jim's car and petrol, so that problem was solved to everyone's satisfaction. Nevertheless that was a lonely and worrying Christmas for Joey, and although she had Christmas dinner with Mary and Jimmy Dewar, she did not want to impose herself on them any more than necessary, as they had already been a great help to her. Jim's skin graft was ultimately successful, but it was necessarily a slow process and he was in hospital for quite a few weeks. As he was not really ill, and had to be in a room by himself because of the danger of further infection, he found time dragged, so we managed to arrange for a television to be provided by a TV-rental shop in Dumfries, and through time, Jim managed with his usual charm to make things more comfortable for himself. He soon had the domestic staff making his tea the way he liked it, and his locker became a wee pantry full of his favourite butter and jam, biscuits and sweets, and so on. The patients were spoiled at Christmas, and even a few wee drams were allowed over the festive season. We managed one or two visits to Jim in hospital and to Joey at home as the weather eased, but it was a great relief to everyone (especially to Mum) when Dad was home again at last, and the remedial work on the house was more or less complete. If he had the trauma of the stay in hospital and the operation he went through, she had the worry and strain of coping at home on her own. The entire episode of the fire took its toll on them both, and it was to prove to be the catalyst that would impel them to decide on a return to Fife.

*Joey and Jim in their "glad rags" at a wedding in 1986*

14 Ford View
Cairneyhill
Fife
Mon 5.1.87

Dear Grandad,

I hope you are feeling better and your leg soon heals. Now that you have your television you will be able to amuse yourself. I should have been at school today but I'm not feeling one-hundred percent after my cold. Mum is not at work today either because she has got the same sort of cold as me so it must be spreading. Did you watch the programme Smeddum on Hogmany? It was about a Scottish farmer and Mum said that you used to plough the fields with a horse and plough. Yesterday we took down the Christmas decorations and the house looks really bare. On Monday I will be going to

*Letter from Donald to his grandad in hospital, January 1987 (page 1)*

The Ardroy Outdoor Centre on the west coast with the school where we'll do absieling, mountain walks, river studies, and animal studies so I'm really looking forward to it. I hope your tea is getting a bit stronger, also don't go chatting up the nurses! The weather here was rotten in the morning but it has cleared up and the sun is shining I hope you're soon home with Gran and get the house back to normal Mum and Dad and Calum all are thinking of you and send you their best whishes

Love
Donald
xxx

P.S Hope ye had a wee nip o' yer bottle on Hogmany!!

*Letter from Donald to his grandad in hospital, January 1987 (page 2)*

# Chapter 36

"Ye ken, it's when ye're fechtin' that ye ken ye're still livin'!"

Within months of the fire, Jim and Joey gradually began to seriously consider coming back to live nearer us all, although it was some time later that they told us of their decision. Towards the end of 1987, they found what turned out to be their last home. Markinch was the obvious choice, of course, and they looked there first, but none of the possible houses was suitable. Passing through the village of Cadham to the north of Glenrothes and between Markinch and Leslie, they noticed some newly built bungalows on Cadham Road, just west of the petrol station at the junction. One was still unsold, and they wasted no time in arranging to view it.

The house seemed to satisfy all their requirements, with three bedrooms and a large combined living and dining room. There was a bathroom, a separate shower room, and a kitchen and utility room, so they had almost the same amount of accommodation as they had in Kirkcudbright, but with the benefit of being on only one level. There was an attached garage and a sizeable garden and room for several cars in the drive. On the west side of the house, there was a lane leading to two small fields at the back belonging to the Tullis Russell paper mill, which was situated beyond them to the south. So there was a sense of space and openness, with views from the back garden to Markinch road-end and in the far distance the distinctive outline of the Haig's of Markinch whisky plant. The possible disadvantage of being on a rather busy road was compensated for by the convenience of bus stops nearby, and the substantial front garden wall shielded the house effectively from traffic noise. This was to become important for Jim and Joey, as in time they could use the bus for local trips when Jim became less and less inclined to drive. Also, they would actually come to enjoy seeing a bit of life from their living room window without in any way being overlooked. So after a satisfactory survey on the property, they wasted no time in making an offer on the house, which was quickly accepted; the move was on!

The apparent suddenness of their decision to move and the swift accomplishment of the new house purchase, followed by an equally efficient sale of the house in Kirkcudbright, took many people by surprise, and the date was soon set for them to move in May 1988. By then they had had twelve years of retirement and had adjusted successfully to a life without the demands of running a business and coping with the hard physical work of farming. They had not been idle, however; it was not in their nature to take things easy, and they were constantly self-motivating in many areas of their day-to-day life. Gardening had become their main interest, of course, but in addition they had spent time improving their home. Joey continued to indulge her passion for reading and had started to do crosswords and other puzzles, while Jim liked the television, watching sport and listening to traditional Scottish music. They had got to know the southwest of Scotland well in their years there and loved the landscapes and seashores of that sometimes overlooked corner of the country. They had always enjoyed spending time with other people, and this had not changed when they left Pitkinny; they had made many friends in Kirkcudbright, friends who were genuinely sorry to see them leave the Stewartry. Some of them would visit them in Cadham, just as other long-standing friends from Fife had visited them when they moved to Kirkcudbright from Fife twelve years before.

The actual move back to Fife was not tinged with the same emotional trauma that had attended the earlier move from Pitkinny. Any misgivings they might have felt were assuaged by the knowledge that they were, in a real sense, returning home, to within a few miles of where they had been born and spent their early years. Also, they were moving closer to us and to all their old friends and contacts. It was all hands to the pump for the actual move. Alison and her boyfriend and future husband, David, went down to help Jim and Joey with the preparations for the move. They found that much of it had been accomplished even before they got there, Joey as usual rolling up her sleeves and getting on with the work and organising Jim into the bargain. She was determined that for once he would not dodge the flitting as he had always managed to do before! By the time the removal vans arrived, much of the packing had been done. What surprised the men was that the second van had to accommodate more garden stuff than household contents! Meanwhile, at the Fife end, we had arranged for carpets to be laid and everything cleaned in the new house to be ready for their arrival. Margaret, John, Pamela, Lynda, Bill, and I, with our boys Calum and Donald, were waiting; when the vans arrived, there were plenty of eager and willing helpers on hand. Joey was stationed on a chair in the hall and forbidden to move, and while she directed operations we all unpacked and distributed their goods and chattels around their new home. Jim, on the other hand, confined himself to the garage, where packing boxes and crates full of his tools and garden equipment were deposited, and he began to arrange his own domain. When I went out at one point to ask for a screwdriver or some other tool for something we were doing in the house, he declared that he knew exactly where to find it, saying, "Ah'm shair that thae boxes kid move on their ain, ye ken, they've been shifted roond this garage that of'en the day!"

Within a few short hours most of the unpacking in the house had been done, the curtains were at the windows, and even the framed photographs and pictures were up on the walls. Their new abode already felt like home, so that it seemed as if they had never lived anywhere else! Joey had come prepared on the catering front and had brought with her quantities of "potted heid," homemade mince pie, and home baking; and David's parents, Anne and David Croal, arrived with a celebration dumpling, so that evening the house was well and truly warmed by a settling-in party, where we all relaxed and tucked into a "flitting feast!" That was one of the happiest days that I can remember with Mum and Dad. The atmosphere was really one of homecoming, not just a house move, and as we left Jim and Joey that evening it was with a feeling that they had completed a journey first begun that Saturday night in 1941, when they had stood at the bus stop at the nearby corner, waiting to embark on their honeymoon. Soon after that happy evening in May 1988, the fitting, finishing touch to their new abode was achieved when its nameplate was fixed above the door: PITKINNY.

There were many people who knew nothing of their move until they were already settled into their new home. One example was Joe Petrie, manager of the agricultural equipment firm Bowen's of Markinch. He had done business with Jim over the years, and he and his wife had once visited Joey and Jim in Kirkcudbright while they were on holiday in the area. They had admired their garden and were especially impressed with Jim's begonias, so when he passed the new house in Cadham one afternoon in the early summer of 1988, Joe said to himself, "Well, there are begonias to rival Jimmy Rutherford's in Kirkcudbright!" He could hardly believe his eyes the next time he passed by, when he saw Jim standing in the drive and realised that the lovely flowers were in fact his after all! So it was with many of their acquaintances in the area around Markinch. Indeed, in addition to seeing more of their family and longstanding friends, they were soon to find that they were meeting up with people they had known in their youth for the first time in all the intervening years. Occasionally passersby would stop to chat with Jim and Joey as they worked in the garden, and they would find that they remembered each other or had mutual friends.

This was the case with some of their neighbours also. Their bungalow was directly across from Cadham Square, now a conservation area, whose houses had originally been planned and built as accommodation for workers in the paper mill. Living in one of the nearest of these houses was the Bell family—John, his wife, Madge, and his brother Andrew. Madge's mother, Mrs Dewar, was the sister of a very old friend of Joey's, Madge Haddow from the early days at Bogside when she lived at Capledrae Row, after whom Madge Bell had been named. Joey hadn't seen Madge Haddow for many years since she had moved down to England with her family. In addition, Mrs Dewar had been nanny many years before in England to Alison, the wife of a colleague of mine, Graham Stewart, my first head of department at Auchmuty High School in Glenrothes. This was typical of the many coincidences that led to the renewing of friendships and the establishment of new ones as Jim and Joey happily enjoyed their new situation. So there were many times when the expression, "Isn't it a small world!" was used. In the case of the Bell family, they were to become very good neighbours, and their substantial local knowledge was of great help to Joey and Jim as they settled in. Andrew in particular was one of nature's gentlemen, and we would be greatly in his debt over the last years of our parents' lives; his kindly, generous, and patient personality meant that he could tolerate Jim's uncertain temper. He had worked for Tullis Russell and other businesses and farms in the area, and his and his brother's undoubted skills in gardening and many other areas of work were often put at Jim's disposal. Joey would see to it that they (and in time, Madge, who helped Joey with some house cleaning) were paid for all the help they gave; and in addition to their practical help, they contributed a great deal in terms of friendship and company to Jim and Joey's years at Cadham.

As always, Joey and Jim relished the empty canvas they were presented with in their new home. The main change they made to the interior of the house was to take down the wall dividing the kitchen from the utility room. This made the kitchen bigger to accommodate a new round kitchen table and fridge-freezer. They decided that the back of the kitchen was crying out for a conservatory, so that was another venture which they embarked on. It maximised the benefit of the open outlook they had at the back of the house, but Jim wasn't long in realising that if the two unused little fields between them and the paper mill were attractive to them, they would be equally so to others, so he embarked on a spoiling operation to prevent them falling into the wrong hands. He could picture what would happen if the fields were let out to the Pony Club or some other horsey organisation. His and Joey's inherent dislike of the "green welly brigade" led them to foresee a situation where the lane beside them would be filled with horse boxes and Range Rovers every weekend. The solution was for Jim to rent the fields from Tullis Russell, and he wasted no time in buying some young beasts, so for the last time in their lives, they could look out the window and see their own livestock grazing. In time, as Jim felt less inclined to have the responsibility of livestock, he would arrange for Mr Paul (the dairyman who supplied their milk) to graze some of his beasts there, but the effect was the same, and so the fields were denied to the equestrian fraternity!

Within their first year at Cadham, much had been achieved by Joey and Jim. Flower beds and lawns were established in the front, side, and back gardens. The conservatory was in place and a greenhouse erected, with a small vegetable plot between it and the back garden wall. Between the greenhouse and the garage there was space for a garden shed with double doors facing west, which they kitted out as a summer house with curtains at the windows and vinyl flooring, shelving for the begonias in winter, and space for other gardening jobs and storage. While Jim and Joey cut back on their vegetable growing, they had enough space for leeks, brussels sprouts, and onion sets, and of course their tomatoes and other salad crops in the greenhouse. "Ye ken, Joey, there's ither folk tryin' tae mak their livin' sellin' timaities!" Jim would say, as it made less and less economic sense to grow your own. Even Joey had to admit that she and Jim were "gettin' on" and slowing down, but she still loved to be able to make her wonderful homemade soup with vegetables they had produced themselves. In later years Jim would declare, "When we cam tae Cadham, Ah kid dae onything!" He was seventy-one and Joey in her seventy-third year, and their achievement during those first years back in Fife would have put many younger folk to shame. I recall one Thursday during the school holidays when I decided to accompany them on their weekly supermarket shopping in Kirkcaldy. I arrived at 1130 a.m. to find them putting away their groceries! They had already been to Kirkcaldy, and that was after they had done their errands at their local shops at Cadham earlier in the morning. Joey had even peeled the tatties, and their twelve o'clock dinner was underway. When I expressed admiration at their efficiency, Jim's reply was, "There's nae hunkerslidin' here, ye ken. Efter a', yer mither's a tough gaffer!" This was around the same time as he made a similar comment when I found him painting the fence and compared him to Tom Sawyer. "Well, Ah never met the chap, but Ah bet ye he didnae hae a boss like yer mither!"

While Jim liked to make out that Joey was a hard taskmaster and, I suspect, left to his own devices would have indulged a desire to be more lackadaisical than she was, he took as much pride in their home and garden as she did; they made a great team. Of course, they would often fall out over some disagreement, being fundamentally very different characters, but what united them was the drive they always shared to enhance and improve their bit of the earth. Prudent stewardship of the land and good husbandry in their methods ensured that they would always struggle to achieve that objective, and it would only be in the last months of her life that physical weakness would eventually put an end to Joey's valiant efforts to tend her home and garden. After she died, Jim lost heart, and his emotional frailty accelerated his physical decline. But all that sadness still lay in the future, as the first few years in Cadham saw them make their unique mark on their last home together.

They continued to derive great pleasure from their grandchildren and were justifiably proud of them all as they grew up. As Pamela, Alison, and Lynda, and later Calum and Donald, passed their driving tests, Jim was only too happy to pay high premiums to add them to his car insurance and loved to have them drive him in his BMW. Driving gave him less and less enjoyment as roads became ever more congested, and he much preferred to be a passenger. He would sometimes use the bus for local journeys, and while he and Joey appreciated, as pensioners, the benefits of free public transport, he couldn't understand how it was possible for the bus companies to survive:

"Ye ken, there's hardly ony bugger peys their fare on thae buses. It's a gey funny wye tae run a business!"

They had the delight of attending all three of their granddaughters' weddings: Pamela to Paul McVey in 1988, Alison to David Croal in 1990, and Lynda to Scott McPherson in 1991, and of seeing them all successful in their chosen careers in teaching, nursing, and banking respectively. They saw Calum and Donald graduate from university, Calum embark on his first post in Hong Kong, and Donald on the first of his post-graduate courses of study. Both Jim and Joey were gratified that all five of their much-loved grandchildren fulfilled their potential and enjoyed the kind of opportunities that were undreamt of when they were young. As Calum set out on his gap year in Mississippi when he was seventeen, his grandad said to him, "Well, Calum, Ah cannae believe that ye're gaun tae be in America afore ye're aichteen. Ye ken, ah was aichteen afore Ah wis in Kirkcaldy!" Joey was always more anxious about the welfare of her young folk as they ventured far from home and would counsel them, "Noo aye mind, ye're Calum Ewing, ye're naebiddy else, and dinnae think ye've tae dae whit a'biddy else does," or "Noo watch fur the bogeymen, Donald. Dae ye ken wha' they are? Dae ye ken whit I mean?" This would be accompanied by a knowing look and a wee nudge in the ribs, and encompassed a world of meaning, none of which was lost on the boys. They and their cousins loved their grandparents dearly and valued their good opinion because they knew how much they were loved in return.

They became great-grandparents with the births of Alison's son Russell in 1992 and Pamela's son Jonathan in 1993, and then with Russell's sister Jennifer and Lynda's first son Stuart in 1996. His little brother Josh, born in 2001, and Donald and Aoife's wee girl Grace, born in 2008, were the only great-grandchildren they would never see, but they would certainly have given them as much joy as the birth of all the others did. Another red-letter day in those years was Joey and Jim's golden wedding in September 1991. They didn't want a big fuss to be made of the occasion, but we had a quiet family party, and they received good wishes from many friends and relatives. I reflected once again on the fifty years that separated them from the shy and anxious young couple who had waited for the bus to take them on their honeymoon and the first step on their life journey together at the corner, only one hundred yards from where their last home would be. It is with bittersweet feelings that I look at those two photographs side by side on our piano and reflect on the fifty years that separate them. One shows a young couple, shy and anxious but strong and upright, about to start a life together; the second the same wife and husband, rather stooped and somewhat diminished by age, but still with the essence of their personalities intact. In those fifty years they had shared a very full life and had much to show for their years, not only in material terms, but in the richness and variety of the experiences they had lived through with family and friends, and in the warmth and affection that had accompanied them on their journey. Their life had never been easy, and there were heartbreaks and problems on the way; but had they been self-regarding enough to look back and weigh up the balance of their years together, I am sure they would have been satisfied with what they saw. I know they took great pride and delight from watching their family grow and develop, but if they were proud of us all, we were equally proud of them and so happy that they were enjoying their twilight years back where they undoubtedly belonged.

It was at this time that their ties to their old home, the original Pitkinny, were finally severed and the lease with the NCB irrevocably relinquished. There was no more coal to be won from under the ground that they had worked, no more black diamonds to be claimed from under the fields they had tended and nurtured with such determination and devotion; within a few years those acres would be reinstated to pasture and crops. Newly planted shelter belts already punctuated the land south of the loan, which had earlier been restored, and now to the unknowing eye, Pitkinny's acreage bears little evidence of the upheaval and violation they had suffered. But on the very occasional approach I have made towards the end of the loan, I am assailed by what feels like an alien environment. The very contours of the old familiar landscape have been altered forever, just as the comfortable landmarks that marked our walk home from Woodend—the coortin' trees and the old tumble-down structures at Cowpour, Auntie Teenie's cottage and the farm at Westfield, and the Redhouse cottages at the corner—have all vanished and remain only as ghostly glimpses in memory. Only Redhouse farm itself still stands, an ever more "Bleak House" looking down the strip to the first of the houses at Woodend. The loan itself is barely distinguishable, as the road into Pitkinny now enters from the north side of the farm.

I have never travelled that road, never returned to Pitkinny, reluctant to witness in closeup the irrevocable changes that have been described to me. The house has been denuded of its chimneys, adorned by a new conservatory at the front, and looks out at the world through new but somehow blank and inappropriate windows. The house is now privately owned and no doubt immeasurably modernised and improved, but I know that the lovingly tended gardens are overgrown and neglected, the steading vastly altered. To my mind, the essence of the Pitkinny I remember exists only in the memories of those people who remember it as I do. There may be ghosts lingering around the house and steading to be glimpsed by those who know where to look and how to see—echoes of the voices of those who lived there for those who know what to listen for and whose ears are attuned to the sounds of laughter, fury, frustration, and friendly conversation that I can still hear when I recall my years of growing up. But I prefer to cherish all these memories myself and with family and old friends, rather than risk returning to find only an arrangement of bricks and mortar, a quiet and empty shell. Let the people who live there now fill the place with their voices and images and make their own memories, and I hope that in the years to come those memories provide them with the same solace and vitality that I gain from my memories of the Pitkinny I knew and loved.

The Pitkinny lease ended finally in 1991, after four years of protracted negotations with the NCB. According to the original terms of his agreement with the Coal Board, Jim and Joey had therefore received an inflation-proof income for sixteen years. So Pitkinny's land had continued indirectly to sustain them with its production of coal from under its acres, if not from its arable and pastoral output. It is ironic, in a way, given Jim's equivocal attitude to the coal industry and his awkward relationship with the miners it employed that it should have been the source of his income during those years. By the time the lease ended, they had come to terms with the fact that their farming life was officially over, and their tenure of the land was now limited to their house, garden, and the two little fields at the back. I do not remember any sense of the sadness there had been when they left Pitkinny, and a last signature was the only physical evidence of that final and technical release of the old tenancy. They were very content in their home at Cadham, and by the time they celebrated fifty years of marriage they had everything as they wanted it in the house and garden. They could see some of their kye grazing at their back door, and Joey could still throw the tattie peelings over the wall as a tasty titbit for the beasts. There was even the occasional crisis that always comes with keeping beasts, as once or twice the cattle strayed and were in danger of getting on to the road, but while this or some problem in the garden could still cause Jim to explode in the old tempestuous way, he would soon calm down and Joey would be relieved to hear him singing again.

Despite the general tenor of contentment, however, there were two real crises which stand out in my memory of those last years in Cadham. Jim had had a long love affair with the car. From his first abortive attempt at buying a car (which he mentions in one of the only two letters he ever wrote to Joey), to that first new Rover 75 that had caused Joey such anxiety as we drove home in it and she made us hide in the back, to the last of his three BMWs that he bought in Kirkcudbright, he had owned many different vehicles. Despite his increasing dislike of the busy roads, he still liked to have a good car and was more than happy to have the family drive him. Sadly, he was to lose his last BMW in a bizarre and traumatic way, which, although in retrospect has a comical side, was anything but funny at the time. The disaster happened without the car even leaving the garage and started in very mundane and innocent circumstances. Margaret, John, Pamela, her son Jonathan, Bill, and I were all visiting Jim and Joey on 18 October 1997. We had all enjoyed a good time together, and Bill and I had left before the others, so it wasn't until the next day that Margaret phoned me to relate the events that unfolded later.

Joey had made soup earlier that day, and she asked Jim to take the tray of filled and cooled containers out to the freezer in the garage. As he had done many times before, he went in the back door of the garage and put the tray on the old kitchen dresser to the left of the freezer while he opened the front door of the garage, as it was necessary to move his car backwards to allow room for the freezer door to open. As it was dark outside, presumably he failed to notice that John's car—a brand new Peugeot—was parked head-on to the garage door. It was some time later that Joey remarked that Jim was taking a long time to come back in from the garage. "I hope he hisnae skailt the soup," she said, so Margaret went out to check. She found Jim standing by the front of his car in the garage with a sweeping brush in his hand and looking completely dazed. The main door of the garage was closed, but Margaret could see at once that the front of the BMW was badly crushed. "What's happened to your car, Dad?" she managed to ask. "Ah dinnae ken whit happened," said Jim in a stunned voice. Then Margaret realised that the space between the car and the back garage wall was no longer occupied by a freezer. Instead, on the floor there was what appeared to be a pile of white cardboard sheets, haphazardly jumbled up with various items of frozen food. It quickly dawned on her that this was all that remained of the freezer, and then she could see that the back wall of the garage was buckled outwards. "Come in to the house, Dad," she urged, and in the time it took for them to walk back through the garden she had to try to plan how to break the news of the accident to Joey.

Joey was in her accustomed place at the kitchen sink when Margaret said, "Mum, come and sit here at the table for a minute." "Whye? Whit's happened?" asked Joey, immediately smelling a rat and not in the least inclined to sit at the table. "Dad's had a wee accident in the garage." Seeing Jim come in the door very sheepishly, Joey turned on him. "Dinnae tell me ye've skailt that soup!" she shouted in exasperation, thinking of all the work she had expended on its preparation. "No, it's no' the soup, Mum," reassured Margaret, picturing the unscathed tray of soup containers sitting on the dresser, and she felt a wave of hysterical laughter come over her as she added, "It's just everything else!" Of course, Joey rushed out to the garage where, understandably, she could hardly believe her eyes: her freezer was completely destroyed, the car smashed up, and the garage severely damaged. How was this possible? As Jim, still in a state of shock, seemed incapable of explaining, Joey immediately latched on to what seemed to her to be the logical explanation. Jim, as usual when they had visitors, took advantage of the company to enjoy a dram or two—or three or four—and that day was no exception, so Joey had no doubt that his whisky intake was directly responsible for what had happened as he had attempted to move the car.

Gradually, however, with Margaret and John and Pamela's mediation, Joey's good sense began to prevail as usual, and she tried to accept a situation that could not be changed. They consoled themselves with the fact that no one was hurt and that there was nothing damaged that couldn't be replaced or repaired. Margaret privately thought there must have been many times when Jim had reversed the car in the garage as Joey stood in front of it, ready to open the freezer, so had the accident happened at such a time, the results would have been far more serious. As John, Margaret, Pamela, and wee Jonathan prepared to leave, it seemed that Jim was recovering from the shock, and they hoped that Joey would not continue to give him too hard a time, although they all agreed that they wouldn't talk about the disaster to anyone outwith the immediate family. Margaret even ventured to make light of the situation by saying to Joey, "Never mind; it could have been worse, Mum." "Hoo the hell could it've been worse, Margaret?" "Well, at least he didnae spill the soup!" For once Joey's sense of humour failed to come to her aid, and Margaret realised it was much too early for Joey to see anything remotely funny in their predicament.

As John went out to put things in his car, he was astounded to find his front number plate lying on the drive just outside the garage. He was unable to see the front of his car properly in the dark, but fearing the worst, he quickly ushered the family into the car, even declining Margaret's offer to drive. Any effects from the whisky he had had earlier had long worn off as a result of the trauma they had all just experienced, and he was relieved that his car seemed to be running all right, as he brusquely cut short their parting with Joey and Jim. "What a hellish day that was," said Pamela as they left Cadham behind. "Aye, and it's not over yet," said John, and he began to tell Margaret and Pamela what he had found. When they got home, they saw by their garage light that the front of their new Peugeot was badly damaged, having presumably been hit by the BMW as Jim reversed it out of the garage. While Jim continued to claim not to know what had happened, we managed to work out the probable sequence of events. To be fair, there were two possible mitigating factors in his favour. Firstly, it had been raining, so the soles of his slippers would be wet, and his foot may have slipped off the brake. Also, the BMW was automatic, and when he reversed and felt the bump with John's car, he must have got such a shock that he may, in response, have put the car into drive and accelerated too hard and hit the freezer and the garage wall.

Nevertheless, it is hard not to believe that he didn't know he had damaged John's car, because, after all, he must have seen it when he closed the garage door after the collision, but whether he deliberately decided to keep quiet about it, or the shock had genuinely affected his memory of that part of the disaster, we will never know. Firstly, he never alluded to it, and secondly, John also refused to mention it to either Jim or Joey. Margaret rightly felt that Jim should confront the full truth of the entire episode, but John would not be persuaded. His car was repaired under the terms of his insurance, and it is to his credit that he preferred doing that to causing Jim and Joey even more worry about the catastrophe. Sadly, the result of Jim's insurance claim was that his beloved BMW was written off, although their house insurance covered the cost of a replacement freezer and the £2,000 repair to the garage.

Few, if any, people outside the immediate family ever knew the details of the accident, and it was seldom referred to by Jim or Joey. He was embarrassed, and she continued to be angry about it, but I am sure, had they been younger or had they had more years to reflect on it, they would eventually have been able to develop a philosophical attitude to it as they had always been able to do with the other serious crises they had met with and weathered in their earlier lives. We have discussed it since and have been able to see the funny side of it, but more than that I find it illustrates how the different personalities and characters of my parents are revealed by the way they dealt with this episode. Jim always enjoyed getting the better of other people, and took a sly and pawky pleasure in getting away with things, whereas Joey was much more strict and honest in her dealings with others and expected everyone to have the same high standards of behaviour as she set for herself. So John was correct in believing that, had she known about the damage to his car, she would have been mortified about his expense and trouble, and so would have taken Jim to task even more than she did. And, of course, as always, she was totally uncompromising in her condemnation of Jim's behaviour when she suspected that the "taking of drink" was implicated in his misdemeanours.

There was an earlier occasion during their years at Cadham when they had a serious row which arose partly from unkind and foolish talk on Jim's part, when he was "the waur o' drink," and Joey's drastic reaction to it. It happened towards the end of what had been a very happy day, the wedding of Lynda and Scott in October 1991. There had been a danger of early frost that autumn, and Joey was worried about some delicate shrubs in the back garden. Ever a genius at improvisation, she had sewn some old shower curtains into covers for the plants. Jim had scoffed at what he saw as an unnecessary precaution. As we were all about to head home from the wedding, Jim was regaling some listeners with story after story—a scenario that Joey had been only too familiar with over the years, and which she hated when she knew that he was well oiled. She overheard him declare to his audience, "Ah've got the cleverest wife in the world, ye ken! Joey can even mak frocks for floors!" She felt, with some justification, that he was ridiculing and mocking her wholehearted attempts to do the best for their garden. This wasn't the first row they had had about the garden, and while Joey tried her best to laugh off his comments at the time in front of the others, she was really hurt; things came to a head a day or two later when I had a frantic phone call from Dad.

"Ye'll hae tae come along; yer mither's gaun aff 'er heid. She's emptying a' thing oot o' the greenhoose an' flingin' it ower the field!" When I arrived at Cadham, sure enough, that was an accurate description of the scene that met me in the back garden. "There'll be nae mair rows aboot the gairden," Joey said when I remonstrated with her about her desperate actions, "because there'll be nae mair gairden!" "Whit a cairry on aboot nuthin'! I didnae mean ony herm," claimed Jim in exasperation. When I eventually managed to get them both to calm down, I tried to have my say. "Can't you live in peace, for God's sake? I've had to listen to your rows for as long as I can remember, and I'm sick of it!" By the time I left to go home, some semblance of peace had been restored, and both of my parents were looking rather shamefaced. Mum never held a grudge for long, and I know she understood how I felt, but Dad's pawky last word as he saw me out to the car was, "Ye ken, it's when ye're fechtin' that ye ken ye're still livin'!"

If there were dramatic incidents like these from time to time, there were many, many more times when we left Pitkinny after happy and harmonious visits. As had always been the case, Jim and Joey had an ever-open door to relatives and friends alike, and they relished the occasions when they had guests, invited or spontaneous. They were never early to bed, and we and others would often leave very late at night; we were always waved off from the front door, as if Mum and Dad were unwilling to let us go. Even as her physical strength began to desert her, Joey would strive to look after her visitors just as she always had, and Jim did his best to help her, although he never really felt at home in the kitchen. Nevertheless, he would often go and put the kettle on and set out the supper things. Otherwise, his strength lay in doing the hoovering and the heavier jobs around the house; and, in time, Madge Bell helped in the house as Andrew and John gave Jim and Joey a hand with the heavier gardening tasks. Margaret, John, Bill, and I had regular visits from Jim and Joey, although these became less frequent as Jim was reluctant to drive far beyond the immediate vicinity of Cadham.

After the loss of his last BMW, they decided that they really didn't need a big, powerful car for the limited driving they did, and I was aghast when Jim bought a Rover 100. It seemed they had gone from one extreme to the other, and I couldn't get used to seeing them in such a tiny wee car. Sure enough, within a few weeks, Jim decided he couldn't stand it either, and bought a new Rover 200. Although slightly bigger, it was still a two-door car, and the crunch came when I picked them up to take them to the funeral of John's father, George French, in Dunfermline. As Joey couldn't manage to get in the back seat, and Jim insisted that I drive, he had to sit in the back. He got in without too much trouble, but when we arrived at the crematorium, he simply couldn't get out! In the end he emerged out of the car on his back in a crab-like motion, all long arms and legs, accompanied by a string of oaths which turned the air blue and attracted some (at best) bemused and (at worst) scandalised glances—the former from people who knew Jim, and the latter from those who didn't! Joey's urgent hushing and my attempts at soothing him made him even more furious, and our arrival was neither dignified nor discreet. So the following week the Rover 200 was returned to the dealership and, third time lucky, as it turned out, a Rover 400 was acquired. This was the last car Jim ever owned and, while not a patch on the first Rover 75 of all those years before, at least it was the same turquoise shade that it had been and had the minimum requirement of four doors!

In the years at Cadham, it seemed that there was hardly a week when Jim and Joey didn't attend a funeral, and Jim especially was a regular attendee at either crematorium or graveyard as older relatives, friends, and acquaintances passed away. Sometimes these occasions would be further afield, and I remember Dad going with his nephew Jim from the Star to a funeral of a farming friend in Perthshire. They made a day of it, of course, and when I asked him about it, Jim was very enthusiastic and reported that he had had a great day out, although he did have the sensitivity to add, "Maybe it's no richt to say that, efter a' the man's deid, but it's true." He once attended a big funeral of someone in the farming fraternity in Kirkcaldy crematorium and was most disappointed that he couldn't get a seat. "That'll no happen again onywye," he declared to Joey; sure enough, the following week as he set out again for another cremation in the same place, he made sure he was really early. As the chapel filled up with mourners, Jim began to realise that he didn't recognise anyone; when the chief mourners appeared, he came to the conclusion that he was at the wrong funeral—in fact, the one before the one he was supposed to be at! When I asked him what he did, he replied, "Whit could Ah dae? I jist sat still and when a'biddy left at the end, Ah jist steyed in me sait until the richt funeral startit."

As Jim and Joey grew older, they began to experience increasing health worries. Joey had developed type 2 diabetes while they were in Kirkcudbright, and after they moved to Cadham her longstanding heart trouble developed into congestive heart failure; she had to be on diuretic treatment. The spondylosis she had had for many years caused her continual and chronic pain, but she was remarkably stoic about it and had learned over the years to manage her pain with a combination of heat lamp treatment, exercise, and the use of a TENS device, all of which were monitored by occasional visits to the chronic pain clinic in hospital. She seldom if ever complained, although we knew there were times when it must have been very hard to remain cheerful. As long as she was able to distract herself from her pain by keeping busy and doing all the things that were important to her, she was able to struggle on, but it was inevitable that this would become more and more difficult. In addition to everything else, she had a hysterectomy at the age of eighty, in 1995, and made a remarkably quick recovery from it, declaring that she had often felt worse with a bad cold! We tried to get her to obey the doctor's orders that she rest in bed every afternoon, but she would have none of it. "If ye come along here some day and fund me in ma bed in the efternain, ye'll ken it's curtains!" she admonished us in no uncertain terms.

Jim joined Joey in a diagnosis of type 2 diabetes and also had a low-grade prostate tumour, which was successfully treated by hormone implants. He would joke, "Dinnae worry aboot hoo ye'll pass the time when ye're auld. Ye'll be that busy keepin' up wi' yer medical appointments!" Additional visits to the chiropodist and the optician meant that Jim and Joey had to strive to keep up to date with everything, but inevitably they did occasionally miss an appointment. When she saw us with Post-It sticky notelets in our house, Joey thought they would be the answer, so I gave her some. The next time I went into their house at Cadham there were wee yellow stickers all over the place with reminders of their various dates and appointments, but even they didn't always prevent them slipping up. Senior moments came thick and fast, and Joey began to find it really difficult when it came to remembering birthdays in the family. She would send a cheque to the birthday girl or boy, but increasingly got muddled up, and we got used to cheques arriving for the wrong person or on the wrong date, so we just developed our own clearing system and exchanged them as necessary, if possible without worrying Mum about her mistake.

During the course of the last decade of the twentieth century, the passing years saw Jim and Joey enter the wintertime of their lives. Looking back now, I can understand that the signs of their growing frailty and increasing dependence on us should have been obvious, but perhaps we never expect our parents to be anything other than the strong, sustaining presence they have always been, and the role reversal that is inevitable as they grew weaker did not sit easily with me. Why would they ask my advice or seek my reassurance when, for most of my life, it had been the other way around? During those last years at Cadham, there were many happy and momentous events as our families celebrated rites of passage that brought great pleasure to Joey and Jim: weddings, graduations, christenings, and career successes for Margaret and me and our families; but it seems to me now that there must have been a sense of winding down for Jim and Joey as the years began to inexorably take their toll on their health and strength. But they gave little or no outward sign that this was so. There was invariably the usual hearty welcome waiting for anyone who arrived at Pitkinny; there was nothing Joey and Jim liked more than an unexpected opportunity for a good blether with old friends, and the kettle and teapot were never cold for long.

As we were still working in those days, we would often visit them at the weekends, arriving during the afternoon and either taking them out for a high tea, or getting fish and chips from the local chip shop to share with them at teatime. Sometimes we would have had a late breakfast or had been too busy to have a proper lunch, and when Jim asked us, as he often would, "So whit did ye hae fur yer denner the day?" Bill would say truthfully, "We haven't really had any dinner." "Havenae hid yer denner?" Jim would repeat in shocked, almost disbelieving tones. "Joey," he would shout, "Anne an' Bill have no had ony denner!" Before we could stop her, Joey would be away getting some soup ready for us and setting the table. It was the devil of a job trying to convince them that we weren't actually starving, and that we were saving our appetites for a high tea later. So we learned that when Jim enquired about our midday meal, we would say, "Mince an' tatties," or "roast chicken," or "stovies," or anything that came into our heads, to satisfy Dad that we had, in fact eaten what to him was sacrosanct: yer denner at twelve o' clock!

WILLIAMSON & HENRY
Solicitors & Estate Agents
(Incorporating: Gibson & Montgomery)

W.D. Henry, LL.B., N.P.
A.C. Henry, LL.B., N.P.
I.N. Steele, LL.B., N.P.

Telephone: Kirkcudbright 30692
(STD Code 0557)

13 St. Mary Street,
Kirkcudbright
DG6 4AA

Rutland Exchange Box No. 813
Kirkcudbright

ACH/JW

13th April, 1988

Mr. and Mrs. James Rutherford,
6 Mount Pleasant Avenue,
KIRKCUDBRIGHT.

Dear Mr. and Mrs. Rutherford,

6 Mount Pleasant Avenue
New Bungalow at Cadham Road, Glenrothes

With further reference to this matter, I am writing simply to confirm that I have now received a letter from Whatlings, on behalf of Mr. and Mrs. Gardner, concluding the contract for the sale of 6 Mount Pleasant Avenue. By the same token, the contract for the purchase of the new bungalow at Glenrothes has also been concluded, and accordingly, that is now both contracts tied up.

The date of entry to the new bungalow at Glenrothes is of course 6th May, and the date of entry to 6 Mount Pleasant Avenue is 16th May, although that date may be brought forward, particularly if you have vacated the house.

Yours sincerely,

PROPERTY OFFICE:
3 St. Cuthbert Street,
Kirkcudbright.
Telephone: (0557) 31049
(Also open Saturday Mornings)

GATEHOUSE OFFICE:
32 High Street,
Gatehouse.
Telephone: (05574) 293
(Tuesdays Only — W.D. Henry)

NEW GALLOWAY OFFICE:
High Street,
New Galloway.
Telephone: (064 42) 440
(Wednesdays Only — I.N. Steele)

*Letter of acceptance to buy house at Cadham, April 1988*

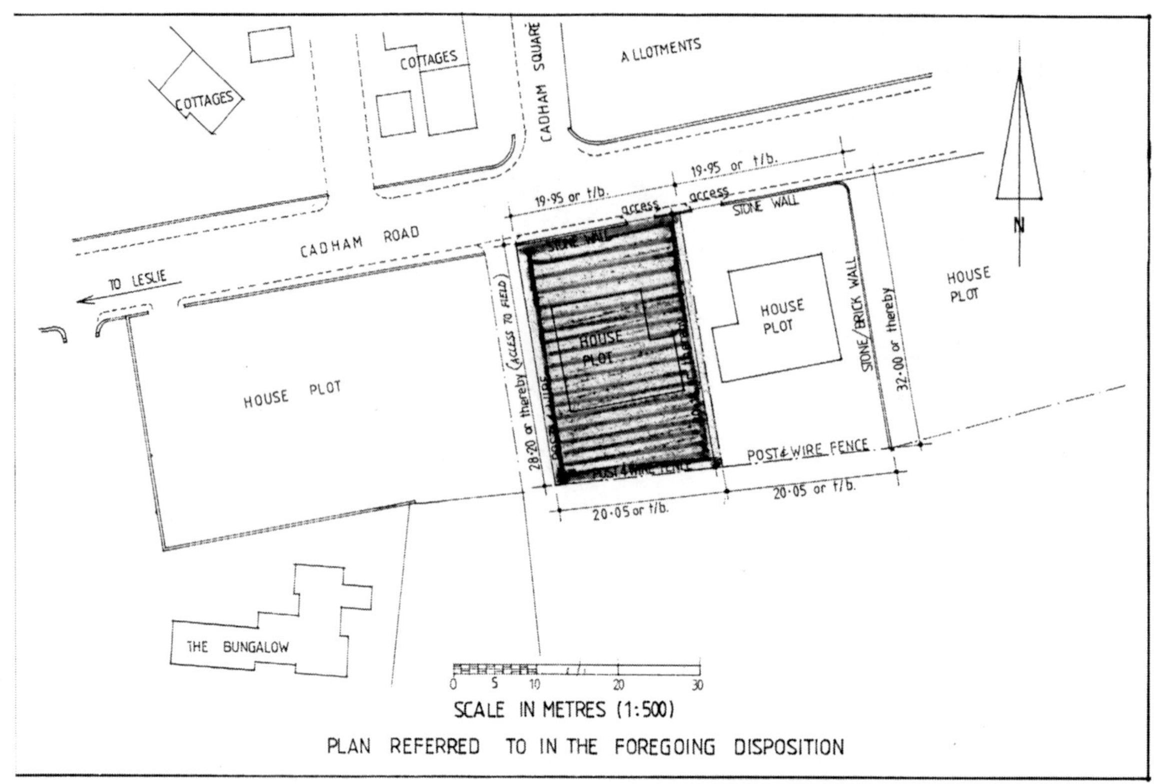


*Plan of house*

*Front of house (Donald, Joey, Anne, Jim, and Calum [sitting])*

*Back garden after the addition of a conservatory, summer house, and a greenhouse*

*First night at Cadham. L to R: David Croal, Anne Croal, Wendy Mitchell, Calum, Cathy Moyes, Joey, Nan Walker, David Croal Senior, Bill*

*Donald (with Tina the dog), Calum, Anne, Margaret, Alison, Uncle James, and David Croal Senior*

*L to R: Nan Walker, Wendy Mitchell, Anne Croal, and Uncle James*

*Christmas 1987. Back Row L to R: Pamela, Alison, Lynda*
*Front Row L to R: Jim, Joey, George and Flo French*

*Reunion of old friends, Summer 1990. Standing L to R: Bill, Lena Imrie, Charlie Hunter, Joyce Thomson (nee Steel), Margaret, Anne, Rob Imrie, Mary Hunter (nee Steel), Jim. Seated L to R: Mrs Page, Joey, and Mrs Steel (This was Mrs Steel's last visit home with daughter Mary and son-in-law Charlie)*

11, Abbey Park Place,
Dunfermline,
Fife, KY12 7PT
Tel: (0383) 722454

SURVEYORS, VALUERS
LAND AND ESTATE SERVICES
R. J. McCrae B.L.E., A.R.I.C.S.
E.D. McCrae B.Sc.(AGRIC)

District Valuers Office,
11 Guildhall Street,
Dunfermline,
Fife.
KY12 7PU

14th December 1987.

Your Ref OGD199/87/Ainslie/MS
Our Ref RJM/MH

Dear Mr. Ainslie,

**Westfield Extension Site**
**North Pitkinny and South Bogside Farms**
**- Tenant on 173 Acres - J. Rutherford, Esq.**

Further to our recent telephone conversations we write to confirm that our client has instructed us to write to you to confirm that he would be prepared to relinquish his tenancy on the above 173 acres, on the following basis:-

1. That he be paid £6,000 as a capital payment immediately for relinquishing his tenants rights on the lands which British Coal are wishing to work in the immediate future. These Westfield Opencast Extension Site lands would not be handed back to our client for some long time in the normal course of events and under this proposal they would never be handed back.

2. That our client continues to be paid the existing loss of profits rental of £14,000 per annum for the next three and three quarter years. This means that he be paid £3,500 on the 1st January 1988 and thereafter every quarter until 1st July 1990 which shall be his last payment.

3. That, for the purposes of doubt, our client's family be paid the above compensation sums even if our client dies prior to July 1990.

4. It is further required that should the above payments be paid late, then, interest should be forthcoming at a rate of 2% above the Bank of Scotland base rate until the matter is settled.

5. That reasonable Surveyors' and Legal Fees be paid in respect of negotiating and administering the above settlement.

In return for the above consideration our client forfeits his right to require British Coal to carry out any reinstatement operations (stonegathering, extra cultivations, drainage, fencing, hedges etc. as he will, of course, have no interest in the lands once they have been reinstated. Similarly, he has no power to veto any works which might be scheduled to take place across the 173 acres (electricity poles, water pipeline, roadways, ditching, or any coal winning operation etc.)

We look forward/

PERTH OFFICE: 3, Comelybank, Perth, PH2 7HU Tel: (0738) 25601

*Jim's offer to relinquish the final tenancy on the remaining 173 acres of Pitkinny, December 1987 (page 1)*

- 2 -

District Valuers Office.

14th December 1987.

**Westfield Extension Site.**

We look forward to your response to the above proposal and would ask that an agreement be forthcoming immediately so that the compensation payment of £6,000 be made on the 1st January 1988 along with the first payment of the reviewed rent.

Yours sincerely,

R.J. McCrae.

Copy to Mr. J. Rutherford, 6 Mount Pleasant Avenue, Kirkcudbright.

*Jim's offer to relinquish the final tenancy on the remaining 173 acres of Pitkinny, December 1987 (page 2)*

. R. Stevenson & Marshall

SOLICITORS
NOTARIES PUBLIC

JOHN CAVERS
JAMES MARSHALL
A. DOUGLAS LINDGREN
DAVID A. HARKESS
ANDREW WEATHERLEY

41 EAST PORT,
DUNFERMLINE, FIFE, KY12 7LG

Telephone: Dunfermline 721141 (5 lines)
(STD 0383)
Rutland Exchange Box No. D.F.13
Fax: (0383) 723779

Your Ref.

Our Ref. H.K.5 (r)-16

27th April, 1989

Mr. J. Rutherford
Pitkinny
Cadham Road
GLENROTHES
Fife

Dear Mr. Rutherford,

We have now received the Agreements in principal which require to be completed in relation to your giving up the tenancy of North Pitkinny. The Agreement is in duplicate. You should read it through carefully and make sure it fully reflects what you wish to happen and thereafter arrange to sign it where shown on Page Fifth and, at the same time, signing the plan where shown as well. You should do this on both Agreements enclosed herewith, both plans, and in the presence of two witnesses who should also sign on Page Fifth where shown. Kindly thereafter arrange for completion of the enclosed Witness Schedule stating, in the places provided, the full names, addresses and occupations of both witnesses, together with the date and place of signature of the deeds. Kindly thereafter return both deeds and the Witness Schedule to us in the addressed envelope enclosed herewith for your convenience.

If, however, it would suit you better to call at the Office and sign the Agreements here this can be completed without any difficulty for you.

Yours faithfully,

Encs.

P.S. We appreciate that some amendment is required to the heading but this will be dealt with later.

AUTHORISED TO CONDUCT INVESTMENT BUSINESS UNDER THE FINANCIAL SERVICES ACT 1986 BY THE LAW SOCIETY OF SCOTLAND

*Covering letter from Jim's solicitor relating to the agreement to relinquish the tenancy of Pitkinny, April 1989*

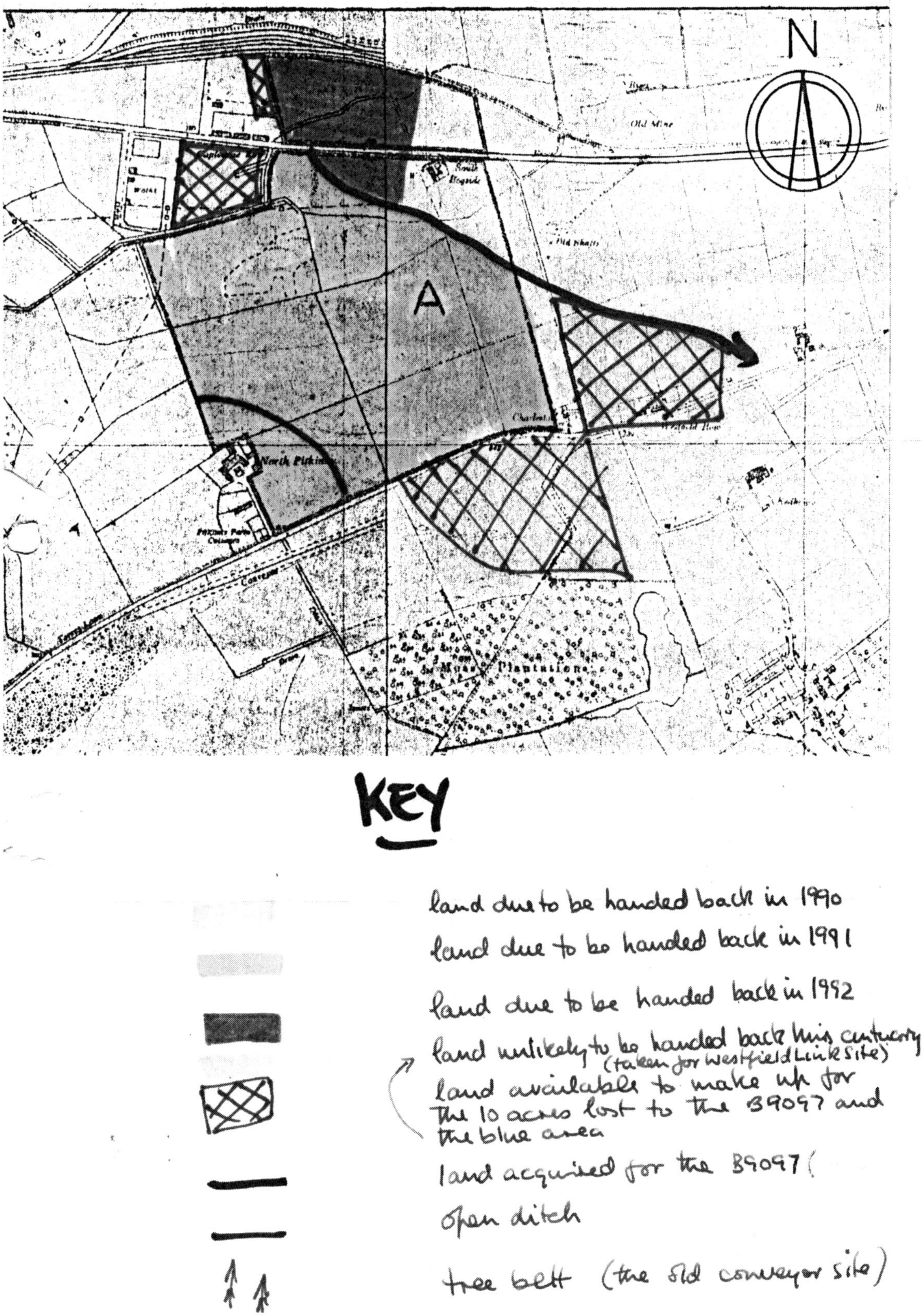

KEY

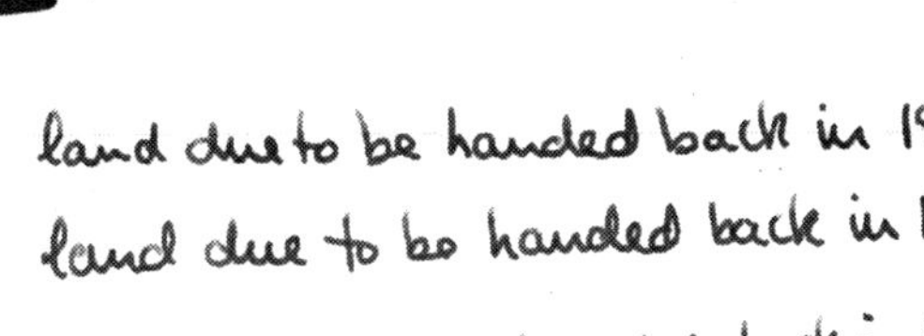


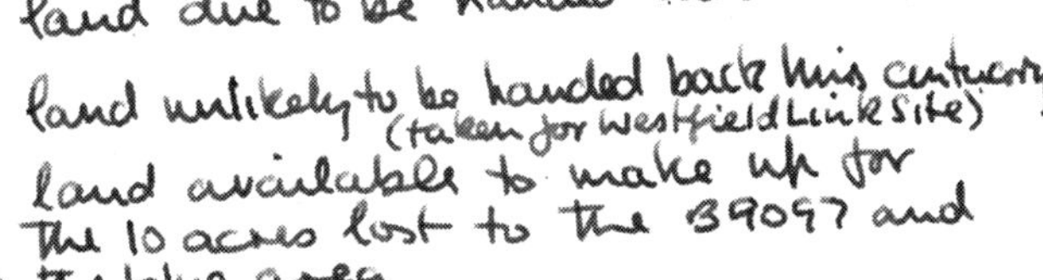

*Plan of reinstatement of opencast site*

TEL. 01592 610071

PITKINNY,
CADHAM ROAD,
GLENROTHES,
FIFE,
KY7 6PE

This is the report concerning accident in garage with my car. I was putting away Soup in a Freezer. To get this done I had to move car. on returing car I don't know. what pathened. It might have been the accelorator jammed or my wet slippers. It was all over so quickly. The Freezer was completely smashed and wall behind burst out.

I enclose receipt of purchase of Freezer. and todays price.

Trust this satisfys You

Yours Truly

Jas Rutherford

*Draft report of accident to BMW car in garage at Pitkinny, Cadham*

# Chapter 37

"Ah'm jist needin' tae be up the road, aside yer mither."

As described in an earlier chapter, Pitkinny had a large number of feline and canine occupants over the years we lived there, but in retirement Jim and Joey had no pets. Occasionally, Joey would express a notion to have a cat again, but nothing ever came of it—that is, until Bill and I acquired a stray cat one day in the garden of our home in Cairneyhill. As Bill dismantled the patio table for the winter, this black and white cat suddenly appeared, and Bill realised that it must have been living under the table, hidden from view by the waterproof cover that came down to the ground. The cat was obviously very distressed at being evicted from his makeshift home, as his vociferous miaowing made clear. Taking pity on the beast, we fed him (the only suitable food to hand was some Marks and Spencer's tuna pate, which he gratefully made short work of) and made a bed for him in the garage.

Attempts to discover who he belonged to or where he had come from proved fruitless, so before contacting the Cat Protection Society, we asked Joey if she wanted him. After some agonising, she decided against giving him a home, so after a few days, we had to drive him over to the Newtongrange branch of the charity, as there was no room in the Fife cat homes. Within a day or two Joey changed her mind and wished that she had decided to have the cat. Finding he was still unclaimed, we returned to Newtongrange and brought the cat to Cadham. We stopped on the way to buy all the necessary accoutrements for a cat: a bed, collar, grooming brush, and of course food, along with a cat flap, which we thought could be fitted into the door of the summer house. This made a suitable and very welcome birthday gift for Joey, coming as it did just before her eighty-second birthday. While a house guest at the cat home, the cat had been given the name of Hughie, and Joey decided that was very appropriate, being the name of her brother who had lived in America for many years.

Their new pet soon made himself at home in Cadham, a close approximation to cat heaven. He made full use of the freedom to roam around the fields and gardens at the back of the house, wisely keeping away from the busy road at the front. He eschewed the custom-made cat bed we had bought him, preferring to sleep on a cushion on the shelf under the window of the summer house, coming and going as he wished through the cat flap fitted in the door. Of course, he also spent a lot of time in the house during the day, and both Jim and Joey enjoyed having a feline companion for the first time in many years. I have heard it said that you do not choose a cat, it chooses you; I think this was undoubtedly the case with Hughie, and in a very short time it seemed like he had always lived with Joey and Jim. As it was to turn out, he more than repaid their hospitality by being a loyal and true companion in the course of the following few years.

Joey and Jim both became octogenarians in the years at Cadham; Joey in November 1995, and Jim in February 1997. The former occasion was celebrated with a family get-together at Balgedie House Hotel in Glenrothes. This was planned by Jim as a surprise for Joey, who believed she was only going out for a quiet lunch with Margaret, John, Bill, and me. In fact, all her grandchildren and her two great-grandsons, Russell and Jonathan, were there, as well as her two brothers, John and James, James's wife May, and her niece, Elizabeth Drennan, from Doncaster. The event almost didn't take place at all. Jim couldn't resist suggesting they have a bar lunch there a few days before, to see what it was like, and while they were there Joey had a bad fall down a few steps while making her way to the ladies' room. This was not the first fall she had had, and as before she was fortunate not to break a limb. Although she was in even more pain than usual, she was able to attend the surprise party a few days later, albeit with a bit of a struggle. This was typical of Joey: in her heart of hearts, she would probably have preferred to stay at home that day, but when she saw that we were going to be disappointed if she missed our lunch, she allowed herself to be persuaded to make the effort to come along. As always, she thought of others before herself, and of course, when she saw the rest of the family waiting for her, she understood our persistence.

When Jim's big day came along, he suggested that he would like to have lunch at the pub in the Star. There had been a public house years before, but for a long time the village was without a hostelry, so when he knew it had reopened, he was keen to try it out, and it seemed a very suitable location for us to celebrate his "coming of age" in his home village. It occurred to me to wonder what his father would have thought if he could have seen us all there. He was never one to enjoy himself and seldom participated in social gatherings or family get-togethers, having more than a little old-fashioned Calvinist distrust of any kind of relaxation or of what he thought of as needless expression of familial affection. One of the very few exceptions had been the time he attended the wedding of Uncle Wullie and Auntie Caroline and insisted on returning home at the earliest opportunity to make sure his treasure trove was still safe underneath the neeps in the shed! Always distrustful of banks and unwilling to have his assets subject to the scrutiny of the tax man, he preferred to keep them where he could keep an eye on them. The idea of having that amount of money in today's value—at least a five- or even a six-figure sum—in the form of ready cash is enough to make your eyes water. No wonder he was worried about it!

There were also sad times in the years at Cadham. In May 1990, Auntie Greta died suddenly and unexpectedly in Doncaster. She suffered a heart attack with no warning, and her loss was devastating to Joey. They had always been very close and had been great support to each other when they were young. Although in later years they were not able to see so much of each other, they were often in touch by phone, and I know how much Joey missed her sister. However, in her usual pragmatic way, she once told me that she found it a comfort to picture Greta going about her housework and looking after Elizabeth and Uncle Bobby in the same way as she always had, and in the countless memories she had of her as they grew up together and then lived parallel lives, becoming wives, mothers, and grandmothers at the same time.

Jim also lost his elder brother Wullie on Christmas Day 1994, and what made that even more unfortunate was that there had been an irrevocable rift between him and his youngest brother Harry. This was caused by the fact that Grandad James had decided to make Wullie and his son Jim his heirs, so when Granddad died in 1972, Harry and his son Jimmy were effectively left out of his estate. Of course, when Jim set up his own business at Bogside in 1941, it was made clear that the help James gave him then would constitute Jim's inheritance once and for all, whereas Harry and Wullie were partners, along with Auntie Nellie, in their father's business at the dairy and Broomfield. In the event, Jim was left £1,000 in his father's will, much to his surprise, and each of his grandchildren was to inherit £100. Margaret and I, with our cousin Isobel, being mere girls, were also surprised that he remembered us at all.

However, none of these bequests could be made, as Harry contested the will, and this was the beginning of years of legal wrangling, which was good news to no one but the lawyers; the whole sorry mess was further complicated when Auntie Nellie died in 1980. Jim did his best to mediate between his two warring brothers, but it did no good and only led to bad feeling on the part of Harry and his wife, Auntie Rina, towards Jim and Joey, as well as towards Wullie and Caroline. It was all very unfortunate and was never completely resolved before first Wullie and then Harry died. The irony is that none of the younger generation has continued the quarrel, and we all get on well together. I believe that is because we all saw too much of the needless heartbreak that comes from family disagreements, and probably all feel that family businesses are more trouble than they are worth. Margaret and I were always so glad that Jim and Joey had struck out on their own when they married and that we were never directly involved with the difficulties that beset "the Star anes."

Despite these unhappy episodes, the years at Cadham were good ones for Joey and Jim as they watched their grandchildren reach maturity and the girls start their own families, while Calum and Donald completed their higher education and set out on their careers. I am sure Joey had qualms about Calum going to work in Hong Kong, and later Jim no doubt worried about Donald being in Japan; still, they were able to suppress their fears, as we did, and were proud of their fortitude and abilities. I know they would have been so content to see the boys happily married and settled—Calum with Maria, and Donald with Aoife and their wee girl, Grace. They were delighted that all their grandchildren loved to visit them whenever they could and did so out of love and genuine interest, never out of a sense of duty or obligation. In turn, Jim and Joey showered their youngsters with warm affection at all times and took great pleasure out of seeing them happy and successful. The special occasions of Christmases shared, birthdays and anniversaries remembered, and weddings and christenings celebrated were of course memorable, but there were innumerable times when we would spend a happy day or even a few hours with Joey and Jim at Cadham or in our own homes. There was always humour, sometimes discussions, or even disagreements, usually interesting news to hear and relate; the one thing you never were was bored. The mutual love and respect we and our children shared with our parents was the result of the kind of people they were, and I consider myself so lucky to have had such parents.

Nevertheless, it would be wrong to present an idealised picture of the last years of their lives, because as the century moved towards its close, time and failing health began to take their toll, especially on Mum. Gradually it became a time of frustration, sometimes verging on despair, well-hidden though she kept it, as she railed against her inevitably increasing weakness, which more and more prevented her from enjoying the physical activity she had always relished. Her housework, cooking, and gardening tasks inexorably became beyond her dwindling strength, but her spirit refused to give in entirely. Her rheumatic heart condition, that unwelcome companion of most of her life, which had developed into congestive heart failure, at last began to catch up with her, as she had two stays in hospital in the autumn of 1998. One November day, her old friend Betty Henderson found her planting bulbs in the garden. Barely able to walk back into the house, she bitterly admitted that she had reached the end of her tether. A few short weeks later, she was hospitalised for the last time on the morning of Christmas Day and died three weeks later on 15 January 1999.

It was left to us, her family, to witness, in spring, the flowering of the bulbs she had planted that day, when she confided to Betty that she knew she would never see them bloom. It was heartbreaking, but also uplifting, that the final flourish of her physical strength was spent doing something she loved which left a legacy for others to enjoy. Joey always put her family before herself, and her greatest pleasure was found in attending to the needs of those she loved.

Calum had planned a visit home from Hong Kong in February, and Joey made me promise that I would not allow him to come home before that. "If Ah thocht that Calum was gettin' on an aeroplane on ma accoont, Ah wid be awfy upset. Tell him he's tae wait and come when he wis meanin' tae', an' tell him Ah mind him fine, wherever he is." A day or two before she died, she could hear that it was very windy outside, but then she added, "Ah dinnae hae tae worry aboot the wither ony mair, dae Ah?" I am certain that she knew she was dying and that she was ready to give up the struggle. I had sometimes heard her say that when there was no more pleasure to be had from living, then it was time to die, and she was reconciled to the ending of her life. She had done her work and she had done it well, and that was always the most important thing for Joey. She was sustained by the love of her family, and she had her wish that Calum did not rush home. He found it hard to be so far away at such a time, but we kept him in touch with all the arrangements and involved him as much as possible in what was happening in the days before and after Mum's funeral. And he came home in time for Dad's birthday in February and had time with his grandad then.

Jim was left alone, bewildered by the loneliness that engulfed him. This unaccustomed solitary existence was an unbearable burden to him. Having always had someone to look after him—his mother, his sister, or his wife—the practical domestic challenges he was faced with were beyond him, despite everything we did to support him. He was desperately lonely, and would sometimes say, "Ah'm jist needin' tae be up the road, aside yer mither." I know that he had regrets that he had not always been easy to live with, and that he had caused Joey much anguish from time to time through their years together. He was heard to say, "Ah jist wish ah could hae ten minutes wi' Joey. Ten minutes wid be enough." In the eighteen months of life that were left to him, you could sometimes catch a glimmer of his old self, but this would happen less and less often. Hughie the cat was a Godsend, inasmuch as Jim had to see to the needs of his pet, and he increasingly spoiled the cat. He was fed on the fat of the land—in fact better than Jim fed himself, I am sure. When I warned him that cats can develop diabetes if they eat too much, he replied, "Well, if he gets diabetes, Ah'll jist gie 'im wan o' ma peels!" He would see that Hughie was tucked up for the night on the shelf in the summer house, with the curtains closed, and then in the morning he assured us he would find the curtains open. "'E's a clever bist, that cat, 'e kin open thae curtains 'issel!"

Slowly but steadily his health deteriorated. His diabetes and prostate condition were both chronic, and in addition he began to complain of pain in his back. He was diagnosed with a degree of osteoporosis, and I wondered how that could be when he had worked hard for most of his life and always had plenty of calcium in his diet. Supper most nights for many years consisted of a jeely piece washed down with a pint of the best milk from his own cows. So he had many different kinds of medication to take, and we worried sometimes in case he would adopt his usual maxim, "Jist anither wan fur luck!" especially since he no longer had Joey there to keep a watchful eye on things. Latterly, he lost his appetite, not just for food, but for life itself.

He told me one day that his doctor had asked him if he thought that he should still be driving. He was obviously taken aback by the question and asked me what I thought. I reminded him how much of a trial he was finding the heavy traffic and remarked that it was not only his own safety that he should be aware of, but that of others on the road, as his reactions were clearly less reliable than when he was younger. He could see my point and said he would give the situation some thought. It was to his credit that he made the decision never to drive again. Thereafter Uncle John, who lived nearby, would be happy to drive him anywhere he needed to go and, in return, he could have the use of Jim's car when he needed transport. Although we felt a degree of relief at this solution, we could understand that this event was a real watershed for Jim. It marked a drastic lessening of his independence and an end to what had been an important part of his lifestyle and a central aspect of his personality. It was inevitable and for the best, but none the less painful for him to experience and for us to witness.

We visited him as often as our busy lives would allow and arranged for a young woman to come in several times a week to help him in the house, and he began to have home care once and then twice a day. He was persuaded to attend the day hospital for the elderly at the nearby Glenrothes hospital, and he enjoyed those visits. Once or twice, there was a pianist who would play for the patients while they had their lunch, and one day Jim was delighted to report that he had sung "The Road and the Miles to Dundee" for everyone. It was heart-rending to see a last flourish of the joy in entertaining people that he had always had, but we knew that he was longing to be free of his lonely struggle, just as he had yearned for physical freedom in his young days. So it was a mercy to him when he suffered a brain-stem stroke and was taken into hospital at the beginning of July 2000. Over the next few days, he gradually lapsed into unconsciousness and died in the early morning of 7 July. As we drove to the hospital in Kirkcaldy, to spend what was to be the last night of his life with him, we passed several tractors and hay tedders turning the hay in the fields of farms that Jim knew well. It was a glorious summer evening, and despite my deep sadness, I was suddenly filled with a conviction that, in spirit, Dad was not an old man, now mercifully unaware of his frailty as his life ebbed away. Rather, he was young again, vigorous and full of life, working the land he loved as he always had. I felt immensely comforted by the certainty that his heart and soul were still those of the callow youth my mother married, striding over the fields with her, surveying the fruits of their labours. I was reminded of the words of Lewis Grassic Gibbon in "Sunset Song":

> And who knows at the last what memories of it were with them; the springs and winters of this land, and all the sights and sounds of it that had once been theirs, deep and a passion of their blood and spirit.
>
> Up through the broom she saw the grass wave with no press below his feet, her lad, the light in his eyes that aye she could bring.

The life Joey and Jim lived together followed the sequence of the seasons and the pattern of the agricultural calendar: Their spring and seedtime of struggle and endeavour were succeeded by the high summer of their middle years as they watched their family and farm flourish, nurtured by their ceaseless efforts in home and field. The autumn days of their lives saw them reach the fulfilment of their hopes and dreams, as they harvested the manifold fruits of all the years of hard work and worry. They were able to settle into an unexpected and consequently all the more comfortable retirement, watching their grandchildren grow up and indulging themselves, not with a release from hard work, but with the joy of choosing the time and pace of that toil. As old age claimed them, they weathered the wintry onset of physical decline and increasing frailty with good grace and their unfailing ability to laugh at their situation and themselves. I remember Jim telling Donald, at a family party, "Ah mind when Ah wis your age, Donald, lookin' at a' the auld men, thinkin', 'See that stupit auld bugger!' Noo Ah ken that Ah'm wan of thae silly auld buggers masel! An' so will you be some day!"

This time it was Donald who was on the other side of the world, in Japan, as we said a last farewell to our father and grandfather, but I was comforted by knowing that he was able to picture the scene at St Drostan's, as Jim was buried beside Joey. They would have been gratified to see so many of their family, old friends, and neighbours gathered together in respect and affection to wish them Godspeed. Now as we stand on the same spot and look at their headstone, we have the solace of knowing that Mum and Dad were reunited that day after the longest separation they had ever tholed since that day they were married nearly sixty years before. Their deaths straddled the end of one millennium and the start of another, marking the end of a century of enormous change and upheaval in the world in general and in the lives of people like them in particular. We have stood there in days of warm summer sunshine and gentle breezes blowing from the west, as it was the day we laid Dad to rest, and on other days when a biting east wind and sleety rain sweeps in from the far shores of the wintry East Neuk of Fife, as they did on that bleak January day when we grieved for Mum. We have heard the skylark in full-throated song soaring high above the places they knew so well as children and young adults, and listened to the sound of trains passing over the viaduct towards the station that saw many of their comings and goings in those years. They are now together for all time in the centre of the landscape that encompassed their birth and early growth and in turn witnessed their decline and deaths. Therein lies our consolation: knowing that there could be no more fitting resting place for them, as in every direction we look, we can trace their footsteps and feel their presence.

*Joey's 80th birthday party. November 1995. L to R: Joey, Lynda, May Mitchell, Elizabeth Drennan, Uncle James*

*Jim's early 80th birthday celebration, Christmas 1996 while Calum was home from Hong Kong and Donald from university*

BALGEDDIE HOUSE HOTEL

**MRS. RUTHERFORD'S 80th BIRTHDAY**

LUNCH MENU

Salad of Avocado & Pink Prawns Marie Rose
Deep Fried Crispy Mushrooms with Garlic Dip
Scotch Broth

xxxxx

Roast Sirloin of Angus Beef with Mustard Grain & Whiskey Sauce
Breast of Chicken with Mushrooms Baked in Crisp Fillo Pastry Served with Maderia Sauce
Deep Fried Lemon Sole Fillets

xxxxx

Ice Cream Profiteroles & Hot Chocolate Sauce
Strawberry Gateau
Cheese Selection

BALGEDDIE HOUSE HOTEL, BALGEDDIE WAY, GLENROTHES (NORTH) FIFE KY6 3ET, SCOTLAND
Tel: Glenrothes (01592) 742511 Fax: Glenrothes (01592) 621702
*Directors:* Mr & Mrs J. CROMBIE

*Menu for Joey's 80th birthday lunch*

*Jim and Russell with the last of Pitkinny's cattle*

*Last visit to Joey and Jim by Aunt Moira and Uncle Jimmy Ewing*

*Last visit to Joey and Jim by Mum Enid Ewing, Christmas 1997*

*Joey's grave and flowers, January 1999*

*Jim and Calum during Calum's visit from Hong Kong, February 1999*

*Margaret, Jim, and Alison, spring 2000*

*Jim's grave and flowers, July 2000*

# EPILUDE

## THE UNFURROWED FIELD

# Epilude

In writing this chronicle of my parents' lives, I hope it will stand as a testament to their steadfastness, not just to each other, but to their family and friends. Just as Margaret and I and our children and grandchildren are part of them, they were part of all the generations that went before. They were shaped by the conditions of the times they lived through, and by the way they responded to the challenges they faced every day. They lived a lifestyle—that of the tenant farmer with a moderate acreage who could still make a good living and enhance the land he stewarded—that has gone forever in the new age of conglomerates and big business in farming. In so doing, they saw the passing of an age. We will never forget them, and we know they are remembered fondly by many. My hope is that, in years to come, further generations of our family may read this, understand, and perhaps also share in that affection.

When I first saw their completed headstone ten years ago and felt that it was all too brief a description of two lives which meant so much to me and my family, I was moved to begin this chronicle. A fitting ending to their epitaph might be the one that adorns the grave of Lewis Grassic Gibbon in Arbuthnott churchyard in the Howe o' the Mearns:

The kindness of friends
The warmth of toil
The peace of rest.

# References


Eric Bogle
"Leaving the Land" from *Singing the Spirit Home*
Greentrax Recordings Ltd., 2005
(Permission to use the title graciously granted after a concert by Eric at Glenfarg Folk Club in Summer 2006)

Bette Boyd and Michael Elder
*A Hantle o' Verse: Poems in Scots for Children*
National Museums of Scotland, 2003
ISBN: 1 901663 73 6
(By kind permission of Nigel Brown, July 2010)

William Fiet
*Old Markinch*
Stenlake Publishing, Catrine, 1998
ISBN: 1 84033 038 4
(By kind permission of David Pettigrew, May 2010)

Lewis Grassic Gibbon
"Sunset Song" from *A Scots Quair*
Canongate Books, Edinburgh, 1995
ISBN: 0 86241 532 2

Dan Imrie
*Around the Farms: 1930s and '40s*
Barr Printers Ltd., Glenrothes
ISBN: 0 9517067 05
(By kind permission of Dan Imrie, May 2010)

Violet Jacob
"The Howe o' the Mearns"
By kind permission of Malcolm Hutton

Simon Taylor and Gilbert Markus
*The Place Names of Fife, Vol 1*
Shaun Tyas, Donington, 2006
ISBN: 1 900289 77 6

Archie Webster
"The Last o' the Clydesdales"
(By kind permission of Peter Shepheard, May 2010)

Lightning Source UK Ltd.
Milton Keynes UK
29 March 2011

170028UK00001B/3/P